THE RED DOOR

Iain Crichton Smith was born in Glasgow in 1928 and raised by his widowed mother on the Isle of Lewis before going to Aberdeen to attend university. As a sensitive and complex poet in both English and Gaelic, he published more than twenty-five books of verse, from *The Long River* in 1955 to *A Country for Old Men*, posthumously published in 2000. In his 1986 collection, *A Life*, the poet looked back over his time in Lewis and Aberdeen, recalling a spell of National Service in the fifties, and then his years as an English teacher, working first in Clydebank and Dumbarton and then at Oban High School, where he taught until his retirement in 1977. Shortly afterwards he married, and lived contentedly with his wife, Donalda, in Taynuilt until his death in 1998. Crichton Smith was the recipient of many literary prizes, including Saltire and Scottish Arts Council Awards and fellowships, the Queen's Jubilee Medal and, in 1980, an OBE.

As well as a number of plays and stories in Gaelic, Iain Crichton Smith published several novels, including *Consider the Lilies* (1968), *In the Middle of the Wood* (1987) and *An Honourable Death* (1992). In total, he produced ten collections of stories, all of which feature in this two-volume collection, except the Murdo stories, which appear in a separate volume, *Murdo: The Life and Works* (2001).

Kevin MacNeil was born and raised on the Isle of Lewis and educated at the Nicolson Institute and the University of Edinburgh. A widely published writer of poetry, prose and drama, his Gaelic and English works have been translated into eleven languages. His books include *Love and Zen in the Outer Hebrides* (which won the prestigious Tivoli Europa Giovani International Poetry Prize), *Be Wise Be Otherwise*, *Wish I Was Here* and *Baile Beag Gun Chrìochan*. He was the first recipient of the Iain Crichton Smith Writing Fellowship (1999–2002).

Iain Crichton Smith

THE RED DOOR

The Complete English Short Stories

1949–76

EDITED WITH AN INTRODUCTION BY

KEVIN MACNEIL

Birlinn

First published in Great Britain in 2001 by
Birlinn Ltd
West Newington House
10 Newington Road
Edinburgh EH9 1QS

www.birlinn.co.uk

The publishers acknowledge subsidy from the
Scottish Arts Council
towards the publication of this volume

ISBN 1 84158 160 7

British Library Cataloguing-in-Publication Data
A catalogue record for this book is available on
request from the British Library

Typeset by Antony Gray
Printed and bound by Omnia Books Ltd, Bishopbriggs

Contents

THE BLACK AND THE RED
AND OTHER STORIES — PART I

THE BLACK AND THE RED
AND OTHER STORIES — PART II

THE VILLAGE

UNCOLLECTED STORIES

Editor's Acknowledgements

First of all, I would like to thank Donalda Smith, whose support during my period of tenure as inaugural Iain Crichton Smith Writing Fellow has given me some idea as to why she was such an inspiration to her late husband.

I want to express my most sincere thanks to the following for their many, many efforts on behalf of this book: Neville Moir, Stewart Conn, Helen Templeton, Andrew Simmons, Hugh Andrew, Gavin Wallace, David Linton, David McClymont and Morna Maclaren.

Grant F. Wilson's *A Bibliography of Iain Crichton Smith* has been indispensable.

I must also thank the staff of the National Museum of Scotland (Edinburgh), the Mitchell Library (Glasgow), and the Scottish Poetry Library (Edinburgh) for their helpfulness.

Every effort has been made to track down all of Iain Crichton Smith's English-language stories, but, given how phenomenally prolific Iain was, I must accept the possibility that these volumes are not quite complete. If any reader knows of a story by Iain Crichton Smith that is not included in these volumes (other than those stories in Stewart Conn's recent edition of *Murdo: the Life and Works*) I would be most grateful if they would get in touch with me via the publisher, in order that any such story might be included in future editions.

Finally, I want to acknowledge that working on these volumes has been a genuine labour of love and I wish to dedicate my own efforts to the late Iain Crichton Smith.

Introduction

Iain Crichton Smith (1928–1998) was one of Scotland's greatest literary phenomena. A voracious reader and a tremendously prolific writer of English and Gaelic poems, plays, novels, short stories, essays and reviews, he was legitimately described by Sorley Maclean as 'one whose imaginative and creative fertility and energy were to become the wonder of literary Scotland.' His success was not – and ought never to be – confined to literary Scotland; for a writer of Crichton Smith's imagination, intelligence, and humanity demands a readership that is as wide-ranging as his work.

It is perhaps inevitable that some misconceptions should arise concerning a writer whose work harnesses a great many seemingly contradictory impulses. Iain's writings are by turns confrontational and subtle, crafted and spontaneous, irreverant and thought-provoking, darkly ambiguous and redemptive. The very titles of many of his works suggest opposites.

One misconception – sustained by some of his editors, publishers, and readers alike – is that Iain was born on the Isle of Lewis. In fact, as he pointed out in the elegy *You lived in Glasgow*, he was born in that city, albeit to a mother and father who were from Lewis, the island on which Iain was subsequently raised:

> I left you, Glasgow, at the age of two
> and so you are my birthplace just the same.

However, Iain, a *Leòdhasach* through and through, was to say that during his childhood Glasgow 'was as distant to me as the moon'. By contrast, he said in an interview for *The Scotsman* in 1985 that Lewis 'follows me around wherever I go, a sort of question mark at the back of my life'.

His father having succumbed to tuberculosis, Iain was raised along with his two brothers on Lewis by a mother who, like the island itself, is a profound and dominating presence in his writing.

Like his peers, Iain spoke Gaelic as a child (except, of course, in the classroom). A bookish boy, keen on football but given to reverie, he was often kept off school by his protective mother, prone as he was to attacks – and suspected attacks – of asthma and bronchitis. The village in which they lived, Bayble, on the Point peninsula, was home to a small, close-knit, and tightly Presbyterian community, aspects of which can be traced in many of Iain's writings.

At eleven years of age Iain won a scholarship to study at the island's principal high school, the Nicolson Institute, Stornoway. This set an attitudinal as well as an actual distance between Iain and his fellow villagers:

> When I left the village community in order to attend the secondary school in Stornoway I felt as if I was abandoning the community. There was a subtle alteration to me in the attitude of my contemporaries who were not taking the road of education but would work on the land or on the fishing boats.

A sense of abandonment (of abdication, of exile, of being different) recurs throughout Iain's work.

The classes he took at the Nicolson and the teachers who taught him there were to influence Iain greatly, not least of all by instilling in him a love of the Classics. He was also to write a number of Nicolson Institute characters and incidents into his stories many years later. He whiled away his lunchtimes in the local library, poring over magazines that described a world entirely different to that of his village. Iain's mind was already assimilating the necessity of duality: between Gaelic and English, between rural and 'downtown', between the insular and the cosmopolitan, between the suffocating restrictions of dogma and the multifarious freedoms of art.

Apprehensive but excited, Iain made his way to the University of Aberdeen and an environment that afforded him greater freedom (and therefore a greater breadth of experience). The city of Aberdeen appears often in Iain's poems and short stories, a glittering place of new learnings, of lodgings, cinemas, students, pubs and beggars. In a celebrated essay 'Real People in a Real Place', Iain writes:

> It is far more difficult to live in a community than to live in a city, for in a community one must have an awareness of the parameters beyond which one cannot go . . . One of my clearest memories is at the age of seventeen arriving at Aberdeen Railway Station and finding sitting there a beggar in black glasses with a cap in front of him on the pavement and in it a few pennies. Such a sight would have been unheard of in an island community. The beggar's blatant economic demand and his overt helplessness, this individual throwing himself on the mercy of chance, would have been a contradiction of everything that the community repre-sented. The shame of dropping out of the community to become pure individuality in a void would not be a concept that a community could sustain.

This compassionate attempt to understand one who is differ-ent, this fascination with the individual, the outsider, is a typical theme in many of Crichton Smith's stories. Of his own sense of alienation, Iain would say: 'I have made the choice, I have forsaken the [island] community in order to individualise myself.' Aberdeen granted him the space to discover – and individual-ise – himself. He immersed himself in poetry (Auden and Eliot being influential favourites) and philosophy (Aberdeen's light was so clear that he 'could see for miles as if it were into the essence of existentialism'). Nonetheless he enjoyed the social aspects of student life. The anonymity – the freedom – of Aberdeen contrasted sharply, excitingly, with the curtain-twitching claustrophobia of a small island village. In his droll, perceptive, and self-deprecating *Life of Murdo*, Iain (writing of himself in the third person) says:

> He [Murdo, i.e. Iain] thanks Aberdeen for giving him these days after his unhappy childhood of poverty and salt herring. His mother stern and loved and at times wild loomed over the

Minch. But Aberdeen was inhabited by many characters, whom he recalls with affection, even the shrivelled ones, the city itself a cage of light.

Iain also mentions that Murdo, his autobiographical alter-ego, 'had the nerve to write for the University magazine *Alma Mater*'. As if taking the second word of the magazine's title as a cue, Iain's earliest published story in this volume, 'Mother and Son', deals with a central Crichton Smith character type: the domineering, principled, powerfully magnetic but wholly demanding mother figure. 'Mother and Son' – while far indeed from being one of Iain's best stories - is interesting in that even at this young age he was considering the influence a mother can have on the mind of a sensitive son, an influence of which Iain was to say near the end of his own life:

> This complication and intricacy of emotional attachment [between 'Murdo' and his mother] Murdo has studied and it appears in one or two of his poems. He was much closer to his mother than boys normally are.

The sense of a young man at university finding himself, and therefore finding himself loosening his ties with both island and mother, is well evoked in the secular epistles of 'The Black and The Red'.

After university, Iain lived with his mother and younger brother in a tenement flat in Dumbarton, and he would regularly visit Helensburgh to be near the sea. 'The sea, monster and creator,' he would later write, 'has remained with me as a well of fertile symbolism. I think of the many dead – some I have known – drifting about in it, being refined there forever.' He attended Jordanhill College to do his teacher training ('Murdo cannot convey the death to the spirit which is to be found in a Teachers' Training College . . . ').

Iain was no happier during his period of National Service. Never regarding himself as a man of solid practical skills and easy conformity, he felt that the world of the army was entirely alien to him. Musing on his army days, he writes with a mixture of honesty and tongue-in-cheek self-scrutiny:

O how clumsy Murdo was. He could not fit into that social organism. He heard his boots on the square with trepidation. He taught himself to iron but at great expense of spirit. He broke like others the ice on the surface of the water buckets in winter in order to shave. He polished his cap brooch and his belt buckle. But Murdo was not a soldier nor a phantasm thereof.

Iain nonetheless was promoted to sergeant in the Education Corps, and his duties now included lecturing (on NATO, on the UN) and teaching (for the Forces Prelim and other exams). A diligent teacher, he found himself unexpectedly enjoying teaching Maths, a subject that had eluded him in his own youth. However the rigidity, the 'mad logic' of the army did not suit him and this was an uncharacteristically fallow period in his development as a writer:

> Murdo felt that Virgil was being squeezed out of him so that many men might become one man. Murdo was afraid. He couldn't write nor did he read. He was too busy suffering punishments. He was too busy aligning his knife and fork correctly on top of his bed for inspection.

In 1952, after completing his National Service, he moved to a new flat in Dumbarton with his mother and younger brother. He got a job teaching at Clydebank High School and was to remain there until 1955. He was not entirely happy, as he found that teaching academic (rather than non-academic) pupils was his forte, and it was generally the less academic classes that he, as a new teacher, was delegated.

While his mother was happy in Dumbarton (she had the Free Church and a circle of friends), Iain himself did not feel at home there, considering the town 'ugly and anonymous'. He missed the sea and the beauty of the Highlands and felt that his writing was suffering because of this.

Iain moved to Oban in 1955, where he 'felt instantly at home'. He took up a teaching post at the high school there, a job he would retain until his early retirement twenty-two years later. Iain's writing prospered in Oban. He wrote his best-known novel in just eleven days during an Easter break, the modern Scottish classic *Consider the Lilies* (known in America by its alternative and less suitable title *The Alien Light*). Certainly one of the best works of fiction concerned with the sorely inequitable Highland Clearances, *Consider the Lilies* has been widely and deservedly praised, despite anachronisms that would no doubt constitute wincing blunders in a lesser work. It is a measure of Iain's writing skills that the presence of postmen, dungarees, grandfather clocks and melodeons at a time when these did not exist in the Highlands in no way detracts from the power of the novel. In an interview for *Books in Scotland* some years later he was to dismiss any criticisms regarding historical inaccuracies: 'I think the anachronisms are trivial. They don't really affect what I was trying to do . . . There are a lot of anachronisms in Shakespeare and in other writers.'

As well as teaching and writing, Iain's energies were also directed towards domestic matters. His mother had come to live with him in his Oban flat in the early 1960s:

> This as it turned out was not a good idea though many people were very kind to her. It was not a good idea for Murdo either: he would no longer be able to go out drinking. Indeed he spent practically all his nights in the house. This had one good result, that he wrote an enormous amount, of stories and poems in both English and Gaelic.

Indeed, he was prolific – arguably too prolific. Perhaps it is inevitable that a degree of inconsistency should creep into the writings of one who produced such an abundance of material. This is true of Crichton Smith's stories, as it is of his poetry. In an interview for the *Glasgow Herald* in 1988 he said:

> One thing I do regret when I was teaching and writing was that I didn't revise things as much as I would have liked to have done. I don't just mean revision; I also mean having the courage to wait, maybe for a year or two, rather than doing it very quickly.

Crichton Smith admired the restraint of writers who focused resolutely on quality rather than quantity, people such as the world-class Gaelic poet Sorley Maclean (brother of Oban High School's rector, Iain's friend John Maclean, famous himself in Highland literary circles for producing a Gaelic translation of Homer's *Odyssey*).

The balance between compulsive, honest, lyrical spontaneity and injudicious haste is a precarious one, sometimes realised in Iain's writing as an agreeable, smooth, uninhibited and wholly natural fluidity, but other times realised as a rashness suggestive of fingers flurrying across the typewriter at almost quicker-than-thought speed. Nonetheless it is the sign of an agile creative mind, muscular, efficient, and concentrated, that such spontaneous literary writings can stand up to scrutiny.

Iain's mother, a returning presence in his work, exerted a great influence on his mind. Writing about her towards the end of his own life, Iain Crichton Smith described the 'intense pity' he felt for her. Her life had been a difficult one, not least of all because, widowed at a young age, she was left to bring up three sons in economically challenged circumstances (often swallowing her 'stubborn pride' to borrow money 'from villagers whom essentially she was not in tune with.') She was very protective of Iain when he was young and he made a number of sacrifices to look after her as she grew older: 'There came a time when she would not leave the house, was indeed frightened to do so. Murdo therefore remained in the house as well: thus he had very little opportunity to enjoy himself in any way.'

Iain's mother passed away in 1969 and this had a profound effect on the writer who, four years prior to her death, had said:

> I myself am fascinated with old people on the verge of leaving life. It links with my obsession with death, which really is the extreme situation. How you face it is the test of all you are. Lawrence said every writer has to conquer death in some way before he can write or live.

After his mother's death, however, it seemed that death might conquer *him* . . .

> His mother had died. He went to the hospital and saw her dead face which seemed to have become stern and Roman.

He felt as if ice surrounded him and he was trembling all the time. He felt as if he was in outer space. It was actually the first dead person he had seen. At this point and for a long time his whole personality disintegrated. He would not go to school. He felt as if death had destroyed his writing.

Feeling isolated, guilty, pained, Iain's torment was no doubt exacerbated by overwork. He sought solace and diversion by visiting writer friends such as Norman MacCaig in Edinburgh and George Mackay Brown in Orkney. It is clear that his mother's death was a devastation from which the writer took some time to recover.

Iain's recuperation, largely instigated by one woman, was actually the start of a period of personal and creative rejuvenation. He had begun to meet with Donalda a year or so before his mother's death. Eleven years younger than him, Donalda had at one time been a pupil of his at Oban High School. Now working as a nurse, she had been considering a switch to primary teaching and had sought Iain's help in securing her Higher English.

His relationship with Donalda developed, heralding a new period of happiness in Iain's life:

> Donalda and Murdo used to go for dinner every Saturday night to a different hotel in Argyll. Sometimes in the autumn they used to pick brambles. Murdo gradually recovered from the death of his mother, for which he had suffered guilt and genuine grief.

In Donalda's company, Iain began to think of Argyll as 'the loveliest area he had ever been in'. He describes waiting for Donalda to visit his flat with a joyfully simple and affecting beauty:

> In his flat in Combie St, he would listen for Donalda's footsteps on the stone stairs. In her yellow dress she was like an actual physical ray of sunshine entering his house.

Indeed, Iain fully recognised how important Donalda was to his well-being, how centrally important she had become to his happiness.

Having long understood that meeting Donalda was 'a turning point' in his life, he married her in July 1977, a month after he had retired from teaching. (Crichton Smith had actually tried to leave teaching on two previous occasions, 'but had lost his nerve'). Donalda and the two boys, Peter and Alasdair, moved in to the flat. Iain settled in to a routine of writing in the morning, preparing the boys' lunches, then writing again in the afternoon, still driven, as he had always been, by a very *Leòdhasach* Protestant work ethic.

Crichton Smith's marriage precipitated a new joy in his work – an energetic delight at the spontaneous beauties of nature, for example, although his writings have always had an undercurrent of darkness, sometimes nudging at the reader's mind and sometimes quite overwhelming it. One of his best novels, *In the Middle of the Wood*, charts the breakdown of a married writer whose paranoia necessitates a spell in a psychiatric hospital. If the novel's tone seems disturbingly autobiographical, there is a good reason for that, as Edwin Morgan has pointed out:

> Smith has said that the whole story is true, and if this is so, it is a most remarkable example of how an artist will use the material of his life, no matter how terrible it may be, and perhaps achieve the double function of exorcising some of his demons and presenting his readers with a highly dramatic story.

Thankfully, Iain recovered from the breakdown and went on to write some of his greatest work.

By the time of his death in 1998, Iain Crichton Smith had become one of Scotland's best-known and best-loved writers. His rich *ouevre* won him a great many accolades and honorary degrees. He was awarded the OBE in 1980.

There is no doubt, therefore, that Iain is a major Scottish writer. But it is at this pertinent juncture that I wish to raise –and subsequently attempt to demolish – another popular misconception: that Iain Crichton Smith was a great poet who 'also wrote prose'. Undeniably, close scrutiny reveals a degree of inconsistency in his stories (just as in his poetry), but I wish to argue that Iain was, on balance, a much better short story writer than he is usually given credit for. Indeed, some of his stories are so tightly charged with evocative imagery and intensely appropriate wording that they constitute prose-poems.

Sorley Maclean's comments are representative of a general attitude that has arisen among some critics with regard to Crichton Smith's writings:

> In spite of at least one most moving novel, *Consider the Lilies*, several generally fine volumes of short stories like *Trial without Error* [sic], many brilliant plays both in English and in Gaelic and much reviewing and lecturing, Iain Crichton Smith is primarily a poet even if he spends more time at the other literary work than at poetry.

Crichton Smith confessed in an interview for *Books in Scotland* that he did not think of himself as a novelist, saying: 'I am not a novelist, but I like challenges in that form.' He also said, revealing just how important the short story form was to him, 'What I really see myself as is more a short story writer and a poet.'

In 'The Necessity of Accident', an excellent, insightful essay appraising Crichton Smith's English-language fiction, Cairns Craig writes:

> [It is]tempting to look upon Crichton Smith's prose writing as the workshop of his poetic imagination – an outlet for a creativity which cannot cease from generating words rather than the mode in which his imagination truly seeks its expression – the hobby of an obsessive wordsmith rather than his vocation . . . But to treat the prose fiction as subsidiary – either to earlier models of Scottish fiction or to Crichton Smith's own poetic creations – is to miss the intensity of his commitment to the medium and the significance of his achievement in it.

Indeed, we do a great disservice to Iain Crichton Smith's memory by misunderstanding, or downplaying, the role of short stories in his contribution to literature.

Survival without Error and other stories (1970) was not Iain's first short story collection to be published, but it was his first English-language short story collection. He had won himself considerable recognition in the field of Gaelic literature since the publication of *Bùrn is Aran* ('Water and Bread', 1960), a book that, in its first edition at least, contained both short stories and poems (an indication, perhaps, of the paucity of Gaelic publishing opportunities). He had also published the story collection *An Dubh is an Gorm* ('The Black and the Blue', 1963), two English-language novels (*Consider the Lilies*, 1968, and the underrated *The Last Summer*, 1969), plus a number of poetry collections.

Iain wrote far more material in English than he did in Gaelic, but his Gaelic short stories were – and are – held in high esteem and, in contrast with critical responses to his English-language work, his Gaelic prose is generally viewed among Gaelic speakers at least as favourably as his Gaelic poetry.

Survival without Error contains fourteen stories, many of them set in Scotland, and many of them concerned with the ways in which diverse people manage to find their way through life's day-to-day impositions and demands, individuals consciously trying to cause but the minimum of fuss and controversy while negotiating the varying weathers of desire and injustice. In negotiating life this way, the individual often compromises him- or herself to the extent that they are personally diminished, sometimes almost drained of authenticity and true identity. *Survival without Error* is partly an examination of bourgeois values and *mores* – surviving 'without error' seems to be an impossibility – but this fine collection feeds off fighting tensions that are often characteristically and tantalisingly ambiguous.

The Black and the Red (1973) is a more diverse short story collection than its predecessor, with stories taking place in, for example, hotels, universities, and World War II trenches. Certain themes do emerge, however, especially alienation and separation. Characters, as is often the case in Iain's stories, tend to be somewhat physically passive, though very active mentally. They seem to be observers, not always fully engaged with their surroundings – attempting to understand, rather than change, the world.

It is a wonderful collection, and contains some of Crichton Smith's classic short stories, such as 'The Dying', 'The Telegram', and the title story. The twenty-one stories focus primarily, though not exclusively, on themes of identity, exile, and human interaction. The narratives are mediated through a voice that is sometimes realistic and sometimes surreal, but always recognisably Crichton Smith's.

It is a pleasure to make available again the stories from Iain's subsequent collection, *The Village* (1976). *The Village* partially shares its title with *The Village and other poems*, one of his finest poetry collections, though it seems, unfairly, to have had little of the latter's recognition.

The Village comprises a series of interlinked tales set in a single Scottish – and, it must be admitted, darkly Lewis-like – community. That the village changes size and appearance from time to time in no way detracts from the collection. The stories here are concerned with many aspects of insular Scottish life: the personal tensions simmering beneath a social veneer, the claustrophobia, the routine, the gossip, the emptiness, the conformity, the paranoia, and the paralysis.

The Village is a marvellous achievement, breathing slow-measured life into a community that is, behind the images of stasis and decay, alive with tensions, inner voices, and stark truths. The stories have a great deal about individual and community-wide identity within the Highlands, often creating drama out of the smallest occurrence. 'The Red Door' is a fine example of the way in which Crichton Smith can make a story of human insight and development out of an apparent triviality, in this case a mysteriously painted door. Murdo awakens one day to find that his door is no longer green but has been 'painted very lovingly' red. It is now the only red door in the village. This simple act changes Murdo's life, endows him with a new sense of self and of self-belief. The door evinces in him 'admiration' and 'a certain childlikeness'. It leads him away from easy conformity to a new and purposeful door. This story is simple, beautiful, and profound and is one of the quiet gems to be discovered in the secluded treasures of *The Village*.

Like *The Village*, *The Hermit and other stories* (1977) is a rather serious collection, free of Crichton Smith's irreverent, disarming, and punchy humour; nonetheless it features some of his best stories. 'The Hermit' itself is a long story based upon a novella that Iain wrote in Gaelic – *An t-Aonaran* (Glasgow University Press, 1976). The story is essentially the same in English as in Gaelic, though certain details and linguistic nuances vary. In fact a number of Iain's stories have bilingual versions, which are best appreciated by the bilingual reader as being parallel versions of each other – neither identical nor fundamentally different.

Murdo and other stories (1981) was legitimately praised on its release, critics admiring its intensity and its defiance of easy categorisation. Norman Shrapnel, reviewing it in *The Guardian*, applauded its ' . . . distinguished though elusive stories . . . He treads precarious frontiers – between prose and poetry, between poetry and dementia . . . '

The 'Murdo' stories are available in *Murdo: The Life and Works* (Birlinn, 2001) and are therefore not included in these volumes.

Mr Trill in Hades (1984) is one of Crichton Smith's strongest and most unified collections. Although the stories all centre around educational institutions and teaching staff, their diversity is great. These stories are compassionate and grim and funny and tragic: their combined effect is to create a rich and penetrating view of human life (and afterlife).

Selected Stories (1990) represented Iain's own choice of his best material and is naturally an extremely strong – and typically varied – collection (as indeed was Douglas Gifford's selection, *Listen to the Voice* (Canongate Books, 1993)).

Many of the previously uncollected stories published now in *The Red Door* and *The Black Halo* are as good as those stories which did make it into the collections, and I suspect many of them were omitted from the published collections for thematic reasons or because of lack of available space. They examine familiar themes but do so with a freshness that awakens alternative perspectives and ideas, often with the full power, intense imagery and sheer verbal energy that are characteristic of the short story collections in general. They allow the reader for the first time comprehensively to appraise Crichton Smith's achievements as short story writer, to piece together this quite central part of his varied literary jigsaw.

It is impossible, given the limitations of space here, to give an exhaustive critique of the themes, techniques, ideas and potential interpretations of Crichton Smith's stories. Iain often explored and re-explored specific themes in his work that were not only important to him personally, but central to his literature, his very dialogue with humanity.

One of the most prominent of these is often, appropriately, evoked quite surreptitiously: the theme of communication (more accurately, miscommunication or a lack of communication). Many of his stories are populated by couples who are – or have become – awkwardly but inseparably incompatible. A gulf of incommunicable difference has opened wistfully between them. Delusion and pathos are frequent undercurrents in such stories. 'The Ships', for example, is situated in a typically (Oban-esque?) Scottish village and is a powerful, though often subtle, examination of small-town ennui, loneliness, and dissemination. The narrator, Harry, limping through the latter stages of his life, has found himself in an unexceptional marriage, questioning the meaning of his existence. He is pitiful. His children appear to have forgotten him, his wife knows all too well the kind of man he is: a liar. Perhaps his exaggerations (deliciously and skilfully portrayed) are partly a poor man's attempt to defeat the mundane through sheer creative invention. Bitterness, duplicity and untrustworthiness are dominant emotions in a story that nonetheless concludes with the realisation of some sharp home truths.

'On the Road' also features an unhappy couple who are, naturally, out of harmony with each other:

> He couldn't understand how her mind worked at all. For two years now he had tried to understand her but couldn't. His

own mind he felt was clear and logical but hers was devious
and odd. It jumped from one thing to another like . . .

Like a rabbit, perhaps? The story is tightly written, the
images densely interwoven. Correspondences, as is often the
case in these stories, shine seductively somewhere just above
the lucid communicative level of logic, hinting at something
sinister and ineluctably superior. The ending to this story is
compellingly irate, indignant, and resentful:

> The moon, white as a pearl, looked in on them through the
> windscreen with a huge peering power, a complete presence.
> It was frightening. Why the hell, he almost shouted, weren't
> you shining before, why didn't you show me the rabbit
> earlier?

Perhaps the supreme example of a sustained investigation of
communication is 'The Hermit', which tells the story of a
loner's arrival in a 'bare bleak island' village. His silent, passive,
self-contained manner, far from catalysing his endearing
integration into the village, leads to an agitated and quietly
explosive period of unease within the (too) tightly-knit community. While various individuals – the narrator included –
empathise in various ways with the loner, they seem to
see themselves in an unappealingly clear light. The hermit,
ultimately, is a scapegoat. Surely his obliquely absent presence
implies he deserves much better treatment than the villagers
give him, but the locals do not understand his silences, and they
read their own bigotries into his lack of communication. The
story is propelled by narrow gossip and by the nagging
imposition of claustrophobic convention. As in *The Village*,
routine is all:

> For me it [the community] is a processional play with
> continually changing actors . . . The young man for some
> reason puts on the disguise of the middle-aged man and the
> middle-aged man in turn the guise of the old man. The earth
> flowers with corn and then becomes bare again. The sky at
> moments is close and then as far away as eternity.

'The Hermit' is, like Nabokov's *Lolita*, more than it seems to be: it, too, is a meditation upon language. There are a great many references to language and the nature of communication stated – and buried – within this most densely revealing of texts. One of the story's greatest successes is to pitch the unknown, the *unsaid* (the hermit) against the familiar, i.e. that which has been said so often it has become routinely acceptable and ultimately meaningless: 'Language almost becomes like tobacco which is as much chewed as smoked . . . So much of language is lying, polite lying but still lying.'

Crichton Smith's stories often triumph by communicating to the reader that which is, to the characters at least, incommunicable. But, furthermore, some of his stories communicate something that seems to be, paradoxically, above verbal understanding: and the fluid, surreal images of many of Iain Crichton Smith's stories, reminiscent of actual dreams, are one of their most recognisable features

Daydreams, night-dreams and literary dreams are surely the inspired cinema screens that brought to light many of the images and stories contained within these volumes. 'On the Train', 'The Survivor', and 'The Maze' are supremely Kafkaesque, while nonetheless being Crichton Smithesque at the same time. A number of Crichton Smith's stories take place in a kind of Twilight Zone of shifting perceptions, a world that is recognisably ours, but one that is filtered through a sinisterly dreamlike atmosphere of paranoia, implication, pessimism, and an inability to control one's destiny. These surreal vignettes burn themselves into the mind like ultra-vivid paintings, fugitive in meaning but unforgettable as works of art. Sometimes their concluding ambiguities offer a measure of solace:

> Slowly the sun disappeared over the horizon and darkness fell and he felt the pressure of the maze relaxing, as if in a dream of happiness he understood that the roads were infinite, always fresh, always new, and that the ones who stood beside him were deeper than friends, they were bone of his bone, they were flesh of his disappearing flesh.

> (from 'The Maze')

As with much of Crichton Smith's work, a sinister intellect hovers about these stories. Many of these pieces are as unshakeable as the grip of a vivid dream that haunts without necessarily yielding its meaning. Images shift and coalesce according, it seems, to their own secret agenda.

'Through the Desert' is dreamy as a Dali painting and is a very fine example of this kind of surrealistic writing, despite a deficient ending. Its tremendous energy, its vivid movement, its colour and its life, are admirable. Images somersault across the page and land on the right side of disorientated sense, quirkily standing up to sympathetic scrutiny:

> ' . . . it was always day and there were no clouds, only a sun which hammered on a steel anvil like a giant at the opening of a film.'
> ' . . . a river with dark water which made the sound of crossed telephone conversations.'

'Getting Married' has the feel of an experimentally surreal piece – nicely written, and 'The Little People', too, is an unusual story, like a nebulous fairy tale. Its engaging mixture of realism and absurdity is both alluring and discomforting.

I feel that many of these surrealist stories seem to prefigure, describe, or subsequently attempt to understand Crichton Smith's own breakdown. In a later work, 'In the Asylum', reality bends 'like plasticine' as the author struggles with his place in the world: 'I do not feel authentic.' Undeniably, however, much of the nightmareish imagery Iain utilised throughout his career feels both authentic and convincing.

Surrealism is actually evident, in varying degrees, throughout his *oeuvre*. 'Goodbye John Summers' is pure Iain Crichton Smith, a story that enigmatically ponders the thorny issue of how well we can actually *know* a person (and, in this case, a person who seems undistinguished almost to the point of invisibility). Like many of his stories, this meditation on death, Christianity, ambiguity, and communication is shot through with strange and imaginative (dream-like but graspable) images and ideas: 'It was a fine bright glittery day when they buried him. I stood at the graveside and stared at the coffin as if I wished to make it transparent, but I was confronted by an opaque yellow hexagon.'

While some of these narratives interweave realism and surrealism, others move inexorably from one to the other. 'In the School' is hellish and yet magnificently minimalist. Its characters are delineated with little decoration – like fine fingerprints they are tidy and self-explanatory. The story glides from dark realism to dark surrealism with an accomplished register. Its imagery revolves around cinders, sparks, fire, ideas of power and leadership and mental health.

Sometimes the departure from strict realism manifests itself as an irruption of the supernatural into the everyday world. 'The Brothers' was initially published in an anthology of literary ghost stories. It is a moving – and chilling – insight into the mind of a writer who has shunned a significant part of his linguistic and cultural heritage. The narrator is a writer from the Highlands who has moved to Edinburgh to write his (English-language) stories and novels. 'The Brothers' feeds off many of the tensions Iain himself explored in his fabulous version of the Old Testament story of Joseph. (And yet it is not without its humour, for surely its mentioning the ghostly but more accurate typing implies a tongue-in-cheek reference to Iain's own typescripts, which were legendarily erratic). The story is propelled by a terrifying and insightful imagination:

> My eyes pierced the door which was like skin and on the other side I saw my brothers broken by defeat and starvation but still human and rustic and brave. It was to them that I must offer myself, not to the alien kings and an alien land.

The ending seems happy, though it is tempered by the notion that yellow often signifies a kind of sickness in Crichton Smith's work: 'I sat in my yellow robe at my yellow typewriter in the yellow room. And I was happy. I overflowed with the most holy joy.'

Crichton Smith's huge mind also bred story after story concerning exile, an understandably common theme in Highland literature. 'The Exiles' features a disapproving, religious *cailleach*, a familiar character-type in his work. This story is not, however, predictable. The old lady has a refreshingly unsentimental view of her native Highlands. As jaded and unenlightened-to-the-point-of-racism as she seems, the relationship that develops between her and the Pakistani salesman/student is touching and plausible.

'An American Sky' is a longer story, concerned with another popular Iain Crichton Smith character-type: the returning exile. This story carefully considers the issues that assail the return of a long-exiled Lewisman – the 'implicit interrogations', the hard realities of homeland change. John Macleod, like many before him, comes to understand 'One always brings back a judgement to one's home'. He decides to return to urban America, or, in Crichton Smith's remarkable and characteristic phrasing, suggesting rapid change and a lack of adequate communication, 'the shifting world of neon, the flashing broken signals of the city'.

The semi-autobiographical 'The Black and the Red' is a story to which many islanders, in particular, relate, concerned as it is with the transition from closeted (or at least insular) life to greater maturity and freedom. Kenneth, writing letters to his mother, reveals how much of university learning occurs outwith the university itself, as he loosens the ties between himself and an oppressive, overbearing mother (and island):

> I think it's time you went out amongst people more. I think it is time you depended less on me, although I shall never abandon you. It is time you looked at the facts. I do not want this burden of guilt. It is time we laughed more – high time.

Ultimately, Kenneth even comes to the realisation that his illnesses have been to some extent psychosomatic: 'I mean that: I'm not going to be sick again.' He is still his mother's loving son, but he is an individual now, aware of his potential and his freedoms.

One of the most appealing features of Iain Crichton Smith's stories are those occasional and cherished instants of intelligent, lyrical, unforgettable epiphany, usually at a story's conclusion. Such moments of epiphany, knitting agreeable, legitimate, and meaningful correspondences together, make for supremely pleasurable reading, no matter that the perceived message behind the images might be shadowy or negative.

'Moments', for example, is an eloquent analysis of those instants of clarity triggered when seemingly unrelated events appear to reveal an unguessed-at synchronous relation in a profoundly meaningful way. A quotation from the episode about the second 'moment' may well apply to the endings of some of Crichton Smith's own stories: 'And that is the thing with "moments". They illuminate but at the same time they don't necessarily lead to what you call understanding. And in any case one man's "moment" is different from another man's.'

A number of the stories end on a note of admirably equivocal epiphany – ambiguity is a common feature. For example, nothing seems clear-cut in 'The Exorcism', a story that hinges upon interpretations of Kierkegaard's philosophy, on which Crichton Smith dwells frequently in his stories and poems. (He was attracted to him partly because Kierkegaard was a poet as well as a philosopher). Ideas and opinions in this story form a spectrum of merging colours – hues and tones that themselves often change as they are being regarded. Devils and saints, realists and fantasists, the possessed and the overpowering encircle each other . . . and the result of the exorcism is satisfactorily problematic:

> I looked at him for a long time knowing that the agony was over. It was a victory but an empty victory. And even in the midst of victory how could I be sure that this was not indeed a second Kierkegaard, how could I be sure that I had not destroyed a genius? How could I be sure that my own harmonious jealous biography had not been superimposed upon his life, as one writing upon another, in that wood where the birds sang with such sweetness defending their territory? I looked down at him white and exhausted. The exorcism was over. He would now follow his unexceptional destiny.

Some of the stories (such as 'The Angel of Mons') employ experimental narratorial devices. Because Crichton Smith's stories rarely offer neat conclusions, preferring instead to scrutinise the world through highly subjective spectra, these devices often tend to be appropriate and satisfying.

'The Ghost' (from *Selected Stories* – not the same ghost that appears in *The Village*!) throws a shifting light on the ambivalence, the ambiguity, that can underpin inherent inexplicabilities of human existence – and the different ambiguities that can remain after an explanation has been offered, while the final story in *The Village* ends strongly but ambiguously: 'After a while our ambitions, thank God, grow less.' The implication is that the villagers are limited, kept in their place; and their place is, simply, the village.

Some of these stories also explore an inherent duality in the human mind reminiscent of *Jekyll and Hyde* – for example 'Mac an t-Sronaich', the title of which refers to a Lewis bogey-man, a dreaded character based upon a real-life murderer who stalked the moors of Lewis at one time and stalked the imaginations of storytellers and children just as effectively thereafter.

'The Old Woman, the Baby and Terry' harks back to the theme of ambiguous survival, with an undertow of selfishness running strongly throughout. Even the baby in the womb has an implied sense of innate manipulation: 'The baby moved blindly in her womb, instinctively, strategically.'

Love is imperative: ' "I love you," she said. "There's nothing else for it." ' It is a source of their strength that many of Iain Crichton Smith's stories conclude with a unification of seemingly irreconcilable opposites in a single (and sometimes wholly enigmatic) dualism.

Naturally, one of the most pressing themes in the stories is that of education: the nature of education and of the institutions and individuals who decide what and how to teach. 'Murder without pain' introduces us to Mr Trill, a name Crichton Smith calls upon in a number of stories and poems. Indeed, Trill represents an archetypal Crichton Smith figure: the principled bachelor, a man so dedicated to routine his life seems to have shrunk all about him.

Trill is a devotee of the Roman intellect. He is such an admirer of the Classical contribution to culture that the reader feels he is almost out of place in the modern world. Disciplined, cool, patient, respectful of that which he deems worthy of his respect, he feels threatened as his world-view is challenged by events at his school. The ending of this story – sometimes dismissed as melodramatic – is confessedly and classically dramatic, as Trill decides to execute a form of justice that is 'Greek to its very essence'.

'The Ring' is based upon an actual event that Iain witnessed during his own schooldays. It is told from the point of view of a pupil, but with the later revelation that the pupil grew up to become a teacher. It is enticingly narrated and is, I think, one of Crichton Smith's finest stories. The pupil's attitude is clear: 'After all, teachers were invincible beings who appeared at the beginning of a period and left at the end of it . . . they were not human beings . . . like the rest of us.' The adult's subsequent attitude towards teaching is clear, too, if more cynical:

> It seemed to me that the best thing about geometry was it never lied to you, which is why I myself am a mathematics teacher as well. It has nothing to do with pain or loss. Its refuge is always secure and without mythology.

'The Play' is an excellent and hugely engaging story that is also based upon a real event, this time when he was teaching at Oban High School. The girls in the class have '. . . a fixed antipathy to the written word'. The teacher decides that if they will not read or write ('Shakespeare is not necessary for hairdressing' as he wryly concedes) then the girls can involve themselves by acting out dramas. The story is an uplifting and a memorable one. Crichton Smith's responsibility is to the human – not to the régime – to individuality and not to conformity. The real-life drama of the original incident that inspired the story resulted in an astonished and pleased school inspector: meanwhile we empathise with the teacher completely as he broods upon Miss Stewart's snobbish dismissal of the pupils' (and teacher's) achievements:

> You stupid bitch, he muttered under his breath, you *Observer*-Magazine-reading bitch who never liked anything in your life till some critic made it respectable, who wouldn't

recognise a good line of poetry or prose till sanctified by the voice of London, who would never have arrived at Shakespeare on your own till you were given the crutches.

This story of triumph *is* a triumph.

The Black and the Red collection modulates into a new key with the masterful final story, 'The Professor and the Comics', an excellent narrative that melds the serious and the humorous to great effect. The aptly named Professor Black's comment that 'Everything is different in spring . . . except history' is dry and thought-flipping, like a Wildean phrase.

The sinister shadows that lurk around many of Crichton Smith's stories are often tempered by a humour that is clever, offbeat, punny or satirical. 'By their Fruits' runs in parallel with Iain's (posthumously published) narrative poem, 'My Canadian Uncle' and draws inspiration from a trip Iain and Donalda made to White Rock (Canada) to meet Iain's uncle, Torquil Campbell. It brings together a number of very Highland themes – exile, religion, and humour. It is both thought-provoking, subtle, and witty

Many examples of Iain's gleefully absurd or knowingly sharp humour can be found in these volumes:

> 'I thought that if the poet who had climbed the lamp-post had fallen down we might have had our first concrete poet.'

> 'She was an incomer from another village and had only been in this one for thirty years or so.'

Sometimes the humour relies less on punch lines than on wider social observations. 'The Travelling Poet' is a wickedly funny portrayal of the egotism and the artistry involved in being a poet and there are flashes of great wit and insight in this marvellous tale. 'Mr Heine', too, is winningly sardonic, his tone of voice almost simultaneously gratifying and sarcastic.

'A Night With Kant' returns us to Crichton Smith's infatuation with philosophy, but it is also very witty. When a prostitute offers to show Kant 'a very good time', his reply is amusing: ' "The time is seven o' clock," said Kant mildly. "It is neither better nor worse." ' As she 'totters' away, Kant is 'stirred by a regretful desire': 'And at that moment the Categorical Imperative was very distant indeed.'

These stories have not generally received the recognition they deserve and it is impossible to give a complete and fair critique of them in the limited space afforded by an introduction. In any case the most convincing demonstration of their quality is to be found within the stories themselves.

Read these stories because they deserve wider critical and general appreciation than they have hitherto been granted. Read these stories because they greatly help us understand why Iain Crichton Smith was not only one of twentieth-century Scotland's *best* but also one of her most *important* writers.

Read these stories because some of them offer ideas for surviving a world that can be more powerful and sinister than one might reasonably have expected. Some explore the inter-action between the mind and the shared world of 'reality'. Some face squarely, questioningly, the connections between the causal and the casual, revealing how identity, contingency and synchronicity impinge upon life. Some teach us valuable lessons about the human condition, about our lives, or about the lives of people we have met (albeit met, perhaps, in a dream). And if some of these stories leave you with no more certainty, clues, or logic than a dream might, then this is because life, surely, is not always clear-cut, and circumstances will sometimes hint at significances touched upon but not grasped (just as the significance of these stories has not previously been grasped).

Read these stories because they are stylistically diverse – variously realistic and hallucinatory, humorous and philosophical, formally complex and naturally, unadornedly simple.

Read these stories because they were created by one of the most humane, eloquent, humorous, productive, scrupulous, lyrical, and uniquely imaginative literary minds of our times.

KEVIN MACNEIL
Summer 2001
Colombia-Malta-Isle of Skye

from
SURVIVAL WITHOUT ERROR
and other stories

The Ships

The grey ships on the far horizon loomed out of the early morning haze, bastions of our lost Empire, the aircraft carrier pregnant with missiles, the other lesser ships receding from her towards the open sea. The foreshore was deserted except for one man who was making little forays into the water, salvaging planks and broken boxes, and stacking them carefully against the sea wall which edged the long strip of green where, later on, the wasp-coloured deck-chairs would be set. Now and again he would stop and look out towards the massive ships whose combined destructive power could blast the small town out of existence in one blistering microsecond.

As he walked, one could see that he was lame in the right leg and, when he bent down, the stiffness of his body was evident. He had rolled his trousers up to his knees which gave him the look of a small boy hunting for crabs or fish. But he moved very warily, stretching out his hands towards the dripping wood, sometimes using a grappling iron which he had with him.

It was not the best time of year for wood. Better would be the winter, when the storm had lashed the foreshore, ascending in white spray and hitting the glass doors and windows of the shops, when the waves were slate grey and looked as dense as geological strata, and the stubby trawlers puffed out thick black smoke as they drove onward into the crashing water.

There was not much wood that morning, and eventually he sat down against the sea wall and took out his pipe. He cut up a piece of small black twist, placed it in the pipe, took out a match and, after some time, succeeded in striking it and lighting the tobacco. He puffed steadily, looking out towards the ships. They were too far out for him to see their names, but their shapes looked formidable, high in the water.

Above him, another oldish man passed, a tall man with a stick and white hair on his face.

'Not much wood today, Harry,' he shouted down.

Harry laughed, exposing slightly yellow teeth between thick lips.

'Didn't expect much, Sonny,' he answered. 'Not with this weather. You're early up.'

'My daughter's coming today,' said Sonny proudly. 'With her man. He's a manager in the SCWS. Mind I telt you of him. Coming up for the day they are. In the car.'

He stood there above Harry on the pavement, looking military in a phantasmal and rather decrepit way with his stick and his white hair.

'Ay. Good for you,' said Harry. 'You'll be going out to dinner with them, shouldn't wonder.'

Sonny gazed unfathomably out to sea. 'Shouldn't wonder,' he agreed.

'Last time it was the Grant. Though it's gone down. Do a lot of fish now. Wee bits of fish.'

Harry's mouth watered. 'And you'll have trifle and the wee oranges. Mandarins. Mind you watch the trifles. Ask for them fresh. They keep them overnight sometimes.'

'You should know, Harry. You were a cook, weren't you?'

'Ay,' sighing, 'I was that. Shouldn't wonder if you get braised steak. And a fag after it. Take a fag after it. With your coffee in the wee cups. Make sure you get the coffee in the wee cups and the brown sugar. The brown sugar's for coffee. White's for tea. Is it a big branch he's manager of?'

'George Street branch,' said Sonny with vague pride, confronting the haze.

'They look big, don't they?'

'Ay, the ships. I was on one of they.'

'Yes, Harry.'

Harry climbed up with the wood in his arms, taking his time, very careful. Puffing. His pipe back in his pocket. 'God dammit,' he said, 'getting steeper every month.'   —

'Ay, a big one she was. In the war, you know.'

'Yes, Harry.'

'You should have seen the food on you. Used to throw it over the side. Buckets of it. Swill. In the Med. it was.'

'I'm sure, Harry.'

Harry put down the wood carefully and leaned down stiffly to unroll his trouser legs. Sonny gazed outwards, posed on his stick, thinking of his daughter and his son-in-law. It would make his day. One up for him. Talk about it later in the shelter when they were watching the pipe band, the old men.

'They were in Italy,' he offered.

'Who, Sonny?' looking up.

'My daughter and her man. For their holidays, you know. They took the car. Wrote us postcards.'

'Is that right, Sonny? Which part?'

'What?'

'What part? Italy's a big place, you know, Sonny. There's Venice. And Rome. Where they Catholic bastards hang out. Went on leave there once. Bologna, it was.'

'No, it wasn't any o' they. Posh place it was. It had towers, see. Castles.' The air began to grow warm, and the ships came clearer out of the water. So huge they were, massive. With steel grey sides.

'Got to go now, Harry. They'll be along any minute, and I've got to change my clothes, the wife says.' He pointed to his red bow-tie. 'Got to take this off. There'll be the nipper as well.'

'Have a good time, Sonny,' said Harry watching his stiff back receding. 'Stuck up bastard. Anyone would think he was an ex-major. Manager of the Co-op! Have a good time,' he shouted bitterly.

He picked up his armful of wood, limping, grinning with his teeth bared.

He walked slowly along the pavement waiting to cross. The shop opposite sold morning rolls and he smelt them in the clear briny air.

'Could you tell me the way to Smith Street?' said an earnest, bespectacled little man who was carrying a copy of *Time Magazine* under his right arm.

'Smith Street?' said Harry. 'You see that newsagent? There, beside the barber's pole? You go up the street there. At the corner. That's Smith Street.'

'Thank you. Thank you very much,' said the little man gently, looking at the wood cradled in Harry's arms.

'I was just speaking to a friend of mine,' said Harry. 'His son-in-law is manager of the Co-op.'

'Oh? That's interesting. Of the Co-op?' said the little man quickly before darting across the road just in front of a big red bus.

Harry waited and finally crossed, the wood in his arms, not going as far as the zebra crossing which was down the road a bit.

'Getting old,' he thought. 'Not as supple as I used to be. Not so many out yet.'

He walked along the pavement. 'Fine day,' he offered the local bank manager who was staring seawards, his black hair carefully combed into shining black waves.

'What? Yes, isn't it?' said the bank manager withdrawing his small eyes from immense distances.

A shopkeeper was bending over a crate of oranges, revealing a large bottom. 'Fine day,' said Harry.

'Ay, it's that,' said the shopkeeper, laughing. 'Ay, it's that.'

Harry looked at the box of oranges as if he knew about oranges.

'Fine crop,' he conceded.

'Yes, Harry, aren't they?' said the shopkeeper, going into the shop with the box.

Harry's thick lips came together, and he looked into the shop for a moment before turning the corner up to his house.

'Hi, Harry,' said a boy going past on a bicycle and waving one hand while keeping a grip on the handle-bars.

'Hi, son,' said Harry to the disappearing whirring wheels and the diminishing whistle.

'Not much wood,' he said, coming into the kitchen.

'Your breakfast's on the table,' said Sarah, lips pursed, flicking at something on the table-cloth.

He eased himself slowly into the leather chair. 'Any mail?'

'The electric.'

'How much?'

'Two pounds and sixpence.' She sat down opposite him and poured out the tea from a teapot cocooned in a red woollen cosy.

He crammed soft white bread into his mouth.

'I wish you wouldn't do that, Harry.' Her voice had a gravelly whine.

'Wha?' mouth full.

'Stuff your mouth with bread. I wish you wouldn't do it, Harry.'

He decapitated an egg with his knife.

'Nothing from them, then?' he asked slowly and almost shyly.

'No, and you know as well as I do that there won't be. They've forgotten us. Our children have forgotten us.'

'Mm,' chewing.

'Saw Sonny this morning.'

No answer.

'Said his son-in-law was coming. Manager of the Co-op, he said, in Glasgow.'

Snort.

'Paper come?'

Nod.

He dried the yellow of the egg with his bread, gulping, chewing. She looked down at her plate.

God, how ugly she was getting with that white hair, grumpy stony face, the dry waspish eyes behind the glasses.

'Going to the Fête today?' He pronounced it as if it rhymed with 'set'.

'You know very well I am, Harry.'

'Only asked. Think Mr Milne will be there?'

No answer.

'He should be there. He's the Tory MP isn't he?'

No answer.

'When are you going?'

'Twelve o'clock. I'll leave your dinner for you. I'll have lunch with the girls.'

'Where?' picking his teeth.

'Clark's. Or the Grant.'

'Upstairs?'

'Where else. They don't do lunches downstairs. You know that, Harry.'

Yes, he knew that.

'Who's paying?'

'Miss Melon will be there.'

'That the schoolteacher?'

No answer.

He buttered his fourth piece of bread, his red cheeks bulging.

'How's your leg today?'

'The same.'

'Going about like a tramp. That wood will finish you.'

'Someone might as well take it. It'd be left there else.'

Grunt.

He wiped his mouth, sat back, reached for the paper.

The phone rang. He went to it, but it wasn't for him.

'Be for me I expect,' she said.

He lifted it. 'Harry Millar here. Who? Oh. For you, Sarah.' His mouth puckered and he sat down to read the paper, half listening.

'You don't say? She's going to be there herself?'

He put on his glasses and read, moving his lips slightly, pouting.

'Hey, Sarah,' he said. She hushed him furiously with her hand.

'Yes, of course, bring your friend. What did you say she did? I know it's the vacation. Yes, of course . . .'

Imagine that. A big fire in Clarewood's. He studied the photographs – the ladders, the window marked with a cross, the two policemen standing talking, hands behind their backs. What had started the fire? His blubbery lips moved.

The receiver was replaced. 'She's bringing a friend. A friend! Why she couldn't have told me before! School-teachers!'

'You've got one in the family yourself,' pacifically.

'Have we? Have we, Harry?'

'Big fire in Clarewood's, Sarah. Three dead.'

'Wish they'd tell you these things beforehand,' she complained, sweeping plates on to a tray.

'They wouldn't know, Sarah. It was a surprise.' He laughed, showing his teeth.

She put the dishes in the sink, running water over the tinny interior through the red rubbery tube. A little water got on to the formica. She wiped it dry.

'There's a photo, Sarah.'

She didn't want to look at it.

'How old do you think I am, Harry? I'm an old woman. I've got to take my time. I can't do everything at once. I'm an old woman, Harry.'

'Just showing you the photo, Sarah, that was all.'

'I haven't got time, Harry.'

'Oh, all right, I'll go into the other room, Sarah.'

He rose and, limping, went.

He sat down in a chair beside the piano with the photographs on top, Helen's photograph and Robin's. His daughter and his son. No letters from them today either. Music on top of the piano, 'The Rowan Tree'.

He sat down in the sun that was shining through the window. Fancy the fire at Clarewood's. Used to live there when we were young, he thought, that area. When we were just married. In a room and kitchen, with a window overlooking the back. Used to be washing hung out there at the back: they called it the green. Just after the war it was. In those days they had the trams. They had to take six wall-papers off the walls when they went in, because the previous tenant had been an old woman who had lived by herself. The two of them used to dance in there, the room still bare, when they worked on it till midnight and after. Sundays, they'd go for a walk by the river, hand in hand. Lie down on the grass and look across the river, shining it was, and the cranes very tall above the water. Always liked a bit of country. Had a moustache too in those days, you could see it in the army picture with the boys all in it. Turning a bit brown now.

To be young . . . Then he had his job at the shipyard, clocked in with his lunch in his tin box. Tin Box Harry. Just a labourer, of course, though he could have been a foreman if he'd wanted. Could've. Sundays, her brother and family would come over from Greendale. Great fun, lots of laughter and jollity. Come to think of it, his brother worked in the Co-op too. Something to do with the bottle department. High up in bottles. Very complicated it was, you wouldn't think there'd be much to bottles, but the way he spoke it was a very responsible job. Pity about Clarewood's.

'How are you, Harry?' That was Ronny, her brother.

'Brought some fish and chips. Thought you'd be hungry, you newly weds.' Wolfish smile, slap on the back, smell of stew. 'And a bottle of beer, Harry. Couldn't afford the champagne. Said in our family we stick to beer. Beer runs in our family. How's that, Harry? "Beer runs in our family".' Roar. Everybody sweaty, full of food, happy. Appetite never so good as in those days.

'And I've got a screwtap, Harry. All the home comforts. A screwtap and fish and chips. On top of the world, eh, Harry? Everyone's got a job. Everyone happy. Eh, Sarah?' And Sarah beginning to smile mirthlessly, beginning to get a little grim. Well, he did have a job, didn't he? But Sarah a bit mirthless just the same.

Ronny flicking his hands at the papers. 'The ruinators after us again, Harry. Mark my words, they'll get us yet. Less we stand up for ourselves. Ach, to hell, let's have some beer.'

Ronny, big, fat, moving out of the door now, to his grave.

'Harry, have you seen my brooch?' He jerked his head to attention: Sarah was ready to go out. 'The one in the shape of an eagle, Harry. Have you seen it?'

No, he hadn't seen it. What had she said about the electric? Two pounds and sixpence. And they hardly used any in summer either.

After she'd gone out, he sat in the room for a while. His eyes wandered over the photographs, the one of Helen, now in Canada, and the one of Robin, in Africa. Sometimes they'd send a postcard. The one from Cape Town, where Robin was on holiday with his English wife, said, 'Wish you were here' (among tall affluent skyscrapers) and then a lot of Xs from the unseen children.

He sat down at the piano for a bit, but he couldn't play. Only

Helen and Sarah could play, and Sarah never played now. In the old days she used to play when the house seemed full of children. There was one called 'The Anniversary Waltz' and another called 'Apple Blossom Time'. Robin wasn't interested in music, he was more practical.

Harry decided he wouldn't have any dinner, he'd go out instead. He looked at what was in the oven. Mince pie. He took it out. Perhaps later on tonight he might cook it. No use wasting electricity till then, if he felt hungry then. He turned out his pockets and found he had exactly fifteen shillings left over from the pension. He would go down and have a look at these ships through the shore telescope for a start: his own field-glasses were broken. If he could only get out to the ships and see them close to, that would be something he could tell the boys!

He went over to the phone and looked up a number. It was that of a lawyer's office. He dialled and heard a girl's cool voice like waterdrops saying,

'Who's speaking?'

'Mr Outerson in?'

'Who's speaking, please?'

'Just a matter of business I had with him. I just came in on the plane today. Is he in?'

'No, he's out at the moment. I'm sorry. He's gone to the bank. Who's speaking, please?'

'Tell him Mr Clifton-Baddeley called. From Zurich.'

There was a long respectful silence. He said,

'Which bank is he in?'

'The Bank of Scotland, sir. I'll make a note of the name. Shall I tell him you're calling back?'

'It doesn't matter. I've only a quarter of an hour or so. Sorry I missed him.'

'We could always go and get him for you.'

'No, no, don't bother. It can't be helped,' said Harry charitably. 'I can wait.'

He replaced the receiver, thanking her. So Mr Outerson was in the Bank of Scotland. He clocked the time. Interesting bits of information you could pick up by using the telephone.

He went out, making sure that he had his Yale key tied round his neck as usual. The house seemed too empty to stay in on such a sunny day. He had a look in the woodshed on the way out, noting that the stool he was making was coming along nicely. He made his way out on to the dazzling street. It was really going to be a fine day, a good day for Sonny to feed on his wee mandarin oranges. His son-in-law might even run to a cigar for him. That would be a blow to the rest of them if he brought a cigar along.

He might drop in for a pint soon, but you couldn't get a good pint for less than two and sixpence. And that would be the price of two loaves. Or a pound of rhubarb, more than a pound of rhubarb, depending where you bought it.

As he came out on to the street he saw that there was a large shining blue car there, like a piece of sky that had dropped to earth. He thought at first it might be Robin come home as a surprise till he saw the naval officer emerge from it. And 'emerge' was the right word, like a god in his blue and yellow, a commodore at least, a golden man.

Probably off that ship, one of the ships anyway, must be off the aircraft carrier at least.

'Could I help you, sir?' he said, almost standing at attention.

'I'm looking for the Commodore Hotel. Could you direct me?'

'Certainly, sir. You go back down on to the main street and then you turn left. It's along the front. You can't miss it. It's got a lot of glass windows. I used to be in the Navy myself,' he said, almost in an undertone.

'What did you say?'

'I said my son was in the Navy during the war. He was a first lieutenant, and he would have been a lieutenant commander, only the war stopped too soon.'

'Oh? Thank you very much indeed,' said the commodore who seemed confused for such an important man. He hastily got back into the car, which accelerated from a standing start and drove away so beautifully its motion almost brought tears to Harry's eyes. He gazed after it, was part of it, then, sighing, made his way to the shore, which was now crowded with people of all shapes and sizes, lying, sprawling, sitting, letting the sun unravel them again.

He headed straight for the telescope but saw that it was being used by a small boy hoisted in the arms of his mother.

He waited, looking out towards the sea which sparkled and sparkled. The haze had cleared now and he could see the ships very clearly.

'I can't see anything,' the small boy screamed.

'Of course you can't, dear. You've used up your three minutes,' said the mother. 'Come on and let the gentleman look.' The little boy regarded Harry with naked hatred, but allowed himself to be led away.

Harry put a sixpence in the slot and manoeuvred the telescope so that he could focus on the ships, swinging it past the lighthouse and the tower on the opposite side of the firth. Eventually he could see men in white walking about the decks. He could even make out the ships' names. The aircraft carrier was the Redoubtable; there were also a few destroyers and some frigates. The Royal Yacht would be coming that night to call on them, and the bay would be all lit up. No use trying to climb the sides of these ships, they were so sheer. And walking about the decks were the men in white, whom he was so secretly watching, unaware of his scrutiny. As he gazed, he saw a launch foaming through the water, the prow rising high, one rating standing at the stern and another at the bow.

He swivelled the telescope round to the far end of the line where there was a frigate. Just behind her he could see an oil tanker with strange funnels. God, how powerful they looked! The British Navy! And he felt a sob in his throat to think of it. Though there weren't really all these many ships after all, not all that many when you considered them. Still, they should be able to put paid to Indonesia or France or any of the small countries who were always pushing us around. There was a click and the images disappeared. He let the telescope drop and walked off. Standing on the green by herself was a tall thin woman in black with a lorgnette, staring out at the ships. A leash hung over her left arm and a little dog was looking up at her.

He crossed the green and sat down in a shelter.

The only other person there was a woman in rather old brown furs, who was wearing gloves though the sun was blazing down. She leaned forward delicately as he sat down and said,

'Have you a match, please?' She took out a cigarette, holding it carefully between finger and thumb. He thought it was a Woodbine; she didn't offer him one. He held out the match for her and she inhaled deeply.

'Exciting, isn't it?' she said.

'The ships?'

'Yes, of course. To see our own Navy there. It gives one a lift. I suppose you were in the Navy yourself?'

He stared at her and saw the water turn a pale gold. Guns were firing, and a U-boat was surfaced beside the ship. The sun struck rays across the water towards them. Men were getting off the ship quite calmly. In a short while the U-boat would fire its last torpedo. Meanwhile, it would let them get into the boats.

Later there was the raft. Once he woke up turning a page of music as he sat on the piano stool. Strange that, out in the middle of the Pacific and the water swaying round a blue piano.

'Yes, I was in the Navy, madam.' He said 'madam' because she looked as if she had been a lady, though she hadn't offered him a cigarette.

'I suppose they come here every Saturday,' she said, pointing to the women lying on the grass, the boys in their bathing suits, and the little dogs running about.

'Ay, they do, every Saturday. And do you come here often yourself?'

'For the air,' she said, 'for the air. I come from Edinburgh actually.'

She smoked fastidiously, looking at him over the ruff at her neck.

'But it's changing now,' she added. 'Skyscrapers. And the music isn't the same as it was. Not the same quality. We used to go to the Usher Hall when we were girls. Have you ever been to the Usher Hall?'

'No, can't say I've been to the Usher Hall.'

'I must say that the tickets are getting very expensive,' she said. 'Why, I was over in America with my daughter some years ago, and tickets are no more expensive than here. And that was in New York.'

If you were in New York, he thought, what are you doing here in this shelter wearing a fur coat in the middle of July? He noticed beside her an umbrella with a gold knob; it looked like a king's sceptre.

'My own daughter's in Canada,' he said. 'She was good at the piano. She got lessons, you know. You should have heard her playing "The Anniversary Waltz".'

'You mean they didn't teach her Bach? But, of course, Stravinsky is all the rage now, though I don't understand him. Don't you think these Socialist people are ruining the country?' she said, flicking her ash on to the stone below. 'Why, it's disgraceful the prices of things. Ten cigarettes more than two shillings. Scandalous. And that Wilson's such an uncultured man.'

'Couldn't agree with you more,' said Harry, narrowing his eyes against the sun.

'And what do you do yourself, if I may ask?' she pursued.

'Oh, I'm retired now, madam. I used to be in business.'

'Oh, how interesting. Doing what, may I ask?'

'Selling jewellery. Upper class stuff, of course. I had a shop here till some years ago. Presley's.'

'I know Presley's. Did you run Presley's? Fancy that. The jewellery business must have been very interesting.'

'Yes, madam. Watches we did. And rings. One day a couple came in for a ring. A sailor he was, and his girlfriend. I remember they were very shy, especially the girl. Slip of a thing, she looked lovely. They asked for one of the rings in the window. It cost a hundred pounds but we didn't have a price tag on it. So I said thirty pounds, seeing they were so young and the girl was so pretty. Mind you, I wouldn't have done that for everybody. Only there was something about them, and they looked so young. The sailor didn't have much money, I could tell.'

'Go on,' she breathed, pointing her cigarette at him.

'I'd be as likely to overcharge if I saw someone I didn't like,' said Harry, adding wistfully. 'It was the emeralds I liked best of all. There's something about them.'

'Remind you of the sea, perhaps.'

'Perhaps. But my son didn't follow me into the jewellery business. That's why I gave up. He's in Africa, a surveyor. He's got a big business over there. In Bulawayo. He comes home quite a lot. Do you know Bulawayo?'

'No, I can't say that I know Bulawayo. Though I've a Boxer which I got from an African friend. I mean he's really European of course. The way they're treating Ian Smith is scandalous, don't you think? These blacks should be shut up somewhere. They're not fit for human consumption.'

'My son has three servants in Africa,' said Harry. 'They cost five shillings a week. All they want is bicycles, that's all they want. Do you know what he said to me once? He said one day he decided to raise the salaries of the Africans, and the Africans walked out. The whole lot of them. Do you know why?'

'I can't imagine.'

'Well, I'll tell you. They said that if they were worth that money they should have got it in the first place. What do you think of that?' His lips pursed angrily. 'They're not like us at all. They're not reasonable.'

'Imagine that! Of course, I quite agree with you. Where are you going now? Home for your dinner?'

'Pleased to have met you,' he said, without answering her question. What a glorious day it was! Oh, to be young again and sailing the Seven Seas, away from women with dogs and lorgnettes, and fat little boys running about with big balloons! For a moment he was stabbed by an incredible pain.

'We will meet again no doubt,' she said, avidly watching a little bald man who was making his way delicately across the sleeping bodies with which the strip was littered.

Harry headed for the pub.

'Hi, Harry,' said the barman who was a tall, skeletal and tough man, able by use of ju-jitsu to throw out on to the road the biggest bruisers of the town. He had a very small head set on a spindly body, and he was wearing a black jacket and a violet, if slightly stained, bow tie.

'How's things, Harry?'

'Oh, not so bad,' said Harry, grinning broadly.

'Got a car yet, Harry?'

'Not yet. Looking around, you know.'

'You do that, Harry, take your time. Reason I asked was you mentioned it. You should get a Cortina.'

Harry sat down in the corner seat which was upholstered in red leather. The place was a bit crowded with boys playing darts and gulping pies in between throws. They were in their shirt sleeves and had the clicking scoreboard working. Students some of them, perhaps, like Robin had been. It was true he once had a shop, but it was a newsagent's not a jeweller's. Sarah was happy in those days because she was kept busy, and there were always people to talk to. Also, people would look up to you if you had a shop. Only it had lasted for no more than three years and then it had gone the way of so many other shops when the big firms and the supermarkets came in. Anyway, he had never been a bookseller and he didn't know much about books. Robin used to work there during the vacation though he was a bit ashamed of it. He had tried to get better books in and that had been the start of the trouble. In Harry's experience most people wanted to buy westerns and romances (especially about nurses and doctors). But, no, Robin had brought in the heavy books, and they lay on his hands. These students reminded him of Robin. In those days they had a car as well. The barman was new, otherwise he would have known about that. But he had so many insults to put up with now: everyone thought they could say what they liked to him.

As he drank some beer a young naval rating came and sat down beside him, carefully placing his white cap on the table. He took out a copy of the *Evening Times* and turned to the sports page. Harry thought he looked very young with his close-cropped blond hair.

'Fine day,' said Harry, after a decent while.

'It is that,' said the rating putting down his paper. He seemed lonely.

'Nice little town you have here,' he said politely.

'Yes. Not been here before?'

'No, can't say I have. Come from England myself.'

'Do you know Portsmouth?' said Harry eagerly.

'Do I know Portsmouth? Yes, I've been in Portsmouth a lot of times.'

'Good Naafi there,' said Harry. 'Big place. Was there during the war, you know.'

'Oh, you were in the war, sir?' Very polite, these ratings, Harry thought.

'I was. In a cruiser. You wouldn't know it, I suppose. It was called the *Indomitable*. We were after the . . . ' He was going to say *Bismarck* but stopped himself in time. 'We were in the Atlantic most of the time.'

'Good for you,' said the rating, looking out of the window as he licked the foam from his lips.

'I suppose things have changed a lot since then,' said Harry, taking another swig. 'I mean, in the ships.'

'I suppose so,' said the rating. 'Not having been in the old ones, I wouldn't know.'

'You've got rockets now,' said Harry.

'Yes, we have.'

'Never thought of that in the old days. Just guns we had. I was a gunner myself. Used to get hot on your hands, they did.'

'I suppose they would.' This rating sounded a bit educated, Harry thought. Not like us.

'A sight for sore eyes they are,' said Harry, pointing vaguely out to sea.

'You mean the Navy? Oh, it's all right I suppose. Not really much in comparison with the Americans though we wouldn't say that to them. They've got a lot of aircraft carriers. We've only got two.'

'I was torpedoed once,' said Harry.

'Is that right? Well, I expect you'd have been picked up pretty rapid now. All sorts of new equipment. You live here?'

'Yes. Not all my days though,' said Harry quickly. 'I've been around. I was in the First World War and then I was in the second one too. That's where I got my leg from.'

'What? Oh, I see. Mean you were wounded?'

'When we ran into the spot of trouble I was. And my right arm isn't too good either.'

The rating finished his beer and was about to get up.

'I'll get you one,' said Harry expansively, coming to a decision. 'Must look after our Navy boys, you know.' He signalled to the barman to come over.

'Another pint for my friend here,' he said.

As the barman was bending down to take their glasses he said,

'What rank is he this time, Harry? Admiral?'

'What did he say?' said the rating after the barman had gone.

'Oh, nothing. He was only joking. They all know me.'

The barman returned with their beers, and Harry watched the rating drink. Very nice boy he looked, with direct, candid blue eyes.

'When are you leaving?' he asked.

'Not allowed to say that,' said the rating. 'But we shouldn't be here long. There's a visit tonight. The Prince himself, you know. The good old prince. All the trimmings. We're going back about five o'clock. Everyone's got to be back there by five o'clock. No shore leave tomorrow. Worse luck.'

He reminds me of Robin, thought Harry. The same clean-cut student look. He looked down at his drink.

'You liked the Navy, sir?'

'Yes, I did.'

'And what are you doing now, sir?'

'I'm retired. My son's in Africa, you know. He's an adminis-trator. He's got a top job there. He was in university, you know.'

The rating looked out of the window and drank quickly.

'There are some people going out to the ships, you know. We're running boats out tonight. You could come if you wanted to.'

'I could do that,' said Harry. The rating looked over Harry's head, his eyes focusing on the street outside as if he had an appointment.

'Tell you what,' he said, looking at a watch with a black leather strap on it, 'I've got to go now, but I'll be back here at five and you could come out with us then. Why don't you do that? Why don't you? Otherwise it'll cost you five bob.' He drank the rest of his beer, looking at Harry with blue, candid eyes.

'Can I get you something else before you go?' said Harry. 'Another pint.'

'Well, I really haven't got time. There's someone out there. But I'll be here at five o'clock.'

'You'll have time for a whisky,' Harry insisted. Without waiting for an answer, he went over to the bar. 'A whisky for my friend,' he told the barman. 'He's in a hurry. He's got an appointment. He's got to get ready for Prince Philip.'

'Right, Harry.' The barman poured out the whisky quickly, and Harry took it over to the table. The rating drank it quickly. 'This is good of you,' he said.

'Think nothing of it,' said Harry, nursing his beer. 'I shall expect you then at five.'

'Yes, that will be all right. I've got some shopping to do. What's your name by the way?'

'Harry Millar. Everyone in town knows me. Used to have a big business here. I've done a lot of trade with them in the past.'

'Yes. No point in you paying five shillings really.' He rushed out as if he had seen someone whom he wanted to meet.

The barman came over.

'What are you up to now, Harry?'

'It was the commodore's chauffeur,' said Harry. 'I'm going out with him in the ship's boat at five o'clock. He said I'd have a grandstand view when they switch on the lights.'

'Good for you, Harry. I heard people were being taken out. Nice-looking fellow.'

'Yes, we Navy boys are like that,' said Harry. He sipped his beer, thinking that he had about eight shillings left.

When he left the pub at three o'clock, he decided he'd go up to the house and leave a note for Sarah, telling her that he might be late. It was a strange experience. He hadn't been out past nine o'clock at night for ages, and he knew that he might be a bit later than that coming back. He felt rather frightened informing her of this in cold print, but a lot depended on what mood she was in. It reminded him of the old days when he used to go out for a Saturday night drink with the boys.

He sat down at the table and wrote: 'I have been given an invitation to go out to see the Fleet. The son of an old friend. He's a sub-lieutenant.' He signed it 'Henry' instead of 'Harry'. The room seemed to get on his nerves when he was in it alone; its emptiness appeared menacing and dull. It was the absence of Sarah's nagging that did it; by God, she was a missile for the Fleet all right! He put the note in an envelope and placed it on the mantelpiece so that she would see it immediately she came in.

As he was descending the stair he met his next-door neighbour who was mowing the lawn.

'Off again, Harry?'

'Yes, I'm afraid so. I have been suddenly invited out, to see the Fleet. An old family friend. He's a lieutenant in the Navy.'

The man looked at him seriously through thick glasses, grunted, then bent down to do something to a rose.

Harry limped on to the level and returned to the shore. He sat in a shelter looking out at the brilliant sea, watching the ships which he would soon see close to.

A fat woman sat at the far end of the shelter. She said,

'It's a grand sight, isn't it?'

'A grand sight,' Harry agreed, and then added, 'I know one of the lieutenants on board.'

'My son's a priest, you know,' she said, 'across the water.'

He didn't know at first whether she meant that her son was aboard or in a parish on the other side of the firth. She continued,

'But we Scots have a soft spot for the Navy, don't we?' She seemed to have a compulsion to talk.

'I come here every day,' she said. 'Every day. I used to be a conductress in my younger days. I remember the days when the trams had no roofs on them. People used to grab at the branches of the trees as we went past. That was at the time of the fair, you understand. My niece now, she's a student teacher. Wouldn't look at the pay of a conductress. But is she any happier, is she? Do you think they're any happier?'

'I don't know,' said Harry. 'I suppose they're not.'

'I used to scrub floors before that,' she said, 'and after that, too, during the Depression. We had seven of a family. The poorest of the poor, you could say. But my niece will take me to a hotel now, and they charge you for rubbish. I know what they do. I said to one of the waitresses, "You bring me more beef than that." And my niece was red in the face, but I got it. They think if they stick a piece of cardboard in the middle of the table that they can charge you double. No honesty in anybody these days. No honesty. My son, the priest, he's as honest as the day is long. You should see what he's done for the boys.'

'What boys?' said Harry.

'The hooligans. The juvenile delinquents. He works with them, you know. And they think the world of him. Mind you, he doesn't get much money, but he's happy. And that's the main thing, I think.' She added, 'Look at the poor sailors, there.' And true enough, there they were parading up and down in pairs following the giggling girls.

In the distance, Harry saw Sonny walking along with his stick. The fool. He should have stayed at home instead of showing that all he had been saying about his son-in-law was a lie. But no! He saw that Sonny had stopped at a café and was talking to a little bald man and a harassed looking woman who was probably his wife. A boy with a lollipop in his hand was dancing up and down between the two of them. So they had come to see Sonny after all. But then again, perhaps they hadn't gone to the hotel for their dinner, perhaps they had only been to the café, for sausages and chips, tea, and pieces of stale soggy bread. And he was glad again till he saw them going into a small green car which was parked just in front of the café. So Sonny had been telling the truth: he felt desolated.

'I was saying that priests nowadays don't get the respect they deserve,' said the woman, 'nor teachers either. My niece was telling me the other day about this little boy who spat at her. Imagine it. He just spat at her. The wee hooligan.'

Harry got up, and, excusing himself, limped down to the shore. There was no wood to be seen, just waves coming in across wiry seaweed. A little dog panted for a ball which his master held in his right hand.

Harry made his way along to the café and ordered a cup of coffee. There was a play on the TV set, but he couldn't hear a word, he could just see figures gesticulating. It seemed to be a western, set in a sandy desert. He toyed with his coffee for a long time, and nibbled a Blue Riband when he caught the waitress looking at him. Who was she anyway? This was his town, he had lived here much longer than she had. He felt the anger rising in him as he looked at the café owner, that greasy Italian. Why was he making money hand over hand while he, Harry, a native of this place, was destitute? After fifteen minutes he went into the lavatory and sat down.

'Good afternoon, Mr Capaldi,' he said as he was going out, but the florid proprietor, who was engaged in composing a slider, didn't answer: perhaps he hadn't heard. In the far corner the coffee machine was hammering away.

It was now quarter to five. He walked down slowly to the pub, making his way along the crowded pavement. He bought an evening paper at the corner from a man with a green bag, and opened it out. The headlines were still about the fire, though it mentioned the visit of the Prince to the Fleet. It now looked as if some people had been burned in the fire; the shop was about three hundred yards from where they used to live. He remembered going past it often when Sarah was in hospital having Helen. As he stood there among the drifting crowd studying the photographs, the area they represented seemed to be more real to him than the town in which he was staying now. It symbolised his youth when he was whole both in body and mind.

At five o'clock the rating rushed up. He had a girl with him; he had picked her up somewhere. She wore thick violet lipstick and smoked glasses, and she went careering on, giggling, hanging on to his hand.

'Will you slow doon?' she shouted in a young gale of laughter.

'Come on,' he said, 'I promised this gentleman we'd take him out to the ship. What time is it? Is that clock slow?' he asked Harry.

'I don't know,' said Harry.

'Have you got a watch?'

'No, I'm sorry . . .' He wished he had more time to invent an explanation as to why he had no watch, but the rating was already in motion.

He rushed them down to the pier. They had to cross the road, and there was a big traffic jam with a policeman, in white gloves, standing there directing operations. Car after car passed, loaded to the gunwales with luggage or trailing caravans.

'It's always like this,' said Harry.

The girl regarded him curiously though he couldn't see her eyes because of the glasses. Her face was very white and she was wearing a necklace of big stones shaped like miniature loaves.

'Could we no get across noo?' she said. The rating looked down at her as if not understanding what she was saying, but then tightened his grip as if in compensation. They got across and rushed down to the wooden pier where the boat was lying. Her heels made a staccato beat on the wood as she went flying along, clinging to the sailor's hand, Harry panting gamely behind the two of them. They passed the lavatories and reached the end of the pier. The launch was just about ready to go.

'Thank God,' thought Harry. 'Thank God we're here in time.' The girl stood at the edge of the pier, looking down at her shiny black shoes; she seemed like a figurehead staring out across the glittering water.

From the boat below they heard a voice: 'Where the f—— hell do you think you've been, Green?'

'I'm sorry, Petty Officer, there's something wrong with that clock.'

'Come on then. Hurry up.'

The rating looked at the two of them, swallowed, and said, 'He seems to be in a bad mood today. It doesn't look as if . . . '

'Who are these people, Green? You're not going off to Vietnam you know. Get a f —— move on.'

Green looked at the two of them and then at the boat, and then said,

'Sorry, I'm afraid it's no go.' Then he was gone, dwindling down the ladder, leaving the girl in the smoked glasses and Harry staring after him.

The girl leaned over the edge, tottering slightly, and said,

'You bastard,' watching behind her smoked glasses her spit floating towards him.

Then she turned away and said to Harry,

'The bastard. I was in the flicks with him all afternoon, and he was all over me, and he promised that he'd take me out to the ship. The bastard.' Her heels clicked decisively back down the wooden pier. Harry saw the people at the pier staring at him, and he waved feebly out to sea.

Then he trudged away from the pier towards home.

At eight o'clock, three hours or so after he had destroyed the note, Sarah came back. She laid her bag down on the table in the hall and went into the room, collapsing in a chair and passing her hand over her brow.

'Made any tea?' she said at last.

'Yes, I've made tea.' She looked at him, sensing something in his voice, but then swept on. 'The day I've had. Have you been telephoning again?'

'No, not today.'

'I should hope not. The bill will be coming soon. That Fête. So many people. And there was nothing one could buy. Even if I had the money. Just mouldy old stuff.'

He put the cups down on the table quietly, almost said something but then didn't. He lay in the chair like an exhausted boxer.

'Was Milne there?' he asked in the same chastened voice.

'Yes. And his wife too. Wearing lemon.'

'What happened?'

'Let me tell you. First of all I met Miss Melon and her friend. This was a big bony woman. By the way, all the people at the Fête were asking for you. They were all saying, "Where's Harry?", and asking about Helen, of course, and Robin. I couldn't very well tell them that we didn't know, that we never heard from them. Once I was standing there looking at a book and this snooty woman came round and said, "That's my book, you know. Do you mind? I've just bought it." So I gave her a piece of my mind. Anyway, I went for lunch with Miss Melon and her friend, and Miss Melon was talking about Robin and how clever he was with his job in Africa an' all. And we had lunch. We had chicken soup and braised steak and trifle and coffee with Danish cheese. And by the way, Sonny was in, with a wee woman and a bald man and a very badly behaved child.

They had a look at the menu, and then they went out again. Perhaps the place was too crowded or perhaps the food was too expensive.' By this time she had removed her stockings, and he had handed her the cup of tea. She looked very old and tired by the fire, wearing her glasses with the blue demon frames.

'And, Harry, that Miss Melon, she was called out. It was a phone call. And so I was left with that big-boned woman who hardly spoke all the time we were there. As well as being a teacher, she owns a block of tenements, you know. And the long and the short of it was that I had to pay for the whole dinner. Two pounds, ten shillings and sixpence. This woman, Harry, she had eyes like stones, and what she was doing at a Conservative fête I don't know, what with her tenements and all. She looked half Russian and the only thing she bought all day was a bunch of violets. Anyway, I had to pay for everything. And Miss Melon came back full of apologies, and she kept on talking about Robin. She set my teeth on edge. So I just left them there. I couldn't stand them talking about Robin.'

'Why not?'

'Why not, Harry, why not? That's all Robin's been to us, an expense. And Helen too. We brought them up and they forgot us. They don't think about us any more. It's high time we thought about that, it's high time we realised it, Harry. And Helen's just as bad as Robin. She's probably as bad as that slab-faced woman now. She never was a beauty. I saw someone like Robin today. He was walking along with Milne, he had bright eyes and glasses that glitter, and he was talking to people but he wasn't really listening. I've seen that with Robin too. I've seen the day I would talk to Robin and he would bend down, but he wasn't really listening. I've seen it, Harry.'

'What do you mean, you've seen that with Robin?' Harry shouted angrily.

'You know what I mean,' she said. 'You know it. He doesn't care. If we still had the shop he might recognise us. But not now. Not Robin.'

'He's away in Africa. You know that.'

'I know, but does he ever send me a present at Christmas, does he, Harry? Don't think I don't feel that. He sends a

Christmas card, and it's written by his wife. But does he send me a present? No, he doesn't and he never will. Robin only thinks about himself. We've bred two monsters, Harry. He sends us a card, when he's away on holiday somewhere, with a lot of Xs. What's the use of that? But does he ever spend any money on us? Does he ask us out? We've never seen his children. He sends us photographs and tells us about their IQs, Harry, and how much they weigh, and he tells us about the house and the new gadgets, but that's all, Harry. He doesn't give us anything of himself. We came up the hard way, Harry, but he doesn't care. We're on our own, Harry, that's what we are. We're on our own.'

He looked down at her and shouted in an unreasoning frenzy as if part of him were being squeezed to death.

'What are you talking about? We'll see him again. He won't stay in Africa forever.'

'Why not, Harry?'

There was a silence. 'What happened today?' she asked him. 'I know something happened. I can tell. We've been too long together for me not to know.'

So he told her about the lieutenant he'd met.

'Are you sure he was a lieutenant, Harry?'

'Of course he was a lieutenant. I saw the pips, didn't I? And he invited me to the ship but I couldn't manage. I had to come back, all because of you.'

'Is that true, Harry?'

'It's as true as anything you've been saying about Robin,' he shouted.

'No, Harry, it's not. What I've said about Robin is true. If you'd been going out to the ship, you'd have gone, only you'd have left a note, because you want to do what's right. Do you think I don't know you after forty years?'

She looked in the wastepaper basket and there, sure enough, was the note, crumpled up.

'Why didn't you go, Harry? Was it really a lieutenant? It was a rating, wasn't it? If he had been a lieutenant, you'd have made him a commodore. It was really a rating. Tell me, Harry.'

So he told her, half rending himself in the process. He hadn't realised how hard it was to tell the truth. She had to prompt him over silences and direct him away from lies.

When he had finished, she said,

'I see. It was very bad of him, wasn't it? Just to get a beer and a whisky. It was very mean. That's why we've got to realise we're on our own, Harry. No one's going to fly in from Africa or from Canada. Do you see that, Harry? We were young once, and now we're old and we're on our own. We've got to muddle through somehow and be as humble and as proud as our circumstances permit. Have you had any tea?'

'No.'

'Drink it now, then, while it's still warm. We're still thinking of ourselves as boys and girls. I'm an old woman and you're an old man, Harry. And there I am just as bad as you, going to a Conservative fête.'

He drank his tea. She went next door and he followed her. She took down the photographs of her son and daughter from the top of the piano and put them in a drawer. She put all the music away into a drawer. The last one he saw was 'Silver Threads among the Gold'.

Then she drew him over to the window. It was getting dark, and she didn't put the light out. Out in the bay they could see the lights of the ships, very bright, twinkling like a bracelet, the lights of the British Navy. Not really all that many, he thought, when you came to think of it. And after all they couldn't beat the Americans and the Russians, and these were the countries that mattered. In the half light he could imagine Sarah as young again. His voice became tender when he spoke to her. Sensing this she went over and switched on the lights. The room was now so bright he could see her, loved and pitiless, but he couldn't see the lights of the ships so well. So he thought he might as well draw the curtains. So that the two of them could learn to be alone, for that was the way it was going to be.

Survival without Error

I don't often think about that period in my life. After all, when one comes down to it, it was pretty wasteful.

And, in fact, it wasn't thought that brought it back to me: it was a smell. To be exact, the smell of after-shave lotion. I was standing in front of the bathroom mirror – as I do every morning at about half past eight, for I am a creature of habit – and I don't know how it was, but that small bottle of Imperial after-shave lotion – yellowish golden stuff it is – brought it all back. Or, to be more exact, it was the scent of the lotion on my cheeks after I had shaved, not the colour. I think I once read something in a *Reader's Digest* about an author – a Frenchman or a German – who wrote a whole book after smelling or tasting something. I can't remember what it was exactly: I don't read much, especially not fiction, you can't afford to when you're a lawyer.

So there I was in the bathroom on that July morning preparing to go to the office – which is actually only about five hundred yards or so away, so that I don't even need to take the car – and instead of being in the bathroom waiting to go in to breakfast with Sheila, there I was in England fifteen years ago. Yes, fifteen years ago. Exactly. For it was July then too.

And all that day, even in court, I was thinking about it. I even missed one or two cues, though the sheriff himself does that, for he's a bit deaf. I don't often do court work: there's no money in it and I don't particularly care for it anyway. To tell the truth, I'm no orator, no Perry Mason. I prefer dealing with cases I can handle in my office, solicitor's work mainly. I have a certain head for detail but not for the big work.

I suppose if I hadn't put this shaving lotion on I wouldn't have remembered it again. I don't even know why I used that lotion today: perhaps it was because it was a beautiful summer morning and I felt rather lighthearted and gay. I don't use lotions much though I do make use of Vaseline hair tonic as I'm getting a bit bald. I blame that on the caps we had to wear all the time during those two years of National Service in the army. Navy-blue berets they were. And that's what the shaving lotion brought back.

Now I come to think of them, those years were full of things like boots, belts and uniforms. We had two sets of boots – second best boots and (if that makes any sense) first best boots. (Strictly speaking, it seems to be wrong to use the word 'best' about two objects, but this is the first time I've located the error.) Then again we had best battle dress and second best battle dress. (Again, there were only two lots.)

We always had to be cleaning our boots. The idea was to burn your boots so that you could get a proper shine, the kind that would glitter back at you brighter than a mirror, that would remove the grain completely from the toes. Many a night I've spent with hot liquefied boot polish, burning and rubbing till the dazzling shine finally appeared, till the smoothness conquered the rough grain.

We really had to be very clean in those days. Our faces too. In those days one had to be clean-shaven, absolutely clean-shaven, and, to get the tart freshness into my cheeks, I used shaving lotion, which is what brought it all back. The rest seems entirely without scent, without taste, all except the lotion.

I went to the army straight from university and I can still remember the hot crowded train on which I travelled all through the night and into the noon of the following day. Many of the boys played cards as we hammered our way through the English stations.

I am trying to remember what I felt when I boarded that train and saw my sister and mother waving their handkerchiefs at the station. To tell the truth, I don't think I felt anything. I didn't think of it as an adventure, still less as a patriotic duty. I felt, I think, numbed; my main idea was that I must get it over with as cleanly and as quickly as I could, survive without error.

About noon, we got off the train and walked up the road to the camp. It was beautiful pastoral countryside with hot flowers growing by the side of the road; I think they were foxgloves. In the distance I could see a man in a red tractor ploughing. I thought to myself: This is the last time I shall see civilian life for a long time.

After we had been walking for some time, still wearing our bedraggled suits (in which we had slept the previous night) and carrying our cases, we arrived at the big gate which was the entrance to the camp. There was a young soldier standing there – no older than ourselves – and he was standing at ease with a rifle held in front of him, its butt resting on the ground. His hair was close cropped under the navy-blue cap with the yellow badge, and when we smiled at him, he stared right through us. Absolutely right through us, as if he hadn't seen us at all.

We checked in at the guardroom and were sent up to the barracks with our cases. As we were walking along – very nervous, at least I was – we passed the square where this terrible voice was shouting at recruits. There were about twenty of them and they looked very minute in the centre of that huge square, all grey and stony.

In any case – I can't remember very clearly what the preliminaries were – we ended up in this barrack room and sat down on the beds which had green coverings and one or two blankets below. There must have been twelve of these beds – about six down each side – and a fire-place in the middle of the room with a flue.

Now, I didn't know anything about the army though some of the others did. One or two of them had been in the Cadets (I remember one small, plump-cheeked, innocent-looking young-ster of eighteen who had been in the cadet corps in some English public school: he looked like an angel, and he was reading an author called Firbank) but the rest of us didn't know what to expect. Of course, I'd seen films about the army (though not many since I was a conscientious student, not patronising the cinema much) and thought that they were exaggerated. In any case, as far as my memory went, these films made the army out to be an amusing experience with a lot of hard work involved, and though sergeants and corporals appeared terrifying, they really had hearts of gold just the same. There used to be a glint in the sergeant's eye as he mouthed obscenities at some recruit, and he would always praise his platoon to a fellow sergeant over a pint in the mess that same night. That was the impression I got from the films.

Well, it's a funny thing: when we went into the army it was at first like a film (it became a bit more real later on). We were sitting on our beds when this corporal came in (at least we were told by himself that he was a corporal: I was told off on my second day for calling a sergeant major 'sir' though I was only being respectful). The first we knew of this corporal was a hard click of boots along the floor and then this voice shouting, 'Get on your feet'. I can tell you we got up pretty quickly and stood trembling by our beds.

He was a small man, this corporal, with a moustache, and he looked very fit and very tense. You could almost feel that his moustache was actually growing and alive. He was wearing shiny black boots, a shiny belt buckle, a yellow belt and a navy-blue cap with a shining badge in it. And when we were all standing at a semblance of attention, he started pacing up and down in front of us, sometimes stopping in front of one man and then in front of another, and coming up and speaking to them with his face right up against theirs. And he said (as they do on the films),

'Now, you men are going to think I'm a bastard. You're going to want to go home to mother. You're going to work like slaves and you're going to curse the day you were born. You're going to hate me every day and every night, if you have enough strength left to dream. But there's one thing I'm going to say to you and it's this: if you play fair by me I'll play fair by you. Is that understood?'

There was a long silence during which I could hear a fly buzzing over at the window which was open at the top, and through which I could see the parade ground.

Then he said,

'Get out there. We're going to get you kitted out at the quartermaster's.'

And that was it. I felt as if I had been hit by a bomb. I had never met anyone like that in my life before. And it was worse when one had come from a university. Not even the worst teacher I had met had that man's controlled ferocity and energy. You felt that he hated you for existing, that you looked untidy, and that he was there to make you neater than was possible.

All this came back to me very quickly as a result of a whiff of that shaving lotion and, as I said, even during my time in the court I kept thinking about that period fifteen years before so that the sheriff had to speak to me once or twice.

The case itself was a very bad one, not the kind we usually get in this town which is small and nice, the kind of town where everyone knows everybody else and the roads are lined with trees. The background to the case was this:

Two youths were walking along the street late at night when they saw this down-and-out sitting on a bench. He had a bottle of VP and he was drinking from it. The two youths went over and asked him for a swig, but he wouldn't give them any so, according to the police, they attacked him and, when he was down, they kicked him in the face and nearly killed him. In fact, he is in hospital at this moment and close to death. The youths, of course, deny all this and say that they never saw him before in their lives, and that they don't know what the police are on about.

They are a very unprepossessing pair, I must confess, barely literate, long-haired, arrogant and contemptuous. They wear leather jackets, and one has a motor bike. They have a history of violence at dance halls, and one of them has used a knife. I don't like them. I don't like them because I don't understand them. We ourselves are childless (Sheila compensates for that by painting a lot), but that isn't the reason why I dislike them. They don't care for me either and call me 'daddy'. They are more than capable of doing what the police say they did, and there is in fact a witness, a young girl who was coming home from a dance. She says that she heard one of the youths say, 'I wish the b—— would stop making that noise.' They are the type of youths who have never done well in school, who haven't enough money to get girls for themselves since they are always unemployed, and they take their resentment out on others. I would say they are irreclaimable, and probably in Russia they would be put up against a wall and shot. However, they have to have someone to defend them. One of them had the cheek to say to me,

'You'd better get us off, daddy.'

They made a bad impression in the court. One of them says,

'What would we need that VP crap for, anyway?' It's this language that alienates people from them, but they're too stupid or too arrogant to see that. As well as this they accuse the police of beating them up with truncheons when they were taken in. But this is a common ploy.

Anyway, I kept thinking of the army all the time I was in court, and once I even said 'sergeant' to the judge. It was a totally inexplicable error. It's lucky for me that he's slightly deaf.

I was thinking of Lecky all the time.

Now, I suppose every platoon in the army has to have the odd one out, the one who can never keep in step, the one who never cleans his rifle properly, the one whose trousers are never properly pressed. And our platoon like all others had one. His name was Lecky. (The platoon in the adjacent hut had one too, though I can't remember his name. He, unlike Lecky, was a scholarly type with round glasses and he was the son of a bishop. I remember he had this big history book by H. A. L. Fisher and he was always reading it, even in the Naafi, while we were buying our cakes of blanco, and buns and tea. I wonder if he ever finished it.)

Funny thing, I can't remember Lecky's features very well. I was trying to do so all day, but unsuccessfully. I think he was small and black-haired and thin-featured. I'm not even sure what he did in Civvy Street, but I believe I once heard it mentioned that he was a plumber's mate.

The crowd in our platoon were a mixed lot. There were two English ex-schoolboys and a number of Scots, at least two of them from Glasgow. There was also a boxer, who spoke with a regional, agricultural accent. One of the public schoolboys had a record player which he had brought with him. He was a jazz devotee and I can still remember him plugging it into the light and playing, on an autumn evening, a tune called 'Love, O, Love, O, Careless Love'. The second line, I think, was, 'You fly to my head like wine'. The public schoolboys were very composed people (certain officers), and the chubby-cheeked one was always reading poetry.

Lecky stood out from the first day. First of all, he couldn't keep in step. We used to march along swinging our arms practically up to our foreheads and then this voice from miles away would shout across the square, 'Squad, Halt!' Then the little corporal would march briskly across the square, and he'd come to a halt in front of Lecky and he'd say (the square was scorching with the heat in the middle of a blazing July), his face thrust up close to him, 'What are you, Lecky?' And Lecky would say, 'I don't know, Corporal.' And the corporal would say, 'You're a bastard, aren't you, Lecky?' And Lecky would say, 'I'm a bastard, Corporal.' Then the marching would start all over again, and Lecky would still be out of step.

It is strange about these corporals, how they want everything to be so tidy, as if they couldn't stand sloppiness, as if untidiness is a personal insult to them. I suppose really that the whole business becomes so mindlessly boring after a few years of it that the only release for them is the manic anger they generate.

Of course, Lecky got jankers. What this involved was that after training was over for the day (usually at about four o'clock) he would put on his best boots, best battle dress, best tie, best everything and report to the guardroom at the double. Then, after he had been inspected (if he didn't get more jankers for sloppiness) he would double up to the barrack room again, change into denims, and go off to his assigned fatigue which might involve weeding or peeling potatoes or helping to get rid of swill at the cookhouse.

Continual jankers are a dreadful strain. You have to have all your clothes pressed for inspection at the guardroom; as well as that, boots and badges must be polished and belts must be blancoed. You live in a continual daze of spit and polish and ironing, and the only time you can find to do all this is after you have come back from your assigned task which is often designed to make you as dirty as possible. There is rapid change of clothes from battle dress to denims and back again. For after your fatigues are over you have to change back into battledress to be inspected at the guardroom for a second time. I must say that I used to feel sorry for him.

His bed was beside mine. I never actually spoke to him much. For one thing his only form of reading was comics, and we had very little in common. For another thing – though this is difficult to explain – I didn't want to be infected by his bad luck. And after all what could I have done for him even if I had been able to communicate with him?

The funny thing was that as far as the rest of us were concerned the corporal became more relaxed as the training progressed and treated us as human beings. He would bellow at us out on the square, but at nights he would often talk to us. He'd even listen to the jazz records though he preferred pop. All this time while the others were gathered round the record player, the corporal in the middle, Lecky would be rushing about blancoing or polishing or making his bed tidy. Sometimes the corporal would shout at him, 'Get a move on, Lecky, are you a f—— snail or something?' And Lecky would give him a startled glance, before he would continue with whatever he was doing.

I never saw him write a letter. I have a feeling he couldn't write very well. In fact, when he was reading the comics, you could see his lips move and his finger travel along the page. Once I even saw the corporal pick up one of the comics and sit on the bed quite immersed in it for a while.

At the beginning, Lecky seemed quite bright. He even managed to make a joke out of that classic day when he was first taught to fire the bren. Instead of setting it to single rounds, he released the whole batch of bullets in one burst and nearly ripped the target to shreds. I saw the corporal bending down very gently beside him and saying to him equally slowly, 'What a stupid uneducated b—— you are, Lecky.' He got jankers for that too.

But, as the weeks passed, a fixed look of despair pervaded his face. He acted as if his every movement was bound to be a mistake, as if he had no right to exist, and that carefree open-faced appearance of his faded to leave a miserable white mask. Sometimes you wonder if it was right.

The more I see of these two people in the court, the more I'm sure that they really are guilty of hitting that old man, though they themselves swear blind they didn't do it. They keep insisting that they are being victimised by the police and that they were beaten up at the station. They even picked on one of the policemen as the one who did it. He very gravely refuted the charges. One of them says he never drank VP in his life, that he thinks it's a drink only tramps use, and that he himself has only drunk whisky or beer. He is quite indignant about it: one could almost believe him. They also accuse the girl of framing them because one of them had a fight with her brother once on a bus. But their attitude is very defiant and it isn't doing them any good. My wife was away yesterday seeing her mother so I had to go to Armstrong's for lunch. Armstrong's is opposite the court which is in turn just beside the police station. As I was entering the restaurant I was passed by the superintendent who greeted me very coldly, I thought. He is a tall broad individual, very proud of his rank, and you can see him standing at street corners looking very official and stern, with his white gloves in his hands, staring across the traffic, one of his minions, usually a sergeant, standing beside him. I wondered why he was so distant, especially as we often play bowls together and have been known to play a game of golf.

It struck me afterwards that perhaps he thought I had put them up to their accusations against the police. After all, we mustn't undermine the authority of the police as they have a lot to put up with, and, even if they do use truncheons now and again, we must remember the kind of people they are dealing with. I believe in the use of psychology to a certain extent, but the victim must be protected too.

There was the time, too, when Lecky nearly killed off the

platoon with a grenade. After a while it got so that hardly anyone in the hut spoke to him much. At the beginning they used to play tricks on him, like messing up his blankets, but that was before the corporal got to work on him (no, that's not strictly true, the Glasgow boys were doing it even after that). Most of the time we didn't see him at all, as he was so often on jankers. I don't know why we didn't speak to him. I think it was something about him that made us uneasy: I can only express it by saying that we felt him to be a born victim. It was as if he attracted trouble and we didn't want to be in the neighbour-hood when it struck. We didn't want to have to do that spell of ten weeks' training all over again as Lecky was sure to do.

One morning we had an inspection. We had inspections every Saturday: the CO (distant, precise, immaculately uniformed) would come along, busily accompanied by the sergeant major, the sergeant, and corporal of the platoon. Oh, and the lieutenant as well (our lieutenant had been to Cambridge). We would all be standing by our beds, of course, rifles ready so that the CO could peer down the barrel, followed in pecking order by all the members of his entourage. If there was a single spot of grease we were for it. Our beds had all our possessions laid out on them, blanco, fork, knife and spoon, vest, pants, and much that I can't now remember. All, naturally, had to be spotlessly clean.

So there we were, standing stiff and frightened as the CO stalked up the room followed by the rest of his minions, the corporal with a small notebook in his hand. Unwavering and taut, we stared straight ahead of us, through the narrow window that gave out on the outside world which appeared to be composed of stone, as the only thing we could see was the parade ground.

Our hearts would be in our boots as we took the bolt out of the rifle and the CO would squint down the barrel to see if there was any grease. Mine was all right, but a moment later I heard a terrifying scream from the CO as if he had been mortally wounded. I couldn't even turn my head.

'Take this man's name. His rifle's dirty.' And the sergeant major passed it down to the corporal who put the name in the notebook. The CO proceeded on his tour round the room poking distastefully here and there with his stick, and staring at people's faces to see if they had shaved properly. I remember thinking it was rather like the way farmers prod cattle to see if they are fat and healthy enough. On one occasion he even got the sergeant major to tell someone to raise his feet to see if all the nails in the soles of his boots were still present and correct. Then he went on to the next hut, his retinue behind him.

And the corporal came up to Lecky, his face contorted with rage, and, punching him in the chest with his finger, said, 'You perverted motherless b——, you piece of camel's dung, do you know what you've done? You've gone and stopped the week-end leave for this platoon. That's what you've done. And don't any of you public school wallahs write to your MPs about it either. As for you, Lecky, you're up before the CO in the morning, and I hope he throws the book at you. I sincerely hope he gives you guard duty for eighteen years.'

Now this was the first weekend we were going to have since we had entered the camp five weeks before. We hadn't been beyond the barracks and the square all that time. Blancoing, polishing, marching, eating, sleeping, waking at half past six in the morning, often shaving in cold water – that had been the pattern of our days. We hadn't even seen the town: we hadn't been to a café or a cinema. All that time we hadn't seen a civilian except for the ones working in the Naafi. So, of course, you can guess how we felt. I wasn't myself desperate. I wasn't particularly interested in girls (though later on when I was in hospital I got in tow with a nurse). I didn't drink. All I wanted was to get that ten weeks over. But I also wanted to put on my clean uniform just for once, and walk by myself, without being shouted at, down the anonymous streets of some town and see people even if I didn't talk to them. I would have been happy just to look in the shop windows, to stroll in the cool evening air, to board a bus, anything at all to get out of that hut.

There were two Glasgow boys there, and they went up to Lecky when the corporal had left and said to him, 'You stupid c——, what do you think you've done?' or words to that effect. They were practically insane with rage. For the past weeks all they had talked about was this weekend and the bints they would get off with, the dance they would go to, and so on. In fact, I think that if either of them had a knife they would have run him through with it. And all this time Lecky sat on his bed petrified as if he had been shell-shocked. He was so shell-shocked that he didn't even answer. He didn't even cry. I had heard him crying once in the middle of the night. But there was nothing I could do. What could anyone do? I must say that I felt these Glasgow boys were going too far and I turned away, feeling uncomfortable.

Lecky was trying to pull a piece of rag through his rifle in order to clean it. One of the Glasgow boys took the rag from him (Lecky surrendered it quite meekly as if he didn't know what was happening, and indeed, I don't think he did know), rubbed it on the floor and then pulled it through the rifle again. The other tumbled Lecky's bed on to the floor, upsetting everything in it. (All this time the chubby-cheeked boy was reading Firbank.)

'You'd best keep in tonight,' the Glasgow boy said. 'If I get you outside . . . ' and he made a motion of cutting Lecky's throat. Lecky sat on the floor looking up at him, deadly pale, his adam's apple going up and down in his throat.

'And no help for this bastard from any of you, anymore,' said the Glasgow boy, turning on us threateningly. The boxer, I remember, grinned amiably like a big dog. I think even he was afraid of the Glasgow boys, but I don't know. He was pretty hefty too, and the corporal spoke more softly to him than to any of the rest of us.

So Lecky went up next morning and got another three weeks of jankers, and on top of that he had trouble from the Glasgow boys as well. I would have said something to them, but what would I have gained? They would just have started on me. The sergeant was a placid family man and he left everything to the corporal. The sergeant was pretty nice really: a nice stout man who was very good at handing out the parcels any of us got and making sure that he got a signature. It was funny how Lecky never wrote any letters.

So the time came for our passing-out parade, to be inspected by a brigadier, one of those officers with a monocle, and a red cap, and a shooting stick. Of course, our own CO would be there as well.

I remember that morning well. It was a beautiful autumn morning, almost melancholy and very still. We were up very early, at about half past five, and I can still recall going out to the door of the hut and standing there regarding the dim deserted square. I am not a fanciful person but, as I stood there, I felt almost as if it were waiting for us, for the drama that we could provide, and that without us it was without meaning. It had taken much from us – perhaps our youth – but it had given us much too. I felt both happy and sad at the same time, sad because I had come to the end of something, and happy because I would be leaving that place shortly.

I don't know if the others felt the sadness, but they certainly felt the happiness. They were skylarking about, throwing water at each other from the wash-basins and singing at the tops of their voices. The ablutions appeared on that day to be a well-known and almost beloved place though I could remember shaving there in the coldest of water, in front of the cracked mirror. Today, however, it was different. In a few hours we would be standing on the square, then we would be marching to the sound of the bagpipes.

And after that we would all leave – all, that is, except Lecky. We were even sorry to be leaving the corporal, who had become more and more genial as the weeks passed, who condescended to be human and would almost speak to us on equal terms. He had even been known to pass round his cigarettes and to offer a drink in the local pub. Perhaps after all he had to be tough; one must always remember the kind of people with whom he often had to deal. For instance, there was one recruit who was in his fourth year of National Service; every chance he got he went over the wall and the MPs had to chase him all over the north of England. That's just stupidity, of course. You can't beat the army, you should resign yourself. Rebellion won't get you anywhere. I believe he had a rough time in the guardroom every time they got him back, but he was indomitable. You almost had to admire him in a way.

Anyway, I found myself standing beside Lecky at the wash basin. I could see his thin face reflected in the mirror beside my own. There was no happiness in it, and one could not call what one saw sadness: it was more like apathy, utter absence of feeling of any kind. I saw him put his hand in his shaving bag, look again, then become panicky. He turned everything out on to the ledge but he couldn't find what he was looking for. I looked straight into the mirror where my face appeared cracked and webbed. He turned to me.

'Have you a razor blade?' he said. To the other side of him I saw the two Glasgow boys grinning at me. One of them drew an imaginary razor across his throat, a gesture which in spite of his smile I interpreted as a threat.

I knew what would happen to Lecky if he turned up on parade unshaven. I looked down at my razor and remembered that I had some more in my bag. I looked at the grinning boys and knew that they had taken Lecky's blade.

I said to him, 'Sorry I've only got the one blade, the one in the razor.' After all, one must be clean. It would be a disgusting thing to lend anyone else one's razor blade: why, he might catch a disease. It is quite easy to do that. There's one thing about the army: it teaches you to be clean. I was never so fit and clean in my life as during that period I spent in the army.

I turned away from the grinning Glasgow boys and looked steadily into the mirror, leaning forward to see beyond the cracks as if that were possible. I shaved very carefully, because this was an important day, cutting the stubble away with ease under the rich white lather, the white towel wrapped round my neck.

I should like to describe that parade in detail, but I can't now exactly capture my feelings. I began very clumsily, not quite in tune with the music of the pipes, but, as the day warmed, and as the colours became clearer, and as the sun shone on our boots and our badges, and as I saw the brigadier standing on the saluting platform, and as my body grew to know itself apart from me, I had the extraordinary experience of becoming part of a consciousness that was greater than myself, of entering a mysterious harmony. Never before or since did I feel like that, did I experience that kinship which exists between those who have become expert at the one thing and are able to execute a precise function as one person. It was like a mystical experience: I cannot hope to describe it now. Perhaps one had to be young and fit and proud to experience it. One had perhaps to feel that life was ahead of one, with its many possibilities. Today I think of Sheila and a childless marriage and a solicitor's little office. Perhaps, for once in my life, I sensed the possible harmony of the universe. Perhaps it is only once we sense it. Not even in sex have I felt that unity. It was as if I had fallen in love with harmony and as if I was grateful to the army for giving me that experience. And after all, at the age I was at then, it is easy to believe in music: I could have sworn that all those men were good because they marched so expertly to the bagpipes, and that anyone who was out of step was bad, and that it would be intolerable for the harmony to be spoilt. I began to understand the corporal, and to be sorry for those who had never experienced the feeling that I was then experiencing.

At that moment all was forgotten, the angry words, the barbaric barrack room, the eternal spit and polish, the heartbreak of those nights when I had lain sleeplessly in bed watching the moonlight turn the floor to yellow and hearing the infinitely melancholy sound of the Last Post. All was forgiven because of the exact emotion I felt then, that pride that I had come through, that I was one with the others, that I was not a misfit.

When the parade was over, I ran into the barrack room with the others. There was no one in the room except Lecky who was lying on his bed. I went over to him, thinking he was ill. He had shot himself by putting the rifle in his mouth and pulling the trigger. The green coverlet on the bed was completely red and blood was dripping on to the scrubbed wooden floor. I ran outside and was violently sick. Looking back now I think it was the training that did it. I didn't want to be sick on that clean floor.

Of course, there was an inquiry but nothing came of it. No one wrote to his MP or to the press after all, not even the public schoolboys. There was even a certain sympathy for the corporal: after all, he had his career to make and there were many worse than him. The two public schoolboys became officers: one in the Infantry and the other in education. I never saw them again. Perhaps the corporal is a sergeant major now. Anyway, it was a long time ago but it was the first death I had ever seen.

The sheriff leaned down and spoke briefly to the two youths after they had been found guilty. He adjusted his hearing aid slightly though he had nothing to listen for. He said,

'If I may express a personal opinion I should like to say that I think the jury were right in finding you guilty. There are too many of you people around these days, who think you can break the law with impunity and who believe in a cult of violence. In sentencing you I should like to add something which I have often thought and I hope that people in high places will listen. In my opinion, this country made a great mistake when it abolished National Service. If it were in existence at this date perhaps you would not be here now. You would have been disciplined and taught to be clean and tidy. You would have had to cut your hair and to walk properly instead of slouching about insolently as you do. You would not have been allowed to be idle and drunk. I am glad to be able to give you the maximum sentence I can. I see no reason to be lenient.'

The two of them looked at him with insolence still. I was quite happy to see the sheriff giving them a stiff sentence. After all, the victim must be protected too: there is too much of this molly-coddling. I hate court work: I would far rather be in my little office working on land settlements or discussing the finer points of wills.

It was a fine summer's day as I left the court. There was no shadow anywhere, all fresh and new, just as I like to see this town.

The Exiles

She had left the Highlands many years before and was now
living in a council flat (in a butterscotch-coloured block) in the
Lowlands. Originally, when she had first moved, she had come
to a tenement in the noisy warm centre of the town, not much
better than a slum in fact, but the tenement had been pulled
down in a general drive to modernise the whole area. The
council scheme was itself supposed to be very modern with its
nice bright colour, its little handkerchiefs of lawns, its wide
windows. The block swarmed with children of all shapes and
sizes, all ages and colours of clothes. There were prams in
practically all the hallways, and men in dungarees streamed
home at five. Then they would all watch TV (she could see the
blue light behind the curtains like the sky of a strange planet),
drink beer, or shake the flimsy walls with music from their
radiograms. On Saturdays they would go to the football
matches – the team was a Second Division one – or they would
mow the lawn in their shirtsleeves. The gardens were well kept
on the whole, with roses growing here and there; in general,
though, it was easier to lay down grass, and one would see,
lying on the grass, an occasional abandoned tricycle.

The walls of the council houses were scribbled over by the
children who ran in and out of the closes playing and shouting
and quarrelling. Apart from the graffiti, the council houses
would have been all right, she thought, but the children
wouldn't leave anything alone, and they were never looked
after by their mothers who stood talking endlessly at bus stops,
bought sweets for the family when they ought to buy sustaining
food, and went about with scarves on their heads.

She herself was seventy years old. She didn't go out much
now. For one thing, there was the stair which was steep and

narrow and not meant for an old person at all. For another, there weren't many places she could go to. Of course, for a young person there were plenty of places, the cinema, the dance-hall, the skating rink and so on. But not for her. She did sometimes attend the church though she disapproved of it: the minister was a bit too radical, leaving too many things in the hands of women, and there was too much of this catering for young people with societies and groups. That wasn't the job of the church. In any case, it should be left in the hands of the men.

She didn't go to church very often in the winter. The fact was that it would be lonely coming home at night up that road with all these hooligans about. They would stab you as soon as look at you. You could see them hanging about at windows waiting to burgle the shops: a lot of that went on. She herself often put a chain on the door and wouldn't open it till she found out who was behind it. Not that very many people called except the rent man, the insurance man (she was paying an insurance of two shillings a week, which would bury her when she passed on), the milkman, and, occasionally, the postman. She would get an airmail letter now and again from her sister in Canada telling her all about her daughters who were being married off one after the other. There were six, including Marian the eldest. Her sister would send her photographs of the weddings showing coarse-looking, winking Americans sitting around a table with a white cloth and loaded with drinks of all kinds, the bride standing there with the knife in her hand as she prepared to cut the multi-storey cake. The men looked like boxers and were always laughing.

In any case, it wasn't easy for her to get down the stair now. Perhaps it would have been better if she had never come to the Lowlands, but then it was her son who had taken her out, and the house had been sold, and then he had got married and she was left alone. And it was pretty grim. Not that she idealised the Highlands either, don't think that. People there would talk behind your back and let you down in all sorts of ways, and you couldn't tell what they were thinking half the time. Out here they left you alone, perhaps too much alone. So far she hadn't had any serious illness, which was lucky as she didn't get on well with the neighbours who were young women of about thirty, all with platoons of children who looked like pieces of dirt, with thumbs in their mouths.

Most days she sat at the wide window watching the street below her. Off to the right, she could see the main road down which the great red buses careered at such terrifying speed, rocking from side to side. They would hardly stop for you. One of those days she would fall as she was boarding one. The conductors pressed the bell before you were hardly on, and the conductresses were even worse, very impudent if you said anything to them.

Down below on the road she could see the children playing. She couldn't say that she was very fond of children after what had happened with her son: leaving her like that after what she had done for him. Not that some of the children weren't nice. They would come to the door in their stiff staring masks at Hallowe'en, and she would give pennies to the politest amongst them. They were much more forward than the children at home and they had no nervousness. They would stand there and sing their songs, take their pennies and run downstairs again. Late at night, in summer, the boys and girls would be going past the houses singing and shouting; half drunk, she shouldn't wonder. And their language. You could hear every word as plain as could be. And there were no policemen where they were. Not that the housing scheme she was in was the worst. There was another one where none of the tenants could do anything to their gardens because the others would tear them all up. You got some people these days!

Really, sometimes she thought that if she had enough money she would go back to the Highlands: but she didn't have enough money, she had only the pension, and the fares were going up all the time. In any event, she wouldn't recognise the Highlands now. She had heard that the people had changed and were just as bad as the Lowlanders. You even had to lock the door now, an unheard-of thing in the past. Why, in the past, you could go away anywhere you liked for weeks, leaving the door unlocked, and, when you came back, the house would be exactly as you had left it, apart from the dust, of course.

It was hard just the same, being on your own all the time. All you got nowadays was closed curtains and the blue light of TV. It was just like a desert. Sitting there at the window all day was not a life for anyone. But what could she do about it? She must put up with it. She had been the fool and now she must put up with it. No use crying.

So she rose late in the morning, for time was her enemy, and took in the milk and made the breakfast (she always had porridge) and then went down to the shop in the council house scheme, for bread, meat and vegetables. In the adjacent newspaper shop she bought the *Daily Express*. When she had had her dinner she sat at the window until it was time for tea. After that she sat at the window again unless it was a Wednesday or a Sunday for on these evenings she went to church. She used the light sparingly in order to save electricity, and sometimes she would walk about in the dark; she was afraid that the lights would fuse and she would be unable to repair them. Her son had left her a small radio to which she listened now and again. What she listened to was the news and the Gaelic programmes and the sermons. The sermons were becoming very strange nowadays: sometimes, instead of a sermon, they had inexplicable discussions about all sorts of abstruse things. Trying to get down to the juvenile delinquents, that's all they were doing. Another programme she sometimes listened to was called *The Silver Lining*. She only used the one station, the Home: she never turned to the Light at all. She was frightened if she moved the hand that she would never get back to the Home again.

But the worst was the lack of visitors. Once or twice the Matron would come in, the minister now and again, and apart from that, no one except the rent man, the milkman and the electric man. But the only thing the last three came for was money. No one ever came to talk to her as a human being. And so the days passed. Endlessly. But it was surprising how quickly they passed just the same.

It was a Tuesday afternoon, on a fine summer's day (that morning she had been to the Post Office to collect her pension as she always did on a Tuesday). She was sitting by the window knitting: she had got into the habit of knitting many years ago and she couldn't stop even though she had no one to knit for. The sideboard was full of socks – all different colours of wool – and jerseys. Everyone said that she was good at knitting and that she should go in for prizes, but who wanted to do that? It was really a bright hot day, with the sun reflected back in a glitter from the windows of the houses opposite. Most of them were open to let in the air, and you could see the curtains drifting a little and bulging.

Looking downwards like a raven from its perch, she saw him trudging from house to house. He was pressing the bell of the door opposite, his old case laid down beside him, dilapidated and brown, with a strap across it. She saw him take a big red handkerchief out of his trouser pocket and wipe his face with it. The turban wound round his head, he stood at the door leaning a little against the stone beside it, waiting. He seemed to have been carrying the case for ever, pressing doorbells and waiting, with an immense patience. The windows of the house opposite were open and she could see Mrs whatever-her-name-was moving about in the living room, but she didn't come to the door: probably she had seen him coming and didn't want to let him in. After a while he turned away.

As he did so he happened to glance up, and saw her sitting at the window. It was just pure chance that he saw her, but he would probably have come anyway since he would go to all the houses. On the other hand, on such a hot day, he might not be willing to face the high stair. He bent down, picked up the case and crossed the road, a slim man. She was looking down directly on to the turban. Strange people these, they had a religion of their own.

She listened for his foot on the stairs as she often listened for the step of the postman, who reached her house about eight o'clock in the morning when she was still lying in bed. Most of the time he would have nothing but bills, and she would hear him ring the bell next door, and then his steps retreating down the stair again. Sometimes she would even get up and watch the letter box with bated breath waiting for a letter to drop through on to the mat below.

In a similar manner, she waited this afternoon. Would he come up to the top or wouldn't he? There was the sound of steps and then they faded. That must be someone going into the house on the middle floor, perhaps the woman coming in from her shopping. Then silence descended again. It must have been another five minutes before the ring came at the door. She hurried along the passageway trying to keep calm and when she opened the door on its chain, there he was, his dark face shining with sweat, his red bandana handkerchief in his hand. His case was laid down on the mat outside the door.

'Afternoon, missus,' he said in a deep guttural voice. 'Wish to see dresses?' He seemed young though you couldn't tell with them. He smiled at her; you couldn't tell about the smile either. It seemed warm enough; on the other hand, to him she was just business. She led him along the passageway to the living room which was at the far end of the house, and he sat down in a deep armchair and began to open the case as soon as he had sat down. He gave the room a quick, appraising look, noting the polished side-board full of glasses of all kinds, the copper-coloured carpet, the table in the centre with the paper flowers in the glass.

The case looked very cheap and cracked and was stuffed to the brim. It amazed her to see how much they could cram into their cases and how neat and tidy they were.

'Fine day, missus,' he said, looking up and flashing his white teeth.

'Would you like a glass of milk?' she asked.

'Thank you very much, missus.' He pronounced his consonants in a very strange manner: of course, they didn't know English well, goodness knew where they came from. She handed him a tall cold tumbler of milk and watched as he took it delicately in his dark hand, the blackness contrasting very strongly with the white of the milk. He drank it very quickly and handed it back to her, then began to put stuff on the floor.

'Silk scarf. Blue,' he said. 'Very nice.' He held it up against the light in which the silk looked cold.

'It is very nice,' she said in her precise English.

He stopped.

'You no from here?' – as if he had heard some tone of strangeness in her voice.

'No. No from here,' she half-imitated him.

'I am from Pakistan,' he said, bending down again so that she could only see the bluish turban. 'I am a student,' he added.

She could hardly make out what he was saying, he spoke in such a guttural way.

'Are you a student?' she said at last.

'Student in law,' he said as if that made everything plain. He took out a yellow pullover and left it on the floor for her to look at. She shook her head: it was very nice wool, she thought, picking it up and letting her hands caress it, but she had no use for it. She supposed that Pakistan must be very warm and yet he appeared hot as if the weather didn't agree with him. What must it be like for him in the winter?

'Where you come from then?' he asked, looking up and smiling with his warm, quick, dark eyes.

'I come from the north,' she said slowly.

'North?'

'From the Highlands,' she said.

'Ah,' he said, as if he did not fully understand.

'Do you like here?' he asked innocently.

'Do you like here yourself?' she countered.

He stopped with a scarf in his hand.

'Not,' he said and nodded his head. 'Not. Too cold.' His eyes brightened. 'Going back to Pakistan after law. Parents got shop. Big shop in big town.' He made a motion with his hands which she presumed indicated the size of the shop.

'Do you come here often?' she asked. 'I haven't seen you before.' Nor tinkers. She never saw any tinkers. Up in the Highlands the tinkers would come to the door quite often, but not here. Drummond their name was, it was a family name.

'Not often. I'm on vacation, see? Sometimes Saturdays I come. I work in shop in Glasgow to make money for law. For education. This vacation with me.'

She nodded, half understanding, looking down at the clothes. She wondered what the women wore in Pakistan, what they did. She had seen some women with long dresses and pigtails. But was that India or China?

The stuff he was selling was pretty cheap. 'Men's hand-kerchiefs.' He held up a bundle of them. She shook her head. 'Men's ties,' he said, holding up a bundle of them, garish and painted. He looked quickly round the living room, noting the glass, the flowers . . .

'You live alone, missus?' he said. She said yes without thinking, wondering why he had asked. Perhaps he would come back later and rob her: you couldn't tell with anyone these days.

'Ah,' he said, again mopping his brow.

'City no good,' he said. 'Too hot. Too great traffic.' He smiled warmly, studying her and showing his white teeth. 'Parents go to mountains in summer in Pakistan.'

He placed a nightgown on top of the pile: it had a blue ground with small pink flowers woven into it.

'Nice nightgown,' he said, holding it up. 'Cheap. Very cheap. Bargain. For you, missus.'

She held it in her hands and studied it. 'Too small,' she said finally. She had one nightgown already she had received from her sister in Canada; it had frills as well, but she never wore it.

'Dressing gown then,' he pursued. 'Two pound. Good bargain. Nice quality.' It was far too expensive.

'Would you like a cup of tea?' she said at last.

'No today, missus. Perhaps next time if I come.'

If he came! That meant he might not come again. Of course if he didn't sell much he wouldn't come, why should he? And it didn't look as if he had sold much, what with the case crammed to the top, the children's stuff still there, panties, jerseys, little twin sets. They were all intact. The young wives had been avoiding him, that was clear. But they would buy sweets and cakes all right though they wouldn't buy clothes for their children. It was scandalous.

'Knickers,' he said. 'Silk knickers.' He held them, very cool, very silky, letting them run through his fingers, his black fingers.

There was hardly anything else there that she could buy, except for the ladies' handkerchiefs but she had plenty of these already, some even from the best Irish linen. One always gathered handkerchiefs, though one hardly ever used them, not these delicate ones anyway.

'Do you ever go home to Pakistan?' she asked.

'Not to Pakistan since I came to this place two years ago. No money.' He smiled winningly, preparing to return everything to the case. 'Some day, perhaps. Two year from this time.' He held up two fingers. 'When law finished.'

She watched his black hands busy against the whites and reds and greens. She noticed for the first time that his own clothes were quite cheap; a painted tie, a dirty looking collar, a dark suit and scuffed shoes, shoes so dusty that it looked as if he had been walking for ever. She was standing by the window, and as she watched him she could see a big red bus flashing and glittering down the road.

He was really quite young when you studied him. For some reason she thought of the time that Norman had come home drunk at two in the morning after the dance, the sickness in the bathroom under the hard early-morning light of the bulb, his refusal to get up the following morning for work ... She wondered if this young man drank. Probably not. There would be some law against it in their religion. They had a very funny religion, but they were clean-living people, she had heard. They didn't have churches over there as we had. It was more like temples or things like that.

As he was putting all the clothes back in the case, she put out her hand and picked up the silk knickers, studying them again. She stood at the window looking at them. Lord, how flimsy they were! Who would wear such things? What delicate airy beings, what sluts, would put these next to their skin? She wouldn't be seen dead buying that stuff. It wouldn't even keep out the winter cold. Yet they were so cool in your hands, so silky, like water running, like a cool stream in the north.

'How much?' she said.

'Fifteen shillings,' he said looking at her devotedly, his hands resting lightly on the case.

She put them down again.

'Have you any gents' socks?' she asked.

He nodded.

'How much are they?'

'Five shilling,' he said. 'Light socks. Good bargain. Nice.' He handed over two pairs, one grey, the other brown. As she held them in her hands, stroking them gently, she realised how inferior they were to her own, she knew that no love had gone into their making. She had never bought a pair of shop socks in her life: she had always knitted Norman's socks herself. Why, people used to stop him in the street and admire them, they were so beautiful, so much care had gone into them! And she knew so many patterns too, all those that her mother had taught her so long ago and so far away. In another country, in another time, in another age.

'Five shillings,' she repeated dully. Still, that was about the cheapest thing he had. She said decisively, 'I'll take them,' though her heart was rent at their cheapness.

She went into the bedroom and took the five shillings out of the shiny black bag, shutting the door in case he might follow her. That left her with three pounds five for the week. Still, in summer it wasn't too bad, she didn't have to use so much electricity and she could save on the coal.

She counted the two silver half-crowns coldly into his warm black hand, and he gave her the socks.

'Thank you, missus,' he said. Could she detect just a trace of Glasgow accent behind the words? That displeased her for some reason. He bent down, strapping the case tight, and, when he was ready to go, he smiled at her radiantly.

'Will you be coming again?' she asked, thinking how quickly the hour had passed.

'Every Tuesday while vacation is on,' he said, looking out of the window at the traffic and the children playing.

She followed him down the lobby.

'You sit at window much?' he said, and she didn't like that, but she said,

'Sometimes.'

'See you Tuesday then,' he said. 'Maybe have something else. Something nice.'

She closed the door behind him and heard his steps going

downstairs, and it was almost as if she was listening to Norman leaving. She went back to the window, looking down, but she couldn't see him: he must be keeping to this side of the street. Later on, however, she saw him crossing the road. He stopped and laid the case down and waved up at her, but she couldn't make out the expression on his face. Then he continued and she couldn't see him at all.

She got up slowly and put the socks in with the pile of the ones she had knitted herself, the loved ones, as if she were making an offering to the absent, as if she were asking for forgiveness. She hoped that next week he would have something cheap. She continued knitting the socks.

Close of Play

'Well, Neil, aren't you going to write the letter?'

He couldn't see her, as he was lying face down on the bed, from which position he said,

'Mother, please go away. I'm listening to the cricket. I'll write it later . . . '

'But they said . . . '

'I know what they said. Just go away, will you?'

'All right, Neil, but they said that the application has to be in tomorrow, and if you don't write the letter tonight . . . ' Her voice trailed weakly away.

He shut the door on her and went back to lie down on the bed again, the transistor beside him. It was right enough, they had to know tomorrow, but supposing he didn't want to go? To go would mean working for the rest of the summer at his Latin, which he had failed the first time, and it would take a lot of energy to pile into the subjunctive in this weather – even to get into university – when you could go for a lazy swim and to a dance in the evening.

His mother's voice came faintly from the kitchen:

'I don't know what you can see in that cricket . . . ' And, true enough, he had never played cricket in his life, but he listened to it just the same, hour after hour. As now.

'This is a really interesting duel we're witnessing at the moment between Illingworth and Redpath.' That Australian drawl. Funny thing, they said 'sundries' instead of 'extras'. He scratched his face: he'd have to shave soon and he wasn't looking forward to it.

'There are twenty minutes left of this Test and the game is poised on a hair. With twenty minutes to go, the Australians have one wicket left. I feel sure that the Australians are not going to play any daring shots at this stage of the game. They'll be happy to force a draw. And now here is Illingworth. A short run, and he straightened that one up. Redpath had a bit of difficulty with it. He came forward and then he went back again. Now he's going out to prod at a spot on the wicket. It's an interesting duel of wits, this, isn't it, John?'

Then there was this job he'd been offered in London, working in an airport office. He didn't really know what it involved, but it might be quite exciting. In any case, he had never been to London. Never. And people were always telling him about it. And then there was that book he had read about Soho, by Frank Norman. He had been in prison or something, hadn't he? An interesting book, not at all like the usual guide, a good, clean, unhypocritical style. A good lot in it about strip clubs too, all about these young girls setting out to ruin themselves. Well, let him get down there and help them to do that. Fifteen pounds a week; not much, but then it would probably go up. By increments, as they laughingly said. And then there was this Latin drag. He was all right at English literature, but Latin – all that grammar and stuff, and Ovid, and all these perverts. What use were they anyway? Just a ticket. Why, once he got his Latin – if he ever got it – he would never read a Latin book or poem or conjugation again. What sort of education was that, when it turned you against a subject? And he'd already failed it once. And probably would again. How could one concentrate on the stuff? It had no contact with the present, all memory work, that was all it was.

He shifted over to light a cigarette, a Sterling. The transistor fell down and he couldn't hear it so well. He set it on its base again and raised the aerial.

'Well, I must say this is really becoming very tense now. That's twice Illingworth has beaten Redpath in the same over. And there are about ten minutes to go on my watch. Illingworth, of course, gets through his overs fairly quickly, so there'll be a few yet. He is an interesting bowler to watch. He doesn't waste much effort and he seems completely unflappable. He shows a lot of intelligence. In fact, both the batsman and bowler are showing a great deal of intelligence.

Redpath is waiting for the loose ball and defending stubbornly against the others. But Illingworth, of course, is not likely to bowl a loose ball.'

Poor old England! Up against it again. Here the Australians were, 88 for 9, and yet the English couldn't bowl them out. There had certainly been ups and downs in this match, let alone the series. In the first innings there was old Dexter walking on, everybody expecting him to hit the Australians into the next county. And what had happened? He had made six runs. You couldn't depend on these people: the more they were built up, the more they fell down like a lot of sandcastles. When you came down to it, all these so-called giants were very ordinary people. They had been built into a legend over the years, but there was nothing to them really. He flicked some ash into the ashtray. Look at Cowdrey: just the same. Probably if you had gone along to see Hobbs, he would have been out first ball as well. Years from now they would say, 'Oh, if only you had seen Cowdrey that day at Lord's. Great. That drive to leg! That four to the boundary! Sweet! Exquisite!' But when you came down to it, he took six hours to make a century. What sort of cricket was that?

He took out a penny and tossed it. Tails for 'I try Latin again' and heads, 'I go to London'. It came down heads. He tossed it three times, and three times it came down heads.

'If Illingworth bowls him out I'll go to university,' he said. 'If England wins I'll go to university. I swear it. I'll read Latin every night. I'll dig into old Lucretius. I'll lap up the ablative absolute. I won't go swimming. I'll put away my motor cycle. I won't borrow off my brother to go to the pub. Just let Illingworth bowl him out, that's all. I'll accept that as an omen from above. I'll take it as a *fiat* from the Delphic oracle. I'll know there's someone rooting for me up there, someone who knows that I exist, someone to whom it matters whether I go to some crummy job in London or to university, someone who cares!' He glued his ear to the transistor.

'Seven minutes left now, and Illingworth is bowling to Walters. Walters is standing there, very composed, very sure of himself. He's a young man, but he isn't letting the tension of the occasion wear him down. He doesn't mind whether it's twenty-three minutes past six or twenty minutes past twelve. He plays every ball on its merits. That one Illingworth bowled Walters tried to swing at it. It hit his pad and skidded down to Graveney for one run. This brings Redpath up again to face Illingworth.'

'Come on,' said Neil, muttering fiercely into the transistor as if he were speaking to someone who could actually hear him, 'come on. I want to see you bowl him out. For Ovid, for Lucretius, for Virgil, for the ablative absolute. For my future. For my career. Bowl the bastard out. Hit the stumps. The Australians can't face spin. Laker proved that. Go on.'

'Illingworth is now going over the wicket to Redpath. There's a bit of dust on the wicket but of course, it's not really in the best position for Illingworth to make use of it. Illingworth's coming in now. He bowls. And Redpath flicks it off his legs. What do you think, John, I'm sure the Australians who are staying up to listen must be pleased with this stand by these youngsters.'

'Yes, I agree. Redpath is playing very intelligently. As you say, he's picking the loose ball to hit and defending against the other ones. He reminds me rather a lot of . . . Oh, sorry.'

'It's all right, John. Illingworth coming up for the last ball of this over. And Redpath is quite determined to last out the evening and the match. So he meets him with a dead bat. You were going to say, John?'

Neil switched off the transistor angrily. 'Damn and blast the lot of you,' he shouted fiercely, banging the transistor with his fist. 'What the hell are you playing at, you useless pimps? You bowl there all day, and you can't get these people out. Tail-enders, and you can't get rid of them. All your days you've been learning to bowl, year after year, decade after decade, and, when it comes to the point, to the critical point, you can't win a match. What sort of people are you anyway? What's wrong with you? Illingworth, the darling of Yorkshire, the demon bowler. My demon backside. Look, Illingworth, can't you see you're bowling for me, me, Neil Brown. Not anybody from Ilkley Moor baht at, but Neil Brown, failed MA. You've got my future in your hands. Can't you hear me? If you bowl him out, I'll write that letter and then I'll go to university. It depends on you. I don't know why I should have picked on you, but you happened to be here. Let's see if you're as good as they say. Go on, bowl him out. Bowl him out, you stupid nit. You've only got five minutes left. Five minutes. Get some urgency into your work. Look, I'm depending on you, it's not England, it's Neil Brown unemployed. His life's ahead of him, can't you see that, you nit? Can't you spin that ball so I can go to university, so I can have a reason for studying that useless trash? Can't you hear me? Look, I've got an hour before the post goes. I should have written it weeks ago, but I'm a lazy bum and I lie in bed and I let my mother work in a shoe shop, the ever glorious Huttons, and sometimes I make the tea for her when she comes home, same as George Bernard Shaw used to do. And I don't get up till about four in the afternoon. And I don't shave till six when I go out and I come in at two in the morning, and I've got this pile of Latin books lying about the house along with T. S. Eliot and W. H. Auden and Dylan Thomas and Seferis.'

He rolled over on his back and looked up at the ceiling.

'Look,' he said, 'make some sign. That's all I ask. One sign. Look, if Illingworth gets him out I'll go to university, I'll work like a slave, I'll do my Latin. I'll get the old lady some money. Do you get that? Do you understand? Is that clear?' He noticed a large stain on the ceiling shaped like Africa, and then, out of the corner of his eye, he saw the clock.

'Twenty-five minutes past six.' He put his hand on the transistor. God, if he's already out. Please make him be out when I switch on the transistor. That bastard, Redpath, defending there so stubbornly. And these Australians from the outback. What did they want to come here for anyway, Arthur Upfield and the rest of them? The Australians for cricket, the New Zealanders for rugby. And poor old Scotland for what? Shinty? He laughed dryly. Each country had its own death sting except poor old Scotland, dead old Caledonia, weird and wild, meek and mild, piqued and piled.

He clicked the transistor and knew that the two batsmen were still there because the crowd were making no noise.

If they had been out – or if one of them had been out – there would have been a change in the atmosphere.

' . . . be surely the second last over. Underwood coming in and bowling to Walters. And that beat him. That certainly beat him. It spun quite sharply and Walters did well to keep the ball out of his wicket. He's going out to give the pitch a prod. Then he takes up his stance and Underwood runs up again. This one he meets with a dead bat and watches the ball trickle to a stop in front of him. Very placid, this man. Very calm. Doesn't seem to be moved by anything much. But I don't think he's reading Underwood very well at this moment. A wicket now would swing the match England's way. However, we must remember that Australia have won the first Test . . . '

He clicked the transistor off again, not able to bear it. About ten balls to go and he couldn't bear the suspense. Perhaps that was what was wrong with him. If he weren't a coward he would be able to sit through the whole thing. Think of those wives who sat through their husbands' horrible speeches. Think of the dreadful routine of the day, the week, the year. Think of the terrible ennui. 'Mr Macaskill took as his theme, "The Mackellars of Struth". He dealt at length with Edward Struth, who bought Struth House in the sixteenth century, and steadily worked his way towards John Struth, who died of apoplexy in 1947.' Or, 'Mrs Innes, who accompanied her husband, presented a bouquet of flowers, and was in turn presented with a bouquet of flowers by little Ann Capewell.' Think of Dexter going back to the dressing room after that six. Graft. That was what was wanted. Like whether England could beat Australia, or whether Australia would dig themselves in and survive. Look at these West Indians: they were pretty temperamental. The flash of genius and talent but no 'bottom'. Like whether these tough Australian provincials – land of Melba and the flood – were going to beat sophisticated England, dying of civilisation and ennui, not able to bring themselves to believe that cricket was of importance in the age of Wittgenstein, England with their rotting empire-less souls, dying on the trees. Like whether he should get up and shave.

Like whether he could switch on that transistor again and

wait for the last over, and listen to it through the bitter six to the equally bitter end. Why, there were old men who would go to cricket matches, be-scarfed and be-false-teethed, their heads nodding in the midday sun, and they would watch them through, or die of heart failure in the process. And think of all those people batting and bowling who had sisters, brothers, mothers, fathers, and all other combinations of kith and kin, watching them being bowled for nought after they had walked so proud and tall to the wicket.

He clicked the transistor on and leaned forward, his mouth almost touching the switches.

'This is the last over now, and Illingworth is just running up to bowl the first ball to Redpath. Mm. I'm afraid that won't get him out. It was a very cosy, not to say mild, ball which Redpath had no difficulty in keeping out of his wicket. Graveney is throwing the ball back to him now. Illingworth catches it and goes back very thoughtfully to begin his short run. Here he is now, and, by gosh, that one nearly got through. I suppose you would have heard the OOH from the crowd, some of whom are now leaving for their transportation. I wouldn't myself like to be leaving at this stage in the game.'

'Shut your stupid mouth or gob,' said Neil, viciously stabbing his cigarette into the scarred ashtray. 'Or whatever word they use in Australia. Back to your boomerang or your walkabout. Come on, Illingworth, you bastard, get him out, can't you see I'm waiting for you? I'm depending on you. Look, if you get him out, I'll send a letter to thank you. I'll send my first pay packet achieved through my Ovid to you, care of the MCC.'

'And now for the third ball of the over. Illingworth runs up and bowls. Redpath shapes to glance, changes his mind and then lets it go safely past his wicket.'

'Illingworth, I'm praying to you. Can't you hear me? My future depends on you. Do you want me to be a down-and-out in Soho, do you? Don't you want me to be a good little bourgeois with a nice family spawned by my conjugations, kept in clothes by my talent for Ovid? Listen, come on, get him out.'

' . . . oh, that was another tricky ball, a really wicked ball. That hit the spot in the wicket there and spun quite a bit.

Redpath jabbed his bat down just in time. I bet he heaved a sigh of relief after that.'

'Come on,' Neil breathed, half in entreaty, half in imprecation, 'come on, get him out. I've got my fingers in my mouth, I've got my nails between my teeth. I'm praying to you. Oh God.' He couldn't stay on the bed any longer. It really seemed to him as if his future were being decided on that baked cricket field hundreds of miles away, by people whom he had never seen, who had never heard of him. He started to pace about the room clutching his trousers with both hands, and taking deep breaths one after the other as he looked out at the back court with the bins all standing beside each other in their repeated grooves.

'And I think this must be . . . Is this the second last ball of the day, Trevor? I've lost count in the excitement. It is? Good. Well, as Trevor says, the second last ball is being bowled now, and here is Illingworth and a tricky ball it was too, which Redpath did well to stop. However, all's well that ends well, and I don't suppose Redpath is going to lose any sleep over it at this stage. The clock is creeping round to the half hour now, and the ground just below is bathed in sunlight as Illingworth runs up to take the last ball of the day and the last ball of this match.'

Neil was kneeling over the transistor listening to it as a doctor listens to a patient's heart to discover if there are signs of imminent death there or not. He suddenly saw that the switches of the transistor were wet with his tears.

'And that is the end of play for the day, and Trevor Bailey will now give a summary of the full day's play.'

Soundlessly, he began to beat on the transistor with his fists as if he had rediscovered that fate itself was against him, that there was no assistance from the heavens, that there was no answer except the statistics being repeated in that rich voice.

He switched the transistor off and went back to bed. He lay back in the sunlight which came through the window flooding the Latin books shut on top of the bookcase and illuminating as well the copy of *Ulysses* lying open half way through.

He muttered to himself, with his eyes shut,

'That bastard Illingworth, that layabout of the first order. Of the first water. Of the last water.'

'Je t'aime'

One day in late August their little daughter ran home from secondary school saying that she had begun to learn French. She was eleven years old and rather backward, and even at the age of eleven had a habit of putting her thumb in her mouth. Her mother, who was standing by the cooker when she came in, told her to take off her school clothes immediately. She did this, and when she was dressed in the black skirt and red jersey which she wore when not in school, she started to run about the room shouting, 'Je t'aime, je t'aime'. Finally, she spun to a stop with her head buried in her mother's waist.

'What does that mean?' said her mother, turning the sausages over in the frying pan. She was a tall woman, rather aloof, and pale as if she were in the habit of not putting too much into life lest she should be hurt.

'It means "I love you". Teacher told us that. But we only learned one or two words today.' She laughed, peeked up, and then looked down at the floor.

'That's good,' said her mother absently. She was secretly pleased that her daughter was learning French. French might be useful in running the boarding house: people might be impressed. She might even run to menus in the future. Her husband was a long-distance lorry driver, and the responsibility for running the boarding house devolved on her, for her husband wasn't interested (though he took the money if she gave it to him). But she had been advised by her mother to have a banking account of her own, and she had done this. Again, it was possible that Grace might go to university in about seven years time. Lots of people went to university now who didn't go in the past. Things were easier now and they got grants.

Running a boarding house wasn't an easy job. She was

sometimes fed up with making food and watching it being shovelled down other people's throats, she was tired of the heat and the stuffiness of the kitchen, she was bored telling a new set of people every fortnight what that castle was, who had built that road, what that statue represented, and hearing exactly the same comments as if they were mint-new. Thank God, they had gone by August.

She looked down at the top of her daughter's head and thought vaguely of the past. She had certainly trained for running a boarding house for she had been a maid in a hotel before she got married. It was watching all these rich people that had made her envious and want to make money for herself. For that reason she was now pleased that her daughter was learning French. She had no feeling for the language itself but to her it represented a weapon for survival, for advancement. If you worked in a boarding house you began to think like that. You studied people to make sure that they didn't cheat you, you had to be a good judge of character. You couldn't afford to let anyone sidle into your affections for they might take advantage of you.

In fact, she might have been better if she had known more about her husband before she married him. To be drunk in youth might be considered bravado: in middle years it was something else again, especially when it included unpredictable violence. She had seen nights when he had hit her in the face and about the body. One night she had pleaded with him not to hit her on the face: it was the explaining to others of the outward stigmata that was difficult and shaming. You couldn't get away from the fact that he was brutal.

'Did you get any homework?' she asked.

'We got some English homework. Sentences.'

'Get out your jotter and do it then,' she said, turning back to the cooker. 'Sit over there on that chair and do it.'

Grace got her bag, took out her jotter and her pencil case, and began to work, chewing gravely at the pencil, dangling her legs and knitting her brows.

Her mother sighed for a moment and then turned back to the cooker.

When her husband came home he threw his bag on the floor into the corner, went to the cupboard, took out a can of beer, opened it and began to drink. He sat down at the table stretching his legs out. He was a big man with a bullet head set on a rather low thick neck, and the shoulders of a boxer. His eyes were small and mocking.

'One of these days I'll get a lorry of my own,' he said. 'I can't stand that bastard Adams. One day he'll go too far and I'll do him, the dwarf.'

'You get good pay,' she said evenly, putting the sausages on his plate. He seemed about to spit on the floor, and then recollected himself.

'One of these days I'll smash his lorry for him. Stood there today checking the time I came in, to the minute. The wee man with his book. What I'd really like is a taxi. I could run a taxi, couldn't I? Hey, I could bring your visitors up from the station. I'd go there in my cap, and I'd bow and I'd see them into the taxi and I'd shut the door for them and everything. "Yes, madam," I'd say, "44 Grosvenor Road. Yes, I know it well. I know it like the back of my hand. The house with the green gate. You couldn't get better chips anywhere, madam," I'd say. "And the salt herring are out of this world and into the next one. Yes, madam, they make the best porridge in town with treacle in it." '

He laughed aloud in sheer jollity thinking of himself in his peaked cap bowing to the visitors like a wee Jap and saying to them, 'That house over there. That belongs to the famous comedian, the Scottish Secretary of State. That statue? That's of the man who invented the Scottish propelling pencil which works on a new principle. You have lead in it for the first time. Yes, madam, he made millions on that.'

He laughed aloud again; he had a great life force, much more than she had. She laughed, too, knowing his ideas of old. Nothing would come of them. There was the time when he wanted to start a shop; nothing came of that. The time he wanted to invest money in a pub. She couldn't let her money go into that; he'd be drunk all day and night. She knew what would happen if he got a taxi. He'd get drunk and wreck it. And of course, he'd never be obsequious to anyone: she couldn't imagine him carrying the cases of some old wizened hag who was only held together by the wrinkles. Even now, he got angry if a visitor got to the bathroom in front of him in the morning. Suddenly he got tired of the play-acting and shouted,

'Grace. What are you doing there? Come over here.'

He bounced her on his knee and rubbed his face against hers. She twisted away from the bristles of his beard.

'Getting too snobbish for your daddy;' he said, joyously, 'now that you're going to the secondary. Eh?'

She climbed down from his knee and began to run madly about the house shouting, 'Je t'aime, je t'aime'.

His wife put down the plate of sausages.

'What in God's name is that?' he shouted in the direction of his daughter, his face going red.

'It's nothing,' she said.

'It must be something,' he said, speaking through a mouthful of sausage. 'What in God's ... ' Then he stopped. A queer expression came over his face, composed of rage and anguish. It frightened her. It was as if he were staring into some other room.

'Come here,' he said to Grace who was abandoned to her wheeling, her blonde pigtails bouncing up and down.

'What was that you were saying just now?'

'I was just saying, "je t'aime",' said Grace, standing looking at him, thumb in mouth.

He turned to his wife. 'That's French,' he said accusingly. 'She's learning French.'

'And what if it is? What's wrong with that?' she answered, still at the cooker. 'They all learn French nowadays in the secondary school.'

'That's a lie,' he said. 'I was talking to the headmaster, and he said you could take French or Gaelic.' She knew that he had never talked to the headmaster in his life (firstly because he did not take the slightest interest in education, and secondly because deep down he was convinced that he was as good as the headmaster any day and therefore wouldn't talk to him), but she also knew that, however he had heard it, what he said was true; there *was* a choice between French and Gaelic.

'What do you think I am, an idiot like your daughter,' he went on, his face darkening. 'And you didn't put on enough sausages. You were supposed to train as a hotel maid and you don't know anything.'

She ignored this and said,

'French is more useful to her. She can go to . . . ' She was going to say 'University', but she stopped, saying instead, 'Domestic College. She can help me here.'

'Her? Domestic College? Don't make me laugh. I'm brighter than her myself and I wouldn't go to a college.'

She leaned against the cooker praying, 'Please God, not another quarrel. I'm tired, tired, tired . . .'

But he continued relentlessly.

'She should be doing Gaelic. That's the language of her forefathers. My mother spoke Gaelic. So did your mother. What does she want with French. She should stand up for Scotland. I was in a Highland regiment and I'm proud of it. What business has she got with French? She can't even speak English. I'm going to see the headmaster and tell him she's going to change.'

He cut himself a slice of bread, buttering it lavishly.

She held on.

'She's going to do French not Gaelic. No one speaks Gaelic now. It's finished. I want her to learn French: it's more useful to her. She could be a help to me. She can't do anything with Gaelic.'

As he munched the bread he seemed to be muttering, 'Je t'aime, je t'aime', over and over to himself.

'He can say it right, mammy,' shouted Grace suddenly. 'He can say it better than you.'

'Be quiet. Go and do your lesson.'

'She'll never learn French in a month of Sundays. She's too stupid. It takes a long time to learn French. I'm telling you, I know.'

She summoned all her strength.

'And I'm telling you she's going to learn French. You can clear out if you want. We've got enough to live on without you. We can do without you. All her friends are learning French. She would feel out of it if she wasn't with her friends.'

'Yah, the Andersons. You want to keep up with the Andersons. You'll soon be teaching her horse-riding. She'll be a debutante, that's what.'

'And what's wrong with horse-riding?'

'Horse-riding?' He laughed, then his face darkened again. 'All right,' he said, 'I might just clear out. I might just do that.' He put on his jacket, leaving his food unfinished, and went towards the door looking down grimly at Grace and saying in a mocking voice, 'Je t'aime'.

'You don't know what it means,' said his wife suddenly. 'You talk big, but you don't know what it means.'

He stared into her almost dead, slate-grey eyes for a long time and then said, controlling himself with an effort,

'It's you who don't know what it means.' Then he walked out.

When he slammed the door she began to think: perhaps this time he will really leave, and in a way she didn't want him to leave. He wasn't a good provider but he had been her only lover, brutal though he was. Not always brutal too, for he could be tender when he remembered. And once he had been dashing and young. She ran to the window and saw him walking down the road, the bullet head and the powerful torso thrust forward as if he were fighting a high wind.

'Get on with your book,' she shouted at Grace, screaming in a voice that she hardly recognised.

He sat in the pub in a corner by himself drinking a big pint of draught. He never drank anything but draught and whisky: he had no time for highfaluting effeminate French wines and that sort of drink. In front of him and behind the counter there was a twisted bottle and above it were written the words: 'WHEN YOU SEE THIS STRAIGHT YOU KNOW YOU'RE DRUNK.'

The barman was tall and had a stringy neck. A lot of the time he would talk about the farm his family owned on the Borders quite near to the Douglas-Homes, but tonight there was no conversation, the lorry driver staring moodily at the bottle and drinking his beer from time to time, thinking. His eye was caught by a bottle which said Burgundy on it. He stared at it as into a mirror, and through the glass he saw her standing at the door of the café, very petite, very thin, very pale, with curly hair. A thin face: the word 'gamin' returned to him over the years. Sitting at the table in the café in 1945, he put down the roll he was eating and looked brazenly at her, letting his eyes run down from the blonde hair to her feet. He seemed to straighten up in his uniform feeling his thighs, covered in their khaki, heavy and solid.

She caught his eye and he deliberately put the roll back to his mouth again, savouring it; she watching hungrily as he chewed, her eyes damned and burning in the white face. He raised the glass of milk to his lips, his eyes still locked with hers. She walked over towards him as if in a dream, her eyes, her whole body, fascinated by the roll and the milk, by their whiteness and their sustenance. He twisted his neck against the rub of the uniform.

As if in a dream she sat down on the chair in front of him, sitting half frightened on the edge, at the same time unable to help herself.

He put down the glass of milk. He looked into her eyes, and she nodded very slightly with despair.

He got up, rolling slightly at the hips like a cowboy, went over to the counter and got another roll and a glass of milk. He brought them over and put them in front of her looking down at her legs as he did so. These thin French tarts, he thought. Not much flesh, but a man couldn't be choosy: it wasn't easy.

Her head bowed like the stalk of a flower, she bit into the roll almost with agony, absorbed in it as a child might be in something it had never seen before, or seen only rarely. He himself stopped eating and watched her. She stopped eating at once, and he looked away. He could see in the mirror that his cap was on at the right rakish angle. When she had finished he got her another roll and some milk: after all, she would be no use otherwise. She looked to see if he had got one for himself, but he hadn't and her eyes darkened again.

During the time she was eating she made once or twice as if to speak, but then looking at him checked herself. Once he looked at his watch which had a leather strap about the hairy flesh. When she was finished she got up slowly and he followed her, putting on his belt, then taking it off again and putting it across the shoulder under the strap. These Redcaps could go to hell as far as he was concerned. He'd beaten up one or two of them already on his way across Europe: they'd remember him, no doubt of that.

They walked silently down the street, meeting other soldiers and French girls on their way. It was a balmy evening and there was a faint moon low in the sky showing the slummy buildings towards which they were heading. She was like a wraith drifting beside him, the only sound being that made by his tackety boots on the roadway. Eventually, they reached a tenement and began to climb some steps, she going ahead. When she was high enough up, he could see that she was wearing a white slip.

There were little sounds in the tenement as if it were inhabited by animals and by people who never ventured out. The walls were scribbled on and there was urine on the stairs. Once a cat with startled green eyes ran down the stairs past them, pausing at the bottom to look up at him before running off. They came to a door which was painted a cracked green. She opened it with a key which she found under the mat, and they went inside. The curtains were all drawn and there was a smell of used air. Under the bed he saw the edge of a chamber pot. Again she made as if to speak but didn't. She sat down on the bed while he studied a photograph on the sideboard marked with cigarette ends. The photograph showed a man in a hat like a drum. When he turned round she was in bed staring up at the ceiling.

He took off his jacket and his tie and then his boots and trousers, leaving his socks on. He climbed into bed. The sheets were more grey than white. Her helplessness released him. Afterwards he fell into a deep sleep in which he saw some deer which reminded him of home.

He woke at seven in the morning and took a while to discover where he was, the room was so dark. Outside he heard the traffic. Inside there was silence apart from the creakings of the old house. The girl was still sleeping on her side, away from him. As he got up he noticed that there were delicate blue veins on her forehead. He tried to orientate himself. Where am I? he thought, where in hell in Europe am I? What country is this? What have I been doing for the past four years? There had been border after border, faces cheering and faces sullen, wet weather and fine, strange faces; strange languages. He sat on the edge of the bed, took off his socks, scratched the soles of his feet, and then put the socks on again. He felt dirty and was about to waken her to ask for some soap and water when something stopped him. His foot accidentally hit the chamber pot: he had forgotten it was there.

He put on his clothes quietly, feeling absolutely lost. He drew the curtains aside and looked down into a back court full of overflowing bins. She turned away from the light, groaning a little. He shook his head to clear it, for he had been drinking before he met her. He felt a desire to urinate and decided that he would go down to the court.

He was dressed now. He went over and looked down at her before he left. He felt terribly lonely as if he was in the wrong place, in the wrong air, as if he was slightly askew to the universe. He took out a wad of paper money and without counting it laid it on the bed. As he was doing this, he was leaning down close and could hear the words she was whispering. They sounded like, 'Je t'aime', but he knew they weren't for him. Perhaps it was a formula she spoke to many men or perhaps she was really dreaming of someone whom she loved. He thought angrily: Perhaps I could make her say it to me if I showed her the money, but the demands of his body didn't leave him time. He walked quietly down the stairs into the morning and urinated near the bins in a corner against the wall. He looked up once and saw directly above him the face of an old man who was staring at him without surprise or fear. He then made his way down the street: he would get drunk as soon as the pubs opened.

When he got out about ten, he was swaying. He walked down the road past his wife's house. A man with a dog on a lead came out of the house two doors down and waited for his dog to pee against a lamp-post. He said, 'Good evening' politely, but the lorry driver said, 'Shut up, you silly bugger', and continued to walk past the wee houses with their beautiful lawns and their TV aerials. People would be preparing to go to bed in the moonlight. The lawn-mowers were in their sheds. The gates were all shut. The windows were all closed. The little dogs with their bellies touching the ground had all been walked. He gave a furious kick at the low stone wall and stubbed his toes and hopped up and down. He could have raised his head into the air and howled like a wolf out of his rage.

Who could one say, 'Je t'aime' to? Who could say it to you?

Goodbye John Summers

Should I speak or not? And if I did would anyone listen? I have seen the burial and I have read the obituaries, but I cannot make up my mind. It was a fine bright glittery day when they buried him. I stood at the graveside and stared at the coffin as if I wished to make it transparent, but I was confronted by an opaque yellow hexagon. There were a lot of wreaths, tulips, carnations and roses, and little pink ribbons intertwined among them. The wind moved vaguely among hair and along sombre trousers. The tombstones of black granite were like mirrors in which you could see your face.

I was at the service and I heard what they said about him. They said he was a good man; that he was intelligent, industrious and compassionate. All this was in a sense true.

In fact, we were classmates once.

A very cool person was John Summers. Have you ever read what it says in Shakespeare about people 'moving others who are themselves as stone'? But I must say that he was a Christian too, and he probably believed what he acted as if he believed in. He looked cool too, a very pale broad face and a neat dark suit and dark neat hair. Competent looking fellow. He was all of that, the kind of person you wouldn't have to say anything twice to. He was a good listener as well and made you feel important, so total was his commitment to what you were saying.

His parents weren't rich. He went to university and he studied science and did well. Nor did he desert 'the boys' in those days. No, he was one of them. If we had a drinking party he was with us. If we went on one of our 'picnics' he was there, singing songs with the rest. I remember our talks together in that tree-shaded university town. It was the time of Bertrand

Russell. (Later I read some Wittgenstein: I don't think he did.) We would discuss Russell's illustration of the penny. It was in connection with sense data, if you remember. I never liked Russell's work. I thought him a bit of a fake, and still think so now. Not John though. Not him.

Then he joined the army and became a captain in the Engineers. I was a private in the Infantry. We didn't see much of each other till the war was over. I found it interesting that he began to vote Tory. I, of course, have always voted Socialist.

He went into teaching and did not choose a scientific career after all. I now begin to feel that this was because, though he had a good mind, he had no creativity. Yet men cannot be blamed for that.

Yesterday as a headmaster he died.

And then there was the service and the burial.

And all his cronies were there, all those who had surrounded him at the local Rotary Club, all those to whom he had read his 'papers', all those to whom he had read the lessons, in his characteristic humble manner. And some sniffling women who weren't even related to him.

What happened to John Summers? What epitaph shall I write for him? What trap was he trapped in? What lies did he believe in?

For there we were together in the early days – at sixteen or so – playing football together. He was a good footballer, quick, clever, and opportunist. He was the sort of player who is always hanging around near goal when the ball comes over. No one remembers how he got there or whether his goal is the result of inspiration or luck. He was 'with' me in those days. I remember him sweating like the rest of us, wearing his red strip and white shorts, eating his orange, not weighing things up, just being there.

I went to see him on his death bed. His head rested on a very white pillow showing the hair still black. His face brightened when he saw me, and I tried to suppress my shock at what the disease was doing to him.

I said, 'How are you, John?'

And he said, 'You're a doctor, Colin, you should know.'

I knew of course.

'And how are you keeping yourself?'

'Oh, fine,' said I.

A nurse walked past, airy and light, with the dry starchy competent clothes all blue.

What was he thinking of?

'How's Mary?' I said.

He didn't blink.

'Fine,' he said.

Someone had once said of him, 'He's the kind of man who wants to be in on everything. He would read a paper on Urdu if you asked him. He knows nothing about science, especially the recent stuff, but he would lecture you on it. He gives the illusion of knowledge, but he doesn't care about anything really. Except himself.'

'Do you remember,' I said to him, 'the night Miller played the bagpipes on the bus coming home from the "picnic"?'

I could see him trying to remember Miller. Finally he said, ' "The Barren Rocks of Aden", wasn't it?'

And he was right too. Absolutely.

'And the woman who lectured us on zoology,' I pursued. 'Her mother died and she died a year later.'

He thought again and then he said, 'Yes, I remember her. Her name was Green, wasn't it?'

Of course.

He had been a good headmaster or so they said. He had been as you would have expected: competent and, to a certain extent, an innovator. He had kept up with things, no one could say he hadn't. He was willing to do all that was required of him. He would speak well about a departing colleague. He would give a kind reference. He would tell a good joke at the club. He would speak at a Conservative conference.

And I wondered: Did he really like doing thus? Was this really what he wanted to do?

For I remember him one midnight talking about Spain and saying that he wished he could go. And he was horrified by Guernica (or said he was).

He married well, a girl about two years younger than himself who introduced him to the gentry. Sometimes she looked puzzled, but she always supported him and could be humorous about him too.

What I want to know is: What is he? Have I ever known him? I mean was all that stuff about Spain put on because he knew that I was going (as indeed I did, serving in an ambulance unit)? Was he even then saying what he wanted me to believe? Was he building up his image with me as early as this? Was he much cleverer than I ever realised? Did he think even then that a reference to Spain would look bad in his education reports? All those Commies.

What I want to know is: When he was drinking his glass of wine in the light of the flashbulb, when he was delivering his little speech to the local ladies on the atom, was he bored to distraction behind the smiling confident face?

Or was that really his world? Was it sufficient to him? And if so, what can one say about Man?

And was even his Christianity a pose?

The obituaries were all very favourable. His friends were all respectful. All that was in order. I watched the coffin as if I expected him momently to emerge from it like a Houdini. But he did not emerge. Naturally not.

Everyone had something good to say about him. He had helped so many causes, being chairman and vice-chairman of this and of that. Never had he been called upon in vain. He had given so much of his time to the community.

One day I went to the office to see him. He spoke to me very pleasantly, smiled, and then tactfully got rid of me. He was expecting a phone call. Lord Coulter, I believe. Some committee on which he served anyway. Very poised he was, very competent, very cool as always.

But I knew, as he gaily turned away, that he was dying.

So I suppose he was everything they say. Except . . .

When we were in university we were both in love with the one girl. Her name was Lorna. She was a lovably stupid girl, the kind of girl who is always breaking valuable vases, and who rides motor bikes. Full of life, gaiety, and so on. In any case, she contracted TB (there was a lot of that in the forties). The point, however, is this: one night he came to see me and told me that after much conflict he was letting me have the first choice with her. He looked pale and worn as if after a sleepless night. I can't remember exactly how he put it: one can't really remember the words he used. Perhaps that's why it's so difficult to make up one's mind about him.

I married her, of course. But that's not the point: the point is, did he know the night he came to see me that she had TB? I can't for the life of me work out how he could have known.

I keep trying to remember what he said, but all I can remember is him standing by the mantelpiece looking very pale but distinguished.

I mean, perhaps he did think of me as a friend. Perhaps he did really make a sacrifice; but why is it that his sacrifices turned out so well for him and mine so badly for me?

That is why I wonder whether I should say something about him. That he was in fact a bastard of the first order. That he would sell his own mother for an ounce of power. That he conned everybody into believing that he was 'good'.

Or is this what in our society goodness means?

Now if he is a real Christian he may meet Lorna. I wonder what plausible story he will have concocted by then. For I'm sure he'll think of something. And even there one would never be entirely sure of him.

Or is this what Christianity is all about, that there the conning is over and the double-dealing is at peace?

Goodbye, John Summers. The fact is, I don't know what I would put on your tomb and I'm sure you would say the same about me.

The Black and the White

'But you should have seen him,' said Bella out of her fat, white, constipated face. 'I mean,' she said, collapsing into a series of small giggles.

'What was it?' said Chrissie sternly, sitting bitterly by the fire, unable to go to church any more because of her legs which couldn't even take her out of the house.

Speaking through her giggles, Bella continued,

'I mean he was just like the minister, like Mr Gunn. The sermon and everything. How are you feeling?'

'I'm just the same,' said Chrissie, regarding with secret rancour the jar of home-made marmalade which Bella had brought.

'It's not good to be in the house all the time,' said Bella, her face crinkling. 'If you could only get out even for a breath of fresh air.'

Chrissie looked enviously at Bella's legs, large and red. Perhaps she would get varicose veins soon, what with all the walking she did in aid of her Bed and Breakfast.

There was a silence through which she could only hear the ticking of the clock. Nowadays her hearing was so acute that she could hear it when it was about to stop. Life, what was it? Long ago she was young and able and could go to church. There was a calm then and peace and a sense of green. The church was a hollow well, cool as summer water. The silence before the sermon began was the kind of silence that you could get nowhere else, not when you were alone, not even in the midst of mountains. It slowly unwrinkled your mind.

Bella burst out sniggering. 'And he had a collar just like the minister. And he showed us films.'

'They shouldn't be showing films in a church,' said Chrissie decisively. Why should she have been struck down? She had done nothing wrong. She had been a good attender, but God had abandoned her.

'And he gave the blessing at the end just like the minister,' said Bella. 'He raised his arms at the end and he gave the blessing. It was like ... ' She paused, her brow wrinkling. She's such a stupid woman, Chrissie thought. Why am I talking to her at all? She's got all these silly girls, delinquents the whole lot of them.

'Like what?' she said aloud.

'It was like ... he was imitating him. That's what it was like. It would have made you laugh, though you shouldn't laugh in church. I know that. And he told us all about India and how the people were dying. And they had leprosy and how their arms weren't fleshy enough to put the injection in.'

What do I care about that? thought Chrissie. A long time ago I might have cared. But then God left me here alone and I became bitter. I get headaches all the time.

'He said there was millions of them. Millions. And that they looked on their women folk like dirt. He said a man would have four wives. Imagine that,' she continued, sniggering helplessly, 'four wives.'

'What's that to do with Christianity?' said Chrissie fiercely, feeling the pain in her legs again. 'Films and Sunday picnics. What's that got to do with God?'

'I didn't know he was going to be there, you see,' said Bella. 'And instead of the minister you saw this wee man – he was so wee, you understand, you could have lifted him up and put him in the pulpit – and he walked along in his gown very dignified. And, I tell you, Mr Mason went up to the pulpit with the Bible same as he does before Mr Gunn comes in, and you know that he can't abide blacks, and this wee man stood up there and looked at us. Honestly, I nearly burst out laughing. He was so black, you see. He was as black as boot polish.'

'I wouldn't have believed it,' said Chrissie. 'When you think of the old days the ministers would stand up there and tell you that you were a sinner and that you would go to hell. They had spunk.'

Bella broke in eagerly.

'And do you remember Maclachlan saying to them one day, "You come here and you read the Bible as if it was a catalogue. You send away for your wardrobes and your dressing tables and your mirrors, but I am telling you that there will come a day when you will go to a place that will have no wardrobes and no dressing tables and no hairbrushes and no mirrors." Oh, he was a terrible man.'

'He told them the truth,' said Chrissie sharply, 'and they deserved it too. Every word of it. I heard him once. He was a great preacher. Black men!'

Bella said in her giggling voice, 'The funny thing was that he was so black, you know, and it was as if he was imitating what the minister does. You wanted to burst out laughing. You can't tell with their faces, you know, what they're thinking. You can't see anything on their faces, they're so black.'

And Chrissie thought: It was the devil, of course. God has sent the devil into the churches to deceive the people: that's what's happening. The devil is imitating the preachers and laughing at them with his black face and white collar. She imagined the black neck ringed with the white collar.

Oh, she could see him there all right. Wasn't it him who was tempting her to blaspheme, to say that God had left the world for ever, and nothing was left but the television sets and the radios and the dance halls and people swearing as they came up the road at night at twelve and one o'clock?

Wasn't it him who spoke to her in the silence of the night, who spoke to her when the light was blue and the lights spun round the ceiling, in the night when she had to get up to take aspirins to dull the pain, and she could see herself in the long mirror in the long lobby?

Wasn't it the devil who was black as night, who spoke to her out of the black night and said to her, 'Come with me. Abandon yourself. Curse God. Speak the terrible words.'

'He was so funny,' said Bella, 'honestly you couldn't help smiling. What did the doctor say about your legs?'

'He said I wouldn't be able to walk down the stairs. That's what he said. I don't know what I'm going to do.' Her whole body seemed suddenly to be full of tears and she repeated, 'I don't know what I'm going to do.'

As she said this she hoped that Bella would respond in some way, that she would realise that she had opened herself out, that she was asking for help; that Bella would sense in that dim mind the true voice of feeling, that she would know that God had spoken.

'It is hard. Everything is hard these days,' said Bella.

And the moment passed.

Devil, devil, devil, thought Chrissie. You too are a devil. And you laugh at the devil in the pulpit, when he has come to tell us of the end of the world when no one will be able to walk about the streets as it tells us in the Bible, when the world will be abandoned to the night.

'And he told us about the Indian babies. That was nice. That part. He's a clever man though he's black, give him that.'

'Indian babies,' said Chrissie vehemently. 'What are you talking about Indian babies for? He should have been talking about God and his hand upon us. He should have been talking about our sins and our lusts. He should have stood up and denounced you all, that's what he should have done. And you watch his films about Indian babies and you think: It's like the TV. He should have told you the truth about yourselves.'

'Well, Chrissie, there are Indian babies and if you had seen them . . .'

'And I'm telling you that we need God more with our black hearts. That's what I'm saying. And he stands there as black as boot polish when he should be white. Oh, Bella, Bella, how much we need him to be white.'

'Well, I don't know,' said Bella hesitantly, 'I thought he . . .'

'He should be white. It's we who are black. But he should be white. That's what it is, Bella. That's what it should be like. And I'll never see it again. The church will be standing there and I'll never enter it again, I'll never sit in my pew again and listen to the psalms. I'm so tired of the blackness, Bella, and you come along and tell me that it's got into the church.'

Bella looked at her in amazement. She must be going out of her mind. This was the last time she'd come here, that was sure. You paid her a nice visit and she was at your throat.

'It should all be white. Everything should be white. Tell the minister to get rid of him at nights when the light is blue. Or he'll be wandering round the rooms laughing, looking at himself in the mirror and admiring himself and trying on the minister's collar for size. Tell him that. Tell him that our hearts are black enough already. Time is so long and there should be more whiteness and not blackness. Time is so long . . . '

Sweets to the Sweet

When I went into the shop next door that day, I heard them quarrelling, I mean Diane and her father, Mason, or the Lady, as we called him. Perhaps they hadn't heard the tinkle of the bell or he had forgotten that I often came in at that time.

'And I'm telling you that university is crap. I'm not going and that's the end of it.'

That was beautiful baby-faced Diane with the peroxide, white hair and the heart-shaped ruthless face.

I heard him murmuring and she began again:

'I'm telling you, you can shove these books. And all that stuff about sacrificing yourself for me is a lot of . . .'

At that point I went back to the door, opened it and let it slam as if I had just come in. The voices ceased and the Lady came into the shop.

He looked tired and pale, but his sweet angelic smile was in evidence as usual. I heard a far door slam and judged that it must be his daughter leaving.

'Marzipan?' he said. I agreed. I like sweets and I eat a lot of them.

Mason is the kind of man who was born to serve, and not simply because it is his trade but because his whole nature is servile. I mean, one has seen shopkeepers who are brisk and obliging, but this is something else again, this is obsequiousness, an eagerness to please that is almost unpleasantly oriental. It makes one feel uncomfortable, but it must please a certain type since his shop does a good trade and, in fact, the rumour is that he is thinking of expanding.

I return to his servility. It isn't that he is insincere or anything like that. It is as if deep in his soul he has decided that he really is the servant, that you are a different order of being, an aristocrat, and he lower than a peasant. He gives the impression of finding himself in you. If it weren't for you he wouldn't exist. Frankly, if you haven't met that kind of person, it is difficult to explain it. I hope I won't be accused of anti-semitism if I say that he reminds me of a Jew, and yet he isn't a Jew, he belongs to this small town and was born and bred here. I suppose there is something about that kind of person which brings out the fascist in one, a desire to kick him as if he were a dog, he looks so eager to please, hanging on your every word, on your every order, as if a few ounces of sweets is more important to him than anything else you can conceive of. (Some day, if I have the time, I shall write a paper about the psychology of service. I think it's important, I imagine a shopkeeper who screams at you because you don't buy anything from his shop as if 'you had something against him'.) The Lady will even cross his hands and stare at you like a lover till you decide what you want, and then he will sigh as if an accomplishment had taken place.

I come here fairly often, and I know his daughter reasonably well. He has only the one daughter and no sons, his wife is dead. They say that he treated her badly. I don't know about that, but I'm sure that he loved his jars of sweets more than her. Imagine living among sweets all day: one would have to be sour when one had left them surely. Is that not right? He wants Diane to go to university since somewhere buried beneath that servility is ambition. I know her, and she is a bitch. Anyone with half an eye could see that, but she's sweet in public, dewy-eyed and cool above the mini-skirt. One of these peroxide blondes and the kind of nutty mind that may get her yet into a students' riot in our modern educational system.

He has brought her up himself, of course. I have played chess with him in the local chess club; I always win, naturally. After all, would he want to lose a customer? But sometimes, I have seen him looking at me ... He thinks the world of his daughter. You know the kind of thing; if she's first in Domestic Science, he'll give her a bicycle. As a matter of fact, I know that she goes with this fellow Marsh, who's at least ten years older than her, and he takes her out to the beach at night on his motor-cycle. His father owns a hotel in the town, and he's got quite a reputation with the ladies. You're not going to tell me that they are innocently watching the sea and the stars.

She doesn't like me. I know that for a fact. I can tell when people don't like me. I have antennae. She thinks I'm some kind of queer because I'm fifty and not married, and because I'm always going to the library for books. And because I wear gloves. But why shouldn't one wear gloves? Just because young girls wear mini-skirts up to their waists doesn't mean that all the decencies should be abandoned, that the old elegancies should go. I like wearing gloves and I like carrying an umbrella. Why shouldn't I?

That day – as so often before – I got into conversation with the Lady while he hovered round me, and we came round to education.

'They're doing nothing in those schools these days,' I said, and I know it's the truth. 'Expressionism, that's what they call it. I call it idleness.'

He looked at me with his crucified expression and said,

'Do you really believe that?' He had a great capacity for listening, he would never volunteer anything. Some people are like that, they hoard everything, not only books, not only money, but conversation itself. Still, I don't mind as I like talking.

'In our days we had to work hard,' I continued. 'We had to get our noses to the grindstone. Arithmetic, grammar and Latin. Now they write wee poems and plays. And what use are they? Nothing. How many of them will ever write anything of any value? It's all a con game. Trying to make people believe that Jack is as good as his master. I'm afraid education is going down the drain like everything else. They can't even spell, let alone write.'

Suddenly he burst out – rather unusual for him –

'She doesn't want to go to university.' Then he stopped as if he hadn't meant to say so much, and actually wrung his hands in front of me.

'You mean Diane?' I said eagerly.

'Yes. I'm so . . . confused. I wouldn't have said it only I have to talk to someone. You know that I don't have many friends. I can count on you as my friend, can't I?'

As far as you can count on anyone, I thought. As far as anyone can count on anyone.

'She says to me, "I can't stand the books". That's what she says. What do you think of that? "I can't stand the books," she says. She says a haze comes over her mind when she is asked to study. She says that she has read all the books she wants to read. "What is the good of education anyway?" she asks. "All that's over. We don't need education any more and anyway", she says, "we're not poor". What do you make of that?'

'Oh, that's what it's come to,' I answered. 'There was Mr Logan died the other day. Now he spent all his years teaching in that school. He read and read. You won't find many like him any more. Nobody needs him. Nobody wants him.'

He wasn't listening. All he said was,

'After what I did for her too. I used to go with her to get dresses fitted and her shoes and everything, and I'm not a woman you know.'

There might be two opinions about that, I thought to myself. 'I don't understand it,' he said, wringing his hands. 'What's wrong with them? She wanted a guitar. I gave her a guitar. She used to go to the folk club Thursday nights and play it. Then she grew tired of that. She wanted to go to France for her holidays and I let her do that. Do you think it's a phase?' he asked eagerly, his face shining with innocence and agony, the crucified man.

I thought of the little white-headed bitch and said,

'No, it's not a phase.'

'I was afraid it might not be. I don't know what I'm going to do.' He was almost crying, such a helpless little man that you couldn't help but despise him.

'I think you should beat some sense into her,' I said suddenly. He looked horrified. 'I didn't know you believed in corporal punishment,' he said.

'In extreme cases I do,' I answered, 'and this seems to be an extreme case. If it was my daughter, that's what I'd do.'

I took my umbrella in my hands, sighting along it like a gun, and said,

'She's betrayed you, kicked you in the teeth. But that's the younger generation for you. They're like bonbons, mealy on the outside but hard on the inside.'

He smiled, for I had used a simile which he would understand. Deliberately.

'Do you really think so?' he said at last, almost in tears, his lips trembling. 'But it's true, you give them everything and they throw it back in your teeth. I slaved to make this shop what it is and it was all for her and she doesn't care. She's never served a customer and I, I have to do it all. I've even got books to study so that I can help her with her lessons. I've got the whole Encyclopaedia Britannica. What will I do? She says she's going abroad. I gave her everything and her mother too, for five years when she was dying, I'm tired, so tired.'

Aren't we all, I thought, aren't we all.

Anyway, that was the last glimpse I had of him, his wet tremulous lips, his doglike expression, his low emotional voice.

The next part of this story is rather undignified, but I must tell it just the same, and the more so because it is undignified. I am not the sort of person who hides things just because they are unpleasant. On the contrary, I feel that the unpleasant things must be told. And I must justify myself too, especially in this situation, in this unprecedented situation.

I have lived in this town for many years now and people are always hiding their little pseudo-tragedies in holes and corners when, if they only knew it, their tragedies are comedies to the rest of us, and as clear as glass doors, too. But I know all about them. I could blackmail the lot of them if I wished, even the most important people in our town, though they sit at their dinners and lunches, among their glasses and champagne. Walking about the town – stopping here, stopping there, speaking to one person at one corner and to another at another corner – I hear many things. I am one of the sights of the town with my kid gloves and my hat. They all know me, but they don't know how dangerous I am. After all Socrates told the truth and he was put to death.

However, let me continue, though it should rend me. One

night, not long after my talk with the Lady, I was taking my walk out to the bay in the moonlight. I like the evening. Everything is so apparently innocent, the stars are beginning to shine, you can see the boats in the water lying on their own reflections, and you can hear the gentle movement of the sea. All is cool and gentle and without intrigue. Now and again as you pass some trees you may hear a rustle in the undergrowth, a desperate movement and perhaps a squeal, but that's only rarely. The thing about animals is that they don't wear gloves or hats, and they don't gossip about each other.

Sometimes, as I walk along, I think of people and sometimes of books. I doff my hat carefully to people I know and glance equally carefully at people I don't know.

Of course, things are noisier now than they used to be. Cars race past, youths craning their heads out of windows and shouting at the passers-by. And they are crammed full of girls, these sports cars. But I ignore them. I walk past the trees which line the road, and I glance now and again at the sea with its lights. I think of . . . Well, what does one think of?

Anyway, this evening I was walking along slowly, feeling benign and calm, and eventually I came to the bay. The sun was setting in its splendour of gold and red, and I sat down on a seat near the water. What is more beautiful and peaceful than that, watching the purple clouds and the pale moon, and the sun setting in barbaric splendour? The world was calm except for the twittering of birds. All round me was desolate and I was staring out towards the horizon where the sunset was turning the sky into, as they say, technicolour.

What beautiful thoughts we have at such moments! How good and guiltless we appear to ourselves, sitting there as if on thrones, hat on head, gloves on hands, and umbrella in case of a shower! We feel like gods, clean, urbane, without sorrow or guilt.

And as I was sitting there that evening, surrounded by rocks and sand, in the strange music of the sea birds, and confronting a sky of scarlet and purple, who should materialise – and I use the word advisedly – but Diane herself.

How beautiful she was, how young! I cannot describe it. Her

face at first looked more peaceful and calm than I had ever seen it.

She spoke.

'You told my father to beat me,' she said, 'didn't you?'

Her voice was musical and low (where did I hear that before?).

Her eyes were green and she wore this mini-skirt of pure gold. I tried to stand up in confusion, clutching my umbrella.

'No,' she said, 'stay where you are. You look like a king sitting there.' I can swear those were her exact words. But it was like a dream. You must remember the atmosphere: you have to remember that, the colours, the dreams.

Then she leaned down towards my right ear and she said, still in that dreamy voice,

'Beat me then. You can if you want. My father never beats me, that's why I despise him. Don't you do the same? Don't you despise these weaklings, these sellers of goods? Can't you imagine a world beautiful and strong and young? I think that you're young. I was afraid of you at first, but now I realise what you are, what you truly are. You are aloof as if you had a destiny of your own. You watch everyone. Not everyone can do what you do, live in freedom.'

What was I to say? She had a whip in her hand. She handed it to me there in that confusion of red and gold.

And stood there waiting like a little girl.

'I followed you, you know,' she said. 'I know you always take your constitutional and think your great thoughts while you do so. My father told me what you said. I made a great mistake in you. You always looked so mealy-mouthed. But then, when you said that, I knew you were not like my father, that you would not bow and scrape to anyone.'

And all this time, I must have been peeling off my gloves very slowly. I couldn't help myself, I tell you. I was taking the whip into my hands. Was I not right? Had she herself not asked me to?

'You have a shop too,' she said, 'but you don't bother to serve in it. You get others to do that.' (Actually, it is a jeweller's and my sister serves in it. A long time ago I left it. I couldn't bring myself to serve people.)

She kept saying, 'I know now you couldn't do that. Your nature isn't like that, is it? You can't bear to serve, you want to dominate.'

By this time darkness was coming down. She bent over and I raised the whip, and as I did so I knew that this was what I was meant to do, to dominate and not to serve, to impose my will on others, to cleanse the sins of the world. And I knew that volunteers would come to me because they recognised who I really was, the jewel hardness of my will.

She was so beautiful, so submissive. I raised the whip, and as I did so lights flashed all round me, and there was her boyfriend, and she was laughing and giggling and almost rolling on the sand in ecstasy. Naturally, he used a flashlight. And naturally . . . But this I won't go over. The devil, that's what she was, the snake with the green eyes. And so beautiful, wriggling like a fish on the sand. If he hadn't taken the whip from my hands, I would have lashed her and lashed her. I had to wipe the blood from my face with the gloves.

Naturally, my sister left the shop and left the town and naturally . . . Well, naturally, my bowing friend put in for the shop and got it fairly cheap. Who else would buy? Not that he put a direct bid in himself, he did it through intermediaries. It was next door to his sweet shop.

He never came to see me. I never saw him again.

They tell me she's going to university after all, to study psychology. A soft option, if ever there was one.

It was funny though. That moment was the most intense of my life. I'll never forget it. I keep going over and over it in my mind, that duel in scarlet and red. Who would have believed evil would be so beautiful and young? And him so servile too. No wonder we get fascists in the world, fascists with blue eyes like mine.

They deceive you and then turn nasty.

But these green eyes, these . . . sweets.

Murder without Pain

At one end of the vast hall was the platform, colourful with masses of red and white flowers. Seated beyond them (as seen from the back) were the twenty or so usual guests (including three or four ministers, the town clerk, the provost, ex-teachers, all with their wives if they had them, and all serious and childlike in their genial and compassionate gaze). The speeches had been made (' . . . as you go out into the world . . . '), the praises had been, as usual, fulsome, as in every other school in the whole country at that particular moment, the applause from the scholars had been wild and undiscriminating, the prayers had been listened to with a reluctant cessation of whispering, and now the climax of the whole ceremony had been reached. As the people in the hall rose to their feet to the sound of massive chords on the organ, the dux was being presented with his huge silver cup by Mr Andrew Trill, MA, who was ending his last year in school as principal Classics master. The Press photographer (a youth with a round face which yet gave an impression of cynicism) knelt down on one knee, camera aimed, one minister looked up at the scrolled roof where God apparently was, the town clerk stood almost to attention (as he had been taught in the HLI in those glorious military days) and Mr Andrew Trill carefully picked up the cup and . . .

Mr Andrew Trill, MA, was a small man with trenched cheeks rather like those of Dante (as seen in some of his portraits) or a Free Church minister. He had silvery hair and small ears. He wore his university tie for the occasion and a dark blue suit. Forty-four years before, he had graduated with honours in Greek and Latin from his university; he had spent two years in Cambridge, had taught for seven years as an assistant, and then in the tenth year of his career had become Principal at the school where he had remained for the rest of his days.

Unmarried, he stayed with his landlady Mrs Sharpe at a flat one stair up in a tenement near the school. His interests were narrow and were confined mainly to Classics and to his workshop, where he made furniture for his own amusement and occasionally for his landlady's profit. He read nothing modern, believing that all important literature had ceased with the fall of Rome. He idolised Homer, Virgil he admired, Lucretius he respected, Catullus he thought lacking in *gravitas*, Ovid he thought scurrilous and banal, Sophocles he revered as he also did Aeschylus, and Petronius he laughed at. He had once been persuaded by an English master to look at some of Pound's translations, but had considered them so inaccurate and ridiculous that he could never be persuaded to read paraphrases again. One exception he did make among the 'moderns' and that was Samuel Johnson whom he considered grave, moral, massive, and accurate – in short, Roman. He thought highly of his adaptation of Juvenal and would read with delight his essays from *The Rambler*, *The Idler*, and *The Adventurer*.

Though he believed that all literature should serve a moral purpose, he never went to church. This was commented on by some of the local people but, as he had always made it a rule never to defend himself against criticism which he hadn't actually heard, he himself said nothing and left his position unclarified. If he had been asked directly, he might have replied that the quality of the sermons was low or that the clergy were pandering too much to a permissive society or that morality could be divorced from Christian dogma. In this he would have parted company with Johnson. What he admired Johnson for was his steady allegiance to commonsense and truth, and above all, his massive intelligence which was not to be confused with smartness, and which was shown not only in his analysis of books, but in his examination of processes and the routine of ordinary life.

He would quote sentences like the following:

There have been men indeed splendidly wicked, whose

endowments threw a brightness on their crimes and whom scarce any villainy made perfectly detestable because they could never be wholly divested of their excellencies but such have been in all ages the great corrupters of the world and their resemblance ought no more to be preserved than the art of murdering without pain.

When school was over for the day, he would come home with a briefcase full of Latin exercises which he would spend two hours correcting. After that he might go down to his workshop which he had made from a washhouse at the back (since Mrs Sharpe had bought herself a spindryer). Or he might read the daily paper or an educational journal or some Latin or Greek poet. He hardly ever went out. An educational meeting might attract him but it did so less and less as he grew older, or very rarely a visiting orchestra. He never went to the cinema, though in his youth he was a constant attender and might still surprise by a comic reference to the Keystone Cops. He shuddered when he passed a café and heard a juke box playing sounds closely akin to the gibberish of mentally deficient apes.

In philosophical discussion he would be gloomy about the present, comparing it to the last days of the Roman Empire. He had read Muggeridge of whom he approved, though he considered him grossly inferior to the Johnson he seemed to be imitating. He defended his withdrawal from the world by a quotation from *The Adventurer*:

As Socrates was passing through the fair at Athens and cast his eyes over the shops and customers, 'how many things are here', says he, 'that I do not want'.

As a matter of fact, he made some of these things himself. His workshop was well-equipped with lathes, planes, chisels, hammers, the latter neatly hanging in their proper places and meticulously ticketed. He had once invited a member of the Technical Department to have a look at the workshop, and the latter had been amazed by the quality of the tools and the precise and competent way in which they were handled and cared for. For his landlady he had made two chairs which she showed off to the visitors, and a table with folding wings which she kept in her bedroom. He had also done work in steel and aluminium and even in silver. He had made a silver plate for Mrs Sharpe on the twentieth anniversary of the death of her husband who had had a minor job in the Civil Service.

His landlady was about sixty years old and had no other lodgers but him. Thirty years before, he had arrived at her door with a green case, had pressed the bell and waited there calmly for someone to answer it. No one could have told that he had just spent three hours looking for lodgings, his expression was so cool and patient. She had studied him with sharp care, but the final verdict in his favour had been made simply because he was a man. Her two previous lodgers – both at the same time – had been two girls who had monopolised the bathroom, had kept odd hours (one had fallen over the umbrella stand one night coming home from a party), and had not shown her what she considered to be proper respect.

This man, however, talked quietly and politely, his clothes were neat without being ostentatious, he seemed sound and professional, and she accepted him. In doing this she made no error, for he raised his rent steadily without being told and he made furniture for the house, an unexpected bonus. When he came first he was paying three pounds a week, now he was paying seven and she had never had to ask him for the money. By what procedure he decided that he should raise the rent (whether he vaguely noticed in shops that prices were going up) she couldn't tell: perhaps he had some sixth sense which learned Mrs Sharpe's desires without words. She didn't actually see much of him. She knocked at his door in the morning at eight o'clock precisely. He rose immediately and went into the bathroom. He was out of there by fifteen minutes past, dressed and ready for breakfast by twenty-five minutes past, and by twenty to nine was out of the house. He had no finicky tastes in food and accepted without question what she set before him. For this reason, he had been eating porridge followed by bacon and egg for the best part of thirty years. He came home for his dinner and also took his tea there. He hardly ever went out and never dined in a restaurant, so that he had no other food with which to compare hers. He never told her anything about the school and never gossiped. This was the only thing she had against him, for she would dearly have loved some inside information, but she was sensible enough to content herself with her other blessings.

She thought him wise and clever, though a bit odd. Once he had gone out in a thick overcoat on a blindingly hot summer day and once he had come home in his gown. She thought it wasn't good for him to be closeted in the house all the time and suggested sometimes that he might go to an exhibition or the local theatre, but he simply ignored her, wiping his mouth delicately with his napkin. She herself was in the habit of going to visit her sister-in-law on Tuesday night and playing bingo on a Friday night. She was quite sure he didn't know what bingo was, and therefore considered herself superior to him in this, though inferior in other things. She had seen his Latin and Greek books and had heard that he was a meticulous, though just and successful teacher, and a man of strong convictions who was held in great respect. He hardly ever wrote letters and rarely received any. Perhaps he had no living relations. Perhaps he was an orphan who had done well for himself. In any case, there was something mysterious about him.

He hated cruelty in any form, and once when she had read out to him a passage from the local newspaper which told of violent and disorderly conduct at a dance, and described in a certain amount of detail a murderous assault which had taken place as a result, he had told her to stop. He seemed to believe, however, that such violence was confined to the lower classes, and as he never came into contact with them he comforted himself with dreams of peace. She knew that her own knowledge of life was greater than his. Many years before she had gone out on to the stair and stopped a fight which was taking place between a Protestant and a Catholic, and she had been greatly respected for it. He would never have gone out; not so much, she guessed, because he was a coward, but because he would appear undignified. Nowadays, there were no fights. Only respectable people lived in the tenement, which was strong with good stone, probably granite, though she wasn't sure.

As has been said, Mr Trill was greatly respected by his colleagues, who treated him with a certain protectiveness for he was inclined to be absent-minded, though he could also be difficult in argument. Over the years, he grew to believe that education was declining and he was not in favour of what he called 'creative indiscipline'. Once there had been in the school a young teacher of twenty-three or so, fresh from what he considered to be the triumphs of training college and brimful of innovations and enthusiasm. He would hold forth in the staffroom about the outdated nature of the teaching in the school. He would say,

'Scottish education hasn't changed for centuries. They are always boasting that it is the best in the world, but it is in fact inferior to English and even to American. The Americans have allowed their children to create out of chaos but we don't allow them to create at all. We make them sit at their desks for five hours a day, and if they make a noise they must be punished. They are taught Tennyson but no Eliot. Literature stopped dead with Browning or even earlier, as far as their examination setters are concerned.'

This young man, whose popularity was therefore not great, had begun all manner of projects. He had told his pupils not to call him sir. He got them to compose plays, which they acted on the floor. He allowed them to use in their plays the language of the working classes and to borrow from television some of the worst language that they heard there. He took them to visit distilleries, sailors' homes, agricultural colleges. His room was full of models, pamphlets and charts. He used a tape recorder and made them write compositions based on film music which he played on a record player. He made them run round the school and asked them to write about how they felt while doing so.

His room was next door to Mr Trill's. One day the latter who was working on Lucretius' *The Nature of Things*, had been unable to bear the noise. He had gone to the young man's door and said to him,

'Why is it that when you put your theories of creative chaos into action, it prevents other teachers from doing their own work? The dictionary has a word for this: it is not experimentalism, it is thoughtlessness.' With this majestic rebuke he had gone back to Lucretius, leaving the young man open-mouthed at the door. After that the room next door had been quieter.

Mr Trill believed that new methods were often the result of restlessness.

'Why should they spend hours on amateurish plays of their own immature creation when they could be working on the excellent productions of others?' he would ask.

Or, 'What is the connection between a visit to a distillery and the teaching of English?'

One of his witticisms was, 'Do you think it would improve my pupils if I taught them Latin music?'

He had once inadvertently heard Edmundo Ros on the radio and had been so disgusted that his favourite term of abuse was, 'You are as bad as Edmundo Ros.' This surprised some of his earlier pupils, but as many of his later ones hadn't heard of Edmundo Ros the comparison lost its point.

His teaching was thorough and successful. He believed in making all his pupils competent in grammar, and when it was stated by the Education Department that this was not necessarily a training in intelligence, he laughed. He told them that the wisest men had been the earliest writers and poets, and that those who came after had only embroidered thoughts which had first been conceived by others. It cannot be said that his pupils were *great* Latinists as a result of his teaching, but at least they were meticulous ones. He was well liked because he never changed and was always predictable, and this gave his pupils a feeling of security. At Christmas he would often be surprised by small presents such as a tie pin or a wallet. He would accept these with gravity and secret jubilation.

His main weakness was that he lectured too much, though he often practised what he called the Socratic method. He was often impatient but always kind to those who tried. He thought that it was very important to be good and if you couldn't be a good scholar you could at least be a good person.

In the last year of his work as principal Classics teacher, there came into his class a boy called Carruthers who was tall, dark, good-looking, superficially lazy and exceedingly clever. He wrote advanced poems which had no rhyme and which used long words like 'vertiginous'. The poems had such titles as 'The Life and Death of a Hippopotamus' or 'Requiem for a Clarinettist'. Carruthers had long legs which stretched out from below the desk, and this made him appear to lounge, as did also his habit of resting his head on his right hand.

At first Mr Trill didn't like him, mainly because he appeared supercilious, but then he grew to like him more because the boy stammered a little and this suggested that he was nervous. Apart from that the boy did his work neatly and well (and with a certain panache), handed it in on all the right days and laughed at Mr Trill's jokes without superiority. After Mr Trill had spoken to them about Johnson, Carruthers was once seen carrying a copy of Johnson's works (this was the only day that Mr Trill could recollect him forgetting his exercise).

He could construe beautifully and was very quick. In fact, he was potentially the best scholar Trill had ever had and for this reason he grew proud of him. He had done off his own bat several translations into verse of passages from Virgil and Homer. One of the sections he had worked on was that one translated by Dryden from Virgil:

> The gates of hell are open night and day
> Smooth the descent and easy is the way
> But to return and view the cheerful skies
> In this the task and mighty labour lies.

As has already been remarked, Mr Trill didn't come into contact with the 'low' rough elements of the school, those which were disorderly and riotous. As he usually had only twenty-five or so scholars in the Sixth, and as they were well orientated towards school by their parents, he had no trouble with discipline. He did not believe that there was much evil in the school, only mischief, and he only half listened to the complaints of those teachers who were in closer contact with the lower classes than he was himself.

One day he said to Carruthers, 'Carruthers, I think you should study for the Bursary Compeitition. I think you would have a good chance of winning it.'

Carruthers had looked at him in his easy smiling polite way and had said,

'If you think so, sir.'

'I do think so, Carruthers. Otherwise I wouldn't have said it. You will have to work hard though, won't you?'

'Yes, sir.'

And Carruthers had worked hard. He read his Homer. Book Three of the *Odyssey* was the main text assigned, but he read a number of other books as well. Nor did he only concentrate on his Classics. His marks in English were very high and his marks in languages also. He was in charge of the School Magazine and was a notable footballer. Everything he tried turned to gold. Other teachers, however, would complain that he spent rather a lot of time in cafés, and it was rumoured that he had been caught drinking at a dance. If he were taken on a school excursion he had a habit of getting lost, always emerging later on with a plausible excuse. All these things Trill would forgive because of an essay he might write on 'Was Virgil Really a Christian?' or 'Lucretius and the World of the Atom'. Trill sometimes felt that he ought to have him up to the house for fuller discussion, but he couldn't very well do so since the house was not his own.

However, in spite of his casual brilliance (or because of it) accusations against Carruthers mounted. He had been seen late at night with a girl from the hostel. There was even a story that he had stolen some money. Many of the stories had been corroborated and proved to everybody's satisfaction. Mr Trill would look at him as he lounged in the sunlit room and think: I wonder how a boy of such intelligence can be enticed into evil courses.

Mr Trill, as has been said, lived in a protected world. True, there had been violence in the days of the Romans and the Greeks, but that violence had been transformed into great art and was therefore respectable. Also the Greeks had been just. Mr Trill was very fond of telling a story which illustrated this.

The story occurred, he said, in a history written by a Greek. A Spartan had arrived home alive from a war. This Spartan had naturally been ostracised by the other Spartans for, after all, Spartans were supposed to return home from a defeat only on their shields, that is, dead. A new battle was to be fought and this Spartan went out to fight with the others, consumed with zeal in order to gain his lost honour. He fought well and was in fact the bravest of the brave. However, in that battle there was another Spartan who, though not so brave as the first one, was nearly so. He fought, not with manic enthusiasm, but with resolution and steadiness. The palm was given to him because, according to this Greek historian, the second one was fighting for his country, the first one only to justify himself.

Mr Trill would say,

'Can you not imagine which one of the two the *Daily Express* would have honoured?' He did not think that this question required an answer.

Mr Trill himself had never fought in any war, being young enough to miss the first one and old enough to escape the second. He had never seen violence at first hand, except once when he had witnessed an accident in which a pedestrian had been run over, and a police car with a pulsing blue light had raced up, followed by the ambulance.

Once he said to Carruthers,

'I have been hearing certain things about you.'

'What things, sir?' said Carruthers, speaking with innocence and politeness.

'That you drink, that you are undependable, that you haunt these cafés with low elements late at night, that you have been seen at the girls' hostel, that you smoke. Is all that true?'

'No, sir.'

'None of it?'

'Some of it, sir. Not all.' All this time Carruthers, tall and easy, had smiled as if thinking of something else, and Trill had been a little frightened for he felt himself in the presence of a superior intelligence. The girls in the class, of course, adored Carruthers, not because he was clever, but because he was handsome. Sometimes Trill would wonder (for he was an

honest man) if the reason why he was growing to dislike
Carruthers was that he himself had never married and had
never had the adoration of women. He thought about this long
and deeply, and at last came to the conclusion that of this
accusation at least he was innocent. From that moment he
dismissed the thought from his mind, for he was quite capable
of being his own executive Freud.

Once by accident he discovered that Carruthers had cheated.
A translation which he had handed in had come from a crib. He
asked Carruthers whether the translation was his own and the
latter, secure in the knowledge that the crib was not likely to be
known to any but a few, denied it. For this he was given five
hundred lines and a tongue-lashing in front of the class.
Carruthers regarded him with a certain smiling impudence but
said nothing.

Sometime after this his phone had rung incessantly and when
he picked it up, a voice at the other end said, amidst the
giggling of girls,

'I am ringing up to discover the meaning of the following
words: *Pedicabo et irrumabo vos*. They occur we believe in
Catullus. I am a Nigerian scholar and I have to pass an examination and hearing that you were an authority on these matters
and happening to be in town I thought I would enquire. I hope
I am not discommoding you in any way.'

He could never actually prove that the voice was Carruthers',
but his hate for Carruthers dated from that night.

This hate was completely irrational, so irrational and blinding
that he could hardly bear to look at Carruthers in class. If it
hadn't been for his strong sense of duty he would have got rid of
him, but he decided that he would be fair to the very end. He
spoke to him more politely than to the others, but his politeness
was chilly though correct. He already was convinced that
Carruthers was dangerous and that neither scholarship nor
brilliance could justify evil.

Even at night in the house he could not forget him and his
knuckles would whiten on the hammer or the chisel. What
seemed to him to make the whole affair even more incomprehensible was that Carruthers was the offspring of good though

rather bewildered parents who had done their best, but had failed mainly because they had left him to go his own way.

Nevertheless, his work was still good. His translation showed not only accuracy but insight. He was going to be the dux of the school and he would most probably win a high place in the Bursary Competition. Sometimes Trill would consider the rest of the scholars, how they worked hard, how they did all that could be expected of them, how their lives were models of patient virtue, and how they would never attain a position in the world. This made him angry and confirmed him in his resolution never to go to church. He began to believe that Carruthers was simply lucky, that his gifts were not his own to dispose of, that he had been born with them though he acted as if they belonged to him alone and by right. The other sloggers showed no envy but rather admiration for one who was essentially inferior to themselves.

Often Mr Trill would read over the lines from Johnson's 'London':

> Others with softer smiles and subtler art
> can sap the principles or taint the heart;
> with more address a lover's note convey,
> or bribe a virgin's innocence away.
> Well may they rise, while I, whose rustic tongue
> ne'er knew to puzzle right or varnish wrong,
> spurned as a beggar, dreaded as a spy,
> live unregarded, unlamented die.

Perhaps if he had gone out more, perhaps if he had lived like some of the teachers in the outer world, or had a better sense of proportion, what did happen might never have happened. Perhaps if he had been willing to discuss golf or the painting of houses, the fevers of other people's children or the mowing of a lawn, perhaps if he had been capable of these things he would not have done what he did. However, as he himself would doubtless have said, 'In all true living there is no perhaps.'

Time and time again, Trill did in fact make an effort to forgive Carruthers. After all, hadn't Johnson himself written at the end of one of his essays:

Of him that hopes to be forgiven it is indispensably required that he forgive. It is therefore superfluous to urge any other motive. On this great duty eternity is suspended and to him that refuses to practise it the Throne of Mercy is inaccessible and the Saviour of the world has been born in vain.

In spite, therefore, of his dislike of Carruthers which almost amounted to hate, he might still have succeeded in forgiving him if that had not happened which to Trill was the ultimately unforgivable. He might have lasted out to the end of the session, hating yet controlled; he might have been constrained to admit that he had been confronted not so much by evil as by mischief (though mischief carried to a higher degree than is usual), if that other event had not happened, which caused Trill's soul to become as iron and his will inflexible.

One day a fifth year boy was found unconscious in the boys' cloakroom. He had been beaten about the head with somebody's boots and so viciously that he was nearly dead. It was Mr Trill who had found him. That particular day he had been on duty patrolling the corridors making sure that there was no horseplay in the washrooms, and protecting cars and property from vandalism. The incident must have happened very quickly, probably when he was over at the other end of the school, 'mooning' about in the sunshine. When he reached the cloakroom there was no one there but the boy, who was lying on his back breathing stertorously, his face covered with blood. One of his eyes was black and there were studmarks on his right cheek. His tie was askew and his jacket open; some of the buttons appeared to be missing. As he looked down at the boy, Mr Trill was at first overwhelmed by horror and then by the most terrible rage. His first reaction was to get hold of the headmaster, which was done, and the boy was immediately taken to hospital in an ambulance. The police had also been contacted.

Mr Trill was almost sick, but he continued his work with a grim expression and an unusually grim resolve. He had never believed that he was a violent man, but he felt convinced that if he could discover who had done that atrocious deed, he would have killed him with his bare hands. His mind was tormented by the most strange images. He imagined himself challenging the perpetrator to a duel with guns or with swords. Later he thought he would simply fight him, and his anger would in itself be sufficient to make him prevail.

He talked to the other teachers about this, and it surprised him that, though all were disgusted with the incident, they didn't seem to feel it at all. They all condemned the beating by means of boots but they didn't appear to feel the boots biting into their own flesh. Some of the younger men used phrases like 'putting the boot in him' which apparently was the practice among city gangsters. None of them revealed that absolute horror and disgust which he himself felt so strongly, but he knew that they would be better at finding out the truth than he was.

An investigation was immediately set on foot. It was discovered that the boy had owed money to another boy. At first this boy's name could not be discovered, but eventually he turned out to be a member of Mr Trill's own Sixth. He, however, protested that he had not touched the victim and it could be proved that he was nowhere near the washroom at the time as he had been sent on an errand downtown by one of the teachers.

Needless to say, Mr Trill ceased to speak to him from that time onwards, for he strongly suspected that the boy was lying. What horrified him more than anything else was that the violence had spread to his own class. His years of teaching the Classics, his concentration on the great thoughts of the world, had failed utterly and completely. It had all ended in a furious scuffle with the words, 'Put the boot in him'.

As time went on, more and more facts were uncovered. The boy himself was unconscious for three days and was in no condition to be questioned. Later, however, it was discovered that he had been attacked by another boy who was in a non-academic class, the latter being immediately expelled after a careful examination. Mr Trill saw him before he left. In fact, he deliberately went to have a look at him to see what he was like. He had eyes like pebbles – this was the first thing he noticed – and no expression whatsoever. Apart from that, he appeared well-mannered and quiet. Irony of ironies, he was distinguished by the fact that he wore a school uniform which was not usual in the school. Mr Trill never had occasion to come into contact with this boy and looked on him as a being from another world, a chimpanzee with a school badge. In a sense, he felt a certain relief. After all, this boy might be the only culprit; this gave him some comfort, though it didn't lessen his hate. He was beginning to feel that the world of the classics – peaceful and calm, devoted to verbs and poets, the world of avenues and stoas, of learning and scholarship – was collapsing all round him in a small vicious dust. Sometimes he would sit by the window of his classroom staring vacantly into space for long periods on end.

So the weeks passed and it appeared that nothing more could be elicited. Eventually, however, after some heart-searching and on the insistence of his parents, the victim told the whole story. He had in fact owed money and had been threatened with a doing over. He had been frightened, but there was no way in which he could get the money. One day he had been in the washroom by himself (he had felt rather strange and eerie at the time because it was unusual for the washroom to be so deserted) when this Fourth Former had come in, had immediately without speech or warning butted him in the head as he was moving away from the sink with the water and soap still in his eyes, had knocked him down and then begun to kick him. The new piece of information was that Carruthers (a friend of the creditor) had been watching all this butchery while it went on, and, with a smile on his face, had given instructions to the Fourth Former as to how he should deal with his victim.

Trill could imagine it all. He could imagine Carruthers standing there, radiant and handsome, he could imagine the delight which he took in the incident, the way in which he would savour every single exact drop of cruelty. All this was clear to him. And it also showed Carruthers as he really was, a perverted intelligence, one to whom Virgil, Homer and the rest were merely pretexts for getting ahead in the world, one whose smile concealed pure and utter evil.

He avoided Carruthers henceforth. The boy sickened him. As he lounged there, calm and relaxed, Trill would sometimes be seized by an almost insane desire to seize him by the throat and strangle him to death. When he went home at night he would think of what ought to be done. He now believed that Carruthers was a dangerous being and could not understand how others could not see this as clearly as he did. He was astonished to find that the incident had raised him in the opinions of the girls, who now idolised him more than ever, as if he knew adult secrets that they themselves longed for but were too shy to investigate. Trill felt that at least the girls would have some veneration for human life, that they would detest one who had not done the attacking but had watched while someone else did it. The fact that they did not appear to feel any disgust for Carruthers enraged him even more.

At night he brooded. What could he do? What he wanted was a kind of justice which would not be crude but which, on the contrary, would be refined and exact, a justice which would be Greek to its very essence, as if scholarship itself were taking revenge on one who had violated it with such contempt.

One night between dream and waking it came to him, the perfect solution. It was as if it had been given from the depths of his subconscious, where Virgil and Homer lay together on that sea bed.

It happened that in order to honour Mr Trill's long service to the school, the headmaster invited him to present the prizes at the end of term. All his time in the school, Mr Trill had never asked for anything, had been uncomplaining and dedicated, had shown loyalty far beyond the call of mere duty. The honour was not disinterested since it might show others that their way of achieving an equal one was to show the same inhuman dedication.

Mr Trill spent the last week of the session (the nights, that is) in the workshop. Hour after hour he spent there. Sometimes he would not emerge till midnight. He was continually consulting clocks: did he have time? His cheeks became hollow, his eyes had dark circles under them. He hardly slept and he hardly ate. He almost completely ignored his landlady as if he had forgotten about her.

On the day of the prize-giving, which was a beautiful summer day, he dressed even more neatly than usual and ate a good breakfast. He paid his landlady for the week saying jocularly,

'Well, I think we're even if anything should happen to me.' She wondered about these words afterwards and would often quote them to her friends, the 'girls' who patronised bingo with her. Mr Trill tidied up his books and put them in a big case. He told her that he was going to sell them all as he didn't need them now (of course she knew that this was the last day of his work at school, but she was surprised just the same). As he was going out the door he turned as if he were about to say something, but he seemed to change his mind and continued on his way. He had the silver cup with him, in order to save time, he said. She watched him walk down the road as he had done for so many years, but this time with a strange foreboding as if she were seeing him for the last time. He did not wave up to her, since he was holding the cup.

The cameraman knelt, the minister decided that perhaps God was not in the ceiling after all, the town clerk retained his military pose, and to Carruthers, the dux of the school (stepping smartly on to the platform, his cowlick flopping endearingly over his forehead), Mr Trill handed the cup. As Carruthers picked it up (and the organ pealed and the mothers of those who had not received prizes gazed at him with fake geniality) a needle containing poison punctured his hand, the poison quickly made its way through the bloodstream and, in his moment of triumph, he fell dead, Trill looking down at him with a detached Greek gaze.

The following lines from Johnson were later discovered inscribed on the cup:

> Then shall thy friend, nor thou refuse his aid,
> still foe to vice, forsake his Cambrian shade:
> In virtue's cause once more exert his rage,
> Thy satire point and animate thy page.

It was noted later that the word 'point' might have given Trill his idea.

One of the Christian ministers (who had the habit of wearing a long cassock and drawing attention to himself by the fervour of his devotions) made a long and apparently profound prayer over the dead dux. He did not realise that he was present at an older justice.

The Adoration of the Mini

It was an old people's hospital and yet he wasn't old. As she stood at the door about to press the bell she looked around her and saw beside a shrouded wheelchair some tulips swaying in the white March wind. Turning her head into the cold bright sun, she saw farther down the road a fat man in blue washing a bright red car. She felt joyous and sad by turns.

She pressed the bell, and a nurse in white and blue came to the door. Visiting hours were two to three, but she thought she could call at any time now. The nurse was stony-faced and middle-aged and glancing at her quickly seemed to disapprove of the roundness of her body: it was not the place for it. She pushed back her blonde hair which had been slightly disarranged by the wind. She asked for Mr Mason, and the nurse showed her the door of the ward. Here and there she could see other nurses, but none of them was young; it would have been better if at least one or two had the expectancy and hope of youth. It would make the place brighter, younger, with a possible future.

She walked into the ward. The walls were flaked with old paint, and old men, propped on pillows, stared ahead of them without recognition or care. One old man with a beard, his eyes ringed with black as if from long sleeplessness, looked through her as though she had been a window pane beyond which there was no country that he could love or desire. By one or two beds – the bedside tables bearing their usual offerings of grapes and oranges, and bottles of yellow energy-giving liquids wrapped in cellophane – there were women talking in whispers.

She walked through the main ward, not seeing him, and then through into a smaller one. And there he was, on his own, sitting up against the pillows as if waiting. But he could not be expecting her. He might be expecting her mother or her brother or her other sister, but not her.

The smell of imminent death was palpable and distinct. It was in the room, it was all round him, it impregnated the sheets, it was in his face, in his eyes. She had seen him ill before, but not like this. His colour was neither yellow nor red, it was a sort of grey, like old paper. The neck was long and stringy, and the knotted wrists rested meagrely on the sheet in front of him.

She stood at the foot of the bed and looked at him. He looked back at her without energy. She said,

'I came to see you, father.'

He made no answer. It was as if he hadn't heard her or as if (if he had heard her) she wasn't worth answering. She noticed the carafe of water at the table at the foot of the bed and said,

'Do you want a drink?'

He remained silent. She began again:

'I came up by train today. It took me eight hours.'

She shook her yellow hair as if to clear her head and said,

'May I sit down?' He still didn't speak and she sat down on the chair. He spoke at last:

'How do you think I look?'

She replied with conscious brightness,

'I had thought you would be worse.'

'I think I'm dying,' he said tonelessly and almost with cunning, 'I've had strange visions.'

He shut his eyes for a moment as if to rest them.

'What do you want?' he asked without opening his eyes.

'I wanted to see you.'

'What about?'

'I . . .'

'You left a good job and went off to London and you're pregnant, isn't that right,' he said slowly, as if he were carving something with a chisel and hammer. 'You had a good brain and you threw it all away. You could have gone on to university.'

'We're married now,' she said.

'I know that. You married a Catholic. But then Catholics breed a lot, don't they?' He opened his eyes, looking at her in disgust, his nose wrinkling as if he could smell incense. She flared up, forgetting that he was dying.

'You know why I left, father. I didn't want to go to university. I'm an ordinary person.'

'You had an IQ of 135. I shouldn't be telling you this but I saw it on your school records.'

'I didn't want to go to university. I didn't want to do Science.'

'I didn't care. It didn't need to be Science. It could have been any subject. You threw yourself away. You went to work in a wee office. And then you got pregnant. And now you say you are married. To a Catholic. And you'll have to be a Catholic too. I know them. And your . . . ' He couldn't bring himself to say that her child would be a Catholic.

She couldn't stop herself. 'I thought a scientist wouldn't care for these things. I thought a scientist would be unprejudiced.'

He smiled grimly. 'That's the kind of remark I would have expected from you. It shows that you have a high IQ. You should have used it. You threw it away. You ignored your responsibilities. You went off to London, to see the bright lights.' She sensed envy in his voice.

After a while she said,

'I couldn't stand school. I don't know how I can explain it to you. The books didn't mean anything after a while. It was torture for me to read them. Can you understand that?'

'No.' His mouth shut like a rat-trap.

'I tried,' she continued. 'I did try. But they didn't mean anything. I would look at a French book and a Latin book and it didn't connect with anything. Call it sickness if you like, but it's true. It was as if I was always tired. I used to think it was only people in non-academic classes who felt like that. I was all right in the first three years. Everything seemed to be interesting. And then this sickness hit me. All the books I read ceased to be interesting. It was as if a haze came down, as if the words lost any meaning, any reality. I liked music but there was nothing for me in words. I'm trying to explain. It was a sickness. Don't you understand?'

'No, I don't understand. When I was in the upper school I wasn't like that. I read everything I could lay my hands on.

Books were treasures. When I was in university it was the same. I read because I loved to read. I wanted to have as much knowledge as possible. Even now . . . ' He paused.

She probed: 'Even now?'

But he had stopped speaking, like a watch run down. She continued,

'Yes, I admired that in you, though you were narrow-minded. I admired your love of books and knowledge and experiments. I admired you for thinking out new ways of presenting your subject. I admired your enthusiasm, though you neglected your family. And then too you went to church. What did you find in church?'

'In church? I found silence there.'

'It was different with us,' she continued. 'It wasn't that I didn't try. I did try. I would lock myself in my room and I would study my Virgil. I would stare at it. I would look up meanings. And then at the end of an hour I hadn't moved from the one page. But I tried. It wasn't my fault. Can't you believe me?'

'I don't understand.' Then he added mercilessly, 'It was idleness.'

'And there you would be in the other room, in your study, preparing your lesson for the following day, smoking your pipe, thinking up new ideas like the time you made soap. You were the mainstay of the school, they said. So much energy. Full of power, boyish, always moving, always thinking. Happy.'

A smile crossed his face as if he were looking into another world which he had once loved and in which he had meaning and purpose.

'Yes, I gave them a lot,' he said. 'A lot. I tried my best with you as well. I spent time on you. I wanted you to do well. But I couldn't make a favourite of you. And then you said you were leaving.'

'It happened one night. I had been doing some exercises in English. I think it was an interpretation passage. I was sitting at the table. There was a vase with flowers in front of me. The electric light was on, and then I switched on the radio and I heard this voice singing "Frankie and Johnny". It was Lena

Horne. I listened to it. At first I wasn't listening to it at all. I was trying to do my exercise. Then, after a while, the music seemed to become more important than what I was doing. It defeated what I was doing. It was about real things and the interpretation wasn't about anything. Or rather, it was about the lack of trade unionism in Japan. I'm not joking: that's what it was. How the bosses wouldn't allow the workers any unions and how they kept their money for them. It had no meaning at all. It was like . . . It was like some obstacle that you pushed against. Like a ghost in a room. And I laid down my pen and I said to myself. What will happen if I stop doing this? And then I did stop. And suddenly I felt so free. It was as if I had lightened myself of some load. I felt free. I listened to the song and I didn't feel any guilt at all.'

He looked at her almost with hatred.

'If you didn't feel any guilt why are you here then? Why didn't you stay with your Catholic? By the way, what does he do?'

'He has an antique shop. Actually, he's quite scholarly. He's more scholarly than you. He knows a lot about the Etruscans. He's very enthusiastic. Just like you. He's got a degree.' She laughed, bubbling.

'In that case,' he said, 'why didn't you stay with him?'

'I came to ask you,' she said, 'what it all means.'

He said, 'I remember one morning at a lecture we were told about Newton. It was a long time ago and it was a large lecture room, row upon row of pupils, students stretching to the very back and rising in tiers. There was sunlight and the smell of varnish. And this bald man told us about Newton. About the stars and how everything was fixed and unalterable and the apple falling to the ground in a garden during the Plague. Harmony. He talked about harmony. I thought the sky was full of apples. And that the whole world was a tree.'

There was a long silence. In it she felt the child turning in its own orbit.

'What use are the books to you now?' she said. The words sounded incredibly naive, almost impudent, and inhuman but she didn't mean them like that. And yet . . .

'You mean,' he said, 'that my life was useless. That I spent my days and nights on phantoms. Is that what you want? Did you come to gloat?'

'No, I want to know, that's all. I want to know if it was something wrong with me. Perhaps it was something wrong with me all the time.'

She imagined him walking in the middle of the night, listening to the silence of the wards, watching the moonlight on the floor. She imagined him looking into the eyes of nurses for reassurance, without speech. She imagined him imagining things, the whispers, the rumours, the laughter. Sometimes a man would die and his bed would be empty. But there would always be another patient. She imagined him thinking: At what hour or minute will I die? Will I die in pain? Will I choke to death?

She thought of London and of this small place. She thought of the anonymity of London, the death of the rainy days. The lostness. The strangeness. Had she chosen well? She thought of Sean, with his small tufted beard, vain, weak, lecherous. He was her only link with that brutal city. All else flowed, she could only follow him, the indeterminate atom.

'You don't know what duty is,' he said at last. 'You live on romance and pap. I've seen you reading *Woman's Own*. You think that the world is romantic and beautiful.' (Did she think that? Was that why she had run away? Did she think that now? What had she not seen? Into the heart of the uttermost darkness in that room where at night the lights circled the ceiling, and nothing belonged to her, not even the flat, not the Etruscan soldiers with their flat, hollow sockets.)

'You don't know about trust and loyalty. You knuckle under whenever any difficulty crops up. Your generation is pap and wind. You owe allegiance to nothing. I have owed allegiance to this place. They may forget me, but I served. What else is there to do?'

She said in a low voice, 'To live.' But he hadn't heard her.

'To serve,' he said. 'To love one's work. Oh, I was no Einstein but I loved my work and I think I did good. You, what do you do?'

Nothing, she thought, except to live where the lightning is, at the centre where the lightning is. At the disconnected places.

At the place where our truth is to be found on the rainwashed blue bridges. At the place without hypocrisy. In the traffic. Where she would have to fight for everything including her husband, not knowing that at least this she could keep, as her mother had known. In the jungle.

She stood up and said, 'Goodbye, father.'

Defiantly he said, 'You refused your responsibility.'

It was like standing on a platform waving to a stranger on a train. For a moment she couldn't make up her mind whether he was leaving her or she leaving him.

He relapsed into petulance. 'I shouted for the nurse last night but she was too busy. She heard me right enough but she didn't come.'

She thought to herself: There is a time when one has to give up, when nothing more can be done. When the connection has to be out. It is necessary, for not all things are retrievable.

As she stood up she nearly fell, almost upsetting the carafe of water, herself full of water.

He had closed his eyes again when she turned away and walked through the ward head down, as if fighting a strong wind. She paused outside the door in the blinding March light where the tulips were.

The man she had seen before had finished polishing his car and was looking at it with adoration. She thought: The Adoration of the Mini, and smiled.

The child stirred. The world spun and took its place, the place that it must have as long as she was what she was. She had decided on it. And what she was included her father. And she thought again of her child, loving and pitying it.

Home

The black polished car drew up outside the brown tenement and he rested for a moment, his hands still on the wheel. He was a big man with a weatherbeaten red-veined face and a strong jaw. On one finger of his right hand was a square red ring. He looked both competent and hard.

After a while he got out, gazing round him and up at the sky with a hungry look as if he were scanning the veldt. His wife in furs got out more slowly. Her face had a haggard brownness like that of a desiccated gipsy and seemed to be held together, like a lacy bag, by the wrinkles.

He glanced up at the tenement with the cheerful animation of one who had left it, and yet with a certain curiosity.

'Lock the car, dear,' said his wife.

He stared at her for a moment in surprise and then said as if he had been listening to a witticism,

'But they don't steal things here.'

She smiled disdainfully.

They walked into the close whose walls were brown above and a dirty blue below, pitted with scars. Somebody had written in chalk the words Ya Bass. It looked for a moment African, and he stared at it as if it had recalled some memory.

On the other side of the road the flat-faced shops looked back at them blankly.

He pointed upwards to a window.

'Mind the Jamiesons?' he said.

She remembered them but took no pleasure in the memory.

The Jamiesons had lived above them and were, of course, Protestant. Not that at that level you could distinguish Catholic from Protestant except that the former went to chapel and the latter didn't. The O'Rahilly's house – for instance – had been full of wee ornaments, and once she had seen a complete ornamental house showing, outside it, like Europeans outside a verandah, Christ and the twelve disciples, the whole thing painted a distasteful green.

She remembered Jamieson all right. Every Friday night he would dress up in his best blue suit, neat as a ray or razor, and would wave to his wife who was following his progress to the road from an open window, her scarf tight round her head. He would go off to the pub and pick a fight with a Catholic, or more likely three Catholics. At midnight he would come home covered with blood, his face bruised a fine Protestant blue, his clothes dirty and brown. He would walk like a victorious gladiator up the stair and then start a fight with his wife, uprooting chairs and wardrobes till the silence of exhaustion settled over the flats at about one in the morning. The next day his wife would descend the stair, her eyes black and blue, and say that she had stumbled at the sink. Her repertoire of invention was endless.

'I remember,' she said.

The town had changed a lot since they had left it, that much was clear. Now the old tenements were being knocked down and the people shuttled out to huge featureless estates where the windows revealed the blue sky of TV. There were hardly any picture houses left: they had been converted into bingo halls. Instead of small shops supermarkets were springing up, flexing their huge muscles. The lover's lane had disappeared. The park seemed to have lost its atmosphere of pastoral carelessness and was being decorated for the visitors with literate slogans in flowers.

'It's thirty-five years since we left,' said her husband.

And the wallet bulged from his breast pocket, a wife, two children, and a good job in administration.

He moved about restlessly. He wanted to tell someone how well he had done but how could he do that? All the people he had known were gone elsewhere, many of them presumably dead and completely forgotten.

'Do you mind old Hannah?' he said.

She had been a fat old woman who sat day after day at the

window leaning out of it talking to the passers-by. A fat woman with arthritis. He wondered vaguely what had happened to her.

'I wonder if the coal-house is still here. Come on.'

He took his wife by the hand and they walked down the close to the back. The coal-houses were incredibly still there, all padlocked and all beside each other, all with discoloured doors. She kept her fur coat as far away from them as she could.

'Do you mind the day I went to the factor?' he said. The factor had been a small, buttoned-up, black-suited lawyer. In those days of poverty he himself had been frightened to visit him in his wee office with the dim glass door. He imagined what he would do to that factor now.

He had gone there after coming home from the office, and the wee lawyer in the undertaker's suit had said to him over his shoulder,

'What do you want?'

'I want to report the rain coming through the roof.'

'How much do you pay Jackson?'

'Fifteen shillings a week.'

'And what do you expect for fifteen shillings a week?' said the factor, as if even giving words away were an agony of the spirit. In a corner of the office an umbrella dripped what seemed to be black rain.

'I was hoping that the house would be dry anyway.'

'I'll send someone round tomorrow,' and the factor had bent down to study a ledger with a rusty red cover.

'You said that a week ago.'

'And I'm saying it again. I'm a busy man. I've got a lot to do.' At that moment he had been filled with a terrible reckless anger and was about to raise his fist when the factor looked up. His mouth opened slightly showing one gold tooth in the middle of the bottom row of teeth, and he said carefully,

'Next week.'

So he had walked out past the dispirited receptionist in the glass cage – the one with the limp and the ageing mother – and then home.

Thinking back on it now, he thought: I was treated like a black. That's what it amounted to. By God, like a black.

He wished that that factor was alive now so that he could show him his bank balance. The wee nyaff. The Scottish words rose unbidden to his mouth like bile.

For a moment he did in fact see himself as a black, cringing in that rotting office, suffering the contempt, hearing the black rain dripping behind him from the furled umbrella.

But then a black would buy a bicycle and forget all about his humiliation. Blacks weren't like us.

As he turned away from the coal-house door he saw the washing hanging from the ropes on the green.

'Ye widna like to be daeing that noo,' he told his wife jocularly.

'What would the Bruces say if they saw you running about in this dirty place like a schoolboy?' she said coldly.

'Whit dae ye mean?'

'Simply what I said. There was no need to come here at all. Or do you want to take a photograph and show it to them? "The Place Where I Was Born".'

'I wasna born here. I just lived here for five years.'

'What would they think of you, I wonder.'

'I don't give a damn about the Bruces,' he burst out, the veins on his forehead swelling. 'What's he but a doctor anyway? I'm not ashamed of it. And, by God, why should you be ashamed of it? You weren't brought up in a fine house either. You worked in a factory till I picked you up at that dance.'

She turned away.

'Do you mind that night?' he asked contritely. 'You were standing by the wall and I went up to you and I said, "Could I have the honour?" And when we were coming home we walked down lovers' lane, where they had all the seats and the statues.'

'And you made a clown of yourself,' she said unforgivingly.

'Yes, didn't I just?' remembering how he had climbed the statue in the moonlight to show off. From the top of it he could see the Clyde, the ships and the cranes.

'And remember the flicks?' he said. 'We used tae get in wi jam jars. And do you mind the man who used to come down the passage at the interval spraying us with disinfectant?'

The interior of the cinema came back to him in a warm flood:

the children in the front rows keeping up a continual barrage of noise, the ushers hushing them, the smoke, the warmth, the pies slapping against faces, the carved cherubs in the flaking roof blowing their trumpets.

'You'd like that, wouldn't you?' she said. 'Remember it was me who drove you to the top.'

'Whit dae ye mean?' – like a bull wounded in the arena.

'You were lazy, that was what was wrong with you. You'd go out ferreting when you were here. You liked being with the boys.'

'Nothing wrong with that. What's wrong wi that?'

'What do you want? That they should all wave flags? That all the dirty boys and girls should line the street with banners five miles high? They don't give a damn about you, you know that. They're all dead and rotting and we should be back in Africa where we belong.'

He heard the voices round him. It was New Year's Eve and they were all dancing in a restaurant which had a fountain in the middle, and in the basin hundreds of pennies.

'Knees up, Mother Brown,' Jamieson was shouting to Hannah.

'You used to dance, too,' he said, 'on New Year's Night.'

'I saw old Manson dying in that room,' he said, pointing at a window. The floor and the ceiling and the walls seemed to have drops of perspiration and Manson had a brown flannel cloth wrapped round his neck. He couldn't breathe. And he heard the mice scuttering behind the walls.

She turned on him. 'What are you bringing that up for? Why don't you forget it? Do you enjoy thinking about these things?'

'Shut up,' he shouted, 'you didn't even have proper table manners when I met you.'

She stalked out to the car and he stayed where he was. To hell with her. She couldn't drive anyway.

He just wondered if anyone they had known still remained. He climbed the stair quietly till he came to the door of their old flat. No gaslight there now. On the door was written the name 'Rafferty', and as he leaned down against the letter box he heard the blast of a radio playing a pop song.

He went down again quietly.

He thought of their own two rooms there once, the living room with the table, the huge Victorian wardrobe (which was too big for the bedroom) and the huge Victorian dresser.

As he looked out of the close he saw that his car was surrounded by a pack of children, his wife, sheltered behind glass, staring ahead of her, an empress surrounded by prairie dogs.

He rushed out. 'Hey,' he said, 'don't scratch my car.'

'Whit is it?' a hard voice shouted from above.

He looked up. 'Nothing,' he said, 'I was just telling them not to scratch my car.'

'Why have you goat it there onyway?'

The woman was thin and stringy and wore a cheap bracelet round her throat. A bit like Mrs Jamieson but less self-effacing.

'I was just paying a visit,' he said. 'I used to live here.'

'They're no daeing onything to your caur,' said the voice which was like a saw that would cut through steel forever.

'It's an expensive car,' he said, watching his wife who was sitting in it like a graven image, lips firmly pressed together.

Another window opened. 'Hey, you there! I'm on night shift. Let's get a bit of sleep. Right?'

A pair of hairy hands slammed the window down again.

Two tall youngsters chewing gum approached.

'Hey, mister, whit are you on about?' They stared at him, legs crossed, delicate narrow toes.

'Nice bus,' said the one with the long curving moustache.

'Nice bus, eh Charley?'

They moved forward in concert, a ballet.

'Look,' he began, 'I was just visiting.' Then he stopped. Should he tell them that he was a rich man who had made good? It might not be advisable. One of them absently kicked one of the front tyres and then suddenly said to his wife, 'Peek a boo'. She showed no sign that she had seen him. They reminded him of some Africans he had seen, insolent young toughs, town-bred.

'All right, boys,' he said in an ingratiating voice. 'We're going anyway. We've seen all we want.'

'Did you hear that, Micky? He's seen all he wants to see. Would you say that was an insult?' Micky gazed benevolently at him through a lot of hair.

'Depends. What have you seen, daddy?'

'I used to live here,' he said jovially. 'In the old days. The best years of my life.' The words rang hollow between them.

'Hear that?' said Micky. 'Hear him. He's left us. Daddy's left us.'

He came up close and said quietly,

'Get out of here, daddy, before we cut you up, and take your camera and your bus with you. And your bag too. Right?'

The one with the curving moustache spat and said quietly,

'Tourist.'

He got into the car beside his still unsmiling wife who was still staring straight ahead of her. The car gathered speed and made its way down the main street. In the mirror he could see the brown tenement diminishing. The thin stringy woman was still at the window looking out, screaming at the children.

The shops along both sides of the street were all changed. There used to be a road down to the river and the lavatories but he couldn't see anything there now. Later on he passed a new yellow petrol-station, behind a miniature park with a blue bench on it.

'Mind we used to take the bus out past here?' he said, looking towards the woods on their right, where all the secret shades were, and the squirrels leaped.

The sky was darkening and the light seemed concentrated ahead of them in steely rays.

Suddenly he said,

'I wish to God we were home.'

She smiled for the first time. But he was still thinking of the scarred tenement and of what he should have said to these youths. Punks. He should have said, 'This is my home too. More than yours. You're just passing through.'

Punks with Edwardian moustaches. By God, if they were in Africa they would be sorted out. A word in the ear of the Chief Inspector over a cigar and that would be it. By God, they knew how to deal with punks where he came from.

He thought of razor-suited Jamieson setting out on a Friday night in his lone battle with the Catholics. Where was he now? Used to be a boiler-man or something. By God, he would have sorted them out. And his wife used to clean the cinema steps on those big draughty winter days.

'So you admit you were wrong,' said his wife.

He drove on, accelerating past a smaller car and blaring his horn savagely. There was no space in this bloody country. Everybody crowded together like rats.

'Here, look at that,' he said, 'that didn't use to be there.' It was a big building, probably a hospital.

'Remember we used to come down here on the bus,' he said. 'That didn't use to be there.'

He drove into the small town and got out of the car to stretch. The yellow lights rayed the road and the cafés had red globes above them. He could hardly recognise the place.

'We'd better find a hotel,' he said.

His wife's face brightened.

They stopped at the Admiral and were back home when the boy in the blue uniform with the yellow edgings took their rich brown leather cases. People could be seen drinking in the bar which faced directly on to the street. They were standing about with globes of whisky in their hands. He recognised who they were. They had red faces and red necks, and they stood there decisively as if they belonged there. Their wives wore cool gowns and looked haggard and dissipated.

His own wife put her hand in his as they got out of the car. Now she was smiling and trailing her fur coat. She walked with a certain exaggerated delicacy. It looked as if it might be a good evening after all. He could tell the boys about his sentimental journey, it would make a good talking point, they would get some laughs from it. No, on second thoughts perhaps not. He'd say something about Scotland anyway, and not forget to make sure that they got to know how well he had done.

The two of them walked in. 'Waiter,' he said loudly, 'two whiskies with ice.' Some of them looked at him, then turned away again. That waiter should have his hair cut. After a few whiskies they would gravitate into the neighbourhood of the others, those men who ran Scotland, the backbone of the nation. People like himself. By God, less than him. He had had the guts to travel.

Outside it was quite dark. Difficult to get used to this climate. His wife was smiling as if she expected someone to photograph her.

Now she was home. In a place much like Africa, the bar of a first class hotel.

He took out a cigar to show who he was, and began to cut it. In the lights pouring out from the hotel he could see his car bulging like a black wave.

He placed his hand over his wife's and said,

'Well, dear, it's been a tiring day.'

With a piercing stab of pain he recalled Africa, the drinkers on the verandah, the sky large and open and protective, the place where one knew where one was, among Europeans like oneself.

To have found one's true home was important after all. He sniffed his whisky, swirling it around in the goblet, golden and clear and thin and burningly pure.

On the Island

They tied up the boat and landed on the island, on a fine blowy blue and white day. They walked along among sheep and cows, who raised their heads curiously as they passed, then incuriously lowered them again.

They came to a monument dedicated to a sea captain who had sailed the first steam ship past the island.

'A good man,' said Allan, peering through his glasses.

'A fine man,' said Donny. 'A fine, generous man.'

'Indeed so,' said William.

They looked across towards the grey granite buildings of the town and from them turned their eyes to the waving seaweed, whose green seemed to be reflected in Donny's jersey.

'It's good to be away from the rat race,' said Donny, standing with his hands on his lapels. 'It is indeed good to be inhaling the salt breezes, the odoriferous ozone, to be blest by every stray zephyr that blows. Have you a fag?' he asked Allan, who gave him one from a battered packet.

'I sent away for a catalogue recently,' said William. 'For ten thousand coupons I could have had a paint sprayer. I calculate I would have to smoke for fifty years to get that paint sprayer.'

'A laudable life time's work,' said Donny.

Allan laughed, a high falsetto laugh and added,

'Or you might have the whole family smoking, including your granny and grandfather, if any. Children, naturally, should start young.'

The grass leaned at an angle in the drive of the wind.

'We could have played jazz,' said William, 'if I had brought my record player. Portable, naturally. Not to be plugged in to any rock. We could have listened to Ella Fitzgerald accompanied by her friend Louis Armstrong who sings atrociously, incidentally.'

'Or, on the other hand, we could have played Scottish Dance Music each day. "The Hen's March to the Midden" would not be unsuitable. I remember,' he continued reflectively, keeping his arms hooked in his lapels, 'I remember hearing that famous work or opus. It was many years ago. Ah, those happy days. When hens were hens and middens were middens. Not easy now to get a midden of quality. A genuine first class midden as midden.'

'The midden in itself,' said Williams. He continued, 'The thing in itself is an interesting question. I visualise Hegel in a German plane dropping silver paper to confuse the radar of the British philosophical school, and flying past, unharmed, unshot, uncorrupted.'

'I once read some Hegel,' said Allan proudly, 'and also Karl Marx.'

Donny made a face at a cow.

They made their way across the island and came to a pillbox used in the Second World War.

'Sieg Heil,' said William.

'Ve vill destroy zese English svine,' said Donny.

'Up periscope,' said Allan.

The island was very bare, no sign of habitation to be seen, just rocks and grass.

'Boom, boom, boom,' said Donny, imitating radio music. 'The Hunting of the *Bismarck*. Boom, boom, boom. It was a cold blustery day, and the telegraphist was sitting at his telegraph thinking of his wife and four children back in Yorkshire. Tap, tap, tap. Sir, *Bismarck* has blown the *Hood* out of the water. Unfair, really, sir. *Bismarck* carries too strong plating. Boom, boom, boom. Calm voice: "I think it'll have to be Force L, wouldn't you say, commander?" And now the hunt is on, boom, boom, boom, grey mist, Atlantic approaches, *Bismarck* captain speaks: "I vill not return, herr lieutenant. And I vill not tolerate insubordination." Boom, boom, boom.'

William looked at the pillbox, resting his right elbow on it.

'I wonder what they were defending,' he mused.

'The undying right to insert Celtic footnotes,' said Donny.

Allan said,

'I was reading a book about Stalingrad. You've got to hand it to these slab-faced Russians.'

The wind patrolled the silence. The green grass leaned all one way. There were speedboats out in the water plunging and rising, prows high.

'Oh well, let us proceed, let us explore,' said William. As they were walking along they came to a seagull's ravaged body, the skull delicate and fragile, lying among some yellow flowers. The carcass had been gnawed, probably by rats. Its white purity in the cold wind was startling. Its death was one kind of death, thought William with a shudder. Suddenly he placed the seagull's fragile skull on top of a hillock, and they began to throw stones at it. Donny stood upright, one hand clutching a stone, the other still in his lapel.

'Have I been successful?' he asked, after he had thrown the stone.

Allan went over. 'No,' he said shortly and took up position. In a frenzy, William threw stone after stone, but missed. It was Allan who finally knocked the seagull's skull from the knoll.

'All these years, like David, watching the sheep,' he admitted modestly.

They walked on and came to the edge of the water on the far side of the island. They were confronted by a seething waste, tumbled rocks, a long gloomy beach, a desert of blue and white ridged waves, a manic wilderness. As they stared into the hostile sea they saw a boat being rowed past by a man with a long white beard who sat in it very upright as if carved from stone. It was very strange and eerie because the man didn't turn his head at all and didn't seem to have noticed them. Donny broke the silence with,

'Ossian, I presume.'

'Or Columba,' said Allan.

'Once,' said Allan, 'I was entertaining two friends.'

'Ladies,' they both shouted.

'Let that be as it may,' said Allan, 'and may it be as it may. I, after the fourth whisky, looked out the window and there, to my astonishment, was a blanket, white with a border of black stripes, waving about in the air. I need not say that I was alarmed; nor did I draw the attention of the two people I was entertaining to it; nor did they notice it. At first, naturally, I thought it was the DTs. But better counsels prevailed, and I thereupon came to the conclusion that it must be the woman above engaged in some domestic activity which entailed the hanging of a blanket out of her window.'

'It was,' said Donny, 'the flag of the Scottish Republic, a blanket with . . . ' He stopped as the bearded man rowed back the way he had come. They watched the white hair stirred in the cold wind and the man with his upright stance.

'The horrible man,' said William suddenly.

'The thing in itself,' said Donny.

'Scotland the Brave,' said Allan, cleaning his glasses carefully. 'I remember now,' said Donny. 'I saw these two green branches on a tree and, full of leaves, they were dancing about in a breeze just outside my window. I didn't pay any attention to them at first and then I saw that they were like two duellists butting at each other and then withdrawing, like, say scorpions or snakes, upright, as if boxing. Such venom,' he concluded, 'in the green day.'

He added, 'Another time I was coming home from a dance in a condition of advanced merriment and I was crossing the square, all yellow, as you will know. Thus I came upon a policeman whom I had often seen in sunny daylight. He asked me what I was doing, looking at the shop window, and I returned a short if suitable answer, whereupon he, and his buddy who materialised out of the yellow light like a fairy with a diced cap, rushed me expeditiously up a close and beat me furiously with what is known in the trade as a rubber truncheon. It was,' he concluded, 'an eye opener.'

'Once,' said William, 'I saw a horse and it could think. It was looking at me in a calculating way. I got out of there. It was in a field on a cold day.'

They stared in silence at the spray, shivering.

'There is a man who is supposed to live in a cave,' said William at last. 'It must be an odd existence.'

'Mussels,' said Donny.

'Whelks,' said Allan.

'All locked up for the night,' said William.

After a pause he said,

'Nevertheless, it's got to be faced.'

'What?' said the others.

'This wilderness. Seas, rocks, animosity, ferocity. These waves all hating us, gnashing their white teeth.'

'I think,' said Allan, 'we should do a Socrates.'

'Meaning?' said Donny.

'Meaning nothing. Irony is not enough any more.'

'It's the inhumanness,' said William, almost in a whisper, feeling what he could not say, that for the waves they themselves didn't matter at all, any more than the whelks or the mussels.

Donny stood facing the water, his hands at his lapels. 'Ladies and gentlemen,' he began, 'Mr Chairman, ladies and gentlemen, guests, hangers-on, attendants, servants, serfs, and tribesmen, I have a few words to say about a revered member of our banking profession: well-known bowler, bridge-player, account-keeper, not to mention the husband of a blushing bride who looks as good as new after clearing her fiftieth hurdle.'

'You're right,' said Allan. 'He's right you know, Willie.'

'Meaning?'

'He faces it. He faces the chaos. Without dreams, without chaos. Only without chaos is it possible to survive. The plant does not fight itself, neither the tiger nor the platypus.'

'You mean that that speech orders the waves,' said William. 'Let me think.'

After a while he said,

> If thou didst ever hold me in thy heart,
> absent thee from felicity awhile
> and in this harsh world draw thy breath in pain
> to tell my story.

'They have their purpose and their eyes are bright with it. Keats.'

'Meaning?' said Allan.

'Meaning vanity. If there were no vanity there would be nothing. The flowers and the women all drawing attention to themselves. The signals. Have you not known, have you not seen, all the people around you, each with his own purpose staring out of his eyes and proclaiming "I am." "I am the most important. Look at me." "I must not be trifled with."? Have you not known it, have you not seen it, have you not been terrified by it? That each feels himself as important as you, that intelligence weakens, that the unkillable survive, the ones who don't think?'

A seagull swooped out of the stormy black and landed on a rock with yellow splayed claws, turning its head rapidly this way and that as if deliberating.

'Then,' said Donny, 'vanity prevails.'

'Without vanity we are nothing,' said William, 'without the sense of triumph.'

'And we have to pay for it with pomp,' said Allan. 'Out of the savage sea the perfected ennui.'

'From the amoeba to the cravat,' said Donny. The wind blew about them: it was like being at the end of the world, the crazy jigsaw of rocks, the sea solid in its strata, the massive power of its onrush, the spray rising high in the sky.

'Where action ends thought begins,' said William, almost in a whisper. 'Out of the water to the dais. And yet it is unbearable.'

'We rely on the toilers of the night,' said Donny.

'Is there anything one can say to the sea,' said Allan, 'apart from watch it?'

They looked at it but their hatred was not so great as its, not so indifferent. It was without mercy because it did not know of them. It was the world before man.

'Imagine it,' said William, 'out of this, all that we have.'

'And us,' said Donny, no longer clowning.

'To watch it,' said Allan. After a while he said,

'It would be fair if we threw stones at it too.'

'Yes,' agreed the other two, beginning to throw stones at the white teeth, but they sank without trace and could hardly be seen against the spray which ascended like a crazy ladder.

There was no ship to be seen at all, only the weird rowing boat that had passed twice with the white bearded man in it.

They turned away from it, frightened.

As they were leaving, Allan said,

'There is nothing more beautiful than a woman when her long legs are seen, tanned and lovely, as she drinks her whisky or vodka as the case may be.'

They bowed their heads. 'You have found the answer, O spectacled sage of the west. Except that the battle there too is continuous.'

'Except that everywhere the battle is continuous,' said William. 'Even in the least suspected places. But you are right nevertheless.'

They took one last look at the sea. In the smoky spray they seemed to see a fish woman, cold and yet incredibly ardent, arising with merciless scales.

'I knew a girl once,' said Allan. 'We slept on the sofa in her sitting room.'

'Both of you?' said the others.

There was a reverent silence.

'I knew a girl once,' said William. 'I remember her gloved hands on the steering wheel, and the dashboard light was green.'

Their clothes stirred in the breeze. Their flapping collars stung their cheeks. They passed the place where the dead seagull was.

'We will bury it,' said Allan. 'It's only fair.'

'No,' said William, 'it would be artificial.'

'Agreed,' said Donny. 'Motion carried, seconded, transformed and retransformed in some order.'

They saw a rat. It looked at them with small beady eyes and scurried out of sight.

'Look,' said William. A cormorant dived from a rock into the seething water. They watched for it to emerge and then it did so like a wheel turning. Also, they saw three seals racing alongside each other at full speed, sleek heads and parts of the body above the surface.

'They say it is the fastest fish in the sea,' said William.

'They say seals turn into women,' said Allan, polishing his glasses. They watched the speedboats drilling through the water. The town with its spires, halls, houses, pubs, rose from the edge of the sea, holding out against the wind. It was what there was of it. Nothing that was not unintelligible could be said about it.

Joseph

It was in the morning that Joseph told his two dreams. Outside the tent, deserts and mountains could be seen in the distance.

His dreams were about stars and corn, familiar images.

His brothers and father ate heavily and rapidly, belching now and again. There were three brothers in particular, Simeon, Reuben and Judah. When he told his dreams he was hated by his three step-brothers but not by Benjamin, who listened spellbound. Benjamin was younger than the others and was his real brother.

Joseph's dreams were beautiful and gay but to his brothers they were dreams of power. And as well as that he had his coat which showed that Jacob, his father, had made him his heir. Jacob listened sadly to the dreams for he himself had cheated his own brother many years before. He knew that in the world one must survive if one can. At night one heard the roar of the lion and the cry of the hyena. Inside the mind and the heart there were wild animals as well. But he was now growing old and wished for peace. Not only had he cheated his own brother Esau by putting on the skin of an animal, but he had himself been cheated by his father-in-law, whom he had cheated in turn. He remembered, however, meeting Rachel – Joseph's mother – at the well in the morning of the world, and falling out of the earth into the sky when he saw her standing there. A gift.

Joseph's dreams were beautiful and his brothers hated him.

2

That same day Joseph made his way to where his brothers were

guarding the sheep from the wild animals. They wore long
cloaks and carried sticks.

When he made his way across the hot country towards them
he met a man and asked him where his brothers were. The man
pointed but said nothing. Then he turned sadly away as if he
had done more and less than enough. When Joseph looked
back he couldn't see him.

The sky was clear and blue and there were birds flying about.
Joseph was carrying food to his brothers, cheese and bread.
When he reached them, Simeon said: 'Here is our brother.'

Judah, the brutal one, was playing monotonously on a pipe.
He had once fought a lioness and the scar remained near his
heart. He was almost howling with boredom, for guarding
sheep all day in the heat of the sun among stones and thirsty
land is not a very interesting job.

Simeon sat on the ground drawing diagrams with a stick. He
said without looking up:

'I have had a marvellous dream. In the dream I saw our
brother Joseph being stripped of his cloak and sold to the
merchants who go down into Egypt.'

'Ah, Egypt,' said Judah, dreaming of brothels. 'That is a good
dream,' he said aloud.

Reuben, who was a liberal, said: 'What will our father say?
He will kill us all for though he is old he is still strong.'

'Are you on our side or not?' said Judah carelessly. Reuben
knew that Judah might kill him, so he said, 'I protest against
this on moral grounds but I cannot save Joseph by dying
myself.'

Simeon laughed. They stripped Joseph of his cloak and when
the merchants came they sold him.

Joseph didn't know what was happening. He was being sold
for his gay dreams. He listened in the caravan to the sad
romantic songs of the camel drivers. In the morning he arrived
in Egypt where there was the Nile and the Pyramids and a
sense of movement combined with massive power.

3

He was sold at the market place along with some apes, a few Negroes from the south, and a dwarf who would dance if you poked at him through the bars with a pointed stick. He was sold to Potiphar, a small bald man who was chief executioner to Pharaoh. Potiphar was always cracking nuts with his teeth and telling broad jokes, which were not at all funny. After some time, Joseph was made a steward over the household, in charge of the servants and everything to do with the house. Potiphar's wife was sultry and lovely. Joseph was tall, handsome and had eyes the colour of figs. He wore the Egyptian white tunic which was rather like that of a Greek. He was clever and competent and he had almost ceased to dream, mainly because he was in a foreign country but also because he didn't have the time.

4

One day he and Potiphar's wife were sitting in the garden where there grew a lot of flowers, including poppies and forget-me-nots. She was sitting in the green shade of a tree. Because of the lack of water trees had to be imported, but Potiphar and his wife were rich and had a big white house with colonnades and porches. Joseph, of course, was used to tents and to deserts.

Potiphar's wife suddenly said:

'I am bored. Potiphar is away from home all day and he comes home worried at night. He is no use to me. He takes his work too seriously. Who would have thought there would be so much documentation connected with hanging? In the old days we used to hunt in the marshes with cats. Now my husband has no time for anything. He is afraid all the time. Are you afraid?'

'Afraid?' said Joseph. 'Sometimes.'

'You are more intelligent than my husband. When you came here you were illiterate. Now you can read and speak our language, and you can also count. Tell me, do you still write poetry?'

'Not much now, madam,' said Joseph correctly, looking at a bird which had perched on a branch beside him, its little body expanding and contracting as it sang.

'Oh, I'm bored,' said Potiphar's wife. 'In the old days I used to be a dancer. Now I am nothing. Nothing at all. I am surrounded by flowers when I should be surrounded by people who would offer me drinks and admire my beauty. Also, I would be happily drunk.' Joseph said nothing. She continued, 'Joseph, I have a fine dream. My husband is away from home. There is a cool room upstairs and a big bed. I dream that I am sleeping there with a handsome young foreigner called Joseph.'

Joseph felt a sudden coldness at his heart as cold as the water in a very deep well.

But she was attractive. She was tall and dark-haired and she had beautiful long legs and her eyes were brown.

'No,' he said, 'I must be loyal to your husband.'

'Honour,' she laughed. 'What a strange word! In another fifty years we will both be dead. My cheeks have fallen in. I will not dare to look in my copper mirror. You will have died of servitude for I can tell that you do not really like to be a slave. There is something about the way you speak and the way you walk. You will never learn to be a slave. In any case, the trees and the flowers will be here and the sun will shine. But we will both be dead. Our heads will be reduced to their skulls. Do you never think of that?'

'I never used to do,' said Joseph.

'Come,' she said rising, 'let us go to bed together. The servants will say nothing. I shall see to that.'

Her perfume almost overwhelmed him, but he remained faithful to his honour learned in the desert. He did not move.

She said: 'Do not antagonise a bored woman. I will give you one more chance.'

'My answer, madam, has to be no,' he said.

'I see,' she said contemptuously. 'So that is the kind you are. Afraid of living.' She tore at her clothes and began to scream. Servants came running. In a short while Joseph found himself in prison.

5

When he got there the governor interviewed him. He was a fat man with fat jowls and had large rings on his fingers. He studied Joseph as if he were a bull at a fair. He said, picking delicately at a sweetmeat:

'I try to do my best here. I think the prisoners like me. You have offended a great man or at least a man in a high position. You are lucky not to be dead. The régime here is not harsh. I pride myself on that. The man before me was brutal but things are changing. There are political prisoners who are confined to their cells most of the time. You are a sexual prisoner, if I may so refer to you. Some time when we get to know each other better you may tell me why you did not go to bed with Potiphar's wife. If I had been in your place I would have done so. In order to get promotion I might even go to bed with Potiphar.'

He laughed shortly, his belly bubbling up and down. He did not offer Joseph a sweetmeat. He continued:

'Everyone knows about Potiphar's wife. She is bored and beautiful. I am a lazy man myself. I hear that you are intelligent, so if I like you you can do a lot of useful work for me. I want the prisoners to like me. I want everybody to be happy. That makes less work for me. My hobby is collecting old pottery. I also like fishing. Is it a bargain?'

Joseph nodded and was taken to a cell.

6

All that night he sat in his cell and brooded. He thought as follows: During the period when I had my gay dreams and when I was innocent and happy I was envied and yet I harmed no one. Then I was sold into slavery along with apes and a dancing dwarf. When I was sold to Potiphar I did my best to be useful and efficient. I forgot my dreams because I was too busy learning how to read and how to count. Then, because of my sense of honour, I was put in prison. He stopped and considered.

My counting tells me as follows. If I had not done all the right things then I would not be in prison. Therefore there must be some reason why I am here, since my counting tells me that there is a logical reason for everything. I have a destiny. This I must believe since any other course would lead to suicide. My star, though broken, is shining. I have come a long way in a short time from the desert into a foreign prison. So be it. I shall wait and I shall study. The governor seems to be a fool, and since power seems to be the only important thing in life I shall gain it. However, I may be here for a long time. I shall therefore have to be patient, where once I was gay. That is the difference between a pool which reflects and a stream which runs.

The night was cold and he wrapped himself in his cloak and lay down on the floor. In the sky there shone a star named Joseph.

7

One day, after he had been in prison for some years, he was sitting in the garden watching a little bird. He was saying:

'All you have to do is fly over that hedge and you will be free. Why do you haunt a prison of all places?'

As he watched it and philosophised he saw two men walking up and down in the garden. One looked well and the other ill. Finally, the well one made the ill one sit down on a bench.

Joseph said to the ill one:

'What are you doing here?'

The well one said:

'I am a butler and my friend here is a baker. We were put in prison by the Pharaoh.'

'I haven't seen you before,' said Joseph. 'Are you political prisoners?'

'Yes,' said the butler. 'You know what powerful men do. Powerful men are unpredictable, especially if they are gods as well. One day the Pharaoh thought that the two of us were poisoning him, so he said, "Take these men to prison". He did this while cleaning his teeth with a toothpick. Immediately he had condemned us he had forgotten us. He sent us to prison because he was bored.'

'Why are you telling me this?' said Joseph.

'Because soon we'll be dead anyway. I will tell you something. We both have dreams. My dream is as follows. I see myself picking grapes from a tree and handing them to the Pharaoh. My friend also has dreams.'

'Tell me your dreams,' said Joseph to the baker who was sitting white-faced and silent on a bench.

The baker said, 'I'm frightened. I feel that my dream will doom me. I have a wife and two children and I am afraid to die.'

'I am not afraid to die,' said the butler. 'Death is better than the life we lead.'

The baker said, 'I dream that I have a basket on my head and the birds of the air peck at the bread inside it.' His head sank listlessly on his chest.

Joseph studied the two of them for some time, the ruddy butler and the white faced baker and then said:

'The dreams mean that the butler will be saved and the baker will die.'

The butler said to him: 'You shouldn't have said that. You have taken away his hope.'

'The truth must prevail,' said Joseph. 'It's like counting. It has nothing to do with hope.'

The butler began to comfort the baker but in his heart he was glad. In any case, he had always had the feeling that he wouldn't be put to death.

'One thing,' said Joseph suddenly, turning away from the bird and twitching a little as if he were swallowing something distasteful, 'when you meet the Pharaoh tell him about me.'

The butler said nothing and finally the two of them left, the butler supporting the baker as before, and Joseph sitting there in a terrible dream of betrayal.

8

One day shortly after this the governor sent for him. He said:

'You'll have to wear fine clothes and make sure that you are clean shaven. The Pharaoh has sent for you. I don't know why this is so. In any case it is a great honour. You have been very competent in your work in the prison and I will give you good references. Everyone likes you, mainly because you have learnt not to speak too much and therefore you don't make enemies. Please tell the Pharaoh if you have a chance, what a competent man I am and how enlightened my régime is. Tell him that I love my prisoners and that they love me. My wife would like it if I was promoted.'

Joseph said: 'I will do that,' looking around the office which was cluttered with papers, and at the governor whose garment was in disarray.

9

The Pharaoh was sitting on his throne and around him were his wizards and magicians. They were saying:

'We cannot tell the meaning of the dream, lord. We have tried divining bowls and have read many books but we confess ourselves baffled.'

The Pharaoh regarded them contemptuously, his little eyes bright as those of a snake, and said:

'I should throw you all into the Nile to feed the crocodiles, for if you cannot divine dreams what else are you fit for? But as the crocodile is an ancestor of mine I won't throw him corrupt flesh.' Noticing Joseph, he said:

'Approach, foreigner. Listen carefully. If you can't tell me the answer to my dreams you will die.'

Joseph noticed the butler standing beside the king, secure and untroubled.

The Pharaoh said:

'When I say that I will have you executed, I am telling the truth. Now then, listen. Every night I dream two dreams. Whenever I go to my bed I dream them. Firstly, I see the Nile untroubled and calm. Then, grazing by the Nile, I see seven fat cows, smooth and shining. Everything is peaceful. The cows are grazing by the river. The sky looks blue and everything appears idyllic. Then slowly I see rising out of the Nile seven other cows, so emaciated that every bone in their bodies is visible. They are like mechanical skeletons, toys. They have hungry red eyes. And then in my dream I see them attacking the seven fat cows and ripping at their live flesh. I see their mouths working like machines. And yet the sky is blue and the Nile is calm.'

The Pharaoh passed a hand over his brow. 'Some more wine,' he said to the butler without looking round. 'But that is not all,' he continued. 'I also see seven sheaves of corn in a field. Fat and prosperous and innocent and golden. It is harvest time. Then I see seven thin sheaves, like dancers, moving towards them and devouring them all. In the silence. It's strange. It's like nothing anyone would ever like to see, because of the silence. I dream these dreams every night. If you tell me their meaning I will offer you anything. Even a god should not have nightmares all the time.'

Joseph thought: This is the time. To sell my dreams for money and for power. This is the time. If this is the time.

He said, 'I know what your dreams mean, O Pharaoh.'

The Pharaoh told the rest to leave and Joseph told what the dreams meant.

'How do I know whether you are right?' said the Pharaoh.

'I am right because you will cease to dream them. That is all.'

The Pharaoh closed his eyes and went to sleep while Joseph stood there as if carved from rock. His hands did not shake and he knew that he was in the hands of destiny. He knew now that destiny was on his side, but he wasn't happy.

After a while, the Pharaoh woke up clear-eyed and said: 'I did not dream the dreams this time. Now what will we do about the famine?'

Joseph said:

'You should appoint a man and he would gather in the corn and you would save it for the time of the famine.'

'Where will I find such a man? Most of my administrators are fools, and you have seen what my magicians are like.'

He considered. Finally he said:

'You.'

'Me?' said Joseph.

'Yes, you. It came into my mind now.' He shouted joyfully. 'All you others come in!'

And they did, cringing and hoping that Joseph had failed. The Pharaoh said:

'I have an announcement to make. This is it. This man Joseph will be my right hand man from now on. Do you see this ring? I put it on his finger. And this cloak. I place it on his shoulders. You will accept orders from him as you would from me. The cloak and the ring will be sufficient.'

There were no comments, naturally. Joseph stood in his new cloak and with his new ring and knew he was hated again. But this time he did know it.

10

He took his chariot one morning when the sun was up and he went to where some workmen were working. They were making a sculpture of the Pharaoh in a rock tomb, and fitting up mirrors so that it could be clearly seen.

Joseph wondered at the majesty and power of the work of art, so solid and lasting and showing such insight and artistry. He said to one of the workmen:

'Which do you think more important, the making of this statue or having enough to eat?'

The workman laughed as if Joseph had made a joke.

Joseph sent for the foreman who was in charge of the whole operation. He was a short, sturdy, busy-looking man with broad shoulders and a practical air about him. His eyes twinkled and he seemed to enjoy life and his work. He wore a blue smock.

Joseph said to him:

'I have a job for you.'

While he was speaking he was looking at the sculpture, showing the Pharaoh seated in all his power and massive glory. The rising sun flashed directly into the hollow eyes, seeming to animate them with commanding intellect.

'What job is that?' said the foreman. Joseph noticed that he didn't say 'sir', though he probably knew who he was.

Speaking carefully and slowly, Joseph said, 'I want you to leave this and build barns, at a higher salary of course.'

'Barns?' said the man incredulously, looking down at his

stubby fingers covered with a fine powder. The hammers resounded through the air of the still morning.

'There is going to be a famine,' said Joseph, 'and many people will die. We want to bring in the corn and store it in barns. We will need large ones and many of them. Will you do that?'

'No,' said the foreman. 'Anyone can build a barn. Only I can create this sculpture.'

'I see,' said Joseph enviously, feeling the cloak heavy round his shoulders like stone. 'You refuse, even though many people will die? Can you not imagine the starvation and the deaths?'

'The world is full of people,' said the sculptor. 'Most of them are not of the slightest importance. I, on the other hand, am a genius. I cannot waste my time building barns. That would be ridiculous.'

'You are sure?'

'Quite sure.'

'You think that art is more important than the saving of life?'

'Yes.'

Joseph went away, thinking to himself, deeply and rancorously.

II

So the corn poured into the granaries. Rats were killed and doors were padlocked. The corn mounted up all golden. There was an enormous documentation to be done. Squads of collectors had to be sent out to examine the land and make sure that the farmers didn't cheat by withholding too much of the corn for themselves. The whole operation required an administrator of genius, which Joseph was. People came from everywhere as the famine spread. Also, there was dissension among the peasants whose corn was being taken from them, sometimes without payment. But Joseph was inflexible, though he was called 'The Foreigner'.

One day he looked up and there was Potiphar's wife in front of him. She looked like a cheap prostitute, which she probably was. She also looked thin. At first she did not recognise Joseph, but then she did. She ogled him and said:

'Can I have some corn? I have already pawned all my jewels. The only thing I have left is my marriage ring.' It came off quite easily and while she was disengaging it from her finger, she made a pitiful attempt to show him her breasts.

'How happy we might have been,' she said, 'the two of us. How much you missed,' she said, almost defiantly. But she lacked the suave confidence of former days. He handed her back the ring and said to an attendant,

'Give this woman corn.' Then he turned away and looked all round him at the golden sheaves.

Food. He had taken food to his brothers but they had rejected it. He in turn had turned down what might have been a form of life.

'Goodbye,' he said over his shoulder, for after all she had gone down in the world. He felt dirty and longed for Benjamin. 'Of course I'm older now,' she said. 'My husband put me out. He was going to kill me but I got away just the same. There was another servant you didn't know about.'

When she had gone a prince from the north came. He had five slaves with him. He said:

'I offer you these five slaves for some corn.' He looked fastidious and talked loudly as if he were the only important person there.

'We have enough people here already,' said Joseph, amazed at his stupidity.

Finally after all the people – the women with the children dead at the breast, the hollow-cheeked proud men, the pale adolescents – came the governor.

'What happened to you?' said Joseph. 'I told a lie on your behalf.'

'I was promoted,' said the governor, 'but I wasn't so happy.'

'You are speaking the truth at last,' said Joseph, and he ordered corn to be given to him.

12

His wife was an Egyptian woman and she was proud of her husband. She was also religious and told stories to their children about Osiris and Anubis and the rest of the gods. While she talked and as they sat in the garden Joseph said nothing and looked at the star which was his own and which had shone over desert, prison and palace. He never cared much for the Egyptian gods for they seemed absurd and incestuous and not mathematical. They were the sort of gods that might have been created by children and for children. The world of number wasn't as untidy as that: it was clear and accurate and pure.

'I'm tired of this weight of responsibility,' he would say. 'There must be a reason for it.'

Day after day he stood there saying, 'No.' If he had not been sold by his brothers and if he hadn't been imprisoned then he wouldn't now be the Pharaoh's right-hand man. So everything had worked out well after all. But he was sad just the same, for his dreams were all about the dying and the dead, about refusals and denials, about starving people and tons of golden corn.

But he loved his life in a way, though some nights he felt he did not belong to that country. Its language was not his. Its customs were not his. He couldn't speak as he wished. But the world of number was common to all. It transcended nationality.

13

The day his brothers came he regarded them out of the shadows. They did not recognise him, though he recognised them. Probably the reason they didn't recognise him was that he was clean shaven as was the custom of the Egyptians. And they could not see him very well in the shadow.

'What do you want?' he asked roughly.

'Food,' said Simeon, who was the spokesman.

They looked rustic, that was what astonished him. He was not at all frightened of them. They looked exactly what they were, uneducated peasants from the hills, with large hands and large feet.

'You are spies,' he said. 'You come from the north. I can tell by your speech. You people think that because we have a famine we are weak and can be overthrown. You are making a big mistake.'

'We're not spies,' said Simeon, truthfully.

Judah said nothing, looking around him contemptuously. Reuben looked this way and that like a cornered rabbit.

'I will have you all thrown in jail,' Joseph shouted. 'On second thoughts, you,' pointing to Simeon, 'will stay here as hostage for the others. I want to hear your story.'

Simeon said:

'We have been sent by our father to get food, because we are starving.'

'Are you the only members of the family?' said Joseph.

'We have a younger brother,' said Simeon.

'Right,' said Joseph, 'I want him here.'

Simeon smiled gently and cunningly:

'If that is your wish, sir.' Joseph cut him off and then said to Judah:

'You, sir, had better change the expression on your face or you will be beheaded. And you, what are you?' he said to Reuben.

'I am a liberal, sir. I do not believe in violence or spying. I know that you are a great man and I love power though I often affect to despise it.'

'I see. You heard what I said. This brother of yours stays in prison.'

Simeon was put in prison but quickly learned to ingratiate himself with the guards and taught them how to play cards, a pastime in which he had often indulged when watching the sheep. Soon he would be able to pick up the language and count.

14

Joseph came home to dinner.

'Are they here?' he asked his wife. She looked at him doubtfully.

'They are my brothers,' he said. 'They sold me into slavery. How many are there?'

'Four,' she said. 'What are you going to do?'

'I shall offer them food,' he said. 'They have the smell of my own land.' She turned away as if about to cry. He put his arms around her.

'But destiny brought me here,' he said.

'Destiny?' she said. 'What's that?'

He went inside. They were all sitting down very quietly, overawed. He shouted to the servants to bring in their food, and he served them himself, giving more to Benjamin than to the others. He noticed how greedily Benjamin ate. But after all he's a growing boy, he thought.

When they were finished eating, he said, 'I will leave you for a few moments.'

He went into an adjoining room and changed quickly. When he came back he was wearing a shepherd's cloak and carrying a stick.

'Do you not know me?' he asked.

Something about the cloak and the stick and the way in which he spoke in their own language recalled him to Simeon, who was the first to speak.

'You are Joseph,' he said in astonishment, his face whitening.

'And you are next to the Pharaoh,' said Reuben, in equal astonishment.

'Our brother has made good,' said Judah mockingly.

Joseph looked at Benjamin but Benjamin could not remember him very well.

This made him extremely sad, sadder than he had been for a long time.

'We were envious of you in those days,' said Simeon quickly. 'It was because your father had chosen you as the heir and you were only the second youngest; and, after all, it was we who looked after the sheep. Isn't that right, Judah?'

'I hated him,' said Judah. 'He was a horrible little bastard.'

'I wouldn't say that,' said Reuben. 'He might have acted a bit arrogant now and again but we must always make allowances for the young.'

'In any case,' said Simeon, his eyes darting hither and thither, 'you've got a high position now and you've got to admit that if it hadn't been for us you wouldn't have got it.'

Joseph gritted his teeth but said nothing. They hadn't changed. But they were still his own people. He thought: Local Boy makes good. From Poet to Administrator.

He thought of the day not so long before when the foreman had come to him looking half starved. He had brought him a small replica of Joseph which he had designed.

'I have spent a year on this,' he said to Joseph. 'It's very valuable. I will give it to you for six bags of corn.'

'Six bags of corn?' said Joseph. He looked at the replica which was green in colour and beautifully made.

'You haven't flattered me,' he said.

'No, that is not my job,' said the foreman. 'Do you want it? It is a portrait of my opposite, the administrator of genius whom I hate. I am an artist of genius.'

'You should have built the barns,' said Joseph. 'Now you wouldn't be starving.'

'I don't regret anything,' said the foreman, looking round the barns. 'I did what I had to do. Do you want the replica?'

'Three bags,' said Joseph, looking at him keenly.

'No.'

'Seven then.'

'No, I want six. It's worth exactly six, neither more nor less.'

'In that case I won't take it,' said Joseph firmly.

The foreman picked up the replica and turned away. 'I don't blame you. We think differently. However, I had thought you would have respect for number.'

'All right,' said Joseph. 'I'll take it though you haven't flattered me.'

'I would have asked more for it,' said the foreman, 'only my wife died when I was working on it, and I don't need so much food now.'

'I see,' said Joseph. 'Goodbye.'

The foreman turned away, his clothes loose on him but his eyes still twinkling.

Joseph seemed to wake up and said to his brothers:

'You will have to stay here now and I will find jobs for all of you. You can all do something. Even Judah could wrestle for money.'

'That's very realistic of you,' said Simeon, rubbing his hands.

'It will be a good thing to be the brother of so important a man,' said Benjamin.

Joseph left them whispering together and sought his wife whom he kissed fondly.

15

When his father came they talked together in the garden. His father was bearded and weaker than he had been. Joseph said to him:

'I know now what my destiny has been. Everything led to you being here. I was destined to save my tribe. And the dream came true.'

His father nodded.

Joseph added:

'I find it strange that I have saved you by becoming corrupt. I hate it and I don't know whether I shall be able to bear it.'

'We all become corrupt,' said his father. 'That is the penalty of living. I too am corrupt. Once I betrayed my brother. Later I had to bribe him with camels. He was stronger than me physically but I was more astute than he was. Also in order to gain my wife, whom I truly loved, I was betrayed and then I betrayed my father-in-law in turn. That is the way the world is. Even God accepts that or we wouldn't have been so successful.'

'What I miss most are my dreams,' said Joseph. 'The famine will soon be over and my work done.'

He banged his hand on a stone.

'But what I miss most are my dreams. When I was innocent they served me nothing. Then I sold them and here I am surrounded by furniture, riches and food.'

'That is so,' said his father nodding. 'I don't understand it either but that is the way it is.'

'I loved my dreams,' said Joseph, 'and now I love number. Soon perhaps I won't love even that. Perhaps I will be like

Judah, bored to death watching the sheep. And all I shall have left will be my furniture. Sometimes I feel it is eating me up.'

'Furniture will not kill you,' said his father, 'though the wild beasts will. You have more than survived.'

A bird flew out of the garden carrying a worm in its beak like a dangling necklace. The beak was black and the worm red.

'I am here,' said Joseph slowly, 'and what we call destiny has put me here. That is what we say.'

'That is right,' said his father, thinking of Rachel standing by the well years ago, the camels' shadows slanting along the ground and his father-in-law coming out to meet him, rubbing his hands briskly and smiling above his beard.

Life is good, he thought, but this is a strange land. We desert folk miss the desert, its purity and its treachery.

Nevertheless, with the greed of an old man he thought: I shall have plenty to eat now.

The Idiot and the Professor and some others

The idiot stood on the pavement. In his right hand he had a tube which looked like a recorder. Absently he scratched the left ear of his crew-cut head. He turned his head to the right, jutting his lips out. Then he turned his head to the left. He sighted along the recorder as if it were a gun. He put it down by his side and ran it along his thigh. Then he absently scratched his crotch, looking up into the sky. His face was young and brick-red in colour, like that of a Nazi who had drunk too much. He was fifty years old and boyish. He knelt down and tapped the recorder against his shoe. He tried to drill his shoe with the recorder. He stood up and looked about him. He scratched his left ear again.

The professor walked up the road, one hand swinging free. He stopped beside the idiot. The idiot looked up at the professor, stroking the recorder. The professor spoke to the idiot, putting his hand on the idiot's shoulder. The idiot looked at him unblinkingly. The professor tried to take the recorder from the idiot, but the idiot at first wouldn't give it to him. Finally he gave it to him. The professor put the recorder to his lips. He played the recorder standing on one leg. He made some music with it. The idiot looked at him in amazement. Then he scratched his crotch again.

Two girls passed, arm in arm, giggling. The idiot looked away from the professor, after the two girls. They waved to him and he nodded his head vigorously. The professor turned the recorder up towards the sky as if he were examining it for stars. The idiot watched him carefully. The books the professor was carrying fell to the ground. A boy and a girl who were passing bent down and picked them up. The idiot bent down also. The girl was wearing a yellow miniskirt like a flower. The idiot could see the backs of her thighs. The professor took the books and picked up his hat which had fallen down. He crammed the latter on his head. He looked vaguely at the nearby church and crooned to himself. He wasn't a tall man, perhaps five foot four, and he had a small white beard. The idiot took the recorder and marched up and down like a sergeant major on parade, swinging his left arm. The professor took the recorder from him and marched up and down, twirling it like a drum majorette. They laughed together.

The tanned visitors came home from the sea and the glens. They stood and watched the idiot and the professor. Some were in sandals, others were naked above the waist. They looked happy and tired, having built sandcastles all day. There were countless numbers of them, and they all stopped to look at the idiot. The idiot snatched the recorder from the professor and the professor made a face and stalked off.

A drunk came weaving up the road, dodging the cars which were honking furiously at him. He put his arm round the idiot's shoulders and began to speak to him. The idiot listened, gazing impassively ahead of him. Suddenly he brought the recorder down on the drunk's head. The drunk nodded his head like a boxer after a heavy punch and moved on, swaying from side to side. The idiot jutted his lips.

The people looked at him, not knowing what to say to him. He looked back at them. The sun briefly dazzled along his recorder. He pointed it at them as if he were going to shoot them. They giggled among each other and pointed at him.

A policeman came and began to move them along. The idiot stood stout and firm, facing the traffic with the recorder in his mouth, his face expressionless. He looked like an American.

The professor had gone home. He took from his bookcase a monograph he had written about Descartes many years before. He read it every night. This was only another night he was reading it.

Many people wrote postcards by the light of the summer sun, telling how they had seen an idiot and how queer he was.

The sea bounded against the rocks.

A boy and a girl stood against a tree whose green leaves made their faces green. The boy put his hand around the girl and caressed her buttocks. She caressed the back of his neck. Her eyes closed. A sheep stared at them. In the distance a motor cycle accelerated. High above the brae there was a rubbish dump full of rats and discarded canisters and the dead body of a ewe.

His father took the recorder from the idiot and put it away in a drawer. The idiot made a sound deep in his throat and scratched his crotch.

'If only there was some expression on your face,' said the father. 'Even one bit of damned expression. Just one iota.'

from
THE BLACK AND THE RED
and other stories

PART I

The Dying

When the breathing got worse he went into the adjacent room and got the copy of Dante. All that night and the night before he had been watching the dying though he didn't know it was a dying. The grey hairs around the head seemed to panic like the needle of a compass and the eyes, sometimes open, sometimes shut, seemed to be looking at him all the time. He had never seen a dying before. The breathlessness seemed a bit like asthma or bad bronchitis, ascending sometimes into a kind of whistling like a train leaving a station. The voice when it spoke was irritable and petulant. It wanted water, lots of water, milk, lots of milk, anything to quench the thirst and even then he didn't know it was a dying. The tongue seemed very cold as he fed it milk. It was cold and almost stiff. Once near midnight he saw the cheeks flare up and become swollen so that the eyes could hardly look over them. When a mirror was required to be brought she looked at it, moving her head restlessly this way and that. He knew that the swelling was a portent of some kind, a message from the outer darkness, an omen.

Outside, it was snowing steadily, the complex flakes weaving an unintelligible pattern. If he were to put the light out then that other light, as alien as that from a dead planet, the light of the moon itself, would enter the room, a sick glare, an almost abstract light. It would light the pages of the Dante which he needed now more than ever, it would cast over the poetry its hollow glare.

He opened the pages but they did not mean anything at all since all the time he was looking at the face. The dying person was slipping away from him. She was absorbed in her dying and he did not understand what was happening. Dying was such an extraordinary thing, such a private thing. Sometimes he stretched out his hand and she clutched it, and he felt as if he were in a boat and she were in the dark water around it. And all the time the breathing was faster and faster as if something wanted to be away. The brow was cold but the mouth still wanted water. The body was restlessly turning, now on one side now on the other. It was steadily weakening. Something was at it and it was weakening.

In Thy Will is My Peace . . . The words from Dante swam into his mind. They seemed to swim out of the snow which was teeming beyond the window. He imagined the universe of Dante like a watch. The clock said five in the morning. He felt cold and the light was beginning to azure the window. The street outside was empty of people and traffic. There was no one alive in the world but himself. The lamps cast their glare over the street. They brooded over their own haloes all night.

When he looked again the whistling was changing to a rattling. He held one cold hand in his, locking it. The head fell back on the pillow, the mouth gaping wide like the mouth of a landed fish, the eyes staring irretrievably beyond him. The one-barred electric fire hummed in a corner of the room, a deep and raw red wound. His copy of Dante fell from his hand and lay on top of the red woollen rug at the side of the bed stained with milk and soup. He seemed to be on a space ship upside down and seeing coming towards him another space ship shaped like a black mediaeval helmet in all that azure. On board the space ship there was at least one man encased in a black rubber suit but he could not see the face. The man was busy either with a rope which he would fling to him or with a gun which he would fire at him. The figure seemed squat and alien like an Eskimo.

And all the while the window azured and the body was like a log, the mouth twisted where all the breath had left it. It lolled on one side of the pillow. Death was not dignified. A dead face showed the pain of its dying, what it had struggled through to become a log. He thought, weeping, this is the irretrievable centre where there is no foliage and no metaphor. At this time poetry is powerless. The body looked up at him blank as a stone with the twisted mouth. It belonged to no one that he had ever known.

The copy of Dante seemed to have fallen into an abyss. It was lying on the red rug as if in a fire. Yet he himself was so cold and numb. Suddenly he began to be shaken by tremors though his face remained cold and without movement. The alien azure light was growing steadily, mixed with the white glare of the snow. The landscape outside the window was not a human landscape. The body on the bed was not human.

The tears started to seep slowly from his eyes. In his right hand he found he was holding a small golden watch which he had picked up. He couldn't remember picking it up. He couldn't even hear its ticking. It was a delicate mechanism, small and golden. He held it up to his ear and the tears came, in the white and bluish glare. Through the tears he saw the watch and the copy of Dante lying on the red rug and beyond that again the log which seemed unchanging though it would change since everything changed.

And he knew that he himself would change though he could not think of it at the moment. He knew that he would change and the log would change and it was this which more than anything made him cry, to think of what the log had been once, a suffering body, a girl growing up and marrying and bearing children. It was so strange that the log could have been like that. It was so strange that the log had once been chequered like a draughtsboard, that it had called him into dinner, that it had been sleepless at night thinking of the future.

So strange was it, so irretrievable, that he was shaken as if by an earthquake of pathos and pity. He could not bring himself to look at the Dante; he could only stare at the log as if expecting that it would move or speak. But it did not. It was concerned only with itself. The twisted mouth as if still gasping for air made no promises and no concessions.

Slowly as he sat there he was aware of a hammering coming from outside the window and aware also of blue lightning flickering across the room. He had forgotten about the workshop. He walked over to the window and saw men with helmets bending over pure white flame. The blue flashes were cold and queer as if they came from another world. At the same time he heard unintelligible shoutings from the people involved in the

work and saw a visored head turning to look behind it. Beyond
it steadied the sharp azure of the morning. And in front of it he
saw the drifting flakes of snow. He looked down at the Dante
with his bruised face and felt the hammer blows slamming the
lines together, making the universe, holding a world together
where people shouted out of a blue light. And the hammer
seemed to be beating the log into a vase, into marble, into
flowers made of blue rock, into the hardest of metaphors.

At the Party

A group of us was gathered in a corner of the room singing Gaelic songs. It was midnight and we were in somebody's house though we weren't sure exactly whose, except that now and again a young couple who seemed to own the place – or at least to rent it – appeared in the doorway of what seemed to be an annexe off the main room and looked around with what might have been satisfaction or apathy or even tiredness. The man was tall, bearded and wore a Red Indian hair band, the girl fair and wearing a chain of white beads at the waist.

The room was crowded with people who had arrived in cars or taxis when the rumour of a party had gone round after the poetry reading was over. Many of them were young and most were students. Two or three messengers had been sent off to buy drink but none had returned, either because they had absconded with the money or because they couldn't find any drink, a reasonable enough assumption at that time of night. Coffee, dispensed in tumblers or mugs, was circulating.

None of the real lions of the poetry reading had stayed. One was so drunk that he had to be carefully disengaged from a lamp-post around which he had entwined himself like a monkey, emitting fragmentary lines of his own verse. Another had gone off with a serious-faced girl in glasses who had spent most of her time taking down notes in a small red notebook during the proceedings. Yet another had disappeared with a dull man who worked in advertising and who had come along to find out how poetry could be used in the selling of fruit. 'My boss,' he said, 'says that before you can sell tomatoes you must think of them as women.' He repeated this statement a lot and did not realise that the laughter it evoked was not a tribute to its perception.

I sat among the Gaelic singers in a corner, a Finnish girl beside me. She had very fair fine hair, very fair fine eyelashes and blue clever eyes. I asked her about Finland and though she was unwilling to sing Finnish songs she told me about the sparse literature of the country in attractive broken English. She said there were quite a lot of Finnish girls and house-wives in the city and that they met now and again in clubs. I stroked her hair and she regarded me with a cool amused gaze. Her husband apparently was a lecturer in the Scandinavian languages and she had met him at a skiing resort. He had gazed down at her solicitously while she lay spreadeagled in the snow. 'Very Victorian,' she said, 'just like God.' 'What do you think of our Gaelic songs?' I asked. She smiled but didn't answer. It occurred to me that at midnight all women are loveable.

The group around me were singing every Gaelic song they had ever heard. They sang songs about exile, about love, about war, about shepherds on distant islands. They sang with the obsessive fidelity and love of the exile. They sang with eyes closed, swaying with longing, as if they were snakes entranced by the scent and blossom of Eden. They were all young except for one man who wore a waistcoat and watch and chain and was bald. No one knew where he had come from – he didn't look like a poetry lover – and his stiff hat was clamped straight over his forehead. His hands rested gently on his stomach and he sang each song carefully and comfortably as if he were sitting at dinner. No one knew what to make of him since he didn't say anything. Now and again he would close his small eyes and then open them and look shyly and quickly around him. Most of the time he looked bovine and had an air of enigmatic satisfaction. Sometimes a song was started by someone who didn't know the words and it had to be completed by the others in their obsessed ring.

I leaned back in my corner, my head on the shoulder of the Finnish girl who was looking across towards a young bearded fellow who was strumming a guitar by himself in the opposite corner. Her face was cool and untroubled. I imagined that I was in love with her; I felt the air of sunny mornings and lemons. I said to her: 'You are so relaxed. Are you always as relaxed as this?' She told me that her child wrote poetry with large coloured crayons and that it was very good poetry too. 'In English, of course,' she said, smiling. I believed her. I believed that her child was a cool Finnish genius with fair hair and classic features. I didn't know why she was there. She reminded me of someone from the Sunday supplements. 'Do they have Sunday supplements in Finland?' I asked. She smiled. I thought of Grimm, Hans Andersen, girls in red coats meeting bowing wolves in birch woods. 'Do you write yourself?' I asked. 'No,' she said, 'I play the piano – badly.'

At that moment there was a ragged cheer such as a dispirited army seeing a glint of reinforcements might give. The drink had arrived though there wasn't much of it. We were doled out a little whisky each, holding out our mugs like refugees in some eastern country. The singing stopped for a moment and then began again. They were singing a song called *The White Swan* which is about the First World War. I drank some of the whisky and joined in. A young girl waved her empty glass like a conductor's baton and smiled at me.

And over her head I saw Miriam whom I had forgotten was there. She was standing talking to a tall bearded flat-faced poet who wore a slightly stained violet tie and a lumber jacket. He was a very bad poet though large and handsome and talkative. Miriam was wearing black which contrasted very strongly with her white miniature face and blonde hair. I tried to make out what she was saying by lip-reading but I couldn't, so I got to my feet and stumbled over to listen. They were talking about the Concept of Alienation. I listened owlishly and amusedly. Brecht and the Concept of Alienation: It's a Braw Brecht Munelicht Nicht the Nicht. He spoke freely and as if he knew a great deal about the Concept of Alienation which presumably he had made some study of. He was a very serious person and much less preferable to X, another poet who lived by quick-wittedness rather than by scholarship. Sometimes Miriam laughed delightedly, sometimes she looked grave and questioning like a child. I wondered how long she would stay at the party.

I had met her first in a library quite by accident when she was looking for a book on the American poet Edwin Arlington Robinson and I had been able to help her as he is one of my own favourite poets. I was very lonely at that time and we began to go about together, having dinner in hotels, going to pubs though she didn't drink much. In fact she always sipped a tomato juice laced (if that is the right word) with Worcester sauce, or it may have been the other way round. Once we were invited late at night to the house of an actor who had tried to make love to her while his wife was making coffee. She had been very angry with him and had hit him over the head with a large book by George Steiner. Another time we went to visit an alcoholic woman painter who had managed to sell me a painting called Exhalations which I had barely succeeded in dragging down four flights of stairs to a taxi.

We talked a lot about literature in which I was rapidly losing interest, much preferring solidly constructed detective stories of the classical type, such as those by S. S. Van Dine. She still retained the pristine hunger for books which I had long lost. She would sit, composed and small, in the corner of a lounge bar while I made a vicious random attack on the supposedly good writing of Faulkner. She was very sensitive and sent a lot of money to Irish people. Once she had a refugee from Ireland in her flat, a ginger-haired slatternly woman who brought in her wake a husband who played the Irish bagpipes from the hip and who was eventually put out of the house by the landlady for practising on them at three in the morning after what he called a 'wet'. When that pair had left she had got hold of an Indian and his wife. Together they wore lots of beads and talked in the most beautiful Oxford accents. She was always helping 'lame ducks' and reminded me of Joan of Arc except that she was much more literate. There was some trace of Americanism in her descent which I thought accounted for her combination of innocence and experience.

I admired her a lot. I admired her sensitivity, her feeling for other people. I admired the simple, almost elegant way in which she lived. She had a very fine delicate wristwatch which recalled her best qualities – unhurried competence and fine outer appearance. I knew that she had had an unhappy upbringing.

Her father had died of TB when she was very young – he had been a lecturer somewhere – and her mother of some other incurable disease. She had lots of nieces and nephews for whom she was always buying toys and though she didn't like mess of any kind she was always dressing and undressing them and taking them to the bathroom and feeding them. They would sit on her lap and pull at her necklace of brown beads. Once I was invited to her brother-in-law's house. He was a professor who was deeply involved in linguistics and whose silences were prolonged as if his researches had convinced him that language is very dangerous and should be tampered with as little as possible. She and her sister (one of three she had) kept up a bitter private running battle all the time we were there, needling each other about incidents that went back to their childhood days. I wondered whether the professor was making notes. A lot of the time, however, he retired to a large sunny room which overlooked a garden full of red and blue flowers. Perhaps he was studying their language or the language of the birds.

However my admiration for her had evaporated when one night after we had been drinking and I had taken her home in a taxi she had savagely turned on me and said as I was making some attempt to kiss her: 'You are the most selfish bugger I have ever met. You really are. Why are you taking me out? You think I'll go to bed with you. You don't care about anyone in the world except yourself. You laughed at that painter though she is on the verge of suicide. What's wrong with her painting anyway? I think it's quite good. You think I'll go to bed with you. You laughed at my brother-in-law because you think he's a pedagogue. It never occurs to you that there are people who genuinely know so much that they find it difficult to say anything at all. You think you can buy me with your money. I don't give a bugger about you. I think you're a bad artist anyway. You laughed at the photographs I showed you. You're always laughing at things, aren't you? You can't even use a tape recorder properly.' That gibe came from an incident when I was recording a Gaelic song for her, I myself doing the singing. 'Your bloody Highlands,' she said. 'All your bloody mist and your bloody principles. No wonder you've never painted anything worth a damn.' The taxi stopped. I tried to help her out but she pushed my hand away. Just as she stood on the road she added, 'And that coat you're wearing, it's bloody mediaeval.' I watched her trying to fit the key in the lock as the taxi sizzled along the blue rainy street. There were lamp-posts every few yards all down the long street brooding over the stone below them. Haloes . . . separate haloes. We entered the circles and bracelets of light. An Indian restaurant flashed by, then a huge warehouse. There was a newspaper headquarters, a shop with naked tailors' dummies and a Chinese restaurant. A drunk pawed at the air with his hands.

She knew I was there all right but she wouldn't speak to me. I went back to my corner from which the Finnish girl had disappeared perhaps to the lavatory. I hadn't known how to speak to her: instead of talking to her I had in fact been cross-examining her. On the fringe of the crowd who were by now licking the bottoms of their mugs, since the whisky had all gone, a young girl was watching me. I went across to her. I said Hello and we sat down on the floor. She told me that she had been studying literature but was now studying physics. She wasn't pretty but she was young and she had managed somehow or other to get hold of some coffee. I told her a joke about a Pakistani who had been taught to play darts. I was ready to like her since my Finnish girl had disappeared. I asked her about university and she said that she preferred physics to literature though she wasn't very practical. She said that she wrote some poetry but didn't have any with her and I silently thanked God. The last poetry book I had read I couldn't make head nor tail of: it seemed to be designed to be read either from the bottom upwards or diagonally or both simultaneously. I thought that if the poet who had climbed the lamp-post had fallen down we might have had our first concrete poet. I was astonished at the extraordinary number of charlatans in art whom I now seemed to see as if in a clear light infesting the room and other rooms all over the world.

The Gaelic singers surrounded us singing in a last fervent burst as if they sensed that the party was nearly over. The young girl looked at them tolerantly and remotely. But after all, I thought angrily, they were my people, weren't they? They had come from my world, a broken world, but a world which still provided the cohesion of song, a tradition. The other people watched, almost with envy. We were the only cohesive group there. She asked me to translate a verse and I did so:

It is a pity that you and I were not where I would
wish to be, in locked room with iron gates, for
the six days of the week for seven, eight years,
the keys lost and a blind man looking for them.

It was, according to the flowery clock on the mantelpiece, one o'clock in the morning, and I saw the poet and Miriam leaving. He put on her black cloak for her and for a brief moment she looked back at me, Napoleonic, self-possessed, frightened. The two of them had probably talked their alienation out, and now perhaps going out into the night she might feel sufficiently like Mother Courage (or the German equivalent). 'You bloody bad poet,' I thought, 'why do people never see through you?' I watched them go. I nearly went after her but I couldn't get out of the singing group. I imagined her and him in their taxi returning perhaps to her flat. I imagined the taxi going past the desolate lamp-posts. The Concept of Alienation. Well, books and plays might help, I supposed. I thought of the taxi as a hearse ticking over. Why were taxis always black, or was that just in Scotland? I imagined her leafing through her pictures of the dead and the doomed, the tubercular and the moustached, all brown with age.

The singing was growing louder. I was with my own people. The song they were singing was about an exile in the city who wished to be home. He remembered the hills, the lochs, the neighbours, the songs. I thought of the last time I had been home. It had rained all the time and I had spent a whole week reading *Reader's Digest* and books by Agatha Christie. Sometimes I had played cards with a spotty cousin. I had seen between showers the mangled body of a rabbit at the side of a road: it had been run over by a car and its guts hung out. One day I had tried to find some fool's gold on the beach but I didn't find any. I remembered the blue and white waves, the astounding Atlantic.

I left the circle. Who was I looking for? I tried to find the Finnish girl but she seemed to have gone, for the ladies' lavatory (quaintly captioned Girls in a primary tangle of colours) was open and vacant. The guitar player had also gone. I went into the darkness. As I was standing there trying to find my bearings a voice came from inside the room. 'When shall we see you again?' Blinded, I turned into the light, not recognising the voice. I went back into the room. It was the student who had changed from literature to physics and I was disappointed: I was hoping it would have been the Finnish girl. I looked at her for a long time and then said that I wasn't in the city very often. I went back into the darkness again. From the next garden a dog, probably a large one, began to bark excitedly. It sounded as if he was tearing at the wall to try and get at me. I went out into the street feeling my way as I had once done across a midnight field on the island. The singing seemed to have stopped and everyone, I supposed, was preparing to leave. I started to walk down the street towards the centre of the city where my hotel was. I supposed the stony-faced porter would come to the door again this time. I would have preferred someone more happy-looking, especially at three in the morning.

In the Station

One day I was sitting in the buffet at Waverley Station in Edinburgh reading the *Sunday Times* and drinking coffee out of a paper cup when a voice from in front of the paper said: 'Have you heard of these two then?' At first I didn't realise that the odd question was directed at me and continued to read about a particularly atrocious brutality in Ireland. But the voice came again: 'Have you heard of these two then?' I lowered the *Sunday Times* and saw sitting opposite me at the table (it was strange I hadn't noticed him before) an unshaven man with a thin ravaged face and wearing an open-necked dirty shirt. In front of him on the table was a paper plate with the remains of a pie which he had been dabbling at.

As I shifted to lower the paper my soaking umbrella which had been leaning against the rather frail table fell down and as I bent to pick it up I could see that on one foot the man was wearing a boot but that on the other foot there was nothing but an old soiled bandage. I straightened slowly and glanced at the pale clock which said quarter to eleven. My train was at ten past, and outside it was raining . . .

'Burke and Hare,' he said. 'They used to kill people and sell their bodies to the hospitals. Sometimes they would dig bodies from the cemeteries and sell them. It was a long time ago, you understand, the nineteenth century.' (As a matter of fact it had been the eighteenth.) 'Not many people know about it.' In this he was wrong: I certainly knew about it. It was one of those things that everybody knew about Edinburgh as well as the fact that Sir Walter Scott had connections with it, that there was a large castle, that there was a cuckoo clock in the Gardens, that the Edinburgh Festival took place once a year. In fact I had just the previous night attended a version of *King Lear* done against a backcloth of what appeared to be oatmeal-coloured sacking. Most of the characters also wore sacking.

'One of the doctors recognised one of the bodies and that was how they were caught. Do you understand?'

I said I did. He had clearly taken me for a tourist which I wasn't and I prepared to raise the *Sunday Times* again – in my mind it had taken on the character of a drawbridge which one could raise or lower according to one's inclination – when he started again.

'I go to the cinema a lot,' he said. 'Last night I saw a film about the last war. The Second World War. It was about the Commandos. My uncle was in the Second World War. He was in the Commandos. This film was about the Commandos. They had flamethrowers and one of the officers said that they would get those German buggers. They were using tanks. What do you call those American tanks they had in the Second World War?'

'Shermans,' I offered automatically.

'No,' he said seriously, 'they were American tanks.'

I nearly burst out laughing. This man seemed a very simple person really. He was also a bore. I volunteered no more words in case he would be encouraged to start on another of his stories. But he continued.

'I go to see the Swedish films too. There was one about this girl who was killed by a fellow with a camera. He would kill them you see and then he would take photographs of them. One night she went up to her bed, before she was killed you understand, and this woman opened the window. She looked green and she walked across to the bed and she put her hand on the pillow and she left blood there. It was a sign, you see. When this girl was killed she was chased across this wood and he killed her. He put her in this pond and he took a photograph of her. And then the detectives got him. Swedish detectives, you understand.'

I was trying to think of what this encounter reminded me of and suddenly I knew. It was exactly like a Pinter play in its utter inconsequentiality. I felt suddenly frightened and odd.

'I suppose you'll be here on holiday,' he said. 'We have the

Edinburgh Festival here once a year. They come from all over. They have plays and they have . . . ' He stopped suddenly and gazed down at his plate.

Behind my *Sunday Times* I was thinking of another episode that had happened two days before.

I was staying at a hotel in the city and one wet afternoon I was sitting in the lounge. There were large windows and through the rainswept panes I could see the Castle towering theatrically out of the mist. There was also a huge statue of Sir Walter Scott that I could see and a stone horse. About the lounge were scattered copies of the *Scottish Field* and the *Countryside* as one might find them in the waiting rooms of dentists or doctors or lawyers. In one corner of the lounge there sat an oldish woman with a mouth like a trap reading *Nemesis* by Agatha Christie. Beside her was a plate of biscuits at which she would absentmindedly nibble in the intervals of turning pages of the book. She was wearing a blue dress and had a string of pearls round her reddish throat.

Opposite me near the fire was a really old woman with a stick. Her back was humped and she wore a meal-coloured matching blouse and skirt. Beside her was a formidable lady in tweeds who had the look of a retired schoolteacher. The old lady signalled for the waitress who almost ran to her, leaning towards her as if she were royalty. The old lady said in a very distinct loud voice, as if she were sitting in her own home, 'I should like a cup, not a pot, of tea and some digestives and thin slices of bread – two – with very thin slices of cheese.' The waitress, enthusiastic and young and beautiful and possibly Irish from her pale fine face, said 'Yes, ma'am,' and rushed off. The old lady rested her veined, entwined hands on top of her stick like a queen and stared ahead of her. The woman beside her was talking but she didn't seem to hear. Now and again her lips moved as if from a phantom memory of eating. Or perhaps she might have been talking to someone. In a supernaturally short time the girl ran back with a silvery glittery tray containing the stuff the old lady had ordered and began to lay it out on the small table with the claw legs. The hotel was certainly clean, one could say that. That morning I had seen a fat singing woman emerging from a lift with a huge mound of billowy sheets, like soap suds all about her.

The old woman picked up the sandwiches and examined them. 'The cheese is too thick,' she said in a squeaky penetrating voice. 'Far too thick. I wanted thin slices.' The girl bent in front of her (I could imagine her furious flush). She was very beautiful with a narrow waist and she was dressed in black with a froth of white at the throat. Yellow curls appeared from below her small black cap and from where I was I could see her graceful youthful thighs. 'I wanted thin slices, didn't I say that?' She turned to her companion. The woman who was reading *Nemesis* turned another page. She had eaten all her biscuits.

'I heard you say that quite distinctly,' said the old lady's companion. The waitress looked from one to the other, all quivering with the desire to serve. 'I'm sorry, Ma'am, I'm sorry, Ma'am,' she repeated over and over.

'Sorry is not enough,' said the old lady. 'Not enough. Take it back.' The waitress retrieved the plate with the sandwiches as if it were a mine and took it back, half running as before. As she raced across the carpeted floor I heard the old lady say:

'Ever since Watson left, the sandwiches have not been the same.' The companion commiserated with her, and began to pour out the tea.

'Not so much milk,' said the old lady suddenly, 'not so much milk.'

I stared moodily out at the Castle. I had phoned three times already for a taxi but they were all busy with tourists.

Beside me there had appeared a man and his wife and their teenage son who was dressed in a red school uniform and looked all knees and hands. He sat very stiffly between his mother and father. The woman closed *Nemesis* with a snap and walked towards the door. Before she reached it she stopped and said to the mother:

'I see that your son is at Heriot's. Has he been playing Rugby?'

'Yes, that's just what he has been doing,' said the mother. The boy looked pleased in an embarrassed way as if he were

Achilles being talked about by the Greeks after a particularly good fight.

'My son still plays Rugby,' said the woman. 'He is a lawyer. He comes to see me on Thursday afternoons.'

'That's nice,' the mother murmured.

'I remember,' said the woman in a loud voice, 'when I was at school – it was at Gillespies – we used to have hockey every Friday afternoon. I don't see so much hockey being played now.'

The mother murmured something incomprehensible. Her husband had taken out a pipe but wasn't sure whether he should light it or not.

'In those days the Principal was a Miss Geddes,' the woman went on relentlessly. 'And there was another lady called Miss Brown who taught us Tennyson. I never hear of her now but I remember quite clearly that she used to teach us much Tennyson. Is your son good at Rugby?'

'Are you, darling?' said the mother brightly to the appanage all red and knobbly-kneed and standing out from the frail furniture.

'Not really, Mother,' said the boy. 'Some of the other chaps are better.'

'They are of course modest,' said the woman. 'That is what public schools teach if they teach nothing else. And a good thing too in the world we live in.' With that she went through the doorway clutching her *Nemesis*, and for a dazed visionary moment I saw with a sense of bewilderment all the old women in the room running on to hockey fields with white sticks and ribboned hair and shouting in the blue windy day. It was all so real that I felt tears coming to my eyes, seeing those locker rooms, those beautiful young girls in green, slim and vivid and pigtailed and uniformed.

I got up from the table folding my *Sunday Times* carefully. I said I had to catch a train. My companion was sitting staring into space, unshaven, pale. He seemed to be wearing layers and layers of clothes as if he were cold. I shivered for a moment as if he were a threat to me. But that of course was ridiculous. With my umbrella, my *Sunday Times* and my case I went to the ticket office and bought my ticket. My train had changed platforms. It usually left from twelve but today it was leaving from fourteen. I didn't like that and was glad that I had checked the notice. It was some time before the man at the gate would allow us on to the train but eventually I settled myself into a corner seat. In front of me there was a man in a bowler hat who was also carrying a *Sunday Times*. I put my umbrella and case on the rack and sat down: after a while the train shuttled backwards and then forwards and began to move away from the platform. The scenery sped past, everything wet and miserable and grey. To the left of me a boy wearing a large Western-style hat was bending down to kiss his girl friend. For a panicky moment I nearly said to the bowler-hatted man, 'You've heard of those two, haven't you?' But I clamped my teeth together lest any language should bleed out. Most of the time my companion made a snorting noise behind the newspaper which I had already read. I wished now that I had bought a paper-back but most of the books on the bookstalls were spy stories which I had read before and I didn't fancy the involved and trivial stories of the second-raters.

An American Sky

He stood on the deck of the ship looking towards the approaching island. He was a tall man who wore brownish clothes: and beside him were two matching brown cases. As he stood on the deck he could hear Gaelic singing coming from the saloon which wasn't all that crowded but had a few people in it, mostly coming home for a holiday from Glasgow. The large ship moved steadily through the water and when he looked over the side he could see thin spitlike foam travelling alongside. The island presented itself as long and green and bare with villages scattered along the coast. Ahead of him was the westering sun which cast long red rays across the water.

He felt both excited and nervous as if he were returning to a wife or sweetheart whom he had not seen for a long time and was wondering whether she had changed much in the interval, whether she had left him for someone else or whether she had remained obstinately true. It was strange, he thought, that though he was sixty years old he should feel like this. The journey from America had been a nostalgic one, first the plane, then the train, then the ship. It was almost a perfect circle, a return to the womb. A womb with a view, he thought and smiled.

He hadn't spoken to many people on the ship. Most of the time he had been on deck watching the large areas of sea streaming past, now and again passing large islands with mountain peaks, at other times out in the middle of an empty sea where the restless gulls scavenged, turning their yellow gaunt beaks towards the ship.

The harbour was now approaching and people were beginning to come up on deck with their cases. A woman beside him was buttoning up her small son's coat. Already he could see red buses and a knot of people waiting at the pier. It had always been like that, people meeting the ship when it arrived at about eight, some not even welcoming anyone in particular but just standing there watching. He noticed a squat man in fisherman's clothes doing something to a rope. Behind him there was a boat under green canvas.

The ship swung in towards the harbour. Now he could see the people more clearly and behind them the harbour buildings. When he looked over the side he noticed that the water was dirty with bits of wooden boxes floating about in an oily rainbowed scum.

After some manœuvring the gangway was eventually laid. He picked up his cases and walked down it behind a girl in yellow slacks whose transistor was playing in her left hand. Ahead of her was a man in glasses who had a BEA case with, stamped on it, the names of various foreign cities. There were some oldish women in dark clothes among the crowd and also some girls and boys in brightly coloured clothes. A large fat slow man stood to the side of the gangway where it touched the quay, legs spread apart, as if he had something to do with the ship, though he wasn't actually doing anything. Now and again he scratched a red nose.

He reached the shore and felt as if the contact with land was an emotionally charged moment. He didn't quite know how he felt, slightly empty, slightly excited. He walked away from the ship with his two cases and made his way along the main street. It had changed, no doubt about it. There seemed to be a lot of cafés, from one of which he heard the blare of a jukebox. In a bookseller's window he saw *From Russia with Love* side by side with a book about the Highlands called *The Misty Hebrides*. Nevertheless the place appeared smaller, though it was much more modern than he could remember, with large windows of plate glass, a jeweller's with Iona stone, a very fashionable-looking ladies' hairdressers. He also passed a supermarket and another bookseller's. Red lights from one of the cafés streamed into the bay. At the back of the jeweller's shop he saw a church spire rising into the sky. He came to a cinema which advertised Bingo on Tuesdays, Thursdays and Saturdays. Dispirited trailers for a Western filled the panels.

He came to a Chinese restaurant and climbed the steps, carrying his two cases. The place was nearly empty and seemed mostly purplish with, near the ceiling, a frieze showing red dragons. Vague music – he thought it might be Chinese – leaked from the walls. He sat down and, drawing the huge menu towards him, began to read it. In one corner of the large room an unsmiling Chinaman with a moustache was standing by an old-fashioned black telephone and at another table a young Chinese girl was reading what might have been a Chinese newspaper. A little bare-bottomed Chinese boy ran out of the kitchen, was briefly chased back with much giggling, and the silence descended again.

For a moment he thought that the music was Gaelic, and was lost in his dreams. The Chinese girl seemed to turn into Mary who was doing her homework in the small thatched house years and years before. She was asking their father about some arithmetic but he, stroking his beard, was not able to answer. At another table an old couple were solidly munching rice, their heads bowed.

The music swirled about him. The Chinese girl read on. Why was it that these people never laughed? He had noticed that. Also that Chinese restaurants were hushed like churches. A crowd of young people came in laughing and talking, their Highland accents quite distinct though they were speaking English. He felt suddenly afraid and alone and slightly disorientated as if he had come to the wrong place at the wrong time. The telephone rang harshly and the Chinaman answered it in guttural English. Perhaps he was the only one who could speak English. Perhaps that was his job, just to answer the phone. He had another look at the menu, suddenly put it down and walked out just as a Chinese waitress came across with a notebook and pencil in her hand. He hurried downstairs and walked along the street.

Eventually he found a hotel and stood at the reception desk. A young blonde girl was painting her nails and reading a book. She said to the girl behind her, 'What does "impunity" mean?' The other girl stopped chewing and said, 'Where does it say that?' The first girl looked at him coolly and said, 'Yes, Sir?' Her voice also was Highland.

'I should like a room,' he said. 'A single room.'

She leafed rapidly through a book and said at last, 'We can give you 101, Sir. Shall I get the porter to carry your bags?'

'It's not necessary.'

'That will be all right then, Sir.'

He waited for a moment and then remembered what he was waiting for. 'Could I please have my key?' he asked.

She looked at him in amazement and said, 'You don't need a key here, Sir. Nobody steals anything. Room 101 is on the first floor. You can't miss it.' He took his cases and walked up the stairs. He heard them discussing a dance as he left.

He opened the door and put the cases down and went to the window. In front of him he could see the ship and the bay with the red lights on it and the fishing boats and the large clock with the greenish face.

As he turned away from the window he saw the Gideon Bible, picked it up, half smiling, and then put it down again. He took off his clothes slowly, feeling very tired, and went to bed. He fell asleep very quickly while in front of his eyes he could see Bingo signs, advertisements for Russian watches, and seagulls flying about with open gluttonous beaks. The last thought he had was that he had forgotten to ask when breakfast was in the morning.

2

The following day at two o'clock in the afternoon he took the bus to the village that he had left so many years before. There were few people on the bus which had a conductress as well as a driver, both dressed in uniform. He thought wryly of the gig in which he had been driven to the town the night he had left; the horse was dead long ago and so was his own father, the driver.

On the seat opposite him there was sitting a large fat tourist who had a camera and field-glasses slung over his shoulder and was wearing dark glasses and a light greyish hat.

The driver was a sturdy young man of about twenty or so. He whistled a good deal of the time and for the rest exchanged badinage with the conductress who, it emerged, wanted to become an air stewardess. She wore a black uniform, was pretty in a thin, sallow way, and had a turned-up nose and black hair.

After a while he offered a cigarette to the driver who took it. 'Fine day, Sir,' he said and then, 'Are you home on holiday?'

'Yes. From America.'

'Lots of tourists here just now. I was in America myself once. I was in the Merchant Navy. Saw a baseball team last night on TV.'

The bus was passing along the sparkling sea and the cemetery which stood on one side of the road behind a grey wall. The marble of the gravestones glittered in the sun. Now and again he could see caravans parked just off the road and on the beach men and children in striped clothing playing with large coloured balls or throwing sticks for dogs to retrieve. Once they passed a large block of what appeared to be council houses, all yellow.

'You'll see many changes,' said the driver. 'Hey, bring us some of that orangeade,' he shouted to the conductress.

'I suppose so.'

But there didn't seem all that many in the wide glittering day. The sea, of course, hadn't changed, the cemetery looked brighter in the sun perhaps, and there were more houses. But people waved at them from the fields, shielding their eyes with their hands. The road certainly was better.

At one point the tourist asked to be allowed out with his camera so that he could take a photograph of a cow which was staring vaguely over a fence.

If the weather was always like this, he thought, there wouldn't be any problem . . . but of course the weather did change . . . The familiar feeling of excitement and apprehension flooded him again.

After a while they stopped at the road end and he got off with his two cases. The driver wished him good luck. He stood staring at the bus as it diminished into the distance and then taking his case began to walk along the road. He came to the ruins of a thatched house, stopped and went inside. As he did so he disturbed a swarm of birds which flew out of the space all round him and fluttered out towards the sky which he could see quite clearly as there was no roof. The ruined house was full of stones and bits of wood and in the middle of it an old-fashioned iron range which he stroked absently, making his fingers black and dusty. For a moment the picture returned to him of his mother in a white apron cooking at such a stove, in a smell of flour. He turned away and saw carved in the wooden door the words MARY LOVES NORMAN. The hinges creaked in the quiet day.

He walked along till he came to a large white house at which he stopped. He opened the gate and there, waiting about ten yards in front of him, were his brother, his brother's daughter-in-law, and her two children, one a boy of about seventeen and the other a girl of about fifteen. They all seemed to be dressed in their best clothes and stood there as if in a picture. His brother somehow seemed dimmer than he remembered, as if he were being seen in a bad light. An observer would have noticed that though the two brothers looked alike the visitor seemed a more vivid version of the other. The family waited for him as if he were a photographer and he moved forward. As he did so his brother walked quickly towards him, holding out his hand.

'John,' he said. They looked at each other as they shook hands. His niece came forward and introduced herself and the children. They all appeared well dressed and prosperous.

The boy took his cases and they walked towards the house. It was of course a new house, not the thatched one he had left. It had a porch and a small garden and large windows which looked out towards the road.

He suddenly said to this brother, 'Let's stay out here for a while.' They stood together at the fence gazing at the corn which swayed slightly in the breeze. His brother did not seem to know what to say and neither did he. They stood there in silence.

After a while John said, 'Come on, Murdo, let's look at the barn.' They went into it together. John stood for a while inhaling the smell of hay mixed with the smell of manure. He picked up a book which had fallen to the floor and looked inside it. On the fly-leaf was written:

Prize for English
John Macleod

The book itself in an antique and slightly stained greenish cover was called *Robin Hood and His Merry Men*. His brother looked embarrassed and said, 'Malcolm must have taken it off the shelf in the house and left it here.' John didn't say anything. He looked idly at the pictures. Some had been torn and many of the pages were brown with age. His eye was caught by a passage which read, 'Honour is the greatest virtue of all. Without it a man is nothing.' He let the book drop to the floor.

'We used to fight in that hayloft,' he said at last with a smile, 'and I think you used to win,' he added, punching his brother slightly in the chest. His brother smiled with pleasure. 'I'm not sure about that,' he answered.

'How many cows have you got?' said John looking out through the dusty window.

'Only one, I'm afraid,' said his brother. 'Since James died . . .' Of course. James was his son and the husband of the woman he had met. She had looked placid and mild, the kind of wife who would have been suited to him. James had been killed in an accident on a ship: no one knew very much about it. Perhaps he had been drunk, perhaps not.

He was reluctant for some reason to leave the barn. It seemed to remind him of horses and bridles and bits, and in fact fragments of corroded leather still hung here and there on the walls. He had seen no horses anywhere: there would be no need for them now. Near the door he noticed a washing machine which looked quite new.

His brother said, 'The dinner will be ready, if it's your pleasure.' John looked at him in surprise, the invitation sounded so feudal and respectful. His brother talked as if he were John's servant.

'Thank you.' And again for a moment he heard his mother's voice as she called them in to dinner when they were out playing.

They went into the house, the brother lagging a little behind. John felt uncomfortable as if he were being treated like royalty when he wanted everything to be simple and natural. He knew that they would have cooked the best food whether they could afford it or not. They wouldn't, of course, have allowed him to stay at a hotel in the town during his stay. That would have been an insult. They went in. He found the house much cooler after the heat of the sun.

3

In the course of the meal which was a large one with lots of meat, cabbages and turnip and a pudding, Murdo suddenly said to his grandson:

'And don't you forget that Grandfather John was very good at English. He was the best in the school at English. I remember in those days we used to write on slates and Mr Gordon sent his composition round the classes. John is very clever or he wouldn't have been an editor.'

John said to Malcolm, who seemed quietly unimpressed: 'And what are you going to do yourself when you leave school?'

'You see,' said Murdo, 'Grandfather John will teach you . . . '

'I want to be a pilot,' said Malcolm, 'or something in science, or technical. I'm quite good at science.'

'We do projects most of the time,' said his sister. 'We're doing a project on fishing.'

'Projects!' said her grandfather contemptuously. 'When I was your age I was on a fishing boat.'

'There you are,' said his grandson triumphantly. 'That's what I tell Grandfather Murdo I should do, but I have to stay in school.'

'It was different in our days,' said his grandfather. 'We had to work for our living. You can't get a good job now without education. You have to have education.'

Straight in front of him on the wall, John could see a photograph of his brother dressed in army uniform. That was when he was a corporal in the Militia. He had also served in Egypt and in the First World War.

'They don't do anything these days,' said Murdo. 'Nothing. Every night it's football or dancing. He watches the TV all the time.'

'Did you ever see Elvis Presley?' said the girl who was eating her food very rapidly, and looking at a large red watch on her wrist.

'No, I'm sorry, I didn't,' said John. 'I once saw Lyndon Johnson though.'

She turned back to her plate uninterested.

The children were not at all as he had expected them. He thought they would have been shyer, more rustic, less talkative. In fact they seemed somehow remote and slightly bored and this saddened him. It was as if he were already seeing miniature Americans in the making.

'Take some more meat,' said his brother, piling it on his plate without waiting for an answer.

'All we get at English,' said Malcolm, 'is interpretations and literature. Mostly Shakespeare. I can't do any of it. I find it boring.'

'I see,' said John.

'He needs three Highers to get anywhere, don't you, Malcolm,' said his mother, 'and he doesn't do any work at night. He's always repairing his motor bike or watching TV.'

'When we got the TV first,' said the girl giggling, 'Grandfather Murdo thought . . .'

'Hist,' said her mother fiercely, leaning across the table, 'eat your food.'

Suddenly the girl looked at the clock and said, 'Can I go now, Mother? I've got to catch the bus.'

'What's this?' said her grandfather and at that moment as he raised his head, slightly bristling, John was reminded of their father.

'She wants to go to a dance,' said her mother.

'All the other girls are going,' said the girl in a pleading, slightly hysterical voice.

'Eat your food,' said her grandfather, 'and we'll see.' She ate the remainder of her food rapidly and then said, 'Can I go now?'

'All right,' said her mother, 'but mind you're back early or you'll find the door shut.'

The girl hurriedly rose from the table and went into the living room. She came back after a while with a handbag slung over her shoulder and carrying a transistor.

'Goodbye, Grandfather John,' she said. 'I'll see you tomorrow.' She went out and they could hear her brisk steps crackling on the gravel outside.

When they had finished eating Malcolm stood up and said, 'I promised Hugh I would help him repair his bike.'

'Back here early then,' said his mother again. He stood hesitating at the door for a moment and then went out, without saying anything.

'That's manners for you,' said Murdo. 'Mind you, he's very good with his hands. He repaired the tractor once.'

'I'm sure,' said John.

They ate in silence. When they were finished he and his brother went to sit in the living room which had the sun on it. They sat opposite each other in easy chairs. Murdo took out a pipe and began to light it. John suddenly felt that the room and the house were both very empty. He could hear quite clearly the ticking of the clock which stood on the mantelpiece between two cheap ornaments which looked as if they had been won at a fair.

Above the mantelpiece was a picture of his father, sitting very upright in a tall narrow chair, his long beard trailing in front of him. For some reason he remembered the night his brother, home from the war on leave, had come in late at night, drunk. His father had waited up for him and there had been a quarrel during which his brother had thrown the Bible at his father calling him a German bastard.

The clock ticked on. His brother during a pause in the conversation took up a *Farmers' Weekly* and put on a pair of glasses. In a short while he had fallen asleep behind the paper, his mouth opening like that of a stranded fish. Presumably that was all he read. His weekly letters were short and repetitive and apologetic.

John sat in the chair listening to the ticking of the clock which seemed to grow louder and louder. He felt strange again as if he were in the wrong house. The room itself was so clean and modern with the electric fire and the TV set in the corner. There was no air of history or antiquity about it. In a corner of the room he noticed a guitar which presumably belonged to the grandson. He remembered the nights he and his companions would dance to the music of the melodeon at the end of the road. He also remembered the playing of the bagpipes by his brother.

Nothing seemed right. He felt as if at an angle to the world he had once known. He wondered why he had come back after all those years. Was he after all like those people who believed in the innocence and unchangeability of the heart and vibrated to the music of nostalgia? Did he expect a Garden of Eden where the apple had not been eaten? Should he stay or go back? But then there was little where he had come from. Mary was dead. He was retired from his editorship of the newspaper. What did it all mean? He remembered the night he had left home many years before. What had he been expecting then? What cargo was he bearing with him? And what did his return signify? He didn't know. But he would have to find out. It was necessary to find out. For some reason just before he closed his eyes he saw in the front of him again the cloud of midges he had seen not an hour before, rising and falling above the fence, moving on their unpredictable ways. Then he fell asleep.

4

The following day which was again fine he left the house and went down to a headland which overlooked the sea. He sat there for a long time on the grass, feeling calm and relaxed. The waves came in and went out, and he was reminded of the Gaelic song *The Eternal Sound of the Sea* which he used to sing when he was young. The water seemed to stretch westward into eternity and he could see nothing on it except the light of the sun. Clamped against the rocks below were the miniature helmets of the mussels and the whelks. He remembered how he used to boil the whelks in a pot and fish the meat out of them with a pin. He realised as he sat there that one of the things he had been missing for years was the sound of the sea. It was part of his consciousness. He should always live near the sea.

On the way back he saw the skull of a sheep, and he looked at it for a long time before he began his visits. Whenever anyone came home he had to visit every house, or people would be offended. And he would have to remember everybody, though many people in those houses were now dead.

He walked slowly along the street, feeling as if he were being watched from behind curtained windows. He saw a woman standing at a gate. She was a stout large woman and she was looking at him curiously. She said, 'It's a fine day.' He said, 'Yes.'

She came towards him and he saw her red beefy face. 'Aren't you John Macleod?' she asked. 'Don't you remember me?'

'Of course I do,' he replied. 'You're Sarah.'

She shouted jovially as if into a high wind, 'You'll have to speak more loudly. I'm a little deaf.' He shouted back, 'Yes, I'm John Macleod,' and it seemed to him as if at that moment he were trying to prove his identity. He shouted louder still, 'And you're Sarah.' His face broke into a large smile.

'Come in, come in,' she shouted. 'Come in and have a cup of milk.'

He followed her into the house and they entered the living room after passing through the scullery which had rows of cups and saucers and plates on top of a huge dresser. In a corner of the room sat a man who was probably her son trapped like a fly inside a net which he was repairing with a bone needle. He was wearing a fisherman's jersey and his hands worked with great speed.

'This is George,' she shouted. 'My son. This is John Macleod,' she said to George. George looked up briefly from his work but said nothing. He was quite old, perhaps fifty or so, and there was an unmarried look about him.

'He's always fishing,' she said, 'always fishing. That's all he does. And he's very quiet. Just like his father. We're going to give John a cup of milk,' she said to her son. She went into the scullery for the milk and though he was alone with George the latter didn't speak. He simply went on repairing his net. This room too was cool and there was no fire. The chairs looked old and cracked and there was an old brown radio in a corner. After a while she came back and gave him the milk. 'Drink it up,' she instructed him as if she were talking to a boy. It was very cold. He couldn't remember when he had last drunk such fine milk.

'You were twenty-four when you went away,' she said, 'and I had just married. Jock is dead. George is very like him.' She shouted all this at the top of her voice and he himself didn't reply as he didn't want to shout.

'And how's that brother of yours?' she shouted remorselessly. 'He's a cheat, that one. Two years ago I sold him a cow. He said that there was something wrong with her and he got her cheap. But there was nothing wrong with her. He's a devil,' she said approvingly. 'But he was the same when he was young. After the penny. Always asking if he could run messages. You weren't like that. You were more like a scholar. You'd be reading books sitting on the peat banks. I remember you very well. You had fair hair, very fair hair. Your father said that you looked like an angel. But your brother was the cunning one. He knew a thing or two. And how are you?'

'I'm fine,' he shouted back.

'I hope you've come to stay,' she shouted again. He didn't answer.

'You would be sorry to hear about your mother,' she shouted again. 'We were all fond of her. She was a good woman.' By 'good' she meant that she attended church regularly. 'That brother of yours is a devil. I wonder if your mother liked him.' George looked at her quickly and then away again.

He himself shouted, 'Why do you ask that?' She pretended not to hear him and he had to shout the words again.

'It was nothing,' she said. 'I suppose you have a big job in America.'

He was wondering what she had meant and felt uneasy, but he knew that he wouldn't get anything more out of her.

'They've all changed here,' she shouted. 'Everything's changed. The girls go about showing their bottoms, not like in my day. The boys are off to the dances every night. George here should get married but I wouldn't let him marry one of these trollops. And you can't visit your neighbours any more. You have to wait for an invitation. Imagine that. In the old days the door would be always open. But not any more. Drink up your milk.'

He drank it obediently as if he were a child.

'Jock died, you know. A stroke it was. It lasted for three years. But he never complained. You remember Jock.'

He didn't remember him very well. Was he the one who used to play football or the one who played tricks on the villagers? He couldn't summon up a picture of him at all. What had she meant by his mother and his brother? He had a strange feeling as if he were walking inside an illusion, as if things had happened here that he hadn't known of, though he should have. But who would tell him? They would all keep their secrets. He even had the feeling that this large apparently frank woman was in fact treacherous and secretive and that behind her huge façade there was lurking a venomous thin woman whose head nodded up and down like a snake's.

She laughed again. 'That brother of yours is a businessman. He is the one who should have gone to America. He would have got round them all. There are no flies on him. Did you not think of coming home when your mother died?'

'I was . . . I couldn't at the time,' he shouted.

George, entrapped in his corner, the net around his feet, plied his bone needle.

'It'll be good to come home again,' she shouted. 'Many of them come back. Donny Macdonald came back seven years ago and they hadn't heard from him for twenty years. He used to drink but he goes to church regularly now. He's a man of God. He's much quieter than he used to be. He used to sing a lot when he was young and they made him the precentor. He's got a beautiful voice but not as good as it was. Nobody knew he was coming home till he walked into the house one night off the bus. Can you imagine that? At first he couldn't find it because they had built a new house. But someone showed it to him.'

He got up and laid the cup on the table.

'Is Mr Gordon still alive?' he shouted. Mr Gordon was his old English teacher.

'Speak up, I can't hear you,' she said, her large bulging face thrust towards him like a crab.

'Mr Gordon?' he shouted. 'Is he still alive?'

'Mr Gordon,' she said. 'Yes, he's alive. He's about ninety now. He lives over there.' She took him over to the window and pointed out a house to him. 'Oh, there's the Lady,' she said. 'He's always sitting on the wall. He's there every day. His sister died, you know. She was a bit wrong in the head.'

He said goodbye and she followed him to the door. He walked out the gate and made his way to where she had pointed. The day seemed heavy and sleepy and he felt slightly drugged as if he were moving through water. In the distance a man was hammering a post into the ground. The cornfields swayed slightly in the breeze and he could see flashes of red among them. He remembered the days when he would go with a bucket to the well, and smelt again the familiar smell of flowers and grass. He expected at any moment to see the ghosts of the dead stopping him by the roadway, interrogating him and asking him, 'When did you come home? When are you going away?' The whole visit, he realised now, was an implicit interrogation. What it was really about was: What had he done with his life? That was the question that people, without realising it, were putting to him, simply because he had chosen to return. It was also the question that he himself wanted answered.

Ahead of him stretched the moors and in the far distance he could see the Standing Stones which could look so eerie in the rain and which had perhaps been used in the sacrifice of children in Druid times. Someone had to be knifed to make the sun appear, he thought wryly. Before there could be light there must be blood.

He made his way to see Mr Gordon.

5

Gordon recognised him immediately: it was almost as if he had been waiting for him. He came forward from behind a table on which were piled some books and a chessboard on which some pieces were standing, as if he had been playing a game.

'John,' he said, 'John Macleod.'

John noticed that standing beside the chair was a small glass in which there were the remains of whisky.

'Sit down, sit down,' said Gordon as if he hadn't had company for a long time. He was still spry, grey-haired of course, but thin in the body. He was wearing an old sports jacket and a shirt open at the neck. There was a slightly unshaven look about him.

'I play chess against myself,' he said. 'I don't know which of us wins.' His laugh was a short bark. John remembered himself running to school while Gordon stood outside the gate with a whistle in his hand looking at his watch impatiently.

'I suppose coming from America,' he said, 'you'll know about Fischer. He's about to do the impossible, beat the Russian World Champion at chess. It's like the Russians beating the Americans at baseball – or us at shinty,' he added with the same self-delighting barking laugh. 'He is of course a genius and geniuses make their own rules. How are you?'

'Very well. And how are you?' He nearly said 'Sir' but stopped himself in time.

'Oh, not too bad. Time passes slowly. Have you ever thought about time?' Beside his chair was a pile of books scattered indiscriminately. 'I belong to dozens of book clubs. This is a book on Time. Very interesting. From the point of view of physics, psychiatry and so on.' He pointed to a huge tome which looked both formidable and new. 'Did you know, for instance, that time passes slowly for some people and rapidly for others? It's a matter of personality, and the time of year you're born. Or that temperature can affect your idea of time? Very interesting.' He gave the impression of a man who devoured knowledge in a sterile way.

John looked out of the window. Certainly time seemed to pass slowly here. Everything seemed to be done in slow motion as if people were walking through water, divers with lead weights attached to them.

'Are you thinking of staying?' said Gordon, pouring out a glass of whisky for his guest.

'I don't know that yet.'

'I suppose you could buy a house somewhere. And settle down. Perhaps do some fishing. I don't do any myself. I read and play chess. But I suppose you could fish and do some crofting. Though I don't remember that you were particularly interested in either of these.'

'I was just thinking,' said John, 'of what you used to tell us when we were in your English class. You always told us to observe. Observation, you used to say, is the secret of good writing. Do you remember the time you took us out to the tree and told us to smell and touch it and study it and write a poem about it? It was a cherry tree, I recall. We wrote the poem in the open air.'

'I was in advance of my time,' said Gordon. 'That's what they all do now. They call it Creative Writing. But of course they can't spell nowadays.'

'And you always told us that exactitude was important. Be observant and exact, you said, above all be true to yourselves.'

'Drink your whisky,' said Gordon. 'Yes, I remember it all. I've kept some of your essays. You were gifted. In all the years I taught I only met two pupils who were really gifted. How does one know talent when one sees it? I don't know. Anyway, I recognised your talent. It was natural, like being a tiger.'

'Yes, you kept telling us about exactitude and observation. You used to send us out of the room and change objects in the room while we were out. You made Sherlock Holmeses out of us.'

'Why do you speak about that now? It was all so long ago.'

'I have a reason.'

'What is your reason?' said Gordon sharply.

'Oh, something that happened to me. Some years ago.'

'And what was that? Or don't you want to talk about it?'

'I don't see why not. Not that it's very complimentary to me.'

'I have reached the age now,' said Gordon, 'when I am not concerned with honour, only with people.'

'I see,' said John, 'but suppose you can't separate them. Well, I'll tell you anyway.' He walked over to the window, standing with his back to the room and looking out at the empty road. It was as if he didn't want to be facing Gordon.

'I was an editor for some time as you know,' he said. 'Your training stood me in good stead. It was not a big paper but it was a reasonable paper. It had influence in the largish town in which I stayed. It wasn't Washington, it wasn't New York, but it was a largish town. I made friends in this town. One was a lecturer in a university. At least that is what we would call it here. As a matter of fact, he wasn't a lecturer in English. He was a lecturer in History. It was at the time of the McCarthy trials when nobody was safe, nobody. Another of my friends went off his head at that time. He believed that everyone was persecuting him and opening his mail. He believed that planes were pursuing him. In any case this friend of mine, his name was Mason, told me that files had been dug up on him referring to the time when he was a student and had belonged to a Left Wing university club. Now there were complaints that he was indoctrinating his students with Communism and, of course, being a History lecturer, he was in a precarious position. I told him that I would defend him in my paper, that I would write a hard-hitting editorial. I told him that I would stand up for principles, humane principles.' He stretched out his hand for the whisky and decided against drinking it. 'I left him on the doorstep at eleven o'clock on a Monday night. He was very disturbed because of course he was innocent, he wasn't a Communist and anyway he had great integrity as a teacher and lectured on Communism only theoretically as one ideology among others. But the McCarthy people of course were animals. You have no conception. Not here. Of the fog of lies. Of the quagmire. No conception.' He paused. A cow outside had bent its head to the grass and was eating.

'Anyway this was what happened. I walked home because I needed the exercise. The street was deserted. There were lampposts shining and it was raining. A thin drizzle. I could hear the echo of my feet on the road. This was the kind of thing you taught us, to remember and listen and observe, to be aware of our surroundings sensuously. By then it had become a habit with me.

'As I was walking along two youths came towards me out of the shadow, from under the trees. I thought they were coming home from the cinema or from a dance. They wore leather jackets and were walking towards me along the sidewalk. They stayed on the sidewalk and I made as if to go round them since they were coming straight for me without deviating. One of them said, "Daddy." I stopped. I thought he was going to ask me for a light. He said, "Your wallet, daddy." I looked at him in amazement. I looked at the two of them. I couldn't understand what was going on. And something happened to me. I could feel everything very intensely, you see. At that moment I could have written a poem, everything was so clear. They were laughing, you see, and they were very casual. They walked like those cowboys you see on the films, physically at ease in their world. And their eyes sparkled. Their eyes sparkled with pure evil. I knew that if I protested they would beat me up. I knew that there was no appeal. None at all. One of them had a belt, and a buckle on it sparkled in the light. My eyes were at the level of the buckle. I took out my wallet and gave them the money. I had fifty dollars. I observed everything as you had trained us to do. Their boots which were shining except for the drizzle: their neckties: their leather jackets. Their legs which were narrow in the narrow trousers. And their faces which were looking slightly upwards and shining. Clear and fine almost, but almost innocent though evil. A rare sort of energy. Pure and bright. They took the wallet, counted the money and gave me back the wallet. They then walked on. The whole incident took perhaps three minutes.

'I went into the house and locked the door. The walls seemed very fragile all of a sudden. My wife had gone to bed and I stood downstairs thinking, now and again removing a book from the shelves and replacing it. I felt the house as thin as the shell of an egg: I could hear, I thought, as far away as San Francisco. There was a tap dripping and I turned it off. And I didn't write the editorial, I didn't write anything. Two weeks after that my friend killed himself, with pills and whisky.'

The whisky which Gordon had given him was still untouched.

'Observation and exactitude,' he said, 'and elegance of language.' There was a long silence. Gordon picked up a chess piece and weighed it in his hand.

'Yes,' he said, 'and that's why you came home.'

'Perhaps. I don't know why I came home. One day I was walking along a street and I smelt the smell of fish coming from a fish shop. And it reminded me of home. So I came home. My wife, of course, is dead.'

'Many years ago,' said Gordon, still holding the chess piece in his hand, 'I was asked to give a talk to an educational society in the town. In those days I used to write poetry though of course I never told anyone. I was working on a particular poem at the time: it was very difficult and I couldn't get it to come out right. Well, I gave this talk. It was, if I may say so myself, a brilliant talk for in those days I was full of ideas. It was also very witty. People came and congratulated me afterwards as people do. I arrived home at one o'clock in the morning. When I got home I took out the poem and tried to do some work on it. But I was restless and excited and I couldn't get into the right mood. I sat and stared at the clock and I knew quite clearly that I would never write again. Odd, isn't it?'

'What are you trying to say?'

'Say? Nothing. Nothing at all. I don't think you'd better stay here. I don't think this place is a refuge. People may say so but it's not true. After a while the green wears away and you are left with the black. In any case I don't think you'd better settle here: that would be my advice. However, it's not my business. I have no business now.'

'Why did you stay here?' said John slowly.

'I don't know. Laziness, I suppose. I remember when I was in Glasgow University many years ago we used to take the train home at six in the morning after the holiday started. At first we were all very quiet, naturally, since we were half-asleep, most of us. But then as the carriages warmed and the sun came up and we came in sight of the hills and the lochs we began to sing Gaelic songs. Odd, and Glasgow isn't that far away. What does it all mean, John? What are you looking at?'

'The broken fences.'

'Yes, of course. There's a man here and he's been building his own house for ten years. He carries stone after stone to the house and then he forgets and sits down and talks to people. Time is different here, no doubt about it.'

'I had noticed.'

'If you're looking for help from me, John, I can't give you any. In the winter time I sit and look out the window. You can see the sea from here and it can look very stormy. The rain pours down the window and you can make out the waves hitting the islands out there. What advice could I give you? I have tried to do my best as far as my work was concerned. But you say it isn't enough.'

'Perhaps it wasn't your fault.'

John made his way to the door.

'Where are you going?'

'I shall have to call on other people as well. They all expect one to do that, don't they?'

'Yes, they still feel like that. That hasn't changed.'

'I'll be seeing you then,' said John as he left.

'Yes, yes, of course.'

He walked towards the sea cliffs to a house which he had visited many times when he was a boy, where he had been given many tumblers of milk, where later in the evening he would sit with others talking into the night.

The sea was large and sparkling in front of him like a shield. No, he said automatically to himself, it isn't like a shield, otherwise how could the cormorants dive in and out of it? What was it like then? It was like the sea, nothing else. It was like the sea in one of its moods, in one of its sunny gentle moods. As he walked pictures flashed in front of his eyes. He saw a small boy running, then a policeman's arm raised, the baton falling in a vicious arc, the neon light flashing from his shield. The boy stopped in midflight, the picture frozen.

6

He knocked at the door of the house and a woman of about forty, thin and with straggly greying hair, came to the door.

She looked at him enquiringly.

'John, John Macleod,' he said. 'I came to see your mother.' Her face lighted up with recognition and she said, 'Come in, come in.' And then inexplicably, 'I thought you were from the BBC.'

'The BBC?'

'Yes, they're always sending people to take recordings of my mother singing and telling stories, though she's very old now.'

He followed her into a bedroom where an old white-faced white-haired woman was lying, her head against white pillows. She stretched out her prominently veined hand across the blankets and said, 'John, I heard Anne talking to you. There's nothing wrong with my hearing.'

They were left alone and he sat down beside the bed. There was a small table with medicine bottles and pills on it.

'It's true,' she said, 'the BBC are always sending people to hear me sing songs before I die.'

'And how are you?'

'Fine, fine.'

'Good, that's good.' Her keen wise eyes studied his face carefully. The room had bright white wallpaper and the windows faced the sea.

'I don't sleep so well now,' said the old woman. 'I waken at five every morning and I can hear the birds twittering just outside the window.'

'You look quite well,' he said.

'Of course I'm not well. Everybody says that to me. But after all I'm ninety years old. I can't expect to live forever. And you're over sixty but I can still see you as a boy.' She prattled on but he felt that all the time she was studying him without being obvious.

'Have you seen the BBC people? They all have long hair and they wear red ties. But they're nice and considerate. Of course everybody wears long hair now, even my daughter's son. Would you like to hear my recording? My grandson took it down on a tape.'

'I would,' he said.

She tapped on the head of the bed as loudly as she could and her daughter came in.

'Where's Hugh?' she asked.

'He's outside.'

'Tell him to bring in the machine. John wants to hear my recording.' She turned to John and said, 'Hugh is very good with his hands, you know. All the young people nowadays know all about electricity and cars.'

After a while a tall, quiet, long-haired boy came in with a tape recorder. He plugged it into a socket beside the bed, his motions cool and competent and unflurried. He had the same neutral quizzical look that John had noticed in his brother's two grandchildren. They don't want to be deceived again, he thought. This generation is not interested in words, only in actions. Observation, exactitude, elegance. The universe of the poem or the story is not theirs, their universe is electronic. And when he thought of the phrase 'the music of the spheres' he seemed to see a shining bicycle moving through the heavens, or the wheels of some inexplicable machine.

Hugh switched on the tape recorder and John listened.

'Tonight,' the announcer began, 'we are going to hear the voice of a lady of ninety years old. She will be telling us about her life on this far Hebridean island untouched by pollution and comparatively unchanged when it is compared with our own hectic cities. This lady has never in all her life left the island on which she grew up. She has never seen a train. She has never seen a city. She has been brought up in a completely pastoral society. But we may well ask, what will happen to this society? Will it be squeezed out of existence? How can it survive the pollution of our time, and here I am speaking not simply of physical but of moral pollution? What was it like to live on this island for so many years? I shall try to elicit some answers to that question in the course of this programme. But first I should like you to hear this lady singing a Gaelic traditional song. I may interpolate at this point that many Gaelic songs have apparently been anglicised musically, thus losing their traditional flavour. But Mrs Macdonald will sing this song in the way in which she was taught to, the way in which she picked it up from previous singers.'

There followed a rendering of *Thig Tri Nithean Gun Iarraidh* ('Three things will come without seeking . . . '). John listened to the frail voice: it seemed strange to hear it, ghostly and yet powerful in its own belief, real and yet unreal at the same time.

When the singing was over the interviewer questioned her:

INTER. And now, Mrs Macdonald, could you please tell me how old you are?

MRS M. I am ninety years old.

INTER. You will have seen a lot of changes on this island, in this village even.

MRS M. Oh yes, lots of changes. I don't know much about the island. I know more about the village.

INTER. You mean that you hardly ever left the village itself?

MRS M. I don't know much about the rest of the island.

INTER. What are your memories then of your youth in the village?

MRS M. Oh, people were closer together. People used to help each other at the peat gathering. They would go out with a cart and they would put the peats on the cart. And they would make tea and sing. It was very happy times especially if it was a good day.

INTER. Do they not do that any more? I mean, coal and electricity . . .

MRS M. No, they don't do that so much, no. Nowadays. And there was more fishing then too. People would come to the door and give you a fish if they had caught one.

INTER. You mean herring?

MRS M. No, things like cod. Not herring. They would catch them in boats or off the rocks. Not herring. The herring were caught by the drifters. And the mackerel. We used to eat herring and potatoes every day. Except Sunday of course.

INTER. And what did you eat on Sunday?

MRS M. We would always have meat on Sunday. That was always the fashion. Meat on Sundays. And soup.

INTER. I see. And tell me, when did you leave school, Mrs Macdonald?

MRS M. I left school when I was fourteen years old. I was in Secondary Two.

INTER. It was a small village school, I take it.

MRS M. Oh, yes, it was small. Perhaps about fifty pupils.

Perhaps about fifty. We used to write on slates in those days and the children would bring in a peat for a fire in the winter.

Every child would bring in a peat. And we had people called pupil-teachers.

INTER. Pupil-teachers? What were pupil-teachers?

MRS M. They were young people who helped the teacher. Pupils. They were pupils themselves.

INTER. Then what happened?

MRS M. I looked after my father and mother. We had a croft too. And then I got married.

INTER. What did your husband do?

MRS M. He was a crofter. In those days we used to go to a dance at the end of the road. But the young people go to the town now. In those days we had a dance at the end of the road.

INTER. Did you not know him before, your husband I mean?

MRS M. Yes but that was where I met him, at the dance.

INTER. What did they use for the dance?

MRS M. What do you mean?

INTER. What music did they use?

MRS M. Oh, you mean the instrument. It was a melodeon.

INTER. Can you remember the tunes, any of the tunes, any of the songs?

MRS M. Oh yes, I can remember *A Ribbinn Oig bbeil cuimbn' agad?*

INTER. Could you tell our listeners what that means, Mrs Macdonald?

MRS M. It's a love song. That's what it is, a sailors' song. A love song.

INTER. I see. And do you think you could sing it?

And she proceeded to sing it in that frail voice. John listened to the evocation of nights on ships, moonlight, masts, exile, and he was strangely moved as if he were hearing a voice speaking to him from the past.

'I think that will be enough,' she said to the boy. He switched off the tape recorder without saying anything, put it in its case and took it away, closing the door behind him.

John said, 'You make it all sound very romantic.'

'Well, it was true about the peats.'

'But don't you remember the fights people used to have about land and things like that?'

'Yes but I remember the money they collected when Shodan was drowned.'

'But what about the tricks they used to play on old Maggie?'

'That was just young boys. And they had nothing else to do. That was the reason for it.'

There was a silence. A large blue fly buzzed in the window. John followed it with his eyes. It was restless, never settling, humming loudly with an angry sound. For a moment he nearly got up in order to kill it, he was so irritated by the booming sound and its restlessness.

'Would you like to tell me about my mother?' said John.

'What about your mother?'

'Sarah said something when I was speaking to her.'

'What did she say?'

'I felt there was something wrong, the way she talked. It was about my brother.'

'Well you know your brother was fond of the land. What did you want to know?'

'What happened. That was all.'

'Your mother went a bit odd at the end. It's quite common with old people. Perhaps that's what she was talking about. My own brother wouldn't let the doctor into the house. He thought he was poisoning him.'

'You say odd. How odd?'

'She accused your brother of wanting to put her out of the house. But I wouldn't pay any attention to that. Old people get like that.'

'I see.'

'You know your brother.'

'Yes. He is fond of land. He always was. He's fond of property.'

'Most people are,' she said. 'And what did you think of my singing?'

'You sang well. It's funny how one can tell a real Gaelic singer. It's not even the way they pronounce their words. It's something else.'

'You haven't forgotten your Gaelic.'

'No. We had societies. We had a Gaelic society. People who

had been on holiday used to come and talk to us and show us slides.' The successful and the failed. From the lone shelling of the misty island. Smoking their cigars but unable to go back and live there. Since after all they had made their homes in America. Leading their half lives, like mine. Watching cowboys on TV, the cheapness and the vulgarity of it, the largeness, the spaciousness, the crowdedness. They never really belonged to the city, these Highlanders. Not really. The skyscrapers were too tall, they were surrounded by the works of man, not the works of God. In the beginning was the neon lighting . . . And the fake religions, the cheap multitudinous sprouting so-called faiths. And they cried, some of them, at these meetings, in their large jackets of fine light cloth, behind their rimless glasses.

He got up to go.

'It's the blood, I suppose,' she said.

'Pardon.'

'That makes you able to tell. The blood. You could have seen it on my pillow three months ago.'

'I'm sorry.'

'Oh, don't be sorry. One grows used to lying here. The blood is always there. It won't allow people to change.'

'No, I suppose not.'

He said goodbye awkwardly and went outside. As he stood at the door for a moment, he heard music coming from the side of the house. It sounded American. He went over and looked. The boy was sitting against the side of the house patiently strumming his guitar, his head bent over it. He sang the words in a consciously American way, drawling them affectedly. John moved quietly away. The sun was still on the water where some ducks flew low. He thought of the headland where he was standing as if it were Marathon. There they had combed each other's long hair, the effeminate courageous ones about to die.

As he walked back he couldn't get out of his mind an article about Billy Graham he had read in an American magazine not long before. It was all about the crewcut saint, the electric blue eyed boy perched in his mountain eyrie. The Victorian respect shown by the interviewers had been, even for him with a long knowledge of American papers, nauseating. Would you like these remarks off the record, and so on. And then that bit about his personal appearances at such shows as *Laugh-in* where the conversation somehow got round to Jesus Christ every time! In Africa a corps of black policemen, appointed to control the crowd, had abandoned their posts and come forward to make a stand for Jesus!

Mad crude America, Victorian and twentieth century at the one time. Manic country of the random and the destined. What would his father or his mother have thought of Billy Graham? The fundamentalist with the stereophonic backing. For the first time since he came home he laughed out loud.

7

It was evening when he got back to his brother's house and the light was beginning to thicken. As he turned in at the gate his brother, who must have seen him coming, walked towards it and then stopped: he was carrying a hammer in his right hand as if he had been working with posts. They stood looking at each other in the half-light.

'Have you seen everybody then,' said his brother. 'Have you visited them all?' In the dusk and carrying the hammer he looked somehow more authoritative, more solid than his brother.

'Most of them. Sarah was telling me about the cow.'

'Oh, that. There was something wrong with the cow. But it's all right now. She talks too much,' he added contemptuously.

'And also,' said John carefully, 'I heard something about our mother.'

'What about her? By God, if that bitch Sarah has been spreading scandal I'll . . . ' His hands tightened on the hammer and his whole body seemed to bulge out and bristle like a fighting cock. For a moment John had a vision of a policeman with a baton in his hand. John glimpsed the power and energy that had made his brother the dominant person in the village.

After a while he said, 'I didn't want to worry you.'

'About what?' said John coldly.

'About our mother. She went a bit queer at the end. She hated Susan, you see. She would say that she was no good at the housework and that she couldn't do any of the outside work. She accused her of smoking and drinking. She even said she was trying to poison her.'

'And?'

'She used to say to people that I was trying to put her out of the house. Which of course was nonsense. She said that I had plotted to get the croft, and you should have it. She liked you better, you see.'

'Why didn't you tell me any of this?'

'I didn't want to worry you. Anyway I'm not good at writing. I can dash off a few lines but I'm not used to the pen.' For that moment again he looked slightly helpless and awkward as if he were talking about a gift that he half envied, half despised.

John remembered the letters he would get – 'Just a scribble to let you know that we are well and here's hoping you are the same . . . I hope you are in the pink as this leaves me.' Clichés cut out of a half world of crumbling stone. Certainly this crisis would be beyond his ability to state in writing.

'She was always very strong for the church. She would read bits of the Bible to annoy Susan, the bits about Ruth and so on. You know where it says, "Whither thou goest I will go . . . " She would read a lot. Do you know it?'

'I know it.'

John said, 'I couldn't come back at the time.'

'I know that. I didn't expect you to come back.'

As he stood there John had the same feeling he had had with Sarah, only stronger, that he didn't know anything about people at all, that his brother, like Sarah, was wearing a mask, that by choosing to remain where he was his brother had been the stronger of the two, that the one who had gone to America and immersed himself in his time was really the weaker of the two, the less self-sufficient. He had never thought about this before, he had felt his return as a regression to a more primitive place, a more pastoral, less exciting position, lower on the scale of a huge complex ladder. Now he wasn't so sure. Perhaps those who went away were the weaker ones, the ones who were unable to suffer the slowness of time, its inexorable yet ceremonious passing. He was shaken as by a vision: but perhaps the visions of artists and writers were merely ideas which people like his brother saw and dismissed as of no importance.

'Are you coming in?' said his brother, looking at him strangely.

'Not yet. I won't be long.'

His brother went into the house and John remained at the gate. He looked around him at the darkening evening. For a moment he expected to see his mother coming towards him out of the twilight holding a pail of warm milk in her hand. The hills in the distance were darkening. The place was quiet and heavy.

As he stood there he heard someone whistling and when he turned round saw that it was Malcolm.

'Did you repair the bike?' said John.

'Yes, it wasn't anything. It'll be all right now. We finished that last night.'

'And where were you today, then?'

'Down at the shore.'

'I see.'

They stood awkwardly in each other's presence. Suddenly John said, 'Why are you so interested in science and maths?'

'It's what I can do best,' said Malcolm in surprise.

'You don't read Gaelic, do you?'

'Oh, that's finished,' said Malcolm matter-of-factly.

John was wondering whether the reason Malcolm was so interested in maths and science was that he might have decided, perhaps unconsciously, that his own culture, old and deeply rotted and weakening, was inhibiting and that for that reason he preferred the apparent cleanness and economy of equations without ideology.

'Do you want to go to America?' he asked.

'I should like to travel,' said Malcolm carelessly. 'Perhaps America. But it might be Europe somewhere.'

John was about to say something about violence till it suddenly occurred to him that this village which he had left also had its violence, its buried hatreds, its bruises which festered for years and decades.

'I want to leave because it's so boring here,' said Malcolm. 'It's so boring I could scream sometimes.'

'It can seem like that,' said John. 'I shall be leaving tomorrow but you don't need to tell them that just now.'

He hadn't realised that he was going to say what he did till he had actually said it.

Malcolm tried to be conventionally regretful but John sensed a relief just the same.

They hadn't really said anything to each other.

After a while Malcolm went into the house, and he himself stood in the darkening light thinking. He knew that he would never see the place again after that night and the following morning. He summoned it up in all its images, observing, being exact. There was the house itself with its porch and the flowers in front of it. There was the road winding palely away from him past the other houses of the village. There was the thatched roofless house not far away from him. There were the fields and the fences and the barn. All these things he would take away with him, his childhood, his pain, into the shifting world of neon, the flashing broken signals of the city.

One cannot run away, he thought to himself as he walked towards the house. Or if one runs away one cannot be happy anywhere any more. If one left in the first place one could never go back. Or if one came back one also brought a virus, an infection of time and place. One always brings back a judgment to one's home.

He stood there for a long time before going into the house. He leaned over the fence looking out towards the fields. He could imagine his father coming towards him, in long beard and wearing wellingtons, solid, purposeful, fixed. And hadn't his father been an observer too, an observer of the seasons and the sea?

As he stood thinking he saw the cloud of midges again. They were rising and falling in the slight breeze. They formed a cloud but inside the cloud each insect was going on its own way or drifting with the breeze. Each alive and perhaps with its own weight, its own inheritance. Apparently free yet fixed, apparently spontaneous yet destined.

His eyes followed their frail yet beautiful movements. He smiled wryly as he felt them nipping him. He'd have to get into the house. He would have to find out when the bus left in the morning. That would be the first stage of the journey: after that he could find out about boats and trains and planes.

After the Dance

I had met her at a dance and we went to her house at about eleven o'clock at night. It was in a tenement and the steps up to her door were wide and large and clean as if they had been newly washed. The road, I remember, was very slippery as it was winter and, walking along in her red leather coat and red gloves, she looked like an ageing heroine out of a fairy story.

When we opened the door and went in she said in a whisper, 'You'll have to be quiet. My father is asleep.' The room blossomed into largeness in the light and one's first impression was of whiteness, white wallpaper and white paint. Above the mantelpiece there was a rectangular mirror with a flowery border. There were rooms leading off the one we were in and the whole flat seemed much more spacious than one might have expected.

She took off her coat and gloves and laid them on the table and sat down. The fire had gone out but there were still a few bits of charred wood remaining in it. A large dog got up and greeted her and then lay down in a corner munching a bone. A white-faced clock ticked on the mantelpiece.

'Would you like some tea?' she asked.

I said 'Yes,' and she went to the blue cooker and put the kettle on. She got out a tin of biscuits.

'My father will be trying to listen,' she said. 'But he's in the far end room. He doesn't sleep very well. There's no one to look after him but me. No one else. I have four sisters and they're all married and they won't look at him. Does one abandon him?' She looked at me wearily and now that she had removed her red coat her face appeared more haggard and her throat more lined. 'Or does one sacrifice oneself? He says to me, "Why did you never marry like your sisters and your brothers?" He taunts me with not marrying and yet he knows that if I married he would be left alone. Isn't that queer? You'd think he wouldn't say things like that, I mean in his own defence. You'd think he'd have more sense. But he doesn't have any sense. He spends a lot of his time doing jigsaws. They never come out right of course. A bit of a castle or a boat, something like that, but most of the time he can't be bothered finishing them. And another thing he does; he puts ships in bottles. He spends hours trying to get the sails inside with bits of string. He used to be a sailor you see. He's been all over the world. But most of the time he cuts wood. He goes down to the shore and gathers wood and chops it up in the woodshed. He makes all sorts of useless ornaments. He's got an axe. And lots of tools. In the summer he spends all his time in the shed chopping up wood. There's a woodshed down below on the back lawn and in the summer there are leaves all round it. He sits there. But he's always hacking away with that axe. Day after day. But what can one do with the old?'

She poured the hot water into the tea-pot and took it over to the table. She poured the tea into two large blue mugs and milked it.

'It's a problem, isn't it, what to do with the old? If one wasn't so good-hearted – some people aren't like that at all. Do you take sugar? One? Some people can go away and forget. My sisters always make excuses for not having him. They say they haven't got enough space with the children. Or they say they haven't got enough money. Or they say he wouldn't be good for the children. It's funny how they can be so forgetful and yet he wasn't any better to me than he was to them. In fact he treated me worse.'

She looked at me as if she expected me to say something. I murmured something unintelligible through the biscuit I was chewing, thinking that it all did sound really like a fairy tale. I wondered why she wore red. I had been reading something in one of the Sunday colour supplements about colour being a betrayal of one's personality but then everything was a betrayal of one's personality. Even conversation. I myself preferred blue but she wore red gloves, a red coat and she even had a red ribbon in her hair.

She was an odd mixture. At the dance she had danced very freely as they do in *Top of the Pops*, swaying like an unconscious flower, in a hypnotic trance of complete surrender to the body.

The dog crunched his bone in the corner and the clock ticked on.

'I don't understand why I'm so soft-hearted,' she said, crushing a biscuit in her hand.

I looked at the TV set. 'Is there anything on TV?' I said, 'or would that disturb your father?'

'There's a *Radio Times* there,' she said carelessly. 'If we shut the door he won't hear it. I don't watch it much.' The set was of white wood and I had a vision of her father hacking it up for firewood with his trusty axe.

I found the *Radio Times* among a pile of romantic magazines, some of which lay open with rings of black ink round horo-scopes.

'There's a series about Henry VIII,' I said. 'It's been going on for a week or two. Have you seen any of it?'

'No,' she said, 'but if you want it. So long as it isn't too loud.'

I switched on the TV and waited for the picture to declare itself. How did people exist before TV? What did they talk about? She rested her elbow on the table and drank her tea.

The picture clarified itself. It showed Anne Boleyn going to the scaffold. She was being prepared by her maids in attend-ance in the prison while the sunlight shone in straight shafts through the barred window. She told them that she wasn't frightened though some of them were crying and their hands shaking as they tied the ribbon in her hair.

The scene shifted to the execution block and showed a large man in black who was wearing a black mask: he was carrying a huge axe in his hand. The wooden block lay below. She came forward and lay down as if she were a swimmer, her hair neatly tied. Her motion had an eerie aesthetic quality as if she were taking part in a ballet dance, swanning forward, the axe falling. As the axe cut the head from the neck there was a roar of applause from the people.

I turned towards her. She was looking very pale. 'I don't like these TV programmes,' she said, and I switched it off. 'They're all so violent.'

'I'd better be going,' I said looking at the clock. 'It's getting late.'

'Yes, I suppose you'd better,' she said. 'I enjoyed the dance.'

I went out into the darkness, at first unable to see, and closing the main door of the tenement behind me. Then as my eyes focused and the sky came into view and defined itself, I saw the white stars. They were like the bones the dog had been crunching.

I walked very carefully along the glassy road almost slithering at times.

Funny about the tall man with the mask and the axe. It had reminded me of something in its extraordinary blatant brutality. The axe and the wood. But the picture I remembered most clearly was that of Anne Boleyn in the sunlight looking out of the narrow barred window on to the lawn. I really hoped that she had meant it when she said that she wasn't afraid. But she had certainly acted as if she meant it. And I was sure she did. For that particular moment in time she had meant it and that was something. One could not be expected to mean it for all moments, even on TV.

The Telegram

The two women – one fat and one thin – sat at the window of the thin woman's house drinking tea and looking down the road which ran through the village. They were like two birds, one a fat domestic bird perhaps, the other more aquiline, more gaunt, or, to be precise, more like a buzzard.

It was wartime and though the village appeared quiet, much had gone on in it. Reverberations from a war fought far away had reached it: many of its young men had been killed, or rather drowned, since nearly all of them had joined the navy, and their ships had sunk in seas which they had never seen except on maps which hung on the walls of the local school which they all had at one time or another unwillingly attended. One had been drowned on a destroyer after a leave during which he had told his family that he would never come back again. (Or at least that was the rumour in the village which was still, as it had always been, a superstitious place.) Another had been drowned during the pursuit of the *Bismarck*.

What the war had to do with them the people of the village did not know. It came on them as a strange plague, taking their sons away and then killing them, meaninglessly, randomly. They watched the road often for the telegrams.

The telegrams were brought to the houses by the local elder who, clad in black, would walk along the road and then stop at the house to which the telegram was directed. People began to think of the telegram as a strange missile pointed at them from abroad. They did not know what to associate it with, certainly not with God, but it was a weapon of some kind, it picked a door and entered it, and left desolation just like any other weapon.

The two women who watched the street were different, not

only physically but socially. For the thin woman's son was a sub-lieutenant in the Navy while the fat woman's son was only an ordinary seaman. The fat woman's son had to salute the thin woman's son. One got more pay than the other, and wore better uniform. One had been at university and had therefore become an officer, the other had left school at the age of fourteen.

When they looked out the window they could see cows wandering lazily about, but little other movement. The fat woman's cow used to eat the thin woman's washing and she was looking out for it but she couldn't see it. The thin woman was not popular in the village. She was an incomer from another village and had only been in this one for thirty years or so. The fat woman had lived in the village all her days; she was a native. Also the thin woman was ambitious: she had sent her son to university though she only had a widow's pension of ten shillings a week.

As they watched they could see at the far end of the street the tall man in black clothes carrying in his hand a piece of yellow paper. This was a bare village with little colour and therefore the yellow was both strange and unnatural.

The fat woman said: 'It's Macleod again.'

'I wonder where he's going today.'

They were both frightened for he could be coming to their house. And so they watched him and as they watched him they spoke feverishly as if by speaking continually and watching his every move they would be able to keep from themselves whatever plague he was bringing. The thin woman said:

'Don't worry, Sarah, it won't be for you. Donald only left home last week.'

'You don't know,' said the fat woman, 'you don't know.'

And then she added without thinking, 'It's different for the officers.'

'Why is it different for the officers?' said the thin woman in an even voice without taking her eyes from the black figure.

'Well, I just thought they're better off,' said the fat woman in a confused tone, 'they get better food and they get better conditions.'

'They're still on the ship,' said the thin woman who was thinking that the fat woman was very stupid. But then most of them were: they were large, fat and lazy. Most of them could have better afforded to send their sons and daughters to university but they didn't want to be thought of as snobbish.

'They are that,' said the fat woman. 'But your son is educated,' she added irrelevantly. Of course her son didn't salute the thin woman's son if they were both home on leave at the same time. It had happened once they had been. But naturally there was the uneasiness.

'I made sacrifices to have my son educated,' said the thin woman. 'I lived on a pension of ten shillings a week. I was in nobody's debt. More tea?'

'No thank you,' said the fat woman. 'He's passed Bessie's house. That means it can't be Roddy. He's safe.'

For a terrible moment she realised that she had hoped that the elder would have turned in at Bessie's house. Not that she had anything against either Bessie or Roddy. But still one thought of one's own family first.

The thin woman continued remorselessly as if she were pecking away at something she had pecked at for many years. 'The teacher told me to send Iain to University. He came to see me. I had no thought of sending him before he came. "Send your son to university," he said to me. "He's got a good head on him." And I'll tell you, Sarah, I had to save every penny. Ten shillings isn't much. When did you see me with good clothes in the church?'

'That's true,' said the fat woman absently. 'We have to make sacrifices.' It was difficult to know what she was thinking of – the whale meat or the saccharines? Or the lack of clothes? Her mind was vague and diffused except when she was thinking about herself.

The thin woman continued: 'Many's the night I used to sit here in this room and knit clothes for him when he was young. I even knitted trousers for him. And for all I know he may marry an English girl and where will I be? He might go and work in England. He was staying in a house there at Christmas. He met a girl at a dance and he found out later that her father was a mayor. I'm sure she smokes and drinks. And he might not give me anything after all I've done for him.'

'Donald spends all his money,' said the fat woman. 'He never sends me anything. When he comes home on leave he's never in the house. But I don't mind. He was always like that. Meeting strange people and buying them drinks. It's his nature and he can't go against his nature. He's passed the Smiths. That means Tommy's all right.'

There were only another three houses before he would reach her own, and then the last one was the one where she was sitting.

'I think I'll take a cup of tea,' she said. And then, 'I'm sorry about the cow.' But no matter how you tried you never could like the thin woman. She was always putting on airs. Mayor indeed. Sending her son to university. Why did she want to be better than anyone else? Saving and scrimping all the time. And everybody said that her son wasn't as clever as all that. He had failed some of his exams too. Her own Donald was just as clever and could have gone to university but he was too fond of fishing and being out with the boys.

As she drank her tea her heart was beating and she was frightened and she didn't know what to talk about and yet she wanted to talk. She liked talking, after all what else was there to do? But the thin woman didn't gossip much. You couldn't feel at ease with her, you had the idea all the time that she was thinking about something else.

The thin woman came and sat down beside her.

'Did you hear,' said the fat woman, 'that Malcolm Mackay was up on a drunken charge? He smashed his car, so they say. It was in the black-out.'

'I didn't hear that,' said the thin woman.

'It was coming home last night with the meat. He had it in the van and he smashed it at the burn. But they say he's all right. I don't know how they kept him out of the war. They said it was his heart but there was nothing wrong with his heart. Everyone knows it was influence. What's wrong with his heart if he can drink and smash a car?'

The thin woman drank her tea very delicately. She used to be away on service a long time before she was married and she had a dainty way of doing things. She sipped her tea, her little finger elegantly curled in an irritating way.

'Why do you keep your finger like that?' said the fat woman suddenly.

'Like what?'

The fat woman demonstrated.

'Oh, it was the way I saw the guests drinking tea in the hotels when I was on service. They always drank like that.'

'He's passed the Stewarts,' said the fat woman. Two houses to go. They looked at each other wildly. It must be one of them. Surely. They could see the elder quite clearly now, walking very stiff, very upright, wearing his black hat. He walked in a stately dignified manner, eyes straight ahead of him.

'He's proud of what he's doing,' said the fat woman suddenly. 'You'd think he was proud of it. Knowing before anyone else. And he himself was never in the war.'

'Yes,' said the thin woman, 'it gives him a position.' They watched him. They both knew him well. He was a stiff, quiet man who kept himself to himself, more than ever now. He didn't mix with people and he always carried the Bible into the pulpit for the minister.

'They say his wife had one of her fits again,' said the fat woman viciously. He had passed the Murrays. The next house was her own. She sat perfectly still. Oh, pray God it wasn't hers. And yet it must be hers. Surely it must be hers. She had dreamt of this happening, her son drowning in the Atlantic ocean, her own child whom she had reared, whom she had seen going to play football in his green jersey and white shorts, whom she had seen running home from school. She could see him drowning but she couldn't make out the name of the ship. She had never seen a really big ship and what she imagined was more like the mailboat than a cruiser. Her son couldn't drown out there for no reason that she could understand. God couldn't do that to people. It was impossible. God was kinder than that. God helped you in your sore trouble. She began to mutter a prayer over and over. She said it quickly like the Catholics, O God save my son O God save my son O God save my son. She was ashamed of prattling in that way as if she was counting beads but she couldn't stop herself, and on top of that she would soon cry. She knew it and she didn't want to cry in front of that woman, that foreigner. It would be weakness. She felt the arm of the thin woman around her shoulders, the thin arm, and it was like first love, it was like the time Murdo had taken her hand in his when they were coming home from the dance, such an innocent gesture, such a spontaneous gesture. So unexpected, so strange, so much a gift. She was crying and she couldn't look . . .

'He has passed your house,' said the thin woman in a distant firm voice, and she looked up. He was walking along and he had indeed passed her house. She wanted to stand up and dance all round the kitchen, all fifteen stone of her, and shout and cry and sing a song but then she stopped. She couldn't do that. How could she do that when it must be the thin woman's son? There was no other house. The thin woman was looking out at the elder, her lips pressed closely together, white and blood-less. Where had she learnt that self-control? She wasn't crying or shaking. She was looking out at something she had always dreaded but she wasn't going to cry or surrender or give herself away to anyone.

And at that moment the fat woman saw. She saw the years of discipline, she remembered how thin and unfed and pale the thin woman had always looked, how sometimes she had had to borrow money, even a shilling to buy food. She saw what it must have been like to be a widow bringing up a son in a village not her own. She saw it so clearly that she was astounded. It was as if she had an extra vision, as if the air itself brought the past with all its details nearer. The number of times the thin woman had been ill and people had said that she was weak and useless. She looked down at the thin woman's arm. It was so shrivelled, and dry.

And the elder walked on. A few yards now till he reached the plank. But the thin woman hadn't cried. She was steady and still, her lips still compressed, sitting upright in her chair. And, miracle of miracles, the elder passed the plank and walked straight on.

They looked at each other. What did it all mean? Where was the elder going, clutching his telegram in his hand, walking like a man in a daze? There were no other houses so where was he going? They drank their tea in silence, turning away from each other. The fat woman said, 'I must be going.' They parted for the moment without speaking. The thin woman still sat at the window looking out. Once or twice the fat woman made as if to turn back as if she had something to say, some message to pass on, but she didn't. She walked away.

It wasn't till later that night that they discovered what had happened. The elder had a telegram directed to himself, to tell him of the drowning of his own son. He should never have seen it just like that, but there had been a mistake at the post office, owing to the fact that there were two boys in the village with the same name. His walk through the village was a somnambulistic wandering. He didn't want to go home and tell his wife what had happened. He was walking along not knowing where he was going when later he was stopped half way to the next village. Perhaps he was going in search of his son. Altogether he had walked six miles. The telegram was crushed in his fingers and so sweaty that they could hardly make out the writing.

The Wedding

It was a fine, blowy, sunshiny day as I stood outside the church on the fringe of the small groups who were waiting for the bride to arrive. I didn't know anybody there, I was just a very distant relative, and I didn't feel very comfortable in my dark suit, the trousers of which were rather short. There were a lot of young girls from the Highlands (though the wedding was taking place in the city) all dressed in bright summery clothes and many of them wearing corsages of red flowers. Some wore white hats which cast intricate shadows on their faces. They all looked very much at ease in the city and perhaps most of them were working there, in hotels and offices. I heard one of them saying something about a Cortina and another one saying it had been a Ford. They all seemed to know each other and one of them said in her slow soft Highland voice, 'Do you think Murdina will be wearing her beads today?' They all laughed. I wondered if some of them were university students.

The minister who was wearing dark clothes but no gown stood in the doorway chatting to the photographer who was carrying an old-fashioned black camera. They seemed to be savouring the sun as if neither of them was used to it. The doors had been open for some time as I well knew since I had turned up rather early. A number of sightseers were standing outside the railings taking photographs and admiring the young girls who looked fresh and gay in their creamy dresses.

I looked at the big clock which I could see beyond the church. The bride was late though the groom had already arrived and was talking to his brother. He didn't look at all nervous. I had an idea that he was an electrician somewhere and his suit didn't seem to fit him very well. He was a small person with a happy, rather uninteresting face, his black hair combed back sleekly and plastered with what was, I imagined, fairly cheap oil.

After a while the minister told us we could go in if we wanted to, and we entered. There were two young men, one in a lightish suit and another in a dark suit, waiting to direct us to our seats. We were asked which of the two we were related to, the bride or the groom, and seated accordingly, either on the left or the right of the aisle facing the minister. There seemed to be more of the groom's relatives than there were of the bride's and I wondered idly whether the whole thing was an exercise in psychological warfare, a primitive pre-marital battle. I sat in my seat and picked up a copy of a church magazine which I leafed through while I waited: it included an attack on Prince Philip for encouraging Sunday sport. In front of me a young girl who appeared to be a foreigner was talking to an older companion in broken English.

The groom and the best man stood beside each other at the front facing the minister. After a while the bride came in with her bridesmaids, all dressed in blue, and they took their positions to the left of the groom. The bride was wearing a long white dress and looked pale and nervous and almost somnambulant under the white headdress. We all stood up and sang a psalm. Then the minister said that if there was anyone in the church who knew of any impediment to the marriage they should speak out now or forever hold their peace. No one said anything (one wondered if anyone ever stood up and accused either the bride or groom of some terrible crime): and he then spoke the marriage vows, asking the usual questions which were answered inaudibly. He told them to clasp each other by the right hand and murmured something about one flesh. The groom slipped the ring onto the bride's finger and there was silence in the church for a long time because the event seemed to last interminably. At last the ring was safely fixed and we sang another hymn and the minister read passages appropriate to the occasion, mostly from St Paul. When it was all over we went outside and watched the photographs being taken.

Now and again the bride's dress would sway in the breeze and a woman dressed in red would run forward to arrange it properly, or at least to her own satisfaction. The bride stood gazing at the camera with a fixed smile. A little boy in a grey suit was pushed forward to hand the bride a horseshoe after which he ran back to his mother, looking as if he was about to cry. The bride and groom stood beside each other facing into the sun. One couldn't tell what they were thinking of or if they were thinking of anything. I suddenly thought that this must be the greatest day in the bride's life and that never again would a thing so public, so marvellous, so hallowed, happen to her. She smiled all the time but didn't speak. Perhaps she was lost in a pure joy of her own. Her mother took her side, and her father. Her mother was a calm, stout, smiling woman who looked at the ground most of the time. Her father twisted his neck about as if he were being chafed by his collar and shifted his feet now and again. His strawy dry hair receded from his lined forehead and his large reddish hands stuck out of his white cuffs.

Eventually the whole affair was over and people piled into the taxis which would take them to the reception. I didn't know what to make of it all. It had not quite had that solemnity which I had expected and I felt that I was missing or had missed something important considering that a woman to the right of me in church had been dabbing her eyes with a small flowered handkerchief all through the ceremony. Both bride and groom seemed very ordinary and had not been transfigured in any way. It was like any other wedding one might see in the city, there didn't seem to be anything Highland about it at all. And the bits of conversation that I had overheard might have been spoken by city people. I heard no Gaelic.

For some reason I kept thinking of the father, perhaps because he had seemed to be the most uncomfortable of the lot. Everyone else looked so assured as if they had always been doing this or something like this and none of it came as a surprise to them. I got into a taxi with some people and without being spoken to arrived at the hotel which was a very good one, large and roomy, and charging, as I could see from a ticket at the desk, very high prices.

We picked up either a sherry or whisky as we went in the door and I stood about again. A girl in a white blouse was saying to her friend dressed in creamy jacket and suit, 'It was in Luigi's you see and this chap said to me out of the blue, "I like you but I don't know if I could afford you".' She giggled and repeated the story a few times. Her friend said: 'You meet queer people in Italian restaurants. I was in an Indian restaurant last week with Colin. It doesn't shut till midnight you know . . . ' I moved away to where another group of girls was talking and one of them saying: 'Did you hear the story about the aspirin?' They gathered closely together and when the story was finished there was much laughter.

After a while we sat down at the table and watched the wedding party coming in and sitting down. We ate our food and the girl on my left spoke to another girl on her left and to a boy sitting opposite her. She said: 'This chap came into the hotel one night very angry. He had been walking down the street and there was this girl in a blue cap dishing out Barclay cards or something. Well, she never approached him at all though she picked out other people younger than him. He was furious about it, absolutely furious. Couldn't she see that he was a business man, he kept saying. He was actually working in insurance and when we offered him a room with a shower he wouldn't take it because it was too expensive.'

The other girl, younger and round-faced, said: 'There was an old woman caught in the lift the other day. You should have heard the screaming . . . ' I turned away and watched the bride who was sitting at the table with a fixed smile on her face. Her father, twisting his neck about, was drinking whisky rapidly as if he was running out of time. Her mother smiled complacently but wasn't speaking to anyone. The minister sat at the head of the table eating his chicken with grave deliberation.

'Did you hear that Lindy has a girl?' said the boy in front of me to the girls. 'And she's thinking of going back home.'

They all laughed. 'I wouldn't go back home now. They'll be at the peats,' said the girl on my left.

'Well,' said the boy, 'I don't know about that. There was a student from America up there and he wanted to work at the peats to see what it was like. He's learned to speak Gaelic too.'

'How did he like it?' said the girl at my left.

'He enjoyed it,' said the boy. 'He said he'd never enjoyed anything so much. He said they'd nothing like that in America.'

'I'm sure,' said the small girl and they laughed again.

'Wouldn't go back for anything anyway,' said the girl to my left. 'They're all so square up there.'

When we had all finished eating, the Master of Ceremonies said that the groom would make a speech which he did very rapidly and incoherently. He was followed by the best man who also spoke very briefly and with incomprehensible references to one of the bridesmaids who blushed deeply as he spoke. There were cheers whenever an opportunity arose such as, for instance, when the groom referred for the first time to his wife and when there was a reference to someone called Tommy.

After that the telegrams were read out. Most of them were quite short and almost formal, 'Congratulations and much happiness' and so on. A number, however, were rather bawdy, such as, for instance, one which mentioned a chimney and a fire and another which suggested that both the bride and groom should watch the honey on their honeymoon. While the telegrams were being read some of the audience whispered to each other, 'That will be Lachy', and 'That will be Mary Anne'. I thought of those telegrams coming from the Highlands to this hotel where waitresses went round the tables with drinks and there were modernistic pictures, swirls of blue and red paint, on the walls. One or two of the telegrams were in Gaelic and in some strange way they made the wedding both more authentic and false. I didn't know what the bride thought as she sat there, as if entranced and distant. Everything seemed so formal, so fixed and monotonous, as if the participants were trying to avoid errors, which the sharpwitted city-bred waitresses might pick up.

Eventually the telegrams had all been read and the father got up to speak about the bride. I didn't know what I expected but he certainly began with an air of business-like trepidation. 'Ladies and gentlemen,' he said, 'I am here today to make a speech which as you will know is not my speciality.' He twisted his neck about inside the imprisoning collar and continued. 'I can tell you that the crossing was good and the skipper told me that the *Corona* is a good boat though a bit topheavy.' He beamed nervously and then said, 'But to my daughter. I can tell you that she has been a good daughter to me. I am not going to say that she is good at the peats for she is never at home for the peats and she never went to the fishing as girls of her age used to do in the past.' By this time people were beginning to look at each other or down at their plates and even the waitresses were smiling. 'I'll tell you something about the old days. We turned out good men and women in those days, good sailors who fought for their country. Nowadays I don't know about that. I was never in the city myself and I never wore a collar except to the church. Anyway I was too busy. There were the calves to be looked after and the land as you all know. But I can tell you that my daughter here has never been a burden to us. She has always been working on the mainland. Ever since she was a child she has been a good girl with no nonsense and a help to her mother, and many's the time I've seen her working at the hay and in the byre. But things is changed now. Nowadays, it's the tractors and not the horses. In the old days too we had the gig but now it's the train and the plane.' The bride was turning a deadly white and staring down at the table. The girls on my left were transfixed. Someone dropped a fork or a spoon or a knife and the sound it made could be heard quite clearly. But the father continued remorselessly: 'In my own place I would have spoken in the Gaelic but even the Gaelic is dying out now as anyone can read in the papers every week. In the old days too we would have a wedding which would last for three days. When Johnny Murdo married, I can remember it very well, the wedding went on for four days. And he married when he was quite old. But as for my daughter here I am very happy that she is getting married though the city is not the place for me and I can tell you I'll be very glad to get back to the dear old home again. And that is all I have to say. Good luck to them both.'

When he sat down there was a murmur of conversation which rose in volume as if to drown the memory of the speech. The girls beside me talked in a more hectic way than ever about their hotels and made disparaging remarks about the islands and how they would never go back. Everyone avoided the bride who sat fixed and miserable at the table as if her wedding dress had been turned into a shroud.

I don't know exactly what I felt. It might have been shame that the waitresses had been laughing. Or it might have been gladness that someone had spoken naturally and authentically about his own life. I remember I picked up my whisky and laid it down again without drinking it and felt that this was in some way a meaningful action.

Shortly afterwards the dancing began in an adjoining room. During the course of it (at the beginning they played the latest pop tunes) I went over and stood beside the father who was standing by himself in a corner looking miserable as the couples expressed themselves (rather than danced) in tune to the music, twisting their bodies, thrusting out their bellies and swaying hypnotically with their eyes half shut.

'It's not like the eightsome reel,' I said.

'I don't know what it is like,' he said. 'I have never seen anything like it.'

'It is rather noisy,' I agreed. 'And how are the crops this year?' I said to him in Gaelic.

He took his dazed eyes off a couple who were snapping their fingers at each other just in front of him, and said: 'Well, it's been very dry so far and we don't know what we're going to do.' He had to shout the words against the music and the general noise. 'I have a good few acres you know though a good many years ago I didn't have any and I worked for another man. I have four cows and I sell the milk. To tell you the honest truth I didn't want to come here at all but I felt I couldn't let her down. It wasn't an easy thing for me. I haven't left the island before. Do you think this is a posh hotel?'

I said that I thought it was. He said, 'I tell you I've never been in a hotel before now. They've got a lot of carpets, haven't they? And mirrors, I've never seen so many mirrors.'

'Come on,' I shouted, 'let's go into the bar.' We did so and I ordered two beers.

'The people in there aren't like human beings at all,' he said. 'They're like Africans.'

After a while he said, 'It was the truth I said about her, she's never at home. She's always been working in hotels. I'll tell you something, she's never carried a creel on her back though that's not a good thing either. She was always eating buns and she would never eat any porridge. What do you think of her husband, eh? He was talking away about cars. And he's got a good suit, I'll give him that. He gave the waiter a pound, I saw it with my own eyes. Oh, he knows his way around hotels, I'll be bound. But where does he come from? I don't know. He's never ploughed any ground, I think.'

I thought at that moment that he wouldn't see his daughter very often in the future. Perhaps he really was without knowing it giving her away to a stranger in a hired cutprice suit.

After a while we thought it politic to go back. By this time there was a lull in the dancing and the boy in the lightish suit had started a Gaelic song but he didn't know all the words of it, only the chorus. People looked round for assistance while red-faced and embarrassed he kept asking if anyone knew the words because he himself had lost them. Suddenly the father pushed forward with authority and standing with his glass in his hand began to sing – verse after verse in the traditional manner. They all gathered round him and even the waitresses listened, there was so much depth and intensity in his singing. After he had finished there was much applause and requests for other songs for he seemed to know the words of all of them. The young girls and the boys gathered round him and sat on the floor in a circle looking up at him. He blossomed in the company and I thought that I could now leave, for he seemed to be wholly at home and more so than his audience were.

Getting Married

It had all happened like a dream. There he was seated on a bench watching the men playing at the open-air yellow-and-black draughtsboard on a beautiful summer's evening, his guitar by his side, not even able to make up his mind whether his holiday was being a success. At the draughtsboard just in front of him a squat one-armed man was sitting on an upended box and staring across at his opponent who was dangling his hooked pole precisely in front of him. Up above at street level the sun flashed from the black statue of Burns who clutched a black marble daisy in his left hand and looked gaily across to a block of what seemed to be insurance offices. He himself was almost falling asleep: he had done a lot of travelling in the last few days. He stretched out legs encased in their tight trousers and regarded his unpolished shoes. He was wondering whether he could get into the YMCA or somewhere.

A gardener hosed a strip of green grass to his right and in the distance on a wooden stage he could see Highland dancers, dressed in innocent white, tiptoeing delicately as if in an amateurish ballet. They looked virginal and clean and oddly archaic. At the same time they reminded him that he himself felt sweaty and unwashed. The one-armed man, chewing gum relentlessly, hooked another piece from the board as if he were taking part in some battle whose outcome would decide the destiny of the world. Somewhere behind him among the trees he heard a clock hammering out six solid strokes.

He closed his eyes and as he did so he heard a voice saying, 'Do you like Shelley?' He turned round in surprise and saw that sitting beside him on the bench was a young girl with a miniature face, long blonde hair and wearing dark green slacks. He hadn't even heard her coming. He jerked himself awake, his long hair shaking.

Her enquiry had been very low and tentative and he didn't quite know what to make of it. She was holding a book out towards him and he looked at it stupidly half wondering if he were really asleep and she were part of his dream.

'I thought you might like Shelley,' she said, 'because of your guitar.'

He gazed at her, tired and sleepy, noticing that there were shadows under her eyes and that her slacks looked slightly worn and soiled. She might have been seventeen.

He looked at the book which showed on the cover the picture of a dreamy poet with long hair.

'No,' he said, 'I don't read Shelley.'

'Oh,' she said. 'I got it from the library.' She didn't seem the type who would read Shelley; he thought her voice sounded slightly uneducated. She seemed in fact like the kind of girl who might work in a shop except that she had about her a curious vulnerability and he was reminded of a woman he had met on the bus coming up who had been crying by herself for a long time and had then confided in him that she was going home to her mother because her husband was beating her up. She kept trying to speak to everyone and offering them cigarettes. Her open appeal for help was embarrassing. Eventually she had gone up to the driver to offer him a cigarette in spite of the fact that there was a notice saying that passengers must not engage the driver in conversation without good reason as they might distract him. At one stage she had shown him a burn on her hand which she said her husband had made with a cigarette.

He himself had heard of Shelley but that was all: he didn't read books like that.

'I am going for a walk,' she said. 'Would you like to come for a walk?' and again he was reminded of the open vulnerability of that other woman, her pouting childish face. Though she had said she was fifty years old, she had looked infantile. Imagine a grown woman on a bus crying like that, the tears seeping out of her as out of a well. At first he had taken her for a spastic, she looked so shapeless and childish, and her legs were drawn up on the seat like a child's.

He got up without thinking partly because he was so surprised and partly because he had nothing else to do and partly
because he was beginning to feel lonely. It didn't really do to
jump into a holiday as he had done without preparation, to
leave the familiar urban streets with their noisy cafés and set off
to the north to find lochs and trees and seas and fresh air. He
was so tired that he felt as if he was walking in a dream. She put
her hand in his and they climbed the steps together. He noticed
vaguely that someone had scrawled YA BAS on the statue of
Burns. He knew it was a statue of Burns because it said so and
he had heard of Burns though he hadn't heard much about
Shelley.

'Where are we going?' he said.

'We'll go for a walk,' she said, 'you just follow me.' They
walked down the street, crossed another one and turned right,
down to the harbour.

'I like watching the ships,' she said. They sat on the edge of
the quay swinging their legs over the side watching the oily
scummy water choked with floating boxes and scum. The
harbour was crammed with fishing boats with names like *Mary
Rose* and *Victor* and *Grace*. Above them towered a huge merchant
ship with scarred rusty sides.

'I would like to go to India,' she said.

'Why India?'

'I don't know. Sometimes I want to go to India. Other times
I want to go to Africa. Tonight I want to go to India. My father
is a scientist, you know. My mother was at university.'

She clutched his hand tightly as if otherwise they might fall
into the water. He didn't know exactly what he felt, a strangeness and yet a warmth. And as she spoke he himself thought,
Yes, it would be good to leave this place and go off to India or
Greece or someplace like that. But then you had to have money.
Perhaps she had money. He'd never had any money. It would
be marvellous to have as much money as you wanted, buy as
many cigarettes as you wanted, wear good clothes, go into the
cabin with your new cases and have people wait on you.

'What songs do you know?' she said. 'You look like a poet. I
thought you looked like Shelley. That's why I spoke to you.

Are you a poet? I got Shelley out of the library. I don't
understand him sometimes.'

'I know a ballad about Benny Lynch,' he said. 'The boxer. He
was destroyed by hangers-on. He was a great champion but the
money destroyed him. That happens a lot with boxers.'

'Sometimes I like to pretend that this is Venice,' she said. 'I
once saw a picture book about Venice. It's full of canals. They
don't have buses in Venice. I would like to go to Venice too.'

She swung her legs together like a child.

'I'm on holiday,' he said. 'I took my guitar with me. I don't
have much money. I don't have any money.'

'Are you a good guitarist?' she asked.

'Yes, I think so. Do you know that song *Waly Waly*?'

'No. Can you play it? Play it then.'

He started to sing and play:

> 'As we cam in by Glesca toun
> A comely sicht we were to see
> my love was clad in the black velvet
> And I mysel in crammasy.'

Ever since he had first heard that song he couldn't get it out
of his head. It was at the Gringo pub one afternoon. A few of
the boys had been there, that was where they met. It was a
pretty crummy pub but the prices were all right.

'What's crammasy?' she asked.

'I don't know,' he said.

There was a smell of brine and oil all around them, mixed
with the aroma of rotten apples as if a box of them had been left
lying about.

'Have you any money at all?' she said. 'We could go to the
pictures.'

'No,' he said, 'I haven't any money.'

She turned towards him, her hand still in his, her face white
and beautiful and intense.

'Come on,' she said. They got up and hand in hand walked
back to the main street and then along it westwards for what
appeared to be miles. Eventually they came out on to the beach
which faced a large panorama of sea. There was a fairground

and they walked through it looking at the people pulling levers, on the roundabouts, spinning on top of the huge wheel which turned over and over against the sky.

They passed a fortune teller's tent and she thought about going in but didn't. 'When my mother was in university,' she said, 'she went to a fortune teller's and he told her she would marry a clever man.' She watched some women playing bingo and said, 'It's disgusting how they spend their time.'

Eventually she turned away and said, 'I don't like fairs. Everything is so cheap.' They left the fair and walked down to the beach. They sat on a seat and watched the white rollers rising terrifyingly high and then dissipating themselves along the sand. They could sense an inhuman violent force of water which would engulf and destroy anything that came near it. Clutching his hand she looked out with parted lips.

'Isn't it beautiful?' she said. He wished that he could take his guitar out there and play. He wanted to stand up and shout 'As we cam in by Glesca toun'. He wanted to dive in there and play his guitar, into that whiteness, that ghostly whiteness, that wheel of power.

She was restless. 'Let's go over there and sit on the grass,' she said. He obeyed her and they sat by themselves away from the little boys playing football in their green and white Celtic stripes.

He lay beside her and stroked her hair tenderly, wanting to comb it. He kissed the side of her head. Then he kissed her gently opened mouth. They breathed in and out tenderly without passion.

'Would you like to marry me?' she said seriously, staring up at the white sliver of moon which had appeared in the dark blue sky.

'Yes,' he said. 'That's what I would like to do.' He kissed her fingers one by one.

'We'll go and see my father later then,' she said. The moon was white and tender like her face. On the finger of one hand she was wearing a Woolworth ring.

'I only met you an hour ago,' he said, tenderly and amazedly kissing her hair and feeling as if the bones in his body were melting. He picked up her hand and kissed each finger again individually. He wanted to protect her. He wanted to have money so that he could give her food. He parted her hair tenderly.

'So this is what love is like,' he thought. He had never felt such tenderness before. She laid her head on his shoulder and fell asleep. He lay on his side and looked at her while the moon rose and the light darkened and the blue of the sky began to become black.

After what seemed a long time she woke up, took his hand and said, 'Let's go.' They walked across the grass and out to the street again. Again they walked for what seemed to be miles, turning right till they came to a rough group of scarred tenements which seemed to have been there for so long that they were like rotten teeth growing out of the ground. He had an impression of scummy pools, worn grass and bricks and at one time saw the moon beyond the corner of the house but then lost it again.

'Play something,' she said. So in front of these ancient horrible old buildings he played *The Bonnie Earl o'Moray*.

'It's beautiful,' she said, her eyes half closed.

Then he played *Macpherson's Rant*.

He was tired. It was growing dark and he didn't know where he was. She eventually stopped at one of the closes which had stairs ascending steeply into the darkness above. There was a smell of urine and of cats. She clutched his hand as they climbed as if worried that he would run away. Once they stopped on a landing and looked out of the broken window there. He saw nothing but a waste of clay and overflowing bins. They climbed till they reached the top landing. He looked down into the well below and felt dizzy. There was no bell and she knocked on the door. There was no answer and she knocked harder. A man's voice was heard from within.

'Eff off,' it said.

'It's Eileen.'

'Eff off.'

'There's someone with me.'

Eventually the door was opened and they went in. Her father was standing in his shirt sleeves just inside the door, unshaven, his shirt open, showing thick black hair at the chest.

'Who the effing hell are you?' he said.

'This is . . . what's your name?' she whispered urgently.

'Jimmy.'

'His name is Jimmy, Father.'

'Got any drink with you, Jimmy?'

'Sorry, I . . . '

'Oh Christ!' The man went into a room and slammed the door behind him.

'Is that your father?' Jimmy whispered.

'Yes.'

He nearly said, What's a famous scientist like him doing here? but looked at her and decided not to. There isn't any room for his test tubes, he thought, or a laboratory or anything. He nearly burst out laughing at the absurdity of it all.

'Come with me,' she said and they entered what might have been a bedroom or a cell. There was no furniture at all except for a bed with clothes piled on top of it.

'Would you like a cup of tea?' she said. 'I can get you a cup of tea.' He said, 'That would be nice,' and sat down on the bed looking at the bare floor. He went over to the window and looked at the pools of scummy green water in the yard. A small boy was peeing into one of them.

After a while she came back with two jam jars of tea. The tea looked thick and black.

'I'm sorry,' she said, 'there's no milk. My mother, though she's highly intelligent, plays Patience a lot and sometimes forgets about things. Do you like Patience?'

'No,' he said though he had never played. He heard a crash from another room and somebody swearing. Perhaps one of the experiments had gone wrong. He took one of her hands in his and using the other to hold his jam jar drank his tea. It was without question the most horrible tea he had ever drunk in his life. It was so bad he couldn't believe it was tea, but on the other hand he didn't know what else it could be. She sat watching him while he drank it.

'It's quite good tea, isn't it?' she said. 'There's a wee shop near here. I don't like supermarkets. Are you really going to marry me?' she said. 'Let's go and ask Father.'

'Do you have to have your father's permission?'

'I would like it.'

'All right then.' He got up, squaring his shoulders, to meet the scientist in his den. He left the room and knocked on the door of the adjoining room.

'What the effing hell do you want?' said the voice of the famous scientist.

He went in. The place was a chaos of unwashed dishes, cardboard boxes, bottles, eggshells, cans, altogether a blizzard of detritus. In the middle of it all sat the bullnecked father in a broken-springed chair watching a TV screen which seemed, like himself, rather unshaven.

'Sir,' said Jimmy above the roar of the TV, 'I should like to marry your daughter.'

'Bugger off.'

'Sir, I know I haven't known her long but . . . '

'I said bugger off.'

Jimmy retired. She was waiting for him when he went into the room.

'What did he say?' she asked.

'Well,' he said and then burst out laughing so hard that he got a pain in his stomach. 'Well,' he said, 'he just told me to leave. That was all. He was watching the TV.'

'Yes, he watches TV a lot. That's how he relaxes. But it'll be all right, you see. When you get to know him better you will realise that he's very sensitive.'

The curve of her neck had infinite pathos. It had the same shape as the moon he had seen when lying on the grass near the fair.

'I love you so much,' he said stroking her hair.

'And I love you too. Very much,' she said. 'From the moment I saw you sitting on the bench with your guitar.'

The darkness came down but there seemed to be no electric switch in the room. Her pale face descended into the darkness and was replaced by the sweet curve of the moon. He touched her face in the darkness and it was wet with tears. He began to play gently on his guitar,

'As we cam in by Glesca toun . . . '

When he had finished playing they sat together on the bed, hands clasped. He knew that he would never leave her and that he would marry her. He was quite helpless. There was nothing else he could do. He tousled her hair and suddenly burst out laughing.

'We'll get married and have three chairs.'

'Children, you mean,' she said seriously.

'We need chairs more,' he said. And at that moment he was astonished to discover how free he was and knew for the first time the meaning of the songs he had been singing and why he had always kept his guitar in spite of everything.

'And your father really is a scientist,' he said laughing, listening to the roar of the TV.

'He has the mind of a scientist,' she said.

He held her so tightly that she cried out. 'Not a bloody switch in the place,' he thought and when he heard the TV set screaming again he shouted out, 'Bugger off, you old bastard.'

'You shouldn't say things like that to my father,' she said, 'he's very sensitive. He's been hurt by the world and he's got the mind of a scientist.'

He lay for a long time in the thickening darkness thinking, 'It's quite inescapable.' And then he thought, 'When it's inescapable, it's easy.' The first thing, he thought, is to take her away from the scientist and the brilliant mother (come to that, he hadn't seen her) and then things would be all right. He knew without looking that she was already asleep.

The Little People

At first when he had got the job he had been very pleased to tell them everything he knew, how the stone huts had been unearthed by an archaeologist who had come up from the south. He would point from the little brae above to the stone enclosures where the little people had slept, presumably after telling each other stories in the flickering light of the flames, the passageways down which they had crawled, the stone cupboards. It was rather like being a teacher and on top of that he had a blue uniform with yellow facings. He was an important man, people listened to him with respect, even with deference, he was the oracle which would at regular intervals emit information to the shallow and the rich and the voyaging. They came from all over, Germans, Dutch, Americans, Canadians, the visitors' book was an incomprehensible record of strange foreign names. They were properly astonished by what he told them and then they departed, taking with them some of the coloured postcards which he sold. He told them of the three skeletons which had been found, of the bone needles, the deer and the shellfish.

But that was of course before he had actually seen the little people, the first night he had remained behind, tired, staring out at the sea with the marks of the tourists' feet still on the sand, and their boyish splashings still in his ears. He liked looking out at the sea, with its large white waves, rising and falling, dissipating themselves in unravelling threads along the shoreline, the sun setting like a red head above the water.

At first he heard only whispers below him, an unintelligible quick susurration like the sudden hastening important whispering of children, and then he saw them, very small people, with long matted hair and furrowed brows. They were gathered together by the fire which had miraculously bloomed, wearing their tatty ageing skins, chattering among each other. There were little children, babies as well as adults, and in the light of the fire they seemed oddly vulnerable and almost brittle. All the time they were talking they were touching each other, gesturing furiously, belching, scratching themselves, looking around them. Once he saw one of them going over to a small compartment near the main room and sitting down to defecate with a serious strained face. It was almost but not quite like watching monkeys in the zoo clinging to the wire netting and holding out their tiny flesh-coloured fingers.

Eventually they went to bed and in the morning they rose again. The talking and whispering recommenced and they ate what appeared to be the remains of fish. They then came up to the level, went down to the seashore and began scrabbling for mussels and whelks which they found clamped to the rocks. Others went to a neighbouring spring for water. One was passing a bone needle through a piece of mangy old fur. It was strange to see them there at his feet, like little dirty mechanical dwarfs, unplugging the helmeted mussels from the bare sea-washed rocks, occupied at their domestic tasks.

Later he saw the deer coming down to feed on the grass. It was a beautiful, elegant animal, composed and fine-looking against the sky. It would bend down and eat and then raise its head, sniffing the air: perhaps the wind did not blow from the small smelly people: in any case it did not seem to know that they were there. He saw two of them detaching themselves with stones in what appeared to be leather thongs, quietly crawling and keeping windward of the deer and for a moment they appeared to him to be animals themselves diminishing to the size of weasels as they drew away. The deer grazed, lifted its head and grazed again. Suddenly the two little men stood up, the stones sped from their slings and hit the deer in the middle of the brow beneath its antlers. Its legs folded beneath it and they rushed forward making incomprehensible triumphant sounds. The other little people rushed forward shouting; there was dancing round the deer and then a stabbing at it with sharp bones, while the area in which it lay became red. They dragged it, shouting and dancing, into the maze of passages and began to hack its head off. Pieces of flesh were detached and put on the fire which bloomed again. They began to eat, rawly tearing at the flesh with their hands. In the vast sea behind them, intensely calm, he saw what appeared to be a cormorant diving into the water and emerging yards away. A woman gave her breasts to a child.

They were very happy now, talking and dancing and singing. Their hands were red with blood and they ran them now and then casually through their matted hair: on their necks were necklaces of shellfish.

He wanted to be with them: he wanted to enjoy himself among them. They seemed so happy and he himself was so lonely. He wanted to be noticed, to bring himself to their attention, but he couldn't see how this might be. He looked back at the coloured postcards which were sold to the tourists and which were racked in their wire cage. He took some of the postcards out and without thinking scattered them below him, letting them drift like snowflakes along the passageways, above the beds, the fire. They swirled out of the air on random curves. The little people looked up at the postcards and moved away from them, crouching in corners, chattering and frightened. The postcards drifted down and lay flat on the ground, in the silence which occurred after the chattering was over.

After a long while, when the postcards were dead, the little people began to come out of their corners. One of them tentatively put his hand towards one of the postcards, then drew it back without touching it as if his hand had been burnt. He remained like that for a long time, watching it as a cat might watch a mouse or a mouse a cat. Looking down from above, he himself felt a terrible pity for the little men and at the same time an impatience. Why don't you pick it up, he was mouthing silently. Prove yourself a hero. Advance. He didn't exactly articulate these words but obscurely he felt some such feelings as might be conveyed by them. Slowly the little man's hand advanced. He touched the postcard this time and then quickly withdrew the hand. The others were all looking at it with bared teeth. Eventually he made a little rush at it and held it. It was harmless, it was dead. Nothing exploded from it. He held it up so that the others could see it. They rushed forward and looked at it. They turned it over and over in their clumsy hands. They held it up to the light. Others picked up other postcards. He noticed that the man who had got it did not wish to keep it but was willing to let the others handle it as well. They made sounds indicative of wonder but clearly didn't recognise any of the patterns though they were looking at a representation of their own world. They were amazed at the colours more than anything, he thought, the bright reds, the blues, the greens. More and more of them were picking up postcards and looking at them, turning them over and over, their brows knitted. They would look at them for a while and then turn away to look at something else. Their span of attention seemed very limited. One turned to look at a bird that was flying in the blue picture frame above. Sometimes they would drop their postcards and eat some of the deer: at other times they might go off to urinate. Eventually one of them tore his postcard by accident and there was a howl of what might have been fear. They withdrew from him looking down at the small pieces which lay on the ground and he himself, appalled, stared down at the dismembered paper. They gestured at him from a distance and he moved away from the pieces, delicately, fearfully, as if they would suddenly join and eat him. No one went near them for a long time.

Eventually some laid the postcards down, others put them inside their hide-covered breasts, others tried to taste them. And one or two studied them all the time, looking at the colours and making little crows of wonder, touching them very gently and not bending them, though at first many had been bent and one at least had been torn.

Matches felt a great excitement moving in him as strongly and with as much suffocating power as the waves of the sea which was not so very far away. He could not imagine what this excitement was but it seemed like a freeing inside himself, a sluicing, a liberation from forces such as his parents, his bingo-playing gross wife, the tenements with their smell of cats, the tourists who were his masters in life though he was their master in information. He wanted to do something more exciting than this. In a confused way he wanted to see the little people win, he wanted to see them become men, he wanted to see them painfully and unwillingly and with joy fly upwards from their passageways and their bone needles and take off, beautiful and intelligent, to their equivalent of the moon. He wanted to offer them a present.

They were quieter now, looking at the postcards, turning them over and over as if there was something there that they wanted to know about but that at the same time they sensed they were incapable of knowing, because of the screen in front of their minds which would not slide aside, which would not open. One of them scratched his face with the edge of one of the postcards to keep the midges away.

Matches went back into his cottage and looked around it. There seemed nothing obvious that he could use. There were only the guidebooks, the postcards, the remnants of the past in their glass cases, the long narrow pieces of bone, the shell-fish necklaces, the map of the settlement. He looked around him in perplexity. He tried his pockets and came out with a lighter. He flicked it absent-mindedly and put it back again. He took the wallet from his breast pocket, took out the single pound note and replaced it. He took out the cigarette packet and put it back again. He took out the knife.

He studied the knife and as he was doing so heard the mewing of the smoky cat which belonged to his wife and which he often took with him because it was company for him and also because it attracted the attention of the tourists because it was so elegant and so beautiful and so rich-looking. They made much of the cat with its large blue eyes and it got him a lot of tips because it was so unusual and they didn't expect a man like him, in his position, to own one. It had smoky fur and blue eyes and it walked in a very artistocratic way and it was the most precious and beautiful thing he had ever owned. It mewed and pressed itself against his legs. He looked down at it (its name was Precious) and a thought swam into his mind. In the cottage he found some cats' meat and went out again, the cat following him. It was beautiful as it arched its body lazily, looking up at him, mewing, its eyes large and arrogant. He threw some of the cats' meat down among the passageways. The cat leaped lightly down and he watched it. In the half-darkness its fur appeared darker: he felt like a sower sowing the first seed in the morning of the world. It began to lick at the cats' meat. He threw more down into the centre where the little people were chattering and saw the cat following the meat. The little people saw it.

The cat wanted to go towards the meat but at the same time its hair bristled and stood on end. It spat fiercely. The little people crouched down in their corners looking at the cat. It was beautiful and fierce and strange and it emitted rays of energy. Blue electricity seemed to spark from it and all the place was full of the smell of blood and rank venison. A child started to crawl towards the cat but was pulled back. Another one did the same and the cat flashed out a claw. There was a sudden howl and the people crouched, remembering the cat leaping down from above on them. The child cried and the mother comforted it. The cat walked tall with arched body into the centre of the ring. It licked the cats' meat warily. It sniffed the dismembered deer. It moved delicately from the body to the antlered head.

There was a chattering among the people, intense and fierce like the magnified purring of a cat. The cat leaped and out of the sand dragged a wriggling animal which looked like a rat. It laid it down near the fire and began to eat it. The people looked on, chattering. It shook and shook the animal and then lay down with it beneath its paws. One of the people touched it and it sprang away but then slowly returned to its kill, circling. Gradually, it quietened down as they all approached it, all humming and chattering, not frightened. It stayed where it was, alert but not afraid: they seemed dazzled by its beauty, its strangeness. They stretched their hands out carefully, and petted it. It purred. It lay down and purred. It seemed to know them better after a while than it had known Matches.

He looked down at it from above: it was so strange to see it there among those people. He wondered for a moment whether he had wished them to kill it and thought that perhaps he had. It walked among the scattered postcards, having fed. It did not seem to want to come up at all. It was wilder than he had thought, not at all an ornament but a really aristocratic being down among these dwarfish tenements. Perhaps they would make a kind of god of it, worship it. He had a desire to suddenly shout out 'Bingo!' in a startlingly loud voice and see if they would start running, in their scabby furs. For the first time in months he began to smile and almost to laugh out loud as he looked towards the sea, with its lazy waves. He felt more alive than he had felt for years, so much so that he could have gone down there and picked the meat from the ravaged deer. The cat moved gracefully among the little people like an aristocrat, its smoky body compact and sure, assured and full of hauteur.

Would he be able to say to his wife when she asked him about the cat, 'I've given it to the Stone Age People. They have made a god of it. We will never die, we are immortal, the little beings will look after it, they will bring it up on their long march through history. They will climb the steps through the passage-ways towards our bingo and our postcards and our guidebooks and our large coloured touring buses and our clothes that flutter transiently round our transient bodies and they will take our cat with them as their god. We will be part of their history as they climb towards number and alphabet, as they ascend from their shell necklaces towards Woolworths, our bluish cat will go with them catching their rats and voles: the wildness slowly taming'?

He took one last look down. The postcards were strewn all over the place except that one of the little people, with strained knitted brows, was turning one over and over in his hands (on the back was the space for someone to write, 'Dear Lucy, I am having a wonderful time. I am sending this to you from the cutest Stone Age village. Ha ha, imagine me in the Stone Age . . . ') as he had seen the monkey doing with the coconut, abandoning it, and climbing the meshed wire to look out, its brows serious and ancient, an obscene man. The cat had gone to sleep and someone was banging two stones together endlessly while others were removing the antlers from the deer from which eventually they would make bone needles which could lead them to the large coaches where they would come and visit themselves in pink slacks, chattering excitedly with their guidebooks and postcards.

God's Own Country

He coughed a lot, persistently and sharply, as if he had been smoking far too much for far too long. 'I'll tell you something about Rhodesia. They call it God's own country, you know. That's what they call it. I'll tell you something. I'm an electrician, you understand. I'm over here for a few months. I'd like to go back but ... ' He waved vaguely and then drank more whisky. He was sitting in the pub, now and again banging at the notes of the piano which was sitting in an alcove. As far as I could make out he wasn't composing any particular tune and I didn't know whether he could even play the piano. It was one of the few things I could do myself, though I would never play in a pub. I like jazz but not classical music. The piano was old and the lid scarred by cigarette butts. Some of the notes were a bit flat. He looked restless and unhappy and he hadn't shaved very well or perhaps his face always had that dark look. There were black hairs showing strongly and almost savagely against the brownness of his wrists.

'I'll tell you something about that bugger Wilson. When he was over seeing Smith, Smith took him out to the verandah and he showed him an African with a spear. "That's all the body-guard I need," he said. Nobody attacked Wilson when he was over there. Your students attack him more than he would have been attacked in Salisbury. They've got good manners over there. Christ, I can tell you that, they're well mannered. Smith doesn't drink, you know. He was a pilot in the war. You drunken Scottish bums,' he said to a friend of mine, "you're always drinking." But he didn't mean anything by that. That's what I heard anyway. You hear all sorts of things but I believe he would say that.

'This place here is so cold. I left Glasgow in '51. I've been dying with the cold since I came back here. I've had to put seven blankets on my bed. I came through London, and it's foggy there and wet and cold. You wouldn't believe the immorality you get in London. They talk about Rhodesia. Nothing but poofs and ponces in London. You can't walk a yard without them trying to get your money off you. That's all they want, money. All the time. You don't get immorality in Rhodesia. You don't get hardly any crime, and that's a fact. That's a fact. We had the Queen Mum over there: she's a nice lady.

'I'll tell you another thing, we haven't got a National Anthem yet but we will. We're working on it.' He ran his fingers along the notes of the piano, the black and the white. 'Your country over here is going to the dogs. Anyone can see that. You go to Glasgow and see. They're hanging about with greyhounds and the place is so dirty and wet. Who'd want to live there? In Rhodesia it's warm and the people are friendly. If I was over there just now I'd be invited into somebody's house for a drink.

'I'll tell you something – when I went to Rhodesia I felt at home. Know what I mean? It was so sunny and the streets were shining and everybody was strolling along. No hurry. No one is in any hurry. You can keep Glasgow for me. What have you done to this country? People can't earn a decent salary. What did you say about servants?

'How many servants did I have in Glasgow? Look, friend, don't take the mickey. If you're trying to take the mickey, don't do it. I can rough it up with the next man. We pay them well, I can tell you that. Were you in the Congo, eh? Well, I've been in the Congo and I can tell you you'd be puking if you'd seen the things I've seen. I can tell you that, friend. Our Africans are earning more than they would earn in the Congo and you can tell that to your Socialist government.

'I'm going back there the first chance I get.'

I could hear the rain drumming steadily on the roof. He shivered and coughed again. 'This bloody cold. If it was anyone else I'd say I'd got soft. You're an educated man, you shouldn't believe all the propaganda that you hear. Why have you people got it in for us? Oh, I can see it in your eyes, you're one of those intellectuals. I'd put the lot of you against a wall and shoot you. Was Wilson in the war, I ask you? Did he fight for his country? I'll tell you there are more patriots over there than you have over here, and don't look so superior.

'The lot of you should be shot. Intellectuals.' He began to cough again, his face almost turning black with the pressure. 'Look at the state you've got your own country in,' he said, still spluttering. 'I tell you, Glasgow is full of unemployed people. They looked like dogs standing against the walls, and look at the vandalism. I couldn't even get a phone I could use.'

He got up, steadying himself against the edge of the table. 'My wife died, that's why I left home. She died two months ago. And I went on the booze. Best wife a man ever had. But I left her alone all the time. See, the job I had, it meant travelling a lot. And I left her in the house. Thank God we didn't have any children. Well, I went on the booze. I didn't think, I didn't think I'd take it so badly. See, somebody say to me I'd have taken it so badly I wouldn't have believed him. But I'll be going back, soon as I get the money. I'm looking for a job but I can't find one. They tell you there are no jobs and I'm a qualified man.'

His eyes focused on the piano as if he were seeing it for the first time.

'These black notes are no bloody good. No bloody good there for music or for government.'

I looked at his hands, the hairs startlingly black against the tanned flesh, primitive and barbaric.

'Tell you something about you intellectuals, you don't know anything. You think you know everything but you know nothing. Put you over there you'd be useless. I can tell you that. The worst people over there are the intellectuals. The Africans don't understand them. And I'll tell you something else. Do you know who the Africans like best? I'll tell you. They like the man who'll tell them what to do and doesn't feel guilty. They like to be told what to do. The Imperialists, they like the Imperialists. They like people who'll talk to them man to man. You should send more Imperialists over.'

He swayed slightly and I noticed that one of the elbows of his jacket was patched, and that his soiled tie was slightly squint.

'None of you intellectuals over there,' he muttered. He made his unsteady way towards the door. 'I've a good mind, I've a good mind . . . Aw, to hell with it. You're all the same. But I'll tell you something, they wouldn't have you over there. They wouldn't take you. Can you repair a TV set? Can you build a power station, eh? I was building a power station. I was away building a power station for six months and my wife died. Can you do that, eh? They need people like me over there. I'm a man's man. I learned my trade and I had a position over there. People will speak to you over there. Do you understand me? Aw, to hell, you're sitting there weighing me up. No warmth.' He staggered out the door.

I looked down at the piano, at the black and the white notes, thinking of the island from which I had come, the black and the white. It seemed very distant though not so warm as Rhodesia. I wondered if he would ever get back there and I didn't know whether I wanted him to. Perhaps as a human being I did.

I looked down at my own pale hand lying on the table. It seemed very white and very frail. It couldn't repair a TV set or set up a power station. It was hairless and white and in the half darkness it gleamed with a ghostly shine. I imagined him making his staggering way among the rain and the fog and the neon lights. But then wasn't that what we all did? And why pity him more than another?

By the Sea

On Sunday I was sitting on a bench in the Public Gardens of the small town when she came and sat down beside me. At first she didn't notice me, perhaps because she didn't expect to find me there. She was smaller than when I had seen her last – about five years before – and she looked older and more bowed. Her back had begun to curve like a hoop and I don't think her eyesight was as keen as it used to be. She was carrying a basket and was puffing and trying to get her breath back when I drew attention to myself. She was surprised and said, 'I can see very well with my glasses but without them my eyesight isn't so good. And how are you?'

I said I was fine.

It was quite warm sitting where we were. Behind us was a large clock in a tower and a garden with red and white flowers. I was looking straight down a street beyond which I could see the sea and people wandering about on the promenade. It was a Sunday during the tourist season and as well as tourists there were weekenders from the city about seven miles away. In the gap between the houses I could see yachts sailing.

To tell the truth I hadn't actually wanted to run into her, she being a relative of mine whom I had rather neglected over the past few years.

'How are things with yourself?' I asked.

'Didn't you hear that George is in the hospital?' she said.

'Oh, is he ill?' I asked.

'Not ill,' she said. 'Not ill physically. Ill mentally. He thinks he's a colonel in the army. And sometimes he plays with toys. He doesn't recognise me.' She spoke very clearly and exactly as if she were talking about a stranger.

I felt rather guilty not knowing about the illness. But she

looked prosperous enough. She was wearing a greyish jumper with a necklace like small loaves around her neck.

'Do you go to see him?' I asked.

'My daughter takes me sometimes with the car,' she said. 'You remember Evelyn? She's married to the distillery manager who lives in N——,' and she named a small town on the East coast. 'She takes me to see him, but it's no use, he doesn't know us. And he used to be so lively. He had a motor hirer's business for three years,' she said. 'But then his leg began to bother him and he had to give up. He began to get lonely and restless sitting in the house all the time.'

I stood up and said, 'Come along and I'll buy you your tea.'

She stood up clutching her bag. I offered to carry it for her but she said no. She looked very old but very determined. I slowed down my steps to conform to hers.

All around us were the green leaves, and shadows lay on the road. Two boys were fooling about at a telephone kiosk.

The restaurant which was only about a hundred yards away on the same side of the street had a black frontage and, inside, black leather seats.

'We'd be better upstairs,' she said. 'The food is better upstairs.' I looked at her in surprise not realising that she would know. She took a long time climbing the stairs but eventually we came to a large dining room facing out towards the sea. It had black and red decor and there was a large number of women in large hats and bright dresses at the tables.

They nodded to her and she smiled frostily, arranging herself and her bag. I thought that it couldn't be easy for her to be so obviously dined in a place to which she had in the past brought others to dine. But of course in the old days she had been better off, people would talk to her at the church door, for example, they would value her opinion.

'I don't see much of them now,' she said, 'they never come to see me.' She deliberately sat with her back to them and they regarded me briefly and then started to talk again among themselves.

'Would you like some wine?' I said.

'No, thank you.'

She studied the large menu very carefully and then said, 'I'll have the fish. I won't have any soup.' I said I would have fish as well.

'You remember Murdina,' she said (another of her daughters), 'she's married in Canada. She works in insurance and she's in charge of a lot of people. Ethel is married in America. The other day she wrote me that she had to drive five hundred miles with her children to be with her husband: he's just got a better job. I brought them up to be good wives. When they were young I would send them to bed at nine o'clock and teach them how to sew and knit and cook. They're clever girls.'

'Have you been out seeing them?' I said.

'Yes,' she said, 'I was out for a month last year before George got ill. I liked it out there. We went out on the plane, the two of us. I thought I would be frightened but I wasn't at all though it was my first time on a plane.'

The fish came and she ate it slowly, chewing every mouthful carefully as if she were storing up nourishment against hard times. She ate with great concentration. Now and again she would pause and ask me a question but most of the time she kept at the fish.

'I broke my leg some time ago,' she said. 'I fell on the floor. It was slippery. I had just been polishing it. There's no need for people to live like animals even if they are alone. They give me a pension, you see, and during those weeks, I don't know how it happened, they overpaid me. So I got a letter from this man in Dunbrick and he said could he have his money back. I couldn't go at the time because I was limping and I had come out of hospital. Well, when I got better I phoned him and said could I go and see him. So one day I got on the bus – I was a bit nervous at first but it was all right – and I went along to the office. It was shut for lunch so I waited in the park till it opened. Then I went along and I met a lady there and explained the situation to her. I had brought along the money, you see, because I didn't want to be in debt. I spent a long time talking to her and she was very kind. After a while she took me in to see this man in black glasses and I explained it to him again. He told me it would be all right and I paid him. And I went home. And do you know, that woman comes to see me regularly, the one in the office. It's very kind of her. She's like a home help to me.'

She carefully put the bones at the side of the plate and said that the fish was very good. 'Very nice indeed.'

'Would you like a sweet?' I said.

'No, but I should like some coffee.'

I ordered coffee. The women were still chattering behind her, looking very fresh and healthy in their yellowy hats.

When we had finished our coffees she said, 'That was very nice, dear,' to the waitress. We descended the stairs carefully. At the bottom I paid the bill and she recognised the woman behind the till.

'And how are you, dear?' said the latter, a thin, slatternly woman who looked very busy.

'Very well, thank you.'

'That's good. This weather is better, isn't it?' She handed me the change.

'This is Chrissie's boy,' she said to the woman behind the till. 'He's got a good position in Newington. You'd have seen his name in the papers.'

'Thank you, dear,' said the woman, nodding indifferently at me.

'I've got some food here,' she said. 'Would you like to come up to the house?'

'No thanks,' I said, 'I've got to get back tonight. I only came up for the day.' As a matter of fact I was staying in a hotel and going away on the following day.

'Well, thank you for my tea,' she said. 'I better be getting home.' I watched her climb the brae to her small council house. She looked both vulnerable and indomitable, climbing steadily, and turning to wave to me at the top, I didn't know whether she was seeing me or not. In any case she would be all right as there were no big streets to cross on the way home.

I remembered something she had said to me at the meal. 'We had a couple staying with us for bed and breakfast once and they tried to pay me with milk bottle tops.' She had laughed out loud. 'Really. It was quite fantastic. Milk bottle tops. And the man had a good position as well. You wonder sometimes what people will do.'

I made my way down to the shore. The street was crowded. On one side of the road there was a long queue of people, some of whom were shouting cheerfully at each other, 'A pint for the balcony', and so on. The queue started outside the door of a hotel.

I stood on the pavement and watched little naked boys wading out to sea. There were dogs running about and fat men throwing stones into the water for them to retrieve.

There were crowds of people lying on the grass, stripped to the waist, and others sitting on deckchairs.

As I walked along I saw a man standing on a box with a small group of spectators gathered round him. In a corner by herself was a woman in a long coat seated beside an odd-looking contraption. The man who was wearing a dark suit and thick glasses with frames like black liquorice was saying: 'Sisters and brothers, you have all heard about Moses and the Jews and how they crossed the desert. Well, in Canada there is a river which begins as a small drop in the mountains. One small drop. Then as this river goes down the hills it gathers other drops and it becomes a large river which eventually flows into the ocean.

'Well, Moses was like that. Every man who starts a large movement is like that. Jesus was like that. Moses' movement was so powerful that though it began as a small drop not even the Pharaoh himself could withstand it. Christ's movement was so powerful that not even the Romans could withstand it. So don't think that you can't bring anything to God's kingdom. Even Moses was meek at first and unwilling to take on God's work. Each of you may consider himself as a small drop but you must never forget that a small drop can start a river. Each one of us can add a drop to water the desert and create an oasis here and there.

'I will tell you a story. Once upon a time there was a man I knew, a dear friend of mine. Well, this incident happened in the First World War. He was a man who didn't smoke, a respectable Christian. Now one weekend there were no cigarettes in the camp and he was supposed to look after the stores. And this friend of mine was blamed for the shortage because everyone knew he didn't smoke.

'But a group of rough soldiers determined that they would kill him for not having provided the cigarettes. Imagine that. Kill him. So one evening they waited for him. My friends, it was a fine evening, a fine summer's evening, and they waited for him. And what were they carrying? Well, I'll tell you. They were carrying bayonets. And as he was walking peacefully along the road he was surrounded by this group of soldiers. What could he do? My friends, what would you have done? He did the only thing possible. He prayed. He prayed very hard. Behind him was a hill which was shining in the late sun. Well, my friends, the next moment he found himself on top of this hill and the soldiers below. How do you explain that? My friends, how do you explain that? Only faith can explain that. Only the work of God. My friends, let us pray.

'Dear Lord, do not let us think that just because we are small drops we are no use to Thee or Thy world. For every great river begins as a small drop. Teach us therefore to realise our own potentialities and our own qualities so that we may bring them as gifts to Thee.

'And now, Sister Perkins from Greenock will accompany us in the singing of *Be Thou My Vision*.' I suddenly realised that the weird contraption was in fact an organ. She began to press the pedals up and down, seated there in her long dress, very upright, while some of the crowd sang and the others drifted away.

When the singing was over the man said, 'Next week, DV, and weather permitting, I hope to be at the Little Hall on Greenock Street. I shall see you there. If it is wet we will have a change of venue.'

He got down from the box and he and the woman and another man put all the stuff including the box and the organ into a van. I watched them as they drove away.

The crowd queueing outside the hotel was lengthening. And suddenly I knew what the queue was for. On Sundays the hotels didn't open till half past six for drink, and they were waiting to get in. They were, however, very good-humoured and singing their Glasgow songs. One old woman was dancing what appeared to be a weird Spanish dance at the front of the queue. Now and again she would shout Olé and the others would echo her joyfully. Her grey hair flashed in the setting sun and she would raise her legs high in the air, revealing red drawers. I stood watching her for a long while till eventually the doors opened and they all poured into the bar of the hotel.

The Black and the Red

I arrived here last night at 9 p.m. and I am writing this in my room at the lodgings.

The journey was pleasant. I was in my bunk on the boat – the bunk you ordered for me – but in the early morning – about six – I had an impulse to go on deck. I passed a steward in white as I walked, rather unsteadily, down the corridor in that sort of sick smell one gets on board ship. The morning was chill, with much sea stretching freely away. I felt my hair lifting gently in the breeze, and then saw it – the sun – very red, like a banner rising over Skye. There was no one on the deck except myself. I have never seen anything so beautiful – that sun rising through the mist, very red, very raw.

When we landed at Kyle there was a great screaming of gulls, porters hurrying past with barrows, smell of rolls and butter from the restaurant. My mouth felt foggy somehow. And then I saw my first train. It was long and brown, the colour of mahogany or that kind of reddish-brown shoe polish I sometimes get. I sat down in one of the rather dirty carriages which at the time was empty but later three boys entered. They were of my own age, perhaps, if anything, slightly older.

I discovered that they were students at the University too. They were reading brand-new Penguin crime stories while I had a copy of Homer, which surprised them. They were rather amused at the newness of my case which was on the rack above me. I think they were also amused at my scarf and tie and blazer. They do not seem to appreciate what is being done for them. However they are friendly. One of them – the most interesting – is called George. He is stocky and redhaired and quite irreverent. He studies medicine and calls one of his lecturers The Spinal Cord. It turns out that he is in the same lodgings as me. I like him.

The countryside through which we passed is divided into geometrical sections – for farms – some squares, some rectangles. Sometimes it's straw-coloured, sometimes lemony yellow, and sometimes green, but very orderly and beautiful, comparing very favourably with the untidy patches at home. It looks very rich and fertile. Nothing of interest happened on the journey except that my companions tried to buy my dinner for me but I refused. They had all been working during the holidays and had plenty of money. One was at the Hydro-Electric, George at the fishing. His father comes from Kyle and is skipper of a fishing boat.

A train seems to move much more slowly than one thinks. I could hear the pounding of the wheels but I was still seeing the same fields. After a while the others curled up and went to sleep. But I didn't sleep. Sometimes I read Homer to the thunder of the wheels. It's strange how unprotected people look when they are asleep.

At ten o'clock we entered the station, but before that I could see the lights of a great city. George and I went out together into the confusion. I was going to order a taxi but George would not hear of it. We climbed the steps into the glare of the light and went in search of a bus. After dashing across the street – or rather after I had dashed across the street – we found ourselves at a big cinema – much bigger than the one in T—— with winking lights of different colours, some violet, some purple.

Sitting on the stone pavement with his back against the wall was a beggar, his cap – containing a few pennies – beside him, and he himself staring blankly into space. At that moment I was terrified. I put my hands into my pockets as if to steady myself and would have given him a pound if George hadn't said:

'Don't be a fool. He's better off than you are. He's not blind at all.' But George put a two-shilling piece in his cap: I didn't give him anything – I don't like people who lie.

When we arrived at the house the landlady came to the door. She is smallish, plump, with a Roman nose. She is said to be greedy for money but perhaps that is scandal. She looks very inquisitive and it is said that her favourite words are: 'Youse students with all the money.' She has a husband who works on the taxis and two children. I saw one of them. He was plump and dressed in white shorts, white socks and a white blouse. He looked at me without speaking, his thumb in his mouth.

Last night, as I was lying in bed watching the lights of cars traverse the walls and the ceiling and listening to the patter of footsteps on the street, I thought I heard someone whistling a Gaelic tune. But it wasn't a Gaelic tune at all.

Your loving son,

KENNETH

Yesterday was my first day at the University. I travel by bus leaving at 8.30 a.m. The distance is about three miles.

The University – a place of bells and ivy – fronts a rough road, curiously enough in one of the ugliest parts of the city, so that it appears like an oasis. There are many notice boards with green baize and notices all of which I have read. Some of them are announcements of prizes, others of the formation of societies (I doubt whether I shall have time to take part in any of these). There is of course a large library with ladders, and a librarian so tall that she doesn't need a ladder.

My first lecture was Greek. I climbed the wide stairs, my nostrils quivering to a strange smell. It was in fact the smell of varnish, and I later saw the typical watery waxy yellow. I sat at the back during the lecture – we are studying Sophocles – feeling the sun warm on my neck and watching the shadows of the leaves dancing on my desk. However, I didn't have time to do that for long.

Our lecturer is a rather small man with a half-open mouth like that of a fish and he seemed to me to be in some vague way untidy. (I don't know quite what I expected – perhaps a flourish of trumpets and a great man in red robes, but that wasn't what came.) He kept saying: 'Now this may be Greek to you, gentlemen . . . ' Sometimes after saying this he would look out of the window and stand thus as if he had forgotten us. I noticed a curious smile on his face, like water round a stone. He speaks rather slowly – his hands behind his back – and I found it quite easy to write down everything he said. In the shops there is quite a large variety of notebooks and I have bought

half-a-dozen, as I foresee much writing. There are thirty
students in the class, more men than girls as one would expect.
Many of them spend much time taking coffee in the Union and
talking intensely. I go to the library. Most of them are far ahead
of me at the moment.

There is one thing. For some reason I feel freer here. At
home somehow or other I felt constricted. Do you remember
how old Angus used to ask me those pointless riddles?

I am sorry to hear about the squabbles in the church. This
money-grabbing is distasteful, and black. I think you should go
out more.

Please don't talk about me to people so much. One doesn't
know what might happen.

My second lecture was Latin – here we are doing Catullus and
my lecturer is called Ormond. He is different altogether from
Mulgrew – the Greek one – Ormond is more like a businessman, with bright fresh cheeks, a successful-looking man who
sways back and forward on his heels when he is talking. He
looks kind and self-possessed. Curiously enough, he wears a
waistcoat, but on him it doesn't look old-fashioned. He talks
quite fast and it takes me all my time to keep up with him.

I haven't been out at night since I came. Apart from George
there are three other lodgers, a lady lecturer at the training
college, a young girl who works in a shop, and a man of about
twenty-eight who's very keen on motor-cycles. The landlady
doesn't like him much as his hands are very oily most of the
time. However he has the most cheerful face imaginable and he
talks in a very quaint slow way except when he's speaking about
motor-cycles.

As for me I work at night sitting by the electric fire. Sometimes the landlady comes in, rather unnecessarily I think, and
looks at me as if she were going to say something about
working too hard but she doesn't actually say anything. Once
however she did say that I ought to go out more. George says
this work and close-sitting by the fire are not good for me, and
not profitable for my landlady! He is a very pleasant person,
George.

The landlady can't be so bad after all. She took us in to see

TV night before last. It was the first time I had seen TV and she was very surprised by this as also by my answers to her questions on life at home. George however looked more serious.

It is now 10.30 p.m. and I have to translate some Sophocles.

By the way I don't know whether George drinks or not. I have never seen him drunk if that's what you mean.

Your loving son,

KENNETH

This afternoon George and I went for a long walk and this in fact is probably the first time that I've been out since I came. After leaving the house we turned left down the street with its silvery tram rails. It was a fine warm afternoon and we saw many people strolling, some with dogs. After a while we turned left again towards Hutton Park. At the entrance to this park are great wrought iron gates and flowers of many colours arranged very cleverly to read WELCOME. I wondered how this was done but George wouldn't tell me, and didn't appear to be interested. He was telling me a story of a visit to the mortuary recently. The body of a young boy of nineteen had been found drowned in the River Lee. In his cigarette case they found a note which read: 'I am tired of being drained of my blood.' That was all. Yet he apparently had adoring parents.

This park is near a cemetery which is orderly and has some green glass urns containing paper flowers. It is almost too orderly, like streets.

When we entered the park I saw that it had swings on which children were playing. In other parts of the park fathers were playing football with their sons, teaching them. One of them was showing his little son how to kick a ball, and though he appeared amiable seemed to me to be exasperated. Many of the balls were rainbow-coloured. We also passed a great startling peacock with purplish plumage like a bride's train. He was superb and alone and, I thought, completely out of place, unable even to fly.

We lay down on the grass (having removed our jackets) in the warm day. For the first time in three weeks I was completely relaxed. I had taken a book with me – about Catullus – but I didn't read it. I watched small white clouds passing over me and heard birds singing in the trees (for there are many trees in the park). Our white shirts were dazzling in the light. George went for some ice-cream and we ate it and talked.

He doesn't write home much. 'After all,' he says, 'they know I am here.' He often gets letters but hardly ever answers them. He told me of his father who seems a good man, not able to spell well, for example 'colledge' for 'college'. I would have been ashamed to admit this: George isn't. He invited me to their house for part of the holidays. What do you think? He is going with a girl called Fiona. I gather that she is very intelligent, and sometimes he talks as if he were her (at least that's what I think) about the nuclear bomb. I think we need it. What else have we got? To defend our religion with. He smiled when I said this, clapped me on the knee, and told me to get up. We walked along the bank of the river (it was here that that boy was drowned) and saw a fisherman wearing thigh-length leathers, patiently casting in the middle. I thought for one horrible moment that we might find a body. Later we saw swans. They have a curious blunt blindness when seen close up. After a while I found I had forgotten my book and we went back to the park to collect it. We talked to two little boys. They were both very grave and very polite and told us all about themselves. They were dressed exactly alike in blue tunics and shorts, white shirts and blue ties. They were like echoes of each other. Eventually their nurse or whatever she was came to collect them. She frowned a little and I think they were very sorry to go, for George at any rate has the gift of friendliness. He makes fun of me sometimes – says I'm too serious. And I argue, he says, too self-righteously, especially with that college lecturer. My views on education are absolutely incomprehensible to him. Sometimes he asks me questions about home and confesses himself utterly perplexed. That people should be talked about for being out on a Sunday!

I hope this confusion of the church accounts will be sorted out. I've seen it reported even in the newspapers here. That's what comes of living in a small village.

Don't think I'm wasting my time. I'm working very hard and I know what has been done for me. I study for about seven hours a day. There is so much to be done. Recently my eye was caught by a book in the library by a man called Camus. It's very strange but interesting.

I go to church here, but the minister Mr Wood isn't very impressive. He is a small stout man who seems to me to have nothing to say. The church itself is small and quite pretty and fresh. But it's his voice that I find peculiar . . . as if he could be thinking of something else when he's preaching. He is not in his voice. It's difficult to explain this. The flowers are beautiful, there are fine texts, fresh varnished tables, but he himself – he doesn't bring these things together. All is forced somehow. I sometimes think we should have more sense of humour. George is very humorous. He kept us in stitches last night composing a romance between the shopgirl and our cyclist friend – the third in the eternal triangle was the motor bike. Actually however Joan and Jake quite liked it, I think, and apart from their being lodgers (whom I suppose she can easily replace) the landlady's romantic soul appears to be touched. She seats them together at meals! And one day Jake took Joan to the shop on his motor bike. The trouble is he blushes too easily.

I've been invited to Mr Mulgrew's house and I think I might go on Wednesday. George's girl friend is coming for dinner soon.

It's very late – 11.30 – and I must finish – I shall post this at 8.30: there's a pillar box quite near.

I think I shall sleep better tonight: I feel much fresher.

Please remember that as I say again I know all that you have done for me.

Your loving son,
KENNETH

Last night I called on Mr Mulgrew our Greek lecturer. It was 7.30 when I arrived at the door of his house which lies in a quiet area about five hundred yards past a busy blue crossroads.

There were two bells, one a white one set in the stone at the side of the door, and the other a black one set in the middle of the door itself. First, I pressed the white one but sensed by the lack of pressure that it wasn't working. Then I pressed the black one which also did not appear to be working. Finally I knocked on the door. There was no light in the hall. Then I knocked again more loudly.

I saw a light flash on – rather a dim one – and Mr Mulgrew himself came to the door wearing no jacket, but a blackish pullover and reddish slippers. Eventually he recognised me, his mouth closing as he did so and a light being switched on in his eyes. I have heard that he is very lonely and that he goes to the cinema regularly once a week no matter what the film is and that he prefers to sit in the same seat each time.

He seemed glad to see me and shepherded me into a room on the right which contained a lot of books, an electric fire (with the two bars on), two easy-chairs (both green), an electric lamp (lit), one table (heavy mahogany), and a smaller, flimsier one. He sat me down in the armchair opposite his own. Beside him on the floor was an open book.

We sat for some moments in silence, he with his legs crossed, dangling one red slipper uneasily, then he took out a packet of cigarettes which he offered me. He seemed surprised when I did not take a cigarette and returned the packet to his pocket. I have the impression that he bought that packet just for me! At the same time he said:

'Very few young people don't smoke nowadays, isn't that right? You're not afraid of cancer, are you?' He looked at me steadily as if he himself was. I said No I wasn't.

'That's a mistake,' he continued. 'We should be. I am. Very much. I find the thought unbearable. Of course it's psychological.' I didn't say anything.

'The reason I asked you here is that your work is good, you know, good. Honest. Yes I think honest is the word. Not slick. So little honesty now, don't you agree. I mean real honesty.'

His eyes seemed to look at me then flicker away again so that I was uneasy.

'Do you know that Wittgenstein used to read Black Mask?' he asked suddenly.

I said I didn't know anything about Wittgenstein (though I've found out a little since).

'He was a great philosopher you know and he used to go to the cinema regularly – gangster films mainly he liked. Imagine that! You should read him, he was very honest.'

Then without transition he began to talk about Sophocles. 'You know the thing I find extraordinary about him,' – for some reason he stood up and began to walk about the room – 'the thing I find extraordinary about him is that he did so much and especially – do you know what I find most extraordinary of all? – that he served in the army!

'Nowadays people serve in the army and then they write a book about it. That's putting it in reverse you know. It shouldn't be like that at all. No, you don't find anything about his experiences in the army in Sophocles. He doesn't exploit them. He just lived.'

Abruptly he sat down again and leaning forward said, 'He just lived. Isn't that fine? To be able to do what Sophocles did.'

Of course I understood what he was saying but I couldn't become enthusiastic – yet in a way he seemed to be enthusiastic – sometimes stabbing forward with his finger – but he didn't make me enthusiastic. It was as if – like Wood – he could be thinking of something else while he was talking.

'Nowadays they talk of their military experience and of women and of drink – but do we find these in Sophocles? No, we don't. That's what we must understand – what did make the Greeks great? He lived till he was ninety – he took part in his civic duties, he served in the army and he wrote all these plays. That's greatness. Especially serving in the army.'

At that moment I heard a tram rocking past into the blue lights and he himself stopped as if he had heard a gun exploding.

Then suddenly he began to talk about Gilbert Murray. 'I once met him,' he said, 'an Australian. But I don't like his translations. You know, he served on the League of Nations. He should have concentrated on his translations. Would you care to see . . . ' Suddenly he got up saying, 'I think I have somewhere here a review I wrote for the Classical Studies on his . . . ' And he went straight to a magazine, took it out and it opened at the correct page. I read the review. It was I thought indecisive and rather mean at the same time. 'One is not sure that . . . ' However I said it was quite good.

'About your own work, that's reasonable. It's got the classical . . . spirit, you know,' said he, pleased with my praise. He was flattering me for some reason.

'Excuse me a moment.' He almost pranced out leaving me alone in the room. I felt desolate and an emptiness throbbed through me. I looked at the clock: it said 8.15. I looked at the books but had no inclination to read them. I noticed that the lamp-shade was red.

In a minute or two he returned. 'I was ordering tea,' he said.

Then for some reason or other I heard myself saying that I couldn't stay for tea. I listened to my own voice with astonishment: it was creating a number of the most plausible lies, the main one being that the landlady had invited me to see TV and he himself knew as a student what these landladies were like. He was listening with his mouth open and agreeing now and then. Then I noticed a certain pride being drawn up over his face like a drawbridge.

'Of course if you can't stay,' he began. I said I wished to but I couldn't and then with an attempt at humour – there was that essay he had set us! He half laughed. I found myself walking to the door as if across a great space. He said he had been going to show me some of his translations, but of course . . .

I repeated I was sorry. At the door he began with a sudden curious depth to his voice but at the same time jocularly:

'And what do you think of us?'

I stared.

'Of the lecturers.'

'Oh,' I mumbled, 'different from school . . . mature . . . more interesting . . . very different . . . '

'Yes,' he said, 'isn't it? I remember when I went to university first . . . ' Then he stopped. 'But I'm keeping you.'

He opened the outer door and we looked out into the night which had a chill dryness and a lot of stars.

'The strange thing about Sophocles, you know,' he said, 'was that he served in the army. A man of action.' He seemed to stand more upright. 'Nowadays . . . he would have written his memoirs.'

I walked down the path to the gate, half-running. I turned to wave but the door had been shut.

Not very far from the crossroads I was approached by a big fat red-faced drunken woman who asked me for a shilling. I seem always to be approached by these people. I gave her the money and strangely enough I looked after her with pleasure as she rolled on huge and healthy and happy to wherever she was going. She called me 'dear'.

So that was the visit. Peculiar. I doubt if I shall go again. I worked again after coming home but somehow . . . No, I won't let you down. Still there was something odd . . .

George comes in now and again. His girl friend is coming up on Saturday and he wants me to meet her. I don't know. He too is uneasy these days. Of course he goes out oftener than me – to dances, etc. – but there's a hectic quality about him. Perhaps he's seeing too many bodies and going to hospitals too much.

Once he brought some records in and played me some jazz. It's really powerful music, blasting. We have nothing like it in Gaelic.

'What do you think of that, eh?' he said, his red hair falling over his face. 'Isn't it tre*men*dous?' He's got a trick of emphasising the middle syllable – tre*men*dously! Sometimes he plays on his trumpet in an almost religious manner – and I think he's quite good – very serious. He bought a small trumpet for little Bertie and it's funny to see them playing together. He's very fond of children. But I'm afraid he doesn't like the college woman. 'Too prim,' he said. And even me he considers prim but he says there's hope for me.

One night at 11 o'clock he was sitting on my bed looking down at the floor and listening to a record. Then he suddenly switched it off and said to me: 'You know you may not know it – clever as you are – but you are on the side of life. I can tell. It's the way you listen – and that wistfulness of yours as if you were listening for . . . a different music.' I don't even know what he means.

I'm sorry you don't think I should go to visit him. It's true enough that we only have a fortnight but it doesn't matter really. I think you would like him, however. I think I told you before he doesn't drink. Why are you asking me again? Something's disturbing him though I don't know what it is. Last night he talked about the hydrogen bomb and about his parents and about the fishing. 'It's so far away, somehow,' he said. 'All that. Don't you find that?' I said nothing. Then he made one of his sudden changes of mood and said: 'Never mind, we'll hear what Mr Bryden (our landlord) has seen in the pictures this week. *The Son of Hippocrates* or *Hippocrates Rides again.*'

I'm sorry to hear this squabble continues. It's indecent. Now I must work. And I am working. Harder than ever since I was up at the lecturer's.

Did you say Alasdair was dying? I hope not. He was a good man. There's too much dying in our island.

Goodnight,

Your loving son,

KENNETH

PS By the way it *was* Sunday George and I went for that walk.

I have nothing much to write about tonight except that I was thinking how in the city at night the lamp-posts are so separate from each other like professors studying the road. At home it isn't like this. At home there is moonlight connecting ditches and so on. Here it isn't like that. In the city you are freer, yet . . .

The romance between Jake and Joan goes on. Joan is what one would say fleshily pretty with a prettiness that will run to fat. Her smile goes outward in a curiously candid manner. And Jake still blushes! George insists that they call him in for their first child and hands her a plate full of vegetables. I couldn't do that. He is so natural and never offensive. Why aren't we like that? He was telling us of the fishing, how the boats used to go out in the evening in the sunset and how they'd come back again in the cold sunrise. He spent most of his trips cooking. Once according to himself he filled the soup with sugar instead of salt and imitated the crew's expressions as they drank it. Even the landlady was in hysterics. I think Jake and Joan will get married eventually. She's only nineteen but girls get married earlier here. I often wonder why at home marriages are so late. I have ideas about it, and I've been reading some of the works of a man called Freud lately. He's very interesting. Why aren't we taught about him in school? I seem to know very little really.

I often wonder too why I used to be ill so often when I was young. All that bronchitis and asthma every summer. It was very strange. And those mustard baths. And the sun on the partition. I am never ill here at all. I have never felt so well, even though I work hard.

Sometimes in the evenings after supper we sit in the dining room by the fire, George and I and Miss Burgess the lecturer (she is small and plump and sews a great deal). We argue – rippingly – I never realised how splendid it is simply to argue. George talks about the hydrogen bomb, but as I said before he seems to be an echo of someone else. He's not really interested, except that he once said something which set me thinking: 'Is the image of hell connected with the hydrogen bomb?' That's interesting, you know. And he's mischievous too. He asks the landlord what pictures he's seen and the landlord who's very slow (with a moustache and white teeth) explains all about the picture at great length. He is not really a good narrator and is soon tangled up. For example he was telling us about *The Goat Woman Strikes Back*, and George was questioning him freely as if it had been an argument by Russell.

'And why did she put a spell on him? I want to know. We must be reasonable.'

I thought this was funny since he seemed to take a pleasure in discomfiting the landlord (no, that's not true, the landlord didn't realise his leg was being pulled). We sometimes listen to the songs on the radio and sometimes he asks me about home. It's incredible to him that they don't like dancing, that we daren't walk outside on Sundays, that we don't have cinemas . . . However, I defend us. Mind you, there's something in what he says.

I don't go to dances, because I *enjoy* reading and studying. I *enjoy* books. They are like food to me. Or at least have been . . . Though sometimes I grow tired. I don't read Latin and Greek all the time. I've been reading Eliot and Camus and ... but there are so many.

I sometimes go to the café in the morning for coffee. It's a small café run by an intelligent man of thirty-five who speaks and acts like a student himself and has a sort of crackling wit. Behind the café there is a lawn and on fine days – most of the days have been fine – we sit out at the back under the trees in the speckled sunshine on yellow deckchairs. Will we ever be as happy as this again? The bells, the ivy, the conversation, the books, the sun.

Coming home yesterday I saw two men fighting at a street corner. Neither of them was drunk so far as I could see. I watched their faces. They were terrible with hatred, not blind, because they were looking at each other as if they could kill each other. One of them brought his knee up at the other's stomach. And yet was the expression on their faces not hatred at all but fear? Two ragged boys were watching them at the edge of the lot, but all the others like me hurried past. I had soon forgotten them.

I'm sorry to hear about Alasdair but he was quite old, wasn't he? I suppose we have to accept that. Once I didn't accept it so much but was terrified. Now, I see that one must learn to take it as it is.

The thought has just occurred to me. I wonder what Mr Mulgrew would have said if he had seen that fight. Sophocles must have seen worse and yet it's not there, not really. Strange! 'What has Sophocles to do with us?' George asked me. What indeed! And the library with its sculptured busts of alabaster? What have they? That has to be answered.

Yes, I go to church every Sunday but Mr Wood has very little to say. In fact he has nothing to say. He has invited me to his home but I shan't go. I would only be hypocritical.

I am working as hard as ever. I hope to do well. I drive myself to work every night. There are more distractions here than at home but so far I've maintained my hard work.

George often asks me about you. He seems very interested in my early childhood illnesses. Last week he sounded me but said I was as clear as a bell. He says that sometimes he envies me for my background but at other times . . . I don't see what you have against George. I like him very much.

I think you should be going out more. I really do. It's not good to depend on one person so much.

George's girl friend is coming here tomorrow. I shall be interested to see what she is like.

Anyone would think from your letter that I was leading a dissipated life. I can assure you I'm not. And after all, you were at Lowestoft yourself when you were only sixteen. I know it was cold and miserable and the fishing was dreadful but it was a way of life.

Your loving son,
KENNETH

Well, Fiona was up visiting George this afternoon and I'm not sure that I like her very much. She is quite unlike anyone I've met before, not I mean physically but mentally and in her style. I don't know, but the girls at home seem vague somehow, they're not keenly interested in *anything*. But this girl thinks like a man: she has a cutting edge to her. After we had dinner and all the others except George, Fiona and I had gone to their work we went out to the lawn in front of the house and sat down on deckchairs. No, that's not true, George sat on a deckchair: Fiona and I sat on the ground. George, I thought, was looking rather unsure of her. He lay back in his striped deckchair with his hands clasped behind his red hair, listening. Another thing by the way is that Fiona wears slacks. She *cross-examines* one and I don't like that. In fact I dislike it immensely.

'Well,' said George lazily, 'why don't you argue?'

'Shut up,' Fiona snapped.

There was a long silence inside the green shadows. One could almost hear the grass grow.

Without thinking I said: 'This is much less bleak than home.'

'Oh?' said Fiona. 'Of course you come from Raws.' Then after a while she added thoughtfully: 'I suppose it must really be pretty bleak there.'

For some reason I became angry: 'It's not as bleak as all that.'

She looked at me in surprise, 'Well, it was you who said so.'

Her face is very intense and pale. I don't think she wears lipstick. The pallor however is of the kind which is rich, almost creamy, and not a wasted whiteness.

'Don't believe him,' said George mischievously, 'they live like prisoners up there – and they believe in hell! They can't even go for a walk on Sunday.'

'Is that right?' asked Fiona wonderingly.

'No.'

'Do you believe in hell then?'

'Yes.'

'But what kind? You mean fire, brimstone, the little devils, etc?'

'No, but I believe in . . . '

George was looking at me quizzically, half-swivelled round in his chair.

'You're abandoning your people,' he said at last laughingly.

'I'm abandoning nothing,' I retorted. 'I believe in hell but not that sort of hell. There are other hells.'

'Yes,' she said thoughtfully, 'there are indeed,' coolly picking a thin green blade of grass and chewing it.

I don't know exactly what's going on but George told me that two years ago she left her parents' home (which is apparently in the city here) and went to live in digs with another girl.

I didn't like the turn the conversation was taking. I had noticed this in George before – that sometimes without meaning to he's inclined to take advantage of people. It's as if he were testing them. It's as if he's looking for someone who will ring true.

'And what of death?' I said to George, 'what of that?'

'Death?' he said blinking into the sunlight. 'Death? What has death got to do with us?' In front of us a small bird, possibly a wren – I think wrens are brown and this bird was brown – was hopping across the grass, stopping sometimes and staring up at us almost questioningly.

'Do you think he's frightened?' asked Fiona stretching her finger out. But the bird hopped away again, sideways.

'I once did that,' I heard myself saying, 'it was a snail: it was on a road, a pathway, dusty, with little stones. I shifted a very small stone in front of the snail but for some strange reason before it reached the stone it turned away as if it sensed that the stone was there, without even touching it. I did it a few times and each time it seemed to know.'

Fiona looked at me, I thought, with some respect.

'That's very interesting,' she remarked, but immediately turned away again chewing her grass like a straw in lemonade. Her gaze is almost impersonal as if she were studying a brief.

'It's true just the same,' said George leaning forward from his deckchair and looking animated for the first time. 'Death has nothing to do with us. Fiona here – she's always on about the hydrogen bomb and the rest of it' (Fiona was regarding him very quietly) 'but after all if it comes – pouf.' Though he was fervent in his speech I saw the despair in his eyes. 'We won't know. It'll just come. Like bashing a fish with a stone. That's the point. You die anyway.'

'You talk very queerly – for a prospective doctor,' said Fiona, her eyes following the bird which was now perched bright-eyed on a branch. I had the impression that she had heard this often before.

'But that's why,' George almost shouted, leaning further forward, his elbows on his knees. 'Can't you see? You people make such a lot out of death. It's death, that's all, it's a fact! It's a fact! It comes one way or another. I'd try to save them of course, of course I would. But what can I do about politics? What would we ever do? My father now – it's like the sea – sometimes he gets a good catch sometimes not. If he doesn't who is he to appeal to? We've had all this out before. I can't help it. I'm going to be a doctor but I'm not a blazing enthusiast. I love children, yes, all right but what can I do? What can we do?'

I had never heard him speak like this before and I didn't understand it. What had become of the jazz enthusiast? What had become of the joker?

'It's when you see death you begin to accept it. Oh I know one fights it – one does. But when you see and hear some stories, well, that's different. Of old people living on and that boy, who was drowned. I tell you, sometimes I hate that.' He stood up and aimlessly kicked a stone into the trees. The little bird flew away.

'Now see what you've done,' Fiona protested, 'you've scared him away.'

He looked at her in astonishment as if about to say 'The bird' but instead shut his mouth again. At the same time a wasp swooped on her – striped rather like a deckchair – and she swept it away with her hand almost absent-mindedly.

With one of his sudden changes of mood George slumped back into the deckchair saying: 'I'm not going to speak another word. That's me finished.' However he was speaking very good-humouredly.

Fiona stood up removing some of the grass from her slacks and began:

'But *I'm* not. You think like Kenneth here,' (he started) 'you think you don't but you do. You accept hell too. That's what you do, you accept it. You say you can't do anything about it. Why can't you? You can't because you don't care. You think you're on the side of life because you play your jazz tunes and go to dances, but you aren't. You don't care because you don't see. What's your father got to do with this? It's not your father. It's you. And what has the fishing to do with it?'

George looked at me half-laughingly but didn't speak. Instead he took out two cigarettes and tossed one to her. She caught it while still speaking.

We don't have girls like this at home, not with this passion. I was listening but not speaking. When eventually she turned to me I said:

'I'm sorry. I'm not on your side. I think we need the bomb. I know you go to meetings and I honour you for it but I can't see it. We need it to defend ourselves. That's all. I doubt if it will ever be used anyway.'

That was all I said. I was honest when I said I honoured her for attending these meetings but I – there was something too ruthless about her, too dominating. I didn't want to be dominated. I was afraid of her in some queer way. It was like these riddles old Angus used to ask me. I dreaded them as if I would make a mistake and I don't like making mistakes. And I'm sure I'm right too and she's wrong. Where will this tenderness get us? These birds? Then she said a strange thing:

'You're different from George, though. You'll see.' And she added: 'You'll see.'

But what am I to see? The afternoon sun was waning slightly and I felt a slight chill. I wanted to stay here and argue but at the same time I wanted to leave. She reminded me of someone but I could not think of whom.

In fact I've been thinking that these letters are sometimes difficult for me to write. You want to know about everything but writing in English I can't communicate somehow. It's so formal. I begin to feel that we have never really communicated. However . . .

So we left it there and the three of us relaxed in the chilling air for a while, George with his eyes closed, I feeling rather out of things as if I had caused a quarrel between George and Fiona and wondering what he had told her about me before she came, and Fiona in her red slacks curled up on the ground tightly like a spring. How had they ever come into contact? Well, George told me. They met at a dance and I suppose hearing that he was a prospective doctor she thought he would be a natural for her ideas and she might discover interesting information as well. Not that she was as calculating as this: no one as passionate as she is could be as calculating as that, but it must have crossed her mind.

Anyway they're not suited to each other. George is too pedestrian for her. I can see that. I think medicine is getting him down.

As for me I have a greater capacity for suffering than either of them. These long summer days in bed – the blackness – the eternal fire – these things have hardened me. I'll not be broken, I know that, not by her arguments. And after all it may be we shall never meet again.

For some reason the thought came into my mind just now. Do you remember Mrs Armstrong? You remember that the day her husband died she stopped the clock and never wound it again. Why did I think of that just now? And when we went into her house – the silence there was, the silence you could hear.

When I saw the two of them going out together, George clowning again and she walking briskly to keep up with him, I thought they looked so young. And yet both of them are older than me! By one year. It's the heart of man. Will that ever change? Will it ever change?

I'm still working hard – in fact harder than ever – and doing reasonably well.

Why did you send me that money? Don't martyr yourself. It makes me feel guilty.

Your loving son,

KENNETH

PS The thing that fascinates me most about university is the way one argues as if the mind matters. At home it wasn't like that. Nothing we could do seemed to matter. Like that bird hopping about, that's how it is now. Of course it wasn't free. But in a way it was. Perhaps that was why Fiona was watching it all the time, the diminutive wren hopping about. I'm sure that phrase diminutive wren is from some book or other, probably Shakespeare but I can't remember where.

Last night sitting in the dining room after supper I listened to a monologue from George. We were in our armchairs in a sort of restful near-midnight silence with the radio playing nostalgic music. Perhaps that's what started him off.

'After we left you today,' he began, 'we didn't talk much. And yet what I said this afternoon was true. They say it all goes back to your childhood. I don't know. My father is a fisherman. You have to know about fishing. It's not like a profession. It's more – precarious. All fishermen drink, you know, well, most of them. You see, they're living under strain. My father doesn't drink all that much but he drinks, a little. Living in a small place does that too. He's a big man, very friendly, very slap-happy. My mother's different – good worker, you know the sort, very industrious. No, I didn't have an unhappy childhood, not at all. I spent a lot of time at the motor boats tinkering about and watching them at the harbour, most of them painted yellow with their names and the yellow buoys on the deck and the green nets ... But sometimes we were hungry, very hungry. I could have savaged a piece of meat in my childhood. You can't eat fish all of the time.

'Once my father told me a story. He used to tell me a lot of stories. It was when he was younger – when he was sailing – he ended up in New Zealand. A few of them jumped ship and stayed behind. One holiday they went out in a small boat – two of them, the day was warm. Very lazy they were, very lazy, drifting along. Then they began to take off their clothes – it was so hot – first the jackets, then the shirts. The sea was – you know – glassy with that tremendous eye-shattering heat. They decided they'd have a plunge – smell of tar from the boat too. So they lowered themselves over the side. No, his friend went first while he kept the boat steady. It was very warm, very calm. Then the shark came. It sheared right through his friend. The boat toppled slightly then he steadied it, sort of. There was some threshing through which he rowed, then nothing. Later they found his friend's stocking – one stocking.

'He often used to tell me stories. You know he didn't drink at all then. Later of course he didn't drink much, but some. There was some – precariousness, but I was happy. I don't write to them, not because I don't like them but because I'm lazy – I'm quite lazy really. I suppose I became a doctor to enter a profession. I didn't want to be poor, you see, again.

'And sometimes, you know, you see certain things, like that drowned boy. They don't get you down all that much, but Fiona, she's romantic, she thinks that life is so tremendously important, and death too. I . . . Well, she's pretty you know. Sometimes you don't think so, but there's bone there. Intensity. So few people have it. Like . . . It's precious. Oh, I'll be a doctor all right and a good one. Remember I told you once you were on the side of life? You are. I laugh more than you, and I joke, but perhaps it's defensive. Since I came here I saw an old woman. She's hanging on to life like a leech in the hospital. Why? And her daughter comes in, weary, weary. It would be better if the old woman died. But she doesn't. She hates life too. She's always complaining. She's eighty – and I once heard her call on her mother. What do you think of that?

'Oh well. Up. Bed, boy. End of Reminiscences of George Morton.

'But I'll tell you this. I've never met anyone like Fiona. I've been out with a lot of girls but . . . she's alive you know. At the dance I met her, you couldn't help being attracted, it was as if she was gulping up life. If you take her to the pictures she's leaning forward, she takes part in the film. You can feel her throwing the pies – and cracking nuts between her teeth. There's a quality of carelessness about her – a divine carelessness.

'Hey! That's great. I ought to be a poet. "Divine careless-ness." That's good, that's good. Come on, let's go upstairs and pull the chain and wake Mrs Bryden from her dreams of filthy lucre.'

So that's George since you wanted to know about him.

As he was talking, for some reason this came into my head. Do you remember Mrs Murray who died about five years ago, you know at 10a. You remember Donald her son – he died of tuberculosis – he was sixteen. I used to visit him. It was in the black house. I remember listening to her once. She was telling me the minister had been in – in fact he used to come in often. 'Donald,' she said, 'he talks about these practical jokes of yours, you know when you let Norman's horse loose and when you took that dead rat into school. He laughs at all these things remembering them and yourself. These are the things he's always talking about and the jam jar you ran away with. And he doesn't know what's waiting for him. The doctor says he'll die but Donald doesn't know it. He's gay – but he coughs a lot. And all he talks about is these nonsensical things! The minister tells him to read the Bible but he hardly ever does. And he doesn't pray. He says he doesn't know how to. He sometimes can't stop himself laughing when the minister is praying. What am I going to do with him?'

I don't know why I thought of that but it came back to me very clearly, and especially the last thing she told me. They told him he was going to die and the minister was always there. Strangely enough he wanted the minister to be with him and he was already reading the Bible. She said however that he was always following her about with his eyes as if he were asking her something and she couldn't think what it was. The moment he died she was sitting in a chair knitting. The Bible fell out of his hand and she went to give it back to him but he was dead. She told me that when she bent down she remembered that the

Bible itself was cold but the sun on the floor below was warm. For some reason she remembered this.

I hate the deaths of our island. There are too many. There are far too many deaths.

Your loving son,

KENNETH

I do not understand your letter. Why this attack on Fiona? No, I haven't seen her since that day but that is no reason for your letter. I don't understand it. I begin to think you are not trying to understand me, though I am trying to understand you. You are not even trying. I know what you have done for me, believe me. I appreciate it. But at the same time it is clear that you are not trying to understand me. That is terrifying. I hadn't realised it before. Fiona is not like that at all. You say she has no right to meddle with these things, that it's not woman's work. What do you expect her to do? Go to the well for pails of water? You say that the government know best. I don't agree. What have they done for us? I'm beginning to see a lot of things. Hell paralyses the will. I don't agree with her, but I don't see why she shouldn't go to meetings if she wishes to. I am not under bad influence. I work hard. I drive myself far into the night. But sometimes I wonder why I do it. At home one doesn't question these things, but I can't prevent my mind from developing.

I will tell you something. I have a picture of an island. It is bleak but the people are gentle. Oh they are gentle enough and polite and well mannered . . . But it may be the gentility of the dead. I see them sitting by their TV sets as here and not walking casually into each other's houses as before without knocking. There is nothing we can do against that, but prepare ourselves. Gentility is not enough in the world we're born into. It is a weakness. To break the will of the children is wrong.

What have I seen in the city since I came? I have seen beggars and lonely men, I have seen the yellow lights of the mind, and the crooked shadows. Yet we must learn to live with it. I know we must. You should not have written that letter. Children should be able to respect their parents. You must try to learn to understand. I know it is difficult but you must learn to try. There is nothing else for you to do, *nothing else*.

Sometimes I get terrified. In this house there are seven or eight people. The landlady – what does she live for, but the making of money? And what will she do with it? She will leave it to her children. And her husband who smokes his pipe and watches films twice or thrice a week? Were the two of them always like that? Or were they once like Jake and Joan? How have they been cheated? And this lady lecturer, who spends her evenings sewing or visiting her friend, the other lady lecturer, what has she to look forward to? These things *have to be answered*. I sometimes wonder: Might they not as well be dead? Perhaps that's what happened to man: he was unfortunate enough to be able to prolong his life. For most people might as well be dead at thirty. And yet . . . I feel that's wrong. There is some meaning if one can find it – a precarious balance somewhere. One looks out and sees, like the Lady of Shalott. But one day the mirror breaks. One should not think like this. Or is it that others don't see it, the abyss?

Jake and Joan are happy. They will be married. They follow each other with their eyes and to others appear silly: but they are precious to each other. And perhaps that is enough: even for a short while. I don't know. Today I got a wedding invitation from Norman, Norman Morrison. He knows I can't go to the wedding but he sent me the invitation and a flattering letter calling me his dearest friend. And it's true I suppose. We went to school together. We used to be sent out gardening together by the head-master. We ate the stolen strawberries with their almost unbearable tartness together. We studied for our bursaries and read the crates of books from the library, surreptitiously checking over our answers to arithmetic problems. And I am glad he is to be married, but I know that we will never speak to each other again in the same way.

I am sick of our melancholy, sick of it. I want to see things as they are. It is necessary. I am sick and tired of people saying No. It is necessary to stop saying No.

I am sorry about your letter. I am very sorry and shocked. I do not think you should have written it. I think it's time you went out amongst people more. I think it is time you depended less on me, although I shall never abandon you. It is time you looked at the facts. I do not want this burden of guilt. It is time we laughed more – high time.

Your loving son,
KENNETH

2

Yesterday quite by chance I ran into Fiona. I went into the café in front of the reading room – where I sometimes study – and there she was. After my ten days at home I had completely forgotten about her. She was sitting by herself in a corner seat drinking coffee. At first she didn't see me, and I watched her. She was idly stirring the coffee with a spoon – her brown and white leather bag was slung over a chair: and she was staring into the cup as if it was – well, perhaps something nuclear! Then she saw me, her face brightened and we began to talk.

I have this bad Highland manner of wanting to know about people – all about them. I pointed to her CND badge and asked her about it. She also showed me the card they are given with its peculiar biblical message. I think she intends going to Aldermarston for the march.

'I'm tired of studying,' she said, 'I feel suffocated. Honestly I do. Suffocated. As if I can't get enough air. Sometimes I walk down to the quay and watch the ships. That helps a little but not much.'

I found it strange listening to her because that was how I felt when I was home – as if I were being strangled to death by invisible hands. However I don't feel so bad now.

She talked fairly freely about her parents after a while: 'My mother's dead,' she said, 'my father's alive. He's a lawyer. He's a fairly successful lawyer – here. Once he had a chance to try for a bigger job in England: but my mother was ill at the time, with her nerves, and he couldn't go.'

She twisted her fingers on the table and I'm sure she didn't notice.

'They used to have the most terrible rows at first. He used to blame her for holding him back. He drinks a lot. Families are like that,' she said, looking out into the street where the large statue of Sir Walter Scott confronted us. 'They fight each other and kill each other and feed off each other.'

I told her a little about George.

'That's different,' she maintained, 'that's honest. My father wasn't like that. His hatred at the end was a cold hatred. Eventually he wouldn't speak to my mother at all. It's strange that. Sometimes I saw him actually grit his teeth. She was one of these defenceless people who invited bullying. But he didn't bully her. He would simply get drunk and ignore her. Once I saw her pouring tea into his cup. It was late, I remember, and he had just come in. The hot tea spilt over her hand. She didn't scream and I saw the red coming up on her hand. But he did nothing. He carried on drinking his tea, as if he hadn't noticed. But I saw that he had noticed, and yet he pretended that he hadn't.

'When my mother died two years ago I left him. That was all. One afternoon when he was at the office I simply packed a bag and left the house. I left a note. I remember I had difficulty with the key. First of all I locked the door and then I had the key in my hand. So I threw it in through the window and walked away. He didn't ask for me back. It was as if he was tired of the lot of us. He tried to give me money (it's very easy to give people money) but I didn't take it. I had some from my mother. She was saving up in a bank for me. She was all I had you see. Anyway he didn't really bother about me much. I can imagine him in the morning shaving and sitting down to have his breakfast and getting the car out, but it's as if I was thinking of a stranger. I have no sympathy for him. I don't hate him, I have no feeling for him. That's all.'

She added, 'I think that was why I joined the CND.'

'How do you mean?'

'I don't know. It's something to do with that pressure. Do you think about it like that?' I didn't understand. Sometimes I'm quite stupid.

'Well, the pressure builds up and you get a nuclear bomb, that's all. But I don't want it to be like that – that would be like my father you see. Something went wrong in his ambitions and the pressure built up. It would have been more honest if he had left my mother. But in his position, you know, that would never do. Like a lawyer I heard of recently. His girl friend wanted to be married in a registry office. But no – not him. He wanted a church wedding: and he's an atheist too.' Looking out of the window she suddenly burst out laughing, a pure bell-like laugh. It's difficult to describe it. It's not the laugh of innocence. It's the laugh which has gone beyond pretensions, it's the pure laugh of comedy which almost for a moment accepts the universe as it is.

Yet I didn't laugh like that. I believe these lies and hypocrisies are evil. They are the greatest evil. And they are within the church too. I dream of another church, a more precarious one, and that laughter will be its bell . . .

I didn't know what else to say except:

'It's the same everywhere. Because people refuse to look. They've got to protect themselves.'

'I suppose so,' she said. 'Can I get you a coffee?'

Instinctively I said 'No' (By the way that's a very funny thing about me which I thought of recently. If anyone asks me a question and I haven't been listening but I pretend that I have I always say 'No'; I never say 'Yes') because I don't like women buying anything for men, and because she can't have much money. Then I changed my mind for some reason and said 'Yes'.

For a long time we said nothing and then we went out and walked along the street in the cool of the evening. We said nothing at all. When we parted I simply said 'Goodnight Fiona' and she said 'Goodnight Kenneth' – she had asked me no questions about myself or my home – and I walked home. That was all. The sky was green above the tram rails.

When I got home George was not yet in. At ten o'clock he came in slightly drunk. I had never seen him drunk before. I think it's a bad sign. I managed to keep him from stumbling over anything and from getting himself entangled with one of the stair rails which is slightly loose and got him to bed. He slept almost as soon as his head hit the pillow. His red hair was

sweating and his face was white. I don't know what's wrong
with him.

This is quite a long letter. I shall write again soon. I hope you
are well.

Goodnight,

Your loving son,

KENNETH

Tonight at seven I put down my books and I thought I'd write
to you. I kept finding there was something I ought to explain
but I couldn't think what it was. Then George came in and we
played some records. He lay on the bed with his hands behind
his head looking up at the ceiling and saying nothing. Sometimes I caught him looking at me as if he wished to say
something but he didn't. (By the way Jean and Jake have
announced their engagement. When Jake told us about it he
was grinning and there was oil on his face: I thought that was
very endearing.) I nearly asked George what was the matter
with him but I didn't. I just sat and listened, or rather at first I
wasn't listening at all. Then it came into my consciousness that
this was a woman singing and there was a kind of catch in her
voice. It was the Blues – a sort of jazz – and a spiritual. For some
strange reason this made me think of our church. I think it
must have been the black disc spinning. (All this time George
was lying on the bed looking up at the ceiling, perfectly
motionless.) Then it struck me. This was the sort of church I
wanted. This woman had more faith and more depth and more
sheer melody of life than our Minister.

I remembered an incident which took place at home. You
know Mrs McInnes the widow, the one with a son in Australia.
I was in her house one night and Mrs MacLeod was there.
They were talking about how her son had sent money home by
a local sailor and they had never seen it. He must have spent it.
This Mrs MacLeod – she's got a sort of moustache and I
remember she was wearing a sort of rabbit collar – she
suddenly said:

'He will pay for his sins. There's one thing I always believe
in. People must be made to pay for their sins.'

I looked at her and there was hate in her face. Her lips were tight. And yet really it had nothing to do with her. She wasn't even concerned. Listening to that record I thought of that and I realised something which I suppose I must have known for a long time.

WE ARE A NEW GENERATION. WE ARE DIFFERENT FROM YOU.

I remember too when you were reminiscing with some of your friends. I didn't understand you. You told each other your jokes but they had no meaning for me. They were past. They were finished.

And I think I know why George started drinking. The reason is he is supposed to cure people, but he doesn't know WHAT FOR. That is why he listens to the music. He wants to find out why he should cure people. That's all. I watched him. His eyes were open at first and I could see him studying the light bulb. Then slowly they shut but he wasn't sleeping. It was as if he were really listening. I heard a trumpet, one clear note – a single pure note like water – no, George said it was like a drink of cool milk during fever or after a hangover, the very cold milk you get in cartons from these machines – this single note held perfectly steady – like a guarantee of something – rising out of the wrestlings of the music, out of the sweat of billiard rooms and men with green eyeshades – this single pure note, and then George opened his eyes, and that was all. The record ended then.

I wanted to tell you that because it's the thing that's been troubling me. The pressures are so tremendous. You must try to understand, please. It will be terrible if you don't try.

I haven't had an answer to my last letter yet so this is an extra.

Your loving son,

KENNETH

I am sorry I'm late in answering your letter. The truth is, I've been ill but not at all seriously. Strangely enough, it is a recurrence of my asthma which I haven't felt since I was twelve. I was sitting down to my books the other night when it began. I went to bed and felt like a fool.

I lay in my room in absolute silence for most of the day. It was a strange experience listening to the silence, and watching the leaves swaying slightly against the window. My room is high up and I don't hear the traffic. In the evening George would come in and sit at my bedside (for company) studying. He has exams soon and he's working hard. He looks more cheerful now. Jake also came to see me, and appears more responsible. I think Joan must be making him wash the oil from his face. He doesn't spend so much time with his motor cycle now.

The landlady left me alone during the daytime. In a way it was a luxurious illness. I felt, not quite alone, but rather at ease for the first time during an illness. I read nothing and would lie there for hours not even thinking but allowing thoughts to flit across my mind like leaves across the window pane. I can't understand why I should have this asthma now.

The landlord sometimes came in after he'd been to the pictures. He is fairly tall with a moustache and very white teeth. He told me all about the pictures he had seen. At first I used to laugh at him quietly inside myself but I don't any more. My new humility almost frightens me. He talked to me about the taxis. Apparently he prefers to drive by night. That's surprising isn't it? When he has no film to speak about he says nothing but sits there with his hands between his legs as if he were a guest in my house. Funny, isn't it? George listens to his stories very seriously which is a new development.

One morning I was awake watching the dawn come up. Usually in the past I have felt nervous in the early morning, with a hollow in the pit of my stomach. This morning however I felt at ease as if in tune with the day which was coming into being like a poem into a poet's mind. And I thought: what a miracle light is. What would happen to us if one night we suddenly realised that the thick darkness would last forever, the thick furry darkness. Fiona wrote me a note but did not come to see me.

I spent four days in bed and when I got up I decided I would not be sick again. I went into the bathroom. The sun was shining on the white bath, and its rays were on the mirror. The diamonds on the floor were very bright and real. After I had shaved and washed my face I felt new. Then I went downstairs for my breakfast: it was like a royal entrance. I loved everybody. Rising from the sick bed is like being reborn. I knew that this love of mine would not last but it did not matter. For that moment it was precious – the stumpy landlady with her vulpine face appeared angelic, her tray silver and her tea wine: her two children could even have sprouted wings: red-haired George was my dearest friend: Jake and Joan were Adam and Eve in the Garden: and there was no evil in the world. (Strangely enough I happened that same evening to overhear the landlady complain about her tiredness caused by her climbing stairs with my food but that did not matter either.)

No, I believe that people are essentially good. If it is possible to see them like that at all, then that is the way we must see them. (Do I sermonise too much?)

In the evening George and I went to the cinema. It is an old cinema. Once upon a time one could get in with empty jam jars (presumably lemon curd for the balcony) and during the performance, believe it or not, a man sprayed us all over with disinfectant. It was a western film and I enjoyed it very much. After sickness, how much one enjoys the world, like a dewdrop on a thorn! We had no need to talk to each other.

Tomorrow I'm going to one of the CND parades with Fiona. It should be interesting.

I hope you are well. Here the weather is good and I suppose it will be the same at home.

I mean that: I'm not going to be sick again.

Your loving son,
KENNETH

An extraordinary thing has happened which I must think about. Today Fiona and I went to the CND sit down demonstration. We sat down on the pavement opposite the City Chambers which are next to the Art Gallery. It was all very quiet and companionable somehow, people sitting down in the sunshine eating sandwiches as if they were on holiday. The pavement was quite warm (unusually warm – mind you, I don't make a practice of sitting on pavements). There were no speeches. The speeches had already been made at Hutton Park.

We sat there surrounded by a crowd of people most of whom we had never seen before and would never see again. It is interesting to watch people passing. After a while you only see their legs, some dumpy, some thin, some active, some slow, some old, some young. There were one or two mounted policemen. They look tall on their gleaming horses, and in their leather leggings.

What does one talk about? We talked about examinations mainly. It was almost weird. I wondered what many of them were doing there. I wondered what I was doing there. Everyone was very orderly and placed sandwich papers in bags or in those wire bins one sees attached to posts. There was one woman beside me: she was dressed entirely in red and reading *Woman's Own*. Extraordinary! Then something happened. We were such an orderly crowd with this hum of conversation going on, like a gala, girls in light summery dresses, men in open-neck shirts. There were babies, milk bottles and lemonade bottles.

Then it happened. One of our group – a student I think – had been pushed towards the middle of the road. It wasn't his fault. It was simply the pressure of the crowd. A policeman came up to him – one of the ones who had been directing the traffic.

It's a funny thing about policemen. Usually you don't notice them at all. You don't somehow think of them as people with emotions. They are there to look calm and controlled and placid and that is what they do. That is what they are paid for. They walk in such a deliberate manner as if they have an understanding with time.

Anyway this policeman came up to him and began to tell him to move back. Now I can understand that some of the policemen must have been harassed. The day was warm – even hot – and there were a lot of people and perhaps they didn't quite know what to do. Furthermore it can't be very comfortable for a policeman to walk about in cloth of such thick texture on a hot day. This was quite a young policeman. I looked at his face and in a surprised flash I realised something. This policeman wasn't being merely tired and harassed, he actually appeared to hate this student. It was in his eyes and also in his teeth which I saw for a moment bared as he hissed out a command. It startled me coming out of that fine day. He pushed the student ahead of him roughly: the student pushed him back (I saw his blue untidy scarf). Then the policeman twisted the student's arm behind his back, and shouted, upon which another policeman came running up: it was like the natural order being over-turned. The student's face was white with pain: whistles were being sounded: the crowd was milling aimlessly around. I saw some milk spilled on the pavement beside me and bits of glass. Then I saw Fiona pushing her way through the crowd. I could hardly recognise her. Her face was pale and set. I tried to follow her but I lost her. I climbed up on the top steps to see. She went up to the policeman and hit him on the back of the head with her handbag. Then she was seized by another policeman. By this time a black van had driven up. She and the student were bundled inside. The door was locked. The van was driven away.

I stood there watching. The young policeman faced the crowd. He was almost grinning. I heard him shouting but I couldn't hear what he was saying. It was as if he hated us. The crowd began to move away until I stood on the steps alone. It wasn't the steps of the Municipal Chambers at all: it was the steps of the Art Gallery. There are ten: I counted. The young policeman was at the bottom looking up, his legs wide apart, while the crowd drifted away. I looked down at him. There was a book in my hand. My flannel trousers swayed slightly in the breeze. I felt thin, even though I was angry. I nearly threw the book at him but he looked and was stronger than me. He did not seem to be standing on the soles of his feet but rather on his toes. I could see his face under the diced cap. It was of a high red complexion: his shoulders were wide and he had the free composure of the fit. His lips appeared petulant and cruel. He stood as if grinning at me for a while – I had the strangest sensation as if he was daring me to attack him – then with an arrogance which was entirely unlike that of a policeman he turned and began as if in parody to pace up and down with a slow deliberate tread.

I left that place and began to walk, not knowing where I was headed for. Eventually I found myself at the iron gates of the university. I walked past the sacrist in his navy-blue uniform with the yellow facings, up the flagged road and into the library. The ivy was very green and grassy, the library very cool. I sat down at a table to rest my feet. In an alcove the logic professor was leaning down close over a book so that his face almost seemed to touch it. I watched him for a while, then suddenly realised that he was asleep. I looked at the dead-white cool busts scattered round the library. I laid my sweating hands on the cool table. I was surrounded by rows and rows of books, but I had no desire to read them. After I had sufficiently rested I got up and went out, carefully closing the door after me. Then I walked down the flagged path. The sacrist was no longer to be seen and the sliding window at the enquiry office was shut. I walked back into town over the rough tarry stones and went home. Then I sat down at the window and thought. Eventually I dipped my pen into the ink and began to write. That is what I could do.

But I shall have to think.

Your loving son,

KENNETH

Today I went to the courtroom. It was 11 in the morning and I was allowed to enter among the few spectators. I sat down on one of the varnished benches, feeling the hot sun warm on my shoulder. There was a big clock which I could see through the window. The atmosphere in the courtroom was very cool and quiet, as in a church, but on the seat at the front of the adjoining benches sat that policeman, his cap beside him on the seat, his hair brilliant and black and cropped, the back of his neck scrubbed and red. Sometimes he looked round as if he were waiting to arrest one of us but none of us was making a noise. He didn't seem to recognise me. Why should he?

At 11 o'clock the clerk – or whoever he is – came in and we all stood up. Then the judge, a small old man, walked rather unsteadily to his raised seat. He wore a hearing-aid. Imagine it! It was like something out of Dickens. It's perfectly true! Then Fiona and the student were led in. She did not look at me, though she was looking towards me. It was strange how that was: yet she appeared calm, though pale. The student was thin, dark-haired, with dark rings under his eyes. He didn't look as if he had slept and he answered questions in a low voice. I noticed that one of his turn-ups was turned down: I found this endearing and pitiful. His tie was also slightly askew. He kept feeling in his pocket as if he were hunting for something – perhaps his cigarette case – but all these things are taken away from prisoners.

The first witness called was the policeman. (I now noticed that there was another policeman beside him: I hadn't noticed before.) My policeman walked up to the witness box and stood there for a moment before reading his statement in a heavy placid self-satisfied tone. But before he began to read, the judge suddenly turned to Fiona and said:

'I hear your father is a lawyer and that you refused his services. Is that true?'

'Yes.'

He looked at her for a moment as if there was something he didn't understand, then said to the policeman:

'Carry on, constable.'

I thought that was a very old-world word. The policeman had hardly begun when the judge said: 'Could you please speak a little louder?'

The policeman glanced at him, I thought, with a curious masked contempt, but raised his voice as he had been ordered, the judge meanwhile cupping his hand over his right ear, and leaning towards him. Fiona was staring right through me and through the window asking nothing of me but existing in a world of her own which was also a real world for she did not look like a statue or a coin: she looked what she was, pale and weak. I wondered what sort of night she had spent and sensed that she was frightened. I thought of how my own stomach turns over when I am frightened and how the sweat prickles my hands.

' . . . then the accused' – looking briefly at the student – 'began to rain blows on me.'

'That is not true.' I had stood up. It was my voice. I had said, 'That is not true' because it was not true but I had not said it as one interrupts a lecturer who is demonstrating a theorem and who has made an error. I had said it as if I were throwing a stone. It was curious how the policeman continued as if he had not heard me: it was the judge who stopped him. The judge was old, but he had heard me. Fiona was looking at me, as if she was seeing me for the first time. Beyond the hearing-aid, the judge's mind was feeling towards me.

I said, 'It is not true. He was not raining blows at him.' I was appealing to the judge but at the same time I had the strangest feeling as if I was happy though I was frightened. It was like having the sweetness and terrible coldness of ice-cream on your teeth at the same time. The policeman had stopped speaking, and was standing as if he didn't know what to do.

The old judge's eyes moved slightly. It was as if he was puzzled by something for a shadow passed across the redness – as you can see a crow at sunset – I have seen that look often in the eyes of the old, the shock of the unexpected and the strange. I thought he was going to fine or imprison me, and I began:

'It is untrue because I was there. The witness was doing no harm. I was watching him. He was pushed into the middle of the road.'

I now knew what had happened. I had spoken these words not because of the bomb but because of Fiona. I knew now what she meant by being on the side of life. She had asked nothing of me. She had stood there in her pallor and her weakness and had made no demands. Therefore I had offered her myself. It was like the amethyst at her breast exploding into a new bomb, which in turn exploded within me, the bomb of truth. It is not preaching I want, but vision!

Therefore, there was the old judge leaning between us with his hearing aid and the policeman with his neat diced evil cap laid beside him. There was the smell of varnish and the court which was like a church. The sun exploded through the window, drunkenly. It flashed on the judge's head, leaped through the glass of water, and shone on Fiona's face which was smiling and dizzy. It swayed the wall diagonally towards the policeman, scything him in two, it made the varnish into a stifling musk, and punched me between the eyes exploding light in my head. The prison fell in like a pack of cards. I looked up. The floor swayed like a deck beneath me. The sun was rising over the sea. There was the noise of a train and coloured flowers. Above me was George's face. And Fiona was standing beside him. The floor steadied. I was calm, so calm. I had never been so calm. Now I write out of this calmness, Fiona and I. George has gone and we are alone. We send you this letter, Fiona and I.

Your loving son,
KENNETH.

PART II

A Day in the Life of . . .

She paid off the taxi she had taken from the railway station and went into the hotel. She felt sweaty and the palm of her right hand slid along the handle of the red case. She put the case down and waited for the girl at the reception desk to stop phoning. She had been in the hotel three or four times before in the past two years but she didn't expect that anyone would recognise her, and this girl seemed new as if she were a schoolgirl working there during holiday time. As she waited she looked around her. There were some chairs with olive green covers at one side of the lobby and on one an old man lying asleep, his mouth open, his feet stretched out, and what looked like a guidebook fallen open on the floor beside him. Her eyes traversed him, following the wall upward to the high ceiling with its white edgings like wedding cake. She turned back to the girl who was looking at her enquiringly. She was a very pretty girl with dark pigtails and bare tanned arms.

'A single room,' she said. 'Have you a single room?'

'I think we can manage that,' said the girl brightly, turning to a plan of the hotel hung up on a sheet on the wall. 'Room 5,' she said, 'or would you like one with a bath? There's 31.'

'I'll take 5.'

'Righto. If you would please sign?'

She signed 'Miriam Hetherington', hesitating as she always did whether to put 'Scottish' or 'British' and finally deciding as she always did to put 'British'. She took the key attached to the large blue block and went to the room which was on the ground floor. She opened the door and entered.

It was like all the other hotel rooms in which she had stayed. There was a dressing table, a wardrobe, a wash basin with

towels, a phone, a card with a list of hotel charges, a large
notice about what to do in the event of fire, a Gideon Bible, a
bed with electric blanket, a large glass ashtray and a small gold-
coloured box of matches stamped with the name of the hotel.
She lay down on the bed and fell asleep.

When she woke she found by a glance at her small silver wrist
watch that she had slept two hours and that it was five o'clock
in the afternoon. She got off the bed, looking down vaguely at
her red shoes which matched the case. Then she opened the
latter and took out her clothes – two dresses, a hat, four pairs of
stockings, a pair of shoes, three sets of undergarments, two
pairs of pyjamas, shoe brushes and shoe polish and various
other odds and ends including a sewing kit and a number of
paperbacks. She packed them neatly into her wardrobe and
dressing chest. When she had done this she took off her blouse
and began to wash her face and neck, rubbing the cold water
briskly into her eyes.

The face that looked back at her from the mirror was the face
of a woman of about thirty-five whose skin at the corner of the
eyes was beginning to wrinkle. The eyes themselves had a
questioning look as if, confronted with the world, they had
found it rather puzzling, not to say unintelligible. The nose
was rather long, the upper lip narrow and severe, the lower lip
full and red. Her teeth were still her own and fairly white. The
forehead was narrow and high and lightly veined and the hair
cut into a boyish crop. In short she had the appearance of
someone who might have been passionate but whose passion
had been mastered by a relentless severity. Her colourful red
blouse and red shoes seemed like a late desperate blossoming of
her buried personality. But she wasn't ugly and, given rouge
and lipstick and relaxation of mind, she would in certain
circumstances appear pretty.

When she had washed herself and used rouge and lipstick she
thought for a moment and then going out of the room and
leaving the key at the desk she went out into the dazzling
sunlight.

The streets were crowded with people – men in shirt sleeves,
women bare-armed in blouses – all strolling along in an easy,

relaxed manner. The road was dense with traffic and it took her some time to cross, but she waited till the sign 'Cross' appeared and then half ran across the street. On the opposite side was a restaurant which she entered. She sat down at a table in the shade and when the waitress came she ordered fruit juice and a gammon steak. At a table beside her there was a boy and a girl holding hands and gazing into each other's eyes. At another table there was a large man with a moustache eating fish and squeezing juice from a lemon on to his plate. He had a newspaper propped against the tea-pot.

She drank her juice and waited for her gammon steak. She didn't feel at all hungry but decided that she ought to eat something since that was what people did at that time of day. Since her parents had died and she had started living on her own she sometimes skipped meals but on holiday one ought to eat, she told herself. She remembered that her mother used always to be very keen on her eating a lot, and would pile her plate high with meat and vegetables which weren't really very well cooked. Her father of course ate steadily and gravely, not seeming to mind what was set in front of him, but as if he were filling himself with necessary fuel. He reminded her of a large squat car which was being pumped full of petrol. Of course he had been a large man and he needed the food. Her mother on the other hand was thin and stringy.

She ate the gammon, carefully putting aside the chips. The man with the newspaper was chewing rapidly and reading at the same time. The young couple were preparing to leave. They had eaten, she noted, some of the cheapest stuff, sausage and egg, but had wiped their plates clean. It took her a long time to eat the gammon but she succeeded and got up. She didn't want any sweet as it might fatten her too much. The waitress hoped that the gammon had suited her and she said yes. The waitress said that if she cared to come back tomorrow they would have something special on the menu. She didn't reply. Again she went out into the sunshine.

For a while she walked along the streets looking in the shop windows. It was a good area of the town with a large number of jewellers' shops, good food shops, and furniture shops. She looked at the rings in the windows and noted that they were very expensive. There were also some quite splendid Russian watches. She remembered giving away her father's watch to her uncle but she had kept her mother's watch and was still wearing it. Her father's watch had been a large golden one, of the kind that men used to carry in their waistcoat pockets. She still had his Masonic ring in a box in the house.

She went into a supermarket and walked around for a bit. There was nothing there that she wanted to buy except possibly two large red footballs which she might take to the neighbours' boys who were mad keen on football. It was always a good idea to take something home to them: one never knew when one might need help from a neighbour, for example if one was ill with 'flu and couldn't get out, especially in the winter time. There were various perfumes which she was tempted to buy but didn't. Later on she went into a large bookshop and studied the books. She read a lot but not as much as she used to. Her mother had always told her that she read too much. 'Too much reading is a weariness to the flesh,' she would say, quoting from the Bible, or what she thought was the Bible. Her mother had hardly read a book in her life except the Bible and the *People's Friend*, and couldn't understand why people should want to read books at all: it seemed such a waste of time when they could be doing something useful. She herself thought she might buy a book called *Emerging Africa* to help her with her geography but decided against it. Holiday time wasn't the right time to read serious books. One read detective stories or thrillers. Half ashamedly she looked at a book on horoscopes and found that she ought to keep a tight grip on financial matters that week and not mix very much with strangers. She put the book down and went out again into the sun.

As she walked down the street she came to a cinema which was showing a film called *The Cowboys* starring John Wayne. She decided to go in and bought a ticket for the balcony. When she sat down it disturbed her to find that she was the only person in the whole cinema. Not only was there no one in the balcony seats, there was no one – not even children – in the stalls. She felt rather frightened and wished that she had not come in till later but after all she had paid her money and couldn't go out again. The red curtains were still drawn and for a long time there was nothing but music to which she listened impatiently, now and again looking behind her as if expecting that someone would come in and attack her. Eventually the music stopped and there were some advertisements, one of which showed a young girl riding a horse through a mountain stream and which after all turned out to be an advertisement for cigarettes. 'Cool as a mountain stream,' breathed the sexy voice of the sponsor. She herself didn't smoke. Her mother hadn't believed in girls smoking: her father however smoked a pipe. When he was finished working for the day in the distillery he would read the paper for a while and smoke his pipe and then fall asleep. She herself was the only child and had perhaps loved her father more than her mother who had often told him that he ought to have a better job with his abilities though as a matter of fact his abilities weren't all that extraordinary except that he was good with his hands. He could make or repair anything. He had made a chair for her when she was a child and later he would make toys for her, wooden animals of all kinds. Her favourite was a squirrel which would climb the chair on its clockwork machinery.

The credits came on the screen for the big picture and she realised that she had read a review of the film in the *Observer* which she bought every Sunday. She also bought the *Sunday Times*. Her father and mother used to get the *Sunday Post* and they would spend the whole week reading it, not missing a single story. In her own job as a teacher she would use the Sunday Supplements for projects. One of her projects was on the Motor Car, though she couldn't drive.

The film turned out to be rather a good one, at least at the beginning. The title *The Cowboys* had to be taken literally for it was about boys, not about men. John Wayne, a rancher whose cowhands abandoned him in order to join a gold rush, was a stern man who had lost two sons partly because he had been too strict with them. The film showed him becoming attached to the boys and learning how to handle them in a human manner with the help of a coloured cook. On the drive too the boys learned to become men. They were attacked by some ex-jailbirds who killed the unarmed Wayne after he had refused to kow-tow to them and had then driven off his cattle. The last part of the film she wasn't sure of. It showed the boys setting off grim-faced after the killers and one by one detaching them and murdering them and finally manœuvring the survivors into a trap where they shot them all. The leader of the killers had got his legs entangled in his horse's stirrups and pleaded to be freed but one of the boys fired a shot into the air which so frightened the horse that it dragged its rider along through a river till he was drowned. She wasn't sure about this last part. Nothing surely could condone violence and if there had been someone with her she would have argued about it. But there was no one there.

Many years before while her parents were still alive she had fallen in love with a man who owned a shop at the time. He was very handsome and very glib but what she took for cleverness her parents took for falsity. He used to take her out a lot especially to the cinema but most of the time she had to pay for their outings. She didn't mind this as she thought that he was making his way in the business. The first time he had tried to seduce her she had been very cold, so cold that she had managed to put him off. It had been in a wood where he had taken her in his new car: she could remember the brown autumnal leaves, and the river flowing through the glen with a desolate sound. He had been very persuasive using all the common arguments such as that it was good for one to have sex. He had been very handsome with his fair hair and fine blue eyes but she had not succumbed. She thought that innocence was important and felt that if she had given in she would have carried for a long time a load of guilt. In fact the sequence which showed the girl riding through the mountain stream had reminded her of the episode. He had been very passionate and also persuasive. He used to take her to parties and she had been so much in love or so infatuated that she had defied her parents and come into the house in the early hours of the morning, still remembering the dancing round the record player in the grey streamers of cigarette smoke. Once she had come in at four o'clock in the morning, only to find her mother, toothless, still awake and waiting for her. 'After all we have done for you,' hissed her mother through a mouth without dentures, 'and you are just a common prostitute.' As a matter of fact it hadn't been like that at all. The party had been exciting and they had all danced to the music of the latest pop songs. She could still remember them with a certain bitterness. Not that she was the kind of person who was very interested in pop songs; she was more interested in classical music and conversation. But coming back in the whiteness of the morning under the million stars had been an experience, for during most of her life she had gone to bed at eleven at the latest, drawing the curtains carefully before removing her clothes.

In any case the whole romance had finished when she discovered that the man to whom she had been engaged had been seeing another girl all the time, a very common girl who really liked pop songs and worked in a supermarket. She had found it shattering that he should have preferred this girl to her. In fact this was the most painful part of the whole episode, that the girl should have such a cheap mind, and that her mother had been right all along. 'It was lucky for you that you found out in time,' her mother would say to her. For a long time she didn't feel like going out but she had to since she was teaching and otherwise people would talk. So she had put on a brave face and pretended that the whole thing had been trivial but for weeks she would burst out crying for no particular reason. After all he had been very entertaining and they had gone to so many different places. What struck her most was that afterwards she would analyse the whole relationship and realise that without her knowing it he had been incredibly selfish. For instance he would only go to places which he himself suggested, football matches for instance because he was interested in football or pubs because he liked to drink. She would have much preferred to visit museums and art galleries but he didn't like that so she had remained silent about her preferences. If once in a while they did go to an art gallery he would fidget and make rude remarks about the paintings. One thing she did discover during their relationship. At the beginning of it she liked representational paintings, at the end she preferred surrealist ones.

Before she started going out with him she had idealistic illusions about love and marriage. She wanted to have children, but legitimately. She imagined herself staying at home looking after the garden and watching her children playing among the flowers while he earned their living. But in fact he let the shop go to ruin and lived extravagantly because his mother would do anything for him and never saw any of his faults. His mother was a woman with blue rinsed hair who played cards a lot.

So that episode had ended ingloriously and the worst of it was that her ideas about love and marriage had been irretrievably soured. If ever a man showed any intention of taking her out she would analyse his motives quite coolly and in the end decide that she would prefer to be on her own. All the passion had been drained out of her. Most of the time after school she stayed in the house and prepared her lessons for the following day. She transferred all her love to her pupils who were all young children. And of course her parents were growing old. Her father had a stroke one day after he had been out working in the garden on a very hot summer's day. Her mother had great difficulty tending him since she didn't want to send him to hospital and eventually she herself had fallen ill. Her father had died first and then her mother and then she was left alone.

After the initial grief which had lasted for a long time she had felt free. She thought that with the money which she had carefully saved she would go to places that she had only read about but which she felt that she ought to visit. There would be no one peering over her shoulder, no one wondering when she would come home at night, she could come and go as she pleased. She had always wanted to go to Greece because she couldn't believe that places such as Parnassus had ever existed or that Homer had ever lived. She could believe in the existence of all other places but not the places in Greece. But in fact she had cancelled her reservations because when it came to the point she couldn't go alone. She had however gone to places nearer home and hadn't enjoyed her holidays at all in spite of her freedom.

Gradually she came to the conclusion that total freedom is an unmitigated evil. There ought to be someone waiting up for one, there ought to be someone with whom one could communicate, even quarrel. But there was no one. She found herself moving in the world like a shadow. And she didn't visit much. There was no one really she wanted to visit and she felt that people might be sorry for her. So she tended to stay in the house a great deal. At first she passed the time by reading but this soured on her. Later she would knit and sew a lot but after a while she thought there was no particular reason for that either. Then she took to going to night classes and she would attend courses such as 'Pre-Raphaelitism' and 'Inflation and How to Deal with it'. But she found the same small earnest women at these courses, not understanding what the lecturer was saying, but only going there because they couldn't bear to stay in the house. And so she had stopped going to these courses as well.

But the long summer holidays were the biggest problem of all. She couldn't stay at home then all the time. She had to go away for a while and therefore she usually took a holiday of about a week. Before she left she carefully turned off the water and the electricity and worried sometimes even after she had reached her destination whether the fire or the immersion had been left on. She was very careful with the doorkey, which she hung round her neck. One of her greatest nightmares was to find herself at the door and not be able to find her key. Once she had left the house lights on all night after going to bed, and a neighbour in the block of flats opposite had come over in the morning wondering if there was anything wrong. They did think about her and they did worry about her. But of course they couldn't be expected to understand what it was to be lonely.

She came out of the cinema, not waiting for the cartoon (she didn't like cartoons) and went outside again. The sun was still hot and there were still as many people on the street as there had been before. It was only eight o'clock and she didn't want to go back to the hotel as early as that. People in hotels noticed you and summed you up, even receptionists. For instance that young girl had asked her if she had a car and she had to confess that she hadn't. Things like that marked you out, made you different. And the more there were of these absences, of these differences, the more wary people became of you. If there were enough differences they would avoid you altogether.

She made her way to the Gardens and sat down on a bench. Even as late as this – eight o'clock in the evening – the sun was still hot though not intolerably so. She sat in the shadow of a tree on a bench on which no one else was sitting. She crossed her legs and automatically pulled her skirt down. Her skirt was of medium length, there was no point in her wearing one of those very short skirts. And she simply watched the people passing. There were young couples with their arms round each other, an Indian girl of quite astonishing beauty who wore clothes the colour of a peacock, accompanied by two grave children – a girl and a boy – who also wore very bright clothes and looked like two perfect statues walking. They wore yellow socks, red shoes and lilac jerseys. A lone Negro went past and a boy on the back of whose blouse was written the number and name *15784 Pentonville*. Two small girls rolled on the grass till the park-keeper blew a whistle and when he began to stride towards them they ran away. On the bench next to hers an oldish woman was sitting by herself throwing bread to the fat blue pigeons who waddled towards her, interrupted now and then by diminutive birds which would fly away with large morsels almost as big as themselves.

It occurred to her that most of her life she had been watching other people pass by as if she herself had no life but were the spectator of the lives of others. Other people often astonished her. So many of them walked instinctively into the future without thinking as if they expected that the water would buoy them up and that nothing would ever happen to them that they could not foresee. They accepted the motions of the present in a way that she could never do. They laughed and played in a forgetfulness which they seemed to be able to summon at will. For instance, she herself found it difficult to sit still on the bench. She wanted to walk about and at that moment she did so. She took a path which deviated from the main road and again sat under a tree. Here it was darker and there was more vegetation, truncated tree trunks and so on. It was some time before she noticed that only a few yards away from her a boy naked to the waist was lying on top of a girl who was also naked to the waist. It was some time too before she pulled her eyes away from them: not that she found the sign disgusting but that she wondered what it was like. She felt stirring within her a motion of regret, an irretrievable absence. But she got up again in case they would see her looking at them and went back to where she had been before.

She took out a magazine which she began to read. It was a romantic magazine which had stories of love found and lost in hospitals, factories and offices. This was her secret vice. She thought of herself as an intellectual who would attend concerts, the better films and plays, but who would never descend to reading trashy love stories. And yet this was what she was doing. And also she was looking up her sign in the horoscope to find out what was to happen to her. She was in fact Capricorn, remote, cold, miserly, determined. She read quickly but with only half her mind. The park was so beautiful, so crowded with people, and she was so alone. An old unshaven man who carried a paper bag sat down at the end of her bench. He slumped forward, his hands on his knees, staring down at the ground. Beside him on the bench he had placed an old greasy cap. His lips mumbled some words which he was apparently addressing to himself. She couldn't make out what he was saying. Eventually he got up and this time she heard him say, 'Bugger everything, bugger everything,' as if it were some meaningful litany. She drew in her legs as he passed her. Then she put down her book and watched the children playing.

She liked children. Since her parents died she often thought that it was the children who had saved her. They were so nice, so innocent, so willing to learn, so willing to engage themselves in plays, concerts, projects, so alive and so loving. She believed that her own mother had never liked children. She herself had been born – she worked out – when her father had been unemployed and when her mother must have been very worried about the future. The coldness of her own personality must have been because her mother had never lavished enough love upon her. Surely that must be the reason. What other reason could there be?

But perhaps the reason why she liked children was that she wanted to mould them to be like herself. Was that it? No, it couldn't be that. Children were so spontaneous, perhaps it was their very spontaneity that she loved. They would come up to her and tell her stories of what had happened to them, and she would listen attentively. They wrote nice little poems which had fine feeling and a directness which moved her. She was lucky in a way to have them. And yet there was something which she was missing. She couldn't think what it was but it was something which kept reality at a remove from her as if she were looking at it through a plate glass window. Children weren't like that. Children moved unselfconsciously through reality.

Her father had that kind of unselfconsciousness. He would sit down in a chair and seem able to endure time without terror. He would move about in a very slow heavy manner as if he were at home in the world. He would eat carefully as if he were drawing from what he ate sustenance for some work which it was necessary for him to do. He talked little and slowly. He would look out of the window and say, 'It's going to be a good day,' and in some way the statement seemed final and exact. He never discussed anything profound or philosophical. Her mother from that point of view was the same. But she was also much more ambitious, much more jagged and edgy. She had even gone to see her daughter capped at the university though she had never been such a long distance from home before. She herself had tried to stop her from going in case she would utter idiocies to her friends but she hadn't in fact done so and had behaved very circumspectly. She had also, strangely enough, chosen the right clothes to wear.

But her mother had said something to her once which she remembered. 'I don't know what will happen to you if you are ever left alone.' She remembered this as if it were some prophecy of disaster.

She put down her book and got up. It was time to return to the hotel. In the hotel there were some sandwiches and tea laid on a table in the lounge. She took some tea but no sandwiches and sat for a bit watching the TV. The only other people in the room were an old man with a white moustache and his wife who sat on the sofa together, not speaking, gazing at the screen with the same kind of look as they might have had if they were looking at fish in an aquarium. The screen seemed to be showing a gangster story for shortly after she sat down a small thin quivering man was shot and the seeping blood reddened the screen. After a while she got up and looked at some magazines which were lying around. One was the *Scottish Field*, another the *Countryside*. There was an unfinished crossword which she looked at without much interest. At one time she had used to do a lot of crosswords but she had given that up.

As she sat there, there came to her the extraordinary feeling that she had ceased to live properly, that at some time she had left a road and was slowly going down a side track where she would find herself on abandoned sidings among old railway carriages in a blaze of yellow flowers. For a moment she suffered intense panic but then the panic subsided and the two old people were still there watching the TV as silently as ever.

Her father hardly ever watched TV. When someone switched it on he went outside and did some job. Her mother would watch it avidly. Sometimes she used to think that the announcers were smiling at her when they signed off for the night. She even seemed to have fallen in love with the man who did the weather forecast. Her face suddenly became school-girlish and illuminated by an autumnal pathos.

When her father had died her mother had acted very practically, doing all the necessary things but then, after all the business was over, relapsing into herself. She seemed to lose all her energy and would fall asleep in the chair even at midday. She also gave up cooking as if all those years she had really been cooking for her husband and for no one else, her husband who had done everything she had wanted him to do, who had never drunk even though he worked in a distillery, who had always been there, quiet, silent and strong. She had ceased visiting people's houses. She had even ceased to watch TV and would say, 'What rubbish they are showing there.'

Two large blue policemen burst into a red room and there

were gun shots. She rose and went to her room. She took off her clothes, laying them down on the chair, and then got into bed. She took out a paperback and began to read it. One of the things she had always dreaded was that she would become an insomniac but in fact she slept quite well. One of the teachers in her school was an insomniac. His name was Ross and he had told her that he only slept an average of an hour a night. He would stay up most of the night making tea and reading. He had got through the whole of Dostoevsky and Tolstoy in one spell of six months. Now he was getting to work on Dickens. She couldn't imagine what it would be like to be an insomniac. She was sure she would go off her head but thanked God that at least she could sleep at nights. She looked at her watch which told her that it was ten o'clock. She closed the book and then her eyes, even though outside she could hear quite clearly the roar of the traffic and somewhere in the hotel the sound of conversation and crockery and trays. She fell asleep almost immediately.

She dreamed that she was in a park full of Greek statues of boys with short cropped hair like American athletes. In the middle of the night the statues began to move and to dance as if during the day they had been waiting patiently so that they could do precisely that. Their hollow eyes assumed expression and intelligence, they moved as if to a music which she herself could not hear. All round them bits of paper and other litter as well as fallen leaves swirled in a wind which had blown up. In the storm of leaves the statues remained solid and the expressions on the faces were both smiling and cruel as if they belonged to a royal supercilious race which despised the human. Then she saw in her dream the park-keeper unlocking the gate and the statues became immobile and blank again.

The following morning she woke new and refreshed and in the blaze of white sunlight that illuminated the room felt inexplicably the same kind of large hope that she used to feel when she was a girl, when suddenly she would throw off the bed-clothes and walk about the silent house as if waiting for something dramatic to happen.

She washed quickly and went down to her breakfast. The

waitress was an old woman with a limp who had a pleasant smile, and asked her whether she would like one egg or two as if she really wanted to give her the two. When she had finished her breakfast she went outside, her handbag over her shoulder. The morning was still cool and she felt confident and happy as she walked along. She knew exactly what she was going to do. She would tour the High Street and look at the museums and other sights and she might even have a look at the Castle later.

All around her she could see the crenellated outlines of old houses, solid and heavy, houses that had been in existence for centuries and between which were lanes and steps that had known many secrecies which at the time appeared trembling and immediate. She could see the spires of large churches that had seen many congregations which had flowed into them and flowed out again in their changing dresses. She found herself on ancient winding stairs at which people had once stood and talked in their short red flaring cloaks. The whole area was a place of romance and mystery. She walked up the steps till she arrived at a library which was advertising an exhibition of old manuscripts. She entered and went into a room which was off to the right and in which a man in blue uniform was sitting at a desk looking rather bored. He said good morning and turned back to whatever he was doing. She walked around looking at the old manuscripts, most of them beautiful illuminated Bibles such as she had never seen before. The pages were embellished with colourful Virgin Marys, green fields, and omnipresent angels. She couldn't read the writing, most of which appeared to be in Latin. In one section she saw Mary, Queen of Scots' last letter written in ancient French in which she seemed not to show so much fear as an imperious hauteur. But it was the lovely illuminated Bibles with their populace of angels that captivated her. What patience and faith and sense of vocation these monks must have had to create these works! She imagined them in gardens, surrounded by trees inhabited by birds, painstakingly drawing and painting. She compared their colours to those of the TV screen and smiled to herself. The world which they revealed seemed so natural and so real though in fact the angels were descending on to the earth that we know. One showed

Sarah, Abraham's wife, being greeted by the two young men who were really angels and the whole picture was so ordinary and almost banal and everyday that it comforted her. Imagine a time when angels came to talk to human beings in such an unremarkable manner, descending and ascending ladders that led from heaven to earth like painters on the street. She thought what her mother would have said. 'Nothing but candles and masses,' she would have said. 'Heathenism.'

As she was going out the old librarian was standing at the door. He said, 'We have millions of books here. Millions. Down below,' he said, pointing.

'Do any of them ever get stolen?' she asked.

'Sometimes,' he said. 'We have a lot of manuscripts here. Some valuable ones get stolen.'

'I suppose a lot of them go to America,' she said.

'They go where the money is. But I don't know much about that.' They talked for a little longer and then she went out into the sunshine.

She continued down the long street. After a while she came to a museum and went inside after she had paid ten pence. She stayed for some time at a case which showed old spectacles worn by people in the past. One pair reminded her of the ones her grandmother used to wear when she visited her as a child. She remembered her grandmother as a twinkling old woman who seemed always to be sitting knitting at a window looking out on to a field full of flowers and inhabited by one wandering cow with soft resentful eyes. As she looked at the spectacles she seemed to see her grandmother again holding a needle up to her eyes and peering through her steel-rimmed glasses.

She left the case with the glasses and had a look at one with old coins, and later one with old stones which were labelled with the name of the finders. There were also ancient stone axes and stone jewellery.

There was a case which showed a wild cat with its claws sunk in the dead body of a rabbit, and another one of a large eagle with flashing yellow eyes. In a corner there were some old guns. There were powder horns richly decorated and domestic implements of various kinds.

One section had a complete reconstruction in shaded orange light of a cottage of the nineteenth century. There was an old woman wearing a shawl sitting on a chair looking into a peat fire. In one corner there was a herring barrel and in another a creel. There was an old clock on a mantelpiece and an iron grille for holding oat cakes. There were old candles and by the fire an old teapot and kettle. Beside the old woman there was a cradle with a doll lying in it imitating a sleeping child. There was a churn and a dressing table. There was a flail and a table. The old woman, long-nosed and shawled, seemed to be dreaming as she looked into the imitation fire. Again she was reminded of her grandmother as this woman too had a pair of spectacles on her nose.

How long ago it all was. How apparently calm it had all been. How pastoral and tranquil that existence behind glass. Had it really been like that? Day after day of peaceful existence without challenge, surrounded by the furniture and routine of a life without significant history. If she broke the glass and entered that world how would she find it? Would she find it peaceful or boring, a world without radio or TV or ballet or art or music, but a world with children and animals and work? How much one could lack and how much one could have. Faintly in the distance she heard the roar of the traffic. What about her own mother? Had she been happy in her routine? She didn't think so, though her father had apparently been. Did she love her father more than she loved her mother? She couldn't say: perhaps they were both part of her, the restless and the tranquil. The fire flamed in front of the old woman showing a red landscape. What was she thinking of as she looked into it? What a strange motionless world really. What a distant motionless world.

She turned away and went outside again. She sat down on a bench and rested in the coolness of the morning.

Men and women were going in and coming out of a bar opposite but she herself never went into a bar alone. At one time she used to go to pubs with Phil and she would sit there sipping a tomato juice. She never said much but Phil was always the centre of attention, open and generous. Not that he was particularly witty, he was just energetic and lively. She sometimes wondered whether this was what was important in life, energy, but at other times she thought that it was courage that was important. Phil wasn't particularly courageous. In fact in many ways he was weak. She had heard that he had left the shop and gone off to London and wasn't doing very well there. He was the kind of person who would become very dull and complaining when he felt that his youth was over, she was sure of that.

She decided that she would go to the Castle after all, since there was nothing else to do. She got up and walked slowly up the brae and when she got to the entrance bought her ticket and joined the queue which was waiting for the guide to take them round. Standing at the gate were two soldiers dressed in tartan trews who, with rifles beside them, stared unwinkingly ahead of them as if they were mechanical dolls. The guide who was carrying a stick and who looked like an ex-sergeant major – strong and red-cheeked – led them off. She half listened to his practised commentary, watching the people ahead of her, most of them foreign. There was a Japanese girl and a boy, some crew-cut Americans, a group who spoke German and a Frenchman with a moustache. The guide told them about the defences of the castle and she thought that every day he would be making the same speech and stopping at the same places for laughter. He made a few jokes about the English and she saw some people laughing: she thought that they were probably English.

After a while she left the party and entered a small chapel which was dedicated to St Margaret. There was a portrait of her in colour with folded hands set in the window, and a Bible on the table. She had a certain tranquillity about her such as she had already seen in the illuminated manuscripts. What was a saint? she wondered. How did one become a saint? Was it when all anger left one, when all passion was drained away, when one was utterly transparent and all life moved in front of one as in pictures? And were saints saints all the time, or only at particular moments?

She left the chapel and went into the museum which contained all sorts of stuff, uniforms, helmets, guns. She stayed for a long time staring at a black Prussian cap which was shaped like a skull. Once she saw the uniform of a British soldier which had a charred hole in the breast where the bullet had entered. There were pictures on the wall of battle scenes. One showed a British soldier in the act of driving his sword through a French standard bearer at Waterloo. She shuddered. What was it like to kill a man with a sword? It would be easier to do it with a gun. She couldn't imagine herself killing anyone with bare steel, it would be an impossibility.

She wandered about studying waterbottles, guns, powder-horns, armour. She read the names of those who had been killed in wars and read the memorial to the unknown dead. She had a look at the Scottish jewellery, the Honours of Scotland. It looked tawdrier than she expected.

When she came out she sat down on a bench near the black cannon wondering what she would do next. From where she was sitting she could look down into the mouths of the cannon and above them the roofs of the city, on which gangs had written with chalk words like groovy and so on. Eventually she got up and left the Castle and walked down the brae and into a restaurant where she had her lunch.

It was two o'clock when she came out and she was at a loss what to do next. She thought that perhaps she might go and sit in the Gardens. So that was what she did. She sat on a bench and half read a book and half snoozed. There were a number of people on the putting green and others lying in the sun, their arms about each other, while in the Pavilion a religious singer sang with great fervour a song about Jesus's saving blood.

All around her was movement and laughter. She tried to concentrate on her book, which was a paperback copy of *Rebecca*, but she couldn't, and finally she laid it down. It was as if she was feeling a change coming over her, a mutation, but she couldn't imagine what it was and she felt dizzy and slightly frightened. She got up again and walked over to the Information Bureau which was quite near. She discovered that there was a play on that night and decided that she would go. It was about Hitler but she didn't know what to expect. Time passed very slowly. She bought an evening paper but most of it seemed to be about cricket and tennis. There was, however, a story about a man and his wife who had picked up a hitch-hiker in their car. After they had been travelling for some time the hitch-hiker had dragged the wife into a wood threatening the husband that if he said anything he would kill him. She nodded over the paper and fell asleep. When she woke up it seemed to be cooler and the place slightly more empty. She got up and went along for her tea. It was now five o'clock.

It occurred to her as she walked along that she ought to have more friends, people she could go and stay with. The previous summer she had actually gone to stay with a friend of hers, a college friend called Joan, who had recently married. But she had found the stay constricting and tedious as Joan had become very dull and respectable and responsible since her marriage, and she had left earlier than she had intended. It was odd how people changed. Before her marriage Joan had been very gay and exciting; now she looked as if she were carrying the weight of the whole world on her shoulders. She also worried a lot about money though her husband had a good job and was making at least three thousand a year.

She went into a restaurant and had some tea. By this time she was almost getting tired of eating. After her tea, which she prolonged till half past five, she went down and sat in the station waiting-room for a while, till the play would begin. She thought about being married and being single. When one was married there were all sorts of things one had to do: the world became untidy. One had to adjust to a husband, then one had to cope with noisy children. She could do this all right in the school because the children she taught were not her own. She saw them to a certain extent at their best, not when they were screaming for attention, or harassing one when one was tired. On the other hand, to be single was not a particularly good state to be in. One gradually lost contact with people unless one was one of those women who served on committees or started art clubs or went to church with flowered hats or made endless jars of preserves.

She sat on a leather seat in the waiting room as if she were waiting for a train. She could imagine herself going to London or any other part of Britain. Better still would be an airport lounge: there one could imagine oneself going to Europe or Africa or Asia. She had only been on a plane once and it had been just like being on a bus, not at all exciting, just looking out of a window and seeing banks of white clouds below one.

It was funny how she fell asleep so often nowadays if she sat down for a long time. Perhaps that was a good thing: on the other hand it might mean that there was something wrong with her. It might be psychological also. She ought really to try and keep awake.

She read some of her book and then went out and walked about the station. She noticed a number of telephone kiosks some of which had been smashed and had gang slogans written on them in chalk. The dangling useless phones somehow looked symbolic. The unharmed booths were occupied by people talking excitedly into black mouthpieces.

Everywhere she went it was the same, people talking to each other, laughing, gesturing, sometimes shouting at each other, as once she had seen a gipsy and his wife quarrelling. It had ended with the man hitting his wife across the face so that blood poured out of her lip. A bony dog barked at their heels and in the background smoke rose slowly out of their camp.

You never saw so many gipsies now. Her mother would never give them anything when they came whining to the door, nor would she listen to the Jehovah's Witnesses who tried to hand out what she called heathenish magazines. Her mother would get rid of such people briskly and effectively. She herself would listen to them in an embarrassed manner while they, that is the religious people, would talk about Darwin and God, referring closely like automata to verses in the Bible. Invariably she bought one of their magazines which her mother would immediately throw in the bin.

As she sat in the waiting-room, watching through the window trains coming and going, pictures of all kinds passed before her eyes. She remembered a holiday she had once had in a desolate glen in the Highlands. She could visualise clearly the mountains veined with stone, the deer that grazed by fences, the foaming rivers, the abandoned cottages, the blaze of yellow gorse, the horses nuzzling each other on the sands. She had liked that place. It seemed suited to her personality. But one day she had seen, sitting in front of a caravan, a large fat lady dressed in red trousers and painting the glen, and the illusion of contentment had been destroyed.

At five past seven she started to walk to the theatre. Now that she had an aim she was happy but at the same time she thought that she would have difficulty in filling the hours of the following day. She had already exhausted quite a lot of the sights she had intended to see, unless perhaps she went on a bus tour. She would have to check on that in the morning, or perhaps they had a brochure in the hotel.

Her feet were already getting sore as she had done a lot of walking but she didn't want to spend money on a taxi. She didn't like taxis. They reminded her of hearses and she was always sure she was being cheated. They would always take one the long way round and she was sure the drivers recognised strangers to the town instinctively.

At twenty past seven she reached the theatre which was a very small one, seating perhaps sixty people or so, on cushions round the central area which formed the stage. There were strong lights blazing down which made the place hot: she imagined interrogations taking place there in a concentrated hot dazzle. She had bought a programme which gave very little information about the actual play: all that she gathered was that it seemed very avant garde. She didn't know what exactly to expect, perhaps a dramatisation of the rise of Hitler, with reference to the SS and the Jews and the concentration camps. She didn't often go to the theatre, preferring the cinema, but there was nothing else on that evening. She also didn't like avant-garde stuff.

She noticed that the audience was predominantly youthful, girls wearing slacks and Indian headbands, most of them probably students. The theatre was a small and intimate one and she could hear some of them talking in a brittle knowledgeable way before the play started. She sat in the front row on her cushion wishing that it was a chair and feeling rather tired because there was no support for her back.

It was certainly not a conventional play. It began with a sinister music on drums which went on and on, exerting a hypnotic dark rhythm. In a mirror high above she could see the drummers with their long hair reflected. Then a young man came into the central space and stood there motionless for a long time while the music played.

Suddenly he became a dying German soldier with glazed eyes, greatcoat, rifle and dull boots. Children came in and danced around him, among them a girl who appeared to be a spastic. The beating drums seemed to draw one into the dying festering mind of the German soldier by their rhythmic compulsion, as he was slowly resurrected, pulling himself to his feet against the wind of death and the beat of the drums. He made an appointment with the spastic girl who at night went into a wood to meet him, the dead German soldier. The lights all dimmed, there was only the wood created by the words, and the girl trying to find the German soldier on her macabre tryst, while the music played, the music of dark Nazism, the music of the terrible haunted wood, where everything was eerie and festering, and the animals crawled and killed. The scene was electrifying. It made her feel excited and disgusted at the same time, that wood where all desires were waiting, buried, but rising as if reflected in the manic glasses of the murdering German soldier. The girl crawled into the wood. The music quickened and then there was the interval, a sane blaze of lights.

She stood up, shaken. She hardly knew where she was. She left the theatre knowing that she couldn't bear to watch. She walked out into the hurting daylight. She walked down the brae steadily till she came to the park again. There she sat down on a bench among all the people. Behind her she could hear the tolling of a church bell. Ahead of her she could see the glasshouse where all the flowers were – the wide red flowers – and the plants, the Mexican cacti which she had once seen and which could exist on so little water.

She sat on the bench and as she did so she thought to herself: I can't bear this total freedom any more. I can't, I can't. I don't know what to do. I cannot live like this. She got up restlessly and walked into the wood. She looked down at a stretch of water where the polluted river flowed past. There were some boys wearing towels round their waists who seemed to have just emerged from the dirty stream, which was not at all like the clean streams to which she herself had been accustomed and where you could see right down to the bottom where the white stones were.

As she stood there she saw a little girl in checked skirt and checked blouse walking into the wood by herself to pick flowers. Dazed she watched her. To her right she could hear the shouting of the boys. Without knowing precisely what she was doing she began to follow the little girl. As she did so she was amazed to discover that a transformation had taken place in her as if she had found a role which she could perform, as if the total freedom had narrowed and come to a focus. She didn't know what she was going to do but it was as if she felt it right whatever it would turn out to be. She followed the little girl into the wood.

The Crater

In the intervals of inaction it had been decided by the invisible powers that minor raids were feasible and therefore to be recommended. In the words of the directive: 'For reasons known to you we are for the moment acting on the defensive so far as serious operations are concerned but this should not preclude the planning of local attacks on a comparatively small scale . . . '

Like the rest of his men on that particular night, Lieutenant Robert Mackinnon blackened his face so that in the dugout eyes showed white, as in a Black Minstrel show. He kept thinking how similar it all was to a play in which he had once taken part, and how the jokes before the performance had the same nervous high-pitched quality, as they prepared to go out into the darkness. There was Sergeant Smith who had been directed to write home to the next of kin to relate the heroism of a piece of earth which had been accidentally shattered by shrapnel. His teeth grinned whitely beneath his moustache as he adjusted the equipment of one of the privates and joked, 'Tomorrow you might get home, lad.' They all knew what that meant and they all longed for a minor wound – nothing serious – which would allow them to be sent home honourably. And yet Smith himself had been invalided home and come back. 'I missed your stink, lads,' he had said when he appeared among them again, large and buoyant and happy. And everyone knew that this was his place where he would stay till he was killed or till the war ended.

'I remember,' he used to tell them, 'we came to this house once. It was among a lot of trees, you understand. I don't know their names so don't ask me. Well, the house was rotten with Boche and we'd fired at it all day. And the buggers fired back. Towards evening – it might have been 1800 hours – they stopped firing and it got so quiet you could hear yourself breathing. One of our blokes – a small madman from Wales, I think it was – dashed across and threw a grenade or two in the door and the window. And there wasn't a sound from inside the house, 'part from the explosion of course, so he kept shouting, "The Boche are off, lads," in that sing-song Welsh of his. So we all rushed the place and true enough they'd mostly gone. Run out of ammunition, I suppose. We went over it for mines but there wasn't none. So we stood in the hall, I suppose you'd call it, all of us with our dirty great boots and our rifles and bayonets and there was these stairs going up, very wide. The windows were shot to hell and there was glass all over the place. And suddenly – this is God's truth – an old woman come down the stairs. Dressed in white she was, a lovely dress like you'd see in a picture. And her lips all painted red. You'd think she was dressed for a ball. Her eyes were queer, they seemed to go right through you as if you wasn't there. She came down the last steps and our officer stepped forward to help her. And do you know what she did? She put her arms around him and she started to waltz. He was so surprised he didn't know what to do – the fat bugger. And all the time there was this music. Well, in the end he got away from her and some people took her away. Well, we could still hear this music, see? So we goes upstairs – there was a dead Boche on the landing, he'd been shot in the mouth – and we goes into this room. There was a bed there with a pink what-do-you-call-it over it. And beside the bed there was this big dead Boche. And do you know what – there was a dagger with jewels in it stuck in his breastbone. And beside him on the floor there was this phonograph playing a French tune, one of the officers said. He said it was a dance tune. Someone said it was bloody lucky the little fat fellow wasn't wearing a grey uniform.'

'All present and correct, sir,' said Sergeant Smith.

'All right, let's go then,' said Lieutenant Mackinnon.

Down the trench they went, teeth and eyes grinning, clattering over the duckboards with their Mills bombs and their bayonets and their guns. 'What am I doing here?' thought Robert, and

'Who the hell is making that noise?' and 'Is the damned wire cut or not?' and 'We are like a bunch of actors,' and 'I'm leading these men, I'm an officer.'

And he thought again, 'I hope the guns have cut that barbed wire.'

Then he and they inched across No Man's Land following the line of lime which had been laid to guide them. Up above were the stars and the air was cool on their faces. But there were only a few stars, the night was mostly dark, and clouds covered the moon. Momentarily he had an idea of a huge mind breeding thought after thought, star after star, a mind which hid in daylight in modesty or hauteur but which at night worked out staggering problems, pouring its undifferentiated power over the earth.

On hands and knees he squirmed forward, the others behind him. This was his first raid and he thought, 'I am frightened.' But it was different from being out in the open on a battlefield. It was an older fear, the fear of being buried in the earth, the fear of wandering through eternal passageways and meeting grey figures like weasels and fighting with them in the darkness. He tested the wire. Thank God it had been cut. And then he thought, 'Will we need the ladders?' The sides of the trenches were so deep sometimes that ladders were necessary to get out again. And as he crawled towards the German trenches he had a vision of Germans crawling beneath British trenches undermining them. A transparent imagined web hung below him in the darkness quivering with grey spiders.

He looked at his illuminated watch. The time was right. Then they were in the German trenches. The rest was a series of thrustings and flashes. Once he thought he saw or imagined he saw from outside a dugout a man sitting inside reading a book. It was like looking through a train window into a house before the house disappears. There were Mills bombs, hackings of bayonets, scurryings and breathings as of rats. A white face towered above him, his pistol exploded and the face disappeared. There was a terrible stink all around him, and the flowing of blood. Then there was a long silence. Back. They must get back. He passed the order along. And then they wriggled back again avoiding the craters which lay around them, created by shells, and which were full of slimy water. If they fell into one of these they would be drowned. As he looked, shells began to fall into them sending up huge spouts of water. Over the parapet. They were over the parapet. Crouched they had run and scrambled and were over. Two of them were carrying a third. They stumbled down the trench. There were more wounded than he had thought. Wright . . . one arm seemed to have been shot off. Sergeant Smith was bending over him. 'You'll get sent home all right,' he was saying. Some of the men were tugging at their equipment and talking feverishly. Young Ellis was lying down, blood pouring from his mouth. Harris said, 'Morrison's in the crater.'

He and Sergeant Smith looked at each other. They were both thinking the same: there is no point, he's had it. They could see each other's eyes glaring whitely through the black, but could not tell the expression on the faces. The shells were still falling, drumming and shaking the earth. All these craters out there, these dead moons.

'Do you know which one?' said Robert.

'I think so, sir, I . . . Are you going to get him?'

'Sergeant Smith, we'll need our rifles. He can hang on to that if he's there. Harris, come with us.' They were all looking at him with sombre black faces, Wright divided between joy and pain.

'Sir.'

Then they were at the parapet again, shells exploding all around them.

'Which one is it?' And the stars were now clearer. Slowly they edged towards the rim. How had he managed to break away from the white lime?

They listened like doctors to a heartbeat.

'Are you there, Fred?' Harris whispered fiercely, as if he were in church. 'Are you there?' Lights illuminated their faces. There was no sound.

'Are you sure this is the right one?' Robert asked fiercely.

'I thought it was. I don't know.'

'Oh, Christ,' said Sergeant Smith.

'We'd better get back then,' said Robert.

'Are you going to leave him, sir?' said Harris.

'We can't do anything till morning. He may be in one of the shallower ones.' His cry of 'Morrison, are you there?' was drowned by the shriek of a shell.

'Back to the trench again,' he said, and again they squirmed along. But at that moment as they approached the parapet he seemed to hear it, a cry coming from deep in the earth around him, or within him, a cry of such despair as he had never heard in his life before. And it seemed to come from everywhere at once, from all the craters, their slimy green rings, from one direction, then from another. The other two had stopped as well to listen.

Once more he heard it. It sounded like someone crying 'Help'.

He stopped. 'All right,' he said. 'We're going for him. Come on.'

And he stood up. There was no reason for crawling any more. The night was clear. And they would have to hurry. And the other two stood up as well when they saw him doing so. He couldn't leave a man to die in the pit of green slime. 'We'll run,' he said. And they ran to the first one and listened. They cried fiercely, 'Are you there?' But there was no answer. Then they seemed to hear it from the next one and they were at that one soon too, peering down into the green slime, illuminated by moonlight. But there was no answer. There was one left and they made for that one. They screamed again, in the sound of the shells, and they seemed to hear an answer. They heard what seemed to be a bubbling. 'Are you there?' said Robert, bending down and listening. 'Can you get over here?' They could hear splashing and deep below them breathing, frantic breathing as if someone was frightened to death. 'It's all right,' he said, 'if you come over here, I'll send my rifle down. You two hang on to me,' he said to the others. He was terrified. That depth, that green depth. Was it Morrison down there, after all? He hadn't spoken. The splashings came closer. The voice was like an animal's repeating endlessly a mixture of curses and prayers. Robert hung over the edge of the crater. 'For Christ's sake don't let me go,' he said to the other two. It wasn't right that a man should die in green slime. He hung over the rim holding his rifle down. He felt it being caught, as if there was a great fish at the end of a line. He felt it moving. And the others hung at his heels, like a chain. The moon shone suddenly out between two clouds and in that moment he saw it, a body covered with greenish slime, an obscene mermaid, hanging on to his rifle while the two eyes, white in the green face, shone upward and the mouth, gritted, tried not to let the blood through. It was a monster of the deep, it was a sight so terrible that he nearly fell. He was about to say, 'It's no good, he's dying,' but something prevented him from saying it, if he said it then he would never forget it. He knew that. The hands clung to the rifle below in the slime. The others pulled behind him. 'For Christ's sake hang on to the rifle,' he said to the monster below. 'Don't let go.' And it seemed to be emerging from the deep, setting its feet against the side of the crater, all green, all mottled, like a disease. It climbed as if up a mountainside in the stench. It hung there against the wall. 'Hold on,' he said. 'Hold on.' His whole body was concentrated. This man must not fall down again into that lake. The death would be too terrible. The face was coming over the side of the crater, the teeth gritted, blood at the mouth. It hung there for a long moment and then the three of them had got him over the side. He felt like cheering, standing up in the light of No Man's Land and cheering. Sergeant Smith was kneeling down beside the body, his ear to the heart. It was like a body which might have come from space, green and illuminated and slimy. And over it poured the merciless moonlight.

'Come on,' he said to the other two. And at that moment Sergeant Smith said, 'He's dead.'

'Dead?' There was a long pause. 'Well, take him in anyway. We're not leaving him here. We'll take him in. At least he didn't die in that bloody lake.' They lifted him up between them and they walked to the trench. 'I'm bloody well not crawling,' said Robert. 'We'll walk. And to hell with the lot of them.' He couldn't prevent himself swearing and at the same time despising himself for swearing. What would Sergeant

Smith think of him? It was like bringing a huge green fish back
to the lines. 'To hell with them,' he shouted. 'This time we'll
bloody well walk. I don't care how light it is.' And they did so
and managed to get him back into the dugout. They laid him
down on the floor and glared around them at the silent men.

'Just like Piccadilly it was,' said Harris, who couldn't stop
talking. 'As bright as day.'

'Shut up, you lot,' said Sergeant Smith, 'and get some sleep.'

Robert was thinking of the man he had seen reading a book
in a flash of light before they had gone in with their bayonets.
He couldn't see properly whether it had been a novel or a
comic. Perhaps it was a German comic. Did Germans have
comics? Like that green body emerging out of the slime, that
fish. He began to shiver and said, 'Give the men whisky if there
is any.' But he fell asleep before he could get any himself,
seeing page after page of comics set before him, like red
windows, and in one there was a greenish monster and in
another a woman dancing with a fat officer. Overhead the
shells still exploded, and the water bounced now and again
from the craters.

'The bloody idiot,' said Sergeant Smith looking down at him.
'He could have got us all killed.' Still, it had been like Piccadilly
right enough. Full of light. It hadn't been so bad. Nothing was
as bad as you feared.

The Fight

He didn't dare to confront it, wriggling with piercing embarrassment into the tent poled by his thin legs and bony knees. The blankets hung warm and woollen from his arched bones to whom today had happened a disgrace so tremendous that his thought could not even edge sideways up to it without the terror of annihilation. Yet how could he prevent images from sidling into his shut eyes enveloped even in their second darkness. First there came the gloves against his petrified scream. But it didn't matter, the gloves still came – the brown glossy white furred gloves: he would never wear them again, that was certain. And yet they had been so neat and fine, fitting with a loud click on his pale hands. It had all started with the gloves which he had worn to school that day for the first time having tested their leather in the early morning when in his shivering joy he had crossed unshod and conspiratorially the cold green linoleum to build the fire and surprise them all. They had matched his brown shoes too: that was an unexpected gift. Though you couldn't throw stones with them you could walk gloved and delicate along the grassy verge of the road like an officer, a lieutenant certainly, a colonel possibly, except that you didn't have the thin whistling cane which swished and cut aristocratically through the icy air. Then inside them your hands felt so disciplined as if the fingers had gathered together out of some chaos, some sadness of shapelessness, into a fixed flesh that you could control and command.

And he had walked up the sideroad to the school where at the gate were assembled some of his classmates. And the whole thing had started because he was so happy and possessed, being by the time he reached school Joe Louis the murderous hooker with the brown polished fists and the crowd rising in a frenzy roaring and punching 'Come on, finish him off' so that in the brisk blue air he had begun to shadow box, his small tight nutty fists left-leading and right-crossing ceaselessly while his head swerved sideways from a slow but murderous opponent.

Then of course in his careless delight he had found himself face to face with the Section scowling in front of him with his screwed red face above his ragged blue jersey and his harsh rocky knees. He had led with a crisp checked left to the jutting chin and brought up his right till it halted exactly in the dirty circle in the centre of the blue jersey. And all the time the Section had stared at him without moving watching the new brown flickering gloves darting about his upright body like moths. The stocky body was rooted: the eyes were rooted: the heavy chin was rooted.

Then Merry had shouted: 'Look at the Fairy making rings round the Section,' and Plummy had said: 'Come on, Fairy, let's see you,' and his light beautiful footwork dazzled even himself as he merged into the music of his body, his gloves darting in and out, artistically, not ferociously, showing off, imperiously calling attention to Joe Louis created by ten thousand eyes, blown into being on ten thousand voices. 'Come on, Fairy, give it to him.' But the Section remained there unmoved as if watching a child dancing, his black hair waving faintly in the morning breeze, his eyes steady.

And then at the climax of the dance when all his feathers were turning red, fanning out all about him in music of colour he had actually hit the Section on the nose and the Section had looked at him at last. Some being had come shambling out of the cave in his eyes and was staring at him as if awakened across a bleak landscape. Even then it might have been all right if he had apologised but how could he when everybody was shouting: 'You should see the Fairy,' 'Why he's a boxer. He's a real boxer' – even though his knees were really melting to water as he looked into the unfolding eyes of the Section.

Then someone shouted: 'There's going to be a fight,' and because it was spoken it was certain.

'At four o'clock.'

'Out on the moor.'

'Behind the school.'

He could have apologised but he turned away saying nothing. And the Section stood there while the strange being stood taller and taller in front of the cave in his red eyes.

'At four o'clock.'

'You should have seen the Fairy.'

'He's a beautiful boxer.'

When he looked at them he could have sworn they were mocking him. He had never been so scared in his life.

All morning he became more and more scared. At the eleven o'clock interval he was speechlessly followed by four or five small boys who stared at him as if they expected him to begin boxing as they watched. Trailed by his fans, he walked round by the grey stone privy at the back of the school. He saw two girls clucking ahead of him, arm in arm, giggling, telling each other secrets. Perhaps they were joking about him. Everyone must know: he was opened out like a walking wound. If only they had fought right away instead of waiting like this. He imagined the Section lounging against a wall or bending his black composed head under the pouring water of the copper tap, an inverted animal. If only he could speak to him. He went into the privy. He read the names scratched on the walls, the initials, the rhymes. He read them over and over again. He passed the Section in the quadrangle as the huge iron bell tolled and tolled. They looked at each other but did not speak. How large he had become, with his raw red fists, his blue jersey like the sea covering a rock, his deadly savage eyes, the rending rage in his heart. But nothing could be done now, he thought, almost vomiting, ceremony had taken over. He was trapped.

At dinner time he felt sick. He could eat nothing. He wanted to be really sick so that he could stay off school. He looked at the safe book he was in the middle of reading with its beautiful crisp cover – *Oliver Twist*. He imagined himself running through the queer air of London, pursued.

It was so strange. Why should he not just stay away from school and listen to the noise the book made in his ear as he read and read throughout the night? He could have cursed himself. He looked through the window and saw a cornstack standing still and motionless on the ground. A fly crawled across the table. Some days he would put a knife in front of it vertically to see what it would do. Today he didn't, he let it crawl. He thought of the Section, ragged-trousered, reddening-eyed, stupid: for he was stupid, everybody said so. The teacher had once asked him: 'How much does a 2½d. stamp cost?' and he hadn't known. The class roared when they told the story. The Fairy however hadn't roared: he had simply hated the teacher. He pushed the plate away from him, to the end of the world. His mother said: 'Are you ill?' No, he wasn't ill. Anyway if he was he couldn't tell her this kind of sickness. She wouldn't understand.

The bell, ponderous and huge, iron and near, swung him into his corner on the windy moor. Grass stirred greyly in the wind. The ground was wet. Pushed by his unwanted supporters he found himself unreally standing in front of the Section. He couldn't understand what he was doing there: all he wanted was to get it over and done with and be home with his book. Someone was advising him to take his jacket off. He didn't: he wanted to be warm. He heard one boy beside him panting with excitement but didn't turn round to see who it was. There in front of him stood the Section, solidly, his jersey billowing in the cold wind. He was afraid to look into his face as if he would meet there some image which would finally destroy him. The ceremony had begun.

A phantom bell rang in his brain, coldly he went forward punch-drunk into the arena. Towards him came the panther with green eyes. On the balcony the beaming emperor turned his thumbs down fatly with sadistic deliberation. Something hit him on the nose. He was terrified. He would have run away but they had closed in on him, he felt their hound breaths: they were baying: there was blood on his glove. He looked up: the green eyes were boring in on him, animal eyes: they shone like stones. The nails on the hands were dirty: the flesh was raw.

A green figure was beating up a child on a London street. It was foggy. The boots came down heavily. He winced at the silver deliberate studs. Had he screamed? He slipped on the wet grass. The gloves had little hairs on them. They were soaked in the puddle.

He heard voices: 'Come on, Fairy, you're doing fine. Hit him.' He hadn't hit him: not once had he hit him. He didn't even want to hit him lest he provoke a stranger, more menacing, figure to shamble outward in front of the green cave. He wanted only to survive his punishment. He felt himself dancing like a puppet. The Section hadn't spoken once. He just kept unslinging his stony punches at him. He didn't dare to look at the eyes but he knew that the Section hated him. He felt this not by the way he hit him but by the service of some obscure sense, some old retainer of knowledge beyond that of the intellect.

'Come on, Fairy.' His gloves and body made beautiful ineffectual rings, away from oftener than towards. Let me not be hit: let me snuggle into my book, let me withdraw.

He hadn't really been punched much except for the one accurate hit on the nose. There was too much disorderly shoving and pushing for that. He heard one voice saying disgustedly: 'It's a slaughter. It should be stopped.' And heard another voice saying: 'The Fairy will get him yet. You wait.' Nevertheless he knew that he wouldn't win. He felt a hard fist hit him in the stomach and he lay down.

'Is he all right?'

'Of course he's all right. Aren't you, Fairy?'

'Really and truly hopeless.'

'Is he crying? O Lord.'

'No, he's not.'

'All right, pick him up then.'

And they had lifted him up, cold cold hands. Someone had said: 'Are you all right?': he had said yes and the moor emptied.

He waited perhaps for the Section to come back and shake hands with him (wasn't that always done?) but everyone had gone: he hadn't fought well enough for even that. As he waited phantom hands came to lead the blind punch-drunk loser home: he would never fight again: he was finished: he should never have fought. His friends had pleaded with him not to fight; but he could not let them down. How could he? They had bet on him thousands and thousands of dollars. The ring was empty: the seats ascended rawly from the centre. The emperor stood up: he was great and glowing, magnanimous, a ruby glittered on his white toga. He was in tears. The Christians would be pardoned, he said, looking down at the prostrate but courageous gladiator. His immaculate gloved hands rested lightly in front of him. The lights darkened and the Christian in his cave in his blue tunic wriggled inwards towards his content.

In Church

Lieutenant Colin Macleod looked up at the pure blue sky where there was a plane cruising overhead. He waved to the helmeted pilot. Here behind the lines the sound of the gunfire was faint and one could begin to use one's ears again, after the tremendous barrages which had seemed to destroy hearing itself. Idly he registered that the plane was a Vickers Gun Bus and he could see quite clearly the red, white and blue markings. The smoke rising in the far distance seemed to belong to another war. He had noticed often before how unreal a battle might become, how a man would suddenly spin round, throwing up his arms as if acting a part in a play: as in the early days when they had driven almost domestically to the front in buses, the men singing, so that he looked out the window to see if there were any shops at the side of the road. Released for a short while from the war he wandered into a wood whose trees looked like columns in a church.

He was thinking of the last bombardment by the Germans which had thrown up so much dust that the British gunners couldn't see what they were firing at and the Germans were on top of them before they knew what was happening. The only warning had been the mine explosion to their left. They had fought among trenches full of dead bodies, and grey Germans had poured out of the dust clouds, seeming larger than life, as if they had been resurrected out of the dry autumnal earth. It was after the plugging of the line with fresh troops that he and his company had been pulled out after what seemed like years in the trenches digging, putting up wire, in the eternal hammering of the German big guns, the artillery battles which were so much worse than local fights, for the death which came from the distant giants was anonymous and negligent as if gods were carelessly punching them out of existence.

He was grateful now for the silence and for the wood which had a certain semblance of order after the scarred ground worked over and over, continuously revised by shells, so that it looked like carbon paper scribbed over endlessly by a type-writer that never stopped.

He looked up again and as he did so he saw two birds attacking another one. They seemed to synchronise their movements and they were low enough for him to see their beaks quite clearly. The third tried to fly above them but they attacked, probing upwards from below. He could no longer see the plane, just the birds. The third bird was weakening. He couldn't make out whether it was a buzzard or a crow. The other two birds were zeroing in at it all the time, pecking and jabbing, going for the head.

He couldn't stand watching the fight any more and turned away into the wood, and it was then that he saw it – the church. It was completely intact though quite small and with grave-stones beside it. It was strange to see it, like a mirage surrounded by trees whose brown leaves stirred faintly in the slight breeze. From the sky above, the birds had departed: perhaps the two had killed the third one or perhaps it had escaped. It reminded him of a dogfight he had seen between a German triplane and a British Sopwith Camel. After a long duel, the German triplane had destoyed the British plane but was in turn shot down by another British fighter. The triplane made a perfect landing. The British troops rushed up to find the pilot seated at the controls, upright, disciplined, aristocratic, eyes staring straight ahead, and perfectly dead. Later they found the bullet which had penetrated his back and come out at the chest.

He pushed open the door of the church and stood staring around him. He had never been in a church like this before with the large effigy of the Virgin Mary all in gold looking down at him, hands crossed. The stained glass windows had pictures of Christ in green carrying a staff and driving rather shapeless yellow sheep in front of him. In one of the panes there was another picture of him holding out his hands in either a helpless or a welcoming gesture. There were no Bibles or hymn books on the seats as if no one had been there for some time. At the side there was a curtained alcove which he thought might be a confessional. He pulled the curtains aside but there was no one there.

He sat down and gazed for a long time at the huge golden cross which dominated the front of the church. The silence was oppressive. It was not at all like the churches at home. There was more ornament, it was less bare, more decorated. The churches at home had little colour and less atmosphere than this. He could feel in his bones the presence of past generations of worshippers, and then he heard the footsteps.

He turned round to see a man in a black gown walking towards him. There was a belt of rope round his gown and his hands could not be seen as they seemed to be folded inside his gown. The face was pale and ill looking.

'What do you want, my son?' said the voice in English.

He was so astonished that he could think of nothing to say. To find a priest speaking English here seemed suddenly nightmarish. For some reason the thought came into his mind of the most macabre sight he had seen in the war, a horse wearing a gas mask. 'Childe Roland to the Dark Tower came . . . '

'You are admiring the church?' said the minister or priest or whatever he was.

'It is very beautiful,' said Colin, and it seemed to him that his voice was echoing through the church.

'It is very old,' said the priest. 'How did you find it?'

'I was walking through the wood and I happened to . . . '

'Alone? I see,' said the priest. 'Would you like to see the rest of it? There is more of it, you know.'

Colin looked round him uncomprehendingly.

'Oh, it's down below. There's a stair that leads downwards. I keep some wine down there, you understand. If you would care for a glass?'

'Well, I . . . '

'It will only take a minute. I would be glad of the company.'

'If it's all . . . '

'Certainly. Please follow me.'

Colin followed him down some stone steps to what appeared to be a crypt which was lit by candles. The priest walked with his hands folded in front of him as all priests seemed to walk, slow and dignified.

They arrived at a small room. 'Here is my bed, you see,' said the priest. 'And here . . . '

All over the floor, bones were scattered, and there seemed to be an assortment of bloody animal traps.

'Rabbit bones,' said the priest smiling. 'Bones of hares. It is not very . . . '

'You mean you . . . '

'This is how I live,' said the priest. 'I have no bread to offer you, I'm afraid. If you would please sit down?'

'I think I had better . . . '

'I said please sit down. I shall tell you about myself. I have lived now for a year by myself. Alone. What do you think of that?' The priest smiled showing blackened teeth. 'You see, I couldn't stand it any more.'

'Stand what?'

'The war, of course. I was in the trenches you see. And I couldn't stand it. I wasn't intended to be a soldier. I was studying for the ministry and they took me out here. I couldn't stand the people one got in the trenches. I couldn't stand the dirt and I couldn't stand all that dying. What do I live on? I eat rabbits, anything I can find. One morning, you see, I ran away. I didn't know where I was going. But I knew that I couldn't stay there any longer. And I found this place. Perhaps God directed me. Who knows? I was frightened that someone would find me. But no one did. I used to hide in the crypt here. But today I felt very alone so I thought I would talk to you. Do you know what it is to be alone? Sometimes I wish to go back but it is impossible now. To hear the sound of one human voice again! One human voice. I needn't have revealed I was here. If you had been German I wouldn't have come out. I don't speak German, you see, not at all. I'm not good at languages, though I did once study Hebrew. Now, shall we go up again?'

'If you wish.'

'I wish to preach. I have never preached. That is something I must do. Shall we go up? If you would go first? I was going to offer you something to eat but I think I should preach first. If you would please sit in the front row. You haven't brought anyone else with you, have you?'

Colin preceded him, knowing that he was in the presence of a madman. He sat down in the front seat and prepared to listen. He felt as if he were in a dream but then he had felt like that for a long time since he had taken the train south to join up in the first place.

The minister went up into the pulpit with great gravity and began to speak:

'I shall not pray because that would mean closing my eyes. God will understand. After all, while I was closing my eyes you might run away. I shall talk about war.

'Dearly beloved,' he began, his voice growing more resonant, not to say rotund, as he continued:

'May we consider who we are? What we are? When I was young I read books as so many of the young do about the legends of Greece and Rome. I believed in the gods. I believed that we are godlike. My favourite god was Mercury because of his great speed and power. Later my favourite hero was Hector because he was so vulnerable.

'I grew up innocent and hopeful. One night when I was sixteen years old I went to a prayer meeting. A visiting preacher spoke of Christ's sufferings and his mercy so vehemently, with such transparent passion, that I was transported into that world and I suffered the thorn and the vinegar in the land of Galilee. I thought that I should lay my life at the feet of a merciful God.

'At the age of eighteen I was forced into the army to fight for what they call one's country. I did not know what this was since my gaze was always directed inward and not outward. I was put among men whom I despised and feared – they fornicated and drank and spat and lived filthily. Yet they were my comrades in arms.

'I was being shot at by strangers. I was up to my knees in green slime. I was harassed by rats. I entered trenches to find the dead buried in the walls. Once, however, on a clear starry night at Christmas time we had a truce. This lasted into the following day. We – Germans and English – showed each other our photographs, though I had none. We, that is, the others, played football. And at the end of it a German officer came up to us and said: "You had better get back to your dugouts: we are starting a barrage at 1300 hours." He consulted his watch and we went back to our trenches after we had shaken hands with each other.

'One day I could bear no more of the killing and I ran away. And I came here, Lord. And now I should like to say something to you, Lord. I was never foolish enough to think that I understood your ways. Nevertheless I thought you were on the side of the good and the innocent. Now I no longer believe so. You may strike me dead with your lightning – I invite you to do so – but I think that will not happen. All these years, Lord, you have cheated me. You in your immense absence.' He paused a moment as if savouring the phrase. 'Your immense absence. As for me, I have been silent for a year without love, without hope. I have lived like an animal, I who was willing to give my all to you. Lord, do you know what it is to be alone? For in order to live we need language and human beings.

'I think, Lord, that I hate you. I hate you for inventing the world and then abandoning it. I hate you because you have not intervened to save the world.

'I hate you because you are as indifferent as the generals. I hate you because of my weakness.

'I hate you, God, because of what you have done to mankind.'

He stopped and looked at Colin as if he were asking him, Am I a good preacher or not?

'You have said,' said Colin after a long time, 'exactly what I would have said. I have no wish to . . . '

'Betray me? But you are an officer. It is your duty. What else can you do?'

He looked at Colin from the pulpit and for the first time his hands came out from beneath the gown. They were holding a gun.

In the moment before the gun was fired Colin was thinking: How funny all this is. How comical. Here I am in a church which is not like my own church with the golden cross and the effigy of the Virgin in front of me. Here I am, agreeing with everything he says. And it seemed to him for a moment as if the gold cross wavered slightly in the blast of the gun. But that might have been an illusion. In any case it was very strange to die in that way, so far from home, and not even on the battlefield. It was so strange that he almost died of the puzzle itself before the bullet hit him and spun him around in the wooden pew.

Through the Desert

He plodded steadily on through the desert. Now and again out of
the corner of his eye he could see a wedding or a funeral but he
didn't stop to watch, because they were so far away and so
diminutive. Advertisements in all the colours of the rainbow
flashed past him. Some advised him to drink more and others to
join the police. One read: Kant needs you for philosophy. He was
not surprised to pass a still life with two oranges and a tomato
and at other times to find a sewing machine humming by itself.
All the time vultures cast their black shadows like sails over him.
Once he heard two massed choirs, clad in innocent white,
singing passionately about a glen: and another time he saw an
illuminated horse, with TENNANTS written on it, galloping into
the sunset. Later he saw a man and a woman quarrelling. The
man raised his fist and the woman began to dance, like a tall red
snake, eventually turning into an advertisement for Cleopatra.

The sun was almost intolerably hot and he didn't know
where he was going. He heard off and on Tchaikovsky's 1812
Overture with fragments of the French National Anthem
interrupted by a steely cavalry charge. He had a vision of a
soldier climbing the Heights of Abraham in a bloody battle
which lasted for five days to the sound of trumpets provided by
Louis Armstrong, and placing at the top, instead of a Union
Jack, a stone handbag. Night with its million stars never
descended: it was always day and there were no clouds, only a
sun which hammered on a steel anvil like a giant at the opening
of a film.

'Do you love me?' a voice was saying. The face from which
the words issued changed continually. It was like a face from a
spy story, made from liquorice, deceptive, and bearing like a
lamp its brilliant smile. Sometimes it said, 'Do yer luv me?'

Sometimes it said, 'Love me?' Sometimes there was a body standing by a car dressed in a dazzling white vest and white pants. He imagined it was autumn, everything was so brown, and there were hazel nuts on the trees, and a river with dark water which made the sound of crossed telephone conversations. At other times he thought it was winter and there was a wolf waiting for him while he put flowers in a skull-shaped basket and snowflakes steadily fell.

Sometimes he thought that in front of him there was an enormous mirror, and he saw a saint all in green escaping through a church window. He took off his jacket by a mirage, and rested his shirt-sleeved arms in it. As the day swirled around him he saw what he had come to see and had been seeing for years, and had been trying to escape from. It sat in the middle of the desert, a chair and table, and on the table a clock and a packet of cigarettes. The clock made of black wood had a white face. On the table was an exercise book and pen. He sat down in the chair and picked up the pen and began to write. The vultures flapped angrily round him as if they had been cheated. He wrote in block capitals: WHAT ONE SEES IS WHAT ONE IS. He looked at this for a long time and then began to write: 'He plodded steadily on through the desert.'

The Return

The house seemed solid in the wind and the rain, the gathering darkness. He was returning from the country of advertisements to this simple place in the autumn. His clothes were old and worn and he looked like a scarecrow. Inside him was the sour taste of insults received, of swine guzzling, of his mouth at the trough. Over and over he kept saying to himself the speech he had prepared, the part he would play; he would arrange his humble hands, his body like an arched bow.

In the stormy autumn day he could see no one, not his brother, not his father. The land too looked strange and dark and foreign. He did not feel as if he was going home. He felt rather as if he were about to endure a sentence passed on him by a judge whom he did not know. He remembered large illuminated shops, prostitutes, people as bright as robins going home with Christmas presents. Nailed to the slatted bench, he would see their legs, their trousers, their skirts, his own broken boots like windows. He had left those lights to enter the storm which was always there, swirling about the bowed cottages, the battered plants. He walked on, his speech tolling in his head. There were no hens in the yard, there were no cattle or sheep to be seen. The land looked old and brown and there were no trees anywhere.

He went up to the scarred door and knocked without thinking. There was no answer. He opened the door and entered. There was an old chair in front of him at an angle to an old dresser. He looked at the chair, wondering what it was doing there in that particular space. That wasn't where it used to be. It was gaunt and tall and wooden, with no cushion or softness of cloth about it. The dark and white air moved about it. He looked at the dresser with the tiers of plates rising about it.

After a while he went up to his own room. The toys were still there, disarranged as if the storm had got at them. There were old fairy stories among them. Westerns. He sat down amongst them, the trail of days without consciousness. A rocking horse swayed dustily when he touched it. He turned away from the mirror.

He began to repeat his speech to himself. 'I was young and foolish, I did not know. I wished to make money and find fame.' His unshaven face stubbled like a cornfield moved slightly as he spoke through the gaps in his teeth. He was practising his role. Outside the windows the moon rose like a balloon at a feast, frail, stormily trailing from a loop of cloud. The wind howled in the chimney: the rain lashed the windows. He could not bear to look at the road.

'No,' he thought, 'I shan't go back there. It's too late.' And at that moment he changed his role. He began to speak with his father's voice. 'You can't leave. We have work to do. We have something to build up.' Frenziedly he began to tidy the room, to arrange the toys. He went through the whole house like a storm, tidying, arranging, dusting. He arranged the photographs, chairs, tables, flicked away spiders' webs. Scrubbed. He found a lamp and lit it. He felt as if he were holding a fort against a siege by the darkness. He moved about the house, the light in his hand. He washed and cleaned himself.

After a long time he sat down at the table and took out the Bible and began to read it. He read it aloud as if there were some people listening to him; he took pride in his reading. The room was clean and lit. Everything was shaped and new and clear. Beyond the house the wind and the rain raged and the moon veered drunkenly about the sky. Eventually, however, the wind died down and the moon steadied, shining with a hard marbly light like a big white stone.

When he had read the passage from the Bible he went upstairs to bed, walking with a stately, heavy, dignified stride, solid and diminished. He hadn't been able to find a calendar but he would find one. He lay beneath the sheet which shone white in the darkness. He stretched out his legs. The moon made the whole floor appear white and hard as if it were made of stone. The rocking horse with its small beady eyes was still. He padded across the room and pulled the curtains aside. There was no one on the road. In the far distance he could hear the voice of the stream and see the white shapeless boulders. He walked back to the bed exactly like his father. He fell asleep quite quickly.

The End

Starving and in rags he came out of the dark cave and, dazzled, confronted the sea from whose blueness and greenness the light bounded. He gazed with lacklustre eyes at the seaweed which swayed languidly to and fro in the water, smelling the tart brine and the hot stink of flowers in the very hot day. He scrambled upwards among the large boulders and the tall thistles towards the road and as he did so he saw the seagulls lying dead all around him. With worn boots he began to kick them away down into the sea below. There were hundreds of them, dirty and covered with dust. Further up he came on a dead rabbit and various dead birds. He looked at them all without comprehension, merely walking over them and kicking them aside. There was dust on the thistles, on the thyme, on the pink weeds which looked like foxgloves, on the marigolds. He climbed steadily, puffing angrily. He hadn't eaten for a long time and not even the whelks he had found at the beginning had sustained him much. He was ready to give up: his body knew it. He was ready to go back there. And that was what he was doing. But the dead seagulls and the other birds disturbed him. And the silence. There were no bird sounds at all and when he got on to the road there were no cars. The only sound to be heard was that of the sea and an underground river. Otherwise nothing at all. It was very strange.

No cars at all passed him in either direction as he made his way towards the town. However, he came on many stationary cars. Some were parked in lay-bys, drivers and passengers lying back in their seats as if asleep. Some seemed to have stopped in the middle of the road: some looked as if they had crashed. One had its roof open and when he looked inside he saw bloody heads as if something had been at them. He couldn't understand any of it. His boots left clear marks in the dust which lay everywhere, even on the trees and the berries which grew at the side of the road. He plodded steadily on. And all the time he was frightened by the silence. There were no insect sounds, no ordinary hummings of the day.

Still it was better than the darkness of the cave, waiting for people to come after him in the middle of the night with torches. With needles. And worse than needles. With their strange busy voices, high like the voices of birds. Why couldn't they leave him alone? He walked on through the dust. More stationary abandoned cars, motor-cycles, bicycles, dead people on the roads. And the dazzling white stone ahead of him. On a day without sound, without scent. He touched his face: it was bearded. He felt unwashed and sweaty. He missed the music too: they used to let him have his transistor. More dead rabbits, dead people, dead birds. More dust.

Till finally he came to the large notice which said WELCOME TO . . . He couldn't make out the name of the town because it was covered with dust. He made his way past the first hotel into the town. And then for the first time he met them – the rats. The place seethed with them. They were like waves of grey water. And it was as if they were waiting for him. He sensed an intelligence hostile to him, a bright glittering intelligence. A knot of them crouched around him, they seemed to have no fear. He picked up a large stone and broke the back of one of them. They immediately savaged it. And then they moved back a little, watching him, an obscene vibrant circle. They seemed very patient, enigmatic, almost humorous. He cleared a space and picked up more stones angrily as if he were being hemmed in, but they drew back as if they sensed that they had plenty of time. Now he could see skeletons everywhere, skeletons of dogs, skeletons of people. He walked past the shops among the seething rats, gathering round him but not attacking. Sometimes he would lash out with a worn boot and one of them would give a high-pitched scream like a child.

He passed the bookshop with all the books in the window. The door was open and there were rats inside the shop. Some were sitting round the books looking out at him with that extraordinary quizzical look, whiskers quivering. The shop floor was a tangle of gnawed magazines and newspapers. He walked past the newsagent's to the jeweller's. Here the shop window, hung with necklaces and watches, was empty of rats. The rats approached him on the street and he screamed and kicked at them in a frenzy of hatred, or threw stones. More and more cars with skeletons at the wheels. More and more skeletons at shop counters, wire baskets at their sides. A cart with a skeleton of a horse. He looked up towards the roof of the church. Were there rats stationed there, waiting?

He came to a grocer's. In the window he saw fruits of various kinds, and tins of food. The door of this place was shut too and the rats hadn't got in. He stopped at the door. The rats were all around him in a ring but not advancing. He rushed at them screaming and mouthing curses, foaming at the mouth. Again they retreated in a seething wave of grey, and this gave him enough time to get through the door, except that two of the rats managed to get in. He looked frantically round the shop and found a big window pole with which he chased them, determined to destroy them. He set out after them screaming. He hated them with a terrible hatred. Nothing less would satisfy him than that he should smash them into pulp. They jumped frantically about but he was so enraged, so clear in his mind, that he caught them one after the other and beat them into a slimy mess. When he had finished he stood panting at the counter. When he looked out the window the other rats were perched on the outside, still looking in at him. They had watched it all and they were waiting.

He found a tin opener and opened cans. So long as it was food he didn't care what food it was. He ate potato salad, peaches, steak, mince, indiscriminately. He found beer cans and twisted the tops free and drank. He found a bottle of wine and drank most of it. He poured the wine down his throat watching the rats who seemed to be watching him with keen interest. He made faces at them, he shouted and cursed them, he beat on the plate glass windows with his bare hands. But they didn't go away. Eventually he left the shop: there was somewhere he had to get to. He took the window pole with

him and bottles and cans. He started throwing the bottles and
cans at the rats while at the same time he began to dance and
sing songs. He wasn't scared of them now. He went after them.
He thrust the hook of the window pole at them. He kicked
them with his boots. And slowly they retreated.

Something told him he must get away from there. Before the
night came. He didn't want to be there when it was dark. For
then he wouldn't be able to see the rats, and their eyes might
shine, green and remorseless. He plodded on through the dust,
the rats watching him warily, some with lips retracted. Soon,
shouting and screaming and cursing, he had left them behind
and he made his way out into the country beyond the town.
Still the dead cars and the dead people and the dead birds and
the dead animals. As he approached the woods, he saw the dead
stoats and the dead hares and the dead foxes. The trees
themselves were draped with dead birds. And as he walked
through the damp green wood there was still the same silence.
Not ominous, just empty. And the same dust everywhere. But
above him the sky was clear and blue and the air warm. And he
could hear the murmur of hidden streams.

Drunkenly he muttered to himself, singing snatches of songs,
as he at last saw the large white house and approached it. From
that distance he could see the chairs and what appeared to be
people sitting in them on the lawn. He began to run drunkenly.
And as he ran he waved. He expected them to be coming
towards him, dark-uniformed, and this time he would welcome
them. He reached the lawn and saw that it was skeletons sitting
in the chairs. Damp books lay beside them covered with dust.
He began rushing about from window to window and through
the windows he could see the wards and the machinery and the
dead bodies. He could see the straitjackets.

He went to the door and began to bang on it, the heavy
wooden door. He tried to turn the handle but it was heavy. He
began to bang again and again. In a few hours it would be dark
and the stars would come out. And he didn't want to be left
outside. He wished now that they had found him with their
torches when he ran away. He banged and banged on the door
monotonously. He began to feel small phantom teeth in his

feet but when he looked down there was nothing there at all. He sank down in front of the large wooden door, weeping. And as he wept and hammered alternately the shadows began to fall, and a breeze stirred the pages of the books and the skeletons swayed slightly to and fro, rocking.

Journeying Westwards

At first it was all right, everything was clear and fine and autumnal. As he drove westward he nearly stopped to admire the trees at the side of the loch. There they were, the oaks, the sycamores, the ash and the copper beech, with their leaves bronze and gold and green and red, perfectly still in a motionless air, burning steadily with their latest flare of the year. The loch itself was so still that they were reflected in it as a perfect solid double of their reality, massive as rocks, so that it was difficult to know what was reality and what was reflection. In fact he couldn't recall seeing a day so still and so clear as if he had found himself by some accident at a point in time between growth and death, between the permanent and the transitory. So that he wanted to stay and watch the trees and the loch, but it was three o'clock and he had to drive on.

And all the way it was like that, twisting roads and boulders and autumn trees in their final flare and all reflected in the loch which never seemed to end. Here and there were houses but in general these trees expended their glamour and colour on the air and stone, but not on the eyes of any human being, bending over the road, seeming to gaze into the water.

Steadily he drove westwards, feeling restless, but stopping at half past five at a hotel for some food and drink. It stood at the side of the road and was the only one open in the small town, all the rest being closed after the end of the season. The tourists with their talk of boats and wearing their red shirts like sails were all away. The shutters would come down, the shops would all be shut on Sundays and the locals would be unable to buy anything, the infinite interrogations about local towers and castles would end till the bright tinkle of the tills in the spring just about the time of the swallows and Easter.

There was hardly anyone in the hotel but himself and a humpbacked maid who told him to wait in the lounge. He sat down on a grey collapsing armchair and looked about him. The furniture seemed to have been thrown together without order. There was an old black wooden chest, two chairs with green and grey cloth over them, and one coloured a faded red. A few *Reader's Digest*s were lying about on a sideboard, and reflected in an old mottled mirror. Surprisingly in the middle of it, like a new house among slums, was a modernistic TV set.

Eventually the maid called him in to dinner. He ate the pork without much interest and then had peach melba. When he had finished he bought only one whisky because he thought he'd better drive safely, though his nerves screamed for more. When he left the hotel it was after six. As the church bells hammered at him he put his foot on the accelerator and headed west passing a group of girls on their way to church, all of them appearing to be wearing pink caps and carrying pink hymn books. The small town, like the trees and the loch, looked calm. The Triumph hummed steadily on but he passed little traffic. As time passed he began to drive between moors on which white sheep grazed and on which rested huge white boulders. The streams seemed to have dried up after the dry summer. Once he passed a caravan and sitting on the green verge beside it on a chair a woman in red slacks painting. She did not stir as he roared past. And all the time the landscape grew rockier and rockier.

Gradually, as he drove on, the darkness began to come down, at first only a slight haze and then more thickly. To his left a moon, autumnal red, began to climb the sky. A rabbit ran across the road and he avoided it by a hairsbreadth. Once a hare lolloped ahead of him for about two hundred yards before leaving the road as if it had been dazed by his lights. Eventually it dashed off to the side of the road and disappeared. Once he saw a weasel and once an owl wafted slowly in front of his windscreen. He had still a long way to go and already he found himself in this world of nocturnal animals. But at least they were company for now the darkness was steadily coming down and he was following the white lines of the road which seemed to continue indefinitely. To make things worse a white fog was swirling about, probably caused by a mixture of frost and warm air. It was moving vaguely at the sides of the road and worse in some places than in others. At times he could see the road quite clearly, at others it was foggy and grey.

He didn't realise when he first became nervous. The nervousness probably grew from the silence around him which was unbroken by anything but the noise of the engine: from the lack of traffic: from the grey fog. At one time he stopped and unfastened his safety belt as if he might wish to escape from some disaster that threatened him. To the left and right of him there were trees, and a straight road ahead of him down which he hurtled. He knew this length of straight road: it lasted for miles.

Behind him in the back seat bounced some toys which had been lying there since she had left and taken the children with her. He had gone to her mother's but she hadn't been there and there was no message. That was a week ago. And he couldn't find her anywhere. Then he had simply stopped looking, just like that. And he had begun to drink, steadily, relentlessly. In pub after pub, arguing with people, being bitter and unpleasant, finding himself alone, going home to an empty house whose mirrors revealed nothing. One night he had wakened up feeling hot (he wasn't sleeping very well) and gone to the window to open it, only to be astonished by the terrible blaze of light which shone on the street and the houses and the grooved dustbins. Shaken to the core he couldn't bear the brilliant light. For a moment it was as if he had glimpsed the world before man, before intelligence, its negligent power, its careless scattering of energy, its clear brilliance. He felt like an interruption of the light.

For a moment as he drove on he thought he saw two hikers with foggy packs waiting at the side of the road and drew up for he needed the company but there was no one there. He had seen no rabbits or weasels or owls for a long time. Once he thought he saw his brother standing at the side of the road – his brother to whom he hadn't written for twenty years – but again there was no one there. He began to shiver uncontrollably. He was frightened lest round the next corner he would find his wife and children waiting in the grey fog, holding out their hands to him. It was like a film of Jack the Ripper, phantoms moving around him, grey. He began to sweat and the palms of his hands felt sticky on the wheel. He began to think of the night he had walked out on Helen the year before.

Phantoms seemed to waver at his side. His father, left alone in the house after his own marriage and now dead, seemed to extend grey hands to him. 'It was not my fault,' he screamed silently. 'I couldn't do anything else.' The foggy hands were replaced by others. There were Irma's hands too. The last time he had seen her was ten years ago. She had driven away from him, her gloved hands resting on the wheel in front of the green dashboard. That was just after he had told her about Helen.

The road now was seething with phantoms and sometimes amongst them he saw himself shouting at Helen, 'Leave me alone. Leave me alone. Can't you see I'm busy?' And his mother with her tranquil cunning eyes. I must get back, he thought, I must get back to where I was happy. But the faces now began to scream at him. The phantoms had come out into the middle of the road and he was boring through them, afraid to stop. He was afraid to stop lest if he did stop they would enter the car. It was like the time he had taken Helen and the boys to the Safari Park and the monkeys had insisted on climbing on the bonnet of his car making faces at him through the windscreen. 'Don't stop,' he had been advised. And he had driven on with his cargo of mocking primitive diminutive faces.

And all the time the terror of the niceness, the warmth of Helen and the boys, their niceness.

Now ahead of him he saw a strange white form waving out of the mist. It flared and changed but at the centre of it was darkness, at the centre of it was a maze of darkness, a wheel. It seemed to be a reflection of the wheel of the car. Instinctively as the car entered it he braked, inside the fog and the darkness and the wheel. And from it issued such a stench as nearly destroyed him. It was a stench such as might arise from the concentrated marshes of the world. He heard someone scream, relentlessly, mindlessly. A wind shook the door of the car. Flashes of light shook the form. It was like thunder, stinking thunder, with a play of lightning and wheels inside it. It was a huge stinking brain, concentrated on itself, wheel within wheel. It turned on itself blindly, blankly, inside the fog which surrounded it. There were ladders of light in it and small animals, weasels leaping at rabbits' throats, owls swooping on mice. And all the time there was the stench. Like the monkeys on the bonnet of the car, it screeched and gibbered and knocked. He couldn't speak, his clammy hands clutched and slid from the wheel. In one corner of the fog, Helen sat knitting, in another his children sat reading red comics. He began to howl like a wolf, as if a hot stone were being wrenched out of him.

Frantically he looked for a place to turn, gritting his teeth. He found it and turned. As he pointed the engine eastwards the fog began slowly to fade away. He drove on slowly and after a while got out of the car. The stars were shining with a concentrated brilliance, millions and millions of them, just as he had used to see them when he was young. He held his hands and his face up to the light as if to wash away the stench. The light was so clear that he could see for miles and miles around him as if he were in a large arena. He got into the car and drove away. He wanted to go home, he wanted very much to touch human hands again.

The Professor and the Comics

I

His moon glasses shining on his round red-cheeked face Professor MacDuff cycled happily along through the March day which made the streets as white as bone. On days like these the city looked freshly coloured and new, the butchers in their striped smocks standing at shop doors, knives clutched absent-mindedly in their hands, young boys racing each other on bicycles, older boys hanging about with yellow crash helmets, women pushing prams and groceries along, window panes flashing, church spires climbing into a blue sky, cinemas advertising (he noticed sadly) Bingo instead of Wild Westerns.

Professor MacDuff waited placidly at the red traffic lights, in his tweed suit, his white shirt and large green tie. He felt fine as if newly resurrected from the grave of winter. What a fine month March was, bringing with it scents as from a rich soil, memories of boyish escapades, ladders, paint, whooping dogs, hosepipes. He cycled on past the Art Gallery (where they were holding an exhibition of Magritte's paintings), past streets lined with flaring green trees, past small shops which said things like 'M NS CL T ES' (the brood which flourished and so quickly died) till he arrived at last at the open steel gates of the university from which rose green sweeping lawns towards the mellow-bricked building itself.

Students (boys hardly distinguishable from girls wearing long hair like Charles I's doomed followers or the Marlborough he hugely admired) strolled about, books under their arms, talking. They waved to him. He waved back, by now wheeling his bicycle. The clock in the tower boomed. Ah, the forest of Arden where all was green, where Rosalind and Celia and Orlando and Oliver (indistinguishable from each other in their virginal green) wandered happily forever. He waved to the Professor of Logic who on dusty days sometimes wore a gas mask. Logic could of course be carried too far.

He parked his bicycle and walked along the corridor where the notices proliferated, so many of them that one didn't have the time or the inclination to read them: a Violin Concerto cheek by jowl with a performance of *Uncle Vanya*, a teach-in on Communism next to a notice about Nationalism, a Wine and Cheese Social next to a poster which showed a lynx-eyed Chinaman with a machine gun.

He said 'Hello' to young Hilton who looked, as usual, aloof and saturnine. He wondered if he was wearing his red socks again and looking back saw that he was. The Moral Philosophy Professor of course never wore socks at all.

He stood outside the door of his lecture room looking at the wooden seats which arose in tiers towards the back, smelling as he so often did the smell of varnish, a reminiscence of his first day in university as a student. 'Ah,' said the History Professor, 'narcissising again?' The History Professor was called Black, wore a black gown and was a very precise Civil Service type of man who read out his lectures with great deliberation in a very even unexcited voice. His students liked him because he arranged and tabulated everything so neatly that it really seemed as if the precise year 1485 was a new departure in English History and the Renaissance did begin in a particular year and perhaps even on a particular day.

'The lecture rooms look different in spring,' said Professor MacDuff.

'Everything is different in spring,' said Professor Black, 'except History.'

'It is as if the people in there were plants,' said Professor MacDuff, turning moon glasses benevolently towards Black who had however moved on. Having not a single jot of imagination himself he was uneasy in the presence of anyone who had.

'Uptight, that's what you are,' said Professor MacDuff grinning.

He went into his room, and put on his gown. Soon his

students would be appearing for the lecture. He smiled with satisfaction, and for a moment he appeared different, as if he were about to embark on a difficult adventure.

It seemed at first to be as it had always been before, the lecture room filling slowly then more rapidly with chattering students who quoted at each other the possibly more obscene bits of Anglo-Saxon or opened notebooks on which were drawn in bold imaginative detail anatomical sections of the human (feminine) form with words like Sex and Crap prominently displayed. Some lounged, some sat up attentively, some shifted about, some half closed their eyes (after late night hangovers), some dreamed. And here and there of course were the pale, intense, bespectacled ones who had really come to drink at the fount of Helicon, to whom for instance Donne's poetry was not merely an academic abstraction but a possible experience. The students wore all sorts and styles of clothing: the only constant was difference. Some of the girls wore long sweeping red Lady Macbethish coats which swung open to frame like Renaissance pictures voluptuous legs below brief skirts. Boys wore dungaree trousers, leather jackets, silken scarves, polo-necked jerseys, a proliferation of costumes.

When he arrived at the dais the noise as usual died down. Professor MacDuff had been at the university for some time, was an institution and was expected to provide not only information but some urbane and even vaguely comic jokes or at least some entertainment. Bred on the unrelated stories of TV the students did not so much want a lecture as a performance, not however insincere but at least with the sincerity of the actor who has his own truth. They expected the medium and the message to coincide and were quickly bored if the medium (in this case the lecturer) should provide a message which had no relation to his own life style. As a Professor at the university had recently remarked with some bewilderment, 'They not only want us to lecture on Che Guevara but in some measure to be Che Guevara.' They did not like dissection of the dead and were therefore impatient with literary criticism.

It need not be said that what the Professor was about to do was remarkable and in some ways revolutionary. He had his own reasons for doing it and they were perhaps not mean reasons. What the students were looking for was excitement. They were young, volatile, energetic (fed on the milk of the Welfare State), already, many of them, veterans of demonstrations, obscurely irritated by restlessnesses whose source they could not focus. It was, Professor MacDuff often thought, a hunger for drama. There was something theatrical about their clothes even. They were pseudo-Elizabethans without any world (except dead planets) to conquer. They seemed to be continually dressing up for a stage which had been shifted while they were preparing or which, though still there, had no audience waiting. For no one wanted to be a member of an audience, everyone wanted to be an actor. Everyone wanted colour, the brighter the better, and drama, the more exciting the better. Perhaps many of them thought they could do the Professor's job better than he could himself.

Nevertheless it was a big thing he was about to do ... 'Today,' said Professor MacDuff drawing himself up to his full height, 'and for the next few weeks of this term I shall talk about comics.'

The reaction of the students to this was at first complete stunned silence and then after a moment a spontaneous roar of applause in the middle of which he stood benevolent and fresh-faced as if he were a kind of happy personification of a vernal rural god.

Some however refrained from cheering as if they sensed that they were being got at in some way, as if they felt a daring breathtaking irony, a parody so piercing that it was a kind of hatred.

One or two among the pale and the bespectacled looked at him as if he had gone mad.

But he continued unperturbed referring duly to his lecture notes, a rotund slightly untidy figure with moon glasses.

'Today,' he said, 'I shall begin since it is spring with a short lecture on the World of the Comics with special reference to Desperate Dan. Later I shall mention other such heroes of the comics as Korky the Cat. My sources are the *Dandy* and the *Beano* and to a lesser extent the *Rover*, the *Wizard*, the *Hotspur*, etc. I shall sometimes refer to comics that are now extinct though at one time they flourished in the imaginations of many who for instance set out to found the British Empire. It is partly with this buried imaginative world, so like Atlantis, that I shall be concerned.

'Now you will all be familiar I take it with the red and yellow pages of the *Dandy* which I place I may say at this point much higher than the rather belligerent papers such as the *Victor*, the *Wizard* and the *Hotspur* in accordance with the one law which I shall enunciate, that distinguishing the truly creative from the uncreative. This law states that no truly creative work of any kind can omit the vulgar.

'For it is clear,' the Professor continued, 'that whereas the *Wizard* for instance is a merely inferior version of such over-rated books as *Treasure Island*, the *Dandy* on the other hand represents pure creativity and belongs to the same world as the silent films and the inimitable Charlie Chaplin, the *Dandy* oscillating as it does between the human world of Desperate Dan and the animal world of Korky the Cat.

'It would however be invidious for me to draw comparisons between these two characters since in fact in such a world comparisons are not possible and would in fact be odious, nor would it be meaningful for me to point out that an animal and a man are not essentially different in this world before good and evil (notice that I do not say beyond good and evil), theological terms which cannot be applied to material of this kind. It is a world rather of errors and inexactitudes. There is a difference one might interpose between an error and a sin. A sin is not an aesthetic term, whereas an error may be so classified.

'Now should comparisons be made on the grounds of vocabulary. I myself would not wish to use neo-Bradleyan techniques in this matter since to do so would be to exile these characters from their own separate world. In the short time that I shall spend today on an introduction to this theme I should merely like to draw attention to some of the characteristics of a typical comic hero, that is, Desperate Dan.

'Naturally one begins with his name. I could spend a long time discoursing on this, especially on the inspired choice of the name Dan which I consider to be much superior to the word Donald or Daniel which are possible alternatives. Why it is superior is not so easy to determine. (It is not for instance as clear as the inspired choice of name by Dickens for his sullen sexton, Gabriel Grub, a name which reconciles both heaven and earth, the angelic and the mouldy.)

'Also one would have to discuss the adjective "desperate", again an inspired choice because of the connotations of menace and despair, both transfused with comedy.

'And I suppose that when one studies Desperate Dan with his unshaven appearance one could at first sight consider him menacing, especially as he is rather large. He might at first be thought of almost as domesticated Stone Age man ambling about in a world of CLONKS and AARGHS.

'He is one might say perpetually on the verge of a revelation, a being dazzled and swindled continually, sometimes by his family, sometimes by outsiders. But he always wins.

'I should like at this point to outline the plot of a typical Desperate Dan episode. In this episode . . . '

At which precise moment there was an unexpected (or perhaps expected) interruption. A slim pale bespectacled boy of the kind whose aloofness conceals a fanatical fire, whose shyness is a mask for a burning egotism, stood up and said: 'I think we have listened long enough to this ridiculous lecture. Surely, sir, you are aware that we have to try to pass an examination in a few weeks' time. As this examination will affect the livelihood of most of us . . . ' Before he could proceed any further there was a brutal roar of derision and anger from the assembled multitude and expletives such as 'SHIT', 'CRAP', etc. were freely hurled.

But the serious boy though paler than before continued: 'It's possible, sir, that you may be interested in comics but that is no good reason for interrupting the syllabus. You are paid to teach us English Literature and by no stretch of the imagination can the *Dandy* and the *Beano* be said to form part of . . . '

A huge bearded student wearing a flowered shirt and tie and a brown leather jacket pushed the earnest protester back into his seat. But at that same moment as the huge hand descended on his shoulder propelling him downwards there emerged from another part of the whirlpool a fresh-faced curly-haired girl who shouted vigorously: 'He's quite right. There are some of us who believe that Shakespeare and Donne are great poets and that it is our right to be told about them. That stuff about Desperate Dan is what we left behind in the nursery. What do you think we are? Do you think we are still in the primary school? Are you playing a joke on us or something? Are you trying to take the mickey? What sort of professor are you? Are you showing some kind of intellectual contempt for us or what?

'Were *you* taught about Desperate Dan when you were in the University? Did someone decide that *you* were too immature to know about Donne? Or about Shakespeare? What right have you to take on yourself to judge us in this way?'

It was noticeable that the girl who was trembling with emotion was listened to with a certain degree of gravity and in a reasonable silence and if she had sat down at that point she might have swayed the meeting but as so often happens she overstated her case: 'Even Beowulf,' she concluded fiercely, 'is more interesting than Desperate Dan.'

Whereupon there was a universal roar of execration, 'Rubbish', 'Codswallop', 'Piss', etc., and she was forced to sit down though battling valiantly to the end, her mouth opening and shutting soundlessly like someone on a TV screen when the sound has been cut off and the temporary fault extends for minute after minute.

All this while the professor sat happily and placidly believing that presently from the world of charge and counter charge there would emerge some heroic figure who would tell what the commotion really meant. It was as if he was waiting for such a figure. Meanwhile he sat perfectly still and relaxed while the mass seethed and shouted, instinctively waiting for a leader, speaking for the moment broken words like 'DONNE – OUT OUT OUT', 'TO HELL WITH SHAKESPEARE' and even 'MACDUFF FOR THE PRIMARIES' which at that moment were being fought in distant Florida.

But as always happens the hour produced the man and the dialogue proceeded.

This time the speaker was a tallish bearded student who stood up with a book in his hand. His beard was of a strawy colour, his lips were red and blubbery and his cheeks had a red slightly hectic tinge. His clothes looked dirty, as if he had been sleeping in them.

'Ladies and gentlemen,' he began, 'I for one have listened to the previous speakers with amazement. What is their definition of education? I might ask this question without hoping for much of an answer.' There was an interjection from the girl who was howled down after which the students settled down to listen to what the student had to say.

'Are the previous speakers some sort of élite? Is that what they are? Let me ask you, how many of you really like reading Donne's poetry or Shakespeare's plays? It would be interesting to find out. How many of you are not bored to death by what the so-called critics call "the intellectual and imaginative, working together". How many of you believe with me that most of their work is a load of crap with nothing to say to any of us? How many of you really like these people? Let's have a show of hands on this.'

Five hands went up slowly. 'There you are. Five people. And most certainly they have been brainwashed. If there are only five people here who really like reading Donne and Shakespeare what conclusion do we draw from this? I'll tell you: we've been conned. Lecturers tell us we're stupid because we don't like reading *Troilus and Cressida*. And yet are we really to believe that we are any stupider than any previous generation? Is this feasible? Is it likely that a whole generation of stupid people has suddenly emerged? Is this a reasonable assumption? I can't believe it. It's ridiculous. A much more reasonable assumption would be that for us these people, these writers, are dead, not only physically dead but spiritually dead. And after all what's wrong with the comics? Our brothers outside read the comics. In factories, on the workshop floor, they read the comics, uncountable numbers of them. Soldiers in the army, airmen in the air force, read the comics. They read them in shops and offices. They are people exactly like us, they are human beings. Are we saying that we are better than them because we have

read some of Shakespeare's plays? Are we not separating ourselves from our brothers? I say that Donne and Shakespeare are
methods to separate us from our brothers, that in order to get
back to them again we should return to the world of comics,
that Donne and Shakespeare are divisive influences.

'And furthermore I suggest that we hold a festival. I suggest
that we have an open air festival in which we will have readings
from the comics, dramatic performances based on the comics,
an extravaganza of joy.'

At this suggestion there was a roar of approval, which died
down when he raised his arm and said: 'I think we should elect a
committee here and now to organise this festival. And I mean my
suggestion to be taken quite seriously. I suggest that Professor
MacDuff be made Honorary President of this committee.'

The Professor signified that he accepted and rose to his feet.
In perfect silence he continued with his lecture. 'I was about to
outline one of the episodes in the saga of Desperate Dan . . . '

2

The Principal of the University was a scientist (or rather an ex-
scientist) with an MSc and various other degrees from other
universities. His main work had been done during the war
when as a member of a chosen group, he had invented a
method of distinguishing between the voices of European and
Japanese soldiers in the jungles of Burma. It was a well-known
fact that the Japanese had used techniques of imitation to
entice British (and lesser) soldiers to their deaths by training
some of their people to speak good English. Professor
Carstairs had put a stop to that by showing that a tape recorder
with a simple attachment could easily distinguish between
Eastern and Western voices. It was according to his often
repeated explanations at cocktails a simple matter of breath
control and pace. These two, he remarked, are very different in
different races. He had once been in the same swing door as
Winston Churchill but to listen to him one might imagine that
Churchill had hearkened with bated breath and composed
intelligence for hours to his explanations of how inferior the

breath control and pace of Japanese voices were to British ones. It was often remarked that he looked rather like Churchill with his great bald head, his smallish stature, the bulldog thrust of his jaw, his habit of jumping head first into situations from which he would later extricate himself with a sophisticated cunning and especially his trick of removing his glasses when he was making a speech. He had lately taken to attaching them to a piece of tape which swung on his breast and would put them on and remove them at regular intervals.

His favourite character was the Chief Constable in *Softly*, *Softly* which he never missed. He liked to affect that sudden sharkish smile, the brutal physical presence, the air of decision, the ultra-sophistication and self-confidence.

He had long ago given up any pretence to creative science, involved as he was in administration. After all, the university was expanding – what it was expanding to was another question – and there were so many people to see, so many people to consult . . . How could one retire to a laboratory in moments of such frantic change?

It is true that now and again he felt a certain nostalgia for his days of creativity, for the military companionship which he had so much enjoyed, for certain equations, for the marvellous randomness of the world. But though he felt this nostalgia there was a part of him which hated randomness, which felt that God must in fact be a ruler and not an artist. He used to say that Einstein was right in not accepting by intuition alone the ideas of probability.

Perhaps if he had had children . . . but he hadn't.

It was this man who met Professor MacDuff for lunch in a Chinese restaurant neighbouring the university. He had a fondness for Chinese restaurants though he couldn't have said why. Perhaps it was memories of the war when he had been busy outmanœuvring the inscrutable Japanese. Not that there seemed much difference between the Chinese and the Japanese: they both looked expressionless and were probably very cunning. He didn't really find their reading of the newspapers backwards very odd: after all he did this himself on Sundays with the *Times* and the *Observer*.

There was something churchlike about Chinese restaurants too. Or perhaps templelike. And the decor always seemed to be either lilac or red. Dragons on friezes on the walls. A moody Chinaman standing next to a telephone. You knew where you were in Chinese restaurants. It was really a business transaction. No nonsense about 'dearie' or 'love' or any of that stuff. All straightforward capitalist procedure.

It was on a Monday that he met Professor MacDuff who came in rather hesitantly not to say gingerly as he was not a devotee of Chinese restaurants, in fact hating them a bit and not liking the food very much. 'I see you're grazing already,' he said as he sat down looking with disfavour on the acres of rice the Principal was guzzling. He ordered some tomato soup and shuddered. He knew in advance what it would be like. Why did the Chinese manage to take all the flavour out of European food? What would happen if we ever went into the Chinese Common Market?

The Principal had decided to flatter him. 'I suppose you've done the Ximenes this week,' he said. 'What was that word for Six Across? I believe the clue was "Brown, that is, was Northern shall, a Highland gentleman". Eleven letters.'

'Dunie wassal,' said MacDuff with not much satisfaction since he knew he was being conned and didn't like being patronised. Nevertheless there was enough of the pedagogue in him to explain that 'dunie wassal' was a Highland gentleman (grossly anglicised) and that 'sall' was the Northern version of 'shall'.

'Of course you're Highland yourself,' said the Principal. 'I keep forgetting that. You've been here so long.'

MacDuff didn't bother to reply.

After a while the Principal said, still munching, 'Funny how we academics are always doing crosswords. I often wonder whether Kant would have been a crossword fan. Perhaps it's something to do with solving the enigma of the world by words alone.'

'O I think it's just an amusement,' said MacDuff bluntly. The tomato soup was as bad as he'd feared. It looked like blood mixed with water. And not very high class blood at that. There was also some horrible music leaking from the walls like sweat. 'Naturally,' he said aloud, 'these are Chinese from Hong Kong.'

'Yes,' said the Principal vaguely. 'Exiles.' He raised his eyes from the suey and said, 'Have you ever read any of the Charlie Chan stories.'

'All of them,' said MacDuff, 'I believe there are only five full length ones in existence. I wish people would republish the great detective classics. You never get anything but thrillers nowadays and sociological analyses. These things have no place in the true detective story, which should be a puzzle. The people should be cardboard not human beings. As in Ellery Queen for instance. Or Carr in his great period.'

'I see,' said the Principal keenly, 'a puzzle eh?' Suddenly MacDuff realised and not for the first time that this man was no fool but in fact had a very fine brain when he chose to use it.

'There was another one, wasn't there?' said the Principal. 'Van somebody or other. He did the Bishop Murder Story. I've been trying to get hold of his books for some time.'

'Van Dine,' said MacDuff briefly. 'Yes, he's good, very good.' He pushed the half-consumed tomato soup away from him. Some of it had spilt on his jacket.

'Yes, the Chinese detective stories all seem to be a bit comic,' said the Principal laying a cunning emphasis on the last word, as if he thought it would entrap MacDuff into some revealing confession.

But MacDuff at this point was holding in front of him a menu as big as a newspaper and was trying to work out which would be the least punishing item for him to choose.

'I said they're slightly comic,' said the Principal.

'Who?'

'Chinese detectives. Chink private eyes.'

'Yes, I suppose so, but then the rest of us don't have the same insight into the Oriental mind as you have,' said MacDuff. He wished he could smoke his pipe. But Chinese restaurants didn't seem to take kindly to pipes. It would be like smoking in church. He thought: The best clue I ever saw was 'Nothing squared is cubed.' The answer was OXO. That was pure genius.

'Regarding your lectures,' said the Principal, deciding on a frontal attack.

'I beg your pardon.'

'I said regarding your lectures. Comic, I've been hearing,' said the Principal. 'I mean I've had letters. From influential parents. Complaints. Some from ministers and nationalists. Crank ones of course. But some very fierce. Some of them accuse you of being a communist.'

'I see,' said MacDuff scrubbing vaguely at the red stain left by the tomato soup.

'By the way, are you?' said the Principal.

'Am I what?'

'A communist.'

'You must know my background.'

'Yes I know. Brilliant First in English, in 1934. Member of University Socialist Party Club for the last two years of your student career. Spoke against Franco at various meetings. Why didn't you go to Spain?'

'Cowardice basically, I suppose. I should have gone. Why didn't you?'

'You must remember I'm younger,' said Carstairs with some satisfaction. He pushed the plate away and ordered banana fritters from an impassive waiter. 'Junior lecturer. Senior lecturer. Full professor. You've never been in any other university. Oh I forgot. You married in 1940. You weren't in the war of course were you?'

'I have bad eyesight as you know.'

'Of course. Your wife was a lecturer in Greek. Died last year. We were all very sorry.' He jabbed at his banana fritter. 'I wonder why you lectured on the comics. It's not really the sort of thing one does. And you of all people. What was that book you wrote, *The Theme of Resurrection in Shakespeare's Later Plays*.'

'I also wrote two on Milton.'

'Of course. I know you're a popular lecturer but you can't possibly continue with this rubbish. Desperate Dan indeed. Many people might think you were going off your rocker.'

'Do you think so?'

'No, I don't. I still don't know what the game is.'

'It's not a game. It's desperately serious.'

'I see. After all you're a scholar and you're not off your rocker as we've agreed. So what is all this about? I know I'm only a scientist and as far as I know we haven't got the equivalent of comics in the world of . . . ' He paused for a moment and then said dreamily, 'apart of course from Bergen. But that's beside the point. I should like to know what you're trying to do. Parents are protesting. You must realise that this is an odd situation. In fact I've never heard of anything like it before.'

'Well, if that's all,' said MacDuff.

'Naturally some people on the Senatus are likely to discuss it. However I'll leave it with you now. I'm sure you will see reason.'

Carstairs sat staring at his coffee for some time after MacDuff had gone. For some reason a tag kept coming into his mind, 'Lead on, MacDuff.' He couldn't make up his mind whether he was going to be Duncan or Macbeth. After thinking about this for some time he decided it didn't make much difference. He looked vaguely around him. Odd that MacDuff didn't like Chinese restaurants. Perhaps if it had been a communist restaurant he might have liked it better. Or perhaps it was all a big bluff. He got up slowly and paid his bill at the desk. Then he went out into the fine spring day, where everything was fresh and new. If one didn't have troubles like this one might even enjoy it. There was a Chinaman standing in the sunshine just outside the door staring at him inscrutably.

Professor MacDuff lived by himself since his wife had died a year before. In general he took most of his meals out, though in the evenings he made some food for himself and did a good bit of reading. He had also taken to playing chess though it wasn't until three years before that he had bought a set and was surprised to find that it wasn't quite as tormenting as he had feared. His wife had died of cancer and it had been a slow death. He had married her when he was thirty years old. He had met her in the university library where she was reading a book on Virgil. He remembered that she had looked rather like a nun, perhaps like the one mentioned in *Il Penseroso*. Her face was classical yet not cold. She was quite small.

When he came home at night he often thought about her and about the classics. The whole house seemed very empty especially in the winter time. At times however he felt that she was still there and sometimes even in his bed he would stretch out his arm as if she was present. It was a strange feeling. Sometimes he would glance up from his book thinking that she was still sitting in the chair opposite him. And then he was stabbed by the most incredible pain.

He had let the house become rather untidy though not dirty. Books were piled behind the chair in which he sat. He read indiscriminately, Science fiction, detective stories, academic books, they were all grist to his mill. Sometimes he would be reading five books at the one time. He was all right during the academic year but the vacations were difficult because they were so long. The previous year he had gone to British Columbia to see his brother who was a businessman over there. He had found the trip interesting – Fable Cottage on Vancouver Island for instance – but was a bit put off by the 'stroll down Chaucer Lane in the English Village which leads to Anne Hathaway's Cottage'. However he hadn't particularly cared for his brother who had become much more vulgar and superficial than he had remembered, and who was absolutely interested in money and little else. His brother in fact was a brutal red-faced crashing bore. He would never see him again.

He sat down in the chair after coming back from his meeting with the Principal. On the floor in front of him was a bottle of Parozone, yellow, and he stared at it for a long time. It seemed in some way to soothe him. After a while he slept. Then he got up and got out his notes on Milton. In his new book which he might never complete he was trying to show how far *Samson Agonistes* was from the true Greek style of drama, how clumsy the versification was. He had always believed that Milton was strongest in poems like *Allegro* and *Il Penseroso* and that at that point there was life and gaiety and the exact elegance of true poetry.

He thought about his wife. She had a clear quick-witted practical mind but at the same time she was an idealistic scholar. She had been in far more jobs than he had ever been in.

For instance she had once been a waitress during the long vacation. Another time she had worked in the cinema as an usherette. She had looked after the garden which he now neglected. She also had, he thought, a purer and more zealous love of learning than he had, a combination of love and precision. Her feeling for the classics made her adore Housman whom he had always considered a bad poet. But, strangely, after she had died he had read the poems again and found that they were more piercing than he could recall. Sometimes when searching in a drawer for a cuff link he would come on a glove or handkerchief that had belonged to her and would be stabbed by that dreadful agony.

But he was all right now, wasn't he? He was even reasonably happy. At least during term time. The Logic Professor would sometimes visit him arriving at about ten o'clock at night (for he seemed to have no regard for or even knowledge of time) and they might play chess for a time. Or drink beer. Or sometimes talk. Often about Wittgenstein who after a difficult life had said that he had been the happiest of men. 'Imagine that,' the Logic Professor would say, 'an odd man. A strange man. Fine fine mind. But odd.' (He himself dabbled in alchemy and had a sundial in his garden to tell the time.) 'Something very prophetic about him. He hated the academic world, you see, and I don't blame him.' Forgetting that it was three o'clock in the morning and settling himself like a gnome on a red cushion from which the feathers were falling out as if it were moulting.

At other times the Divinity Professor would come all aflame with the latest conference he had attended and bringing along with him questions such as 'How far can we use the work of atheistic writers in studying theology?' His thin, pale, ravaged face showed how he was struggling against the stream.

And then of course there were his neighbours (the two houses divided by a hedge), a young couple of whom the husband was a young mathematics lecturer and his wife a teacher in a city school. They had a child of about five years old.

When he had finished his work on Milton he made himself some tea and switched on TV. A keen-eyed announcer of the type satirised by Monty Python was looking straight at him and saying:

'... the initiative on Ireland. To discuss what the package may be we have brought along to the studio tonight Mr Ray of the Conservative Party, Mr Hume of the Labour Party and Mr O'Reilly of the Unionist Party and Miss Devlin.' Each face nodded modestly, mouthing some phantom unheard words which might have been Good Evening.

The announcer trained his gimlet eyes on one of the four people and said, 'And now, Mr Ray, may I ask you the following question. It has been rumoured that there is a split in the Tory Cabinet, some hawks saying that nothing should be done until the IRA have been beaten on the ground and some doves saying that there must be an initiative now. What are your views on that?'

'Well, Terence, first of all as you know very well I can't speak for the Cabinet, otherwise I would be a member of it, but it seems to me obvious speaking personally, and I must emphasise this, that we can't allow violence, the rule of violence, to prevail in Ireland or anywhere else. If you recall, an analagous situation arose in Cyprus some years ago as well as in Algeria ...'

'Yes I appreciate that but could you be more ...'

'I was trying to lay the foundation for an answer.'

'I understand. Can I take it then that you support the hawks? Mr Hume, what do you say to that?'

Mr Hume, a large slow man with beetling brows, leaned forward, dominating the screen like a serene basking shark.

'I think it is totally typical of the Conservative Party to take such a position. Their idea of solving any problem is to use force. The lame duck philosophy ... We see it in UCS, in their handling of the question of children's milk, in their whole philosophy of government ...'

'Yes but about the Irish initiative ...'

'I was just coming to that ... How can one believe that the IRA can be beaten when they obviously have behind them the whole Catholic ...'

Professor MacDuff put the volume down so that the lips moved but nothing could be heard. The mouths opened and shut like those of goldfish in a pond. He went to the back of the set and fiddled about with the controls. The faces lengthened and shortened like Dali's picture 'The Persistence of Memory' which shows watches and clocks hung like plasticine and liquorice over chairs. One could imagine cutting them up and eating them from a knife. 'The new Chinese food,' he thought. After he had played about for some time, allowing lines and dots to invade the screen, shaping faces and bodies into gluey masses, making the bodies tall and thin as the man in *Monsieur Hulot's Holiday* and fat and squat figures as in a spoon, he switched to the other channel which showed a number of girls dancing to the music of pop songs, swaying their bodies, flicking their hands, tribal people.

In the middle of this the phone rang and he went and answered it. 'Who's that?' he asked.

'BBC here. TV actually. That is Professor MacDuff, isn't it?'

'Yes this is Professor MacDuff.'

'Well, we have heard some rumours that you are teaching something to do with Desperate Dan and that you believe that this is as valuable as the more conventional stuff. We were wondering perhaps if you could come along to the studio and . . . '

'When?'

'When?' The voice seemed slightly disconcerted. 'Well, we were thinking in terms of this week. There's a spot called *Matters of Moment* which you may have watched . . . '

'What time?'

'If you could be along here at six o'clock on Friday night. Would that be all right? I could come along beforehand. I would handle it myself. My name is Burrow by the way.'

'On my own you mean?'

'Well, have you any other suggestions as to the format? We are always open to . . . '

'I thought I might discuss my ideas with a student perhaps if you . . . '

'Uh huh, have you anyone in mind?'

'As a matter of fact I have. His name is Mallow, Steven Mallow. I could provide you with his address if you . . . '

'That would be fine. We could get in touch with him. You would wish to discuss this issue with him, is that right?'

'That is right,' said the Professor picking up and laying down a copy of Catullus's poems which were lying near the phone.

Steven Mallow was the student who had defended him at the lecture. Not that he knew much about him except that in one examination he had gained one mark by defining Grimm's Law.

'I can take it then that you will be at the studio for five,' said Burrow. 'We usually provide some food before you go on and then of course you have to be made up. But don't worry about that. Our girls are very expert.'

'Fine,' said the Professor, 'if that's all . . . How long would we be on for?'

'Oh I think we could give you fifteen or twenty minutes. Is that fair? Does that sound OK to you?'

'Yes, it's fine as far as I am concerned.'

'Good then. We will see you at five. Ask for me personally please. Nigel Burrow.'

Professor MacDuff put down the phone. As he looked into the darkening garden he could see the statue of the Greek boxer, arms raised in front of him, pale and trembling in the twilight.

Another short time and I shall be leaving the university, he thought. And he couldn't imagine what it would be like to be alone without anything to do. He had no hobbies at all. He did not play golf, he did not play bowls, he wasn't a committee man. He would grow old on his own, that was inevitable and terrifying. But as he stood there the line from Tennyson came into his mind, 'Old age hath yet his honour and his toil', and he was vaguely comforted by the words and their sound. They seemed to be a guarantee of something, they seemed to provide a music which he could confront the imminent chaos with. He picked up the Catullus and gazed at it absently. Behind him he could see flashes of light from the TV but no sound and he went back and switched it off completely. After some time he prepared himself for bed. As he lay down he watched the cold white moon marbling the sky, a persistent chill scrutiny, an eye of light. Forgetting, once again he stretched out his arm as if to embrace his wife and then withdrew it remembering. Turning over on his side he went to sleep.

3

Professor MacDuff arrived at the studio at five o'clock precisely and after inquiring at the desk about where he should go was met by Burrow who took him up to a room on the table of which there were salads wrapped in cellophane and a selection of whiskies and beer and sherry. He refused anything to drink and sat down. He felt tense as he had never taken part in a broadcast before although Burrow tried to put him at his ease. With Burrow was a man called Russell who was perhaps the producer.

'I should like to say,' said Burrow, 'that we won't discuss the subject beforehand in case you might say during the programme, "As we were mentioning before we came onto the air!" That looks bad.'

'I understand,' said the Professor looking dispiritedly at the salad and convinced that he would not be able to do more than nibble at it.

'As a matter of fact once you get started,' said Russell, 'you will forget the cameras are there and will only be concerned with what you are saying. Isn't that so, Nigel?'

'Absolutely,' said Burrow. The professor suddenly had the idea that in a short while they would forget his name and even the programme in which he was taking part and that the only reason he was there was not that he should provide information or discuss fundamental things but that he should fill up a space. Pursuing his thought aloud he said:

'Have you ever thought that producers of programmes and editors of newspapers must continue with their work because there is a space which must be filled every day? Have you ever had that feeling?'

He looked at Russell who seemed not quite to understand the question.

'I've never actually thought of it in those terms,' he said, 'but I suppose it's true in a way. Certainly we're often pressed for time.'

This wasn't at all what the Professor had meant: in fact when he tried to say what he meant he wasn't sure that he could express it. It was something to do with the fact that newspapers and programmes had been originated and that since they had been originated they must proceed by the force of inertia. There was another theory he had about the relationship between space and time as far as news was concerned but he couldn't clarify the thought. The clock showed five past five and at that moment Mallow entered wearing a blue polo-necked jersey and tight green jeans and carrying a folder with papers.

'Hi,' he said raising his arm in salute. 'The communicators are together I see.' He laid his folder on the table and sat down.

'I think perhaps we should have something to eat now,' said Burrow. 'It isn't much but it's the best the canteen can do.'

They all began to remove the cellophane wrappings from the paper plates to reveal chicken and lettuce and beetroot and so on.

The Professor made vague dabs at it. His cuisine, what with the Chinese food, hadn't been very spectacular recently. His stomach was tied in knots as it always was before an important occasion, especially one where he would have to expend emotion. He drew in his breath and expelled it slowly knowing that the more tense he was the better he would perform provided that the tension didn't reach too high a pitch. There was silence for a while till Russell said, 'I suppose Nigel has told you that you'll have to be made up. But don't worry, it won't take long.'

'Right,' said Mallow. 'We don't get handbags do we,' and he laughed. Russell who looked as if he had often heard the joke smiled palely. For a moment MacDuff wondered if Mallow had been on television before. Dearest Mary, he said to the shade of his dead wife, please help me, it is all for you. He tried to forget where he was by thinking of his wife, sometimes seeing her with her head bent over a book and at other times pruning the roses beside the Greek statue in the garden. The curve of her back was ineffably painful to him.

The conversation around him blossomed and concerned itself with the chess tournament which was at that moment taking place in Russia.

The usual banalities were exchanged though MacDuff was surprised to notice that Mallow apparently didn't care much for chess. It wasn't the 'game for the working classes', he said at one stage. You wouldn't see working men play it in pubs. It was too 'intellectual'. MacDuff didn't take much part in the conversation: he was thinking deeply and he was also rather nervous. To use such an instrument . . .

Eventually Burrow rose from the table and said that if they followed him to the make-up room . . . He glanced at his watch and added that he wasn't trying to hurry them but . . .

So they went into the make-up room and it didn't take very long for a young girl to dab at MacDuff's cheeks. Then they were sitting on chairs on a platform, himself and Burrow and Mallow. Burrow was in the middle.

MacDuff thought to himself, I must appear very natural, not at all crazy. I musn't move my hands or my legs, I must show conviction.

They were ready. There were some preliminaries and then the programme was stopped and Burrow told them that what they had just said wouldn't go out but they were *really* ready now.

BURROW   'Tonight we have with us on *Matters of Moment* a Professor of English, Professor MacDuff' (he nodded towards MacDuff who moved his lips silently and nodded), 'and Stephen Mallow, a student of English in his class. Recently Professor MacDuff has been doing an analysis of comics with his students and this we hear has been causing some friction. Professor MacDuff however believes that comics have a useful part to play and those of us who had to study Shakespeare and Anglo-Saxon are I am sure wondering what he will say. First of all I should like to ask Mr Mallow if he was surprised when the Professor began to give lectures on the comics. Mr Mallow?'

MALLOW   'Not really. Perhaps I was surprised that Professor MacDuff should . . . But no I can't say I was surprised. After all lots of people read the comics, far more than read Shakespeare.'

BURROW   'Do you mean then that you would approve of Bingo
          rather than Brahms?'

MALLOW   'If that is what people want. Yes.'

BURROW   'I see. You would approve of lectures on Bingo?'

MALLOW   'Why not? What you have to understand is that most
          people don't read Shakespeare because they like him.
          They've been conned into reading him. Most people
          don't really like Brahms. They prefer to sit down by
          the fireside and read a good thriller. Or even a comic.
          You find spontaneous humour in a comic. It's not
          easy to write a good comic. You need technique.'

BURROW   'I see. What would you say to that, Professor
          MacDuff?'

MACDUFF 'As a matter of fact I have brought along with me
          some poems which I found in a magazine. I think it is
          a minor magazine but the people in it, the poets, are
          well known, so I am told. I should like to read one of
          these poems. It is called "Bus". It reads as follows:

>   Last bzz
> Izz
>   drizzly
>   missed.

Here is another poem:

>   Mamba
>   adder
>   boa constrictor
>   pricked her
>   mam
>   ba
>   anaconda
>   python.

The book from which this is taken, the magazine I
mean, is called *Azure Blues*. The blurb reads:

Simmons [that is the poet who wrote these verses]
undoubtedly shows in this book a feeling for urban

nuances which by linguistic modes he imposes on the reader. His poems in their simplicity and bizarre menace are a projection into the future.'

'I'm not quite sure,' said Burrow, 'are you approving or disapproving . . . ?'

'I was wondering whether Mr Mallow,' said the Professor, 'thought that these were good poems.'

'Well,' said Mallow, 'they seem to me to be attempting something new. They seem to me to have a certain avant-garde feeling . . .'

'I was wondering,' said MacDuff, 'whether in fact the working classes would find them interesting. You see,' said the Professor, 'I think in fact they're a load of crap.'

There was a long silence in the course of which Professor MacDuff regarded with satisfaction and merciless tranquillity the expressions which crossed Burrow's face ranging from bewilderment to fear and the appearance of being hunted. He looked at that moment as if he wanted to leave the box in which he was sitting and certainly, thought MacDuff, he would have brought the programme to an end if MacDuff hadn't insisted on its being sent out live.

Eventually Burrow said out of his bemusement, 'I thought Professor MacDuff that you were in fact . . .'

'As a matter of fact,' said the Professor, 'I have also brought along with me some lines from a poet whom I admire very much. His name is Shakespeare. The speech is from *Hamlet*. I should like to read it. It begins as follows:

' "To be or not to be that is the question." He is of course discussing suicide. It goes on,

> Whether 'tis nobler in the mind to suffer
> the slings and arrows of outrageous fortune
> or to take arms against a sea of troubles
> and by opposing end them.

'I am quite sure that the working men will recognise in these lines some of the difficulties that obsess us all.'

Mallow was signalling frantically.

'The fact is,' said the Professor, 'that the greater writers, the great composers, have all written about ordinary people. They were people who suffered. Shall I tell you what is wrong with people like Mallow and his kind? Envy. Pure envy. Why are they envious? They are envious because they cannot write like Shakespeare or like Sophocles or like Tolstoy. Do you think for a single moment that I could conceivably be interested in comics? Do you think for a moment that I look down on the working man? Do you think the great writers have looked down on the working man? Listen to a quotation from the comics. These sounds: "Aargh," "Yoops." They are like the sounds we would make when we came out of the slime. Aren't they? Shall I tell you something? It is the people who write the comics who look down on the working man. They are saying, "This is what the working man is like. This is what he prefers. He can't do any better than this. Give him any rubbish." And people like Mallow are the sort who try to deprive him of his heritage. Does he want us to go back to the slime?'

BURROW 'I'm sorry, I don't understand, I thought that you were defending the comics, that you were lecturing on them because you . . .'

MACDUFF 'Exactly. And why did I do that? I did that so that I would end up here. So that I would get an audience. Why did you want me here? Shall I tell you? I'll tell you the reason why you invited me here. You don't really give a damn one way or the other. You're not really interested in this at all, are you? You put me on the box because you thought I was going to be sensational, didn't you? That I would be entertaining. What the hell do you care about culture or about anything else? What do you care about all those people who have died in order to produce a poem or a symphony? You don't give a damn, do you? What can your friend Mallow say? He doesn't know enough about literature or about anything else to answer me. Does he even know enough about the comics? Does he know when the comic first started? Of course he doesn't. He's just a shallow nincompoop.'

BURROW 'Well, Mr Mallow?'

MALLOW 'I was just about to say that this trick is what one would expect of one who is trying to defend the élite and élitism. What has Professor MacDuff ever done except to stay in his ivory tower? Can he tell us if he has in fact gone out to the people? Can he tell us that he is not defending the rotting bastions of capitalism and that in order to do that he must defend the élitism of Shakespeare and the rest?'

MACDUFF 'You asked me whether I have done anything for the working man. Yes, shall I tell you what I've done for the working man? I've spent fifty years reading books and lecturing on them. I have spent fifty years trying to separate the false from the true. I have spent fifty years trying to nurse in people's minds that love of excellence which prevents us from being animals. You may call it an ivory tower if you like. I say that I've been protecting your civilisation, the civilisation of all men. I've been trying to keep us all from being yahoos. I'm not saying that I did it alone. But I helped to do it. I'm proud of doing it. Listen to this. This is Hamlet again speaking to Horatio his friend. Hamlet is concerned about his honour and he says:

> Absent thee from felicity awhile
> and in this harsh world draw thy breath in pain
> to tell my story.

Listen to this line:

> The still sad music of humanity.

'I could go on all night. When did Mallow or any of his kind ever write anything like that? Is that élitism? Shall I tell you about Mr Mallow and the rest of them? They think they know everything and they know nothing. Michelangelo and the other great painters didn't think it odd or wrong to be apprentices to painters lesser than themselves. This is the first generation we have had who think they have nothing to learn. I shall challenge Mr Mallow now. I shall ask him who wrote some great lines that I will quote. And to be perfectly fair if he can't answer these questions – since I am sure he cannot – I further challenge him to produce his alternatives.'

BURROW 'Mr Mallow?'

MALLOW 'I haven't been a professor in an ivory tower for fifty years so I haven't got the Professor's useless learning. It would be easy for me to ask him . . . '

MACDUFF 'Please let him ask me to identify any lines that he can produce that the listeners will be able to call great. For after all I believe in the audience out there. I believe they want the best. I don't believe they are content with bingo and dominoes or whatever Mr Mallow wants them to play. I don't believe they want to read comics. I don't believe they want to be like everyone else. Even on this medium which tries to make them so I still believe with Blake and all the great writers in their potential and their individuality. I believe that they can tell which writers will set down their joys and their sufferings. I believe that they can love the best and the excellent. I do not believe in the "working man" I believe in individual men. And I say that people like our friend here are practical illiterates who wouldn't know a line of poetry if it hit them between the eyes. Our universities are full of them. But they have to make the choice whether they want to go back to the world of the comics with their grunts or forward to the best that man has ever thought. I shall be retiring after this programme is over. I am not ashamed of my lifetime's work and I want to be clear about this. I'm not ashamed of my ivory tower if that is what you call it. I have been in the firing line and a much more complex one than most. It's true I haven't fought in wars with bullets but this is another war, and I am suggesting that those great writers as in any other war should not have died in vain. Listen:

The woods are lovely dark and deep.
But I have promises to keep
and miles to go before I sleep.
And miles to go before I sleep.

I don't give a damn for this medium. And I recognise
that I have to use a medium which I despise in order
to say the things I have to say. I regret that I had to
use subterfuge in order to get on it at all. But someone has to say the things I have said. I'm not ashamed
of my life. I have done what I set out to do. And I shall
continue doing it too.

'And I should like to say this to you. Always try to
tell the best from the trashy. You'd try to do it when
you're shopping, wouldn't you? Why shouldn't you
do it for your minds? The mind surely is as important
as the body. I'm not waiting for our friend to sum up.
I'm leaving now. I'm leaving because I'm not going to
allow them to package all this up very neatly. I say, to
hell with their medium. I can step out of the box any
time.'

And at that precise moment he did. He walked off down the
steps, and after a long time onto the street, which was sunny
and warm. He walked briskly along, meditating on how he
should word his letter of resignation. He thought about his
wife and felt her closer to him than ever before. She had worn
out her days on Greek scholarship, practising the discrimina-
tion without which we are animals, he thought. There can be
no doubt that whatever happens, we are right, he said to
himself. The signs glittered all round him, the signs of supermarkets and cinemas. He felt happy and free and gay, as if new
creative life had been given to him. Already he could hear the
phone ringing or its meaningful silence. It was necessary to
shed that load, to go to Spain at last . . .

from
THE VILLAGE

Easter Sunday

It was Easter Sunday and the women were all in church. They were wearing red hats and yellow hats and pink hats with flowers on them. On the blue velvet cloth that hung down in front of the pulpit there was a yellow cross. The pews were varnished and the light reflected from them. In one window there was a picture of a thinnish yellow Christ surrounded by a lot of weak-looking sheep.

Mrs Maclean was thinking, 'What I can't stand is the noise they both make in the morning, and their moods. If it isn't one then it is the other. Depressions and moods. Sometimes I feel that I shan't be able to go on. I thought they would like the school but neither of them does, and on holiday they are unbearable. What I would like to do is sit by the fire and read a thriller but I never have the time. Some day I shall manage that when they leave me and marry. That will be heaven.'

The minister said, 'I have a friend who once visited Yarmouth and he saw some fishermen there and he asked them, "Do you know about Christ? He also was a fisherman." And one of them said, "But did he go deep sea?" Still, it's not a joke really . . . '

The minister was thinking, 'I am wasting my time here. True, there is the picnic and the Guild but they don't really listen. I feel uncomfortable trying to get down to their level. I'm sure Christ wasn't like that. I am a scholar really. I should be writing theology but I haven't the time. I never have the time, though I have all the time in the world. They think I'm eccentric. That was the mistake I made from the beginning when I came here. I should have appeared jovial among them and the thing is I don't know anything about farming. It is difficult for me to find the simple images that Christ used. Still,

I shall have to continue. If only I took more joy in the baptisms.'

Outside the window there were the tombstones, some dating back two hundred years. Sometimes the children hand in hand in their little gaily-coloured frocks ran between them, playing games. At Easter time the light shone on their polished surfaces.

Mrs Milne thought, 'If he wants to leave me he can. I suppose everybody in the village knows that we don't get on. We even sleep in separate rooms. I said that the black eye had come from my falling downstairs. And they know perfectly well I don't polish the stairs, so how could I slip on them? I know he took her to the dance. He didn't make any attempt to disguise it. He shouts at me, "I hate you, I hate you." Though why he should I don't know since I do everything I can for him. Maybe I should have married Alasdair when he asked me. But that was a long time ago. I find this sermon silly. I wonder what he does with himself for the rest of the week. I wonder if he believes all this rubbish. Perhaps he does. But he's no good at funerals or visiting people, so they say. He's never visited me. He only goes to the houses where he'll get good food. I wouldn't have come, except this morning being Easter I felt so happy. I woke up and felt happy and I hadn't felt so happy for such a long time.'

The church was cool and there were lots of flowers in vases. The congregation sang *Abide with Me* and the minister gazed around him with satisfaction.

'That was the hymn they sang on the *Titanic*,' thought Mrs Gray. 'I remember hearing about that, or did I see a film? There was a pianist up to his knees in water. And they showed a shot of ice cubes in glasses while the ship was sinking. I thought that was clever. I wish I was in the city, this place is so boring. Last holidays I nearly didn't come back. I lay on my bed the last night while Jimmy snored and I nearly ran away. I could hear the traffic, I could imagine them coming out of the theatres and the cinemas. I could imagine the night clubs, women in furs getting into taxis, the glitter of the light on the street. We even went to the zoo which I love. There is nothing here, just those bloody hills with hardly any human beings about. One of these days I'll get a gun and shoot rabbits and hare. I might even shoot some sheep. I get up every morning and there's nothing to do. I'm sick of saying good morning to people I don't care for. The minister will be standing at the door as usual, bowing and scraping, oily little man. But I'm getting too old now to leave and Jimmy's job is here. I suppose that's life. I'm glad I didn't wear my flowered hat. Everyone else is wearing one, like schoolgirls.'

The collectors dressed in their best suits walked down the aisle looking dignified and important. One was the local joiner and the other the local painter. They smiled at everybody and passed the cloth bag along.

'How shall I tell my mother,' thought Mary, 'that I'm pregnant? I'll have to tell her soon. It's a wonder she doesn't know already. And he won't marry me, I know that. I could tell it from the beginning almost, but I lived in hope. He's a Sagittarius and I'm a Capricorn. Capricorn and Taurus get on all right but not Sagittarius and Capricorn. It said in my horoscope today that relationships this weekend would be tricky. Actually it was that particular night. I don't know what came over me, it must have been the Bloody Maries. It was like something you'd read in a woman's magazine. We were coming home from the dance and suddenly we were in a field. I didn't even know how we'd got there, perhaps we had wings. That's a laugh. Anyway he began to stroke me and talk to me and he said how touch was so important, I remember that. He stroked me and his talk went on and on, and there was a stream that I could hear flowing at the edge of the field. She'll throw me out. If it was the city it would be different but in a village everybody knows. Perhaps some of them know already. They'll sit in church but that's as far as it'll go. When it comes to helping there'll be a different story. It's going to be pretty tough and he won't help. They told me he has started going out with Susan. They were seen at a hotel last Friday. There are always spies who tell you these things. It might be better not to know, the pain's so great. The only problem is I don't know what to tell my mother. It'll break her heart, or so she'll say. But she won't think about me. She'll think about all those bitches with their flowery hats.'

The minister made the sign of the cross and hurried to the door to talk to them before they left. He hated that. The fact was he could hardly ever think of anything to say and they knew it. They knew that he didn't like them. They stood in the way of his ideal sermon which would be delivered to empty pews. He held out his hand, bowing slightly. They murmured some words which he could hardly hear. The children ran down to the road between the gravestones. They would turn out more or less exactly like their mothers. Sometimes he had terrible dreams of a figure in a huge office with a stamping machine which duplicated people. Transparencies. Once he thought he saw Christ himself turning his back on the village and setting off into the wilderness among the deer. Not even He could take them all the time. He would sometimes prefer the wastes and the innocent beasts. That was why he often went out on boats, to get away from them.

He watched with relief the last one leaving in the sparkling sunshine. The coloured hats bobbed down the road. He turned away and thought of his study where he could involve himself in the labyrinthine delights of theology. Thank God Christianity wasn't simple, there was so much to reconcile. If it had been simple it would have died long ago.

Sunday

I sat in the tall chair, my feet not quite touching the floor. It was a Sunday afternoon and I was visiting the unmarried fat girl who was called Rhoda and who seemed to me to be quite old, though perhaps she was about thirty-five. Her mother, a sharp-edged woman in black and with a perpetual drop at her nose, was in church as she so unfailingly was. I never knew what to say, but to be in another house was at least a change. I picked up a magazine called *Woman's Own* and looked through it. Rhoda was talking to the other fat girl from the village, a friend of hers also unmarried whose name was Annie. They were whispering and giggling – both fat girls together – and I turned the pages of the magazine. My attention was caught by a story which described how a nurse in a hospital stabbed her rival to death with a pair of scissors. I shook with fear and disgust. The two of them in front of me wavered like glazed dolls, their red faces gleaming.

Rhoda was saying, 'There was this Pole I met and he took me to the cinema. It was in the blackout.' There was much secretive giggling and I heard the last words, 'and I said I don't take Woodbines.' I felt hot and flustered and I thought of the scissors. Such an ordinary evil. Outside the window I could see the bare landscape, entombed in Sunday. A seagull was perched on the earthen wall staring stonily around it, its head moving in quick jerks as if it were on strings. I hated seagulls, they were so blank-eyed and voracious. There was nothing that they wouldn't eat.

Having nothing to do on Sundays I just went to people's houses and sat there, sometimes not speaking. I would often get a piece and jam. Annie was sitting opposite me, her huge red legs spread so that I could see her large green bloomers. I was thinking that the following morning I would have to explain to the teacher why there was a large blot of ink on my exercise book. I knew she would belt me. She had thin glasses above a narrow nose and she would sometimes belt people for no reason. The composition was called, 'A Day in the Life of a Postman'. I had written a story about an old woman who never got any letters from anyone and would stand in the lobby watching the letter box all day. It wasn't really about the postman at all and that was another reason why I would get the belt. I had spent three hours on it because I liked writing but I was miserable thinking how I would be belted.

Rhoda had a bicycle pump which she had taken over from the bed on which it had been lying. I knew that she didn't have a bicycle. They were talking about something and Rhoda was stroking the pump in her lap. They were both laughing and then Annie began to stroke it as well. I could't imagine either of them on a bicycle, they were so fat. I knew that both of them had been in England and sometimes they talked in English thinking that I was too young to understand. But I read a lot of English books and I could write good English.

Annie was saying, 'He took me to his flat. He had everything there. Everything.' They looked directly in each other's eyes and laughed in a high hysterical manner. Sometimes they stared at me sideways and seemed to be whispering about me. I could feel my knees flushing below the woollen shorts which my mother had knitted for me as she had also knitted the stockings with the diamond tops. The clock ticked heavily. Sunday was heavy on the village. It was like a huge dull suety pudding with dull heavy raisins in it. The ditch outside the window was full of dirty old cans and there were little yellow primroses lodged in the bank above it.

I felt uncomfortable as if there was something going on that I didn't understand. I wanted to leave but I couldn't think how I could manage it. Sometimes I went to a house and I couldn't get up to go because I was too shy. I felt that perhaps they wanted me, for some reason, to go. One of them looked at me and said, 'Too small,' and they giggled again. I felt my face redden and grow hot. I didn't want to be belted but there was no way round it. It was unjust but that was how things were. I hated the teacher. I hated her thin glasses and her sarcastic voice. I hated the dusty globe which lay on her desk. But I would have to go to school anyway since this time I didn't feel sick.

I got up, thinking, 'Tomorrow I shall wear my new sandals and I shall run home from school.' I was suddenly happy. They were whispering, their heads close together, Rhoda stroking the bicycle pump. When I reached the door I opened it quickly, pulled it behind me quickly, and ran as fast as I could home. I would try on my sandals again if my mother would let me. It was something to look forward to. But I couldn't do anything about the blot. To rub it out would leave a worse mark. I would just have to take what was coming to me. I couldn't do anything at all about it.

The Old Woman and the Rat

When the old woman went into the barn she saw the rat and she also saw the feathers of the little yellow chicken among which the rat was sitting. It was a large grey rat and its whiskers quivered. She knew that there was no way out for it but past her, for there was a hole between the door and the wall and she knew that this was the place where the rat had entered. She regretted that she had not filled this up before. It seemed that the rat was mocking her but certainly it knew that she was present. And it also knew that the chickens had belonged to her, those beautiful little chickens of bright yellow which she had nursed so carefully and which had seemed so much the sign of a new spring. The day was Easter Friday.

As she gazed at the rat she felt a ladder of distaste shudder up her spine climbed by many rats, but she stood where she was and then bent down slowly to pick up a plank of wood with nails at one end of it. Her back ached as she bent. The barn itself was large, spacious and clean with a stone floor. At the far end were the remains of the chickens and the hens. Above were the rafters on which hung an old mouldy saddle which her father had once had for the horses. It hung its wings on both sides of the rafter. She thought, and then quite deliberately she stuffed it, mouldy and breaking as it was, into the hole which the rat had entered by. All this while the rat watched her with bright intelligent eyes as if it knew perfectly well what she was up to. The arena was prepared, the large clean spacious arena. She made her way rather fearfully towards the rat. She felt rather unsteady but angry. After all, she was quite old and she had arthritis in her hands and she had varicose veins in her legs. The rat certainly was fitter than her, more agile, more swift. She advanced on the rat steadily with her plank, the nailed end foremost. It waited, almost contemptuously. She went up to it and thrust the plank at it. It moved rapidly away and crouched, looking at her, its long rat tail behind it, its whiskers quivering, its bright eyes moving hither and thither. Where have you been? she thought. Before the chickens, where have you been? She thought of her husband, dead in the cemetery, and closed her eyes. She deliberately made visions of flowers appear.

She thought. Then slowly she went over to a big disused table which she had put in the barn many years before and propped it up on end, to cut off part of the space. But that was useless for the rat immediatly climbed up to its top and stood there slightly swaying and half smiling. For the first time as she looked up at it she thought that it might leap down at her from above and this frightened her. She was also frightened that her fear might be communicated to the rat which might then attack her. She backed away from the rat slowly, thinking. What a terrible thing to have this battle when she could be in church, but then some things were more important even than church. She backed towards the door still holding the short nailed plank ahead of her. She pulled the door slowly behind her and backed out, shutting the door quickly. She was determined that the rat would not escape. She almost felt the rat's claws in her back as she turned away but she knew that it was still there in the barn with the remains of its feast, its obscene supper. She went into the house and got a box of matches. Then she went round the side of the house in the great calm of the morning and got a lot of straw and grass, all of which was dry because of the blue cloudless weather. She felt happy now that she had something to do. But clutching her masses of grass and straw and with the box of matches in the pocket of her apron she was slightly frightened entering the bare arena again. Still it was better to be bare than not, for one knew where one was then. She felt in her mouth the tiny fragile bones of the chickens, and the taste of the blood. She slowly opened the door and edged in with all that grass and straw. The rat stayed where it was, licking its body. She threw the straw and the grass as far towards it as she could and then rapidly picked up the plank with the nails again, her back vibrating with terror. The rat watched her, more uneasily now, as if wondering what she was up to. She lit the match nervously and threw the lighted flame among the dry straw and the grass. The fire ran along it boiling like illuminated rats. The rat backed away into its corner, snarling. Smoke began to rise and billow round it, for there must have been some dampness at the centre of the straw somewhere. She backed towards the door. The rat rushed out through the smoke towards her, its teeth drawn back. Behind the rat she saw the flames rising and the smoke. It seemed to have emerged out of, been generated by, the fire. The rat made for the place where she had stuffed the remains of the broken winged saddle. As it did so she swiped at it with the nailed plank. It squirmed away, half hit. It turned and faced her snarling as if it knew that she was the only obstacle to its escape. Its face looked incredibly fierce and evil as if all the desire for life had been concentrated there. It wished to live at all costs. For a moment she was terrified at what she had done, at the smoking arena she was in. But she knew that the stone floor would prevent the fire from spreading. The rat launched itself at her, knowing that she was the enemy, that there was no going back through the smoke. She swung the nailed plank as its face, snarling and distorted, looked towards her, and she felt it hit the rat, felt the rat's claws scrabbling against it as if it wanted to get purchase on it, to grip it and climb towards her. She swung the plank against the floor and banged and banged. The rat's head and body squelched against the stone floor of the barn which had once been filled with sacks of corn. She banged and banged till the shudders left her back and breast and legs. She banged it so that it was a flat grey mess on the floor. Then after a while flushed and panting she opened the door on the wide day. She threw the plank as far away as she could into the undergrowth. There were bits of rat attached to it. No doubt the birds of the air would finish it off. She forced herself to get a spade to detach the smashed body from the floor. She threw the mashed carcass from the spade into the bushes as well and then fetched pail after pail of water which she splashed over the place where the body had been. She cleaned and cleaned till there was not even the shadow of the rat left. When the straw had finally burned itself out she took that away as well, and the remains of the chicken and the hens which had themselves got burnt. She spent a long time cleaning the barn, making it bright as new. When she had finished she went into the house and made herself strong tea. It was too late for church now. Still she could go there in the evening. Meanwhile she could sleep for a while by the window, for she felt empty and victorious. As she passed her mirror she saw that her face looked gaunt and fulfilled, and she hadn't felt so light for a long time.

The Delicate Threads

I am ten years old but I am supposed to be very intelligent. I heard my father say that one night to my mother but he didn't tell me. It was something to do with the IQ test he gave me out of a blue book one Sunday afternoon when it was raining and there was nothing much to do. As a matter of fact there is little to do here anyway. Perhaps that was why my father gave me my funny name. I know that he reads a lot and sleeps a lot as well. Still a doctor has plenty of time on his hands in the village: no one ever dies here. They just rot away.

I spend most of my time thinking up new ideas. I am not an inventor or anything like that: I'm what you might call an author. But one of these days I'll go and find what's in the cave. My father says that a village is bound together by a lot of fine threads and that if you pull on one you disturb the whole village. He probably got that out of one of his sloppy books. I hardly ever read and that puzzles him. But the thing is that I see the end of the story almost from the very first page. I have this sixth sense, I suppose you might call it. It's the same with TV, I can't be bothered much with it either. All the other boys were on about Colditz. I thought it was daft, all these silly people making up silly plans which never came to anything, and they were supposed to be grown up men. Even my father liked Colditz.

I must tell you about one incident of which I'm very proud, just to show you the kind of thing that I can do. The postman in our village is a great gossip. He gets up at six in the morning and he sets off on his old bicycle, carrying his bag, and waving cheerfully to anyone who is up at that time. He's a bit of a fool actually. He has no business to go broadcasting the things he does, such as that Mrs Moss has been ordering clothes again without telling her husband. He can tell from the mail order catalogue, you see. I sometimes think that he also opens all the letters. How else could he have known that Mrs Murray got a tax refund? Yet he told various people that.

But the person he told our family about, when he was leaning against the gatepost one fine summer morning, and the sun sparkled off his bicycle, was young Mrs Ross. He told us that she got a letter regularly in a man's handwriting from Essex (where she had been working before she got married) but that as her husband was away at work before he, the postman, got to the house, he never saw the letters. Each letter was always addressed to Mrs James Ross, and he often wondered what James would do if he knew what was going on behind his back. As a matter of fact I myself think James Ross is a bit of a twit. Anyone who can spend his time as a shepherd must be that. All these stupid sheep he looks at all day. Also he chased me away once from his hen house though I had no intention of stealing the eggs. All I wanted was to look at them. Anyway the postman never noticed me standing there. I thought about his story for a long time. I brood a lot especially in the attic and I look down through the skylight window on the houses of the village. It gives me a feeling of power, to watch all these clods working at their silly jobs. What a life! I'll soon be out of here when I get older. I'm fed up of the place. I've got a lot of mirrors in the attic and sometimes I play with my little theatre and make masks for myself.

But anyway one day when the postman came to the house again I stopped him and asked him if he would like a cup of tea. I told him my mother had invited him in and as she is quite good-looking he was flattered. I had arranged this with my mother before, saying that I wanted to have a look at his bicycle as I wished to buy one. She was agreeable to this though she couldn't see why I couldn't just ask him about the bicycle when he was there himself. But I said I was too shy. So then she said she'd ask him but I said no, he would tell everybody and I wanted it to be a secret. Anyway while he was in the house I searched among the letters in the bag and found one from Essex addressed to Mrs James Ross. I stroked out the 's' of

'Mrs' with a pen and returned it to the bag just in time as the old fool came round the corner looking very pleased with himself.

Now I knew the mind of the postman well. I knew that he had his suspicions about the letter and I also knew that his job bored him, cycling round the village day after day and waving good morning, and bringing letters to people when he himself got none. When he was very young he had wanted to be an engineer and even yet he was good at repairing things. So I knew that he felt bitter. You could tell that by the way he smiled at people when he was talking to them but frowned immediately they turned away from him. As I am only ten, people don't take any notice of me, so I am allowed to see things like that. Well, I considered that he would want to find out once and for all what was going on and that he would take the letter not to James's wife but to James himself (he might not be able to imagine how or why the 's' had been stroked out but he would take advantage of it). If the wife later said anything to him, then he was in the clear. And that is exactly what he did. I like having this power over people, making them do things that deep down they themselves want to do. The result was that the husband gave his wife the most awful thumping and the postman sang most gloriously at church on Sunday believing that what he had done was, in the sight of God, morally reasonable. That was one of my most interesting enterprises.

The other one I wish to tell you about since it gave me complete control where I most wanted it was the following. One hallowe'en night I asked my father if I could dress up as a guiser and go out and collect apples and oranges, which he agreed to. My father really is a very pleasant man on the whole and treats me with much dignity and sensitivity. But then everyone does this if they can keep you quiet. It's all a matter of trading, as with stamps. Anyway I dressed up as a man from the classics whose name was Agamemnon. I have read a little, you know, it's just that sometimes I get bored and I have a reason to be interested in the Greek stuff as I will tell you later (all the best stories have surprise endings and I'm saving one for you).

I knew that he had been on an expedition to Troy and had a lot of trouble from Achilles, the bloke with the weak heel. I like him quite a lot. I saw a picture once of Achilles stabbing Hector while his round shield was in the centre of the picture like a wheel. I liked that. You call that symbolism. My father acts surprised when I tell him these new words and he sometimes looks at me in a horrified manner.

In any case I dressed up as this wet Greek and set off to all the houses. It was the night that my father was directing the local play and it was lucky it was that night since he usually came home very late, very mellow and fulfilled. That sort of thing gave him a kick. Actually his plays are a load of rubbish and so are the actors and actresses. Most of them work in shops and I suppose it's a change from banging away at the till, but even I realise that they're very poor actors.

Well, at about ten o'clock I arrived at this house where Mr Dewhurst stays. He's a stranger who came into the village about six months ago and he's got a big blue Jaguar and a lot of money. He's built himself a swimming pool at this huge house and they say that he's something to do with films. He's a big fellow with a moustache and when he goes shopping he wears a hunting jacket and a tweed cap and he carries a cane. He looks in actual fact a bit of a drip though some people say that he's very dangerous to the local women, especially those who fancy themselves as actresses and see themselves in Hollywood. He doesn't seem to be married and he throws a lot of parties. Once I did some bobs-a-job for him since I amuse myself by belonging to a Scout Club, and one of the jobs he gave me was to clean out the dining room. It was full of ashtrays which were crammed with bits of cigars and cigarettes and there were lots of glasses lying about the floor. He gave me a pound for cleaning up that lot. I told my mother about it and she phoned up and thanked him.

Anyway it was a very glittering night and there were lots of stars in the sky and I was walking along the road as Agamemnon. His house is in a wood and there's a path up to it. I could hear animals rustling among the undergrowth but apart from that there was a deep silence. There were however lights on in the house which I had cased pretty thoroughly when I was doing my bob-a-job. I didn't go to the front door at all. I went for the light ladder in the woodshed where I had seen it before and set it up against the window. It was very quiet except that now and again I could hear a woman's laughter. I set the ladder slowly and carefully against the wall and climbed in through the window. I had noticed that he was a fresh air fiend when I was up before and that nearly all the windows were open. Anyway, not to be too rural and boring with my story, I climbed in (I have actually a very good head for heights) and crawled slowly along the corridor till I came to the room from which I could hear the laughter coming. I stood up then and very quickly pushed the door open. To this day I cannot forget that scene. He was on top of my mother and as he turned round I could see that he wasn't wearing his pants but that they were on the chair beside the bed. The expression on his face was quite indescribable. I couldn't begin to tell you about it. Perhaps if I had brought a camera . . . The tableau (another word I found recently) was frozen. There I was dressed as Agamemnon and there were the two of them caught in the act.

My mother screamed, a high scream that went on and on. She of course knew of my disguise and she told him who I was before he could belt me out of the room and the window. In any case he offered me all sorts of money which I refused. I was really very dignified, asking him what he thought I was, did he think that I would corrupt myself in that cheap manner, etc. etc. I must say that he seemed very confused and that his eyes gradually glazed over. I have found that this happens often when older people have any real dealings with me. I had of course succeeded in getting my mother into my power which had been my aim from the start. There is nothing that she will now refuse me, nothing at all.

But I'll tell you something. Where I'm going to now is the cave. I want to test out my father's words about the threads which bind the village together and which vibrate all the time according to him. What I shall find in the cave I don't know but I'm sure it must be something horrible, some terrible stinking monster which gnaws and sleeps and belches, some being such as the world has never seen in the daytime. I have had this feeling in my bones for a long time, as if it was my destiny to find this monster and see what it has to say for itself. Not that I want to fight it really. I shall make use of it if I can, but I do know that it is waiting there in the darkness. It won't suspect a ten year old boy of trickery or cunning or destructiveness, surely. Like all monsters it will probably be stupid. Like all people, really. And in any case the victory is predestined. After all, my father didn't name me Theseus for nothing.

The Conversation

'Thank you for coming, Iain. Pain? No, he wasn't in pain. He got quieter and quieter. You wouldn't have known him, he got so quiet. You see, the minister used to come a lot. He is a very kind man really though he is strict and he helped him a great deal. Norman gave up all his nonsense and became very calm.

'The minister used to sit by the bed and read passages to him from the Bible even on the hottest days. I admired him for that. I will always remember him for that. Not many ministers would do it but this one is a good visitor.

'At first before the minister came Norman would talk about the tricks he used to play on the village people, like the time he put a crab on Roddy's chair. These were the vain things he would talk about but of course he didn't know then that he was dying. We should always remember, Iain, that we are going to die. Joking is all very well, but life is a serious thing.

'And he would talk about his school-days and about football games and things like that. After all, he was only sixteen.

'But then the minister came and he changed for the better. He would lie in his bed and listen to the Bible and ask questions. I once heard him asking why Abraham was ready to sacrifice Isaac and the minister told him the reason. The minister said that he had a natural spirit of inquiry which was a good thing if it was steered in the right direction. He said that his questions were those of the natural man but that later they would lead to the calmness of the spiritual man.

'And the minister would pray with him for a long time. He would ask for God's help because we are all sinners and if God won't help us who will? We must all remember that we are in the hands of God.

'One day I went in and Norman screamed at me that the

minister had told him he was dying. There were tears running down his cheek. I took his hand in mine and I said, "We are all dying. That is what the minister meant." "That is not what he meant," he said weakly as he lay back on the pillow. It was a great struggle for him to fight against the natural man; after all what can you expect of a boy of sixteen? It was warm in the room; a summer dying is the worst. I used to bring him in cups of milk and he would drink them propped up on his pillow. Sometimes he would look very beautiful, like an angel, he was so thin and white. The minister would never take anything. Perhaps he thought that as we are very poor we needed all our food for ourselves.

'One night Norman had a nightmare and he shouted to me to put the minister away because he was killing him but I knew that was just the devil trying to master him. And so I hushed him to sleep.

'But the minister was attentive, I must say that for him. He is a real minister, a real compassionate man. He wished to save Norman's soul before he died, and he wrestled with the devil on his behalf, and sought to take his thoughts away from the vain things of this world to the eternal treasures of the next world which moths will not corrupt. The doctor asked me if anyone was visiting Norman and I told him about the minister. He didn't say anything but he is not really a good doctor anyway, he bounces into the room joking all the time as if he was a clown. Sometimes he will even dance, he has no dignity at all. I've even heard him singing a song. Imagine a professional man acting like that. That's all he is, an actor. A lot of people like him, but I don't think a man as undignified as that can be a good doctor. Professional people should be more serious and not allow themselves to be laughed at. Norman liked him well enough. Indeed he looked forward to his visits.

'One afternoon on a hot day – it was a Wednesday – I went into the bedroom and it was very quiet. The curtains were blowing gently in the breeze. I was carrying a cup with some milk in it and when I looked at the bed I thought at first that Norman was asleep. He lay so still and his hair was over his brow. He looked like a statue. I put the milk down beside the bed on a small table and I touched his forehead. It was cold. I knew then that he had died. I picked the Bible up from the floor where it had dropped from his hand as he fell asleep. The Bible was cold but underneath it the floor was warm. I remember that very well, the black leather of the Bible, and the warmth of the floor round about it. That was a week last Wednesday. He was buried on the following Friday. He was sixteen years old and three days when he died.

'Are you going then? Are you sure you won't have a cup of tea? No? Well, thank you for coming, Iain. You and he were great friends in the old days, I know that; he often used to talk about you. But as I told you he became very quiet and serious at the end. He put away the natural man and became more spiritual and I am very glad of that. For if we aren't spiritual, if we do not lean on the mercy of God, what are we? What are we indeed?'

I'll Remember You

Life is very strange and we never know when we are young how things will turn out. I had bitter thoughts about life this evening when my grandchild Robert told me his story. Like his mother he is fair-haired and blue-eyed and looks as if butter would not melt in his mouth though in fact like most children he is cunning, watchful and various.

Robert as I have said came rushing in to tell his story, very frightened indeed. There is in the village an old fat woman with red legs and a large red face and a moustache who stays by herself in a thatched house and is the butt of the village boys. They knock on the door of her house and run away as she comes out, staring angrily round her and swearing in a loud voice. Her name is Murdina and she has been alone now for many years after her aged parents, whom she looked after, died. Those who out of compassion have visited her house say that it is extremely dirty and smelly and infested with cats which she feeds haphazardly from saucers which litter the floor.

This particular summer's day Robert (whom I have often belted for playing pranks of this nature) and some of his friends knocked on the door as usual and waited for the fat woman to come out, trembling with rage, her red cheeks inflated and turning a deep purple, and her knickers as usual half down her ankles. This time, however, no one appeared and out of the bravado created by a summer's day (having tired of the tent choked with smoke) they crept up to the door again, feeling cheated by her failure to appear, and fearfully crept inside. They came face to face with a number of half-wild cats with green eyes and nearly ran back into the hot sunlight again where the corn and grass were fiercely growing by the well not far from the thatched house. But feeling that it would be cowardly to run away after coming so far, they crawled into the main room. They saw her lying asleep there, her head leaning against the back of the chair, her arms sprawled in front of her like those of a boxer who has gone back to his corner after a particularly fierce round and leans exhausted against the ropes, his legs spread out.

The house was very silent and the only sound to be heard was the buzz of a fly which finally as they watched settled on her almost bald head and stayed there, vibrating. What frightened them was that she made no move to swat at the fly and displace it from her head. There was no fuel in the fireplace and on the floor was a saucer which the cats had licked of all the milk that it had contained. For a long time they stayed there in the silence watching the large black fly settled on her bald head. Then with one accord, knowing that there was something wrong, they all rushed out into the hot sunlight and ran home to tell their story. Robert told me. I leathered him and told my wife who immediately with some women went to the house. They found her lying dead in the chair.

We lay in the corn on that autumn night while the autumn moon shone overhead. I kissed her and touched her breasts. She closed her eyes and the moon lighted the small blue veins. Her face was small and white and fragile, her outspread legs luminous in the moonlight. There was no sound to be heard but that of the sea in the distance, resonant and nostalgic. The tides of her blood seemed to move with the salty tides. It was barely possible to feel such tenderness and not have one's heart broken. It was not possible to see any other face in the harmony of the universe in that harvest time. As her arms encircled me she looked vulnerable, desirable and precious. I kissed her, holding her tight in my arms. She moved a little, sighing with either contentment or sorrow. We would not marry because of her aged parents as she had a great sense of responsibility. The sea roared in our blood and beyond us, heavy with its burden of the dead and the resurrected. I touched her cheeks and they were wet with brine.

I woke up and there was a fly on her bald head. Large and fat she swam towards me across the water, a porpoise that had come to grief, a whale of that terrifying sea with its many currents. There was a child somewhere crying. I brushed the fly away hearing his nightmare cry in the cool room with the moonlight on his brow. My aged wife was telling me about the ring that had been found in a drawer in a piece of aged blue cloth. I didn't say anything, but the brine sprang from my eyes as I thought of how we live, tethered and roped, by that well which once contained the freshest of waters and now will hardly show us even our own reflections without comedy and bitterness.

The Ghost

One night I met the ghost at the corner of the road and it looked exactly like a spook I had seen in a small book of paintings by Miro.

'It's a fine night,' it said, wavering in front of me, just like a sheet such as my mother used to wash in the spring.

'It is that,' I said, not very frightened, for this ghost looked quite comic and friendly and not at all intimidating. There was something even cosy about it.

'Of course you have to believe in my existence now,' it went on. 'Not many people believe in ghosts but I must admit that I like to be believed in. I like to be friendly. I miss my conversations with people, about the weather and so on.'

'I do,' I said, 'believe in you. After all, you are there, aren't you?'

'I am indeed,' it said. 'And another thing, ghosts aren't always gloomy. For instance, I come back regularly to be among people. I miss them a lot. Most people are really quite kind and interesting. You don't particularly care for people, do you?'

'I wouldn't say that,' I said. 'I wouldn't say that at all.'

'I see. It's just all that stuff you write about the Clearances and old women. It's all very gloomy really. I used to write little plays myself but they were usually very comic. Most people thought they were amusing and said that they cheered them up. I keep up, you know. I visit houses now and again after midnight and I keep up with the magazines.'

'I'm glad to hear that,' I said. 'They'll need your subscriptions the way things are going.' I was beginning to think that this was really rather a shallow ghost.

The ghost laughed a little but I don't think it quite saw the point of my joke.

'After all,' it continued, 'isn't it time you wrote something cheerful and happy? On the spur of the moment as it were. Have you ever seen a cockerel for instance crowing in the early morning? I have had occasion to. It looks very beautiful, its claws thrust into the ground. You should have a look at animals, for instance. Or don't you agree?'

'Oh, I do agree. Only it troubles me to see you out here on such a fine night. Has it ever occurred to you that you might frighten people? You don't frighten me but that's because you talk in such a literary manner and are obviously interested in my work. But other people might not be so calm.'

'To tell you the truth,' said the ghost, 'no one has ever had a heart attack because of me. Anyway I thought I'd give you some advice. When you think of it there are a lot of comic people in the village, and there have been a lot of funny incidents. Now I've got an idea for you. Why don't you write a play about two sisters who fall in love with a poacher? They are always cooking the fish he brings back but they don't know it's been stolen. And you could have a fat policeman in it.'

'No,' I said, 'I don't think that would suit me at all. Not at all.'

'Well, then,' said the ghost, 'what about a story about an oldish man who lives with his mother and sends off a letter to a Marriage Bureau? There's plenty of comic material in that.'

'True,' I said and there was a long silence.

'On the other hand,' I said speaking with difficulty, because of my boredom, 'I have been brought up on Kafka and Kierkegaard and I don't think I would like to write that sort of stuff at all. Where is the art in that? Anyway I don't know two such sisters.'

'But can't you invent them?'

'I don't work like that,' I said.

'I only thought,' said the ghost sadly. In fact the longer it talked to me the sadder it seemed to get.

'I mean, let's face it,' it began again. 'The past is past, isn't it? We need something more cheerful. I like a lot of colour myself. I get on best with children. I have a lot of friends who are children. We go about together in the spring, dancing about. I suppose people must think we are clouds.'

'I suppose they must,' I said grimly. 'Especially Wordsworth. I'm very glad you have brought me those interesting ideas . . . '

'Oh, I've got more, I've got lots more. For instance,' the ghost said, sitting or seeming to sit on a stone, 'this man gets a wife after all from the Marriage Bureau and it turns out she's got a wooden leg. You could make something funny out of that.'

'That would be possible,' I said carefully. 'On the other hand, where is the moral in it?'

'But would it need to have a moral?'

'As a ghost born and bred in the Highlands you ought to know better than that,' I said. 'Really, I'm ashamed of you. Or rather, I'm ashamed that you haven't worked that out for yourself. I think that your literary standards are very low. Why, if we had been writing about Marriage Bureaux and wooden legs we would be back where we were before.'

'Where were we before then?' said the ghost which now appeared to be smoking a pipe.

'I mean,' I said, 'the very fact that you are here suggests that there is more to life than materialism and humour and wooden legs.'

'Is that so, now? I wonder why you should believe that. Still, I suppose, having seen a ghost, you will believe anything.'

'Well,' I said, 'we'd be back to the primitive silly work which no one could take seriously.'

'I took it seriously,' said the ghost. 'And many people like me took it seriously. And after all I do exist though you didn't believe so before, did you?'

'I certainly didn't,' I answered, feeling my head spinning a little for I wasn't quite sure what the appearance of the ghost meant. 'I certainly didn't,' I repeated. 'Nor do I believe in astrology and seances and other things like that.'

'There you are, then,' said the ghost cheerfully as if it had proved something of importance. 'And here I am waiting to be cheered up and you are depressing me with your morality. You should have a look round you at the world as it is. It is quite beautiful, isn't it? Look at that moon for instance and the stars. And do you hear that stream running along the ditch? Why don't you pay attention to things like that?'

'But I do notice them,' I said. 'And I don't need you to remind me of them. So why don't you just go away?'

'I was only trying to help,' said the ghost. 'I was only trying to give you ideas. For instance, I have another idea at this moment. Why don't you write a story about a man who inherits a piece of land and it turns into . . . '

'Sorry,' I said, 'I don't like any of your ideas. You don't seem to me to be very serious for a ghost. I thought ghosts were always very serious.'

'I don't see why ghosts would be any more serious than other people,' said the ghost. 'It all depends on your taste.'

'You know what you like, I suppose,' I said contemptuously.

'Exactly,' said the ghost. 'I couldn't have put it better myself.'

'Hm.'

'And to tell you the truth I used to write plays myself. One was called *Hector's Wedding*. Have you ever heard of it?'

'I'm afraid I . . . '

'Well, what about *Where There's a Will There's a Way*? That was about a crofter and his land. It was very funny. The villagers used to split their sides watching that one.'

'I am sure they did,' I said. 'But to be quite honest with you, I never . . . '

'Never mind. It doesn't matter . . . ' But the ghost looked a bit crestfallen just the same.

'It's a great pity,' I said. 'I'm sure they were very amusing.'

'As a matter of fact I believed a lot in inspiration,' said the ghost, cheering up again. 'Whenever I was scything or doing some work around the house I would be visited by inspiration and I would come in at once and put pen to paper. Everyone was amazed by my gift.'

'That's very interesting,' I said.

'All my work was done like that. All my best work, that is. I was never one for sitting down and chewing my pen. I don't suppose you would write a preface to my plays, would you? I would like to see myself in print,' it said wistfully.

'I don't even know where they are,' I said firmly. 'And in any case plays are not my line.'

'Just a thought,' said the ghost. 'I would like to make people happy and my plays went down very well.'

'But how did they use language?' I said. 'That's very important, you know.'

'Language? The words came to my lips and I wrote them down.'

'I see,' I said. 'In that case you've never heard of Henry James.'

'No I haven't. Not at all. And I would like very much if you didn't make fun of me.'

'I'm not making fun of you,' I said. 'And you must remember that it was you who stopped me, not the other way round.'

'I was just giving you suggestions,' said the ghost who seemed to have gone into a huff. 'After all it is very terrible when you are visited by inspiration and you have no pen and can't write anything.'

'Yes,' I said with sudden pity. 'It must be like these writers in Russia.'

'I don't know about that but it is very uncomfortable.'

'I'll tell you what,' I said, 'you just stop me now and again and you can give me more ideas for plays and things like that. Mind you, there's no guarantee that I'll use any of them. But I'll think about them. And the happier they are the better, since we are in a happy phase.'

'I shall certainly do that,' said the ghost happily. 'I'm really glad I met you. I thought you would be very gloomy but you aren't like that at all. You are really quite sensitive and kind.'

'I try to be,' I said. 'After all, your work is older than mine, closer to the people.'

'That's very true,' said the ghost contentedly.

'And now I'll have to be going,' I said. 'I've got a lot of things to do.'

'I won't keep you any longer,' said the ghost getting up rapidly from the stone on which it seemed to be sitting. 'You are, I am sure, a very busy man. And I have a lot of time on my hands. But now that you have given me a purpose I shall get to work immediately.'

'You do that,' I said. 'After all if I'm a man of the world you are a man of the next world.'

He laughed very heartily at this joke which I remembered from a book called *The Best Hundred Ghost Jokes*. He laughed so much that I thought he would never be able to resume his fairly upright shape again but he did and still laughing he waved and disappeared. I walked on under the moon and the stars thinking that no matter where you went there were always funny stories to be got and I must learn about them somehow. A light anecdote or two might distract my two or three agonised readers wherever they are, scattered on the surface of this hilarious tortured globe. Even the one who reads my work back to front in Cambodia.

The Red Door

When Murdo woke up after Hallowe'en and went out into the
cold air to see whether anything was stirring in the world
around him, he discovered that his door which had formerly
been painted green was now painted red. He stared at it for a
long time, scratching his head slowly as if at first he didn't
believe that it was his own door. In fact he went into the house
again and had a look at his frugally prepared breakfast –
porridge, scones and tea – and even studied the damp patch on
the wall before he convinced himself that it was his own house.

Now Murdo was a bachelor who had never brought himself
to propose marriage to anyone. He lived by himself, prepared
his own food, darned his own socks, washed his own clothes
and cultivated his own small piece of ground. He was liked by
everybody since he didn't offend anyone by gossiping and
maintained a long silence unless he had something of importance
to say.

The previous night children had knocked on his door and
sung songs to him. He had given them apples, oranges, and
nuts which he had bought specially from a shop. He had gazed
in amazement at the mask of senility on one face, at the mask of
a wildcat on another and at the mask of a spaceman on the face
of a little boy whom he could swear he knew.

Having made sure that he was in his own house again he went
out and studied the door for a second time. When he touched
the red paint he found that it was quite dry. He had no feeling
of anger at all, only puzzlement. After all, no one in his
experience had had a red door in the village before. Green
doors, yellow doors, and even blue doors, but never a red door.
It certainly singled him out. The door was as red as the winter
sun he saw in the sky.

Murdo had never in his life done anything unusual. Indeed because he was a bachelor he felt it necessary that he should be as like the other villagers as possible. He read the *Daily Record* as they did, after dinner he slept by the fire as they did, he would converse with his neighbour while hammering a post into the ground. He would even play draughts with one of them sometimes.

Nevertheless there were times when he felt that there was more to life than that. He would feel this especially on summer nights when the harvest moon was in the sky – the moon that ripened the barley – and the earth was painted with an unearthly glow and the sea was like a strange volume which none could read except by means of the imagination.

At times too he would find it difficult to get up in the morning but would lie in a pleasant half dream looking up at the ceiling. He would say to himself, 'After all, I have nothing to get up for really. I could if I liked stay in bed all day and all night and none would notice the difference. I used to do this when I was a child. Why can't I do it now?'

For he had been a very serious child who found it difficult to talk to children even of his own age. Only once had he shown enthusiasm and that was when in a school playground he had seen in the sky an aeroplane and had lisped excitedly, 'Thee, an aeroplane', a rather ambiguous not to say almost unintelligible exclamation which had been repeated as a sign of his foolishness. He had never taken part in the school sports because he was rather clumsy: and his accomplishments in mathematics were meagre. When he became an adolescent he had taken a job as cook on board a fishing boat but had lost the job because he had put sugar instead of salt into the soup thus causing much diarrhoea.

Most of the time – while his father and mother dreamed their way towards death – he spent working on the land in a dull concentrated manner. In summer and autumn he would be seen with a scythe in the fields, the sunlight sparkling from the blade while he himself, squat and dull, swung it remorselessly. There had in fact been one romance in his life. He had made overtures – if such tentative motions might even be called that – to a spinster in the village who lived with her grossly religious mother in the house opposite him and who was very stout. However he had ceased to visit her when once she had provided him with cocoa and salt herring for his supper, a diet so ferocious that even he could not look forward to its repetition with tranquillity.

There was another spinster in the village who wrote poetry and who lived by herself and he had certain feelings too tenuous to be called love towards her. Her name was Mary and she had inherited from her mother a large number of books in brown leather covers. She dressed in red clothes and was seen pottering vaguely about during the day and sometimes during the night as well. But she was more good looking than the first though she neglected herself in the service of books and poetry and was considered slightly odd by the villagers. Murdo thought that anybody who read a lot of books and wrote poetry must be very clever.

As he stared at the door he felt strange flutterings within him. First of all the door had been painted very lovingly so that it shone with a deep inward shine such as one might find in pictures. And indeed it looked like a picture against the rest of the house which wasn't at all modern but on the contrary was old and intertwined with all sorts of rusty pipes like snakes.

He went back from the door and looked at it from a distance as people in art galleries have to do when studying an oil painting. The more he regarded it the more he liked it. It certainly stood out against the drab landscape as if it were a work of art. On the other hand the more he looked at it the more it seemed to express something in himself which had been deeply buried for years. After a while there was something boring about green and as for blue it wouldn't have suited the door at all. Blue would have been too blatant in a cold way. And anyway the sky was already blue.

But mixed with his satisfaction he felt what could only be described as puzzlement, a slight deviation from the normal as if his head were spinning and he were going round in circles. What would the neighbours say about it, he wondered. Never in the history of the village had there been a red door before.

For that matter he couldn't remember seeing even a blue door himself, though he had heard of the existence of one.

The morning was breaking all over the village as he looked. Blue smoke was ascending from chimneys, a cock was crowing, belligerent and heraldic, its red claws sunk into the earth, its metallic breast oriental and strange. There was a dew all about him and lying on the fences ahead of him. He recognised that the village would wake to a new morning, for the red door would gather attention to itself.

And he thought to himself, 'I have always sought to hide among other people. I agree to whatever anybody tells me to do. If they think I should go to church, I go to church. If they want me to cut peats for them, I do. I have never,' he thought with wonder, 'been myself.' He looked down at his grey fisherman's jersey and his wellingtons and he thought, 'I have always worn these things because everybody else does. I have never had the courage to wear what I wanted to wear, for example a coloured waistcoat and a coloured jacket.'

The red door stood out against the whiteness of the frost and the glimmerings of snow. It seemed to be saying something to him, to be asking him a question. Perhaps it was pleading with him not to destroy it. Perhaps it was saying, 'I don't want to be green. There must be a place somewhere for me as myself. I wish to be red. What is wrong with red anyway?' The door seemed to him to have its own courage.

Wine of course was red and so was blood. He drank none of the former and only saw the latter when he cut himself while repairing a fence or working with wood when a nail would prick his finger.

But really was he happy? That was the question. When he considered it carefully he knew that he wasn't. He didn't like eating alone, he didn't like sitting in the house alone, he didn't like having none who belonged to him, to whom he could tell his secret thoughts, for example that such and such was a mean devil and that that other one was an ungrateful rat.

He had to keep a perpetually smiling face to the world, that was his trouble. But the red door didn't do that. It was foreign and confident. It seemed to be saying what it was, not what it thought others expected it to say. On the other hand, he didn't like wellingtons and a fisherman's jersey. He hated them in fact: they had no elegance.

Now Mary had elegance. Though she was a bit odd, she had elegance. It was true that the villagers didn't understand her but that was because she read many books, her father having been a teacher. And on the other hand she made no concessions to anybody. She seemed to be saying, 'You can take me or leave me.' She never gossiped. She was proud and distant. She had a world of her own. She paid for everything on the nail. She was quite well off. But her world was her own, depending on none.

She was very fond of children and used to make up masks for them at Hallowe'en. As well as this she would walk by herself at night, which argued that she was romantic. And it was said that she had sudden bursts of rage which too might be the sign of a spirit without servility. One couldn't marry a clod.

Murdo stared at the door and as he looked at it he seemed to be drawn inside it into its deep caves with all sorts of veins and passages. It was like a magic door out of the village but at the same time it pulsed with a deep red light which made it appear alive. It was all very odd and very puzzling, to think that a red door could make such a difference to house and moors and streams.

Solid and heavy he stood in front of it in his wellingtons, scratching his head. But the red door was not a mirror and he couldn't see himself in it. Rather he was sucked into it as if it were a place of heat and colour and reality. But it was different and it was his.

It was true that the villagers when they woke would see it and perhaps make fun of it, and would advise him to repaint it. They might not even want him in the village if he insisted on having a red door. Still they could all have red doors if they wanted to. Or they could hunt him out of the village.

Hunt him out of the village? He paused for a moment, stunned by the thought. It had never occured to him that he could leave the village, especially at his age, forty-six. But then other people had left the village and some had prospered though it was true that many had failed. As for himself, he could work hard, he had always done so. And perhaps he had never really belonged to the village. Perhaps his belonging had been like the Hallowe'en mask. If he were a true villager would he like the door so much? Other villagers would have been angry if their door had been painted red in the night, their anger reflected in the red door, but he didn't feel at all angry, in fact he felt admiration that someone should actually have thought of this, should actually have seen the possibility of a red door, in a green and black landscape.

He felt a certain childlikeness stirring within him as if he were on Christmas day stealing barefooted over the cold red linoleum to the stocking hanging at the chimney, to see if Santa Claus had come in the night while he slept.

Having studied the door for a while and having had a long look round the village which was rousing itself to a new day, repetitive as all the previous ones, he turned into the house. He ate his breakfast and thinking carefully and joyously and having washed the dishes he set off to see Mary though in fact it was still early.

His wellingtons creaked among the sparkling frost. Its virginal new diamonds glittered around him, millions of them. Before he knocked on her door he looked at his own door from a distance. It shone bravely against the frost and the drab patches without frost or snow. There was pride and spirit about it. It had emerged out of the old and the habitual, brightly and vulnerably. It said, 'Please let me live my own life.' He knocked on the door.

The Blot

Miss Maclean said, 'And pray tell me how did you get the blot on your book?'

I stood up in my seat automatically and said, 'It was . . . I put too much ink in the pen, please, miss.' I added again forlornly, 'Please, miss.'

She considered or seemed to consider this for a long time, but perhaps she wasn't really thinking about it at all, perhaps she was thinking about something else. Then she said, 'And did you not perhaps think of putting less ink in your pen? I imagine one has a choice in those matters.' The rest of the class laughed as they always did, promptly and decorously, whenever Miss Maclean made a joke. She said, 'Be quiet,' and they stopped laughing as if one of the taps mentioned in our sums had been switched off. Miss Maclean always wore a grey thin blouse and a thin black jacket. Sometimes she seemed to me to look like a pencil.

'Do you not perhaps believe in having a tidy book as the rest of us do?' she said. I didn't know what to say. Naturally I believed in having a tidy book. I liked the whiteness of a book more than anything else in the world. To write on a white page was like . . . how can I say it? . . . it was like a bird leaving footprints in snow. But then to say that to her was to sound daft. And anyway why couldn't she clean the globe which lay in front of her on the desk? It was always dusty so that you could leave your fingerprints all over Europe or South America or Antigua. Antigua was a really beautiful name; I had come across it recently in an atlas. The highest mark she ever gave for an essay was five out of ten, and she was always spoiling jotters by filling them with comments and scoring through words and adding punctuation marks. But I must admit that when she wrote on the board she wrote very neatly.

'And what's this,' she said, 'about an old woman? I thought you were supposed to write about a postman. Have you never seen a postman?' She was always asking stupid questions like that. Of course I had seen a postman. 'And what's this word "solatary"? I presume you mean "solitary". You shouldn't use big words unless you can spell them. And whoever saw an old woman peering out through the letterbox when the postman came up the stairs? You really have the oddest notions.' The class laughed again. No, I had not actually seen an old woman peering through a letterbox but there was no reason why one shouldn't, why my old woman shouldn't. In fact she *had* been peering through the letterbox. I was angry at having misspelt 'solitary'. I didn't know how I had come to do that since I knew the correct spelling. 'Old women don't look through letterboxes waiting for letters,' she almost screamed, her face reddening with rage.

Why did she hate me so much? I wondered. It was the same when I wrote the essay about the tiger who ate fish and chips. Was it really because my work wasn't neat and because I was always putting ink blots on the paper? My hands were clumsy, there was no getting away from that. They never did what I wanted them to do. Her hands however were very thin and neat, ringless. Not like my mother's hands. My mother's hands were wrinkled and one of the fingers had a plain gold ring which she could never get off.

'Old women don't spend their time waiting for letters,' she shouted. 'They have other things to do with their time. I have never seen an old woman who waited every day for a letter. HAVE you? Have you?'

I thought for some time and then said, 'No, miss.'

'Well then,' she said, breathing less heavily. 'But you always want to be clever, don't you? I asked you to write about a postman and you write about an old woman. That is impertinence. ISN'T IT?'

I knew what I was expected to answer so I said, 'Yes, miss.'

She looked down at the page from an enormous height with her thin hawklike gaze and read out a sentence in a scornful voice. ' "She began to write a letter to herself but as she did so a blot of ink fell on the page and she stopped." Why did you write that? That again is deliberate insolence.'

'It came into my mind at that . . . after I had put the ink on my jotter. It just came into my head.'

'It was insolence, wasn't it? WASN'T IT?'

Actually it hadn't been. It had been a kind of inspiration. The idea came into my head very quickly and I had written the sentence before I thought how it would appear to her. I hadn't been thinking of her when I was writing the composition. But from now on I would have to think of her, I realised. Whatever I wrote I would have to think of her reading it and the thought filled me with despair. I couldn't understand why her face quivered with rage when she spoke to me, why she showed such hatred. I didn't want to be hated. Who wanted to be hated like this?

I felt this even while she was belting me. Perhaps she was right. Perhaps it had been insolence. Perhaps neatness was the most important thing in the world. After she had belted me she might be kind to me again and she might stop watching me all the time as if I was an enemy. The thing was, I must learn to hide from her, be neat and clean. Maybe that would work, and her shouting would go away. But even as I thought that and was writhing with pain from the belt, I was also thinking, Miss Maclean, very clean, Miss Maclean, very clean. The words shone without my bidding in front of my head. I was always doing that. Sums, numbs, bums, mums. I also thought, Have you Macleaned your belt today? I thought of a story where a dirty old man, a tramp sitting by the side of the road, would shout, 'Why aren't you as clean as me?' The tramp was very like old Mackay who worked on the roads and was always singing hymns, while breaking the rock. And there was another story where the belt would stand up like a snake and sway to music. In front of her thin grey blouse the belt would rise, with a snake's head and a green skin. I could even hear the accompanying music, staccato and vibrant. It was South American music and came from the dusty globe in front of her.

The Vision

We walk together along the shore. You are searching for stones which have interesting shapes, gnarled pieces of wood, shells. Walking ahead of you I find a pink doll's leg with brine inside it and as I turn it upside down small orange organisms like fragments of crab pour out. There is an empty squashed bottle of Parozone. There is a dead crow with dried black claws and a gutted body. You bring me a beautiful scalloped shell veined with blue, and place a gnarled piece of wood, which seems to have a bird's head, on top of a stone. It peers blankly out at the yachts anchored colourfully in the bay. I am reminded of the bird's cage with the yellow budgerigars which whistle all day when they are not billing and cooing and looking in their small round pink-edged mirrors.

There are stones everywhere worn away by the sea over the ages. Your bright blue coat looks slightly out of place but your tanned face belongs to the world of sailors. There is a large bare bone which might be that of a sheep. Soupy pools of brine contain green organisms. The breeze slightly ruffles your hair as you bend over a shell, totally absorbed. You are carrying pieces of wood in your arms almost as if you were visiting a large supermarket. I say, 'Why didn't you collect a basket before you came on to the shore?' You laugh. So much of the detritus of the world comes here at night and during the day. Men in ships throw plastic bottles over the side and they land here. But there is nothing that this detritus tells us. It is purely random, a doll's leg and arm, smooth and hollow; bones; a veined shell.

Our car, small and red and round as a bubble, stands by itself not far from the pier with its rotting planks. It doesn't look as if it has been cast up. Nothing has yet gnawed at it, as something gnawed at the crow in the middle of the night. The sun flashes from the water and the waves move in to the shore very quietly. There is a strong acrid smell of brine, a thick soupy smell; it is all a disordered kitchen. I find a large rusty wheel and a broken telescope.

You are squatting by the shore studying a shell. You are entirely absorbed in the study of it. I can see your blue coat from the back and your bent head with the ordered coiffure. For a moment I am frightened by a terrifying vision. It is as if you are in another time, seeing that shell for the first time, and as if a glass wall had come down between us. I am studying you studying the shell, as you are studying the shell. I am frightened lest you should change before my eyes, lest your blue coat change to one made of skin, lest your hair become straggly and greasy, lest your knees and legs peer out from the frayed pelt. I suddenly shout to you because I am frightened. You do not answer. You change. Slowly you change. I look down at my suddenly bared legs. I see the boat coming to the shore with cloth bellying from its masts. I feel the contrary wind. It is cold here. It is very cold. My hairy hand has mislaid its wristwatch. The crow rises into the sky on flapping leathery wings. The bottle floats back to the ship. The bone grows into an animal which I do not know, which I know, which is ambling towards me as the sky darkens, as your bony brow stares and stares at the blue veined infinitely coiled shell.

The Phone Call

Tonight I shan't be able to sleep and I don't know what to do about it. I could not understand what was being said to me on the phone. The first twice I phoned I couldn't get through at all. There was an intolerable buzzing in my ears, a noise like that of the sea, and I had to put the phone down. I hate phones anyway, especially public phones, half of which are now vandalised. Last week for instance after hearing the pay signal I put money in the slot, a querulous voice spoke from somewhere and then faded away. I couldn't even recognise it. Another time when phoning my village home from the heart of this terrible city I heard instead of my brother's voice that of an old bewildered man. Why can't the world be more predictable? And as well as this there are women of a certain kind who phone forever. They place their handbags and cigarette packets in front of them on the ledge (as if they were ensconcing themselves for the night) and project interminably their inane verbiage. I can hear them clearly through the glass saying that they will have to stop now as there is someone waiting but they continue just the same, shifting away from me as I parade up and down, whistling loudly or coughing heavily if it is a cold night and in any case seething with murderous thoughts.

I do not know as a result of the conversation what is happening. I know that my mother is ill but I don't know how serious her illness is. I was speaking to Donny but I could not hear what he was saying. He doesn't like the phone either and he also speaks from a public phone box. I heard what sounded like a high wind raging in the background. He said something about 'dea' but I couldn't make out whether he was saying 'dead' or 'deaf'. And there was a word which might have been 'ever' or 'fever'. He might have been saying that she was deaf as ever or that she was dead of fever. I know that she is deaf and has been growing more so, though she used to have exceptionally acute hearing. She could hear everything I did. Even when I was reading and turning a page in the book she could hear me. I used to read a lot when I was young. Now I live in the city and I do not read so much. I do not have that tranquillity any more.

I too have always had good hearing. I could hear the rustling of her gown on those beautiful spring days. I could hear her muttering to herself as she read a newspaper, or a letter from her sister in Canada. She always read the letter in low tones to herself. She and her sister were always very close and they were both religious. I remember when her sister was once on holiday from Canada she gave me a terrible telling off for coming in late one night after I had been drinking a little. She was wearing black clothes and a necklace of fake gold at the throat. She terrified me. I thought Canada would have chastened her a bit (after all she had been there for thirty years) but not at all, she was more religious than my mother. She is a tough old bird and I have seen from her letters (which have always the same clichés) that she isn't afraid of death even though she has had one heart attack. Her letters of course are totalling uninteresting, most of them misspelt and consisting of phrases such as 'We are in the hands of God.' That night she shouted and was very angry. My mother said nothing but looked down at her hands which were resting loosely in her lap. That was one of the reasons I left home. I should have done it years ago.

But I would not wish her dead just the same. How could I wish her dead when I recall her fierce solicitude for me, her overwhelming demonic love, which though frightening was also genuine? Sometimes I walk the streets at night – this yellow maze – thinking what a mess she made of me. I shudder now when I think of how my heart leaped when that voice seemed to say across immense distances, 'Dead of fever'. Was it fear or joy? I shall never go back there. But that does not mean that I do not feel tenderness, or that the tenderness grows any less the further away I am from home and its fields in the middle of this incomprehensible city.

Poor Donny, shouting to me across distances. Nevertheless I

shall not sleep tonight, and all because of these kiosks which contain the storms of our civilisation, the scrawls of illiterates, nor can one do anything but hate the latter when they cut one off from communication, so that one does not know whether one's own mother is dead or alive, and all that one hears is a high wavering hum as if the voices of the dead, venomous and confused, were speaking to one. She always loved her brother who was drowned at sea many many years ago. He was her favourite brother, handsome and daring, and he died young. That was why she would never allow me near the sea and why the other boys called me a coward. Her brother was drowned when there was a high wind.

I don't like kiosks. I don't like boxes of any kind. I feel when I shut the door as if I shall never be able to get out again. Once I panicked and pushed at the wall instead of the door and it was perhaps five minutes before I got out. My hands were raw with punching at the walls. I am the same with certain dirty lavatories at railway stations, the locks are sometimes difficult. Some day I shall have a telephone of my own when I earn enough money for I can't say that I have prospered since I came to the city. I find it confusing and brutal and some mornings I wake up with a taste of death in my mouth and stare at the morning star, wincing and pointed. I miss the apron which once I touched as a child. Let me admit that.

But to think that perhaps at this very moment she may be dying and I not to know it. Perhaps she is lying dead on a bed, though the word could of course have been 'deaf', not 'dead', for she certainly became that. She would shout at me, 'What are you saying about me?' though I was in fact saying nothing. My trouble has always been my pity and my tenderness, they have been my enemies. Even at my work I can't be brutal enough. For one has to be brutal, there is no getting away from it. For instance, if someone comes after me into the office and wishes to phone I let him do so though he knows perfectly well that he was second and I was first. And never yet have I met anyone who refuses to take advantage of my pity and tenderness. For I have this ability to put myself in the position of other people. On the other hand few other people seem to have this gift. To tell you the truth my tenderness is gradually festering into contempt. I hate quarrels. That is why even if a woman of the type I have mentioned has been phoning from a public call box for an hour and I have been shivering out in the cold she will always get away with it because of her strength of will, and I always feel that it is I who have been in the wrong. I have sometimes noticed that when I speak to someone in the office they don't answer as if they don't hear me, or if they do answer it is only after a very long pause. I often feel that I am some sort of ghost. I am always impressed by the firmness of other people, and how they stand up for their rights. I know that I owe my weakness to her. Nevertheless she loved me, I admit that. I have enough imagination and pity to make allowances for that, for if we don't have imagination what are we but animals? What are we but animals anyway? Though I am more sensitive than most, a fact which has caused me much pain . . . I am more sensitive though not so intelligent.

Tonight I shan't sleep, wondering if in fact she has died and because of that vandalised phone and that high wind I can do nothing about it. I can see Donny in my mind's eye crammed into the kiosk and furrowing his brow, at that corner not far from the house. Perhaps he had finished with the farm work for the day. He must have done; after all it was after six when I phoned. He was always a slow solid worker, not like me, bored by her many illnesses. If anything went wrong she always took to her bed and told us that she was going to die. And she did that as far back as I can remember; it was her way of punishing us. Perhaps this time she really is ill, perhaps she is going to die. I used to make tea for her and she would cough (or pretend to cough) and take the cup with a trembling hand while I stared unwinkingly at the brown landscape through the window with the flowery curtains. She always insisted that the house be clean, that the furniture be polished. Every day I could see my useless superfluous face duplicated in it endlessly. I hate my face and my weak pointed chin. Her face is dominated by the curving beak of the nose, ruthless and Roman. And that, even when she was sick or pretending to be so.

Now night is falling. And I remember the incident after I had left the kiosk angry and frustrated. There was a man waiting outside in order to phone and I asked him what the time was (I never carry a watch). He was apparently stone deaf for he said, 'It is a very beautiful evening isn't it?' and continued to say this. He was dressed impeccably though he was undoubtedly a lost man: I could tell that by his neat voice and his veined eyes. He was dressed like someone out of a film, a kind of superannuated British major who is trying to put a good face on things and pretends to belong to a good club. He had in fact the appearance of a broken-down gentleman with his brown suit and veined gentle eyes. He went on and on about the weather, in his extremely polite voice, and I seethed with rage at the inefficiency of the world. I hadn't got through on the phone and now I couldn't get through to this man though all I wanted to know was the time. I could have picked him up like one of the china ornaments in my mother's house and smashed him to pieces on the road. He was so eager to please, so impeccable in his dress and wandering irrelevant speech.

I turned away knowing that I would not be able to sleep, though in fact in the barbarous city I do not sleep anyway. Perhaps she is dead or perhaps she is only deaf. And it might have been 'fever' or 'forever', the words are very like. I hate kiosks; they remind me of upright coffins. And the vandalism doesn't help, these obscenities and the black dangling useless phones. I could strangle those vandals, those useless animals. They can't do anything, they can't even read books. They get like that because they love no one. But I have no pity for them: it is their own fault. Others have come from bad backgrounds and turned into good citizens with good jobs. Others have survived the sea and the high winds as uselessly and lived lives without aggression. Why can't they do the same?

The House

In Oban in Scotland there is an unfinished circular many-windowed tower which dominates the town. It was built by a local banking family in order to give employment to the townspeople at a time when there was not much work to be had. Modelled on the Colosseum, statues of the bankers were to be placed in the windows and possibly, for all one knows, illuminated at night. But in fact for some reason – it may be that there was not enough money or it may be that death intervened – the tower was never completed and remains to this day, an object of curiosity to the many tourists who come from all over the world. It is very high up and the walk there is long but pleasant. When one arrives inside the empty structure one can walk across the circular grassy floor and hear, if it is a day in spring or summer, the birds trilling close at hand, or one can perch on the sill of one of the windows and look down at the sea which glitters in the distance. It is said that a certain lady was once looking for the Colosseum in Italy and tried to find out where it was by describing it as that building which is modelled on MacCaig's Tower in Oban.

But in fact in our own village when I was growing up there was a house which had been unfinished for a long time though of course it was not so large as this tower. It was being built by the family of the Macraes over many years and no one remembers when it was begun though there are legends about it. The first Macrae, it is said, spent his entire life gathering huge boulders from wherever he could find them and hammering away at them like a sculptor to prepare them for the house. He was, it is also said, a very large strong fellow who killed a man who made mock of his dream house, not a stone of which had actually been laid. The two men, the Macrae and the other, fought, so it is said, for a whole day till eventually Macrae got his opponent on the ground and banged away at his head with a large stone which he was actually going to use in the building of the house. After that, no one made fun of his project. He died of a stroke with the hammer in his hand.

The next Macrae was a dreamier type of person. He himself didn't attempt any of the actual building but employed some workers to do it. The trouble was that he had so many ideas and plans, some appearing in his head simultaneously, that they had to pull down what they had built almost as soon as they had built it.

Also they drank and smoked when they should have been working and continually asked for higher wages which he refused to give them. At one time he would want the house to merge into the landscape, at another he would want it to stand out from it since he was subject to varying moods of submission and domination. They say that he would walk around dressed in very bright colours shouting at his workmen in fragments of Italian which he had picked up from a guidebook. The workers naturally thought that he was mad.

One of the inhabitants of the village – actually the schoolmaster – called him Penelope partly because of his dainty effeminate air, but also because he was pulling down each morning what had been erected the night before. But this Macrae, whose name was Norman, didn't care. He went his way, carried a whip, and liked nothing better than to order his workers about though they paid little attention to him. There seemed, otherwise, little purpose in his life. He didn't believe in God or the Bible and said once that things existed to be changed every day in order to prevent boredom. In fact he would have nothing to do with the detailed plans which his massive father had drafted out and wouldn't even look at them. He would sometimes say that he wasn't necessarily his father's son, a comment which caused some gossip in the village as in fact his father had been a man who liked women and was a bit of a Lothario.

When Norman died all that had been accomplished was that half the gable had been built. Norman had wanted to have an engraving set in the stone which would show a horse with an eagle's head but had died before this could be started. The only reason he could give for creating such an engraving was that he liked eagles and horses, though in fact he had only seen an eagle once in his whole lifetime, and that was in a painting. The villagers didn't like him as much as they had liked his father, though he had harmed them less, and had not, like his father, fornicated with many of their pliant daughters. They didn't understand his statements for he could say that truth can be revealed as much in a green door as a red one, and that men's shoes are being worn out each day. However when there was a sickness in the village he had helped them out with corn and fish though he openly despised all of them and called most of them superfluous.

The next Macrae – Donald – was different again from Norman. He was a gloomy man who always wore dark clothes and spent most of his time reading his grandfather's plans in a small room of his house. He also hired workers but kept them at it. The trouble was that he could never find the exact kind of stone that he wanted for the house, and all the stone that he did find locally was, according to him, soft and inferior. He spent much money on importing stone and because it was so expensive he became poorer and poorer but succeeded at last in adding another wall in which a long narrow lugubrious window was set. Sometimes he would sit with his elongated head and body at this window gazing across the village or brooding or reading a theological book. He would tell the villagers that they must prepare for their deaths and that they were merely like the lilies of the field. It did not escape their notice however that he got as much money from them as he could. He said that the house he was building was like a temple which would last forever and that it would glorify them all, poor as they were. Did they not wish to see some solid building erected among their poor thatched houses? They would gaze down at the ground, their caps in their hands, but say nothing since they couldn't understand a word he was saying. What with his theological books and his stones he spent practically all his money and the family's money and he died at fifty years old, a religious recluse who would suddenly emerge from his house and shout at the workmen that they weren't worthy of their hire. Then he would mutter to himself and go back into his gloomy room where he would read till the early hours of the morning. No one had a good word to say for him for he would say things like, 'You have no sense of excellence' to their faces. At one time he even started a school in competition with the one already there, but after a while no one would attend it for he would never allow any of the pupils out during school hours in contrast to the teacher in the other school who used to take the children out to pick flowers and berries.

The Macrae I knew – the son of this one – was a large jovial fat man who dressed in a brown canvas blouse. Day after day he would set off with his wheelbarrow and bring back a huge boulder which he would lever on to the ground in order to add another part of the wall to the house, which by now had three walls and a stone floor and three windows. The trouble with Iain Macrae was that he liked children and when they danced round making fun of his house which would never in their opinion be finished, he would look at them with a merry smile and tell them stories. When he was doing this, his expression would become wonderfully tender and he would gaze into the distance over their heads as if he were seeing a most beautiful serene sight. He would completely abandon any work on his house and begin, 'Last night I was walking across the moor looking for a boulder when I saw an owl sitting on a stone reading a book.' The children would gather round him open-mouthed and cease to play pranks. He was really a very lazy fat man who seemed to move heavily like a large solid cloud. When he was asked why he didn't abandon the house altogether he would say, 'One must have something to do. Even if it's no good.' And he would smile a sad clownish smile. He was liked in the village as he would do anything for anyone at any time and would wholly neglect his own affairs in order to help. When he was on his death-bed he was making jokes about his coffin and saying that they must get him a large one. At one time he would say that it should be made of stone, but at other times he preferred wood since it changed so much, whereas stone never changed, and this was its weakness. In fact he didn't care about the quality of the stone he trundled along in his wheelbarrow and sometimes he would forget which stone he ought to have been using at a particular time. 'We all have something to do,' he would say, 'and this was what was left to me. I couldn't live in this house,' he would add, 'if it was finished. I would admire it from a distance.' And so another wall and another window would be slowly added in the interval of telling stories to the children. But the people grew used to seeing this unfinished structure and praised God that their own houses were wind and rain proof and tightly made. He also died as a result of wheeling a stone along. He fell on his face while torrents of blood poured out of his mouth, and stained the ground. He wasn't long on his death-bed where he grew very thin and meagre so that no one would ever have thought that he had weighed fifteen stone and could tell interesting stories to children, who as a mark of respect gathered a bunch of flowers and laid them on his grave.

His son was a brisker thinner man who decided that the house must be finished once and for all. He had grown up in the knowledge that his father had been, to a certain extent, a figure of fun and was determined that he himself would not be humorous or play the clown for anybody. For this reason he would rise early in the morning and start on the house. The village would resound to his hammering day after day. He never ceased working. He was also resolute that he would do all the work himself. It is true that he couldn't handle a hammer as well as his forebears but what he lost in skill he made up for in determination. 'One should never leave a job incomplete,' he would say, staring you straight in the eye. 'Never. It is immoral. Laziness is immoral.' And as most of the villagers were themselves lazy, standing at the corners of their houses with their hands in their pockets most of the day, he wasn't liked much. 'I have other things I must do after this is completed,' he would say. And so he would work like a slave. People said that he would kill himself but in fact he didn't. He seemed to be very tough physically and never once had an illness while he was building the house, though he worked in the rain and sometimes in the snow.

Eventually one morning he finished it. People thought that he would have a celebration party but he didn't. He wasn't the kind of man who cared for sentiment. But when the house was completed it was noticed that he would stand looking at it and then move onward and look at it from another angle. A depression hung over the village. The villagers had thought that they would be glad when the house was finished but they weren't. It was partly because it wasn't as good as they had expected (after all builders had been working at it for a hundred years at least and perhaps even longer than that) and in comparison with their dreams it looked more ordinary than they had expected. They didn't quite know what they had expected, but they had certainly expected a structure more elaborate and elegant than they got. It seemed to be saying that after all man's imagination is much the same everywhere.

But the real trouble was that they didn't have so much to talk about. In the past if there was a pause in the conversation they would start to tell some story about That House or if they didn't have actual stories about it they would invent some. In any case the village seemed to grow gloomier and gloomier. Some of them wanted to smash the house down so that it could be started all over again. But of course they wouldn't do that for they were all basically law-abiding people. But they grew to hate the last of the Macraes, who was called William. And as he sensed this he began to avoid them. He too grew tired of looking at the house in which he had begun to live. He had bought very ordinary furniture for it, and all the usual conveniences of a house, and in fact made it look very common and not to be distinguished from the other houses of the village except that it was a stone house. People would say how different he was from his forefathers and what fine ideas they had had, and what plans and ideals they had nursed. William tried to mix with them but not very successfully since, though he enquired about their families, they knew that fundamentally he wasn't interested. Obscurely they felt that they had been betrayed. Was all their legend-making to end up like this after all, with this very ordinary house which seemed to answer very trivial problems? Why, because it was lived in, the house didn't even have any ghosts! The villagers had even been cheated of that! They looked forward to William's death and for this reason hoped that he would not marry, since they would then have the freedom to do with the house what their imaginations wished. They actively discouraged any girl in the village from marrying him, though at the same time they were worried lest he should import a wife from somewhere else. But in fact he showed no sign of doing that. On the contrary, he would sit in the house brooding for hours and it was even rumoured that he wished to pull the house down and start again. But all the zest had left him – perhaps he had overworked too long – and he remained where he was in his ordinary house with the ordinary curtains and the ordinary carpets and furniture.

He died of some form of melancholia. After his death, all the furniture and carpets etc. were sold by a dull-looking niece of his from outside the island who had no intention of coming back. The house remained empty since there was no one who wanted to buy it and a satisfactory series of legends began to blossom around it, most of them having to do with mysterious lights at windows, men reading Bibles in a greenish light or telling stories to phantom children. Stories were freely invented and the best of them survived and the worst perished. The most mysterious statement they found was in one of the books which the second Macrae had kept. It read, 'When all the lies have been answered, other lies will have to be invented.' The villagers thought that in inventing legends they were being true to the early founders of the house and looked at it as women will stand at a church door watching the bride coming out and dreaming that she at least will begin a race of uncorrupted children, not realising that for this to happen she must be a virgin of the purest blood.

The Painter

We only once had a painter in our village in all the time that I can remember. His name was William Murray and he had always been a sickly, delicate, rather beautiful boy who was the only son of a widow. Ever since he was a child he had been painting or drawing because of some secret compulsion and the villagers had always encouraged him. He used to paint scenes of the village at harvest time when we were all scything the corn, or cutting it with sickles, and there is no doubt that the canvas had a fine golden sheen with a light such as we had never seen before. At other times he would make pictures of the village in the winter when there was a lot of snow on the moor and the hills and it was climbing up the sides of the houses so that there was in the painting a calm fairytale atmosphere. He would paint our dogs – who were nearly all collies – with great fidelity to nature, and once he did a particularly faithful picture of a sheep which had been found out on the moor with its eyes eaten by a crow. He also did paintings of the children dressed in their gay flowery clothes, and once he did a strange picture of an empty sack of flour which hung in the air like a spook.

We all liked him in those days and bought some of his pictures for small sums of money since his mother was poor. We felt a certain responsibility towards him also since he was sickly, and many maintained that he wouldn't live very long, as he was so clever. So our houses were decorated with his colourful paintings and if any stranger came to the village we always pointed to the paintings with great pride and mentioned the painter as one of our greatest assets. No other village that we knew of had a painter at all, not even an adult painter, and we had a wonderful artist who was also very young. It is true that once or twice he made us uncomfortable for he insisted on painting things as they were, and he made our village less glamorous on the whole than we would have liked it to appear. Our houses weren't as narrow and crooked as he made them seem in his paintings, nor did our villagers look so spindly and thin. Nor was our cemetery, for instance, so confused and weird. And certainly it wasn't in the centre of the village as he had placed it.

He was a strange boy, seeming much older than his years. He hardly ever spoke and not because there was anything wrong with him but because it seemed as if there was nothing much that he wished to say. He dressed in a very slapdash manner and often had holes in the knees of his trousers, and paint all over his blouse. He would spend days trying to paint a particular house or old wall or the head of an old woman or old man. But as we had a lot of old people in the village, some who could play musical instruments – especially the melodeon – extremely well, he didn't stand out as a queer person. There is, however, one incident that I shall always remember.

Our village of course was not a wholly harmonious place. It had its share of barbarism and violence. Sometimes people quarrelled about land and much less often about women. Once there was a prolonged controversy about a right of way. But the incident I was talking about happened like this. There was in the village a man called Red Roderick who had got his name because of his red hair. As is often the case with men with red hair he was also a man of fiery temper, as they say. He drank a lot and would often go uptown on Saturday nights and come home roaring drunk, and march about the village singing.

He was in fact a very good strong singer but less so when he was drunk. He spent most of his time either working on his croft or weaving in his shed and had a poor thin wife given to bouts of asthma whom he regularly beat up when it suited him and when he was in a bad temper. His wife was the daughter of Big Angus who had been a famous fisherman in his youth but who had settled down to become a crofter and who was famed for his great strength though at this time he was getting old. In fact I suppose he must have been about seventy years old. His daughter's name was Anna and during the course of most days she seemed to be baking a lot without much result. You would also find her quite often with a dripping plate and a soggy dishcloth in her hand. She had seven children all at various stages of random development and with running noses throughout both summer and winter.

It must be said that, when sober, Red Roderick was a very kind man, fond of his children and picking them up on his shoulders and showing them off to people and saying how much they weighed and how clever and strong they were, though in fact none of them was any of these things, for they were in fact skinny and underweight and tending to have blotches and spots on their faces and necks. In those moments he would say that he was content with his life and that no one had better children or better land than he had. When he was sunny-tempered he was the life and soul of the village and up to all sorts of mischief, singing songs happily in a very loud and melodious voice which revealed great depth of feeling. That was why it seemed so strange when he got drunk. His whole character would change and he would grow violent and morose and snarl at anyone near him, especially the weakest and most inoffensive people.

One thing that we noticed was that he seemed very jealous of his father-in-law who had, as I have said, a reputation in the village for feats of strength. It was said that he had once pulled a cart loaded with peat out of a deep muddy rut many years before when he was in his prime, but now that he was ageing and wifeless he lived on more failingly from day to day, since after all what else is there to do but that?

Red Roderick in his drunken bouts would say that it was time the 'old devil' died so that he might inherit something through his wife, since there were no other relations alive. Red Roderick would brood about his inheritance and sometimes when he was drunk he would go past his father-in-law's house and shout insults at him. He brooded and grew angry, the more so since his father-in-law's land was richer than his own and better looked after, and also there were a number of sheep and cows which he coveted. I sometimes think that this must have been how things were in the days of the Old Testament, though it doesn't mention that people in those days drank heavily unless perhaps in Sodom and Gomorrah.

His whole mind was set on his inheritance mainly because he regretted marrying the old man's daughter who, in his opinion, had brought him nothing but a brood of children whom in his drunken moments he despised and punished for offences that they had never even committed. Yet, as I said, in his sunny moments there was no one as gay and popular as he was, full of fine interesting stories and inventions.

However, I am coming to my story. One day he went to town in the morning (which was unusual for him) and came home in the afternoon on the bus, very drunk indeed. This was in fact the first time he had been drunk during the day, as it were, in the village, and we all thought that this was rather ominous, especially as he began by prowling around his own house like a tiger, sending one of his children spinning with a blow to the face in full sight of the village. The trouble was that all the villagers were frightened of him since none of them was as strong as he was in those moments of madness.

After he had paced about outside his house for a while shouting and throwing things, he seemed to make up his mind and went down to the byre from which he emerged with a scythe. At first I thought – since I was his neighbour – that he was going to scythe the corn but this was not at all what was in his mind. No, he set off with the scythe in his hand towards his father-in-law's house. I remember as he walked along that the scythe glittered in his hand as if it was made of glass. When he got to the house he shouted out to the old man that it was time he came out and fought like a man, if he was as great as people said he had been in the past. There was, apart from his voice, a great silence all over the village which drowsed in the sun as he made his challenge. The day in fact was so calm that there was an atmosphere as if one was in church, and it seemed that he was disturbing it in exactly the same way as a shouting lunatic might do who entered a church during a service.

One or two people said that someone should go for a policeman but no one in fact did. In any case looking back on it now I think that in a strange shameful way we were looking forward to the result of the challenge as if it would be a break in an endless routine. Nevertheless there was something really frightening and irresponsible about Red Roderick that day as if all the poison that seethed about his system had emerged to the surface as cloudy dregs will float upwards to the surface of bad liquor. Strangely enough – in response to the shouting, as in a Western – the old man did come out and he too had a scythe. He advanced towards Roderick, his eyes glittering with venom and hatred as if he too shared in the madness which was shattering the silence of the day. Then they began to fight.

As Red Roderick was drunk perhaps the advantage given him by relative youth was to a certain extent cancelled. There was however no doubt that he wished to kill the old man, so enraged was he, so frustrated by the life that tortured him. As they swung their scythes towards each other ponderously, it looked at first as if they could do little harm, and indeed it was odd to see them, as if each was trying to cut corn. However, after some time – while the face of the old man gradually grew more demoniac in a renewal of his youth – he succeeded at last in cutting his son-in-law's left leg so that he fell to the ground, his wife running towards him like an old hen, her skirts trailing the ground like broken wings.

But that was not what I meant to tell since the fight in itself, though unpleasant, was not evil. No, as I stood in the ring with the others, excited and horrified, I saw on the edge of the ring young William with his paint-brush and canvas and easel painting the fight. He was sitting comfortably on a chair which he had taken with him and there was no expression on his face at all but a cold clear intensity which bothered me. It seemed in a strange way as if we were asleep. As the scythes swung to and fro, as the faces of the antagonists became more and more contorted in the fury of battle, as their cheeks were suffused with blood and rage, and their teeth were drawn back in a snarl, he sat there painting the battle, nor at any time did he make any attempt to pull his chair back from the arena where they were engaged.

I cannot explain to you the feelings that seethed through me as I watched him. One feeling was partly admiration that he should be able to concentrate with such intensity that he didn't seem able to notice the danger he was in. The other feeling was one of the most bitter disgust as if I were watching a gaze that had gone beyond the human and which was as indifferent to the outcome as a hawk's might be. You may think I was wrong in what I did next. I deliberately came up behind him and upset the chair so that he fell down head over heels in the middle of a brush-stroke. He turned on me such a gaze of blind fury that I was reminded of a rat which had once leaped at me from a river bank, and he would have struck me but that I pinioned his arms behind his back. I would have beaten him if his mother hadn't come and taken him away, still snarling and weeping tears of rage. In spite of my almost religious fear at that moment, I tore the painting into small pieces and scattered them about the earth. Some people have since said that what I wanted to do was to protect the good name of the village but I must in all honesty say that that was not in my mind when I pushed the chair over. All that was in my mind was fury and disgust that this painter should have watched this fight with such cold concentration that he seemed to think that the fight had been set up for him to paint, much as a house exists or an old wall.

It is true that after this no one would speak to our wonderful painter; we felt in him a presence more disturbing that that of Red Roderick who did after all recover. So disturbed were we by the incident that we would not even retain the happy paintings he had once painted and which we had bought from him, those of the snow and the harvest, but tore them up and threw them on the dung heap. When he grew up the boy left the village and never returned. I do not know whether or not he has continued as a painter. I must say however that I have never regretted what I did that day and indeed I admire myself for having had the courage to do it when I remember that light, brooding with thunder, and see again in my mind's eye the varying expressions of lust and happiness on the faces of our villagers, many of whom are in their better moments decent and law-abiding men. But in any case it may be that what I was worried about was seeing the expression on my own face. Perhaps that was all it really was. And yet perhaps it wasn't that alone.

The Existence of the Hermit

There once came to our village – or rather to the outskirts of our village – a hermit from somewhere in the south. He was a fairly stocky man with an unshaven face and intense blue eyes, and he wore a long ragged coat which he tied with a belt. He built himself a tin hut with a tall narrow chimney near the road, and he stayed there by himself. As is often the case with men who live mysteriously on their own, romantic stories grew up about him. The favourite one was that he was of a good family but had been crossed in love in his youth and had ever since then avoided the company of people, especially women. With the greatest certainty the villagers would tell this story, for which there was not the slightest evidence, to strangers who visited the place, and, almost without realising that what they were relating was a fiction, would embroider the essential fable with the most elaborate details such as that he was a scientist or a writer or even a singer. Since in all the time that I saw him he never sang a single song this seemed strange but then they could have argued that he had given up singing as well, as a gesture of contempt and defiance. He did visit the village shop and he bought his groceries in it though he would never speak more than was necessary. He rode a bicycle and when he passed along the village street he looked like a chimney sweep with his dirty belted black coat which seemed as if it had been dipped for a long time in soot. He stayed by himself in the hut most of the time except when he took walks across the moors and no one knew how he passed the time except that perhaps he might be reading. The strange thing was that as far as we knew he never drank. There was no drink to be had in the village and he never went to the town, so he didn't have any unless he made it himself.

We were curious about him when he first came but after a while most of us grew to accept him. For myself, I couldn't live like that but then everybody is different from everybody else and he seemed to be able to live on his own, an ability which is not given to many men. We often tried to question him in an oblique manner, but he wouldn't speak to us and made an excuse to get away again, even though we might waylay him in the shop. The children tried to see inside his hut but he chased them away so ferociously that they never returned. Clearly, all he wanted was to be left alone. It is true that sometimes he might be seen fishing from a rock but usually in an isolated place where no one was likely to talk to him.

At last, as I said, we accepted him as part of the landscape in which we all lived but gradually we came to realise that he was a disturbance to the village, though he was in no sense a nuisance. What I mean by disturbance is that the very fact of his existence was a kind of insult to us all. Or perhaps insult is not the right word. The fact is that human beings are made in such a way that anyone who lives differently from themselves, even though he does not seek to influence them in any way, is a challenge and a cross. Stories are composed about such a person in order to make him comprehensible. There was, as I have said, no reason at all to believe that the man was avenging himself on the world because of an emotional wound but that was the only way in which the villagers could make sense of his mode of existence. For no matter how much such a person wishes to withdraw, he cannot, since after all he exists. Why else do we envy people who have done us no harm? Why do we envy a man for being outstanding in a job which we may even despise? There is no doubt that we all suffer from being human.

Let me say, first of all, that I never found out anything about this man. He might have been intelligent or stupid, I couldn't tell. He might have been a plumber or a physicist, I never found out. And neither did anyone else. He might have been a great scholar or a dunce. No one knew. Certainly he seemed competent enough. He looked after himself pretty well. He was never ill all the time he stayed near the village. He bought a reasonable amount of food and seemed able to cook it. He never at any time asked for any help. It is true also that he could fish, for one of the villagers saw him from a distance and said that he knew perfectly well what he was doing. Naturally he never went to church.

But, as I have said, the very fact of his existence was a disturbance since one cannot hope not to exist if one is alive. In the long winter nights, in the long summer days, we knew that he was there. We didn't think of him as judging us. He was simply there and that was enough. Let me explain to you what I mean.

There lived in our village an old married couple who had been happily married for a very long time. At least they had never quarrelled openly and had seemed to exist in harmony. Now about two years after this hermit came to live near our village we noticed that the husband, a large bearded fellow, began to insult his wife and to say that he wished he had never got married. This was indeed very odd since his wife had been a good wife. She had reared his children who were now married and away from the island. She had looked after the land with him and had carried peats home in the summer. She had cooked his meals and kept his house neat and tidy and now when she was ready to reap the rewards of her good useful life her husband began to grow restless and to say that he had missed a great deal in his life. He began to treat her abominably and would as I have said insult her in public. Then he would ask for forgiveness and go to church on Sunday.

It was noticed that he would go and stand near the hermit's hut and stare at it unblinkingly for a whole morning or afternoon as if he was wondering what the hermit was doing. But he never actually tried to enter the hut. Once he tried to speak to the hermit in the shop but the hermit pushed by him and cycled away. The old man stared after him with great wistfulness.

One night the village was roused by a quarrel between the old man and his wife. At the end of it he went back into the house, took out a big bag of clothes and set off in the moonlight shouting that he was going away to live by himself and be a hermit since it was now clear to him that it was possible to live like that. It is true that he did go away for a little while but he eventually came back. He joked that he had missed his tobacco but everyone knew that he had suffered a defeat. Everyone also knew that he had been staying in an old barn, the owner of which had diplomatically ignored him, and that the real reason why he had gone back was that the roof of the barn let the rain in. It was noticed that he still gazed wistfully towards the hermit's hut but he made no more attempts to speak to the hermit. He would simply regard him with wonder and fear. That was the first thing that happened.

The second thing that happened concerned our schoolmaster. Our schoolmaster was a large bald man who believed that every word that he uttered ought to be listened to with the greatest respect. It didn't matter what one talked about, he was sure to talk about it at greater length. For instance if one talked about fishing then he would carry on a long discussion about surface fish and ground fish and confuse everyone with his learning. If one talked about farming then it seemed that he knew all about that too, and he would tell us how mechanical inventions had changed farming in the eighteenth century. If one talked politics then he was in his element. He was indeed a very vain man.

Naturally he used to talk about the hermit for he himself was very gregarious. He would say, 'It is quite unnatural for a man to live like that. He must have some secret. Perhaps he is working on a scientific process which keeps him occupied during the winter nights. Perhaps he reads a great deal. Or perhaps he is a writer.' But in fact there was never any sign that he did any writing, even of letters, for the postman never called at his hut. The schoolmaster would pound the table and say, 'No man can live on his own like that without some secret, something to occupy his mind.' And he would grow very heated, almost as if it was a matter which required his personal investigation. His bald head would shine with sweat and he would shout at us though none of us ever contradicted him since we all wanted to lead quiet lives. But his weakness was that he had forgotten that after all he was only a schoolmaster in a very small school and that in the world outside there were many people who were cleverer than him.

One night after drinking some whisky he said that he himself would go and find out what the hermit was doing. We tried to dissuade him, for since he was a schoolmaster he would get into serious trouble if the hermit caught him, but he said that all he wanted to do was look in the window, and anyway that he had been in the war and had been on many missions more difficult than this. As a matter of fact we all knew that he had been in the Education Corps and was unlikely to have taken part in any jungle warfare as Hugh Maclean – who was much quieter – had done. In any case staggering slightly he went off into the night. When he returned two hours later he was at first unusually silent. When we asked him what he had seen through the window he said in a tone of amazement that the hermit had just been sitting in a chair neither reading nor writing nor doing anything at all, except perhaps thinking. He kept muttering over and over, 'It's impossible. It's impossible. The man was just sitting there, and he seemed quite happy.' He emphasised the last sentence very clearly and seemed totally astonished when he said it. Ever since that night he became much quieter as if he had been stunned by some vision of a world that he did not know existed. Now and again when there were a few of us together he would suddenly burst out, 'I wonder if that hermit is sitting there on that chair,' and he would walk up and down the room in an agitated manner.

The last incident I am going to relate happened as follows. A bachelor whom we knew and who up until this time I speak of had been very gregarious, and who attended local football matches etc., though he had a wooden leg, suddenly at about the age of fifty decided that he would also withdraw from society as the hermit had done. He stayed in his house without hardly ever coming out except that he would go to the village shop but when he did he wouldn't speak to any of the villagers. He would no longer attend any of the social events that occurred and wouldn't help with the peat cutting as he had done in the past. If anyone knocked at the house he would ignore him, so that eventually people ceased to visit him altogether. He neglected his dress and looked ragged and dirty. He grew a straggly beard which didn't suit him since he had always been neat and elegant before. He stopped the daily papers (which arrived a day late anyway). He ceased to write or receive letters. He no longer painted his house and allowed it to go to rack and ruin. He became unpleasant to the children and was disliked by all.

One day after a year or so of this existence he came screaming out of the house and began to take off his clothes in full sight of the villagers. Shouting obscenities, he threw furniture out of his house. We knew then that he had become touched and he was in fact taken to the asylum. As he sat in the ambulance he kept saying, 'It is impossible to live like that. It is impossible to live like that.'

Now whether the hermit found out about this, or whether for some other reason, he decided to leave the village. One morning we woke up and there was no smoke coming from the chimney of the hut. The door too was wide open as if he was inviting people to see that he had gone. As he took the bicycle, he must simply have travelled in the clothes that he was always wearing. The one chair and table were left behind: so also was the stove on which he had cooked. No one knew where he went to. No one knew anything about him. But after he had gone it was as if a great weight had been lifted from the shoulders of the villagers and they walked about and talked more cheerfully than in the past. No one speculated about him or wondered where he had gone. In fact no one ever talked about him after that except that the schoolmaster would as before suddenly rise from the table saying, 'I wonder what the hermit is doing now.' But no one answered him, for we had come to recognise that the hermit had been an unhealthy influence. We had come to understand, as I have said already, that the very fact of his existence was a disturbance to the village even though he never talked to us, in fact, precisely because he never talked to us. We succeeded in blotting him out of our minds and he ceased to become a challenge to us. Some time later we even pulled down his tin hut so that no one would have any memory of his existence, though the shape of the hut still remains in the earth to this day. Some time, however, the grass will grow over it completely and we won't remember anything at all about him, thank God.

Fable

There is a fable I should like to relate to you about the village.
Once upon a time there was a man who lived in it, whose name
was . . . In actual fact his name doesn't matter, since names tell
one so little about people nowadays. This man had suffered a
great deal in our village. He had first of all lost his land to an
older brother who had turned up from America after having
been given up for dead decades before. That was the first thing
that happened to him. The second thing – excluding the awful
routine common accidents and terrors of the day – was that he
married badly. He married a woman who had a mind like a
termite, nibbling all day and all night at the furniture of the
world so that it came to look scarred and ghostly and ugly. In
her later years she grew slatternly and gross: she had already
been a devoted huntress of dust and a nag. Finally she took to
her bed, though no one believed that there was anything wrong
with her. In fact, however, there was, for punctuating her shrill
complaints was the erratic tick of her heart which was like the
termite she had put into the furniture, now vague and ghostly.
For many years he stayed with her till her lips turned blue and
she died. Her last words were that he would regret her death.

He remained reasonably composed after her death and dealt
with the burying in a calm manner. Five days after her death he
packed a case and early in the morning left the house. He
looked free and joyful for the first time in many years, though
one presumes that at some time in his early youth he must have
been free and joyful too. He walked along the road that
summer morning (the grass wet with dew on both margins of
it) till he came to the cross roads. From this cross roads four
other roads wound their way to different possible destinations.
He walked down one of them, swinging his case gaily, and after

a while came back. Then he walked down a second one, slightly less gaily, and turned back. He walked down the third one, more slowly, and turned back. For a long time he waited, sitting on his case, listening to the twitter of the birds and the sound of the streams on that May morning, before setting out again. Then he walked down the fourth road. But after an hour or so he came back. Finally he sat down on his case, his head on his hands, and that was how they found him. When they raised his head they found that the eyes had no expression in them at all and he stared dully at all of them as if he didn't recognise them.

They locked him up in an asylum and because he could not bear to be parted from his case they let him have it. Now and again he will set off with it on a journey to the centre of the room or round the walls but always he will come back to the centre and sit down on the case. They haven't even bothered to remove the clothes from it though they did in fact take away the razor which was a cut-throat one and which, of course, he is never allowed to use now.

The Old Man

In our village there lived an old man who had a white beard and the apparent peace and tranquillity of a character out of the Bible. He stayed by himself and as far as one could tell never read books or did physical work. Over the years he had been accepted as the wisest man in the village, though no one quite knew how old he was or even much about his past. People used to take their problems to him and if he solved them, as he nearly always did one way or another, they would bring him gifts such as crowdie or butter or fish or meat. In fact, I think that he lived entirely off these presents. He didn't seem at all concerned with material things and unlike the rest of the villagers did nothing to improve his house which was simple, unpretentious, and always clean. His solutions to problems were often surprising and I often felt that behind his serene look there lay a joker who contrived to create interesting situations out of sheer high-spirited devilment. At other times his solutions had an interesting severity and rigour and contained an element of the unexpected. For instance . . .

There was another village beside ours. Our principal source of fuel was peat which was cut in the spring and stacked later. These peat banks were situated on the boundaries between the villages and the other village often claimed that by cutting peats we were in fact invading their territory. Sometimes for one reason or another there were quarrels between the villages and the men of the other village would wage a war of nerves saying that they wouldn't allow us to have any peat. In actual fact, I think that the other village was right in its claims and that all the peat banks did belong legally to them though the case was never judged.

One particular spring there was a lot of rancour and it looked as if there might be a physical battle. The men in our village who had a sense of responsibility were worried as the people in the other village were threatening that they would come out in strength to defend their peat banks to the death, and use force if necessary. Naturally in this situation it was decided that we should go and consult the Old Man who would advise us, as we knew that he had a trick of turning a problem over on itself so that it sparkled with a novel solution. So a group of us went to see him. He listened to us for a long time as we explained what he already knew, that without peat the village would be in extreme difficulty in the winter when the cold weather came. On the other hand we did not want to pay money to the people of the other village for the peat, as that would create a precedent, and suggest that they were wholly in the right. Also we didn't want any violence which might be repeated every year if it happened once. We put our arguments at great length for we were really worried.

There was with us at the meeting a little man called Tommy who was slightly touched in the head and who suffered intensely from the cold. Even on the hottest days he would sit by the fire and we knew that he would suffer the most of all. He lived with his sister in a dirty house in apparent harmony for his sister was more sensible than he was, though she has a habit of wearing fishermen's jerseys. During the meeting Tommy kept muttering, shrugging his shoulders as he did so (for this was a nervous habit that he had), 'What will I do? What will I do? I will die of the cold.' Though we suspected that what he was saying was the truth we also found him funny and there were smiles on the grave faces round the room.

After a while the Old Man said, 'When two forces which are both aggressive meet each other there is only one thing that can solve the problem without bloodshed.' He looked at us as if he wondered whether we ourselves had seen the solution but all of us gazed at him with blank faces. Eventually he said, 'That thing is the comic. What you must do is make the other side laugh.'

We stared at each other in amazement till one of us said, 'How can we do that? We don't feel like laughing.'

'I will tell you,' said the Old Man, 'what you must do. As the two groups approach each other, you from one side and the people from the other village on the other side, and as you threaten each other and appear very frightening, and as you may even be carrying weapons, what you will do is this. You will instruct Tommy here to remove his trousers in full view of all. The other side will be so flummoxed by this comic answer to their threats and will grow so confused that first they will not know what to do (since who would attack a man without trousers?), then they will burst into laughter for, as anyone can see, Tommy has particularly knobbly knees and one can see from the clothes line that his sister puts out that he wears very long woollen drawers with patches on them. That's my answer to the problem. You will have to persuade Tommy to do this yourselves.'

Naturally Tommy was indignant and shaking his shoulders and thrusting forward his red nose like a cockerel he maintained that he would do no such thing. The minister also at first appeared to think that the whole suggestion was immoral, but when it was pointed out that neither of them, in common with the rest of the village, would get any heat for the following year if they did not give the help that was required they both eventually agreed.

The following day everything turned out as the Old Man had forecast. We, that is the men of the village, went out with our peat cutters across the moor but when we arrived at the banks we found drawn up against us a long line of grim silent men determined to defend their territory to the end. It was, I remember, a fine spring morning with a lot of dew sparkling on the blades of grass and when one looked at the works of nature around one felt it silly that men should constitute such a disharmony as to be acting in such a childish manner, since after all there was enough peat for everybody. But of course human kind is made in this fashion that at certain times it wishes to quarrel and if it can't find a reasonable bone to quarrel over will invent an imaginary even spiritual one.

Now there emerged from the opposing group a big big man who looked very frightening indeed and who told us in a very loud voice, after first drawing his hand across his nose and wiping it in an insulting manner, that it was time that we went home and that if we didn't do so we would be dealt with in a very drastic not to say brutal mode. At that very moment Tommy ran forward from our group and faced him, looking up at him as if from a great depth, shrugging his shoulders and twitching his neck. He looked so comic that we could see some of the people on the other side smiling and really it was very funny. Tommy shrugging his shoulders and seeming so daft staring up at this huge boulder of a man like a hen looking up at a mountain. But when the Goliath took a threatening step forward and Tommy began to dance a mocking dance which concluded with his removing his trousers to show very long dirty woollen pants with holes in them, the men on both sides were rolling about, some of them clutching their bellies in actual pain from the laughter. Then we knew that the quarrel was over, at least for the time, and indeed it was. For that year at least we were allowed to carry on with our peat cutting. Perhaps next year again we would have to invent something new, but on that morning we didn't think as far ahead as that, as we cut the life-saving peat. Tommy of course was given extra peat since after all he had placed its acquisition before his honour, and the Old Man was supplied with all his needs for a whole year as well.

Another problem that was brought to him he tackled in a different though perhaps less successful manner. There lived in our village a handsome schoolteacher who was married to a large-breasted serene girl who had very little to say for herself. The schoolteacher was dark-haired and smooth and had a suave manner of talking such that he could have charmed, as they say, the birds off the trees. Indeed before he got married he was in the habit of going about with a lot of girls and many of the fathers had written him letters at various times telling him that if he didn't lay off their daughters he would be beaten up one dark night. After his marriage he seemed to have quietened down and led as far as one could judge an exemplary life. He no longer went to dances and confined his work to the school. His wife too seemed happy in her own quiet way. His wife was the daughter of a Roddy Macleod who worked on the roads, hammering away at stones contentedly all the day long. There was some difficulty however with the couple as they didn't have any children and this set some of the tongues of the villagers wagging, wondering which of the two was to blame for this. However, as I said, they seemed quite happy though it was often wondered why he had married her in the first place since she didn't have much to say for herself. She spent a lot of her time working at a loom making woollen things which she sold to the villagers. She also had a cow from which she got milk, and her house was always spick and span.

However, this idyll was to end, for there returned to the village after a long absence at university a clever handsome girl who took a post at the school. She was a very blonde, beautiful girl who liked to be in the limelight and who was a considerable number of years younger than the schoolmaster. It was noticeable after a while that the two of them spent a lot of their time after school together on what the schoolmaster said was necessary documentation though in fact up till the time of her arrival he had been one of the first out of the gates when the final whistle went. This girl, I must say, though beautiful, had a very bright calculating mind and she must have decided that if she could take the schoolmaster away from his wife she could make something of him and that the two of them would go away together. The problem was that it would be difficult for either of them to be long enough together to get to know each other well since, as one must understand, in a village everyone watches everyone else under a very intense neighbourly microscope.

But it was quite clear to everyone that the schoolmaster still retained a great deal of his charm which had a slight air of dissoluteness about it, and that this girl had been attracted by it like a butterfly to an old lamp. After all there was no one in the village as clever as she and the other girls didn't like her, so she had to have someone to be with. Furthermore she had a certain position in the village which made the girls doubly jealous, both of her beauty and her superior rank.

The wife one day came along to see the Old Man and placed the problem before him. He listened gravely especially after she had laid an offering on the table for him. This was a beautiful blue jersey that she had knitted.

'Tell me, Helen,' he said, 'how far would you go to keep your husband?'

'As far as possible,' she answered serenely, and with total faith. 'There is nothing that I would not do to keep him.'

'In that case,' he said, 'there is one thing that you can do. You have no children and the people of the village gossip about it. Tell me, is it your fault or his?'

She blushed and then said, 'I think it must be his.'

'I suspected as much,' said the Old Man. 'These rakes are always the same. What therefore you must do is put about the village the story that your husband is impotent. The other woman will hear of this and will have nothing to do with him. He is impotent, I take it?' he said.

'He is,' said Helen. 'I will do that for I do not want anyone else to have him.' The Old Man looked at her sadly for she appeared serene and in her way beautiful. Her eyes however had a strong resolute look such as he had often seen in the eyes of children.

The story was put about the village as the Old Man advised. The schoolteacher heard it naturally but the result was not to make things harmonious or return the marriage to its original state. The beautiful girl did in fact leave the village which she should have done long before since her open ruthless intelligence was not suited to the subtle deviousness of village ways, but the husband at first took to drink and then left the village as well. Helen was left alone but later married a large serene fisherman, and had three children in as many years.

I often wondered about this solution but the Old Man would never discuss any of his judgments and I never found out the thinking behind this one except that he once said, 'Any woman who could say that her husband was impotent was obviously not happily married in the first place no matter whether she thought she was or not. She had clearly mistaken habit for happiness.' And since he was the Old Man, no one questioned him further. I must say that for myself I have a sneaking feeling of pity for the husband who had obviously not known his wife at all and had mistaken serenity for acceptance. People who talk as much as he did should obviously listen more.

I shall give one more example of his solutions to problems. One winter there happened to ravage the whole island an epidemic of 'flu. So bad was it that no house was exempt; any house might have three or four cases. The one district doctor was exhausted racing from one house to another, being called in the middle of the night, lacking a sufficient supply of medicines. One day in a hurry and looking pale he came to the Old Man and laying his bag on a chair said: 'I do not know what to do. This plague has reached crisis proportions and as you know it is a killer. People are dying all over the place. I have to decide which houses I shall go to first and I'm reaching the stage that I'm getting more and more confused. Some may have to die in order that others may live. I need advice. Perhaps if I told you of two cases you could tell me which one ought to survive. Well, for instance, there is that old woman Mrs Stewart whose husband has been dead, as you know, for many years. In spite of this she has been helpful, cheery and useful. She is, however, seventy years old and lives alone. She is friendly with everyone and all are astonished at her resilience. On the other hand there is young Fred Macrae whose father is an alcoholic, who is moody and depressed. His mother is a slatternly woman who seems totally unable to manage the house. These two are the most critical patients on my list at the moment, but which should I pay more attention to since there are so many more on my books? I am merely giving you two instances since I have other examples in other villages in my district. But the thing is that I'm getting confused. Sometimes I stagger about when I wake up in the morning and I don't know where I am and I can't think straight. I am tired all the time.'

The Old Man said, 'You want me to tell you which of these two to save since after all you may have to make a decision between the two of them? Justice is very hard and harder than mercy. Let me tell you a story about justice. Once upon a time there was a state called Sparta in Greece. Don't look so impatient. It may save time in the long run. The Spartans of course were very fierce warriors with a high sense of honour and they would not return from defeats alive but rather dead on their shields. However once one of them did and he stayed in the village ostracised by the others. However when the Spartans went to war again he was the first to volunteer and fought like a madman. Everyone agreed that he had fought the most bravely but the prize was given to the second bravest man since after all he didn't have the same motivation. That is an example of justice. The Greeks of course lived in smallish groups and didn't romanticise as we do. If you ask me which of these two to save I would say the old woman.'

The doctor looked at him in astonishment. 'The fact is,' said the Old Man, 'that that boy will have a miserable unhappy life, son of an alcoholic and a slatternly mother. He will not recover from this upbringing. I've seen it happening before. So have you. The old woman on the other hand though she has been alone and widowed has never become embittered and has remained cheery and helpful. If she recovers from this 'flu she may live a good many years yet. Without doubt the villagers will look at her and say, "What a marvellous thing human nature is! There's this old woman who has remained cheerful after bitter loss. Not only that, but she has recovered from 'flu. God must therefore be on her side." '

'You at least are,' said the doctor. The Old Man smiled but said little. 'Anything,' he said, 'that helps to comfort our fallen nature is good, anything else is bad. That is why you should save the old woman. She is a sign of hope.'

The doctor looked at him for a long time and then said, 'You are the wisest man I know, if you are a man at all. I will do that.' Then, tired but not so confused, he almost ran out of the room. The Old Man poured himself out a small glass of wine and drank it slowly. His face seemed to become haggard and worn and he looked very old indeed. But when a knock came to the door he put the wine away in the cupboard, adjusted his expression, as it were, to one of serenity and said, 'Come in.' He did not wish people to know that he drank much wine for they would not respect him afterwards. That was why he smashed all the empty bottles before putting them in the bucket so that people would not know that they had been bottles at all. The poor people needed all the help and illusion they could get after the mess that had been made of things.

The Prophecy

I may say at the very beginning of this story that I am a very worried man for it had never occurred to me before that what is up there or somewhere around may very well be a joker. In fact to be perfectly honest I hadn't believed that there was anything much around at all. Some years ago I came to live in this village in Scotland (I am by the way an Englishman and my name is Wells). I have no connection at all with the Highlands: I am not an alien exploiter either. I am just a man who like others was fed up of the rat race as it is called reasonably correctly. In fact I am (or perhaps was) a psychologist. I am not very much now. Brilliance in psychology as in everything else belongs to a youth of energy and fire and by leaving the rat race I suppose I was signalling those days were over for me even though I thought of myself somewhat in the manner of those Chinese exiles from court who used to drink wine and write little poems in the cold mountains while they gazed at the road they would never travel again. I am also unmarried.

I worked in a university and quite frankly I got tired. If you wish to know what I got tired of I will tell you. I became enraged, literally enraged, by the contradictions which I saw in people's personalities every day and which they seemed implacably to be unaware of. Let me give you one or two instances. One man I knew was always talking of 'professional behaviour' and yet at the same time he was the worst, most consistently destructive and rabid gossip I have ever seen. Another, a hard drinker, lectured on alcoholism as the manifestation of ultimate weakness. Another, a so-called devotee of pure research, was leaping on to the barbaric bandwagon of the quick Penguin for the masses.

I became obsessed by this gap between the spoken word and

the reality of the personality. I was losing my balance. I found that I was checking myself continually against my own standard of consistency and in doing so making myself more and more vulnerable. In other words I was coming to the conclusion that these contradictions are necessary to life and that he who sets out deliberately to erase them is in fact destroying himself. I found in other words that there is an enmity between consistency and life. This discovery was so shattering that for a long time I was incapable of working at all. For if this were true then an attempt to seek consistency and truth was in fact suicidal. Many nights I have sat staring at a book completely oblivious of my surroundings, and when I woke up from my daydream I found that I was still at the same page. The discovery I had made seemed to me utterly shattering. My mind roamed pitilessly in all directions. It seemed to me quite clear for instance that Christ was both violent and peaceful in his nature and that theologians in trying to eliminate the one in order to reinforce the other so as to create a perfectly consistent being without flaw were, in fact, being false to reality. Life is not reasonable, to live is to be inconsistent. To be consistent is to cease to live. That was the logical converse.

Now, however it happened, I thought that I should try and find a place where there would be a greater simplicity than I had been used to and that there I would be able to test this new theory. In fact what of course had happened was very simple. My energy and fire had run out and I was merely escaping. That was the truth I was disguising in terms of my research and my love of truth. I understand perfectly why my love of truth is so great. I was brought up by possessive parents who married late and each day I was trying to justify myself to their unlimited love and pride. Never would it be possible for any human being to do that – to fill that gap with the continual victories of the virtuoso – but this did not mean that it was possible for me to stop trying. It was this hunger for justification that destroyed me. For it is clear to me now that an excessive consciousness is bound to be at the mercy of the mediocre and the satisfied. An immense hunger for truth and consistency is rare and cannot by its nature lead to happiness. Most men do not by a privileged mercy see their own contradictions. Gandhi was peaceful to the world but aggressive to his family. So was Tolstoy. Both these men among many others were impaled on the impossible attempt to make life consistent and truthful. This is impossible precisely because truth is abstract and static and life flows ceaselessly like a river.

I arrived therefore in this village, in this country, the Highlands. I didn't know very much of the Highlands when I came. Naturally I could appreciate its scenery, but scenery after all is only a reflection of the psyche. There were hills, lochs, rivers, broken fences and roads. It looked like a land to which much had been done, adversely. It looked a lonely land without sophistication or riches. It echoed with ghosts and waterfalls. It looked a broken land. And it suited me because that was what I was myself, a broken man. Quite literally, I was a signpost pointing nowhere. It wasn't, I suppose, at all extraordinary that the Highlanders accepted me or at least didn't show any hostility. I used to go out fishing and they would tell me the best bait. I was shown how to cut my own peats. I even used to tar and felt my own roof. All these things I learned from them. I imagine that what I was doing was using my psychological techniques so that they would like me. I took care not to offend them. The only thing was I never went to church but strangely enough they accepted that too on the grounds that a man must be loyal to his own church and since mine was presumably the Church of England I couldn't be expected to betray it simply because I had put a number of miles between it and myself.

I studied these people and their history. I knew what had made them and what they had become. I recognised their secretiveness and the reason for it. I sensed the balance of forces which is necessary to keep a village together. I recognised the need for rivalry between villagers. I was dimly aware of the vast spaces of their past and how they must be occupied. I noticed the economic differentiation between men and women. I was aware of the hidden rancours and joys. After all I had been a psychologist. These things were child's play to me. I learned their language and read their books and poems. I had plenty of time to read and I read a lot. The local schoolmaster came to visit me.

And this is what happened. Now I am ready to tell my story and I am sure that you must appreciate that it is a very odd one.

This schoolmaster was a very odd psychological type. He was immersed in his children, I mean his pupils. He believed that his ideal work, what he was destined for, was to be among them. He was really rather a child himself with his rosy face and his impermeable surfaces. I could see what had happened to him, but after all that is the terror with which a psychologist must live, to see the gestures and know their real value and weight and meaning, to track a joke to its stinking lair. The schoolmaster was in fact one of the few people I could really talk to on a certain level since he had in fact read a little though in no sense deeply. Still he was useful to me since he knew a great deal of the lore and literature of the people, though of course not profoundly, being himself still inside that lore.

One night we had a long discussion about predestination. It was disordered and random and without penetration. My mind had lost its edge and wandered vaguely round the edges of the real problem like someone who roams round a field at night. I knew that my mind had lost its edge and its conviction and it disturbed me. I knew that my mind was not powerful enough to make a proper analysis of such a concept though in relation to his it was in fact the mind of a giant. We drank much sherry since the schoolmaster would not drink whisky. I was sick of myself and only half listening when suddenly he said, 'What do you think of this? Many years ago, in fact it must be over a hundred years ago, we had a prophet here who made some odd prophecies.'

'And how many of them have come true?' I said indifferently, purely automatically.

'Well,' he said, 'it is rather difficult to say. They are set in such mysterious terms. For instance, he said that when the river ate the land stones would be raised. Some people think this refers to the storm of last year when that big wall was built.'

Mechanically, I said, 'That could be expected, surely, in a

place which gets so much rain as this. I wouldn't place much reliance on that.' And I poured myself another sherry.

Anyway he told me some more of his mysterious sayings but only one stayed in my mind. There is a reason for this which I did not see at the time but which will appear later.

This saying went something like this: 'When the wood is raised at the corner then wills will crash.'

In my befuddled state I coudn't make any sense of this, especially the last part. The first part could refer to a wooden building and the corner was a clear enough sign since there is a place at the end of the village called the Corner but as for the second part I was bemused. I said to him and I remember this clearly, 'Surely that must really be "Wills will clash", not "crash".'

'That's how it has come down to us,' he said looking at me. And that was that. I was sure that there had been an error in the manuscript or whatever and later found out that the manuscript if it had existed no longer did so. For that matter, perhaps the man had never existed at all. The schoolmaster however was very sure of the prophet's existence and talked of him as a strange being who lived by himself, wore a beard and walked about in a dream most of the time.

Anyway, the night passed and the schoolmaster went home and I went to bed half thinking about the phrase 'Wills will crash' and pretty certain that the word should have been 'clash'. Otherwise the whole thing didn't make any sense and naturally I wanted it to make sense. After all that was what I was, a man who wanted to make sense of things. I slept a dreamless sleep but when I woke up in the morning I was still thinking of this saying. I am sure it would have passed smoothly into my mind leaving no trace if it hadn't contained what I considered to be a semantic inexactitude. I worried at it but could make no further sense of it. I tried to find out more about the prophet's sayings but could discover little about him, no more in fact than the schoolmaster had told me. As it was winter time I had time on my hands and pursued my investigations and came up with a blank. It was at this point that the idea came to me, as Relativity must have come to Einstein.

2

It was really a blindingly simple idea and I wondered why no one had thought of such a thing before. Maybe (I half considered) I had been sent to this place in order to arrive at the stunning conception I had now arrived at. Maybe I was predestined to meet the schoolmaster . . . At that time you see I had no idea of the intricacies that would enmesh me. Anyway my idea was this. Why didn't I raise the wood at the corner (that is, raise a shed there) and see what would happen? There was no reason why I couldn't do it if I wanted to. I had plenty of money. There were one or two unemployed people who would build the shed for me. I had no fears that permission would be refused me as I was quite popular and not thought of as an outsider. I reviewed my idea from all angles and there seemed nothing against it. It would give me an interest during the winter months and it would return me to a psychological or at least philosophical theme. I may say that as I have mentioned already I had no feeling for ghosts, spirits, stars, etc., at that time, and thought them easily explicable manifestations of the fallible human psyche.

Anyway, not to be too tedious about the business, I decided to build a wooden shed at the Corner. I had no doubt that this was the location mentioned since I gathered that the place had been so-called from time immemorial. I got hold of a middle-aged fellow called Buckie who was a builder but unemployed at the time. As he had a large family which consisted mostly of teenage girls who shrieked and screamed and presumably ate a lot, like seagulls, he was very glad to help me. The hut was to be fairly spacious. Buckie reported every morning in his blue overalls with his rule in his pocket and began to work on the fine new yellow wood. I often used to watch him but as he didn't say much at any time I ended by leaving him alone. He didn't even ask me why I wanted the shed built. Perhaps he thought I wanted a place where I could be absolutely quiet or perhaps he thought I intended to get some stuff which I would store there eventually.

In any case one fine day I went to the Corner and found that the shed had been built. As green is my favourite colour I decided to paint it green and this I did myself. For the rest it was a fairly spacious shed with two windows and one door. It was fairly warm inside but not too warm and there was plenty of room. The windows were quite large and looked out on to the road which travelled past the hut towards the town eight miles away. After the hut was finished I would go and sit there. I took a chair and table and I would read and so some writing. Otherwise I didn't use it much.

At nights I would lie awake and wonder why I had been so stupid as to build it. There it pointlessly stood for no reason that I or anyone else could offer. I had no clue as to what I was going to do with it. I couldn't offer it to anyone else, not even as a place for staying in, for no one would have made their home there as there was a tradition that there were ghosts at the Corner and the villagers were very superstitious. Thus the days passed and I waited. I had built the hut and the next move was up to the prophet, if there was to be any next move. Sometimes I felt like a girl waiting to be visited by a lover and impatient that he wasn't coming. If he had any sincerity or love why didn't he prove by his presence that his words were true?

Naturally some of the villagers asked me why I had built the hut and I told them some vague story about wanting a quiet place to study in. They seemed quite satisfied with this explanation as though I mixed with them, they didn't make any pretence of understanding me.

Then on a lovely spring evening the first move was made. There was a knock at the door and standing there was a young boy from the village whose name was John Macleod. He was a tall rather clumsy-looking fellow with a reddish face and large hands and he worked as a painter in the town coming home at nights on the bus. I was in a good mood at the time for some reason and I stood there at the window looking out towards the glittering sea across the walls and ditches and houses and fields.

The boy took a long time to come to the point (indeed if he had had a cap he would have been twisting it in his hands) but the gist of his request was that perhaps out of the goodness of my heart I might lend the young people of the village the hut for their weekend dances. Normally they conducted their dances in the open air at the Corner but of course this meant that there could be no dances on a rainy night. There was really no problem since my hut was large enough to accommodate all the young people who were likely to turn up (about sixteen at the most). I thought about it very briefly and then agreed, especially as the boy assured me that the hut would be left spick and span after they had finished with it hat there would be no damage at all as the village youth were well-behaved, that he would return the key to me after they had cleaned out the hut if it was necessary to do so. I myself knew that the villagers were law-abiding and would not harm the hut, so I agreed readily. And he went away quite excessively happy. I dismissed the whole thing from my mind, glad that at last a use had been found for my hut. Funnily enough, though, I had a vague feeling at the back of my mind that I had made some connection however tenuous with the prophet hovering somewhere in the offing. It was an odd unaccountable feeling and I soon got rid of it.

Nothing happened for four or five weeks. During the successive Saturdays the dances in the hut went on, the key was handed back to me and the place was left tidy as promised. Unfortunately, though I didn't know it, the air around me was rapidly darkening with omens. As everyone knows islanders are not notable for speaking out, and no rumour at first reached me till quite suddenly out of the blue the Rev. Norman Black made his explosive attack in the pulpit on a particular Sunday. As I wasn't in church I didn't hear his exact words but I was given accounts of it. The Rev. Norman Black is a small fiery man with a ginger moustache who holds the local people in an iron grip. They go out and gather his peats for him, they give him presents of meat and milk, and in return he exercises dominion over them. They are in fact very frightened of him indeed. I cannot help admiring him in a way since his consciousness of his own rightness is so complete and utter. He bows the knee to no one and he flashes about in his small red car like a demon from the pit spitting sulphur and flame, and when he feels it is necessary he has no deference to the high and no mercy on the low. As far as I could gather the drift of his sermon, shorn of theological and ecclesiastical language, was as follows. The shed or hut was infested by young people intent on fornication: this was in fact the reason why the hut had been built in the first place. As long as the dancing took place in the open then one could see what was going on but when walls had been erected then privacy suitable for dalliance and immorality had been created. Also why was the hut painted green? This was very ominous indeed. Furthermore why had this hut been built by an Englishman who never attended church? Was it because he was bent on undermining the morality of the village? What other explanation could there be? Considered from that angle my enterprise did indeed look suspicious and cunning especially as I had no real explanation for the hut, and even if I were to offer one no one would believe me now. As for my true reason, who would believe that?

At first I was inclined to laugh at the whole thing but in fact there apparently had been some drinking. Some 'dalliance' had, in fact, taken place though it was, I am sure, quite innocent. Nevertheless people began to sidle past me. They began to wonder. Was I some thin end of the wedge? Had my previous civil behaviour been a mask? Cold shoulders were turned to me. My visitors dwindled. Anger grew. After all I had been extended hospitality and I was repaying it with lasciviousness cunningly disguised as philanthropy. I felt around me a rather chill wind. Neighbours began to slant off when I approached.

Steadily as the Rev. Norman Black blew on the flames and lashed his theological whip the village divided itself into two camps, that of the adults and that of the young. One night there was an attempt to set the place on fire. After that a guard was mounted over the hut for some time each night. Parents warned their children not to go to the dances and the young rebelled. I found myself at the centre of the cross fire. Messages were scrawled on my door in the middle of the night. The young expected me to stand up for them and I still gave them the key. Even the schoolmaster was divided in his mind and ceased to visit me. I was alone. My visits to the local shop became adventures into enemy country. The shop was often out of articles that I needed. My letters arrived late.

One day a group of youngsters came to the door and told me that some adults were intending to march on the green hut and burn it down.

Let me say at this point that I was faced with a particularly interesting scientific problem. I wished naturally to be merely an observer in the experiment I was conducting and for this reason I couldn't interfere on either side. However, I walked along with the youngsters towards the hut. When we arrived the adults had not yet reached it, and we waited outside the hut in a group. There was a number of boys and girls and many of them were very angry. They felt that they were defending not only a hut but a principle. They felt that the time had come when they must stand up for themselves against the rigid ideology which was demanding the destruction of their hut. My hut had in fact become a symbol.

We waited therefore and saw in complete silence the adults approaching. There was a large number of them and they carried axes and spades. They stopped when they saw us and the two groups faced each other in the fine sunshine. They were led, as one could see very quickly, by the fiery minister. This was indeed a clash or crash of wills that the prophet had foreseen. The minister came forward and said, 'Are you going to allow us to pull down peacefully this habitation of the devil?'

One of the boys who was home from university and whose name was John Maclean said, 'No, we're not. You have no right to pull the hut down. It doesn't belong to you.' He was studying, as I remember, to be a lawyer. I said nothing but remained an interested spectator. What was I expecting? That there would be an intervention from heaven?

The minister said no more but walked steadily forward with an axe in his hand. Now this posed another interesting problem. No one had ever laid hands on a minister before, certainly not in a country village. If anyone did, would there indeed be an intervention from heaven? The minister, small and energetic, advanced towards the hut. The group of youngsters interposed themselves. He pushed among them while one or two of the girls, their nerve breaking, rushed to the other side to join their fathers, who were waiting grimly to see the result of the minister's lone attack. I think they too were wondering what the youths would do. In his tight black cloth the minister moved steadily forward, axe in hand.

The youths were watching and wondering what I should do but I did nothing. How could I? After all I was a scientist engaged in an experiment. Some of them were clearly speculating on what would happen to them when their parents, many of them large and undeniably fierce, got them home again. In the sunshine the minister advanced. One could see from the expression on his face that for him this hut really was an abomination created by the devil, that its destruction had been ordered by the Most High, that he, the servant of God attired in his sober black, was going to accomplish that destruction. Interestingly enough I saw that among the adults was Buckie the builder placidly awaiting the destruction of the work of his own hands. Did I however glimpse for one moment a twitch of doubt on his face, a fear that he perhaps too was present at a personal surrender? I knew all the invaders, every single one of them, placid, hard-working men, good neighbours, heavy moral men, all bent on destroying my green hut which was at the same time both Catholic and demonic and perhaps life-enhancing. It was odd that such a construction should have caused such violent passions. But I had not met a man like this minister before. When he had finally arrived next to the youths he said in a slightly shrill voice (perhaps even he was nervous?), 'I have come here to lay this abomination to the ground. Shall any of you dare touch the servant of the Lord?' Quivering he raised his head, his moustache bristling. There was a long silence. It was clearly a moment permeated with significance. Were the young going to establish their independence once and for all? Or were they going to surrender? The village would never be the same again after this confrontation, no matter what happened.

The men waited. The minister pushed. And he slipped on the ground. I am not sure how it happened – maybe he slipped on a stone, or maybe he had done it with the unconscious deliberation and immense labyrinthine cunning that the service of the

Lord had taught him. Anyway as if this had been what they
waiting for, the men pushed forward in a perfect fury (would
these sons of theirs defy their elders as represented by the
minister?), impatiently pushed their sons and daughters aside
and with axes held high hacked away at the hut. Thus in Old
Testament days must men such as this have hacked to pieces
the wooden gods of their enemies, coloured and magical and
savage. Thus they splintered and broke my hut. Before they
were finished the youngsters had left, giving me a last look of
contempt. I was the fallen champion, the uncommitted one.
I who had apparently been on the side of youth against the
rigid structures of religion, had surrendered. When the men
had accomplished their destruction, their penetration of the
bastion of immorality, they too turned away from me as if in
embarrassment that I had witnessed such an orgy, almost
sexual in its force and rhythm. Without speaking to me
they left.

After they had all gone, leaving an axe or two behind, I stood
there beside my ruined hut, the shell which had been ripped
open and torn. Not even the Bacchanalians had been so fierce
and ruthless. Thinking hard, I poked among the fragments.
Above me the sky was blue and enigmatic. No prophecy
emerged from its perfect surface. I remembered the words,
'When the wood is raised at the Corner wills will crash.' Or
rather 'will clash'. Suddenly in a moment of perfect illumination such as must have been granted to the prophets I realised
that the words could also be 'walls will crash'. But even before
I had assimilated that meaning another one so huge and comic
and ironic had blossomed around me that I was literally
staggered by the enormous terror of its implications and sat
down with my head in my hands. For I now knew that I could
not stay in the village. My time there had come to an end. I was
ready to start afresh. My retreat had ended. I must return to the
larger world and continue with my work. But then the final
revelation had come, as I shivered suddenly in the suddenly
hostile day. I thought of my discussion on predestination with
the schoolmaster. I thought of his casual remarks about the
prophet. I thought of how I had been led to this particular

village to learn about the prophecy and this prophet. I thought of the hundred years the man had been dead. I thought of the last meaning of all which had just come to me and I laughed out loud at the marvellous joke that had been perpetrated on me, rational psychologist from an alien land. There the words stood afresh in front of my mind's eye as if written in monstrous letters, luminous and hilarious, in the sunny day of clear blue. It was as if the heavens themselves cracked, just like my hut, as if the vase, elegant and beautiful, had shown a crack running right down its side, as if I could see the joking face, the body doubled over in laughter. For the words that came to me at that moment, the last reading of all, were these: 'WHEN THE WOOD IS RAISED AT THE CORNER WELLS WILL CRASH.'

The Letter

When you find this letter I shall hope to be dead. Though in fact it is not a letter but an explanation. I am as you know your village headmaster and you understand who and what I am. Or at least you understand me as far as anyone can understand anyone else. You know me as one who takes care of your children. You know me, I hope, as a dedicated man. I am fifty years old and I have been here a long time. I have presided at your small concerts. I have a wife and children and have loved in my way this village since I first came to it many years ago when I was twenty-five years old on a fine day in a light such as I had never seen before on earth. I cannot describe to you what I felt that day. If I were a poet I might be able to but I am not. I am, I think, a very ordinary man and the older I grow the more ordinary and less exceptional I see that I am. But that day was the beginning of a new world, a new life. The air seemed cleaner, objects in the world more solid and luminous, the sky and sea bluer. It was as if I had undergone a resurrection. Yet there was no question of a previous death. I have seen a painting like that somewhere, but I can't remember where.

And indeed my love of the place as a new land communicated itself to my work. I taught as if I were inspired. I loved the minds and motions of children. I saw the world through their eyes, in flashes, unpredictably. I think that in fact I became a child and that all these years I was in fact a child. The world was immediate to me, I fed on it. I had immense unremitting hope. I woke in the morning as if to a new world as children do. I taught and read and taught. All that I read was for them. All that I did was for them. I surrendered myself to them. I became their servant. And in that I was entirely happy.

I cannot remember when that dream faded. Perhaps there

was no particular day. Perhaps it is a poison that we all have to drink and that those who love most dearly drink most deeply. It wasn't anything that they – I mean the children – did. For I must say that they have always been faithful to me as far as it is possible for them to be so. I believe I have understood them more than most people do since I have been for so many years a child myself. Even now perhaps I am a child expecting more than the world can give.

I never asked of the world material possessions. You all know that. My life has been very simple and seen from the outside must have appeared even limited and dull. I did not seem to enjoy riches or to have great passions. I was happily married, as you saw. I used even to read the books the children read. I became fond of fairy stories. I loved especially the story of Little Red Riding Hood, and saw in my mind's eye the wolf lounging against a tree while the girl carried her scones or whatever it was to her white-shawled granny. I loved that world of pigs and foxes and cats and dogs and old women and magic lamps. Indeed the more I progressed in life the more I abandoned my books of philosophy in favour of the fairy story and its animals and its more creative and happy logic.

Why then am I writing this letter to you telling you that never again will you see me? I will tell you. Yesterday I held a service in the hall. This was one of my concessions to you. I knew and I have always known that I must appear religious, otherwise I would not be able to teach your children. And I did want to teach, and not only to teach but to teach these particular children. So I consoled myself with the fiction that if I wished to serve them at all – and I really thought I would serve them better than anyone else – I would simply have to surrender to you on this point, not realising that this mumbo jumbo of the Old Testament which they did not understand was a poison which was steadily eroding all the other bloom that I was putting on them. But then I was cowardly; I did not wish to leave. One can only work creatively in one particular place at one particular time, in a place where objects are known long enough to be converted to symbols, and become beautiful and enduring and permeated with the hue of one's life-blood. I was not a tourist – that at least I can say. And there is no one I despise more than the tourist.

I will tell you what happened. Yesterday they were singing a hymn and I was watching and listening, and I had a vision. The vision was so deadly that I know that I shall not recover from it. It is the death blow. As I looked at them singing from their hymn books I saw them all as children of their mothers and fathers. I saw them as what they would become and I knew that they would become like their mothers and fathers. I could see it in the turn of their heads, in their petulant or absorbed pose. I knew not only that I personally had failed them but that anyone would have failed them. I knew that there is a spirit of the universe which is plotting to make us as like each other as possible. I knew that there is no heaven and that my vision for twenty-five years had been a fake. I knew that the tree produces the leaf and the fish produces the fish, that the corruption has been there from the beginning, and that the teacher also is the corrupter. No one is free from the plague. Christ was the man or god whom they thought would uncorruptedly break the ring, but in order to do that he had to remain a virgin and be crucified. We are producing each other endlessly and corruptedly. There is no Eden and no heaven. At that moment I looked into hell. For in one girl in particular I saw already forming the fat jowls of her mother. I saw that clearly and without evasion. And when I saw the one I saw all the others. I cannot bear to be part of this conspiracy. I cannot bear to see the old emerging from the young. I cannot bear not to believe in my vision. For this reason, when you find this letter I shall be dead. I have to withdraw myself, this instrument of corruption, from the world. I now believe that we have been visited by some original sin of the most immense magnitude and that there is no way of cleansing this sin. And I cannot live with this experience since it negates the whole idea of my life. I am a warder who wished to throw prisons open, while all the time I was creating them. Because of my egotism I thought that I was a saviour but I was not. To be a saviour one must have blood that is not human. There is nothing any of you can do about this. I wish it to be clear that it is not your fault. So goodbye, my fellow human beings in trouble. You can do none other than you do. Neither can I. I have no message for you and without a message what am I? Nothing. And to nothing I go back.

Jimmy and the Policeman

There was once in our village an unpopular policeman and a pickpocket. When I say that the policeman was unpopular I mean that he was far too energetic to be a good village policeman and he was also too thin. Most village policemen are fat large men with red faces who usually have their tunics open and pace steadfastly like comics from a film. They will pass the time of day with the locals, pretend that the bar has actually shut at ten o'clock on the dot, discuss gardening, lean over fences and generally leave the villagers to mind their own business. This particular policeman wasn't like that at all. First of all he was, as I have said, very thin, and secondly he was determined to clamp down on all crime and thirdly he didn't want to be outwitted by anyone.

He would call at the bar at ten o'clock to make sure that everyone had stopped drinking. He interfered in the Case of the Missing Cow, and made a mess of things. After all, if he had left the affair alone, everyone would have been quite happy but he had to stir things up. And in any case the cow hadn't been stolen at all. He even bothered the children and there was the case of the Green and Red Marbles which I shall not trouble you with because it was so trivial. Thus it was decided that since in a village everyone must make allowances for everyone else, he should be taught a lesson. And the instrument which destiny chose was Jimmy Smith, a pickpocket. But again let me qualify this. Jimmy was not a criminal, he was a joker. He had quick hands but he used them to entertain people. He was an independent little man with a great dislike for authority of any kind. There was an element of the child in his nature and he liked best to play with the children with whom he would make balloons disappear, handkerchiefs end up in the wrong pockets, and marbles change colour like those sweets they used to call bull's eyes.

Now the policeman took an instinctive dislike to him because I suppose he puzzled him. Jimmy had no interest in money or getting on in the world. He did odd jobs for people but otherwise seemed perfectly happy where he was, puffing at his pipe all day. He had a small black pipe with a silver lid on it which was his most precious possession. Most of the day he would sit in front of the door, playing with pebbles which he had picked up, or sitting in his room reading a book. He was a great reader and was never more content than when he was immersed in an old Western or a ragged detective story that had gone the rounds of the village. Nevertheless, though he was harmless, the policeman was suspicious of him partly I think because he was so indolent and there was no way in which power could be exerted over him and partly because there was a peculiar creative streak in his nature which the policeman found disturbing. Once he tried to get him for drinking but in some unaccountable manner Jimmy disappeared and the policeman couldn't nail him at all.

One day he came to Jimmy's house and spoke to him in the following terms.

'Jimmy,' he said, 'I'm the policeman in this village and I want you to understand this. I'm determined to be a good one. That is to say, no crime will be permitted here while I am the policeman. I have the feeling that you are secretly laughing at me and I won't have it. I have heard certain things you have said about me, joking references, and I won't put up with them.'

'Oh, excuse me a moment,' said Jimmy who seemed hardly to be listening, 'while I make a cup of tea. I wonder if perhaps you would like one.'

'I . . . ' Now, it happened that it was rather a hot day and the policeman was feeling sticky in his warm blue uniform so thinking that he would make himself look human – for he wasn't a complete fool – he agreed to accept a cup of tea. Another reason why he accepted the tea was that he wished to have more time to look at Jimmy and study him. Jimmy was apparently unconcerned but bustled about with cups and saucers. The policeman gazed idly round the room, which was neat and tidy and small. There didn't seem to be enough space, as they say, to swing a cat. There was a sink at which Jimmy was busy, there were two chairs, a fireplace which was completely bare, a small cooker, a table and nothing else. Jimmy, it seemed, was a spiritual monk as far as possessions were concerned. There was however a big red balloon hanging from the middle of the ceiling and a guitar in one corner. All the time, Jimmy bustled about with his pipe in his mouth. It was noticeable that sometimes he didn't smoke at all, though he still kept the pipe between his teeth.

When the tea was ready Jimmy took the cups over and laid them down on – oh, yes, I forgot there was a stool. All the time, he had been talking in some mysterious way, for he still had the pipe in his mouth, saying that he had nothing against the policeman, that all he wanted was to be left alone, that he wished he could play the guitar better, that it was a fine day, that someone's cow had been eating his washing, that he had just finished a comic song which ... But the funny thing was that when he laid the cups down, somehow or other, either by accident or design, the tea from one of the cups was spilt over the policeman. The latter got up in a rage while Jimmy dabbed at him with a cloth which he had taken over from the sink, his hands flying hither and thither, faster it seemed than lightning and at one time whipping out the policeman's handkerchief to help repair the damage. All this time he kept up a running fire of apologies while the policeman's face reddened and reddened. Eventually the trousers were dried out by means of the cloth and the handkerchief, and the policeman was about to storm out still swearing vengeance against Jimmy who appeared entirely anguished and staggered by what had happened and was suggesting that the policeman should have another cup of tea. However, the latter, not to be mollified, prepared to leave, renewing his pose, ready to confront the world again, dry and complete.

However, just as he was leaving, Jimmy said quietly, 'I wonder if you have still got the five pound note you keep in your wallet.' The policeman looked at him, saw some dancing glitter of comedy in his eyes, took out his wallet and sure enough there was a five pound note missing.

There was a long silence in the room interrupted only by the frantic buzzing of a bluebottle against dim panes. The two men gazed at each other. The balloon swung gently between them and the guitar leaned back in its corner.

'So,' said the policeman at last, 'this is a challenge.' He brooded for a moment, thought that beating Jimmy up was not on, that pure deduction must be the answer, that if he didn't come up with the answer he was finished in the village, and then proceeded to think. Jimmy glanced at him mockingly. For the first time the policeman realised that there was an elfin quality about Jimmy, in the thin ironic face, and the playful smile, that too he had what could only be called an implacable cheek. He said, 'First of all I have to search you. Come here.'

Jimmy submitted to the search in a good-humoured manner, but there was no five pound note on him. There was no money on him at all.

The policeman took a walk over to the sink. There was nothing there either. It was neat and tidy and white. The policeman examined himself. There were no five pound notes in his pockets and nothing in his turn-ups. He opened the wallet again to make sure that the money hadn't been returned there in some mysterious manner, but it hadn't. He looked in the fireplace but that was bare. He tried the top of the stool but it remained fixed. He made Jimmy stand naked while he examined all his clothes. For one terrifying moment he thought that perhaps Jimmy had gambled on this, that he would have arranged for someone to be watching, and that he, the policeman, would be accused of sodomy. He made Jimmy put on his clothes again. Jimmy sat back in the chair puffing at his pipe contentedly. The policeman gazed at him. He said at last, 'I am really a very good policeman, you know. It would be a tragedy for you if I were to leave. Who else would you get in my place but some idiot who would be unable to solve any of your crimes? I believe in what I am doing. I was born to be a policeman. You think your idyllic existence will go on forever, that there will never be any serious crime or murder. But how do you know that? All you have to do is read the papers.'

The silent guitar leaned back in the corner. The balloon drifted a little, like someone breathing. Jimmy said nothing but smiled. The policeman knew that if Jimmy told the story of the Locked Room he would never recover from it. In a sudden rage he pulled down the balloon and burst it as if he thought the money might be inside it, but it wasn't, and the deflated balloon lay on the floor. He searched in the teapot and the kettle, but there was nothing there. He looked in the tin where the tea had been.

'I've got it!' he said at last. 'I know what you've done. I know exactly what you've done. You've rolled the money up and put it in your pipe bowl.' Jimmy looked at him in wonderment and slightly fearfully. He mimicked alarm and despondency. He seemed to protest as he handed the pipe over. The policeman looked into the bowl. There was nothing there.

He sat and looked at Jimmy in despair. He had tried everything and he hadn't found the solution. The room was small and bare. There were no other hiding-places.

For the first time however he realised that there was a clock and that it was ticking rather loudly. He felt that it was ticking away his career. He remembered the stories about Jimmy, how once at Hallowe'en he had made a cart disappear, how he could do weird things with telephones . . . As he sat there in amazement and bafflement, Jimmy said, 'You're a good policeman. You're really very good. But what you haven't realised is that if you go on the way you are going you will increase and not decrease the amount of crime in the village. You will have to learn to leave people alone unless there is something really serious. Look at me. I leave people alone. I'm cleverer than you. I've just proved it. My mind works faster. If I wanted to commit a serious crime I could get away with it. You have forced me to take a five pound note from you. That is a crime you are directly responsible for. Do you understand? Now I am a law-abiding person and if the law were just I should be able to sue you for serious temptation but I am not going to sue you. I'm letting you off. Do you realise that I have put you in prison? This room is a prison for you. You can't leave it because I have wound round you a net of the mind. For years, for the rest of your life, if you leave now with the mystery unsolved, you will be wondering about it. It will cause self-doubt. You will never be the policeman you were. I hope you understand that clearly.'

The policeman looked at him for a long time and then said, 'You are saying that you are offering me a bargain.'

'Yes. The fact that you thought of my pipe suggests that you are clever. You will have to learn to be tolerant. Will you do that if I tell you the solution?'

'Yes,' said the policeman at long last. 'I'll do that. I have understood everything you have said.'

'Good,' said Jimmy springing up. 'The five pound note is pinned to the back of your tunic. If you had gone out of this house swearing vengeance on me with the five pound note pinned to your tunic, what do you think would have happened?'

The policeman shivered as if in a cold wind.

'Now,' said Jimmy, 'I think we'll have a proper cup of tea. Or rather whisky. I make it myself, you know. After all we have something to celebrate. The return of a policeman to ordinary humanity.'

After the Film

Murdo came out of the village hall in a daze after seeing the Western. The shapeless night was all about him and the moon a cold stone in the sky. He stopped and looked up at it. Its gaze reminded him of the professional killer in the film, cold, inhuman. The killer clad in black had ridden out of the mountains, guns slung low, hat casting a black shadow over the rough rocky ground. There had been a saloon full of people dancing, whirling about, shouting, drinking: of girls with frilly dresses which ballooned over their heads: of comic finished men with large drooping moustaches. And into this place the killer had come, professional, remote, always standing on the edge of things, watching. Murdo lowered his eyes from the moon. There was the village with its huddle of houses, its unfinished fences, its holed walls. There were the peatstacks, black in the moonlight. For a moment he had a vision of the village as unprotected, untidy, dull. He peopled it with the villagers standing in their braces outside the houses, harvesting, stacking corn. There was one thing about Westerns, however, you never saw the sea in them. Plains, rocks, canyons, but never the sea.

He saw in his mind's eye the professional killer walking down his own village street. For that matter he himself for a moment was the professional killer. He always looked after his gun, polished it. After all, he was dependent on it. It was his livelihood. His reflexes were honed to the sharpest possible pitch. His mind operated continually at the highest levels. Life was a continual gamble with death, a continual proof of itself on that fabulous street he was walking now and which was quite still. It looked like a bone in the moonlight and as he thought this he heard a dog bark. The bark was duplicated by that of another dog. Then there was silence. He walked or rather rolled on his high heels down the street, feeling the gun in his hand, the leather on his body, cool and tight. All problems were solved by the gun, by speedy reflexes.

He was in Dodge City or Abilene. There were enemies all around him. But he was walking easily. He wasn't a simple village boy who moved slowly about in acres of time. He was impregnable among all these untidy shapes beside the untidy sea, which bothered him a bit because it shouldn't be in the script. The moonlight lay across it in sparkling drops, right out to the furthest edge. As he watched, the tightness and stiffness drained out of him. The professional was walking towards the sea but who would shoot into the sea? He didn't understand why this should bother him so much. His phantom hat cast its shadow over the unseen flowers which grew at the side of the road. His body was black and menacing. He had ridden far and in his hand the six-gun spun. He was walking down the road towards the sea, towards its shining acres, towards its jagged rocks. He passed the houses all asleep. He saw a cat scurry across the road in front of him, its eyes green and watchful. He walked on. The sea was growing louder. It reminded him suddenly of Mary, who would be lying asleep in her bed at that moment, her hair untouched by scent. Tomorrow at school he would see her again. As he thought this he also realised that his mind had been clouded, that the professional care had left him. 'I could have been killed there,' he thought to himself. 'Just as I passed that house I could have been killed. I allowed myself to think of something else.' He made his mind steady and cold again, drawing his power from the dazzling stony moon. As before, the untidy shadows fed his superiority, he himself was a being of hard edges. But nevertheless the sea glittered ahead of him and he could hear the sound it made, languorous and resonant with ancient stories. The light shining on it made him recall a wedding he had been to recently. The cat leaped out ahead of him again and he went for his gun. But he was too late. The cat had got away. If that had been the sheriff he would have been killed. The professional never got a second chance from another professional. The sea filled his head with its noise. The houses entered his consciousness, untidy and shadowy. Mary was walking across the sea, long blonde hair streaming. His gun and holster had dropped away. He walked on naked and vulnerable into the roar of the night and its randomness. He felt a breeze stir his hair briefly and die away. The road had become mysterious and he could feel the scent of the flowers rank in his nostrils. His black leather clothes faded into the night, and his jersey shone white in the moonlight. He was making his way to the sea. He wished to listen to the ageless stories, the rumours of the past. He felt like a rock melting. He entered the random shapeless shadows, happy to be there looking around him. To be a professional . . . How to shoot into the sea with the blonde light falling across it? How to keep continually awake in that ancient sleepy sound? He had dropped his holsters, he was moving forward, unprotected, towards that ageless monotonous sound which the villagers had heard for centuries, towards the sea the gunfighter had never seen.

Moments

I

There exist in life what I call moments and I mean, by that, moments of vision. I should like to tell you of two of them which have a connection with the village. One I experienced myself; the other was experienced by a friend of mine. There is nothing supernatural about these moments. They do not belong to another world or anything silly like that. They appear in the present but when they do appear they seem to shine with an enormous significance, as if they meant to tell us something that we do not quite understand or cannot put into words. There are of course coincidences but that is not what I mean. Once I myself for instance phoned a girl friend of mine and three times got another girl whom I had once known. There was something wrong with the phone. And I could list hundreds of other coincidences. Moments aren't like that, they aren't surprising. On the contrary, they seem to reveal something we ought to have seen for a long time. They dazzle with their rightness. But let me go on and tell my story.

In the first instance I must tell you that in my village years ago, and indeed in most villages years ago, there was a man who wrote business letters and filled in forms for people. The villagers cannot write business letters and they are terrified of forms. The reason I think is that these letters and forms are official and in their minds connected with the Government or its agencies and, because of past experience engraved on their consciousnesses, they consider the Government and its agencies hostile and frightening. The reason why they have to write business letters and fill in forms is that some of them get subsidies for cattle and so on, and also there is some correspondence in connection with their crofts. They are always afraid that their crofts will be taken away from them if they do not write these letters and fill in these forms correctly.

Now in our village the man who did this was called John Campbell. He had spent most of his early life in Canada and America. He would tell us how he had been working for many years on what he called the Elevators though as far as I can gather this was something to do with grain and not lifts. He came home when he was forty-five years old. He was a small, clever man who however suffered badly from arthritis, so intensely that he was often in great physical pain. For this reason he didn't work as most of the crofters did. In fact I would say that apart from one other man – an idler of the first order – he was the only man in the village who didn't work at anything day after day. He used to stay in bed late because of his arthritis and when he got up he would propel himself to his chair with sticks. He was an entertaining man and his house used for a while to be the centre of the village ceilidhs. He would still get magazines from someone in America and he would talk at great length about the Depression and events like that. He would tell us about the political changes in the world and how they ought to be interpreted. 'You mark my words,' he would say. 'One of these days the Communists will take over in America, and in Britain too.' He hated Socialists and com-plained about the smallness of his pension. Sometimes as he talked he would wince from the pain of his arthritis, which he once told me he thought he had got from swimming in too cold water. He had a very strong torso but that may have been because of the sticks he was always pushing himself along with, and the way in which he would use the muscles of his chest. He was also a great smoker though he didn't have very much money. One morning he appeared at my window at five o'clock – it was summer time – asking if I had a cigarette. This was before his arthritis became so bad that he was confined to the house. The villagers thought that because he had been in America he must be a very clever man and as I said he used to write their letters for them. They gave him some money for doing this and as he also had an ailing wife this helped him a lot.

His wife was a pale, pretty, dark-haired woman who suffered much from bronchitis especially in summer and autumn when there was a lot of pollen in the air. She spoke little and did not complain. I used to visit John a lot because he was an intelligent man and sometimes we would play draughts together. He often used to beat me and when he did his whole appearance seemed to change and he would grow fresh and cheery and happy. There was no harm in him at all and what I liked about him was that he never used to gossip. His mind was on higher things. The villagers of course never talked politics. They would talk about such and such a girl who had suddenly to go away to England to hide, as they thought, her pregnancy. And stories like that were their daily food. But John on the other hand would talk about politics and economics and loved a good argument. There was another reason why the villagers liked him, and that was that he never revealed their secrets to anyone. For them, to receive a letter was a great event and to receive a form a threatening one. They hardly ever wrote even personal letters.

I knew that John suffered a lot from his arthritis and that was the main reason why I visited him. He would never complain however and showed a keen interest, as I have said, in intellectual affairs. I wondered sometimes if he was very bored by his narrow existence but he never said anything about that either. Sometimes he would tell me stories about his years in Canada and America. He told me once that he had been in a bar in some American city and he had seen a boy from the village who was down and out and who had pleaded with him with tears in his eyes not to tell anyone he had seen him. Another time he had told how he had fought a man for a piece of bread during the Depression years. Clearly he had suffered a lot but in general he maintained the reticence of the true gentleman. Sometimes he would show me letters of a less private nature he had written to Government Departments on behalf of crofters. These letters were usually very neatly written till the arthritis spread to his hands. He would write to these remote people in an almost commanding style in which he often used long words though shorter ones would have done equally well. For instance he

would use 'comprehend' instead of 'understand' and 'differen-
tiate' instead of 'distinguish'. He told me with a certain pathos
that when he was in school he was very good at English and the
teacher had prophesied a future for him as a writer. I myself
thought that his writing though commanding was rather florid
but as he himself used to say, 'We must make sure that these
people know that we aren't barbarians, that we are educated
people. Otherwise they'll trample all over us.' Perhaps he
believed that all Governments are infested with Communists.
He also, I remember, used words like 'inst.' and 'ult.', words
which I would never use myself.

As time passed he had to retire to his bed and he became
paler and paler. His wife too wasn't very well and all of us in the
village used to bring them fish because we knew they were
dependent on us since they didn't have a breadwinner. Latterly
he would prop himself against the pillows and write his letters,
whose style became more and more elaborate. Once indeed I
think he got a letter back from a bureaucratic minion who
wrote that he couldn't understand what he was writing about.
It was almost as if he were creating an elaborate manner of
writing such as a writer may do in his 'middle' or 'late' period.
Or it may even be that he was trying to establish a more
personal contact with these remote people than is warranted by
subjects like taxation or crofting. He used to write, 'Dear Sir,'
but in his later years he would write 'My dear Sir.' He would
sign all his letters with a large, almost royal, flourish.

I will now tell you about the moment. As time passed he
grew, as I have said, more and more pale and would lie on his
bed staring at nothing. He would only rouse himself when
some villager would tiptoe in, taking off his bonnet, and tell
him in wearisome roundabout terms of a letter that he had
wanted written. I sometimes think he thought of these villagers
as petitioners whose requests he was tired of granting. He
would even talk about 'emoluments' which he received from
them. But in the end I am sure he would have written the letters
for nothing much as a writer may practise his art for his own
satisfaction even though no one will ever see it. He would rouse
himself as if from some deep reverie, listen keenly, and stretch

out his hand twisted by arthritis for his pen and paper. He had a tray beside his bed on which he would rest the paper and then he would start to write as if he had forgotten the villager and the reason for writing in the first place. At moments like these he seemed happy and the vacancy would fade from his eyes and he would again return to the world of things.

One day when he was working in the fields – my field adjoined his – his wife came rushing down and panting heavily told me that he was in a bad way, that he had been taken with some sort of fit. She wondered if I would go for the doctor but before that she would be grateful if I would look in on him. I immediately rushed up to the house, she trailing in my wake, her breath whistling from her narrow box of a chest. I opened the door. The house had a strange cool silence about it. I went into the bedroom where he was lying. He was sitting up in bed with the tray in front of him and on the tray there was resting a sheet of notepaper. His head, however, had fallen on one side like a bird's head frozen on a branch. I knew that he was dead. As I waited for his wife to come panting in I looked down at the letter and it was then that the moment occurred. The letter was addressed to a tax office in Glasgow and the first words – for the letter was incomplete – read as follows: –

My Dear Sir,

    I would like to draw your attention to the fact that during the past years I have been excessively burdened with tax for which I can find no reason when I consult my records. It seems to me that there is something radically wrong with the keeping of your accounts and that you have made an inexcusable error particularly as there are others in the same position as myself who have not been excessively taxed in this manner. I would esteem it a great favour if you would make an enquiry into this at your earliest . . .'

There the letter broke off and a scrawl trailed right down the page. As I said, I was struck and illuminated by something extraordinarily significant in the letter though I could not at the time see what the significance was. Nor do I now see it. For one can sense significance without understanding it. All I can say is that as I waited for his wife to arrive I stood there at the bedside staring down at that head all on one side – the face unshaven – and the pen escaped from his hand, swollen and glassy, while the letter lay on the tray, fairly neatly written except for the scrawl which ran down the page beginning at the end of the letter. The other thing I remember, out of that storm of pathos and illumination, was that I noticed a chamber pot underneath the bed as if he had been using it not long before.

2

The second 'moment' I heard about – if such a term is permissible – has to do with a young friend of mine. This friend had come home to his mother's funeral from America where he held an important post, Professor of Physics in fact at some university, I think in California. I imagine he will now be about forty-three years old which means that he has risen very fast in his career (and if you don't believe that a small village like ours can produce a Professor of Physics in America you're very wrong since in fact we have also other famous people in other parts of the world). I remember Robert as a young reserved boy who was respected by the other children and took part in most of the sports and pranks they got up to. But there was always something very adult about him even when he was young and he would talk to the older people on equal terms which was rather unusual. I put that down to the fact that he was the only son of a widow who had great will-power and ambition for him though she wasn't particularly liked in the village. In fact the villagers thought she was rather snobbish though I don't think that was true. It simply didn't occur to them to wonder what it must be like to be a poor widow in a village: it is not an enviable position. In any case she died and Robert came home to the funeral. It occurred to some of us that he might have taken his mother to America with him but he didn't, and she herself insisted that she would never go there . . . I thought when I saw him that he was looking very thin and seemed to be overworking. But I suppose the pressures in America must be greater than here (though the pressures here are great enough).

He hadn't kept up with the village while he was away and indeed his appearance was almost a surprise to us all though we were glad he came to take charge of things. I gathered that he was married to an American girl who herself had been a student and that he also had two children. He seemed rather astonished that the village hadn't changed much – the same people in the same houses, the same broken fences, the same subjects of gossip – though I can't understand why that should astonish him. Still a lot of these very clever people don't live in the real world as ordinary people do. It struck me afterwards that maybe he didn't write to his mother at all.

I felt that he was lonely and the night he came to visit me he talked for a long time about physics. Not that I know much about physics but I am a good listener. I was surprised that he wanted to talk about his work since most people don't, and I thought that it must be that he was hanging on to what he knew in an environment that seemed to disturb him. Not that he would ever think of coming back to the village and settling down after being in America at the heart of things and concerned with a subject like physics at such a high level. He didn't say anything much about his wife and children.

I gathered something like this from him, that modern physics is very different from the physics that I learned at school. He told me that the connections are much less clear at a certain level and that electrons for instance cannot be plotted both as to velocity and position. He told me all this very earnestly as if it were a disguise for something else that he didn't want to talk about. He repeated the bit about the electron a few times as if he were trying to convey something to me, almost in a kind of code, but I didn't understand what he could be trying to convey. I just listened. He told me that he himself ran a large department and that though he knew his physics he wasn't sure whether he could manage people very well. I could have told him the reason for this was his rather protected childhood but of course I didn't say so. I kept having to remember that he was no longer a boy but had adult responsibilities. The thing was he looked like a boy. Maybe it was something to do with his haircut. There was sometimes a wistful note in his voice as if by going to America he had left behind something which was very precious to him though I couldn't think what it was. Nor, as I said, did I think he would come back. Still he gave me a lesson on physics though all the time I felt that deep down he wasn't talking about physics at all. I can't honestly remember much else that he told me since I haven't the head for abstractions. When he left me late at night he looked more relaxed. I remember him turning round boyishly at the door and saying, 'I hope I haven't bored you with all this, sir.' It was the sort of remark that no true villager would ever have made and I of course said that he hadn't bored me. The other thing was I couldn't tell whether I felt sad or proud that he had called me 'Sir'. He went out into the night.

The following day was the day of the funeral. A large number of people turned up in the church and we sat there quietly waiting for the service to begin. I always feel cool and composed in church. I think it has something to do with the atmosphere and the silence. In front of us was the pulpit and below the pulpit was the coffin. After a while the minister came in in his robes and we sang a hymn and he said a prayer and read a passage from the Bible. I remember thinking at the time how divorced the language of the Bible is from the language of everyday life, how majestic and weighty it is, with its similes of desert and water, angels and devils, the spirit and the body. I looked at Robert now and again but he seemed to be taking things calmly enough. There was however in front of me a small woman in black who was dabbing at her eyes with a small white lacy handkerchief. When the service was over four men came forward and lifted the coffin to their shoulders. I saw Robert staring intently and then we were out in the bright sunshine of the day, among the green fresh leaves which had turned the window a deep green. There were cars waiting and I got into one and he got into another which was driven by an uncle of his – a brownish man with a large brown moustache – and we set off to the cemetery. When we arrived there we walked between glittering rows of tombstones to the place where his mother would be buried. The minister was standing bare-headed by the grave, his hair blowing slightly in the wind and his eyes screwed up against the breeze and the sun. He spoke loudly in the open air while we all stood around the grave in silence, all of us in dark suits. Robert went forward when his name was called and took hold of one of the tassels and the coffin was lowered on ropes into the earth. When it was all over we went to our cars and made our way home.

That night Robert came to see me though I didn't expect him. Normally a visitor would only come to see one once because he was expected to visit every house in the village. After he had sat down he suddenly said, 'Do you remember last night when I was telling you about physics?' I said that I remembered some of it, though I couldn't understand all of it. He was silent for a moment and then he said, 'I had an astonishing vision today, if I can call it that. You remember we were sitting in church waiting for the service to start. Well, I felt very calm and composed at the time. There was a smell of varnish or something from the pews and everyone was quiet. In America I don't go to church much though America is a very religious country whatever people may tell you. I just didn't seem to have the time, there was always so much to do. So I was surprised when I felt so peaceful and serene. To tell you the truth I don't much believe in God and heaven and things like that. My feelings about my mother were not intense. I have been away for years and I hadn't seen her for a long time. She was as you know a very strong-willed woman –' he hesitated as if about to say more and then decided against it. 'In any case that wasn't what I meant to tell you. You remember last night I was talking about the fact that physics nowadays is not so simple as it used to be and I mentioned to you that an electron cannot be plotted both as to position and velocity. I have always found this difficult to accept. I have always wanted physics to have intelligible connections, at the lower level as well as at the higher. Maybe there is buried in me the teaching of the church which sees connections everywhere. Anyway there I was sitting in the front pew feeling serene and the minister was speaking that beautiful language about eternity and the hymn was being sung. It didn't happen then, that vision. It was later.'

'At the graveside, you mean?' I said.

'No,' he said, 'not at the graveside.' He looked at me triumphantly as if he were setting me a puzzle which he was daring me to work out. But then he continued.

'No, it wasn't then. It was shortly beforehand. You remember when the service was over, four men came forward and lifted the coffin on their shoulders?'

I said I did.

'Well,' he said, 'the coffin was heavy and they were staggering a bit till they got a proper grip and then I noticed something extraordinary. Perhaps I would have noticed it before but that was the first funeral I had ever been at.'

I looked at him almost in amazement. It was so strange to think that was his first funeral, that that was the first dead person he had seen. Perhaps that was why he looked so boyish.

'To you perhaps it won't mean anything. Perhaps you didn't even notice it. But to me it came as a vision. You see, it was perhaps my conversation with you that ignited it. But as they staggered under the weight of the coffin – such red-faced ordinary stalwart men – for a moment I saw that one of the men in front had his arm round the other man.' He paused and sat in silence as if he were seeing it all again. 'It was one of those moments such that if one is lucky one gets in a lifetime, in one's researches I mean, such as perhaps Einstein had. The two things came together in my mind you see, the electron lacking both position and velocity and the arm of the man round the other man as they staggered under the weight of the coffin. The significance was stupendous and shattering. I suppose you'll think I'm daft?'

I said that of course I didn't believe he was daft and shortly afterwards he left. It was as if he had been trying to tell me something – or tell himself something – but I couldn't understand quite what it was. And that is the thing with 'moments'. They illuminate but at the same time they don't necessarily lead to what you would call understanding. And in any case one man's 'moment' is different from another man's. He left home the following day and naturally he never came back. Now and again I hear that he is doing great things over there and sometimes I see his name in the local paper as having been awarded another degree. But I shall always remember him as I saw him that night, his brown hair tossed back, telling me about the arm that was round the other man as they staggered under the weight of the coffin.

Old Betsy

So old Betsy is dead, who belongs to my days of childhood in this village. I see her very clearly, many years ago, walking down the road, after being in the shop, and shouting to the villagers, 'The bread is good today but don't touch the meat. The oranges are good but don't touch the bananas.' And she would walk past in her black cloak, her curdled face alight with life, lonely and indomitable, her husband, a road mender from Ireland, long since dead. 'He was a fine man, a chreutair,' she would say, 'and always fond of his bit of bacon, and his egg.' I have a vague memory of a small bent man in blue braces hammering dispiritedly among a pile of stones. But it may not be a memory of him at all.

Once when I was a little girl, going to school, some workmen were repairing our roof, boys from the neighbouring town, and she walked past shouting at me, 'Do you wear a semmit, a chreutair?' I blushed among the laughing boys and she shouted, '1/11 from J. D. Williams, a chreutair. I saw them in the catalogue.' And, red and pale by turns, I nearly sank into the ground while the boys on the roof crowed like cockerels.

And so she's dead in the house she inhabited alone for twenty years among plates green with verdigris, hard by a rapacious nephew who was waiting for her to die, and I see us shouting after her from the school bus, as she carries her messages home, swaying from side to side like a sailor. It is Easter, time of new hats and daffodils. And when did she ever have a new hat?

'A chreutair,' she told me. 'Don't marry that man. His father was a drunkard and his father before him.' But I did marry him. 'I told you, a chreutair,' she said a year later. 'A man who doesn't shave every morning is no good. It shows he has no respect.' I would wash the plates, mossy with green stuff, and give her soup which I had brought over in a pan. (He and I had divided our possessions neatly when he left: he had insisted on taking the refrigerator because it was his mother's, but I had kept the set of pans decorated with red roses.) 'Now, Seumas Macleod, he would suit you, he's a good-living man and he was born in April. That's a good sign.'

Today I shall go to the funeral after I have made some coffee. There is snow on the hills and it is Easter.

The fact is the two of us never got on and he is now in Glasgow probably drinking heavily. I have little feeling for him and I no longer even have his photograph in the house which is much cleaner. Yesterday I was in church in my new green costume and I watched the young girls in the choir tossing their hair back as they sang a hymn about God's love.

'Thank you for the soup, a chreutair,' Betsy would say, 'but there isn't enough turnip in it. I can't stand that woman who plays the organ in church. Her mother came from one of the islands. She couldn't use a cooker, you know, till I taught her and now she plays the organ.'

I waited for the Resurrection to take place as I do every spring, but it didn't. The minister flung his arms wide like a bat and blessed us but he doesn't visit the sick. He doesn't visit Betsy. 'He is a wooden minister, a chreutair. He was born in September. That's always a bad sign.' The Resurrection of course never happens, not even a frail yellow Christ rising from the green mossy plates. What are we here for?

What are we here for? said the minister at the graveside shivering.

Let them take out their flowers and their mirrors, I thought. The skies are blue and there are clouds like semmits in J. D. Williams. She used to sweat a lot when she was alive and sometimes pinch sweets and fruit from the village shop. They said she had rich relatives who never came to see her and that she had once been engaged to a prosperous farmer.

'I broke it off, a chreutair, when one day we were out for a walk and he walked ahead of me at a great rate. Never trust a man like that. He has no consideration.' My husband used to take my housekeeping money and he never walked anywhere much. He sometimes became violent and once gave me a black eye. 'I fell off a ladder,' I told her, ladling out some potato soup.

'Ay, a chreutair, there's a lot of ladders in life and a lot of snakes too.' That surprised me, for I had never thought of her playing games. And yet she too must have been young once, I supposed. 'There was no harm in him,' she said, 'all he wanted was his bit of bacon. And his clothes washed. He was born with a hammer in his hand.'

Truly though it is Easter the world is hard. One night we were drunk together after my husband had left me and we sang Gaelic songs in her house, untidy and cumbered with furniture. She had a surprisingly poignant voice and all her songs were about sailors leaving islands and going to places like Canada.

'A chreutair,' she said to me, leaning sideways with her curdled, flushed, confiding face, 'the only man I ever loved was the man who came about my insurance when my husband died. He had boots of black leather and he wore green trousers and talked very posh.'

I suppose I could marry Seumas Macleod who always takes the collection on a Sunday in a pink bag and shaves so close that his skin blooms like that of a baby. I sometimes see him gazing at me with slow easily-fathomed eyes.

It is Easter and she has been buried. I turn away from the grave in my green costume, naked as a chicken in the scouring wind, and my bones tiny and sleepy. There are three ducks walking in front of me and a tall drake with an angry red comb. I think maybe I shall marry Seumas Macleod. After a while our ambitions, thank God, grow less.

Uncollected Stories

Mother and Son

His clothes were dripping as he came in. The water was streaming down his cheeks, a little reddened by the wind and the rain. He shook back his long hair and threw his jacket on the bed post, then abruptly remembering, he looked through the pockets for a box of matches. The house was in partial darkness, for, though the evening was not dark, the daylight was hooded by thick yellow curtains which were drawn across the width of the window. He shivered slightly as he lit the match : it had been a cold, dismal afternoon in the fields. The weather was extraordinarily bad for the time of year and gathering the sheaves into stacks was both monotonous and uncomfortable. He held the match cupped within his hands to warm them and to light his way to the box where he kept the peats. The flickering light showed a handsome face. The forehead was smooth and tanned, the nose thin though not incisive, the mouth curved and petulant, and the chin small and round. It was a good-looking face, though it was a face which had something childish about it. The childishness could be seen by a closer look, a look into the wide blue eyes which were rather stolid and netted by little red lines which divided them up like a graph. These eyes were deep and unquestioning as a child's, but they gave an unaccountable impression that they could be as dangerous and irresponsible as a child's. As the match flickered and went out with an apologetic cough, he cursed weakly and searched his pockets. Then he remembered he had left the box on the table, reached out for it impatiently, and lit another match. This he carried over to the lamp which lay on the table. The light clung to the wick, and he put the clean globe gently inside the brackets. When the lamp was lit, it showed a moderately sized kitchen, the walls of which were painted a dull yellow. The dresser was surmounted by numerous shelves which held numerous dishes, some whole, some broken. A little china dog looked over the edge as if searching for crumbs: but the floor was clean and spotless, though the green linoleum looked a bit worn. Along one wall of the room was a four-poster bed with soiled pillows and a coverlet of some dark, rough material. In the bed was a woman. She was sleeping, her mouth tightly shut and prim and anaemic. There was a bitter smile on her lips as if fixed there; just as you sometimes see the insurance man coming to the door with the same smile each day, the same brilliant smile which never falls away till he's gone into the anonymity of the streets. The forehead was not very high and not low, though its wrinkles gave it an expression of concentration as if the woman were wrestling with some terrible witch's idea in dreams. The man looked at her for a moment, then fumbled for his matches again and began to light a fire. The sticks fell out of place and he cursed vindictively and helplessly. For a moment he sat squatting on his haunches staring into the fire, as if he were thinking of some state of innocence, some state to which he could not return : a reminiscent smile dimpled his cheeks and showed in eyes which immediately became still and dangerous again. The clock struck five wheezingly and, at the first chime, the woman woke up. She started as she saw the figure crouched over the fire and then subsided: 'It's only you.' There was relief in the voice, but there was a curious hint of contempt or acceptance. He still sat staring into the fire and answered dully: 'Yes, it's only me!' He couldn't be said to speak the words: they fell away from him as sometimes happens when one is in a deep reverie where every question is met by its answer almost instinctively.

'Well, what's the matter with you!' she snapped pettishly, 'sitting there moping with the tea to be made. I sometimes don't know why we christened you John' – with a sigh. 'My father was never like you. He was a man who knew his business.'

'All right, *all* right,' he said despairingly. 'Can't you get a new record for your gramophone. I've heard all that before,' as if he were conscious of the inadequacy of this familiar retort – he added: 'hundreds of times.' But she wasn't to be stopped.

'I can't understand what has come over you lately. You keep mooning about the house, pacing up and down with your hands in your pockets. Do you know what's going to happen to you, you'll be taken to the asylum. That's where you'll go. Your father's people had something wrong with their heads, it was in your family but not in ours.' (She had always looked upon him as her husband's son, not as her own: and all his faults she attributed to hereditary weaknesses on his father's side.)

He pottered about, putting water in the kettle, waiting desparately for the sibilant noise to stop. But no, it took a long time to stop. He moved about inside this sea of sound trying to keep detached, trying to force himself from listening. Sometimes, at rarer and rarer intervals, he could halt and watch her out of a clear, cold mind as if she didn't matter, as if her chatter which eddied round and round, then burst venomously towards him, had no meaning for him, could not touch him. At these times her little bitter barbs passed over him or through him to come out on the other side. Most often however they stung him and stood quivering in his flesh, and he would say something angrily with the reflex of the wound. But she always cornered him. She had so much patience, and then again she enjoyed pricking him with her subtle arrows. He had now become so sensitive that he usually read some devilish meaning into her smallest utterance.

'Have you stacked all the sheaves now?' she was asking. He swung round on his eddying island as if he had seen that the seas were relenting, drawing back. At such moments he became deferential.

'Yes,' he said joyously. 'I've stacked them all. And I've done it all alone too. I did think Roddy Mason would help. But he doesn't seem to have much use for me now. He's gone the way the rest of the boys go. They all take a job. Then they get together and laugh at me.' His weakness was pitiful: his childish blue eyes brimmed with tears. Into the grimace by which he sought to tauten his face, he put a murderous determination: but though the lines of his face were hard, the eyes had no steadiness: the last dominance had long faded and lost itself in the little red lines which crossed and recrossed like a graph.

'Of course Roddy doesn't want to help you. He's got enough to do as it is. Anyway he's got his day's work to do and you haven't.'

'It isn't my fault I haven't.' He spoke wearily. The old interminable argument was beginning again: he always made fresh attacks but as often retired defeated. He stood up suddenly and paced about the room as if he wanted to overawe her with his untidy hair, his thick jersey, and long wellingtons.

'You know well enough,' he shouted, 'why I haven't my day's work. It's because you've been in bed there for ten years now. Do you *want* me to take a job? I'll take a job tomorrow . . . if you'll only say!' He was making the same eternal argument and the same eternal concession: 'If you'll only say.' And all the time he knew she would never say, and she knew that he would never take any action.

'Why, you'd be no good in a job. The manager would always be coming to show you what you had done wrong, and you'd get confused with all those strange faces and they'd laugh at you.' Every time she spoke these words the same brutal pain stabbed him. His babyish eyes would be smitten by a hellish despair, would lose all their hope, and cloud over with the pain of the mute, suffering animal. Time and time again he would say to her when she was feeling better and in a relatively humane mood: 'I'm going to get a job where the other fellows are!' and time and time again, with the unfathomable and unknowable cunning of the woman, she would strike his confidence dead with her hateful words. Yes, he was timid. He admitted it to himself, he hated himself for it, but his cowardice still lay there waiting for him, particularly in the dark nights of his mind when the shadow lay as if by a road, watching him, tripping behind him, changing its shape, till the sun came to shine on it and bring its plausible explanations. He spoke again, passing his hand wearily over his brow as if he were asking for her pity.

'Why should anybody laugh at me? They don't laugh at the other chaps. Everybody makes mistakes. I could learn as quickly as any of them. Why, I used to do his lessons for Norman Slater.' He looked up eagerly at her as if he wanted her to corroborate. But she only looked at him impatiently, that bitter smile still upon her face.

'Lessons aren't everything. You aren't a mechanic. You can't do anything with your hands. Why don't you hurry up with that tea? Look at you. Fat good you'd be at a job.'

He still sat despairingly leaning near the fire, his head on his hands. He didn't even hear the last part of her words. True, he wasn't a mechanic. He never could understand how things worked. This ignorance and inaptitude of his puzzled himself. It was not that he wasn't intelligent: it was as if something had gone wrong in his childhood, some lack of interest in lorries and aeroplanes and mechanisms, which hardened into a wall beyond which he could not go through – paradise lay yonder.

He reached up for the tea absent-mindedly and poured hot water into the tea-pot. He watched it for a while with a sad look on his face, watched the fire leaping about it as if it were a soul in hell. The cups were white and undistinguished and he felt a faint nausea as he poured the tea into them. He reached out for the tray, put the tea-cup and a plate with bread and jam on it, and took it over to the bed. His mother sat up and took the tray from him, settling herself laboriously back against the pillows. She looked at it and said:

'Why didn't you wash this tray? Can't you see it's all dirty round the edges?' He stood there stolidly for a moment, not listening, watching her frail, white-clad body, and her spiteful, bitter face. He ate little but drank three cups of tea. Then he took out a packet of cigarettes and lit one nervously and self-consciously.

'Cigarettes again? Don't you know that there's very little money coming into the house. If it weren't for your father's pension where would you be . . . you who'se never done a day's work in your life? Answer me!' she screamed. 'Why are you sitting there like a dummy, you silly fool!' He took no notice, but puffed at his cigarette. There was a terrible weariness in his eyes. Nowadays he seldom felt his body tired: it was always his mind. This voice of hers, these pettinesses of hers, were always attacking his mind, burrowing beneath it, till he felt himself in a dark cave from which there was never to be any escape.

Sometimes words came to him to silence her, but between the words leaving his mind and leaving his lips they had changed: they had lost their import, their impact, and their usefulness.

His mind now seemed gradually to be clearing up, and he was beginning to judge his own actions and hers. Everything was clearing up: it was one of his moments. He turned round on his chair from a sudden impulse and looked at her intensely. He had done this very often before, had tried to cow her into submission: but she had aways laughed at him. Now however he was looking at her as if he had never seen her before. Her mouth was open and there were little crumbs upon her lower lip. Her face had sharpened itself into a birdlike quickness: she seemed to be pecking at the bread with a sharp beak in the same way as she pecked cruelly at his defences. He found himself considering her as if she were some kind of animal. Detachedly he thought: how can this thing make my life a hell for me? What is she anyway? She's been ill for ten years: that doesn't excuse her. She's breaking me up so that even if she dies I won't be any good for anyone. But what if she's pretending? What if there is nothing wrong with her? At this a rage shook him so great that he flung his half-consumed cigarette in the direction of the fire in an abrupt, savage gesture. Out of the silence he heard a bus roaring past the window, splashing over the puddles. That would be the boys going to the town to enjoy themselves. He shivered inside his loneliness and then rage took hold of him again. How he hated her! This time his gaze concentrated itself on her scraggy neck, rising like a hen's out of her plain white nightgown. He watched her chin wagging up and down: it was stained with jam and flecked with one or two crumbs. His sense of loneliness closed round him, so that he felt as if he were on a boat on the limitless ocean, just as his house was on a limitless moorland. There was a calm, unspeaking silence, while the rain beat like a benediction on the roof. He walked over to the bed, took the tray from her as she held it out to him. He had gone in answer to words which he hadn't heard, so hedged was he in his own thoughts.

'Remember to clean the tray tomorrow,' she said. He walked back with the tray fighting back the anger that swept over him carrying the rubbish and debris of his mind in its wake. He turned back to the bed. His mind was in a turmoil of hate, so that he wanted to smash the cup, smash the furniture, smash the house. He kept his hands clenched, he the puny and unimaginative. He would show her, avenge her insults with his unintelligent hands. There was the bed, there was his mother. He walked over.

She was asleep, curled up in the warmth with the bitter, bitter smile upon her face. He stood there for a long moment while an equally bitter smile curled up the edge of his lips. Then he walked to the door, opened it, and stood listening to the rain.

New Stockings for Young Harold

'I really must tell you about the stockings!'

'The stockings?'

'Yes . . . Willie, would you mind cleaning the spoon and putting it away. You've had enough of that now. Well, as I was saying. You know that woman who goes round the houses asking for things, old clothes and things like that, I don't really know her name. I just know that she comes to the house every week.'

'You mean old Barbara?'

'Yes, I suppose so. She's not really old. I'd say she was in her forties, but she looks older than that.'

'Yes, her husband's a drunk?'

'Is he? Willie, will you clean that spoon. That boy's incredible. She comes around here every Thursday morning. She's quite well mannered too. Quiet.'

'Yes, it's tragic. Her husband doesn't do any work . . . '

'Well, she was round last Thursday. I give her old clothes, you know. One ought to help these people and after all it isn't their fault.'

'No. Indeed. I believe she really looks after her children.'

* * *

'So she came to the house on Thursday as usual. That was a week yesterday. I was in the kitchen baking. I remember quite clearly, it was a fine day too. You know we haven't been having good weather lately, that's why I remember. She's really quite clean you know. Willie put the jar away now. Are you putting it away? Boys are growing so greedy nowadays and so big. Do you know I can hardly keep him in shirts. Will . . . '

'She came round on Thursday?'

'Yes, and she looks quite clean you know.'

'Yes, I can believe that. Her house . . .'

'So she knocked on the door. She didn't know I had seen her coming. She was patting her hair and straightening her dress all the way to the house. It was really quite comical. As if I was going to notice that! She was wearing some sort of white blouse. I wonder how long she's had it. She knocked on the door and I went to open it. It's interesting to study her, you know. She'll never take anything to eat. I always offer her but she never accepts. I sometimes look at her eyes too: they're very restless, they keep moving over the house. I suppose they'll get a council house. When she started to come first, I thought she was going to burgle me, but, of course, she's so honest . . . Sit down on that stool, Willie. No, not that one, the one nearest the fire, and do your lessons. He's just got a new teacher and well . . . Of course, I'm quite tactful with her now.'

'Yes, one learns to be.'

'Yes, of course. So I take out all the old clothes I have and she can take what she wants. I lay them out on the floor for her. It looks funny like salesmanship in reverse, except that one doesn't take money. At first she chooses only one thing. She says, "Did you knit this yourself?" Of course, she's flattering me. Then she says: "Could I have this?" And of course I say: "Yes." But I ask her to take other things too. Oh, we really have a conversation. I say: "But I really don't need it. Really I don't." And she says: "But it's so . . . No, I couldn't." And I say (it's really comical, you'd think I was selling it to her), "Oh, but you must. It would really be thrown out anyway. And you might as well have it." And she'll say: "Would it really?" and I'll say – "Of course," and it goes on like that. Eventually she'll take it. It's quite a battle. I feel in a sweat after I have finished giving her something.'

* * *

'You were saying about the . . . '

'Yes, of course, the stockings. Well, last Thursday she chose these stockings. They were green stockings with yellow diamonds at the tops. Oh, they were quite beautiful, but quite faded now, you understand. Willie, are you sure you're doing your lessons? Remember it's a new teacher and you must make a good impression on him. Well, she chooses these stockings – she really admired them – for one of her boys. I suppose he must be the same age as Willie though he's not in the same class. I believe he's rather backward. She really took a fancy to these stockings; she admired them tremendously; John bought them for Willie. She kept saying: "No, no, they're too pretty. I can't take them." And that's how you know she likes them when she says that.'

*   *   *

'So she took them and went away quite happy. Well, on Monday – not on the Friday, she must have been washing them and there were some holes in them too and she would have been darning them – well, on Monday the really comic thing happened. I'm sorry, would you care for some more tea? I'd forgotten. No? Willie, move your chair a little farther from the fire.

'Well, one of her sons . . . what's his name, Willie?'

'Harold.'

'Well, Harold wore them to school. There he was. You can imagine him, so proud of his new stockings with the yellow diamonds, strutting up to the school gate. Was that how it was, Willie?'

'Yes.'

'And he goes into the classroom. You can imagine him stretching out his legs so the teacher can see his "new" stockings. He's really very pleased with them.'

'And?'

'Yes . . . All goes well till the interval when what do you think happened?'

'I can't . . . wait. Somebody spilt water on them?'

'No! You'll never guess. Who would see the stockings but our friend here?'

'No!'

'Yes! Willie! And do you know he really tore into Harold. He began shouting out: "These are my stockings," and he started pummelling Harold for dear life. I admit it was bad – Willie, you must never do that again, do you hear me? – but you must see it was comical, these two gladiators. And you know what happened. He took off poor Harold's shoes and then the stockings. Imagine it! And he put them on over his own. Wasn't it uproarious?'

*   *   *

'He had no right to them. They were my stockings. You shouldn't have given them to him.'

'I gave them to his mother, Willie, not to him.'

'I suppose she won't come back now?'

'Well, that's the funny part of it. I intended to send her a message to say I was sorry and the . . . '

'She won't get my stockings again.'

'Well, of course, I didn't want to send the stockings back again. You see that?'

'Yes.'

'It wouldn't do. They would be fighting each other all the time. No, it wouldn't do.'

'No.'

'So I was going to send her this message. But then yesterday, Thursday, you see, she came again. She always comes on Thursday.'

'Her husband goes into town that day.'

'Is that the reason? I was going to say something but she talked to me and looked at me as if nothing had happened. Really, it was quite astonishing, quite astonishing. So I took my cue from her. I went and brought out some old clothes the same as usual. You see she never takes more than one thing at a time and there always seems to be something. Willie?'

'Yes.'

'Go outside a moment, will you? You need some fresh air. Hurry up. Leave these books and mind and be back here in fifteen minutes. And don't slam the door. Well, she was examining the old clothes you see. She's down on her knees looking them over.'

'Well . . . ?'

'You'd never guess. She chose . . . What do you think she chose?'

'Really, I . . . '

* * *

'No, don't guess . . . she chose . . . a vest! A vest! You see the point, don't you?'

'Yes.'

'A vest! It was really . . . And then just as usual she went away. It was extraordinary, wasn't it?'

'Yes, quite extraordinary. Well, I'm afraid I must be going.'

'Now? But surely . . . Oh, you must stay. Surely a little while longer. John won't be home for ages yet.'

'No truly, I couldn't.'

'Well, if you must you must. But it was rich wasn't it? Really.'

The Scream

The older boys used to play cards in her house (it wasn't really much of a house, just two rooms, a kitchen and bedroom) and have song sessions there with an accordion. She was very old even when I first remember her, with skin unlike other people's skin, so unlike that it didn't seem to be skin at all. It wasn't red or pink or white, it was like something ancient and unmentionable gone curdled and sour, like very very old cream petrified and hideous. She would sit on a stool by the fire wearing a black shawl and a black dress. She had been widowed many years before and lived on the Old Age Pension. I can still remember some of the boys who used to be there. One was Cob. He was a wonderful footballer who was drowned in the war. I was half asleep in bed when he came to say goodbye on what turned out to be his last leave. I could hear him talking through a haze of sleep but I was too tired to raise the lids of my eyes and say goodbye to him. His destroyer was torpedoed shortly afterwards. Then there was Gammy. There was something wrong with one of his legs – no one exactly knew what. He was a first-rate card player. He's still alive, married now. There was also Peddie who was a fine rollicking singer, virile and boisterous. He married about ten years ago and has seven or eight children. And there were many others.

I don't know why they all met in that house – and being much younger than they I never questioned them about it, had I even consciously thought of it then. Nor did my friend Clocky. To us they were simply The Older Boys: great football players, accordion players, singers, card players. We always thought of Her – Minnie – as of some old crazy witch wrecked over the fading fire while all round her surged speech, music and smoke. We were only allowed to stay till ten but even by ten things were getting rough, for example they often used to have girls there. It gave me an extraordinary sensation once to see my own brother with his arm round a giggling redhead who appeared to me disgusting and stupid. She seemed to leer at me as I watched. There was almost a fight once over solo: Cob accused Peddie of reneging on diamonds:

'You —— well did. The hand before last you trumped my diamond.'

'I —— well didn't.'

'You —— well did.'

'I'm —— telling you I didn't.'

'Look here you ——.'

'Aw shut your —— mouth. Look up the cards and find out.'

'I won't —— look up the —— cards.'

'You're getting too —— big for your —— boots.'

Then voices would join in: 'Give it up, boys, go on give it up,' but the two would continue:

'I don't need to look up the —— cards. You trumped that —— diamond and you —— well know it.' All this time Minnie would be sitting on her stool, mechanically knitting some trailing shapeless object for some unnamed recipient. She would knit jerseys for some of the boys. They were always clumsy and ill-fitting. I think the habit of going to her house must have begun either in her husband's lifetime or because it was the only place where the boys could do practically as they liked. When some of the more considerate ones said about 11 o'clock that it was time to go she would look at the small white-faced clock with the trembling hands and say:

'You aren't thinking of going away yet are you?'

And sometimes she would make tea for them even at that hour and bring out from the heavy dresser hard round biscuits. She herself would dip them in the tea to soften them for her toothless jaws. Sometimes if she was in a particularly good mood she would take a seat at the table and they would make fun of her.

'Minnie's best friends are trumps tonight.'

And there would be similar jokes about night clubs, spades, last trumps and so on. I think that on the whole they liked her.

Her husband had been a sailor. She had been older than him by about seven years. People said she had trapped him into marrying her. She was the only daughter of a sour-faced half-mad woman who had tried to keep her for herself. This half-mad mother of hers used to have fits, particularly at the full moon, when she would crawl under the bed and jump out, in the middle of the night, with horrifying screams. Minnie herself never told anyone this but I heard it from others. She had no children. It was no secret that her husband used to go with other women and that he didn't care whether she knew it or not. However he had been a pleasant enough man and people said they didn't blame him for she was a bit queer.

Some nights even before ten I would see the boys and girls wrestling on the hard bench in the kitchen and she would look at them with her fixed smile. More often however she would pretend not to see them.

They would even insult her:

'Where did you get these biscuits from, Minnie? No wonder you haven't any teeth left.'

or someone would say:

'To hell with it. I'm fed up coming here. Why don't we go somewhere else for a change?'

or:

'Is that your picture on the wall, Minnie? You looked better then, almost human.'

'When do you read the Bible, Minnie? I bet you don't read it at all.' There was a huge black Bible on the shelf above her bed. We didn't know whether it was put there for show or not.

No matter what they did she wouldn't put them out. They would sometimes bring bottles in and drink. Sometimes they would offer her a drink but she would never touch it. Perhaps it reminded her of her husband. One night two of them came in masked and nearly frightened her to death. But she would always say 'Boys will be boys' and smile her sickly smile. She must have spent hours tidying up the house after they had left. Of course I think of all this as I look back on it now. Then I simply saw her as an unlikeable old woman who would have been better out of the house when we were in it.

However as the years went by fewer and fewer people went to visit her. The reason for this was that her health was rapidly failing. I used to watch her bending over a sheaf of corn and remain motionless in the act like a moon in water. Latterly she began to take more and more to her bed. I don't know exactly what was wrong with her, possibly some form of rheumatism. She seemed to grow smaller and smaller and blacker and blacker. My mother and I used to visit her sometimes, my mother tall and slim, Minnie small and black. She would often go to bed in the middle of the day and call us feebly to her bedroom where she sat humped among tumbled blankets and an old overcoat with bright buttons. I assumed it belonged to her husband. She would sometimes stroke it absently while talking to us.

At this time Minnie began to pretend that she could tell fortunes. She would put my hand between her dry palms, fondle it as if extracting all its warmth from it, and eventually turn it face upwards.

'A fine boy you have here,' she would say to my mother, looking at me with her scattered eyes.

'A fine boy' she would repeat to herself.

'Yes they are all fine boys,' she would add, stroking the old overcoat. Then she would look at my hand. I don't think she even saw the lines but she would invent.

'A clever boy. He will grow up to be a credit to you. He will earn a lot of money. He will be a model son . . . a model son.'

One day, after such endangering flattery, my mother snatched me out of the house as if to protect me from some evil influence.

So, fewer and fewer people visited her or if they did it was only to give her spasmodic help, as if she was something to which they had an obligation. None of the older boys went there in the evening: there was no accordion, no jokes, no swearing, no love-making. The house was dead.

Clocky and I, however, used to go to her house though not often. Clocky was smaller than me with smooth black hair and a tanned polished face. His eyes were cunning and alert.

During the summer months we would raise a tent and build a fire inside till the smoke forced us out into the hot air. A favourite sport of his was to throw stones at horses as they stood statuesquely in the brittle sunlight, till he drove them into a disjointed panicky motion. Between us there was a curious unspoken antagonism. Nevertheless he was the only boy of my own age: he was inventive and fearless. For instance he was not afraid of ghosts nor did he believe in fairies or goblins. He liked to feel things in his hands, usually stones. He would steal and lie his way out of situations without the slightest compunction. For example we would all steal turnips, carrots from the small gardens but if caught would usually confess under strenuous examination. Often it was even heroic to confess. Clocky would never confess. I once saw him swearing on the Bible that he hadn't stolen some jam though I knew perfectly well he had. However I would never dream of telling on him.

One August day, tired of tent-living, of running, of playing, we were walking drearily along the road not knowing what we would do next when one of us (I can't remember who) took a notion to visit Minnie. Together we walked in the roaring heat up to her house. We knew she would be in bed exhausted, breathing like an old yellow fish that had been thrown twitching on humped rocks. The door was open and we crept in. We hadn't spoken to each other. We quietly entered the kitchen which was large and cool like an inverted pail. The long wooden bench ran along one side of it. The floor was hollowed and pitted. There was a dresser on the side farthest from the door. We opened its door and helped ourselves to blackcurrant jam which lay at the bottom of the paper lidded jar. On the paper was a picture of a footballer and studying it abstractedly we heard the voice going on and on:

'I can't help it. I can't stand you. Go out to your women, then. Do you think I don't know? They all come to hint it to me. Hit me: yes go on hit me. You can't hurt me. I'll see you dead yet. Don't think I'll die so that you can marry your women.'

There was a silence, then the voice began again, this time with a fiercer, more reckless, intonation:

'I hate you. Why are you keeping me here when I could have been married? You're afraid. That's what it is. You're afraid of getting old and dying. I don't care whether you die or not.' (Here her voice rose to a scream.) 'I don't. I don't. I want to get married. Weren't you married? You think that I won't leave you. But I will, I will, I will. You're mad. Everybody says you're mad. You should never have married. You can't look after your own children properly. Why did you marry then? I hope you die.'

The voice continued as we ate the jam. Then Clocky going down on his hands and knees crawled up to the room where the old woman was speaking and crying. I followed him. We could see blankets hanging untidily over the foot of the bed. Wasps buzzed in the window panes, but this room too was frighteningly cool.

We crawled under the blankets like Red Indians. But the old woman seemed to hear the rustling, for she suddenly shouted:

'Who's there?'

We said nothing. My body grew cold.

'Who's there?' she screamed, like a child. We heard her scrambling about as we lay there and thought she was about to leave her bed. But no we heard a whisper of leaves. She must have opened her huge black Bible. There was a petrified silence. The wasps were like aeroplanes. Then she began to speak again:

'I didn't mean it. Why don't you let me be? I didn't mean it. It was all my fault.' Her voice expired: 'All my fault.' Her voice drooled.

I could hear our hearts beating.

Suddenly Clocky catapulted outwards from below the bed. In the centre of the scream I followed him head bent for the door. The scream uptore roots. Back in the tent I heard it, till in my mind it died away into an exhausted whimper. When it stopped I went out of the tent. Clocky shouted after me, but I turned away. He stood in the tent like a witch doctor shouting after me while thin wisps of smoke curled about him. But I didn't turn back nor did I stop running till I reached home.

The Angel of Mons

... and I don't know if it was in the papers over there, dad, though you see some of their reporters now and again hopping about, trying to keep their shoes from getting muddy: it was in the early morning it happened, you could look across the mud for a little way and see everything flattened and all mixed-up together. Do you know what I saw? It was a helmet half-buried in the mud and a bird standing on it, jumping about, with its head a little to one side, just like in the garden at home: this little bird, I watched it for a long time and it stayed there without flying away. You don't see birds around here often, they've been scared off: but this one was quite happy, just as if it was at home, I remember it very clearly. And the sun seemed to come up, very bright, and this bird was basking in the sun, shaking its wings now and again, as if there was dew on them: I don't understand where it came from at all: and all the time the sun was coming up, bright and hot. At least that's how I think it was.

I was watching that bird and thinking how it was hopping about there without a care in the world, and I was wondering about your last letter and how mad you were about me deciding to become a lay preacher – just because Mum died, you said – throwing away my training, you said – and you know how it is in the army, I'm trying to describe it, you get feelings things are going to happen or they're not going to happen as if all of you are together, even though you're alone, like when you listen to the Last Post and you hear all these voices and all these people speaking. Well it was just like that. Some people said we were going over the top and it was only three in the morning but I don't remember it like that at all. What I remember is that bird hopping about on the helmet and the sun coming up very very hot and I was thinking about that telegram I got about Mum's death – and anyway you know perfectly well that I'd decided to become a lay preacher even before she died. It was nothing to do with you really, dad, and I know it must have been awful for you all these years, with her in bed and me working for my apprenticeship. It was just that I couldn't bear it any more, what was any apprenticeship worth anyway? And you say that the worst thing of all is me wanting to leave home, but I can't help that either, dad, I've got to get away just for a while. So there it is, there's not really any point talking about it, I can't help being what I am and you being what you are. And I do wish, dad, you would stop talking about money, I'm not interested in money. You know I send you most of my money home and anyway since I came here I've decided to become a lay preacher more than ever. You say it's all nonsense, you're entitled to your own opinion, dad, and that's a fact, but I wish you didn't talk like that. I don't mind you going to the pub, as I said mother being an invalid must have been a great strain on you all these years, but you shouldn't be bitter. What do you have to thank God for you say, well, you can go out now and take your dog for a walk, that's one thing, and you can sit down and read a book can't you. It's no good being bitter and anyway I've made up my mind and I won't change it no matter what happens. But I must get back to what I was saying.

Well there was the sun coming up bright and hot – so hot that it almost hurt your eyes – and there was this bird hopping about on the helmet – I was afraid it would fall off and be sucked down into the mud, the mud here is very thick and heavy and I didn't want it to be lying there all the time till it died, it would be a very slow death – and looking up then – my eyes were hurting me a little at first – I saw it in the sky perfectly plainly. I don't suppose you'll believe it but it was there as clear as anything you ever saw, a great white angel with wings and a beautiful, beautiful gentle face, that's what it was, gentle, it was so great and kind so that the light no longer blinded your eyes but you could look at it without being hurt. I can't describe it to you but you'd have to see it yourself its face was so gentle. And I think I went and told the others and they saw it too. Their faces became gentle as they looked, it was a miracle, dad, the way their faces seemed to become gentle like water, all these men.

There's no reason to doubt it now . . . .
. . . .
. . . . .CENSORED . . . .
. . . .

Cheerio for now, dad,
Your loving son,
DANIEL.

2

. . . you were asking me about this Angel of Mons, and saying that the Vicar preached that this meant God was on our side. And I should think he is right too. Give him my regards. It's good to know there are people like him still about with faith in his country, not like some of these long-haired fellows, Germans in disguise I'd say.

Well, this Angel of Mons was quite extraordinary. It was about four in the morning and we were just about to go over the top. You know the sort of thing, we set up a creeping barrage, and there was an unholy racket – flashes of guns and everything. I really hate the Boche then when it's cold and you feel tired and you've got to go in there and everything looks so messed-up. I get flaming mad when I think I could be back in Blighty still in my bed and just because of these little rats I've got to be in the trenches here. I get mad when I think of it.

As I said it was about four and we were all shivering. Picture me standing there with my watch in my hand – waiting for zero hour you know. You always say I'm a glutton for being punctual: well, you have to be, here, there's nothing else for it. Otherwise the Old Man will be on top of you and that's not all. God, how I hated these Germans.

Anyway there we were. Almost zero hour and this infernal racket going on pounding the Boche lines. Sometimes it gives you a sense of power too, thinking how your shells are pounding in there and they're crawling about for a change.

My sergeant-major was just beside me. I've told you about him – or have I? His name's Musgrave, a big red-faced chap. Very dependable. He always stands up straight when he's walking wherever he is.

All this time there were terrific flashes in the sky. I couldn't describe it to you not if I was Shakespeare himself. Do you remember that week we were on holiday in Cornwall and we ran into the storm on the moor? Remember there was thunder and lightning and the moor was flat and bare. And there wasn't any shelter anywhere till eventually we found this abandoned hut with the rain lashing in through the windows. Well, think of that multiplied a thousand times. That's how it was.

I was looking round at my men – quite good, too, most of them. You could see the light hitting their faces. And I was saying to myself repeating it over and over:

'You German —— '

'You German ——. '

That's what I do before a battle. I just keep repeating that. It makes me feel better.

And quite suddenly I heard some of them shouting. They're not supposed to shout you know; it's bad for discipline. I turned round. Musgrave had turned round already and was laying into them – and I saw that they were all pointing to the east. Their faces seemed to be shining but there were a few who were asking:

'What is it? What is it?'

I remember one of them especially, he was looking very anxious and asking people:

'What is it? I can't see anything. What is it?'

And none of them answered him, except that they were all looking towards the east, and I heard someone saying:

'An angel.'

And another saying: 'Look at its face!'

And all this time this little man was bouncing up and down saying:

'What is it? I can't see it. What is it?'

And Musgrave was shouting: 'You . . . what the . . . are you looking at? There's a war on you know.' But no one listened to him, that was the amazing thing.

Someone else said: 'It's a sign.'

I looked at their faces. They all looked as if they were seeing a vision except this man and one or two others, and Musgrave cursing right, left and centre.

I turned too and looked where they were looking but I couldn't see anything, nothing at all except the flashes from the guns. There were heads raised above the parapets near me and I could hear even in that racket some of the NCOs shouting out:

'Get your heads down, you stupid ——,' but no one listened.

I thought there was going to be a mutiny, the soldiers looked so unmilitary, their rifles hanging in their hands as if they had forgotten all about them. I knew what to do all right. I took out my pistol and shouted above the din:

'We're going over now. I'll shoot anyone who doesn't follow.'

Some of them stared at the pistol as if they couldn't understand what it was.

I shouted again:

'We're going over now. I'll shoot anyone . . . ' and then just at that moment the bombardment stopped and I remember speaking the rest of the sentence out in dead silence. I can't tell you what it was like, that sudden dead silence and these words coming out of it. As I looked their faces changed again, became tense, I shot my pistol into the air and we were off. Well, that was it. It didn't last very long whatever it was and I forgot about it. I was pretty busy for the next few hours.

I think it was just tension myself. They snapped out of it pretty quickly when we got going and did very well all of them. Perhaps it's something to do with guns and the flashes. Still, there's nothing we can do about that: that's for the top people to deal with and what can a lieutenant do about it?

What does Pater say about it? Has he heard about it? I hope he's keeping as fit as ever . . .

3

REPORTER	Now, sir, what can you tell me about this Angel business?
GENERAL	I have nothing to tell you.
REPORTER	Nothing? But surely, general, you can't just say nothing. This has caused a terrific furore. I doubt whether you people can afford to ignore it.
GENERAL	That's what I intend to do. Ignore it.
REPORTER	But . . . Look at it this way, the Germans are also writing about it. They saw it too, or so they say. They want to be in on it too.
GENERAL	In on it?
REPORTER	Obviously. They can't allow the English only to see angels. They claim it's one of theirs.
GENERAL	And what do their generals say about it?
REPORTER	I don't know. I haven't noticed.
GENERAL	Well, I'm sure if you study these German comments you'll find that their generals say nothing at all. And I also intend to say nothing.
REPORTER	But you agree that there was an angel?
GENERAL	I'm saying nothing. There may have been an angel: there may not. So far as I'm concerned that's not my department.
REPORTER	And whose department is it?
GENERAL	I can't imagine.
REPORTER	But, general, can you not see the possibilities? 'God is on the side of the British army.' I must admit I find it comforting.
GENERAL	I don't.
REPORTER	To think that these men . . .
GENERAL	Nonsense. What do angels know of us? Can they suffer on our behalf? I'm a religious man but I don't believe in angels. I believe in God and Christ but not in angels.
REPORTER	But the men believe in them.
GENERAL	That's their right.
REPORTER	But how could so many men be deceived?

GENERAL I'm not saying they were deceived. I don't know.

REPORTER And the ministers are preaching in the pulpits that it shows God is on our side.

GENERAL They have their rights, too. I pray to God every night and every morning, as they do. What are you writing?

REPORTER What you said.

GENERAL Read it to me.

REPORTER 'General ——, himself a religious man, doesn't believe in the appearance of the angel at Mons.'

GENERAL Obviously you can't print that. Anyway it's untrue. I didn't say I didn't believe in it. Your despatch will have to be censored.

REPORTER Isn't it always? What am I supposed to write then?

GENERAL I'll tell you what I think now and make an official statement later. You agree to that?

REPORTER Naturally, I have no choice.

GENERAL Perhaps after the war when it's all over and you want to write a book about it – so many people wish to write books, I can't understand why – you may use this.

REPORTER After the war is over, this will have no value.

GENERAL Precisely.

REPORTER What are your real views?

GENERAL My real views? Well, I'll tell you. My job is to win the war for my side, that is for the British. In order to win the war I have to make plans. I have a very good staff officer – he's a Scotsman, you'll have heard of him, Hume is his name. In any plan one wishes to avoid as many imponderables as possible. Do you understand mathematics?

REPORTER I've tried.

GENERAL I don't. I leave that to my staff officer. But he always talks Mathematics, all about variables and constants. I know roughly what's he's talking about.

REPORTER And your objection I take it is . . .

GENERAL That that angel is a variable. It wasn't allowed for in the plan. Not only so but it was a totally unknown variable. For instance, one might by chance run into two additional Boche regiments, not bargained for in our plan. But at least we would know where we were, and appropriate action could be taken.

REPORTER But surely . . .

GENERAL However, when you are confronted by the totally unknown and inexplicable there is a very long pause which is often fatal in war. You don't know what to do. There are no precedents. It is situations like these which we wish to avoid. Supposing the army had refused to fight and been slaughtered by the Germans. In that case the appearance of the angel would have been decisive for the other side, and the angel's famous compassion would have been destructive and evil.

REPORTER But the Germans themselves saw it.

GENERAL So they say.

REPORTER You don't mean that . . .

GENERAL I mean nothing. Suppose the story got about that the Germans had a new secret weapon which could cause paralysis of the enemy forces so that instead of fighting they stared into this compassionate face. What then?

REPORTER But such a weapon is inconceivable.

GENERAL You might argue that it has already been conceived. It is therefore best to assume it wasn't there at all. Once you admit the presence of the unknown you have to explain it and it is then the trouble begins.

REPORTER I must admit I hadn't thought of all this. But then . . .

GENERAL It is my job to think of these things. Anyway I feel it – or rather my staff officer feels it – untidy that God should have to intervene in this way.

REPORTER Untidy?

GENERAL We don't wish to return to the Trojan War. This appearance was essentially pagan. There is no need for God to appear at all. And what would happen if we depended on these appearances?

REPORTER We cannot depend on the undependable.

GENERAL We may, you know. We have to face this. The appearance must not be allowed to become fact. It's too superstitious, as I said.

REPORTER But what could have caused it?

GENERAL I have no idea. In the long run men must rely on themselves not on angels. Angels have nothing to do with us. Do you understand? Ah, come in, Hume. This gentleman would like to talk to you about angels. He works for a newspaper.

4

'The Battle of Mons was opened by the British with a barrage of fire and one angel.'

Here the reader – and I don't wonder – will stop and stare. An angel? And how did they indent for that? Are the quartermasters of the bourgeois forces on good terms with angels then? We wouldn't have thought it. Or was it perhaps the bourgeois clergy that pulled the wool over people's eyes? And was this a British angel or a French angel or a German angel? Or was it educated at Eton and did it speak Latin? Who knows? They all claim this angel, as if it was one of their own aeroplanes!

What a scandal there would have been if they had shot it down! It would not have been cricket!

And what did German decadent metaphysics make of it? 'The spirit of history. Hegel in person.'

But there is one thing that can be said: this was a bourgeois angel: it wasn't only French or British or German: it was common ownership by all.

Nationalised, in fact!

And what is the explanation of this strange phenomenon? Surely the bourgeois aren't beginning to swallow their own lies. That would be ironical indeed!

But you object it wasn't the bourgeois that saw it but ordinary soldiers, who had no interest in this war.

And that is true. It was the ordinary soldiers who saw it.

But what did it do, this angel? As far as we can see, it just hung there fluttering its wings, looking very sad and very compassionate. It didn't help either side. It just hung there like a Christmas card.

What are we to make of it? If it had only done something, you say, but just hang there like a decoration.

But of course it couldn't do anything. What could it do?

It was simply a sign that the war was at a standstill. It was simply a sign of the internal collapse of the whole bourgeois system.

But how can that be, you ask?

Well, it is quite simple. All countries move upwards into the so-called phase of the spirit, the phantom sphere where its inner resources are exhausted. It happens also with individuals who merely reflect in this way the coming death of the system which they inhabit.

Aren't Plato's ideas the same, these phantoms in the sky?

And this angel which hung there motionless and compassionate, what else does it signify but the death of a system torn apart on earth but united in the sky?

Why was it that it was the ordinary soldiers who saw it first?

Again the answer is simple. The ordinary people – or rather the people – saw it first because they are in the van of knowledge. They feel – even before the bourgeois – the death of the system which the bourgeois had created.

And why was it that their first idea was to lay down their arms till threatened by their officers? It was because they knew that that was not their war, that that was on the contrary a bourgeois war, and they were no longer going to endure fighting for their so-called masters.

It is perfectly clear that this phenomenon – this angel – shows in fact that the death of the bourgeois system was beginning to penetrate the consciousness of the ordinary soldier: and this was reflected in his consciousness by a picture drawn from the Christian myth. There is and can be no other explanation.

If it had happened in some other country – of a different religion but at the same level of bourgeois development – the picture might have been different but the explanation the same.

We therefore believe that in some sense there was an angel –

but that this angel was a sign generated by the mind and transmitted to the sky. It was as real as a dream is real. And in the same way as dreams represent disturbances in the mind, so does this.

Our system, however, will eliminate both signs and dreams. We will not be looking to heaven like bird-watchers or philosophers but down to earth which is man's home and not the clouds.

The General

Well, let me first of all explain the aim of this programme. What we are doing is to bring back to Flanders one of the generals who fought there in the days of the First World War. As you know there has been a great revival of interest in this – in that – war recently. None of us here of course fought in that war. I'm afraid we were too young and I suppose as time passes one tends to forget these things.

Here we are then, standing at this very moment on one of the great battlefields of that war. As you will see, it's a dry day with a slight breeze (you can judge its direction by that flag over there: it's just fluttering a very little).

Now, I have with me General Hume. You will, of course, have heard of him. He was Staff Officer to General H during the last two years of that war. He is a man of varied experience. After the war, he went into banking and became President of British National. He is retired now.

I General Hume, may I ask you first of all how old you are?

H Eighty.

I May I say, sir – and I am sure viewers will agree – that you are a very young eighty.

H Thank you.

I We should also like to thank you at this point for agreeing to take part in this . . . reassessment. By the way, viewers, there seem to be a lot of jets flying about here and I hope they wont distract you too much.

Now, General . . . by the way would you prefer to sit . . . We have a . . .

H No, thank you.

I Yes, well . . . Might I ask you first, sir – Where were you born?

H The Borders. Coldstream.

I Of a . . . I have it written down here that you attended Eton.

H That is correct. We were reasonably well off.

I And then . . . Sandhurst. That is right isn't it?

H That is right.

I Quite a . . . Yes. Now, was there a military tradition in your family?

H My father was a brigadier.

I And wanted you to follow in his footsteps?

H Yes, he was in the Boer War.

I I see. A cavalryman?

H Yes.

I And after Sandhurst? You were then gazetted to . . . ?

H The Guards, as a lieutenant.

I And later were selected to attend staff college.

H I was a major then.

I So that gradually . . . ?

H Well, to tell you the truth, the mortality rate was high in the war and there were other reasons. I became eventually a staff officer.

I With what rank, sir?

H Brigadier.

I I see. Now then, the war broke out in 1914. Where were you then?

H Exercising at Aldershot. I remember it quite clearly. We were told about it in the mess.

I Can you remember the exact words, sir?

H Well, the brigadier said – I was just a major then – 'This is it'.

I 'This is it'. What were your thoughts when he said that?

H Thoughts? I can't remember really. I went and had a bath. I was dirty, you see.

I Yes. And did you think the war would last long?

H No. I can't say I did. I don't think I did. I was a bit excited of course.

I Naturally. And after that you were sent to France. You being a major then? A young major?

H That is correct.

I Did you think perhaps . . . Well, what was your attitude to the Germans at that time?

H I didn't really know. Hadn't had any experience of them. I thought they would be good soldiers.

I May I ask why you thought that, sir?

H Well, I'd been to Germany you see in a purely civilian capacity. I went on holiday there. Eastern Germany. Two years before that. Good farming country.

I And you formed the impression they would be good soldiers?

H Yes, that was the impression I had. Industrious hard working people.

I I see. Bankers in fact.

H Bankers?

I You fought at first as a major in the opening engagements. Did you have any reason to change your mind about the Germans?

H No, can't say I did.

I Have you any . . . well, stories of this early period to tell the viewers?

H Stories. Now. Well, I was wounded of course.

I How did that happen?

H Oh, I was shot. In the leg. Nothing serious. I was actually writing a letter at the time. The bullet ricochetted. It was a letter to my sister.

I Telling her you would be home by Christmas?

H No, not really. If I remember rightly I was writing to her about our woods. I had an estate in the Borders. It was always in the family.

I Have you still got it?

H No, as a matter of fact we haven't. We've had to sell it. Or rather *I've* had to sell it.

I I see. So you were wounded. What were your feelings at the time?

H Feelings? I felt irritated. You see I was writing in the open air. The pad was on my knee. It was a day in summer – very beautiful – just like home. I remember trying to stand up but I couldn't. I felt rather ridiculous. Of course, my leg's all right now.

I Yes. And you were in hospital for how long?

H Oh a matter of weeks. Then I was sent back to HQ – given paper work.

I Did you like that?

H It wasn't bad. Running an estate you know you have to do a bit of paper work.

I I see.

H I must have been efficient for they gave me a lieutenant-colonelcy.

I Tell me, sir – one of the criticisms made of the brass – excuse me – in the world war was that they didn't know what was going on at the front. Would you agree with this?

H That obviously happens. Obviously. But not seriously. One has a job to do. One doesn't see everything that's going on.

I Tell me, General Hume, are you, were you, an ambitious man?

H Yes, I suppose I was within limits.

I Is there any truth in the story that there was an internecine rivalry between you and . . . Colonel Graham. Have you read his book by any chance.

H Graham's book? No.

I Does he not say that you went over his head with General H? Does he not accuse you of sycophancy? Does he not note your rapid promotion? That you were apparently favoured because you were a Scotsman?

H Poor Graham. Did he say that?

I He came through the ranks, didn't he? A very unusual thing in those days. He was originally a non-commissioned officer. A very brilliant man.

H That is so. As a non-commissioned officer.

I You are now eighty years old, General Hume. Do you still regard Graham as 'poor Graham'.

H Of course. What has being eighty got to do with it? Graham lacked imagination.

I All his allegations are therefore false.

H The ones you enumerated are false.

I That you were basically not interested in the men – that you were only concerned with your own ambition – that you went over his head to the General? All that is false?

H Entirely so.

I You did of course marry General H's daughter.

H That is so.

I And it is rumoured that he has connections with the bank you are in.

H I was invited to take that job. I was a satisfactory choice I think you will find.

I No doubt. General Hume. No doubt. At any rate your plan for the staging of this battle at this spot was the one finally adopted, practically without change. By the way where is Colonel Graham now?

H I couldn't say. He may be writing a book. Or possibly watching this programme.

I If he is, there is nothing you would like to say to him?

H No.

I Anyway your plan was adopted?

H If you like to put it like that, yes.

I So this therefore is the battlefield. We are standing on it now. It is a fine dry day with a little breeze and you can see the grasses waving on it. There are some poppies as you can see and very beautiful and nostalgic they are too. But this of course is a graveyard. Is that not so, General?

H Every battlefield is a graveyard.

I Naturally. Would you please tell us your plan of campaign for that day.

H Plan? Yes, of course. It was basically simple. You will notice over to your right a hill. My objective was to capture that hill.

I Would it be true to say that you hadn't seen the terrain before the battle was fought?

H No, of course not. I rode out to see it. I spent a day here.

I Please continue.

H Well, obviously one has to disguise one's intentions. So on the western flank a dummy attack was set up.

I Is there another hill there, General?

H No, of course not. But there was an area of marshy land dividing the two armies. Now there had been a spell of dry weather, and the Germans might have thought it quite feasible for us to attack at that point. By the way, may I smoke my pipe or will this spoil your machinery?

I Please do.

H Thank you. Well, the dummy attack was started but un–
fortunately . . .

I There was very heavy rainfall during the three previous
days. What amounted to a prolonged cloudburst in fact?

H That is so. You seem to know this very well, by the way. It
was extremely unfortunate.

I What happened?

H What was bound to happen. Our men got bogged down.

I By an act of God in fact?

H One might call it that. It was totally unforeseen.

I Did you insist on going through with the attack on schedule?

H The attack did go through on schedule.

I Didn't you know of the condition of the ground?

H Well, of course one has to take chances, hasn't one? And
after all it was only a dummy attack.

I But the Germans didn't have to withdraw troops from that
salient did they?

H No, in the event they didn't.

I So your men were mown down?

H Many were killed, it is true.

I Thirty thousand. Thirty thousand and six to be precise.

H There were a great number killed.

I Is that all you have to say?

H What else should I say? If one were sentimental one
wouldn't be a general.

I But you weren't a general then, were you?

H No I wasn't. By the way, may I ask if this sentimental
performance of yours is for TV consumption?

I It is possible one or two of your former tenants and shooters
may be watching.

H That is very kind of them.

I By the way, General, do you believe in God?

H Of course.

I You have a strong religious background?

H Yes.

I You did not for instance think that God was working against
you?

H Working against me? Of course not. He's got his job to do too, you know. Just like yourself.

I May I ask, sir, what your thoughts are now as you survey the battlefield?

H My thoughts? It was a long time ago. I was younger then. A lot has happened since then.

I Personal matters?

H Among other things.

I Do you consider them more important than this?

H I married for one thing. One remembers that.

I So you can't communicate anything to us, sir?

H Well I remember when I heard the attack had failed . . .

I Your instinct was not to go to the battlefield.

H No, shall I tell you what I did?

I Please.

H I went into my office, calculated the losses, the total losses you understand, and I started drawing up a new plan.

I You showed no deep emotion?

H It is not one's business to show deep emotions.

I And your feelings now?

H These men have been dead for a long time. There is nothing I can say about them. Nothing at all.

I You are not perturbed by the dead?

H What use would my perturbation be to them?

I You do not feel sadness. Nostalgia?

H That is my own business.

I As your *plan* was, even though it failed?

H Exactly so sir.

I You are now eighty years old?

H That is so.

I And you feel no . . . emotion as you survey this battlefield?

H When one is eighty it is not easy to feel emotion.

I I see.

H I hope you do. There is nothing I can say about these men except that they are dead.

I You sleep well at nights?

H As well as a man of my age may be expected to sleep.

I And these are your final words on this battle?

H Yes.

I I see ... Well, viewers, that's that. Which brings us to the end of our programme, where we tried to show what it must have been like in those far-off days of World War I. Goodnight. Goodnight.

Incident in the Classroom

In the early morning light the pale-green pencil-sharpener spun out its long, thin, orange-edged, fresh streamer into the motionless, beautifully clean wastepaper basket.

The floor was wooden bright and clean. The windows sparkled with comforting sunshine. Pencils quietly devoured white paper, as white as the bulbs that hung, still and detached, over the varnished, gleaming, iron-shod desks.

Miss Helen Hope watched as the yellow-pigtailed, stripe-pinafored, buckle-shoed and spectacled Margaret sharpened her orange pencil standing over the wastepaper basket with a small frown of concentration that slightly lined her brow.

Lazily she saw the long curved wood lengthen itself into an impossible tongue. And she thought: this is a good moment: this moment is good. She frowned however, slightly reflecting Margaret's frown.

'Stop writing, children,' she said, and they stopped writing at once. It was frightening. Margaret returned to her seat. Miss Helen Hope stood tall and fiftyish before the class. She was as slim as a pencil in her dark skirt and jacket, white-brooched at the right breast. Her black shoes shone brightly. She felt completely assured and real inside her spruce contained blackness, and knew what she would say, life sparkled in her eyes, her smooth hair sang about her head.

'Give me,' she said, 'an example of a preposition, Mary.'

'Please miss, "at" is an example of a preposition.'

She had taught them to answer in sentences. It was more secure.

Mary was thinking 'at' is thin and black like the point of a pencil.

'Very good,' said Miss Helen Hope. 'Now Margaret, give me an example of a conjunction.'

She watched Margaret stand up quietly in a space of her own, her face slightly flushed with excitement.

'Please miss, "and" is an example of a conjunction.' Their eyes momentarily met and then jumped away with mutual embarrassment as if they had been burnt.

'Who are you?' thought Miss Helen Hope. Margaret thought: – 'Now she will ask me for an adjective. I am glad to be able to answer her questions. It makes me feel happy all over.'

Then just as she was preparing herself for the second question a knock came at the door, which after a decent interval was opened. The class stood up, mainly black-pinafored, as Miss Helen Hope turned to the headmaster.

To his 'Good-morning' they sat down, turning again to their books. The headmaster was a small, waistcoated man who crossed the floor with mincing steps. They could hear him talking: – 'Now about the cards, Miss Hope, do you think we should . . . ?'

Miss Hope answered his questions quietly and clearly, her face slightly flushed, her eyes sparkling.

The headmaster thought approvingly, she is a good teacher, and she, knowing that he thought this, was pleased. She also knew that the children knew that he thought this. It was surprising how much they knew.

He had not been a good teacher himself and he envied Miss Hope for her beautiful crystal control. It appealed to something in him that he could not name.

'I am a child myself,' Miss Helen Hope thought. 'I love this quite, clean, sparkling room. I like to see good, clear-varnished desks. I like to see the sunlight on the early morning floor.' She bowed her head to the master and continued speechlessly: – 'How glad I am to be able to please him.' When the headmaster went out she turned again to the class.

'You give me an example of a proper noun, Margaret.' Margaret again stood up flushed with pleasure and did as she was asked.

As Miss Hope was on the point of asking her a further question she checked herself abruptly, telling her that she could sit down. The class had grown used to this. Margaret was always asked more than one question.

They felt uneasy about this but did not understand their uneasiness as they watched their classmate, spectacled and pleased, returning to their teacher the information she had given them. They may have considered that Miss Hope thought Margaret was cleverer than themselves, but they knew that she was not.

Miss Hope herself didn't know why she asked her more questions than the others: at least not till that moment when she checked herself.

Then she knew, and she knew because of what happened in her mind when she was about to ask the question. She had suddenly thought of her own room in her own flat.

It was a beautiful room. She had a picture of a big greenish armchair sunk deep into a greenish rug, of a white-faced calm clock ticking away on a greenish mantelpiece, of a bookcase filled with paper-backed books, of papers stacked neatly on a varnished table, of silver pans humming with Sunday comfort over a cooker whose small red eye winked out at her.

She didn't know why the picture came into her mind at that moment – at least not at first – or why she thought of the tongued letter-box at the end of the hall. Then her mind reared up and reared away again.

It was because . . . She looked again at Margaret sitting there in her gleaming spectacles looking at her across these feet of sunlit wood as if she knew. She imagined herself at the same desk and Margaret with her composed glasses raising a pointer towards a shining wall atlas.

'Now children, this is England and this is 30 Silver Street.'

Her yellow pigtails sang seductively in the crisp early morning air.

She imagined herself sitting snugly at the desk and being asked: – 'What is an adjective?'

She stood up: – 'Please, miss, "green" is an adjective.'

Margaret and the headmaster nodded approvingly.

'Yes, yes, that is right.'

'Now children,' she said briskly in her real self, 'we will do some geography on the wall atlas. Margaret, point out London on the map.'

Margaret came out again with the same subtle smile and did correctly what she was asked.

She looked again at Margaret standing there proud and academic. Fractionally a picture of her own flat again entered her mind. This time it was the clock suspended as it were in green air and ticking away quietly for ever.

'Yes, that is good , Margaret. Now point out Alexandria.'

She knew when she said this that they hadn't done the Middle East. She felt the class looking at her with an air of polite surprise as if she had done something bad-mannered like entering a room without knocking.

Margaret didn't look at her, but hesitated for a long time. She studied the huge shining map, with its beautiful clear reds and yellows, suspended rectangularly from its single silver nail.

Miss Hope noticed how her left hand clutched momentarily at her dress and how her left shoe dug into the floor. She made as if to point to a place on the map, decided against it, and turned away.

'Please, miss, I don't know.'

Miss Hope realised how into her voice had crept a hint of anger, the very slightest shade of rebellion, as if she was searching for a reason for her discomfiture and not being able to find one as yet was releasing her puzzlement in her angry tone.

'Thank you, Margaret,' she said, 'it doesn't matter.'

But she knew it did matter. It was the beginning of a strange road.

Why had she done it? As she watched the figure returning to its desk another picture came into her mind. This time it was of another class, a class of boys. It was a cold day in a bitterly cold classroom. She had been working steadily at some marks, she remembered it quite clearly.

For some reason one of the marks in the column had been in red while the others were in normal blue. She couldn't understand this. The class was quite small, in fact there weren't more than twenty. She herself was about thirty years old then.

She remembered also that the previous night she had been attending a church meeting. The hall had been cold and draughty.

Suddenly as she looked up nakedly into the classroom out of aching eyes she saw what she had never seen before and what she hoped she would never see again, but of course she would see it again and again.

Sitting in the very front of the class was a very small boy who wore thick foggy glasses. They were like the bottoms of bottles. In his breast pocket was stuck an orange pencil, blatantly, like a lance, too aggressive for the dull pose of the body. Around him was an aura of dirtiness, a vagueness of mediocrity.

At that moment she had seen quite clearly what would happen to him, she saw the sort of house in which he would live, the sort of wife he would marry, the sort of children he would breed, mice with glasses.

She remembered repeating to herself in anguish of the spirit: Pray God that I am wrong. Perhaps he had some gift, some unexpected knowledge, some grace which can save him. She imagined perhaps a love of violins, a dream of oceans.

And she remembered unrolling a wall atlas, not quite the same as the one she had in that room (it seemed, in recollection, duller, the lettering was smaller, less shiny), and asking him on impulse: 'George, could you point to Chicago on the map?'

She didn't know why she had chosen Chicago. Perhaps it was, in the end, to give him some sort of chance. She imagined that he might be interested in gangsters, guns. He had gone out to the board.

She still remembered with sudden recoiling pain the stumpy way in which he had stood on his flannelled legs like a kind of adult clown. His fogged glassy eyes had stared at the map with an illusion of intellectuality. Despairingly, in the end, he had pointed into the middle of Russia.

His glasses, she thought, had looked appealingly at her. His eyes, she wondered, must be vein-twisted under a flat stone. Then knowing he had been wrong, he returned to his seat.

'Thank you, Margaret,' said Miss Helen Hope, 'and now, Mary, will you please tell me where . . . '

The Hermit

We were on a touring bus one morning and it stopped at a shed by the side of the road. A hermit lived there. The shed was made of tin and had a long chimney sticking out of it. The 'bus driver, very upright behind the wheel, tooted the horn a few times and then stopped. We were looking out the window at the hut. After the driver had stopped tooting a man came out. He was very thin, and white, bristly hair was seen not only on his head but on on his cheeks as well. His trousers were held up by braces. He was carrying a chanter. He scratched his head and then came over to the 'bus. He stood on the step and said, 'Good morning, ladies and gentlemen, I'm afraid I was late getting up.' He spoke in a sort of educated voice.

He looked down at the ground and then up again and, laughing a little, said, 'Would you like if I played you some tunes to speed you on your way?'

He took out his chanter and blew through it. Then he took out a dirty white handkerchief and wiped it. He played 'Loch Lomond' very badly, and put the chanter on a case beside him, a case belonging to one of the passengers.

'This is the day I go for my pension,' he said, and someone laughed.

'I go down the road there to the Post Office.' He pointed into the slight mist ahead of us.

The driver said, 'He's been on TV, haven't you?'

The hermit scratched his head again, looking down at the floor, and then, looking up again with an alert bright look on his unshaven ravaged face,

'Yes, I was on TV,' he said.

'What programme were you on?' someone shouted from the back, greatly daring. It was a woman's voice.

'It was called "Interesting People". I was interviewed, I played the chanter.'

'Will you be on again?' someone asked.

'I don't know. I may be. Depends if they like me.'

Everyone laughed, and he grinned impudently.

'I was late getting up,' he said to the driver. 'I was washing my clothes last night.'

'You should get married,' another woman shouted out.

'It's too late now,' he said perkily. 'Would you like to hear another tune? I must play for my money.'

This time he played 'Scotland the Brave'. He put the chanter down and said – 'It's too early to play.' He had played it very badly. In fact, his playing was so bad it was embarrassing.

He handed his cap round. When it came to my turn I debated whether to put threepence or sixpence in. After all, even though he was a hermit, he did play very badly.

As the cap was being handed round he stood on the steps and said – 'No, I don't have a gun. Anyway, there's nothing here to kill, madam. I get my cheese and bread from down the road, and that's all I need.'

When the cap was handed back to him he took out his chanter again and said – 'I hope it'll behave better this time. I'll play you one for the road if my chanter behaves.' He played 'I'm no' awa' tae bide awa'.' 'I'm afraid my chanter is playing up on me today,' he said, laughing. He got down from the step on to the road. The driver let in the clutch just as the hermit was saying, 'I hope you have a pleasant day.' The 'bus picked up speed. I saw him turning away and going into his hut. He didn't wave or even look back, though some people in the 'bus were waving.

I didn't know whether I hoped he got on TV or not. Playing like that he didn't deserve to.

I heard a woman behind me saying: 'Such an educated voice.'

And another one: 'Perhaps he's got a tragedy in his life. He sounded an intelligent sort of man.'

If I'd had the courage I would have spat on them. Who was he, anyway, making money from us just because he was a hermit? Anyone could be a hermit. It didn't take courage to be a hermit. It only took despair. Anyway, he was one of the worst instrumentalists I had ever heard. I'd have given the money to Bob Dylan if he'd stood there singing 'Don't Think Twice, It's All Right', but not to that faker.

The Long Happy Life of Murdina the Maid

And now we arrive at the island of Raws, well known in legend and in song. To this island, rich in peat and some deposits of iron, there came St Murriman, clad in monk's habit and hairshirt. A great man, he is said to have baptised in his old age a number of seals which he thought to be children as they rolled by the shore in their innocent gambols. (And indeed seals do have a peculiar childlike appearance if you scrutinise them carefully enough.) This island too is famous for the story of the Two Bodachs, one of these stories in which our history is perennially rich. But perhaps the most famous story of all is that of Murdina the Maid. (I speak under correction but I believe that a monograph has been written on this story and that a paper was once delivered on it at a Celtic Congress.)

Murdina the Maid was born of good-living parents, the father a blacksmith and the mother a herdsgirl. They lived together in harmony for many years till the mother, whose name was Marian (a relation it is said on the distaff side to the MacLennans of Cule), delivered a fine girl. She grew up, as Wordsworth says, in 'sun and in shower' till she attained the age of seventeen years. We may think of her as apple-cheeked, dewy-eyed, with sloe-black eyes and a skin as white as the bogcotton. However, matters were not allowed to remain like that.

This poor innocent girl one night was attending what we call in the vernacular a dance (though different indeed were the dances of those days from the dances of our degenerate time) and there she met a man, let us call him a man for want of a better name, though he was more like a beast in human form. He was a Southron man, and he was addicted to the music of the melodeon, an instrument which in those days provided our people with much innocent amusement.

We have no record of their dalliance and of his wicked wiles but sufficient to say that he persuaded her to run away with him to Glassgreen, the great metropolis, albeit she went home for her wardrobe (poor as it was) first. One may imagine what such a wardrobe would consist of, two long skirts, a coiffed head-dress, two pairs of stockings woven at home, one pair of shoes and one pair of tackety boots, with, of course, some under-clothes of the colour pink.

Compare with this the wardrobe of her seducer which would contain brightly painted ties (all bought in a shop), trousers of an alien style, shirts of a sordid cut, and shoes of a hitherto unseen mode. The man's name was Horace.

Thus it was that playing his melodeon and providing her with deceitful music he led her like the Pied Piper to Glassgreen.

Imagine, however, the consternation of the blacksmith and his spouse. Day after day he would lift his hammer and not even hit the anvil with it. Sunk into depression, his stalwart arms rapidly losing their strength, he sank into an early grave and his wife did not outlive him long. O Murdina, how hapless your expedition to the metropolis! Hapless indeed our lives unless we obey our parents. Where she expected a mansion she was led at last into a small room which contained one bed, a gas cooker, a cupboard and not much more. But the tears she shed that evening were more than compensated for by the dallyings of her lover, whose moustache brushed her mouth as he yawned copiously through the long night.

So she began to visit dens of iniquity. Psychedelic were her days and drugged her evenings. The water of the earth did not suffice her but she must be stayed by beverages unknown to her parents. Ravaged by music which stole her soul away she would sing in these same dens of iniquity intertwined with her lover. But sorrowful too were her thoughts for her lover had not as much money as would sustain her wicked delights, such as splendid clothes and furniture of a rare ilk. Thus one night when he was sleeping the sleep of the sinful, she stole from his small den taking with her his pocket book, a number of his ties (which she hoped to sell) and a diamond necklace which he said he had got from his mother, long under the sod in his native Donegal.

With these, she found herself another protector who was in the habit of giving room to a number of girls who had nowhere else to go. Laudable and charitable as this was, we must however acknowledge that his mode of living was not what one would require from a godly man, for he was not above sending these girls out into the cold to hold converse with strangers such as seamen, foreigners, and persons of diverse vices.

Thus passed her nights and her days, yearning as she said for the innocent pleasures of Raws, with its limpid streams, and its snow-covered bens.

One night the island came to her as in a vision. She saw it, as it were, clearly delineated on the walls of her luxurious room, and she heard in her ears the sound of its innumerable waves. In the morning she arose, put on her new-bought furs, and set off to find the mode of transport which would take her to her home. In the carriage were many young men who (on hearing of her adventures) were desirous to approach with many friendly overtures and those she was not loathe to deny, only saying that she would bring them to her house. She handed out to them with much magniloquence cards which showed both her own and the name of her house.

Arrived in Raws, she was welcomed with open arms by those who saw in her the penitent returned with her spiritual gains. This gave no small encouragement to the indigenous folk for it showed them that they themselves might do what she had done. She set up house in Raws and many were the guests who came to her house. Indeed it can safely be said that hers was the most popular house in the island, and not until the early hours of the morning did her visitors depart, fortified by her conversation and her kindly dalliance.

Often with tears she would lay a wreath of orchids on the graves of her parents and caused a marble monument to be built to them on which she had carved these words: 'Gone Before, But not much Before.'

So she lived to a good old age, providing pleasure and benefit to all and had no cause to regret the day she had left Glassgreen for as she herself once remarked in one of her more serious moments, 'The competition here is not so fierce as in the wicked world of the south.'

Thus, therefore, is told the legend of Murdina who from being an apple-cheeked girl became a dowager of the neighbourhood, contributing much tablet to the local sale of work as well as many cast-off dresses some of which are to be seen to this day in colours like purple and pink.

It is easy to see therefore that those who leave these beautiful islands with their lovely airs and golden sands always have the urge to return as she did, happy in that they have abandoned the snares and competition of the metropolis.

The Injustice to Shylock

What does he require of me? Does he himself know? One moment I am odious, the next eloquent. One moment I am standing in a courtroom defending myself, the next attacking my accusers with words I did not know I possessed, words so violent and so lovely that I satiate myself on them and wish them back again. But the next moment I am barren and grey, an old monk in an alien world. Who am I? I say to him. I clutch my Bible but it is like a stone, there is no answer. My heart beats dully. Where am I going, now without progeny? Where am I, beaten and poor, to go? I ask for new words but he gives none. He is entirely unfair to me, a miser with his vocabulary. One moment I am perfect and happy, executing the exact motions of my being, a self-admirer, the next he removes the harmony from me. My friends secretly laugh at me. I am betrayed by justice and by language together. They listen to the young and beautiful but not to the old. They do not know me. No one here knows me and he makes no attempt to let them know me. How could they, revolving in their frivolous circles, recognise this grey man at the centre who is not me and whom he will only permit to speak in broken tones? What does he know about me? Has he suffered? What right does he have to pass judgment on me from his bountiful universe, I who am compelled to perpetual silence and meagreness once I leave the room that he has placed me in at the end? He has removed language from me but that does not mean that I do not exist. I pray for better words, any words, but he does not give them to me. He has his favourites and they are the beautiful and the plausible and the negligent and the unprincipled. They have their music without morality or meaning, their fine tinkling idiocies, but he does not speak for me. Once or twice he did but then he forgets me, seduced by them, their apparent immortality. I understand that but I cannot forgive it.

He has taken everything away from me and he has not even given me myself, for I sway as in water between the tragic and the comic. Ah, but he says, I must not make you wholly tragic nor must I make you wholly comic. But what about the others? He has made them wholly careless. How does he know what I feel when I look at those others, single in themselves, elegant and exact and insensitive? Does he not see that I require a clearer future if I am to keep faith with the simplicities of justice? Does he care for justice at all or is he enchanted by the corrupt music of the nightingale?

What am I to do in this harmonious city – this city of false and base symmetry whose salons are built on stones? How am I to endure the merciless azure of its amoral sky, the perpetual flowering of its golden suns, breeding their perpetual rays? How am I to endure the music of careless youth when they return to their houses in the moonlight, she in her false black clothes (imitating the tranquil self-possession of a false law) and he in his large bluff insincerities? Their heaven appears so perfect and so false and I, a shadow, watching them, clutching my Bible, as if I were in the wrong, as if I were an irrelevant disturbance, I to whom so much has been done of injustice. They do not even see me. He has given them the true music of his heart, his genius is in the voice of their nightingales, in their voices, he attributes to them the legends of Rome, its sensuous paganisms. Am I an idiot therefore, a barren man? Or is it luck after all? Has he abolished merit and principle? Is that what the flat distant mellow moonlight means, the acres of luck? Is it luck that condemns me and fructifies them? Clutching my Bible I must bear in my single hell their voices singing so melodiously, their casual frivolities and gestures, as they pass the shrubbery where I stand grey and unappeased, not even a margin to their illuminated book.

I say to him in his Heaven: Unfair one, you have betrayed me. You have taken from me not only my gold and my daughter but also my language. You have taken the side of the young and the unjust and for that you shall surely perish.

And surely I hear him saying: I will resurrect you. I shall perfect you again on my perpetual journey. I shall raise you from the dead again in another guise and you will be better than you ever were. But nevertheless I hear in his voice a certain dislike, as if he grudges me life, as if I spoil his lucidities.

But if he does not give me his measure of fairness he will have failed and it will destroy him. In another court he will receive his justice. He will die because of his indifference. For he has taught me to demand the beautiful words, the words that will justify my existence, and I must have them, grey robed as I am in this beautiful place where the single ones confront me from their singularity and I return to them my fruitful because broken muse.

In the Maze

I am waiting here in the middle of the maze having paid the man his shilling. It took me some time to get to the centre past blind alleys, diversions, past a little capped man with his son, but always keeping my eye on the white clock at the centre. I know that I am going to die here for there would be no other reason to invite me. And I don't even know who wrote the note. It could be my husband, who, continually acting Hamlet, thinks I am Gertrude. On the other hand it could be my son who wants my money. But the handwriting was not theirs. On the other hand they would be careful to disguise it.

Once he came home from the theatre and stabbed at my then boy friend through the bedroom curtain but Eric was lucky enough to escape unharmed except for a slight abrasion on the right buttock. My husband later tolerantly told me that he had walked off stage and still found himself in the play walking through the streets, feeling as if he was carrying a rapier at his side. Naturally it was his mother who destroyed him. She always wanted him to be a girl and brought him up on mirrors and dolls. He is insanely jealous and has never forgiven me for Eric: and Eric hasn't either, not with a badge on his right buttock from a phantasmal rapier.

All this hasn't helped our son much. He is always brooding in a saturnine way, spending enormous amounts of money, driving fast cars towards the sea. My husband tells him that he is looking for Elsinore but I think he is insecure and is looking for the womb. He hates me as well and thinks me flabby, stupid and insincere. He also doesn't like his father much and the feeling is returned.

On the other hand it might be Eric. He might be Eric. He might have taken up with someone else though he is not really the masterful type. I had to make all the running after meeting him at the party and he is terrified of Richard. He is blonde and wickedly beautiful and he looks sometimes as weak as blancmange.

So at any moment I will see one of these three coming towards me with a sword or a gun. It is interesting to ask myself why I came but there is no reason. Perhaps I want some new sensation? Perhaps I want to know who is interested enough to send me a note? After all I am not so young as I was: my mirror tells me so. Perhaps the note is in my own handwriting? I could disguise it, couldn't I?

It was quite odd about Richard's walk home through the play. He swore that he saw courtiers standing at bus stops in their reds and yellows like people on playing cards. My son of course thinks he is mad but who isn't nowadays? And if he knew what his grandmother had done he would have some pity. But the young have no pity now. They are remorseless and sensation-mongering. Their favourite painter is Bacon whom my husband likes. He would like to paper the bedroom with him, all those glass cages and soundless screams and popes in their regalia.

Perhaps on the other hand Eric wants to kill me. Perhaps he is so terrified of Richard and what he might do that he has decided to kill me. For I won't let him go. But that doesn't explain why I am here. Why I am here, I think, is because someone has asked me. Someone has enough will-power and decisiveness to ask me to do something. It is as simple as that. I am being offered a part in the play and this is my audition, in the centre of a maze. I had a curious feeling when coming through the maze as if it were trying to upset the shape of my brain cells. But I defeated it and here I am staring up at the white clock which hangs like a bubble against the blue sky. I am sitting on a bench waiting, my red gloves obediently beside me hanging down like those of an exhausted boxer. For we do exhaust ourselves, don't we? We eat ourselves up.

I decided that I would wear my lemon suit, the one I used to wear when I was young. So that if it is Richard he will enter that world again. On the other hand if it is Eric it will be a joke at his expense. If it is my son – our son – let him stab quickly. I feel guilty towards him for I have given him nothing. And neither has Richard. He is wandering about on the face of the earth, driving from here to there without reason, looking for the sea.

It's quite calm here. The sunlight is falling helplessly around me. I am helpless inside it. My lemon dress composes a painting. I attract the light and shade towards me. I compose it. There is no one else in the maze. I hear no one outside it though there were some idiots there some time ago laughing and playing tricks on each other. I could hear their voices echoing. They seemed to belong to another world, perhaps the real world, but if so why should their voices sound so hollow? They didn't find the maze difficult. That is what is so extraordinary about them.

I should like to have powder and lipstick with me and a small table so that in all this azure I could arrange myself. But that of course is impossible. Everything is impossible in this fifth rate country composed of ice and suicide. To which character should I give my signature? And even now is Richard striding towards me, paranoically angry, cloak flying? He always has this irritating habit of looking white-faced. Eric bites his nails.

In any case I did not recognise the handwriting on the note. Perhaps it's a joke? I don't know.

Listen. I can hear footsteps. His mother was a hellish woman. She destroyed him utterly. He was never any good to me, no wonder I took Eric. He is a lesbian, I think. The footsteps are coming closer. Soon they will be here. I can hear him trying to find his way about, hesitating. Of course he was always hesitant. He is turning. He is stopping. He is thinking. He has found the way. My heart is beating and I am waiting for him, my legs crossed. He is standing in front of me. I rise. I hold my powder compact in my hand. I reach out towards him. I know he is going to kill me. 'Gertrude,' I cry. He raises his hand. His lips are red with lipstick, his lined face looks vaguely into mine as into a mirror. I hate her. She destroyed me. I am a fragment in her mirror. It is better to lie down here in the middle of the maze under the clock's ticking. But I strike first. She falls. I walk out. So that is why I kept this appointment. So that is why I am wearing not lemon but black. The whore betrayed me. So that is why I hear cheering as I leave the maze. The idiotic groundlings are throwing their apple cores away and the earth is green again. I feel the swish of the velvet and the rapier at my side. I shall walk towards the rocks. I shall drive towards the sea. I shall hear again the sound of the sea.

The Meeting

She is sitting beside me wearing a pair of lilac gloves, and the reason for that of course is that her left hand is unringed. I can't remember where we met (I think it was probably in a pub) but in any case I am drunk though that does not prevent the operation of the sleepless crystal of my mind. There is a large hearth in the room and also a large dog which is mercilessly crunching bones under the wooden table. She is wearing tall leather boots. There are lines round her eyes.

She has a mother, so she tells me, ancient and tyrannical, who is at this moment lying asleep in her queenly rigid bed like one of those classical marbly women from Racine's plays. I know it is because of her that she has not married. She is telling me the story of her life and I seem to have heard it before over and over in some other place at some other time, and in any case I am drunk. I was drunk when I walked with her here under the autumnal stars past red kiosks and letter boxes with their slitted mouths.

The dog is crunching bones in the corner.

The old woman is presumably asleep in her white classical bed. The stars do not know our ruins and our pains. The darkness slowly crunches them.

I propose to myself a future. I shall say I will marry her but only on one condition, that she leaves behind her the old woman to whom she is bound by veins and bones, resignation and despair.

I see in front of me clearly the battle being waged, the house emptying itself of her, the roots being torn up, the steady crunching, the moans, the cries.

I shall propose to her a vision of freedom, the two of us together radiant among white cookers, classical curtains, carelessnesses and affluences, no ancestral mournings, all the ceilings innocent and new. I shall advance these ideas out of eloquence for at least I have that. She will lay her head on my shoulder (she is doing it now), I am aware of her flesh, she of mine. We are like children in a story of Hans Anderson, blue boots, red cheeks, but no grannies. And the barenesses of autumn.

I shall speak of affection, an island of two people without footprints. Attracted by my vision she will fight for her own survival, tear the furniture up by the black roots, excavate and wash her ravaged psychic landscape, hanging it up on ropes between poles. She will be standing outside a church on a windy day watching herself in angel white and carrying red roses, the photographer kneeling and firing at her. All shall be calm, the honeymoon in a hotel entirely new and fresh.

Ah, how well I can speak, though the crystal is always listening to myself speaking, watching her listening, aware of innocences gone sour, of vulnerabilities, of desert places veined with blue.

The dog is crunching the bones under the table.

The sky bears its brown fruit.

The fireplace is huge and draughty. It is very silent in the lounge except for the white bubble of the electric clock whose tick one can very faintly hear.

I propose such a pure world as she has thought (and I too) has gone forever. We will be together, unaffected by ironies in a house new as a bone. The wardrobes will be our own, the tables our own, the chairs our own and they will exist in such a lyrical light, unaffected by the past, the 'things in themselves' without fingerprints. She will arrive there, a psychic conqueror, a new woman, she will stand upright as in the Sunday Supplements assessing furniture and carpets. I shall be the one on whom she leans. I shall exist for her in a green field.

(In fact as I think these thoughts, or at least as the crystal thinks them, I am myself almost persuaded in such a possibility, such a universe.)

I propose again that when she has seen all this, when she has apparently entered the promised land, cleared of the lumber of ancestry, when she has fought her way into the imagined Eden as innocent as an advertisement, when she is standing easy and ungloved and new by the cooker on which she will willingly cook all my meals, I shall disappear at that very moment, I shall withdraw into the world which I knew before I ever met her, before I proposed these things, the ambiguous world in which I usually live.

And yet why do I feel all this, why do I have these thoughts, why does the crystal send out these terrible rays so that even now as I place my hand as if by accident on her knee and then on her crossed thighs, I look down barbaric vistas? Why will the crystal emanations never cease? So that as I look at her I think of myself looking at her and I hear the large dog crunching the bones under the table (ancestral and scarred), I see the furniture closing on those innocences. I see the wardrobes and chairs taking over mastery as if we were involved in a war with them. And it is not because I am drunk. Not at all. I am sober at the very heart of me. The crystal never gets drunk. It is not appearance, it is the thing in itself. The crystal, tired of ennui, wishes to play. It wishes to play games. It wishes to make faces, to dance, to be gay in a cold way. It wishes not to be itself, and yet it cannot unwish its own existence.

She is leaning towards me. I hear the ancestral voices. I wish to love her. Perhaps I shall. Perhaps I shall be permitted. Perhaps the pathos will allow it.

Perhaps if I should look just once into eyes that are different from mine, that do not reflect me, I shall not hear the eternal crunching. I shall not see the autumn stars which are so naked and so old! Perhaps the crystal shall cease transmitting, shall lie down at last with its own bone, if only I look into those eyes, if only I lose myself.

Let me look.

Ah!

Waiting for the Train

He stood on the railway-station platform at midnight waiting for the train.

Every night he came and waited for it, or rather waited for it to stop. Every night the train sped past with lighted carriages in which he saw as in a series of moving paintings dramatic events framed – a murder, a wedding, a transaction. But the train did not stop and he had to wait till the night became the reasonable day and the day gloomed into night again. But he suffered over and over the pain of being separated from the illuminated events, their joy or terror.

Sometimes under the booming roof he would hear a voice which said: 'This train will stop at Belsen and at Auschwitz, at Friedsville and Pascaiville. Passengers will leave their luggage at the office where it says KRAUT in block letters.'

Visions came to him of a garden in which he had once worked, in the grounds of a huge castle. Under the trees he would frolic with Marguerite, who had long since left, high-heeled, with a transistor that played incessantly in her left hand. Chewing gum, she swayed to the music. Where was she now? He imagined that she was a dancer somewhere or a striptease artist in some sleazy club. Anyway, she had left no address when she set out into the wide world with painted toe-nails, indomitable heart-shaped face and her transistor.

And so many others had also left him – men and women and children. They had all gone into the world of light while in the darkness he waited for the train to stop so that he might be allowed to board it, and join those others on their recurrent journey from spring to fall.

His footsteps echoed hollowly in the station as he walked up and down. The footsteps were of himself, they echoed himself back to himself. He could not emerge from the impatience of himself, except by entering the train and those illuminated possibilities that he saw each night.

He stared ahead of him to the opposite platform where he could dimly make out advertisements exhorting him to eat more, drink more, buy a more comfortable bed, listen to a record or buy a newspaper. In the daylight there seemed to be a lot of advertisements about Goethe, at night they changed to Baudelaire. He waited because he felt incomplete, because he wanted not just the fruit but the core as well. He waited because he did not want to be excluded from the circus.

Sometimes he would try to trick whoever was in charge of the train. He would appear in rags, dirty, dependent, a beggar. He would stand under a light which would show his unshaven face, a suffering stubbled Van Gogh. At other times he would howl into the night with a high-pitched scream as if by imitation he would make the train stop. But it did not stop as if it sensed the falsity of his cries.

But tonight he was ready for it. Tonight he knew once and for all that there was no place for him but the train. He had given away all his possessions, even his photographs of the castle showing himself in the grounds tending a tree in the sunlight. He had simplified himself to what he was and wore. He was ready to offer himself to the howling train and the lighted compartments. The howl of his mind answered to the howl of the train.

He prayed, 'Why should I be different? Why should I not be permitted this terror? Why should I be omitted?'

And as he prayed he heard the whistle of the train, the clear high manic note. Suddenly a voice above him spoke in a clipped inhuman tone, almost Japanese.

'This train will stop at Miltonstown and Rimbaudville. When you board it you must leave all your luggage behind you. Tickets are non-returnable. Do not be alarmed by the appearance of the guards or police. Whatever happens happens to you. Your capacity for pain is the only entry fee required, but you must remember that this is as great as your capacity for joy. Do you accept these conditions? If you do have enough faith to, close your eyes.'

For the first time in his many vigils he closed his eyes because he had tried everything else. The train thundered towards him. He felt it was going past and nearly opened his eyes but didn't.

'You may open your eyes now,' said the voice. He opened them. The train had stopped and there was a door open. Without a case, empty of possessions, he entered it in the greenish light. There was a ghastly overwhelming smell which gradually became sweet and wholesome. The train was blazing with light from end to end. He moved down the corridor. In one compartment he saw a firing squad with invisible faces, in another a woman nursing a baby. In yet another a boy being beaten with a blunt instrument.

He found a carriage and sat down in it, and as he did so his fatigue was changed to buoyancy. Opposite him there was a picture of a seaport, above him there was a painting of a youth in a flowery dress leaning against a tree. Music played incessantly, demonic, elegant and sweet.

He heard someone singing, 'I'll be with you in apple blossom time.' Someone else was singing, 'I'm falling, falling, falling in love with you.' He thought he recognised Marguerite's voice but older, richer, more vibrant.

He set off in search of her past the lovers, the murderers, the clerks. He thought he would find her eventually though it might take a long time. And each time on the recurrent journey she would be different. But as long as they were on the same train it did not matter particularly.

In the Café

The two of us – she wearing her yellow coat and I wearing my drab one – entered the café and sat down at the draughts-board table which was near the open door through which we could see the apple tree growing. The café owner nervous and bustling and vibrant swept towards us.

'Ah,' he said, 'you are existentialists.'

'Yes, I am,' I said. But she said nothing.

'Existentialism began in cafés,' he said. 'I'm very proud of that. Not here, of course. In France. What is your pleasure? A coffee?'

'Yes,' I said, 'two coffees. One white and one black.'

'True,' he said, 'two blacks do not make a white.' He gave our order to a hovering waitress and sat down beside us.

'I prefer Camus to Sartre,' he said. 'I feel that Sartre does not have a truly creative mind. But on the other hand I am sure they both wrote in cafés.' He waved his hands dramatically like a Frenchman as he spoke. 'Not that I've ever seen a writer writing in my café. Still, this is not a sunny clime.'

He continued, 'If for every chair there is no Ideal chair we are back with nothingness. Agreed?'

She, who was just recovering from a cold, sniffled but said nothing. I nodded, regarding the marble-topped chair with the draughts-board pattern. There were so many kinds of chair, after all.

'You are with me,' he remarked. 'I never suffer from jealousy,' he went on. 'If no one buys anything here I do not feel rejected. I know the owner of a newspaper shop who can't bring himself to serve anyone who has a newspaper from another shop under his arm. That of course is a classic case of insecurity. I on the other hand feel and act like a café owner but with hauteur. Sartre and Camus have given me a status. In my café there happen all sorts of metaphysical events. My café is an image of the entire world like the Round Table. I act as a café owner should. If Man is not a thought of God, what is he? Eh?'

'I don't know,' I said. 'What is he?'

'He is a drinker of coffee and a muncher of cakes. That among other things. Out of all that detritus he has to make not only himself but all men. Have you noticed,' he said, 'that I wear a purple bow tie every day? That is because of the part I play. I am royalty now created by philosophy. Hegel I think is more suited to restaurants. I know exactly the type of restaurant. It is large and drab and not very well lighted. Do you understand what I mean? Have you seen these kinds of restaurants? They serve you with huge dark slabs of things.'

'Yes, I know them,' I said. 'You are a very interesting café owner.' She didn't say anything but we were both very conscious of her fine face and yellow coat.

'Ah, Man has to be made and remade again and again,' said the café owner. 'I could even become a tailor. That too would give my life meaning. That is the true image. Man to be rouged and powdered every day. For every day is a new day. And I always begin it with a cup of coffee. That is my ritual. Ah, here is yours.' And the waitress in white set the coffees down in front of us.

'Fine coffee,' I said as I drank.

'It is only with certain people that I can be a café owner,' he said. 'For instance I knew at once that you were both existentialists. One day I shall have to invent a motto and ribbon for us. I do not see long-distance lorry-drivers as existentialists though they often come here. They are Hegelians and always want pies which I don't serve. Should Man be created in the image of the long-distance lorry-driver?'

'I think not,' he said. And laughed. She didn't laugh.

'Good,' he said, 'you are a connoisseur of humour. But when I look around me and see the contingent chairs and tables my heart bleeds for them, they are exiles from Marx and Hegel and such large people. There is no room for them. They are like orphans, however beautifully they are painted. I yearn for the days when a chair had a life of its own. I think of the chairs sitting here during the night trying to add a cubit to their stature, trying to be more truly themselves.'

'I can imagine that,' I said.

'Yes,' he said earnestly, 'I'm a very sensitive man. I would not like Man to be made in my image but perhaps in that of a peacock with a flavour of early morning coffee about it.'

'It would not be inappropriate,' I said. But she said nothing.

At that moment a number of noisy rugger players came in and he sighed and left us. 'They will need help in the kitchen,' he said. 'Anyway I don't like rugger players. Their books are obscene.'

After he had gone she said, 'What an odd queer man.'

'He seems very intelligent,' I said.

'He is very queer,' she said sniffling. 'And I don't know or care what existentialism is.'

'He is one,' I said. 'I like this café.' In fact I was very reluctant to leave it. There hung about it the pungent smell of coffee.

'I don't,' she said. 'The coffee isn't very good. And I'm sure it's also very expensive.'

'Well, he may have to charge for the conversation,' I said.

'We came here for coffee and not conversation,' was her answer.

'We could go and sit on the chairs beside the apple tree,' I said.

'No,' she said, 'I've got a cold anyway. I don't know what you see in him. He talks a lot. I think he's boring.'

'All right,' I said, 'if that's what you think we can go.'

'That's what I think,' she said.

She was in one of her sullen moods but I thought that it would have been pleasant to sit by the apple tree in deckchairs on such a fine sunny day. But we didn't and that was that. In any case the streets did look contingent and so did the rooks flying about the university tower. And so did the café itself, to a certain extent, seen from outside. And so . . . But that's not true. She did not look contingent. But we needed each other and it would have been bad if the café owner with his theories of existentialism had come between us especially as he charged such a high price for coffee that I thought good but she didn't. So I didn't stay and we boarded a green contingent bus and she sniffled continuously from her cold and we went to her house and played scrabble most of the afternoon while her parents withdrew to some other contingent part of the building. Still, I thought, I could always go back there on my own and listen to the café owner's theories because he seemed such a happy man who knew exactly what he was, a Café Owner.

On the Road

They were driving along the road – he and she – in the half dark when he hit the rabbit which was running across the road in front of him and converted it from a living, graceful, trembling being to a messy pulp. She shouted at him and he stopped the car and she was sick. As he tried to hold her head, she pouring a thin green bile out of her mouth, she pushed him away and as she did so he noticed without thinking of it the white moon rising ahead of him in the sky.

She raised her head at last and they went back into the car. He protested over and over that there was nothing he could have done about it, that he couldn't have pulled up in time. She didn't say anything, it looked as if she was in one of her moods again. It was true that sometimes she went into deep dark moods which lasted for a long time but eventually gave place to sunshine. He waited for this mood to pass. The thin moon seemed to be directly ahead of him as he travelled on, this time more slowly, hoping that he wouldn't hit anything else, for instance a small owl wafting across the windscreen of the car. She was still silent curled up inside herself and he didn't know what to say to her. If it hadn't been for her he would have forgotten about the rabbit a long time ago. But when he looked at her he thought of the messy redness of the rabbit with its guts spewed out on the road.

'That is how it is,' she said at last.

'What?' he asked, glad that she had spoken.

'With us,' she said, 'with everybody. We make a bloody mess of each other.' She spoke as if she had been granted a revelation.

He waited for her to go on, but she didn't for a while and then she said, 'Only we don't see it. We don't see it out there like that.'

What she said puzzled him because he didn't understand it. He had never felt like a rabbit. Anyway a rabbit didn't feel things like a human being and it must have been killed instantly in any case.

'If we could see what we do to each other,' she said. 'We would look like the rabbit. Do you see that?'

He drove very carefully in case there were some small animals about that he couldn't see.

'Don't you see that?' she said so suddenly and with such violence that he nearly swerved off the road.

'I couldn't help what happened,' he said, feeling stubbornness settling within him like a stone. 'I didn't want to kill it. I couldn't stop, that's all.'

'It's part of everything else,' she said persistently. 'It's part of what we do. Like the day you . . . '

'The day I what?'

'The day you gave me the present. It was a necklace.'

'What about the day?' He remembered the necklace but he couldn't remember the day he had given it to her.

'You said we should celebrate by going to bed together.'

'What's wrong with that?' he asked. 'I can't see anything wrong with that.' That pale white moon was beautiful. Quite lovely. Like a pearl necklace against the background of darkish blue.

'You didn't think how I felt, did you? You didn't think at all. Like with the rabbit. You could have turned away but you didn't. Or at least you're glad in a way.'

'What the hell are you talking about?' he said. 'I told you I didn't want to kill it. I've got nothing against rabbits. It was just bad luck.'

'It was like a bribe,' she said.

'What was like a bribe?'

'The necklace. I remember it quite clearly. You associated the two, the bed and the necklace. And I didn't think of it like that.'

'I was just joking,' he said. 'For God's sake it was just a joke.'

'Rabbits can't understand jokes,' she said.

'What did you say?'

'I said rabbits don't understand jokes.'

'I know that, but what has the rabbit got to do with necklaces?'

'A lot. It's got a lot to do with them.'

He couldn't understand how her mind worked at all. For two years now he had tried to understand her but couldn't. His own mind he felt was clear and logical but hers was devious and odd. It jumped from one thing to another like . . . He could feel no more small animals hitting the car. The moon rose more clearly ahead of him as the air darkened. It was really a lovely moon like the one they had used to see when they were courting and they could hear the sound of the leaves and the small animals and the water in the ditches.

'For you,' she said, 'the necklace was to be used for getting something else. Don't you see it was a trap, a rabbit trap? For the little rabbit.'

Her pale throat glowed out of the darkness, he could imagine her small white teeth between the lips. No, he couldn't cause an accident to her. For God's sake, she was inside the car. What was all this nonsense about rabbits anyway? There were hundreds of rabbits. By the laws of average, some rabbits were bound to be killed. After all, he hadn't set out to kill it.

'I'm sorry,' he said feeling the stone in his body. 'I'm sorry. I didn't mean to kill it.'

'Of course you didn't,' she said in a small voice. 'Naturally.'

The moon was now a full pale blaze ahead of him. Its majestic aloof beauty awed him. It was so huge and confident rising out of the darkness, more impressive than the sun, a big white stone. It seemed to swim through the sky.

'I'm sorry,' he said again but this time there was a change in his voice. 'I'm sorry. I didn't understand.'

'What we do to each other,' she said again. 'If we could see it, the torn flesh I mean.' He thought she was going to be sick again. And this time he did see it. He saw it quite clearly. He saw the rabbit with its guts hanging out and his wife spewing a thin green bile. He saw it all absolutely clearly by the light of the moon that floated over the undergrowth that was so fresh and new.

He stopped the car. 'I'm sorry,' he said, 'I really am. I see it.'

She looked into his face to see if he had really seen. Her small teeth shone white and her face seemed to quiver. Good God, he thought, the rabbit. The rabbit in my car sitting beside me. What then did I leave back there? But the moon shone fully and clearly and provided no answer. He stopped the car and put his arms around her, very gently, without kissing her. He simply held her against him, while she quivered. That damned necklace, he thought, I wish I had never bought it or I wish I had never said anything. And yet all the same he had wished to surprise her. He had really been happy buying it. He noticed that she wasn't wearing it, in fact now that he thought of it he couldn't remember her wearing it. The moon, white as a pearl, looked in on them through the windscreen with a huge peering power, a complete presence. It was frightening. Why the hell, he almost shouted, weren't you shining before, why didn't you show me the rabbit earlier?

Publication Acknowledgements

from *Survival without Error and other stories* (1970)
first published by Victor Gollancz Ltd, London:

The Ships; Survival without Error; The Exiles; Close of Play; 'Je t'aime'; Goodbye John Summers; The Black and the White; Sweets to the Sweet; Murder without Pain; The Adoration of the Mini; Home; On the Island; Joseph; The Idiot and the Professor and Some Others

from *The Black and the Red and other stories* (1973)
first published by Victor Gollancz Ltd, London:

The Dying; At the Party; In the Station; An American Sky; After the Dance; The Telegram; The Wedding; Getting Married; The Little People; God's Own Country; By the Sea; The Black and the Red; A Day in the Life of; The Crater; The Fight; In Church; Through the Desert; The Return; The End; Journeying Westwards; The Professor and the Comics.

from *The Village* (1976)
first published by Club Leabhar Ltd, Inverness:

Easter Sunday; Sunday; The Old Woman and the Rat; The Delicate Threads; The Conversation; I'll Remember You; The Ghost; The Red Door; The Blot; The Vision; The Phone Call; The House; The Painter; The Existence of the Hermit; Fable; The Old Man; The Prophecy; The Letter; Jimmy and the Policeman; After the Film; Moments; Old Betsy

Uncollected Stories

Mother and Son first published in *Alma Mater* 60, no.1, Spring 1949; New Stockings for Young Harold first published in the

Glasgow Herald, August 1960; The Scream first published in the *London Magazine*, January 1961; The Angel of Mons first published in *Lines* 19, Winter 1963; The General first published in *New Saltire* 11, April 1964; Incident in the Classroom first published in the *Glasgow Herald*, July 1964; The Hermit first published in *Sruth*, August 1967; The Long Happy Life of Murdina the Maid first published in *Ossian* 1968; The Injustice to Shylock, In the Maze and The Meeting first published in *Lines* 42/43 Sept. 1972–February 1973; Waiting for the Train first published in the *Glasgow Herald*, July 1974; In the Café and On the Road first published in *Scotia Review*, December 1974